ALSO BY GARDNER DOZOIS

ANTHOLOGIES

A Day in the Life
Another World
Best Science Fiction Stories of the Year
  #6–10
The Best of Isaac Asimov's Science
  Fiction Magazine
Time-Travellers from Isaac Asimov's
  Science Fiction Magazine
Transcendental Tales from Isaac
  Asimov's Science Fiction Magazine
Isaac Asimov's Aliens
Isaac Asimov's Mars
Isaac Asimov's SF Lite
Isaac Asimov's War
Isaac Asimov's Planet Earth
  (with Sheila Williams)
Isaac Asimov's Robots
  (with Sheila Williams)
Isaac Asimov's Cyberdreams
  (with Sheila Williams)
Isaac Asimov's Skin Deep
  (with Sheila Williams)
Isaac Asimov's Ghosts
  (with Sheila Williams)
Isaac Asimov's Vampires
  (with Sheila Williams)
Isaac Asimov's Moons
  (with Sheila Williams)
Isaac Asimov's Christmas
  (with Sheila Williams)
Isaac Asimov's Detectives
  (with Sheila Williams)
The Year's Best Science Fiction, #1–18
Future Earths: Under African Skies
  (with Mike Resnick)
Future Earths: Under South American
  Skies (with Mike Resnick)
Future Power
  (with Jack Dann)

Aliens! (with Jack Dann)
Unicorns! (with Jack Dann)
Magicats! (with Jack Dann)
Magicats 2 (with Jack Dann)
Bestiary! (with Jack Dann)
Mermaids! (with Jack Dann)
Sorcerers! (with Jack Dann)
Demons! (with Jack Dann)
Dogtales! (with Jack Dann)
Ripper! (with Susan Casper)
Seaserpents! (with Jack Dann)
Dinosaurs! (with Jack Dann)
Little People! (with Jack Dann)
Dragons! (with Jack Dann)
Horses! (with Jack Dann)
Unicorns 2 (with Jack Dann)
Invaders! (with Jack Dann)
Angels! (with Jack Dann)
Dinosaurs II (with Jack Dann)
Hackers (with Jack Dann)
Timegates (with Jack Dann)
Clones (with Jack Dann)
Armageddon (with Jack Dann)
Modern Classics of Science Fiction
Modern Classic Short Novels of
  Science Fiction
Modern Classics of Fantasy
Killing Me Softly
Dying for It
Immortals (with Jack Dann)
Roads Not Taken (with Stanley
  Schmidt)
The Good Old Stuff
The Good New Stuff
Explorers
Slow Dancing Through Time
  (with Jack Dann, Michael Swanwick,
  Susan Casper, and Jack C.
  Haldeman II)
Isaac Asimov's Werewolves
  (with Sheila Williams)
The Furthest Horizon

FICTION

Strangers
The Visible Man (collection)
Nightmare Blue
  (with George Alec Effinger)
The Peacemaker
Geodesic Dreams (collection)

NONFICTION

The Fiction of James Tiptree, Jr.

Worldmakers

SF ADVENTURES IN TERRAFORMING

Edited by Gardner Dozois

St. Martin's Griffin

New York

www.stmartins.com

Copyright acknowledgments appear on pages v–vi.

Library of Congress Cataloging-in-Publication Data

Worldmakers : SF adventures in terraforming / edited by Gardner Dozois.
    —1st ed.
        p.   cm.
    ISBN 0-312-27570-6
    1. Science fiction, American.   2. Space colonies—Fiction.   I. Dozois,
Gardner R.

PS648.S3 W649   2001
813'.0876208358—dc21

                                        2001041957

10 9 8 7 6 5 4 3 2

Contents

Preface

Even by the early middle of the twentieth century, it was becoming uneasily obvious—to those who kept up with science, anyway—that the other planets of our solar system were not likely abodes for life. Previous generations of science-fiction writers, the pulp-era "Superscience" writers of the 1930s and 1940s, had been free to use the solar system as their playground, and to populate Mars, Venus, and even Mercury or the Jovian moons, with oxygen-breathing humanoid natives (who conveniently all spoke English, or at least an understandable pidgin) that you could have swordfights with and/or fall in love with; in their hands, the solar system was as crowded and chummy as an Elks' Club picnic, chockablock with alien races and alien civilizations—affording plenty of scope for Story.

By the early fifties, however, influenced by the Campbellian Revolution in science fiction, circa 1939, when the new editor of *Astounding* magazine, John W. Campbell, began downplaying the melodramatic pulp stuff in favor of more thoughtful material that actually made a stab at rigor and scientific accuracy (and perhaps influenced as well by visionaries such as Konstantin Tsiolkovsky, Herman Oberth, Robert Goddard, Werner von Braun, Willy Ley, and the founding fathers of the British Interplanetary Society, people who actually wanted to *go* into space, for *real*, and who were carrying out the first crude experiments that might someday make that a possibility), we began to get the *realistic* space story, stories that took the idea of space exploration *seriously*, as something that might *actually happen*, that treated space as a real frontier that one day could be explored, rather than just as a setting, a colorful backdrop for chase-and-fight pulp fantasies.

Ironically, the realistic space story came along at just about the same time that scientific investigation was making it clear that there was no place in the solar system where you could *set* a realistic space story, realistically speaking—at least not one that didn't feature the characters lumbering around in space suits for the entire arc of the plot. As the century progressed, and space probes actually began to *visit* other planets to collect hard data, it became harder and harder to get away with a Mars that was crisscrossed with canals and swarming with sword-swinging, six-armed green warriors and beautiful egg-laying princesses in flowing diaphanous gowns, or a Venus that was covered deep with broad oceans in which swam giant dinosaur-like beasts. At last, it became impossible. The planets simply weren't *like* that. And although the dream of life on Mars has hung on even to the present day, in an increasingly more pallid and less hopeful form (now we'd be overjoyed to find *lichens* . . . or even fossil microbe evidence that there *once had been* life there, millions of years ago), it was obvious by the middle of the century that Dejah Thoris wasn't going to be there to greet the boys when they stepped off the spaceboat. By the late 1960s and early 1970s, space probes had "proved" that the solar system was nothing but an "uninteresting" collection of balls of rock and ice, or hellholes of deadly heat and pressure with atmospheres of poisionous gas. No available abodes for life. Dull as a supermarket parking lot.

So where were the space colonists going to *go*? And where were the SF writers going to set their "realistic" tales of space exploration and colonization?

Some writers immediately whisked themselves and their stories away to other solar systems or even to other Galaxies, far outside the writ of embarassing and hampering Fact, where they could set up whatever worlds they chose. To many writers, though, especially those with a "hard science" bent who were the very types to want to write a "realistic space story" in the first place, this was cheating: The now more widely understood limitations of Einsteinian relativity seemed to say that Faster Than Light travel was impossible (although even some of the hardest of the hard-science boys would be having second thoughts about this by the end of the century) and therefore that interstellar travel itself (let alone far-flung interstellar empires) would be difficult or impossible to achieve.

Faced with unlivable, deadly, unEarthlike conditions on all the actual real estate within practical reach, it became obvious that there were only two ways to go (unless you ignored the problem altogether, which many writers blithely did and do, and create a magic Faster Than Light drive or spacewarp device with a snap of your authorial fingers), and the "realistic space story" from then on tended to follow one or the other of them.

Science-fiction writer James Blish described those two ways rather succinctly: You can change the planet to accommodate the colonists, or the colonists to accommodate the planet.

The first of these methods, changing the planet to provide more Earthlike conditions for the colonists, has become known in the genre as "terraforming," and it is the territory explored in the anthology you hold in your hands, which deals with the creation of new, inhabitable worlds out of old, uninhabitable worlds by science and technology.

The second method, redesigning humans so that they are able to survive on alien planets under alien conditions, has become known as "pantropy" (a word coined by Blish himself), and is the territory explored (along with other deliberate, engineered changes to the human form and nature) in the upcoming companion anthology to this one, *Supermen: Tales of the Posthuman Future*, also from St. Martin's Griffin.

●

Although a (rather thin) argument could be made for the "atmosphere plants" that kept Edgar Rice Burroughs's Mars from dying, it's more likely that the notion of terraforming an alien world was first introduced into the genre, as fiction, at least, by Olaf Stapledon's monumental work of imagination, *Last and First Men*, in 1930 . . . although the term "terraforming" itself was coined by Jack Williamson, in a series of stories (in which terra-forming would actually play a rather minor role) published in 1942 and 1943, later melded into the novel *Seetee Ship*. The early 1950s saw the first detailed "modern" terraforming stories, including stories such as Walter M. Miller's "Crucifixus Etiam" and Poul Anderson's "The Big Rain" and Isaac Asimov's "The Martian Way." (Asimov's novella is mostly concerned with the politics involved in liberating a Martian colony from the political domination of mother Earth, although it *does* feature the first suggestion in SF—as far as I can tell, anyway—that Mars could be supplied with water by bringing ice asteroids to it . . . although Asimov has them landing gently rather than smashing catastrophically into it, as later terraformers would have it.) Some of the best novels to deal with the theme, such as Arthur C. Clarke's *The Sands of Mars* and Robert A. Heinlein's *Farmer in the Sky*, also appeared in the early 1950s, followed, a few years later, by novels such as Poul Anderson's *The Snows of Ganymede*.

As the sixties progressed and eventually turned into the seventies, terra-forming stories would tend to retreat from the foreground of the field and instead become part of the genre's background furniture—so that while many stories and novels would casually mention that they were taking place on a world that had been terraformed, few would deal centrally with the problems and consequences of the terraforming process *itself*. There were exceptions, of course, including Roger Zelazny's *Isle of the Dead*, Gregory Benford's *Jupiter Project*, David Gerrold's *Moonstar Odyssey*, George R. R. Martin's *Tuf Voyaging*, and Andrew Weiner's *Station Gehenna*—but, by and large, that was the way to bet it.

Then, in the late 1980s and early 1990s—perhaps because of new data from new generations of space probes that made it clear just how bizarre, complex, surprising, and mysterious a place our solar system *really* is—science-fiction writers (following the lead of somewhat earlier pioneers such as John Varley, Gregory Benford, Bruce Sterling, Michael Swanwick, and others) began to become interested in the solar system again, finding it lushly romantic *just as it was*, lifeless balls of rock and all. Suddenly, we were seeing stories and novels again that dealt centrally with terraforming, instead of reducing it to a background enabling-device, including the launch of two major series of terraforming novels that treated both the scientific and the social problems involved in creating a new world in considerable detail and with great gravitas, Kim Stanley Robinson's *Mars* trilogy (*Red Mars, Green Mars, Blue Mars*), and Pamela Sargent's *Venus* trilogy (*Venus of Dreams, Venus of Shadow,* and *Child of Venus*), as well as singleton novels such as Greg Bear's *Moving Mars*, Ian McDonald's *Desolation Road*, and Jack Williamson's *Beachhead* (part of an explosion in the nineties of novels about a colonized Mars, many of which, such as Paul J. McAuley's *Red Dust* and Alexander Jabiokov's *River of Dust*, mention terraforming schemes at least in passing). There was a rush of terraforming short stories as well in the last years of the nineties, one that has as yet showed no sign of slowing down here at the beginning of a new century.

That's quite a bit of literary ground to cover, more than fifty years' worth, and, as usual with these retrospective anthologies, there were many more stories that I would have *liked* to use than I had *room* to use. Winnowing-screens were clearly called for.

In many current stories, terraforming is accomplished at the wave of a hand by posthumans who have been given the powers of gods by incomprehensibly advanced science and technology, but that's the territory which will be covered in the follow-up volume to this one, *Supermen: Tales of the Posthuman Future*, and not the sort of thing I wanted for *this* anthology, which I intuitively felt should deal centrally with the problems that ordinary humans, people not unlike you and me, would have to face in terraforming a world, and with the social and political and personal consequences of the success of such a project—or of its failure. So that was one winnowing screen.

With an anthology entitled *Worldmakers*, I could almost certainly have gotten away with including some stories set in Virtual Reality surrounds, or in artificial simulation–worlds inside computer systems, but that seemed wrong to me for this particular book too (and besides, I've already edited three anthologies which cover those sorts of stories, *Isaac Asimov's Cyberdreams* and *Isaac Asimov's Skin Deep*, with Sheila Williams, and *Hackers*, with Jack Dann). So that was another screen.

The last winnowing-screen will probably be the most controversial: I decided not to include any stories about space stations or "O'Neill"-style orbital L5 colonies. For one thing, because there's been a recent rush of anthologies full of such stories—including *Skylife*, edited by Gregory Benford and George Zebrowski, and *Star Colonies* and *Far Frontiers*, edited by Martin H. Greenberg and John Helfers—but also because "L5 colony" stories have a dated smell to them now, to me, anyway. There was a glut of such stories in the late seventies that persisted throughout much of the eighties, a fad that dominated the field for several years, but now, more than fifteen years later, that particular concept seems faded to me, dusty, an SF dream of the future that's never going to come true, receding into distance, much like domed cities and continent-girdling slidewalks and automated highways. (My own opinion, for whatever it's worth, is that deliberately planned and created all-in-one-shot space cities of the "L5 colony" type are unlikely, anytime in the reasonably foreseeable future—enormously too expensive, for one thing, and, as many stories, such as Paul J. McAuley's recent "Quiet War" stories, have shown, too vulnerable to a million forms of sabotage and terrorism to be really practical; easier by far to create bases dug into the sheltering rock of the Moon, or Mars, or even to hollow out an asteroid. We probably *will* get space cities eventually, but they won't be *planned*, as such; instead, my guess is that they'll accrete slowly and gradually, haphazardly, bit by bit, around space factories and other installations that have a practical *reason* for being there, like company towns springing up around a mine or a military base, and although the inhabitants may *be* de facto colonists, in the long run, they won't *think* of themselves as such until several generations have gone by—they'll just be people who work in space, until their children or grandchildren decide not to go home.) And that was the final screen.

➤

Will we terraform other worlds? Science-fiction writers seem to vacillate between optimism and pessimism on the subject, with the last few years seeing a number of stories about *failed* or failing terraforming projects, perhaps as the realization of just how immense and complicated a job it would be sinks in, perhaps in part in reaction to the relative optimism (at least in terms of saying that it *can* be done) of books such as Kim Stanley Robinson's *Mars* trilogy. (On the other hand, the two most recently published stories included here are reasonably optimistic about the chances of a terraforming project succeeding, so perhaps the pendulum is swinging again.) Perhaps, to people raised in an immediate-gratification society, the idea of starting a project that you won't live to see completed, that won't come to fruition until hundreds of years after your death, seems alien and unnatural, sadly pointless, something not worth doing at all. I think that many people dismiss terraforming on those grounds, as something we'll never have the patience or continuity or dedication to actually *finish*. So why start at all? On the other hand, the people who started raising the great cathedrals of Europe knew they were embarking on projects that wouldn't be completed for hundreds of years, long after their own deaths, and that didn't stop them from starting the work necessary to raise them. So such selfless dedication and no-immediate-result long-term planning *is* possible, *is* a part of the spectrum of possible human behaviors. Once, people had a vision intense enough to help them sustain organized community effort over a span of centuries. Who can say they won't find such a vision again? (Perhaps religious Faith helps in making a generations-long perspective of this sort possible, and Mars will end up being terraformed by Baptists or Mormons or Hindus or Buddhists, or by the sons of Islam.)

My own guess is that, if the human race survives and our technological civilization doesn't crash disastrously, terraforming of some sort will become a reality, sooner or later. After all, we've already inadvertently "terraformed" *our own Earth*, radically changing our climate and ecosystem, and we didn't even mean to *do* it! It wasn't even all that *difficult*, was it, given a few hundred years of time for many small, almost-unnoticeable-at-first effects to multiply and set up self-reinforcing, escalating feedback loops? I suspect that somebody's bound to try it deliberately somewhere else one of these days—if anyone lives through humanity's first, blundering, inadvertent "experiments" in terraforming in the first place, that is!

In the meantime, while we're waiting for the Final Results to come in (perhaps you'll be lucky enough to become one of the "Posthumans" who are the subject of this anthology's follow-up volume, and will be able to afford to wait hundreds of years to See For Yourself!), here are some of the best guesses by some of SF's most gifted dreamers about what it would be like to attempt to build a brave new world out of dust and poison and ice, to create a new home for yourself and your children and your children's children where there was nothing before but desolation and ashes and death . . . to *dream* fiercely enough to make your dream a reality.

Enjoy.

—GARDNER DOZOIS

Worldmakers

The Big Rain

POUL ANDERSON

One of the best-known writers in science fiction, Poul Anderson made his first sale in 1947, while he was still in college, and in the course of his subsequent career has published almost a hundred books (in several different fields, as Anderson has written historical novels, fantasies, and mysteries, in addition to SF), sold hundreds of short pieces to every conceivable market, and won seven Hugo Awards, three Nebula Awards, and the Tolkien Memorial Award for life achievement.

Anderson had trained to be a scientist, taking a degree in physics from the University of Minnesota, but the writing life proved to be more seductive, and he never did get around to working in his original field of choice. Instead, the sales mounted steadily, until by the late fifties and early sixties he may have been one of the most prolific writers in the genre.

In spite of his high output of fiction, he somehow managed to maintain an amazingly high standard of literary quality as well, and by the early to mid-1960s was also on his way to becoming one of the most honored and respected writers in the genre. At one point during this period (in addition to non-related work, and lesser series such as the "Hoka" stories he was writing in collaboration with Gordon R. Dickson), Anderson was running three of the most popular and prestigious series in science fiction all at the same time: the "Technic History" series detailing the exploits of the wily trader Nicholas Van Rijn (which includes novels such as The Man Who Counts, The Trouble Twisters, Satan's World, Mirkheim, The People of the Wind, *and collections such as* Trader to the Stars *and* The Earth Book of Stormgate); *the extremely popular series relating the adventures of interstellar secret agent Dominic Flandry, probably the most successful attempt to cross SF with the spy thriller, next to Jack Vance's "Demon Princes" novels (the Flandry series includes novels such as* A Circus of Hells, The Rebel Worlds, The Day of Their Return, Flandry of Terra, A Knight of Ghosts and Shadows, A Stone in Heaven, *and* The Game of Empire, *and collections such as* Agent of the Terran Empire); *and, my own personal favorite, a series that took us along on assignment with the agents of the Time Patrol (including the collections* The Guardians of Time, Time Patrolman, The Shield of Time, *and* The Time Patrol).

When you add to this amazing collection of memorable titles the impact of the best of Anderson's non-series novels, works such as Brain Wave, Three Hearts and Three Lions, The Night Face, The Enemy Stars, *and* The High Crusade, *all of which were being published* in addition to *the series books, it becomes clear that Anderson dominated the late 1950s and the pre–New Wave sixties in a way that only Robert A. Heinlein, Isaac Asimov, and Arthur C. Clarke could rival. And like them, he remained an active and dominant figure right through the seventies, eighties and nineties.*

In the gritty, hard-hitting, and powerful story that follows, he gives us a vivid impression of the amount of sheer, backbreaking, hands-on, physical work it would take to terraform a world; and an unsettling reminder that one person's vision of what Utopia should be like, and how much you're willing to pay to achieve it, may differ irrevocably from another's—with fatal results.

Anderson's other books (among many others) include The Broken Sword, Tau Zero, A Midsummer Tempest, Orion Shall Rise, The Boat of a Million Years, Harvest of Stars, The Fleet of Stars, Starfarers, *and* Operation Luna. *His short work has been collected in* The Queen of Air and Darkness and Other Stories, Fantasy, The Unicorn Trade *(with Karen Anderson),* Past Times, The Best of Poul Anderson, Explorations, *and, most recently, the retrospective collection* All One Universe. *His novel,* Genesis, *was published in February 2000. Until his death on July 31, 2001, Anderson lived in Orinda, California, with his wife (and fellow writer), Karen.*

I

The room was small and bare, nothing but a ventilator grill to relieve the drabness of its plastic walls, no furniture except a table and a couple of benches. It was hot, and the cold light of fluoros glistened off the sweat which covered the face of the man who sat there alone.

He was a big man, with hard bony features under close-cropped reddish-brown hair; his eyes were gray, with something chilly in them, and moved restlessly about the chamber to assess its crude homemade look. The coverall which draped his lean body was a bit too colorful. He had fumbled a cigarette out of his belt pouch and it smoldered between his fingers, now and then he took a heavy drag on it. But he sat quietly enough, waiting.

The door opened and another man came in. This one was smaller, with bleak features. He wore only shorts to whose waistband was pinned a star-shaped badge, and a needle-gun holstered at his side, but somehow he had a military look.

"Simon Hollister?" he asked unnecessarily.

"That's me," said the other, rising. He loomed over the newcomer, but he was unarmed; they had searched him thoroughly the minute he disembarked.

"I am Captain Karsov, Guardian Corps." The English was fluent, with only a trace of accent. "Sit down." He lowered himself to a bench. "I am only here to talk to you."

Hollister grimaced. "How about some lunch?" he complained. "I haven't eaten for"—he paused a second—"thirteen hours, twenty-eight minutes."

His precision didn't get by Karsov, but the officer ignored it for the time being. "Presently," he said. "There isn't much time to lose, you know. The last ferry leaves in forty hours, and we have to find out before then if you are acceptable or must go back on it."

"Hell of a way to treat a guest," grumbled Hollister.

"We did not ask you to come," said Karsov coldly. "If you wish to stay on Venus, you had better conform to the regulations. Now, what do you think qualifies you?"

"To live here? I'm an engineer. Construction experience in the Amazon basin and on Luna. I've got papers to prove it, and letters of recommendation, if you'd let me get at my baggage."

"Eventually. What is your reason for emigrating?"

Hollister looked sullen. "I didn't like Earth."

"Be more specific. You are going to be narcoquizzed later, and the whole truth will come out. These questions are just to guide the interrogators, and the better you answer me now the quicker and easier the quiz will be for all of us."

Hollister bristled. "That's an invasion of privacy."

"Venus isn't Earth," said Karsov with an attempt at patience. "Before you were even allowed to land, you signed a waiver which puts you completely under our jurisdiction as long as you are on this planet. I could kill you, and the U.N. would not have a word to say. But we do need skilled men, and I would rather okay you for citizenship. Do not make it too hard for me."

"All right." Hollister shrugged heavy shoulders. "I got in a fight with a man. He died. I covered up the traces pretty well, but I could never be sure—sooner or later the police might get on to the truth, and I don't like the idea of corrective treatment. So I figured I'd better blow out whilst I was still unsuspected."

"Venus is no place for the rugged individualist, Hollister. Men have to work together, and be very tolerant of each other, if they are to survive at all."

"Yes, I know. This was a special case. The man had it coming." Hollister's face twisted. "I have a daughter— Never mind. I'd rather tell it under narco than consciously. But I just couldn't see letting a snake like that get 'corrected' and then walk around free again." Defensively: "I've always been a rough sort, I suppose, but you've got to admit this was extreme provocation."

"That is all right," said Karsov, "if you are telling the truth. But if you have family ties back on Earth, it might lessen your usefulness here."

"None," said Hollister bitterly. "Not anymore."

The interview went on. Karsov extracted the facts skillfully: Hollister, Simon James; born Frisco Unit, U.S.A., of good stock; chronological age, thirty-eight Earth-years; physiological age, thanks to taking intelligent advantage of biomedics, about twenty-five; Second-class education, major in civil engineering with emphasis on nuclear-powered construction machines; work record; psych rating at last checkup; et cetera, et cetera, et cetera. Somewhere a recorder took sound and visual impressions of every nuance for later analysis and filing.

At the end, the Guardian rose and stretched. "I think you will do," he said. "Come along now for the narcoquiz. It will take about three hours, and you will need another hour to recover, and then I will see that you get something to eat."

The city crouched on a mountainside in a blast of eternal wind. Overhead rolled the poisonous gray clouds; sometimes a sleet of paraformaldehyde hid the grim red slopes around, and always the scudding dust veiled men's eyes so they could not see the alkali desert below. Fantastically storm-gnawed crags loomed over the city, and often there was the nearby rumble of an avalanche, but the ledge on which it stood had been carefully checked for stability.

The city was one armored unit of metal and concrete, low and rounded as if it hunched its back against the shrieking steady gale. From its shell protruded the stacks of hundreds of outsize Hilsch tubes, swivel-mounted so that they always faced into the wind. It blew past filters which caught the flying dust and sand and tossed them down a series of chutes to the cement factory. The tubes grabbed the rushing air and separated fast and slow molecules; the cooler part went into a refrigeration system which kept the city at a temperature men could stand—outside, it hovered around the boiling point of water; the smaller volume of superheated air was conducted to the maintenance plant where it helped run the city's pumps and generators. There were also nearly a thousand windmills, turning furiously and drinking the force of the storm.

None of this air was for breathing. It was thick with carbon dioxide; the rest was nitrogen, inert gases, formaldehyde vapor, a little methane and ammonia. The city devoted many hectares of space to hydroponic plants which renewed its oxygen and supplied some of the food, as well as to chemical purifiers, pumps and blowers. "Free as air" was a joke on Venus.

Near the shell was the spaceport where ferries from the satellite station and the big interplanetary ships landed. Pilots had to be good to bring down a vessel, or even take one up, under such conditions as prevailed here. Except for the landing cradles, the radio mast and the GCA shack in the main shell, everything was underground, as most of the city was.

Some twenty thousand colonists lived there. They were miners, engineers, laborers, technicians in the food and maintenance centers. There were three doctors, a scattering of teachers and librarians and similar personnel, a handful of police and administrators. Exactly fifteen people were employed in brewing, distilling, tavern-running, movie operation, and the other nonessential occupations which men required as they did food and air.

This was New America, chief city of Venus in 2051 A.D.

Hollister didn't enjoy his meal. He got it, cafeteria style, in one of the big plain mess halls, after a temporary ration book had been issued him. It consisted of a few vegetables, a lot of potato, a piece of the soggy yeast synthetic which was the closest to meat Venus offered—all liberally loaded with a tasteless basic food concentrate—a vitamin capsule, and a glass of flavored water. When he took out one of his remaining cigarettes, a score of eyes watched it hungrily. Not much tobacco here either. He inhaled savagely, feeling the obscure guilt of the have confronted with the have-not.

There were a number of people in the room with him, eating their own rations. Men and women were represented about equally. All wore coveralls of the standard shorts, and most looked young, but hard too, somehow—even the women. Hollister was used to female engineers and technicians at home, but here *everybody* worked.

For the time being, he stuck to his Earthside garments.

He sat alone at one end of a long table, wondering why nobody talked to him. You'd think they would be starved for a new face and word from Earth. Prejudice? Yes, a little of that, considering the political situation; but Hollister thought something more was involved.

Fear. They were all afraid of something.

When Karsov strolled in, the multilingual hum of conversation died, and Hollister guessed shrewdly at the fear. The Guardian made his way directly to the Earthling's place. He had a blocky, bearded man with a round smiling face in tow.

"Simon Hollister . . . Heinrich Gebhardt," the policeman introduced them. They shook hands, sizing each other up. Karsov sat down. "Get me the usual," he said, handing over his ration book.

Gebhardt nodded and went over to the automat. It scanned the books and punched them when he had dialed his orders. Then it gave him two trays, which he carried back.

Karsov didn't bother to thank him. "I have been looking for you," he told Hollister. "Where have you been?"

"Just wandering around," said the Earthling cautiously. Inside, he felt muscles tightening, and his mind seemed to tilt forward, as if sliding off the hypnotically imposed pseudopersonality which had been meant as camouflage in the narcoquiz. "It's quite a labyrinth here."

"You should have stayed in the barracks," said Karsov. There was no expression in his smooth-boned face; there never seemed to be. "Oh, well, I wanted to say you have been found acceptable."

"Good," said Hollister, striving for imperturbability.

"I will administer the oath after lunch," said Karsov. "Then you will be a full citizen of the Venusian Federation. We do not hold with formalities, you see—no time." He reached into a pocket and got out a booklet which he gave to Hollister. "But I advise you to study this carefully. It is a résumé of the most important laws, insofar as they differ from Earth's. Punishment for infraction is severe."

Gebhardt looked apologetic. "It has to be," he added. His bass voice had a slight blur and hiss of German accent, but he was good at the English which was becoming the common language of Venus. "This planet vas made in hell. If ve do not all work together, ve all die."

"And then, of course, there is the trouble with Earth," said Karsov. His narrow eyes studied Hollister for a long moment. "Just how do people back there feel about our declaration of independence?"

"Well—" Hollister paused. Best to tell the unvarnished truth, he decided. "Some resentment, of course. After all the money we . . . they . . . put into developing the colonies—"

"And all the resources they took out," said Gebhardt. "Men vere planted on Venus back in the last century to mine fissionables, vich vere getting short efen then. The colonies vere made self-supporting because that vas cheaper than hauling supplies for them, vich vould haff been an impossible task anyvay. Some of the colonies vere penal, some vere manned by arbitrarily assigned personnel; the so-called democracies often relied on broken men, who could not find vork at home or who had been displaced by var. No, ve owe them notting."

Hollister shrugged. "I'm not arguing. But people do wonder why, if you wanted national status, you didn't at least stay with the U.N. That's what Mars is doing."

"Because we are . . . necessarily . . . developing a whole new civilization here, something altogether remote from anything Earth has ever seen," snapped Karsov. "We will still trade our fissionables for things we need, until the day we can make everything here ourselves, but we want as little to do with Earth as possible. Never mind, you will understand in time."

Hollister's mouth lifted in a crooked grin. There hadn't been much Earth could do about it; in the present stage of astronautics, a military expedition to suppress the nationalists would cost more than anyone could hope to gain even from the crudest imperialism. Also, as long as no clear danger was known to exist, it wouldn't have sat well with a planet sick of war; the dissension produced might well have torn the young world government, which still had only limited powers, apart.

But astronautics was going to progress, he thought grimly. Spaceships wouldn't have to improve much to carry, cheaply, loads of soldiers in cold sleep, ready to land when thermonuclear bombardment from the skies had smashed a world's civilization. And however peaceful Earth might be, she was still a shining temptation to the rest of the System, and it looked very much as if something was brewing here on Venus which could become ugly before the century was past.

Well—

"Your first assignment is already arranged," said Karsov. Hollister jerked out of his reverie and tried to keep his fists unclenched. "Gebhardt will be your boss. If you do well, you can look for speedy promotion. Meanwhile"— he flipped a voucher across—"here is the equivalent of the dollars you had along, in our currency."

Hollister stuck the sheet in his pouch. It was highway robbery, he knew, but he was in no position to complain and the Venusian government wanted the foreign exchange. And he could only buy trifles with it anyway; the essentials were issued without payment, the size of the ration depending on rank. Incentive bonuses were money, though, permitting you to amuse your-self but not to consume more of the scarce food or textiles or living space.

He reflected that the communist countries before World War Three had never gone this far. Here, everything was government property. The system didn't call itself communism, naturally, but it was, and probably there was no choice. Private enterprise demanded a fairly large economic surplus, which simply did not exist on Venus.

Well, it wasn't his business to criticize their internal arrangements. He had never been among the few fanatics left on Earth who still made a god of a particular economic setup.

Gebhardt cleared his throat. "I am in charge of the atmosphere detail in this district," he said. "I am here on leafe, and vill be going back later today. Very glad to haff you, Hollister, ve are alvays short of men. Ve lost two in the last rock storm."

"Cheerful news," said the Earthman. His face resumed its hard wooden-ness. "Well, I didn't think Venus was going to be any bed of roses."

"It vill be," said Gebhardt. Dedication glowed on the hairy face. "Someday it vill be."

II

The oath was pretty drastic: in effect, Hollister put himself completely at the mercy of the Technic Board, which for all practical purposes was the city government. Each colony, he gathered, had such a body, and there was a federal board in this town which decided policy for the entire planet.

Anyone who wished to enter the government had to pass a series of rigid tests, after which there were years of apprenticeship and study, gradual promotion on the recommendation of seniors. The study was an exhausting course of history, psychotechnics, and physical science: in principle, thought Hollister, remembering some of the blubberheads who still got themselves elected at home, a good idea. The governing boards combined legislative, executive, and judicial functions, and totaled only a couple of thousand people for the whole world. It didn't seem like much for a nation of nearly two million, and the minimal paperwork surprised him—he had expected an omnipresent bureaucracy.

But of course they had the machines to serve them, recording everything in electronic files whose computers could find and correlate any data and were always checking up. And he was told pridefully that the schools were inculcating the rising generation with a tight ethic of obedience.

Hollister had supper, and returned to the Casual barracks to sleep. There were only a few men in there with him, most of them here on business from some other town. He was awakened by the alarm, whose photocells singled him out and shot forth a supersonic beam; it was a carrier wave for the harsh ringing in his head which brought him to his feet.

Gebhardt met him at an agreed-on locker room. There was a wiry, tough-looking Mongoloid with him who was introduced as Henry Yamashita. "Stow your fancy clothes, boy," boomed the chief, "and get on some TBI's." He handed over a drab, close-fitting coverall.

Hollister checked his own garments and donned the new suit wordlessly. After that there was a heavy plasticord outfit which, with boots and gloves, decked his whole body. Yamashita helped him strap on the oxygen bottles and plug in the Hilsch cooler. The helmet came last, its shoulderpiece buckled to the airsuit, but all of them kept theirs hinged back to leave their heads free.

"If somet'ing happens to our tank," said Gebhardt, "you slap that helmet down fast. Or maybe you like being embalmed. Haw!" His cheerfulness was more evident when Karsov wasn't around.

Hollister checked the valves with the caution taught him on Luna—his engineering experience was not faked. Gebhardt grunted approvingly. Then they slipped on the packs containing toilet kits, change of clothes, and emergency rations; clipped ropes, batteries, and canteens to their belts—the latter with the standard sucker tubes by which a man could drink directly even in his suit; and clumped out of the room.

●

A descending ramp brought them to a garage where the tanks were stored. These looked not unlike the sandcats of Mars, but were built lower and heavier, with a refrigerating tube above and a grapple in the nose. A mechanic gestured at one dragging a covered steel wagon full of supplies, and the three men squeezed into the tiny transparent cab.

Gebhardt gunned the engine, nodding as it roared. "Okay," he said. "On ve go."

"What's the power source?" asked Hollister above the racket.

"Alcohol," answered Yamashita. "We get it from the formaldehyde. Bottled oxygen. A compressor and cooling system to keep the oxy tanks from blowing up on us—not that they don't once in a while. Some of the newer models use a peroxide system."

"And I suppose you save the water vapor and CO_2 to get the oxygen back," ventured Hollister.

"Just the water. There's always plenty of carbon dioxide." Yamashita looked out, and his face set in tight lines.

The tank waddled through the great air lock and up a long tunnel toward the surface. When they emerged, the wind was like a blow in the face. Hollister felt the machine shudder, and the demon howl drowned out the engine. He accepted the earplugs Yamashita handed him with a grateful smile.

There was dust and sand scudding by them, making it hard to see the mountainside down which they crawled. Hollister caught glimpses of naked fanglike peaks, raw slashes of ocher and blue where minerals veined the land, the steady march of dunes across the lower ledges. Overhead, the sky was an unholy tide of ragged, flying clouds, black and gray and sulfurous yellow. He could not see the sun, but the light around him was a weird hard brass color, like the light on Earth just before a thunderstorm.

The wind hooted and screamed, banging on the tank walls, yelling and rattling and groaning. Now and then a dull quiver ran through the land and trembled in Hollister's bones, somewhere an avalanche was ripping out a mountain's flanks. Briefly, a veil of dust fell so thick around them that they were blind, grinding through an elemental night with hell and the furies loose outside. The control board's lights were wan on Gebhardt's intent face, most of the time he was steering by instruments.

Once the tank lurched into a gully. Hollister, watching the pilot's lips, thought he muttered: "Damn! That wasn't here before!" He extended the grapple, clutching rock and pulling the tank and its load upward.

Yamashita clipped two small disks to his larynx and gestured at the same equipment hanging on Hollister's suit. His voice came thin but fairly clear: "Put on your talkie unit if you want to say anything." Hollister obeyed, guessing that the earplugs had a transistor arrangement powered by a piece of radioactive isotope which reproduced the vibrations in the throat. It took concentration to understand the language as they distorted it, but he supposed he'd catch on fast enough.

"How many hours till nightfall?" he asked.

"About twenty." Yamashita pointed to the clock on the board, it was calibrated to Venus' seventy-two-hour day. "It's around one hundred thirty kilometers to the camp, so we should just about make it by sunset."

"That isn't very fast," said Hollister. "Why not fly, or at least build roads?"

"The aircraft are all needed for speed travel and impassable terrain, and the roads will come later," said Yamashita. "These tanks can go it all right— most of the time."

"But why have the camp so far from the city?"

"It's the best location from a supply standpoint. We get most of our food from Little Moscow, and water from Hellfire, and chemicals from New America and Roger's Landing. The cities more or less specialize, you know. They have to: there isn't enough iron ore and whatnot handy to any one spot to build a city big enough to do everything by itself. So the air camps are set up at points which minimize the total distance over which supplies have to be hauled."

"You mean action distance, don't you? The product of the energy and time required for hauling."

Yamashita nodded, with a new respect in his eyes. "You'll do," he said.

The wind roared about them. It was more than just the slow rotation of the planet and its nearness to the sun which created such an incessant storm; if that had been all, there would never have been any chance of making it habitable. It was the high carbon dioxide content of the air, and its greenhouse effect; and in the long night, naked arid rock cooled off considerably. With plenty of water and vegetation, and an atmosphere similar to Earth's, Venus would have a warm but rather gentle climate on the whole, the hurricanes moderated to trade winds; indeed, with the lower Coriolis force, the destructive cyclones of Earth would be unknown.

Such, at least, was the dream of the Venusians. But looking out, Hollister realized that a fraction of the time and effort they were expending would have made the Sahara desert bloom. They had been sent here once as miners, but there was no longer any compulsion on them to stay; if they asked to come back to Earth, their appeal could not be denied however expensive it would be to ship them all home.

Then why didn't they?

Well, why go back to a rotten civilization like— Hollister caught himself. Sometimes his pseudomemories were real enough in him and drown out the genuine ones, rage and grief could nearly overwhelm him till he recalled that the sorrow was for people who had never existed. The anger had had to be planted deep, to get by a narcoquiz, but he wondered if it might not interfere with his mission, come the day.

He grinned sardonically at himself. One man, caught on a planet at the gates of the Inferno, watched by a powerful and ruthless government embracing that entire world, and he was setting himself against it.

Most likely he would die here, and the economical Venusians would process his body for its chemicals as they did other corpses, and that would be the end of it as far as he was concerned.

Well, he quoted to himself, *a man might try.*

⬤

Gebhardt's camp was a small shell, a radio mast, and a shed sticking out of a rolling landscape of rock and sand; the rest was underground. The sun was down on a ragged horizon, dimly visible as a huge blood-red disk, when he arrived. Yamashita and Hollister had taken their turns piloting; the Earthman found it exhausting work, and his head rang with the noise when he finally stepped out into the subterranean garage.

Yamashita led him to the barracks. "We're about fifty here," he explained. "All men." He grinned. "That makes a system of minor rewards and punishments based on leaves to a city *very* effective."

The barracks was a long room with triple rows of bunks and a few tables and chairs; only Gebhardt rated a chamber of his own, though curtains on the bunks did permit some privacy. An effort had been made to brighten the place up with murals, some of which weren't bad at all, and the men sat about reading, writing letters, talking, playing games. They were the usual conglomerate of races and nationalities, with some interesting half-breeds; hard work and a parsimonious diet had made them smaller than the average American or European, but they looked healthy enough.

"Simon Hollister, our new sub-engineer," called Yamashita as they entered. "Just got in from Earth. Now you know as much as I do." He flopped onto a bunk while the others drifted over. "Go ahead. Tell all. Birth, education, hobbies, religion, sex life, interests, prejudices—they'll find it out anyway, and God knows we could use a little variety around here."

A stocky blond man paused suspiciously. "From Earth?" he asked slowly. "We've had no new people from Earth for thirty years. What did you want to come here for?"

"I felt like it," snapped Hollister. "That's enough!"

"So, a jetheading snob, huh? We're too good for you, I guess."

"Take it easy, Sam," said someone else.

"Yeah," a Negro grinned, "he might be bossin' you, you know."

"That's just it," said the blond man. "I was born here. I've been studying, and I've been on air detail for twenty years, and this bull walks right in and takes my promotion the first day."

Part of Hollister checked off the fact that the Venusians used the terms "year" and "day" to mean those periods for their own world, one shorter and one longer than Earth's. The rest of him tightened up for trouble, but others intervened. He found a vacant bunk and sat down on it, swinging his legs and trying to make friendly conversation. It wasn't easy. He felt terribly alone.

Presently someone got out a steel and plastic guitar and strummed it, and soon they were all singing. Hollister listened with half an ear.

> "When the Big Rain comes, all the air will be good,
>   and the rivers all flow with beer,
>   with the cigarettes bloomin' by the beefsteak bush,
>   and the ice-cream-bergs right here.
> When the Big Rain comes, we will all be a-swillin'
>   of champagne, while the violin tree
>   plays love songs because all the gals will be willin',
>   and we'll all have a Big Rain spree!"

Paradise, he thought. *They can joke about it, but it's still the Paradise they work for and know they'll never see. Then why do they work for it? What is it that's driving them?*

◆

After a meal, a sleep, and another meal, Hollister was given a set of blueprints to study. He bent his mind to the task, using all the powers which an arduous training had given it, and in a few hours reported to Gebhardt. "I know them," he said.

"Already?" The chief's small eyes narrowed. "It iss not vort vile trying to bluff here, boy. Venus alvays callss it."

"I'm not bluffing," said Hollister angrily. "If you want me to lounge around for another day, okay, but I know those specs by heart."

The bearded man stood up. There was muscle under his plumpness. "Okay, by damn," he said. "You go out vit me next trip."

That was only a few hours off. Gebhardt took a third man, a quiet grizzled fellow they called Johnny, and let Hollister drive. The tank hauled the usual wagonload of equipment, and the rough ground made piloting a harsh task. Hollister had used multiple transmissions before, and while the navigating instruments were complicated, he caught on to them quickly enough; it was the strain and muscular effort that wore him out.

Venus' night was not the pitchy gloom one might have expected. The clouds diffused sunlight around the planet, and there was also a steady flicker of aurora even in these middle latitudes. The headlamps were needed only when they went into a deep ravine. Wind growled around them, but Hollister was getting used to that.

The first airmaker on their tour was only a dozen kilometers from the camp. It was a dark, crouching bulk on a stony ridge, its intake funnel like the rearing neck of some archaic monster. They pulled up beside it, slapped down their helmets, and went one by one through the air lock. It was a standard midget type, barely large enough to hold one man, which meant little air to be pumped out and hence greater speed in getting through. Gebhardt had told Hollister to face the exit leeward; now the three roped themselves together and stepped around the tank, out of its shelter.

Hollister lost his footing, crashed to the ground, and went spinning away in the gale. Gebhardt and Johnny dug their cleated heels in and brought the rope up short. When they had the new man back on his feet, Hollister saw them grinning behind their faceplates. Thereafter he paid attention to his balance, leaning against the wind.

Inspection and servicing of the unit was a slow task, and it was hard to see the finer parts even in the headlights' glare. One by one, the various sections were uncovered and checked, adjustments made, full gas bottles removed and empty ones substituted.

It was no wonder Gebhardt had doubted Hollister's claim. The airmaker was one of the most complicated machines in existence. A thing meant to transform the atmosphere of a planet had to be.

The intake scooped up the wind and drove it, with the help of wind-powered compressors, through a series of chambers; some of them held catalysts, some electric arcs or heating coils maintaining temperature—the continuous storm ran a good-sized generator—and some led back into others in a maze of interconnections. The actual chemistry was simple enough. Paraformaldehyde was broken down and yielded its binding water molecules; the formaldehyde, together with that taken directly from the air, reacted with ammonia and methane—or with itself—to produce a whole series of hydrocarbons, carbohydrates, and more complex compounds for food, fuel and fertilizer; such carbon dioxide as did not enter other reactions was broken down by sheer brute force in an arc to oxygen and soot. The oxygen was bottled for industrial use; the remaining substances were partly separated by distillation—again using wind power, this time to refrigerate—and collected. Further processing would take place at the appropriate cities.

Huge as the unit loomed, it seemed pathetically small when you thought of the fantastic tonnage which was the total planetary atmosphere. But more of its kind were being built every day and scattered around the surface of the world; over a million already existed, seven million was the goal, and that number should theoretically be able to do the job in another twenty Earth-years.

➡

That was theory, as Gebhardt explained over the helmet radio. Other considerations entered, such as the law of diminishing returns; as the effect of the machines became noticeable, the percentage of the air they could deal with would necessarily drop; then there was stratospheric gas, some of which apparently never got down to the surface; and the chemistry of a changing atmosphere had to be taken into account. The basic time estimate for this work had to be revised upward another decade.

There was oxygen everywhere, locked into rocks and ores, enough for the needs of man if it could be gotten out. Specially mutated bacteria were doing that job, living off carbon and silicon, releasing more gas than their own metabolisms took up; their basic energy source was the sun. Some of the oxygen recombined, of course, but not enough to matter, especially since it could only act on or near the surface and most of the bacterial gnawing went on far down. Already there was a barely detectable percentage of the element in the atmosphere. By the time the airmakers were finished, the bacteria would also be.

Meanwhile giant pulverizers were reducing barren stone and sand to fine particles which would be mixed with fertilizers to yield soil; and the genetic engineers were evolving still other strains of life which could provide a balanced ecology; and the water units were under construction.

These would be the key to the whole operation. There was plenty of water on Venus, trapped down in the body of the planet, and the volcanoes brought it up as they had done long ago on Earth. Here it was quickly snatched by the polymerizing formaldehyde, except in spots like Hellfire where machinery had been built to extract it from magma and hydrated minerals. But there was less formaldehyde in the air every day.

At the right time, hydrogen bombs were to be touched off in places the geologists had already selected, and the volcanoes would all wake up. They would spume forth plenty of carbon dioxide—though by that time the amount of the free gas would be so low that this would be welcomed—but there would be water too, unthinkable tons of water. And simultaneously aircraft would be sowing platinum catalyst in the skies, and with its help Venus' own lightning would attack the remaining poisons in the air. They would come down as carbohydrates and other compounds, washed out by the rain and leached from the sterile ground.

That would be the Big Rain. It would last an estimated ten Earth-years, and at the end there would be rivers and lakes and seas on a planet which had never known them. And the soil would be spread, the bacteria and plants and small animal life released. Venus would still be mostly desert, the rains would slacken off but remain heavy for centuries, but men could walk unclothed on this world and they could piece by piece make the desert green.

A hundred years after the airmen had finished their work, the reclaimed sections might be close to Earth conditions. In five hundred years, all of Venus might be Paradise.

To Hollister it seemed like a long time to wait.

III

He didn't need many days to catch on to the operations and be made boss of a construction gang. Then he took out twenty men and a train of supplies and machinery, to erect still another airmaker.

It was blowing hard then, too hard to set up the seat-tents which ordinarily provided a measure of comfort. Men rested in the tanks, side by side, dozing uneasily and smelling each other's sweat. They griped loudly, but endured. It was a lengthy trip to their site; eventually the whole camp was to be broken up and reestablished in a better location, but meanwhile they had to accept the monotony of travel.

Hollister noticed that his men had evolved an Asian ability just to sit, without thinking, hour after hour. Their conversation and humor also suggested Asia: acrid, often brutal, though maintaining a careful surface politeness most of the time. It was probably more characteristic of this particular job than of the whole planet, though, and maybe they sloughed it off again when their hitches on air detail had expired and they got more congenial assignments.

As boss, he had the privilege of sharing his tank with only one man; he chose the wizened Johnny, whom he rather liked. Steering through a yelling sandstorm, he was now able to carry on a conversation—and it was about time, he reflected, that he got on with his real job.

"Ever thought of going back to Earth?" he asked casually.

"Back?" Johnny looked surprised. "I was born here."

"Well . . . going to Earth, then."

"What'd I use for passage money?"

"Distress clause of the Space Navigation Act. They'd have to give you a berth if you applied. Not that you couldn't repay your passage, with interest, in a while. With your experience here, you could get a fine post in one of the reclamation projects on Earth."

"Look," said Johnny in a flustered voice, "I'm a good Venusian. I'm needed here and I know it."

"Forget the Guardians," snapped Hollister, irritated. "I'm not going to report you. Why you people put up with a secret police anyway, is more than I can understand."

"You've got to keep people in line," said Johnny. "We all got to work together to make a go of it."

"But haven't you ever thought it'd be nice to decide your own future and not have somebody to tell you what to do next?"

"It ain't just 'somebody.' It's the Board. They know how you and me fit in best. Sure, I suppose there are subversives, but I'm not one of them."

"Why don't the malcontents just run away, if they don't dare apply for passage to Earth? They could steal materials and make their own village. Venus is a big place."

"It ain't that easy. And supposin' they could and did, what'd they do then? Just sit and wait for the Big Rain? We don't want any freeloaders on Venus, mister."

Hollister shrugged. There was something about the psychology that baffled him. "I'm not preaching revolution," he said carefully. "I came here of my own free will, remember, I'm just trying to understand the setup."

Johnny's faded eyes were shrewd on him. "You've always had it easy compared to us, I guess. It may look hard to you here. But remember, we ain't never had it different, except that things are gettin' better little by little. The food ration gets upped every so often, and we're allowed a dress suit now as well as utility clothes, and before long there's goin' to be broadcast shows to the outposts—and someday the Big Rain is comin'. Then we can all afford to take it free and easy." He paused. "That's why we broke with Earth. Why should we slave our guts out to make a good life for our grandchildren, if a bunch of freeloaders are gonna come from Earth and fill up the planet then? It's *ours*. It's gonna be the richest planet men ever saw, and it belongs to us what developed it."

Official propaganda line, thought Hollister. It sounded plausible enough till you stopped to analyze. For one thing, each country still had the right to set its own immigration policies. Furthermore, at the rate Earth was progressing, with reclamation, population control, and new resources from the oceans, by the time Venus was ripe there wouldn't be any motive to leave home—an emigration which would be too long and expensive anyway. For their own reasons, which he still had to discover, the rulers of Venus had not mentioned all the facts and had instead built up a paranoid attitude in their people.

☞

The new airmaker site was the top of a ridge thrusting from a boulder-strewn plain. An eerie coppercolored light seemed to tinge the horizon with blood. A pair of bulldozers had already gone ahead and scooped out a walled hollow in which seal-tents could be erected; Hollister's gang swarmed from the tanks and got at that job. Then the real work began—blasting and carving a foundation, sinking piers, assembling the unit on top.

On the fourth day the rock storm came. It had dawned with an angry glow like sulfur, and as it progressed the wind strengthened and a dirty rack of clouds whipped low overhead. On the third shift, the gale was strong enough to lean against, and the sheet steel which made the unit's armor fought the men as if it lived.

The blond man, Sam Robbins, who had never liked Hollister, made his way up to the chief. His voice came over the helmet radio, dim beneath static and the drumming wind: "I don't like this. Better we take cover fast."

Hollister was not unwilling, but the delicate arc electrodes were being set up and he couldn't take them down again; nor could he leave them unprotected to the scouring drift of sand. "As soon as we get the shielding up," he said.

"I tell you, there's no time to shield 'em!"

"Yes, there is." Hollister turned his back. Robbins snarled something and returned to his labor.

A black wall, rust-red on the edges, was lifting to the east, the heaviest sandstorm Hollister had yet seen. He hunched his shoulders and struggled through the sleetlike dust to the unit. Turning up his radio: "Everybody come help on this. The sooner it gets done, the sooner we can quit."

The helmeted figures swarmed around him, battling the thunderously flapping metal sheets, holding them down by main force while they were welded to the frame. Hollister saw lightning livid across the sky. Once a bolt flamed at the rod which protected the site. Thunder rolled and banged after it.

The wind slapped at them, and a sheet tore loose and went sailing down the hill. It struck a crag and wrapped itself around. "Robbins, Lewis, go get that!" cried Hollister, and returned attention to the piece he was clutching. An end ripped loose from his hands and tried to slash his suit.

The wind was so deafening that he couldn't hear it rise still higher, and in the murk of sand whirling about him he was nearly blind. But he caught the first glimpse of gale-borne gravel whipping past, and heard the terror in his earphones: "Rock storm!"

The voice shut up; orders were strict that the channel be kept clear. But the gasping men labored still more frantically, while struck metal rang and boomed.

Hollister peered through the darkness. "That's enough!" he decided. "Take cover!"

Nobody dropped his tools, but they all turned fast and groped down toward the camp. The way led past the crag, where Robbins and Lewis had just quit wrestling with the stubborn plate.

Hollister didn't see Lewis killed, but he did see him die. Suddenly his airsuit was flayed open, and there was a spurt of blood, and he toppled. The wind took his body, rolling it out of sight in the dust. A *piece of rock*, thought Hollister wildly. *It tore his suit, and he's already embalmed—*

The storm hooted and squealed about him as he climbed the sand wall. Even the blown dust was audible, hissing against his helmet. He fumbled through utter blackness, fell over the top and into the comparative shelter of the camp ground. On hands and knees, he crawled toward the biggest of the self-sealing tents.

There was no time for niceties. They sacrificed the atmosphere within, letting the air lock stand open while they pushed inside. Had everybody made it to some tent or other? Hollister wasn't sure, but sand was coming in, filling the shelter. He went over and closed the lock. Somebody else started the pump, using bottled nitrogen to maintain air pressure and flush out the poisons. It seemed like a long time before the oxygen containers could be opened.

Hollister took off his helmet and looked around. The tent was half filled by seven white-faced men standing in the dust. The single fluorotube threw a cold light on their sweating bodies and barred the place with shadows. Outside, the wind bellowed.

"Might as well be comfortable," said Johnny in a small voice, and began shucking his airsuit. "If the tent goes, we're all done for anyhow." He sat down on the ground and checked his equipment methodically. Then he took a curved stone and spat on it and began scouring his faceplate to remove the accumulated scratches in its hard plastic. One by one the others imitated him.

"You there!"

Hollister looked up from his own suit. Sam Robbins stood before him. The man's eyes were red and his mouth worked.

"You killed Jim Lewis."

There was murder here. Hollister raised himself till he looked down at the Venusian. "I'm sorry he's dead," he replied, trying for quietness. "He was a good man. But these things will happen."

Robbins shuddered. "You sent him down there where the gravel got him. I was there, too. Was it meant for me?"

"Nobody could tell where that chunk was going to hit," said Hollister mildly. "I could just as easily have been killed."

"I *told* you to quit half an hour before the things started."

"We couldn't quit then without ruining all our work. Sit down, Robbins. You're overtired and scared."

The men were very still sitting and watching in the thick damp heat of the tent. Thunder crashed outside.

"You rotten Earthling—" Robbins' fist lashed out. It caught Hollister on the cheekbone and he stumbled back, shaking a dazed head. Robbins advanced grinning.

Hollister felt a cold viciousness of rage. It was his pseudopersonality he realized dimly but no time to think of that now. As Robbins closed in, he crouched and punched for the stomach.

Hard muscle met him. Robbins clipped him on the jaw. Hollister tried an uppercut, but it was skillfully blocked. This man knew how to fight.

Hollister gave him another fusillade in the belly. Robbins grunted and rabbit-punched. Hollister caught it on his shoulder, reached up, grabbed an arm, and whirled his enemy over his head. Robbins hit a bunkframe that buckled under him.

He came back, dizzy but game. Hollister was well trained in combat. But it took him a good ten minutes to stretch his man bleeding on the ground.

Panting, he looked about him. There was no expression on the faces that ringed him in. "Anybody else?" he asked hoarsely.

"No, boss," said Johnny. "You're right, o' course. I don't think nobody else here wants twenty lashes back at base."

"Who said—" Hollister straightened, blinking. "Lashes?"

"Why, sure. This was mutiny, you know. It's gotta be punished."

Hollister shook his head. "Too barbaric. Correction—"

"Look, boss," said Johnny, "you're a good engineer but you don't seem to understand much about Venus yet. We ain't got the time or the manpower or the materials to spend on them there corrective jails. A bull what don't keep his nose clean gets the whip or the sweatbox, and then back to the job. The really hard cases go to the uranium mines at Lucifer." He shivered, even in the dense heat.

Hollister frowned. "Not a bad system," he said, to stay in character. "But I think Robbins here has had enough. I'm not going to report him if he behaves himself from now on, and I'll trust the rest of you to cooperate."

They mumbled assent. He wasn't sure whether they respected him for it or not, but the boss was boss. Privately, he suspected that the Boards must frame a lot of men, or at least sentence them arbitrarily for minor crimes, to keep the mines going; there didn't seem to be enough rebellion in the Venusian character to supply them otherwise.

Chalk up another point for the government. The score to settle was getting rather big.

IV

Time was hard to estimate on Venus; it wasn't only that they had their own calendar here, but one day was so much like another. Insensibly and despite himself, Hollister began sliding into the intellectual lethargy of the camp. He had read the few books—and with his trained memory, he could only read a book once—and he knew every man there inside out, and he had no family in one of the cities to write to and think about. The job itself presented a daily challenge, no two situations were ever quite the same and occasionally he came near death, but outside of it there was a tendency to stagnate.

The other two engineers, Gebhardt and Yamashita, were pleasant company. The first was from Hörselberg, which had been a German settlement and still retained some character of its own, and he had interesting stories to tell of it; the second, though of old Venus-American stock, was mentally agile for a colonist, had read more than most and had a lively interest in the larger world of the Solar System. But even the stimulation they offered wore a little thin in six months or so.

The region spun through a "winter" that was hardly different from summer except in having longer nights, and the sterile spring returned, and the work went on. Hollister's time sense ticked off days with an accuracy falling within a few seconds, and he wondered how long he would be kept here and when he would get a chance to report to his home office. That would be in letters ostensibly to friends, which one of the spaceships would carry back; he knew censors would read them first, but his code was keyed to an obscure eighteenth-century book he was certain no one on Venus had ever heard of.

Already he knew more about this planet than anyone on Earth. It had always been too expensive to send correspondents here, and the last couple of U.N. representatives hadn't found much to tell. The secretiveness toward Earthmen might be an old habit, going back to the ultra-nationalistic days of the last century. Colony A and Colony B, of two countries which at home might not be on speaking terms, were not supposed to give aid and comfort to each other; but on Venus such artificial barriers had to go if anyone was to survive. Yamashita told with relish how prospectors from Little Moscow and Trollen had worked together and divided up their finds. But of course, you couldn't let your nominal rulers know—

Hollister was beginning to realize that the essential ethos of Venus was, indeed, different from anything which existed on Earth. It had to be, the landscape had made it so. Man was necessarily a more collective creature than at home. That helped explain the evolution of the peculiar governmental forms and the patience of the citizenry toward the most outrageous demands. Even the dullest laborer seemed to live in the future.

Our children and grandchildren will build the temples, read the books, write the music. Ours is only to lay the foundation.

And was that why they stuck here, instead of shipping back and turning the whole job over to automatic machinery and a few paid volunteers? They had been the lonely, the rejected, the dwellers in outer darkness, for a long time; now they could not let go of their fierce and angry pride, even when there was no more need for it. Hollister thought about Ireland. Man is not a logical animal.

Still, there were features of Venusian society that struck him as unnecessary and menacing. Something would have to be done about them, though as yet he wasn't sure what it would be.

He worked, and he gathered impressions and filed them away, and he waited. And at last the orders came through. This camp had served its purpose, it was to be broken up and replanted elsewhere, but first its personnel were to report to New America and get a furlough. Hollister swung almost gaily into the work of dismantling everything portable and loading it in the wagons. Maybe he finally was going to get somewhere.

He reported at the Air Control office with Gebhardt and Yamashita, to get his pay and quarters assignment. The official handed him a small card. "You've been raised to chief engineer's rank," he said. "You'll probably get a camp of your own next time."

Gebhardt pounded him on the back. "Ach, *sehr gut!* I recommended you, boy, you did fine, but I am going to miss you."

"Oh . . . we'll both be around for a while, won't we?" asked Hollister uncomfortably.

"Not I! I haff vife and kids, I hop the next rocket to Hörselberg."

Yamashita had his own family in town, and Hollister didn't want to intrude too much on them. He wandered off, feeling rather lonesome.

His new rating entitled him to private quarters, a tiny room with minimal furniture, though he still had to wash and eat publicly like everyone else except the very top. He sat down in it and began composing the planned letters.

There was a knock at the door. He fumbled briefly, being used to scanners at home and not used to doors on Venus, and finally said: "Come in."

A woman entered. She was young, quite good-looking, with a supple tread and spectacularly red hair. Cool green eyes swept up and down his height. "My name is Barbara Brandon," she said. "Administrative assistant in Air Control."

"Oh . . . hello." He offered her the chair. "You're here on business?"

Amusement tinged her impersonal voice. "In a way. I'm going to marry you."

Hollister's jaw did not drop, but it tried. "Come again?" he asked weakly.

She sat down. "It's simple enough. I'm thirty-seven years old, which is almost the maximum permissible age of celibacy except in special cases." With a brief, unexpectedly feminine touch: "That's Venus years, of course! I've seen you around, and looked at your record; good heredity there, I think. Pops okayed it genetically—that's Population Control—and the Guardians cleared it, too."

"Um-m-m . . . look here." Hollister wished there were room to pace. He settled for sitting on the table and swinging his legs. "Don't I get any say in the matter?"

"You can file any objections, of course, and probably they'd be heeded; but you'll have to have children by someone pretty soon. We need them. Frankly, I think a match between us would be ideal. You'll be out in the field so much that we won't get in each other's hair, and we'd probably get along well enough while we are together."

Hollister scowled. It wasn't the morality of it—much. He was a bachelor on Earth, secret service Un-men really had no business getting married; and in any case the law would wink at what he had done on Venus if he ever got home. But something about the whole approach annoyed him.

"I can't see where you need rules to make people breed," he said coldly. "They'll do that anyway. You don't realize what a struggle it is on Earth to bring the population back down toward a sensible figure."

"Things are different here," answered Barbara Brandon in a dry tone. "We're going to need plenty of people for a long time to come, and they have to be of the right stock. The congenitally handicapped can't produce enough to justify their own existence; there's been a program of euthanasia there, as you may know. But the new people are also needed in the right places. This town, for instance, can only accommodate so much population increase per year. We can't send surplus children off to a special crèche because there aren't enough teachers or doctors—or anything, so the mothers have to take care of all their own kids; or the fathers, if they happen to have a job in town and the mother is a field worker. The whole process has *got* to be regulated."

"Regulations!" Hollister threw up his hands. "Behold the bold frontiersman!"

The girl looked worried. "Careful what you say." She smiled at him with a touch of wistfulness. "It needn't be such a hindrance to you. Things are . . . pretty free except where the production of children is involved."

"I—this is kind of sudden." Hollister tried to smile back. "Don't think I don't appreciate the compliment. But I need time to think, adjust myself— Look, are you busy right now?"

"No, I'm off."

"All right. Put on your party clothes and we'll go out and have some drinks and talk the matter over."

She glanced shyly at the thin, colored coverall she wore. "These are my party clothes," she said.

Hollister's present rank let him visit another bar than the long, crowded room where plain laborers caroused. This one had private tables, decorations, music in the dim dusky air. It was quiet, the engineer aristocracy had their own code of manners. A few couples danced on a small floor.

He found an unoccupied table by the curving wall, sat down, and dialed for drinks and cigarettes. Neither were good enough to justify their fantastic cost but it had been a long time since he had enjoyed any luxuries at all. He felt more relaxed with them. The girl looked quite beautiful in the muted light.

"You were born here, weren't you, Barbara?" he asked after a while.

"Of course," she said. "You're the first immigrant in a long time. Used to be some deportees coming in every once in a while, but—"

"I know. 'Sentence suspended on condition you leave Earth.' That was before all countries had adopted the new penal code. Never mind. I was just wondering if you wouldn't like to see Earth—sometime."

"Maybe. But I'm needed here, not there. And I like it." There was a hint of defiance in the last remark.

He didn't press her. The luminous murals showed a soft unreal landscape of lakes and forests, artificial stars twinkled gently in the ceiling. "Is this what you expect Venus to become?" he asked.

"Something like this. Probably not the stars, it'll always be cloudy here but they'll be honest rain clouds. We should live to see the beginning of it."

"Barbara," he asked, "do you believe in God?"

"Why, no. Some of the men are priests and rabbis and whatnot in their spare time, but—no, not I. What about it?"

"You're wrong," he said. "Venus is your god. This is a religious movement you have here, with a slide rule in its hand."

"So—?" She seemed less assured, he had her off balance and the green eyes were wide and a little frightened.

"An Old Testament god," he pursued, "merciless, all-powerful, all-demanding. Get hold of a Bible if you can; and read Job and Ecclesiastes. You'll see what I mean. When is the New Testament coming . . . or even the prophet Micah?"

"You're a funny one," she said uncertainly. Frowning, trying to answer him on his own terms: "After the Big Rain, things will be easier. It'll be—" She struggled through vague memories. "It'll be the Promised Land."

"You've only got this one life," he said. "Is there any sound reason for spending it locked in these iron boxes, with death outside, when you could lie on a beach on Earth and everything you're fighting for is already there?"

She grabbed his hand where it lay on the table. Her fingers were cold, and she breathed fast. "No! Don't say such things! You're here too. You came here—"

Get thee behind me, Satan.

"Sorry." He lifted his glass. "Here's freefalling."

She clinked with him smiling shakily.

"There isn't any retirement on Venus, is there?" he asked.

"Not exactly. Old people get lighter work, of course. When you get too old to do anything . . . well, wouldn't you want euthanasia?"

He nodded, quite sincerely, though his exact meaning had gone by her. "I was just thinking of . . . shall we say us . . . rose-covered cottages, sunset of life. Darby and Joan stuff."

She smiled, and reached over to stroke his cheek lightly. "Thanks," she murmured. "Maybe there will be rose-covered cottages by the time we're that old."

➴

Hollister turned suddenly, aware with his peripheral senses of the man who approached. Or maybe it was the sudden choking off of low-voiced conversation in the bar. The man walked very softly up to their table and stood looking down on them. Then he pulled out the extra chair for himself.

"Hello, Karsov," said Hollister dully.

The Guardian nodded. There was a ghostly smile playing about his lips. "How are you?" he asked, with an air of not expecting a reply. "I am glad you did so well out there. Your chief recommended you very highly."

"Thanks," said Hollister, not hiding the chill in his voice. He didn't like the tension he could see in Barbara.

"I just happened by and thought you would like to know you will have a crew of your own next trip," said the policeman. "That is, the Air Control office has made a recommendation to me." He glanced archly at Barbara. "Did you by any chance have something to do with that, Miss Brandon? Could be!" Then his eyes fell to the cigarettes, and he regarded them pointedly till Barbara offered him one.

"Pardon me." Hollister held his temper with an effort and kept his voice urbane. "I'm still new here, lot of things I don't know. Why does your office have to pass on such a matter?"

"My office has to pass on everything," said Karsov.

"Seems like a purely technical business as long as my own record is clean."

Karsov shook his sleek head. "You do not understand. We cannot have someone in a responsible position who is not entirely trustworthy. It is more than a matter of abstaining from criminal acts. You have to be with us all the way. No reservations. That is what Psych Control and the Guardians exist for."

He blew smoke through his nose and went on in a casual tone: "I must say your attitude has not been entirely pleasing. You have made some remarks which could be . . . misconstrued. I am ready to allow for your not being used to Venusian conditions, but you know the law about sedition."

For a moment, Hollister savored the thought of Karsov's throat between his fingers. "I'm sorry," he said.

"Remember, there are recorders everywhere, and we make spot checks directly on people, too. You could be narcoquizzed again any time I ordered it. But I do not think that will be necessary just yet. A certain amount of grumbling is only natural, and if you have any genuine complaints you can file them with your local Technic Board."

Hollister weighed the factors in his mind. Karsov packed a gun, and— But too sudden a meekness could be no less suspicious. "I don't quite understand why you have to have a political police," he ventured. "It seems like an ordinary force should be enough. After all . . . where would an in-surrectionist go?"

He heard Barbara's tiny gasp, but Karsov merely looked patient. "There are many factors involved," said the Guardian. "For instance, some of the colonies were not quite happy with the idea of being incorporated into the Venusian Federation. They preferred to stay with their mother countries, or even to be independent. Some fighting ensued, and they must still be watched. Then, too, it is best to keep Venusian society healthy while it is new and vulnerable to subversive radical ideas. And finally, the Guardian Corps is the nucleus of our future army and space navy."

Hollister wondered if he should ask why Venus needed military forces, but decided against it. The answer would only be some stock phrase about terrestrial imperialists, if he got any answer at all. He'd gone about far enough already.

"I see," he said. "Thanks for telling me."

"Would you like a drink, sir?" asked Barbara timidly.

"No," said Karsov. "I only stopped in on my way elsewhere. Work, always work." He got up. "I think you are making a pretty good adjustment, Hol-lister. Just watch your tongue . . . and your mind. Oh, by the way. Under the circumstances, it would be as well if you did not write any letters home for a while. That could be misunderstood. You may use one of the standard messages. They are much cheaper, too." He nodded and left.

Hollister's eyes followed him out. *How much does he know?*

"Come on," said Barbara. There was a little catch in her voice. "Let's dance."

Gradually they relaxed, easing into the rhythm of the music. Hollister dismissed the problem of Karsov for the time being, and bent mind and senses to his companion. She was lithe and slim in his arms, and he felt the stirrings of an old hunger in him.

●

The next Venus day he called on Yamashita. They had a pleasant time together, and arranged a party for later; Hollister would bring Barbara. But as he was leaving, the Venusian drew him aside.

"Be careful, Si," he whispered. "They were here a few hours after I got back, asking me up and down about you. I had to tell the truth, they know how to ask questions and if I'd hesitated too much it would have been narco. I don't think you're in any trouble, but be careful!"

Barbara had arranged her vacation to coincide with his—efficient girl! They were together most of the time. It wasn't many days before they were married. That was rushing things, but Hollister would soon be back in the field for a long stretch and—well—they had fallen in love. Under the cir-cumstances, it was inevitable. Curious how it broke down the girl's cool self-possession, but that only made her more human and desirable.

He felt a thorough skunk, but maybe she was right. *Carpe diem.* If he ever pulled out of this mess, he'd just have to pull her out with him; meanwhile, he accepted the additional complication of his assignment. It looked as if that would drag on for years, anyhow; maybe a lifetime.

They blew themselves to a short honeymoon at a high-class—and expensive—resort by Thunder Gorge, one of Venus' few natural beauty spots. The atmosphere at the lodge was relaxed, not a Guardian in sight and more privacy than elsewhere on the planet. Psych Control was shrewd enough to realize that people needed an occasional surcease from all duty, some flight from the real world of sand and stone and steel. It helped keep them sane.

Even so, there was a rather high proportion of mental disease. It was a taboo subject, but Hollister got a doctor drunk and wormed the facts out of him. The psychotic were not sent back to Earth, as they could have been at no charge; they might talk too much. Nor were there facilities for proper treatment on Venus. If the most drastic procedures didn't restore a patient to some degree of usefulness in a short time—they had even revived the barbarism of prefrontal lobotomy!—he was quietly gassed.

"But it'll all be diff'rent af'er uh Big Rain," said the doctor. "My son ull have uh real clinic, he will."

More and more, Hollister doubted it.

➤

A few sweet crazy days, and vacation's end was there and they took the rocket back to New America. It was the first time Hollister had seen Barbara cry.

He left her sitting forlornly in the little two-room apartment they now rated, gathering herself to arrange the small heap of their personal possessions, and reported to Air Control. The assistant super gave him a thick, bound sheaf of papers.

"Here are the orders and specs," he said. "You can have two days to study them." Hollister, who could memorize the lot in a few hours, felt a leap of gladness at the thought of so much free time. The official leaned back in his chair. He was a gnarled old man, retired to a desk after a lifetime of field duty. One cheek was puckered with the scars of an operation for the prevalent HR cancer; Venus had no germs, but prepared her own special death traps. "Relax for a minute and I'll give you the general idea."

He pointed to a large map on the wall. It was not very complete or highly accurate: surveying on this planet was a job to break a man's heart, and little had been done. "We're establishing your new camp out by Last Chance. You'll note that Little Moscow, Trollen, and Roger's Landing cluster around it at an average distance of two hundred kilometers, so that's where you'll be getting your supplies, sending men on leave, and so forth. I doubt if you'll have any occasion to report back here till you break camp completely in a couple of years."

And Barbara will be here alone, Barbara and our child whom I won't even see—

"You'll take your wagon train more or less along this route," went on the super, indicating a dotted line that ran from New America. "It's been gone over and is safe. Notice the eastward jog to Lucifer at the halfway point. That's to refuel and take on fresh food stores."

Hollister frowned, striving for concentration on the job. "I can't see that. Why not take a few extra wagons and omit the detour?"

"Orders," said the super.

Whose orders? Karsov's? I'll bet my air helmet!—but why?

"Your crew will be . . . kind of tough," said the old man. "They're mostly from Ciudad Alcazar, which is on the other side of the world. It was one of the stubborn colonies when we declared independence, had to be put down by force, and it's still full of sedition. These spigs are all hard cases who've been assigned to this hemisphere so they won't stir up trouble at home. I saw in your dossier that you speak Spanish, among other languages, which is one reason you're being given this bunch. You'll have to treat them rough, remember. Keep them in line."

I think there was more than one reason behind this.

"The details are all in your assignment book," said the super. "Report back here in two days, this time. Okay—have fun!" He smiled, suddenly friendly now that his business was completed.

V

Darkness and a whirl of poison sleet turned the buildings into crouching black monsters, hardly to be told from the ragged snarl of crags which ringed them in. Hollister brought his tank to a grinding halt before a tower which fixed him with a dazzling floodlight eye. "Sit tight, Diego," he said, and slapped his helmet down.

His chief assistant, Fernandez, nodded a sullen dark head. He was competent enough, and had helped keep the unruly crew behaving itself, but remained cold toward his boss. There was always a secret scorn in his eyes.

Hollister wriggled through the air lock and dropped to the ground. A man in a reinforced, armorlike suit held a tommy gun on him, but dropped the muzzle as he advanced. The blast of white light showed a stupid face set in lines of habitual brutality.

"You the airman come for supplies?" he asked.

"Yes. Can I see your chief?"

The guard turned wordlessly and led the way. Beyond the lock of the main shell was a room where men sat with rifles. Hollister was escorted to an inner office, where a middle-aged, rather mild-looking fellow in Guardian uniform greeted him. "How do you do? We had word you were coming. The supplies were brought to our warehouse and you can load them when you wish."

Hollister accepted a chair. "I'm Captain Thomas," the other continued. "Nice to have you. We don't see many new faces at Lucifer—not men you can talk to, anyway. How are things in New America?"

He gossiped politely for a while. "It's quite a remarkable installation we have here," he ended. "Would you like to see it?"

Hollister grimaced. "No, thanks."

"Oh, I really must insist. You and your chief assistant and one or two of the foremen. They'll all be interested, and can tell the rest of your gang how it is. There's so little to talk about in camp."

Hollister debated refusing outright and forcing Thomas to show his hand. But why bother? Karsov had given orders, and Thomas would conduct him around at gunpoint if necessary. "Okay, thanks," he said coldly. "Let me get my men bunked down first, though."

"Of course. We have a spare barracks for transients. I'll expect you in two hours . . . with three of your men, remember."

Diego Fernandez only nodded when Hollister gave him the news. The chief skinned his teeth in a bleak sort of grin. "Don't forget to 'oh' and 'ah,' " he said. "Our genial host will be disappointed if you don't, and he's a man I'd hate to disappoint."

The smoldering eyes watched him with a quizzical expression that faded back into blankness. "I shall get Gomez and San Rafael," said Fernandez. "They have strong stomachs."

◆

Thomas received them almost unctuously and started walking down a series of compartments. "As engineers, you will be most interested in the mine itself," he said. "I'll show you a little of it. This is the biggest uranium deposit known in the Solar System."

He led them to the great cell block, where a guard with a shock gun fell in behind them. "Have to be careful," said Thomas. "We've got some pretty desperate characters here, who don't feel they have much to lose."

"All lifers, eh?" asked Hollister.

Thomas looked surprised. "Of course! We couldn't let them go back after what the radiation does to their germ plasm."

A man rattled the bars of his door as they passed. "I'm from New America!" His harsh scream bounded between steel walls. "Do you know my wife? Is Martha Riley all right?"

"Shut up!" snapped the guard, and fed him a shock beam. He lurched back into the darkness of his cell. His mate, whose face was disfigured by a cancer, eased him to his bunk.

Someone else yelled, far down the long white-lit rows. A guard came running from that end. The voice pleaded: "It's a nightmare. It's just a nightmare. The stuff's got intuh muh brain and I'm always dreamin' night-mares—"

"They get twitchy after a while," said Thomas. "Stuff *will* seep through the suits and lodge in their bodies. Then they're not much good for anything but pick-and-shovel work. Don't be afraid, gentlemen, we have reinforced suits for the visitors and guards."

These were donned at the end of the cell block. Beyond the double door, a catwalk climbed steeply, till they were on the edge of an excavation which stretched farther than they could see in the gloom.

"It's rich enough yet for open-pit mining," said Thomas, "though we're driving tunnels, too." He pointed to a giant scooper. Tiny shapes of convicts scurried about it. "Four-hour shifts because of the radiation down there. Don't believe those rumors that we aren't careful with our boys. Some of them live for thirty years."

Hollister's throat felt cottony. It would be so easy to rip off Thomas' air hose and kick him down into the pit! "What about women prisoners?" he asked slowly. "You must get some."

"Oh, yes. Right down there with the men. We believe in equality on Venus."

There was a strangled sound in the earphones, but Hollister wasn't sure which of his men had made it.

"Very essential work here," said Thomas proudly. "We refine the ore right on the spot too, you know. It not only supplies such nuclear power as Venus needs, but exported to Earth it buys the things we still have to have from them."

"Why operate it with convict labor?" asked Hollister absently. His imagination was wistfully concentrated on the image of himself branding his initials on Thomas' anatomy. "You could use free men, taking proper precautions, and it would be a lot more efficient and economical of manpower."

"You don't understand." Thomas seemed a bit shocked. "These are enemies of the state."

I've read that line in the history books. Some state, if it makes itself that many enemies!

"The refinery won't interest you so much," said Thomas. "Standard procedure, and it's operated by nonpolitical prisoners under shielding. They get skilled, and become too valuable to lose. But no matter who a man is, how clever he is, if he's been convicted of treason he goes to the mine."

So this was a warning—or was it a provocation?

When they were back in the office, Thomas smiled genially. "I hope you gentlemen have enjoyed the tour," he said. "Do stop in and see me again sometime." He held out his hand. Hollister turned on his heel, ignoring the gesture, and walked out.

Even in the line of duty, a man can only do so much.

◆

Somewhat surprisingly Hollister found himself getting a little more popular with his crew after the visit to Lucifer. The three who were with him must have seen his disgust and told about it. He exerted himself to win more of their friendship, without being too obtrusive about it: addressing them politely, lending a hand himself in the task of setting up camp, listening carefully to complaints about not feeling well instead of dismissing them all as malingering. That led to some trouble. One laborer who was obviously faking a stomachache was ordered back to the job and made an insulting crack. Hollister knocked him to the floor with a single blow. Looking around at the others present, he said slowly: "There will be no whippings in this camp, because I do not believe men should be treated thus. But I intend to remain chief and to get this business done." Nudging the fallen man with his foot: "Well, go on back to your work. This is forgotten also in the records I am supposed to keep."

He didn't feel proud of himself—the man had been smaller and weaker than he. But he had to have discipline, and the Venusians all seemed brutalized to a point where the only unanswerable argument was force. It was an inevitable consequence of their type of government, and boded ill for the future.

Somewhat later, his radio-electronics technie, Valdez—a soft-spoken little fellow who did not seem to have any friends in camp—found occasion to speak with him. "It seems that you have unusual ideas about running this operation, señor," he remarked.

"I'm supposed to get the airmakers installed," said Hollister. "That part of it is right on schedule."

"I mean with regard to your treatment of the men, señor. You are the mildest chief they have had. I wish to say that it is appreciated, but some of them are puzzled. If I may give you some advice, which is doubtless not needed, it would be best if they knew exactly what to expect."

Hollister felt bemused. "Fairness, as long as they do their work. What is so strange about that?"

"But some of us . . . them . . . have unorthodox ideas about politics."

"That is their affair, Señor Valdez." Hollister decided to make himself a little more human in the technie's eyes. "I have a few ideas of my own, too."

"Ah, so. Then you will permit free discussion in the barracks?"

"Of course."

"I have hidden the recorder in there very well. Do you wish to hear the tapes daily, or shall I just make a summary?"

"I don't want to hear any tapes," stated Hollister. "That machine will not be operated."

"But they might plan treason!"

Hollister laughed and swept his hand around the wall. "In the middle of *that*? Much good their plans do them!" Gently: "All of you may say what you will among yourselves. I am an engineer, not a secret policeman."

"I see, señor. You are very generous. Believe me, it is appreciated."

Three days later, Valdez was dead.

➤

Hollister had sent him out with a crew to run some performance tests on the first of the new airmakers. The men came back agitatedly, to report that a short, sudden rock storm had killed the technie. Hollister frowned, to cover his pity for the poor lonely little guy. "Where is the body?" he asked.

"Out there, señor—where else?"

Hollister knew it was the usual practice to leave men who died in the field where they fell; after Venusian conditions had done their work, it wasn't worthwhile salvaging the corpse for its chemicals. But—"Have I not announced my policy?" he snapped. "I thought that you people, of all, would be glad of it. Dead men will be kept here, so we can haul them into town and have them properly buried. Does not your religion demand that?"

"But Valdez, señor—"

"Never mind! Back you go, at once, and this time bring him in." Hollister turned his attention to the problem of filling the vacancy. Control wasn't going to like him asking for another so soon; probably he couldn't get one anyway. Well, he could train Fernandez to handle the routine parts, and do the more exacting things himself.

He was sitting in his room that night, feeling acutely the isolation of a commander—too tired to add another page to his letter to Barbara, not tired enough to go to sleep. There was a knock on the door. His start told him how thin his nerves were worn. "Come in!"

Diego Fernandez entered. The chill white fluorolight showed fear in his eyes and along his mouth. "Good evening, Simon," he said tonelessly. They had gotten to the stage of first names, though they still addressed each other with the formal pronoun.

"Good evening, Diego. What is it?"

The other bit his lip and looked at the floor. Hollister did not try to hurry him. Outside, the wind was running and great jags of lightning sizzled across an angry sky, but this room was buried deep and very quiet.

Fernandez's eyes rose at last. "There is something you ought to know, Simon. Perhaps you already know it."

"And perhaps not, Diego. Say what you will. There are no recorders here."

"Well, then, Valdez was not accidentally killed. He was murdered."

Hollister sat utterly still.

"You did not look at the body very closely, did you?" went on Fernandez, word by careful word. "I have seen suits torn open by flying rocks. This was not such a one. Some instrument did it . . . a compressed-air drill, I think."

"And do you know why it was done?"

"Yes." Fernandez's face twisted. "I cannot say it was not a good deed. Valdez was a spy for the government."

Hollister felt a knot in his stomach. "How do you know this?"

"One can be sure of such things. After the . . . the Venusians had taken Alcazar, Valdez worked eagerly with their police. He had always believed in confederation and planetary independence. Then he went away, to some engineering assignment it was said. But he had a brother who was proud of the old hidalgo blood, and this brother sought to clear the shame of his family by warning that Valdez had taken a position with the Guardians. He told it secretly, for he was not supposed to, but most of Alcazar got to know it. The men who had fought against the invaders were sent here, to the other side of the world, and it is not often we get leave to go home even for a short while. But we remembered, and we knew Valdez when he appeared on this job. So when those men with him had a chance to revenge themselves, they took it."

Hollister fixed the brown eyes with his own. "Why do you tell me this?" he asked.

"I do not—quite know. Except that you have been a good chief. It would be best for us if we could keep you, and this may mean trouble for you."

I'll say! First I practically told Valdez how I feel about the government, then he must have transmitted it with the last radio report, and now he's dead. Hollister chose his words cautiously: "Have you thought that the best way I can save myself is to denounce those men?"

"They would go to Lucifer, Simon."

"I know." He weighed the factors, surprised at his own detached calm. On the one hand there were Barbara and himself, and his own mission; on the other hand were half a dozen men who would prove most valuable come the day—for it was becoming more and more clear that the sovereign state of Venus would have to be knocked down, the sooner the better.

Beyond a small ache, he did not consider the personal element; Un-man training was too strong in him for that. A melody skipped through his head. *"Here's a how-de-do—"* It was more than a few men, he decided; this whole crew, all fifty or so, had possibilities. A calculated risk was in order.

"I did not hear anything you said," he spoke aloud. "Nor did you ever have any suspicions. It is obvious that Valdez died accidentally—too obvious to question."

Fernandez's smile flashed through the sweat that covered his face. "Thank you, Simon!"

"Thanks to *you*, Diego." Hollister gave him a drink—the boss was allowed a few bottles—and sent him on his way.

The boss was also allowed a .45 magnum automatic, the only gun in camp. Hollister took it out and checked it carefully. What was that classic verdict of a coroner's jury, a century or more ago in the States? "An act of God under very suspicious circumstances." He grinned to himself. It was not a pleasant expression.

VI

The rocket landed three days later. Hollister, who had been told by radio to expect it but not told why, was waiting outside. A landing space had been smoothed off and marked, and he had his men standing by and the tanks and bulldozers parked close at hand. Ostensibly that was to give any help which might be needed; actually, he hoped they would mix in on his side if trouble started. Power-driven sand blasts and arc welders were potentially nasty weapons, and tanks and dozers could substitute for armored vehicles in a pinch. The gun hung at his waist.

There was a mild breeze, for Venus, but it drove a steady scud of sand across the broken plain. The angry storm-colored light was diffused by airborne dust till it seemed to pervade the land, and even through his helmet and earphones Hollister was aware of the wind-yammer and the remote banging of thunder.

A new racket grew in heaven, stabbing jets and then the downward hurtle of sleek metal. The rocket's glider wings were fully extended, braking her against the updraft, and the pilot shot brief blasts to control his yawing vessel and bring her down on the markings. Wheels struck the hard-packed sand, throwing up a wave of it; landing flaps strained, a short burst from the nose jet arched its back against the flier's momentum, and then the machine lay still.

Hollister walked up to it. Even with the small quick-type air lock, he had to wait a couple of minutes before two suited figures emerged. One was obviously the pilot; the other—

"Barbara!"

Her face had grown thin, he saw through the helmet plate, and the red hair was disordered. He pulled her to him, and felt his faceplate clank on hers. "Barbara! What brings you here? Is everything all right?"

She tried to smile. "Not so public. Let's get inside."

The pilot stayed, to direct the unloading of what little equipment had been packed along; a trip was never wasted. Fernandez could do the honors afterward. Hollister led his wife to his own room, and no words were said for a while.

Her lips and hands felt cold.

"What is it, Barbara?" he asked when he finally came up for air. "How do we rate this?"

She didn't quite meet his eyes. "Simple enough. We're not going to have a baby after all. Since you'll be in the field for a long time, and I'm required to be a mother soon, it . . . it wasn't so hard to arrange a leave for me. I'll be here for ten days."

That was almost an Earth month. The luxury was unheard-of. Hollister sat down on his bunk and began to think.

"What's the matter?" She rumpled his hair. "Aren't you glad to see me? Maybe you have a girl lined up in Trollen?"

Her tone wasn't quite right, somehow. In many ways she was still a stranger to him, but he knew she wouldn't banter him with just that inflection. Or did she really think—"I'd no such intention," he said.

"Of course not, you jethead! I trust you." Barbara stretched herself luxuriously. "Isn't this wonderful?"

Yeah . . . too wonderful. "Why do we get it?"

"I told you." She looked surprised. "We've got to have a child."

He said grimly, "I can't see that it's so all-fired urgent. If it were, it'd be easier, and right in line with the Board's way of thinking, to use artificial insemination." He stood up and gripped her shoulders and looked straight at her. "Barbara, why are you really here?"

She began to cry, and that wasn't like her either. He patted her and mumbled awkward phrases, feeling himself a louse. But something was very definitely wrong, and he had to find out what.

He almost lost his resolution as the day went on. He had to be outside most of that time, supervising and helping; he noticed that several of the men had again become frigid with him. Was that Karsov's idea—to drive a wedge between him and his crew by giving him an unheard-of privilege? Well, maybe partly, but it could not be the whole answer. When he came back, Barbara had unpacked and somehow, with a few small touches, turned his bleak little bedroom-office into a home. She was altogether gay and charming and full of hope.

The rocket had left, the camp slept, they had killed a bottle to celebrate and now they were alone in darkness. In such a moment of wonder, it was hard to keep a guard up.

"Maybe you appreciate the Board a little more," she sighed. "They aren't machines. They're human, and know that we are too."

" 'Human' is a pretty broad term," he murmured, almost automatically. "The guards at Lucifer are human, I suppose."

Her hand stole out to stroke his cheek. "Things aren't perfect on Venus," she said. "Nobody claims they are. But after the Big Rain—"

"Yeah. The carrot in front and the stick behind, and on the burro trots. He doesn't stop to ask where the road is leading. I could show it by psychodynamic equations, but even an elementary reading of history is enough to show that once a group gets power, it *never* gives it up freely."

"There was Kemal Ataturk, back around 1920, wasn't there?"

"Uh-huh. A very exceptional case: the hard-boiled, practical man who was still an idealist, and built his structure so well that his successors—who'd grown up under him—neither could nor wanted to continue dictatorship. It's an example which the U.N. Inspectorate on Earth has studied closely and tried to adapt, so that its own power won't someday be abused.

"The government of Venus just isn't that sort. Their tactics prove it. Venus has to be collective till the Big Rain, I suppose, but that doesn't give anyone the right to collectivize the minds of men. By the time this hellhole is fit for human life, the government will be unshakeably in the saddle. Basic principle of psychobiology: survival with least effort. In human society, one of the easiest ways to survive and grow fat is to rule your fellow men.

"It's significant that you've learned about Ataturk. How much have they told you about the Soviet Union? The state was supposed to wither away there, too."

"Would you actually . . . conspire to revolt?" she asked.

He slammed the brakes so hard that his body jerked. *Danger! Danger! Danger! How did I get into this? What am I saying? Why is she asking me?* With a single bound, he was out of bed and had snapped on the light.

Its glare hurt his eyes, and Barbara covered her face. He drew her hands away, gently but using his strength against her resistance. The face that looked up at him was queerly distorted; the lines were still there, but they had become something not quite human.

"Who put you up to this?" he demanded.

"No one . . . what are you talking about, what's wrong?"

"The perfect spy," he said bitterly. "A man's own wife."

"What do you mean?" She sat up, staring wildly through her tousled hair. "Have you gone crazy?"

"*Could* you be a spy?"

"I'm not," she gasped. "I swear I'm not."

"I didn't ask if you were. What I want to know is could you be a spy?"

"I'm not. It's impossible. I'm not—" She was screaming now, but the thick walls would muffle that.

"Karsov is going to send me to Lucifer," he flung at her. "Isn't he?"

"I'm not, I'm not, I'm not—"

He stabbed the questions at her, one after another, slapping when she got hysterical. The first two times she fainted, he brought her around again and continued; the third time, he called it off and stood looking down on her.

⬢

There was no fear or rage left in him, not even pity. He felt strangely empty. There seemed to be a hollowness inside his skull, the hollow man went through the motions of life and his brain still clicked rustily, but there was nothing inside, he was a machine.

The perfect spy, he thought. *Except that Karsov didn't realize Un-men have advanced psych training. I know such a state as hers when I see it.*

The work had been cleverly done, using the same drugs and machines and conditioning techniques which had given him his own personality mask. (No—not quite the same. The Venusians didn't know that a mind could be so deeply verbal-conditioned as to get by a narcoquiz; that was a guarded secret of the Inspectorate. But the principles were there.) Barbara did not remember being taken to the laboratories and given the treatment. She did not know she had been conditioned; consciously, she believed everything she had said, and it had been anguish when the man she loved turned on her.

But the command had been planted, to draw his real thoughts out of him. Almost, she had succeeded. And when she went back, a quiz would get her observations out of her in detail.

It would have worked, too, on an ordinary conspirator. Even if he had come to suspect the truth, an untrained man wouldn't have known just how to throw her conscious and subconscious minds into conflict, wouldn't have recognized her symptomatic reactions for what they were.

This tears it, thought Hollister. *This rips it wide open.* He didn't have the specialized equipment to mask Barbara's mind and send her back with a lie that could get past the Guardian psychotechnies. Already she knew enough to give strong confirmation to Karsov's suspicions. After he had her account, Hollister would be arrested and they'd try to wring his secrets out of him. That might or might not be possible, but there wouldn't be anything left of Hollister.

Not sending her back at all? No, it would be every bit as much of a giveaway, and sacrifice her own life to boot. Not that she might not go to Lucifer anyhow.

Well—

The first thing was to remove her conditioning. He could do that in a couple of days by simple hypnotherapy. The medicine chest held some drugs which would be useful. After that—

First things first. Diego can take charge for me while I'm doing it. Let the men think what they want. They're going to have plenty to think about soon.

He became aware of his surroundings again and of the slim form beneath his eyes. She had curled up in a fetal position, trying to escape. Emotions came back to him, and the first was an enormous compassion for her. He would have wept, but there wasn't time.

⬭

Barbara sat up in bed, leaning against his breast. "Yes," she said tonelessly. "I remember it all now."

"There was a child coming, wasn't there?"

"Of course. They . . . removed it." Her hand sought his. "You might have suspected something otherwise. I'm all right, though. We can have another one sometime, if we live that long."

"And did Karsov tell you what he thought about me?"

"He mentioned suspecting you were an Un-man, but not being sure. The Technic Board wouldn't let him have you unless he had good evidence. That— No, I don't remember any more. It's fuzzy in my mind, everything which happened in that room."

Hollister wondered how he had betrayed himself. Probably he hadn't; his grumblings had fitted in with his assumed personality, and there had been no overt acts. But still, it was Karsov's job to suspect everybody, and the death of Valdez must have decided him on drastic action.

"Do you feel all right, sweetheart?" asked Hollister.

She nodded, and turned around to give him a tiny smile. "Yes. Fine. A little weak, maybe, but otherwise fine. Only I'm scared."

"You have a right to be," he said bleakly. "We're in a devil of a fix."

"You *are* an Un-man, aren't you?"

"Yes. I was sent to study the Venusian situation. My chiefs were worried about it. Seems they were justified, too. I've never seen a nastier mess."

"I suppose you're right," she sighed. "Only what else could we do? Do you want to bring Venus back under Earth?"

"That's a lot of comet gas, and you'd know it if the nationalist gang hadn't been censoring the books and spewing their lies out since before you were born. This whole independence movement was obviously their work from the beginning, and I must say they've done a competent job; good psychotechnies among them. It's their way to power. Not that all of them are so cynical about it—a lot must have rationalizations of one sort or another— but that's what it amounts to.

"There's no such thing as Venus being 'under' Earth. If ready for independence—and I agree she is—she'd be made a state in her own right with full U.N. membership. It's written into the charter that she could make her own internal policy. The only restrictions on a nation concern a few matters of trade, giving up military forces and the right to make war, guaranteeing certain basic liberties, submitting to inspection, and paying her share of U.N. expenses—which are smaller than the cost of even the smallest army. That's all. Your nationalists have distorted the truth as their breed always does."

She rubbed her forehead in a puzzled way. He could sympathize: a lifetime of propaganda wasn't thrown off overnight. But as long as she was with his cause, the rest would come of itself.

"There's no excuse whatsoever for this tyranny you live under," he continued. "It's got to go."

"What would you have us do?" she asked. "This isn't Earth. We do things efficiently here, or we die."

"True. But even men under the worst conditions can afford the slight inefficiency of freedom. It's not my business to write a constitution for Venus, but you might look at how Mars operates. They also have to have requirements of professional competence for public schools—deadwood gets flunked out fast enough—and the graduates have to stand for election if they want policy-making posts. Periodic elections do not necessarily pick better men than an appointive system, but they keep power from concentrating in the leaders. The Martians also have to ration a lot of things, and forbid certain actions that would endanger a whole city, but they're free to choose their own residences, and families, and ways of thinking, and jobs. They're also trying to reclaim the whole planet, but they don't assign men to that work, they hire them for it."

"Why doesn't everyone just stay at home and do nothing?" she asked innocently.

"No work, no pay; no pay, nothing to eat. It's as simple as that. And when jobs are open in the field, and all the jobs in town are filled, men will take work in the field—as free men, free to quit if they wish. Not many do, because the bosses aren't little commissars.

"Don't you see, it's the *mass* that society has to regulate; a government has to set things up so that the statistics come out right. There's no reason to regulate individuals."

"What's the difference?" she inquired.

"A hell of a difference. Someday you'll see it. Meanwhile, though, something has to be done about the government of Venus—not only on principle, but because it's going to be a menace to Earth before long. Once Venus is strong, a peaceful, nearly unarmed Earth is going to be just too tempting for your dictators. The World Wars had this much value, they hammered it into our heads and left permanent memorials of destruction to keep reminding us that the time to cut out a cancer is when it first appears. Wars start for a variety of reasons, but unlimited national sovereignty is always the necessary and sufficient condition. I wish our agents had been on the ball with respect to Venus ten years ago; a lot of good men are going to die because they weren't."

"You might not have come here then," she said shyly.

"Thanks, darling." He kissed her. His mind whirred on, scuttling through a maze that seemed to lead only to his silent, pointless death.

"If I could just get a report back to Earth! That would settle the matter. We'd have spaceships landing U.N. troops within two years. An expensive operation, of doubtful legality perhaps, a tough campaign so far from home, especially since we wouldn't want to destroy any cities—but there'd be no doubt of the outcome, and it would surely be carried through; because it would be a matter of survival for us. Of course, the rebellious cities would be helpful, a deal could be made there—and so simple a thing as seizing the food-producing towns would soon force a surrender. You see, it's not only the warning I've got to get home, it's the utterly priceless military intelligence I've got in my head. If I fail, the Guardians will be on the alert, they may very well succeed in spotting and duping every agent sent after me and flinging up something for Earth's consumption. Venus is a long ways off—"

He felt her body tighten in his arms. "So you do want to take over Venus."

"Forget that hogwash, will you? What'd we want with this forsaken desert? Nothing but a trustworthy government for it. Anyway—" His exasperation became a flat hardness: "If you and I are to stay alive much longer, it has to be done."

She said nothing to that.

His mind clicked off astronomical data and the slide rule whizzed through his fingers. "The freighters come regularly on Hohmann 'A' orbits," he said. "That means the next one is due in eight Venus days. They've only got four-man crews, they come loaded with stuff and go back with uranium and thorium ingots which don't take up much room. In short, they could carry quite a few passengers in an emergency, if those had extra food supplies."

"And the ferries land at New America," she pointed out.

"Exactly. My dear, I think our only chance is to take over the whole city!"

◆

It was hot in the barracks room, and rank with sweat. Hollister thought he could almost smell the fear, as if he were a dog. He stood on a table at one end, Barbara next to him, and looked over his assembled crew. Small, thin, swarthy, unarmed and drably clad, eyes wide with frightened waiting, they didn't look like much of an army. But they were all he had.

"Señores," he began at last, speaking very quietly, "I have called you all together to warn you of peril to your lives. I think, if you stand with me, we can escape, but it will take courage and energy. You have shown me you possess these qualities, and I hope you will use them now."

He paused, then went on: "I know many of you have been angry with me because I have had my wife here. You thought me another of these bootlickers to a rotten government"—that brought them to full awareness— "who was being rewarded for some Judas act. It is not true. We all owe our lives to this gallant woman. It was I who was suspected of being hostile to the rulers, and she was sent to spy on me for them. Instead, she told me the truth, and now I am telling it to you.

"You must know that I am an agent from Earth. No, no, I am not an Imperialist. As a matter of fact, the Central American countries were worried about their joint colony, Ciudad Alcazar, your city. It was suspected she had not freely joined this confederation. There are other countries, too, which are worried. I came to investigate for them; what I have seen convinces me they were right."

He went on, quickly, and not very truthfully. He had to deal with their anti-U.N. conditioning, appeal to the nationalism he despised. (At that, it wouldn't make any practical difference if some countries on Earth retained nominal ownership of certain tracts on Venus; a democratic confederation would reabsorb those within a generation, quite peacefully.) He had to convince them that the whole gang was scheduled to go to Lucifer; all were suspected, and the death of Valdez confirmed the suspicion, and there was always a labor shortage in the mines. His psych training stood him in good stead; before long he had them rising and shouting. *I shoulda been a politician*, he thought sardonically.

"... And are we going to take this outrage? Are we going to rot alive in that hell, and let our wives and children suffer forever? Or shall we strike back, to save our own lives and liberate Venus?"

When the uproar had subsided a little, he sketched his plan: a march on Lucifer itself, to seize weapons and gain some recruits, then an attack on New America. If it was timed right, they could grab the city just before the ferries landed, and hold it while all of them were embarked on the freighter—then off to Earth, and in a year or two a triumphant return with the army of liberation!

"If anyone does not wish to come with us, let him stay here. I shall compel no man. I can only use those who will be brave, and will obey orders like soldiers, and will set lives which are already forfeit at hazard for the freedom of their homes. Are you with me? Let those who will follow me stand up and shout 'Yes!'"

Not a man stayed in his seat; the timid ones, if any, dared not do so while their comrades were rising and whooping about the table. The din roared and rolled, bunk frames rattled, eyes gleamed murder from a whirlpool of faces. The first stage of Hollister's gamble had paid off well indeed, he thought; now for the rough part.

He appointed Fernandez his second in command and organized the men into a rough corps; engineering discipline was valuable here. It was late before he and Barbara and Fernandez could get away to discuss concrete plans.

"We will leave two men here," said Hollister. "They will send the usual radio reports, which I shall write in advance for them, so no one will suspect; they will also take care of the rocket when it comes for Barbara, and I *hope* the police will assume it crashed. We will send for them when we hold New America. I think we can take Lucifer by surprise, but we can't count on the second place not being warned by the time we get there."

Fernandez looked steadily at him. "And will all of us leave with the spaceship?" he asked.

"Of course. It would be death to stay. And Earth will need their knowledge of Venus."

"Simon, you know the ship cannot carry fifty men—or a hundred, if we pick up some others at Lucifer."

Hollister's face was wintry. "I do not think fifty will survive," he said.

Fernandez crossed himself, then nodded gravely. "I see. Well, about the supply problem—"

When he had gone, Barbara faced her husband and he saw a vague fright in her eyes. "You weren't very truthful out there, were you?" she asked. "I don't know much Spanish, but I got the drift, and—"

"All right!" he snapped wearily. "There wasn't time to use sweet reasonableness. I had to whip them up fast."

"They aren't scheduled for Lucifer at all. They have no personal reason to fight."

"They're committed now," he said in a harsh tone. "It's fifty or a hundred lives today against maybe a hundred million in the future. That's an attitude which was drilled into me at the Academy, and I'll never get rid of it. If you want to live with me, you'll have to accept that."

"I'll . . . try," she said.

VII

The towers bulked black through a whirl of dust, under a sky the color of clotted blood. Hollister steered his tank close, speaking into its radio: "Hello, Lucifer. Hello, Lucifer. Come in."

"Lucifer," said a voice in his earphones. "Who are you and what do you want?"

"Emergency. We need help. Get me your captain."

Hollister ground between two high guntowers. They had been built and manned against the remote possibility that a convict outbreak might succeed in grabbing some tanks; he was hoping their personnel had grown lazy with uneventful years. Edging around the main shell of the prison, he lumbered toward the landing field and the nearby radio mast. One by one, the twenty tanks of his command rolled into the compound and scattered themselves about it.

Barbara sat next to him, muffled in airsuit and closed helmet. Her gauntleted hand squeezed his shoulder, he could just barely feel the pressure. Glancing around to her stiffened face, he essayed a smile.

"Hello, there! Captain Thomas speaking. What are you doing?"

"This is Hollister, from the Last Chance air camp. Remember me? We're in trouble and need help. Landslip damn near wiped our place out." The Earthman drove his machine onto the field.

"Well, what are you horsing around like that for? Assemble your tanks in front of the main lock."

"All right, all right, gimme a chance to give some orders. The boys don't seem to know where to roost."

Now! Hollister slapped down the drive switch and his tank surged forward. "Hang on!" he yelled. "Thomas, this thing has gone out of control—Help!"

It might have gained him the extra minute he needed. He wasn't sure what was happening behind him. The tank smashed into the radio mast and he was hurled forward against his safety webbing. His hands flew—extend the grapple, snatch that buckling strut, drag it aside, and *push!*

The frame wobbled crazily. The tank stalled. Hollister yanked off his harness, picked up the cutting torch, whose fuel containers were already on his back, and went through the air lock without stopping to conserve atmosphere. Blue flame stabbed before him, he slid down the darkened extra faceplate and concentrated on his job. Get this beast down before it sent a call for help!

Barbara got the bull-like machine going again and urged it ahead, straining at the weakened skeleton. The mast had been built for flexibility in the high winds, not for impact strength. Hollister's torch roared, slicing a main support. A piece of steel clanged within a meter of him.

He dropped the torch and dove under the tank, just as the whole structure caved in.

"Barbara!" He picked himself out of the wreckage, looking wildly into the hurricane that blew around him. "Barbara, are you all right?"

She crawled from the battered tank and into his arms. "Our car won't go anymore," she said shakily. The engine hood was split open by a falling beam and oil hissed from the cracked block.

"No matter. Let's see how the boys are doing—"

He led a run across the field, staggering in the wind. A chunk of concrete whizzed by his head and he dropped as one of the guard towers went by. Good boys! They'd gone out and dynamited it!

Ignoring the ramp leading down to the garage, Fernandez had brought his tank up to the shell's main air lock for humans. It was sturdily built, but his snorting monster walked through it. Breathable air gasped out. It sleeted a little as formaldehyde took up water vapor and became solid.

No time to check on the rest of the battle outside, you could only hope the men assigned to that task were doing their job properly. Hollister saw one of his tanks go up under a direct hit. All the towers weren't disabled yet. But he had to get into the shell.

"Stay here, Barbara!" he ordered. Men were swarming from their vehicles. He led the way inside. A group of uniformed corpses waited for him, drying and shriveling even as he watched. He snatched the carbines from them and handed them out to the nearest of his followers. The rest would have to make do with their tools till more weapons could be recovered.

Automatic bulkheads had sealed off the rest of the shell. Hollister blasted through the first one. A hail of bullets from the smoking hole told him that the guards within had had time to put on their suits.

He waved an arm. "Bring up Maria Larga!"

It took awhile, and he fumed and fretted. Six partisans trundled the weapon forth. It was a standard man-drawn cart for semiportable field equipment, and Long Mary squatted on it: a motor-driven blower connected with six meters of hose, an air blast. This one had had an oxygen bottle and a good-sized fuel tank hastily attached to make a superflamethrower. Fernandez got behind the steel plate which had been welded in front as armor, and guided it into the hole. The man behind whooped savagely and turned a handle. Fire blew forth, and the compartment was flushed out.

There were other quarters around the cell block, which came next, but Hollister ignored them for the time being. The air lock in this bulkhead had to be opened the regular way, only two men could go through at a time, and there might be guards on the other side. He squeezed in with San Rafael and waited until the pump cleaned out the chamber. Then he opened the inner door a crack, tossed a homemade shrapnel grenade, and came through firing.

He stumbled over two dead men beyond. San Rafael choked and fell as a gun spat farther down the corridor. Hollister's .45 bucked in his hand. Picking himself up, he looked warily down the cruelly bright length of the block. No one else. The convicts were yammering like wild animals.

He went back, telling off a few men to cut the prisoners out of their cells, issue airsuits from the lockers, and explain the situation. Then he returned to the job of cleaning out the rest of the place.

It was a dirty and bloody business. He lost ten men in all. There were no wounded: if a missile tore open a suit, that was the end of the one inside. A small hole would have given time to slap on an emergency patch, but the guards were using magnum slugs.

Fernandez sought him out to report that an attempt to get away by rocket had been stopped, but that an indeterminate number of holdouts were in the refinery, which was a separate building. Hollister walked across the field, dust whirling about smashed machines, and stood before the smaller shell.

Thomas' voice crackled in his earphones: "You there! What is the meaning of this?"

That was too much. Hollister began to laugh. He laughed so long he thought perhaps he was going crazy.

Sobering, he replied in a chill tone: "We're taking over. You're trapped in there with nothing but small arms. We can blast you out if we must, but you'd do better to surrender."

Thomas, threateningly: "This place is full of radioactivity, you know. If you break in, you'll smash down the shielding—or we'll do it for you—and scatter the stuff everywhere. You won't live a week."

It might be a bluff—"All right," said Hollister with a cheerful note, "you're sealed in without food or water. We can wait. But I thought you'd rather save your own lives."

"You're insane! You'll be wiped out—"

"That's our affair. Anytime you want out, pick up the phone and call the office. You'll be locked in the cells with supplies enough for a while when we leave." Hollister turned and walked away.

He spent the next few hours reorganizing; he had to whip the convicts into line, though when their first exuberance had faded they were for the most part ready to join him. Suddenly his army had swelled to more than two hundred. The barracks were patched up and made habitable, munitions were found and passed about, the transport and supply inventoried. Then word came that Thomas' handful were ready to surrender. Hollister marched them into the cell block and assigned some convicts to stand watch.

He had had every intention of abiding by his agreement, but when he was later wakened from sleep with the news that his guards had literally torn the prisoners apart, he didn't have the heart to give them more than a dressing-down.

"Now," he said to his council of war, "we'd better get rolling again. Apparently we were lucky enough so that no word of this has leaked out, but it's a long way yet to New America."

"We have not transportation for more than a hundred," said Fernandez.

"I know. We'll take the best of the convicts; the rest will just have to stay behind. They *may* be able to pull the same trick on the next supply train that our boys in Last Chance have ready for the rocket—or they may not. In any event, I don't really hope they can last out, or that we'll be able to take the next objective unawares—but don't tell anyone that."

"I suppose not," said Fernandez somberly, "but it is a dirty business."

"War is always a dirty business," said Hollister.

He lost a whole day organizing his new force. Few if any of the men knew how to shoot, but the guns were mostly recoilless and automatic so he hoped some damage could be done; doctrine was to revert to construction equipment, which they did know how to use, in any emergency. His forty Latins were a cadre of sorts, distributed among the sixty convicts in a relationship equivalent to that between sergeant and private. The whole unit was enough to make any military man break out in a cold sweat, but it was all he had.

Supply wagons were reloaded and machine guns mounted on a few of the tanks. He had four Venusian days to get to New America and take over—and if the rebels arrived too soon, police reinforcements would pry them out again, and if the radio-control systems were ruined in the fighting, the ferries couldn't land.

It was not exactly a pleasant situation.

The first rocket was sighted on the fifth day of the campaign. It ripped over, crossing from horizon to horizon in a couple of minutes, but there was little doubt that it had spotted them. Hollister led his caravan off the plain, into broken country which offered more cover but would slow them considerably. Well, they'd just have to keep going day and night.

The next day it was an armored, atomic-powered monster which lumbered overhead, supplied with enough energy to go slowly and even to hover for a while. In an atmosphere without oxygen and always riven by storms, the aircraft of Earth weren't possible—no helicopters, no leisurely airboats; but a few things like this one had been built as emergency substitutes. Hollister tuned in his radio, sure it was calling to them.

"Identify yourselves! This is the Guardian Corps."

Hollister adapted his earlier lie, not expecting belief—but every minute he stalled, his tank lurched forward another hundred meters or so.

The voice was sarcastic: "And of course, you had nothing to do with the attack on Lucifer?"

"What attack?"

"That will do! Go out on the plain and set up camp till we can check on you."

"Of course," said Hollister meekly. "Signing off."

From now on, it was strict radio silence in his army. He'd gained a good hour, though, since the watchers wouldn't be sure till then that he was disobeying—and a lovely dust storm was blowing up.

Following plan, the tanks scattered in pairs, each couple for itself till they converged on New America at the agreed time. Some would break down, some would be destroyed en route, some would come late—a few might even arrive disastrously early—but there was no choice. Hollister was reasonably sure none would desert him; they were all committed past that point.

He looked at Barbara. Her face was tired and drawn, the red hair hung lusterless and tangled to her shoulders, dust and sweat streaked her face, but he thought she was very beautiful. "I'm sorry to have dragged you into this," he said.

"It's all right, dear. Of course I'm scared, but I'm still glad."

He kissed her for a long while and then slapped his helmet down with a savage gesture.

The first bombs fell toward sunset. Hollister saw them as flashes through the dust, and felt their concussion rumble in the frame of his tank. He steered into a narrow, overhung gulch, his companion vehicle nosing close behind. There were two convicts in it—Johnson and Waskowicz—pretty good men, he thought, considering all they had been through.

Dust and sand were his friends, hiding him even from the infrared scopes above which made nothing of mere darkness. The rough country would help a lot, too. It was simply a matter of driving day and night, sticking close to bluffs and gullies, hiding under attack and then driving some more. He was going to lose a number of his units, but thought the harassing would remain aerial till they got close to New America. The Guardians wouldn't risk their heavy stuff unnecessarily at any great distance from home.

VIII

The tank growled around a high pinnacle and faced him without warning. It was a military vehicle, and cannons swiveled to cover his approach.

Hollister gunned his machine and drove directly up the pitted road at the enemy. A shell burst alongside him, steel splinters rang on armor. Coldly, he noted for possible future reference the relatively primitive type of Venusian war equipment: no tracker shells, no Rovers. He had already planned out what to do in an encounter like this, and told his men the idea—now it had happened to him.

The Guardian tank backed, snarling. It was not as fast or as maneuverable as his, it was meant for work close to cities where ground had been cleared. A blast of high-caliber machine-gun bullets ripped through the cab, just over his head. Then he struck. The shock jammed him forward even as his grapple closed jaws on the enemy's nearest tread.

"Out!" he yelled. Barbara snatched open the air lock and fell to the stones below. Hollister was after her. He flung a glance behind. His other tank was an exploded ruin, canted to one side, but a single figure was crawling from it, rising, zigzagging toward him. There was a sheaf of dynamite sticks in one hand. The man flopped as the machine gun sought him and wormed the last few meters. Waskowicz. "They got Sam," he reported, huddling against the steel giant with his companions. "Shall we blast her?"

Hollister reflected briefly. The adversary was immobilized by the transport vehicle that clutched it bulldog fashion. He himself was perfectly safe this instant, just beneath the guns. "I've got a better notion. Gimme a boost."

He crawled up on top, to the turret lock. "Okay, hand me that torch. I'm going to cut my way in!"

The flame roared, biting into metal. Hollister saw the lock's outer door move. So—just as he had expected—the lads inside wanted out! He paused. A suited arm emerged with a grenade. Hollister's torch slashed down. Barbara made a grab for the tumbling missile and failed. Waskowicz tackled her, landing on top. The thing went off.

Was she still alive—? Hollister crouched so that the antenna of his suit radio pocked into the lock. "Come out if you want to live. Otherwise I'll burn you out."

Sullenly, the remaining three men appeared, hands in the air. Hollister watched them slide to the ground, covering them with his pistol. His heart leaped within him when he saw Barbara standing erect. Waskowicz was putting an adhesive patch on his suit where a splinter had ripped it.

"You okay?" asked Hollister.

"Yeah," grunted the convict. "Pure dumb luck. Now what?"

"Now we got us one of their own tanks. Somebody get inside and find some wire or something to tie up the Terrible Three here. And toss out the fourth."

"That's murder!" cried one of the police. "We've only got enough oxy for four hours in these suits—"

"Then you'll have to hope the battle is over by then," said Hollister unsympathetically. He went over and disentangled the two machines.

The controls of the captured tank were enough like those of the ordinary sort for Barbara to handle. Hollister gave Waskowicz a short lecture on the care and feeding of machine guns, and sat up by the 40mm cannon himself; perforce, they ignored the 20. They closed the lock but didn't bother to replenish the air inside; however, as Hollister drove up the mountainside, Waskowicz recharged their oxygen bottles from the stores inside the vehicle.

⬬

The battle was already popping when they nosed up onto the ledge and saw the great sweep of the city. Drifting dust limited his vision, but Hollister saw his own machines and the enemy's. Doctrine was to ram and grapple the military tank, get out and use dynamite or torches, and then worm toward the colony's main air lock. It might have to be blown open, but bulkheads should protect the civilians within.

An engineer tank made a pass at Hollister's. He turned aside, realizing that his new scheme had its own drawbacks. Another police machine came out of the dust; its guns spoke, the engineers went up in a flash and a bang, and then it had been hit from behind. Hollister wet his teeth and went on. It was the first time he had seen anything like war; he had an almost holy sense of his mission to prevent this from striking Earth again.

The whole operation depended on his guess that there wouldn't be many of the enemy. There were only a few Guardians in each town, who wouldn't have had time or reserves enough to bring in a lot of reinforcements; and tanks couldn't be flown in. But against their perhaps lesser number was the fact that they would fight with tenacity and skill. Disciplined as engineers and convicts were, they simply did not have the training—even the psychological part of it which turns frightened individuals into a single selfless unit. They would tend to make wild attacks and to panic when the going got rough—which it was already.

He went on past the combat, towards the main air lock. Dim shapes began to appear through scudding dust. Half a dozen mobile cannon were drawn up in a semicircle to defend the gate. That meant—all the enemy tanks, not more than another six or seven, out on the ledge fighting the attackers.

"All right," Hollister's voice vibrated in their earphones. "We'll shoot from here. Barbara, move her in a zigzag at 10 KPH, keeping about this distance; let out a yell if you think you have to take other evasive action. Otherwise I might hit the city."

He jammed his faceplate into the rubberite viewscope and his hands and feet sought the gun controls. Crosshairs—range—*fire one!* The nearest cannon blew up.

Fire two! Fire three! His 40 reloaded itself. Second gun broken, third a clean miss—*Fire four! Gotcha!*

A rank of infantry appeared, their suits marked with the Guardian symbol. They must have been flown here. Waskowicz blazed at them and they broke, falling like rag dolls, reforming to crawl in. They were good soldiers. Now the other three enemy mobiles were swiveling about, shooting through the dust. "Get us out of here, Barbara!"

The racket became deafening as they backed into the concealing murk. Another enemy tank loomed before them. Hollister fed it two shells almost point blank.

If he could divert the enemy artillery long enough for his men to storm the gate—

He saw a police tank locked with an attacker, broken and dead. Hollister doubted if there were any left in action now. He saw none of his own vehicles moving, though he passed by the remnants of several. And where were his men?

Shock threw him against his webbing. The echoes rolled and banged and shivered for a long time. His head swam. The motors still turned, but—

"I think they crippled us," said Barbara in a small voice.

"Okay. Let's get out of here." Hollister sighed; it had been a nice try, and had really paid off better than he'd had a right to expect. He scrambled to the lock, gave Barbara a hand, and they slid to the ground as the three fieldpieces rolled into view on their self-powered carts.

The stalled tank's cannon spoke, and one of the police guns suddenly slumped. "Waskowicz!" Barbara's voice was shrill in the earphones. "He stayed in there—"

"We can't save him. And if he can fight our tank long enough— Build a monument to him someday. Now come on!" Hollister led the way into curtaining gloom. The wind hooted and clawed at him.

As he neared the main lock, a spatter of rifle fire sent him to his belly. He couldn't make out who was there, but it had been a ragged volley—take a chance on their being police and nailing him—"Just us chickens, boss!" he shouted. Somewhere in a corner of his mind he realized that there was no reason for shouting over a radio system. His schooled self-control must be slipping a bit.

"Is that you, Simon?" Fernandez's voice chattered in his ears. "Come quickly now, we're at the lock but I think they will attack soon."

Hollister wiped the dust from his faceplate and tried to count how many there were. Latins and convicts, perhaps twenty—"Are there more?" he inquired. "Are you the last?"

"I do not know, Simon," said Fernandez. "I had gathered this many, we were barricaded behind two smashed cars, and when I saw their artillery pull away I led a rush here. Maybe there are some partisans left besides us, but I doubt it."

Hollister tackled the emergency control box which opened the gate from outside. It would be nice if he didn't have to blast— Yes, by Heaven! It hadn't been locked! He jammed the whole score into the chamber, closed the outer door and started the pumps.

"They can get in, too," said Fernandez dubiously.

"I know. Either here or by ten other entrances. But I have an idea. All of you stick by me."

The anteroom was empty. The town's civilians must be huddled in the inner compartments, and all the cops must be outside fighting. Hollister threw back his helmet, filling his lungs with air that seemed marvelously sweet, and led a quick but cautious trot down the long halls.

"The spaceship is supposed to have arrived by now," he said. "What we must do is take and hold the radio shack. Since the police don't know exactly what our plans are, they will hesitate to destroy it just to get at us. It will seem easier merely to starve us out."

"Or use sleepy gas," said Fernandez. "Our suits' oxygen supply isn't good for more than another couple of hours."

"Yes . . . I suppose that is what they'll do. That ship had better be up there!"

The chances were that she was. Hollister knew that several days of ferrying were involved, and had timed his attack for hours after she was scheduled to arrive. For all he knew, the ferries had already come down once or twice.

He didn't know if he or anyone in his band would live to be taken out. He rather doubted it; the battle had gone worse than expected, he had not captured the city as he hoped—but the main thing was to get some kind of report back to Earth.

A startled pair of technies met the invaders as they entered. One of them began an indignant protest, but Fernandez waved a rifle to shut him up. Hollister glanced about the gleaming controls and meters. He could call the ship himself, but he didn't have the training to guide a boat down. Well—

He pulled off his gloves and sat himself at the panel. Keys clattered beneath his fingers. When were the cops coming? Any minute.

"Hello, freighter. Hello, up there. Spaceship, this is New America calling. Come in."

Static buzzed and crackled in his earphones.

"Come in, spaceship. This is New America. Come in, damn it!"

Lights flashed on the board, the computer clicked, guiding the beam upward. It tore past the ionosphere and straggled weakly into the nearest of the tiny, equally spaced robot relay stations which circled the planet. Obedient to the keying signal, the robot amplified the beam and shot it to the next station, which kicked it farther along. The relayer closest to the spaceship's present position in her orbit focused the beam on her.

Or was the orbit empty?

". . . Hello, New America." The voice wavered, faint and distorted. "*Evening Star* calling New America. What's going on down there? We asked for a ferry signal three hours ago."

"Emergency," snapped Hollister. "Get me the captain—fast! Meanwhile, record this."

"But—"

"Fast, I said! And record. This is crash priority, condition red." Hollister felt sweat trickling inside his suit.

"Recording. Sending for the captain now."

"Good!" Hollister leaned over the mike. "For Main Office, Earth, United Nations Inspectorate. Repeat: Main Office, U.N. Inspectorate. Urgent, confidential. This is Agent A-431-240. Repeat, Agent A-431-240. Code Watchbird. Code Watchbird. Reporting on Venusian situation as follows—" He began a swift sketch of conditions.

"I think I hear voices down the hall," whispered Barbara to Fernandez.

The Latin nodded. He had already dragged a couple of desks into the corridor to make a sort of barricade; now he motioned his men to take positions; a few outside, the rest standing by, crowded together in the room. Hollister saw what was going on and swung his gun to cover the two technies. They were scared, and looked pathetically young, but he had no time for mercy.

A voice in his earphones, bursting through static: "This is Captain Brackney. What d'you want?"

"U.N.I. business, Captain. I'm besieged in the GCA shack here with a few men. We're to be gotten out at all costs if it's humanly possible."

He could almost hear the man's mouth fall open. "God in space—is that the truth?"

Hollister praised the foresight of his office. "You have a sealed tape aboard among your official records. All spaceships, all first-class public conveyances do. It's changed by an Un-man every year or so. Okay, that's an ID code, secret recognition signal. It proves my right to commandeer everything you've got."

"I know that much. What's on the tape?"

"This year it will be, ' 'Twas brillig and the slithy toves give me liberty or give me pigeons on the grass alas.' Have your radioman check that at once."

Pause. Then: "Okay. I'll take your word for it till he does. What do you want?"

"Bring two ferries down, one about fifty kilometers behind the other. No arms on board, I suppose? . . . No. Well, have just the pilots aboard, because you may have to take twenty or so back. How long will this take you . . . Two hours? That long? . . . Yes, I realize you have to let your ship get into the right orbital position and— All right, if you can't do it in less time. Be prepared to embark anyone waiting out there and lift immediately. Meanwhile stand by for further instructions. . . . Hell, yes, you can do it!"

Guns cracked outside.

"Okay. I'll start recording again in a minute. Get moving, Captain!" Hollister turned back to the others.

"I have to tell Earth what I know, in case I don't make it," he said. "Also, somebody has to see that these technies get the boats down right. Diego, I'll want a few men to defend this place. The rest of you retreat down the hall and pick up some extra oxy bottles for yourselves and all the concentrated food you can carry; because that ship won't have rations enough for all of us. Barbara will show you where it is."

"And how will you get out?" she cried when he had put it into English.

"I'll come to that. You've got to go with them, dear, because you live here and know where they can get the supplies. Leave a couple of suits here for the technies, pick up others somewhere along the way. When you get outside, hide close to the dome. When the ferry lands, some of you make a rush to the shack here. It's right against the outer wall. I see you're still carrying some dynamite, Garcia. Blow a hole to let us through. . . . Yes, it's risky, but what have we got to lose?"

She bent to kiss him. There wasn't time to do it properly. A tommy gun was chattering in the corridor.

Hollister stood up and directed his two prisoners to don the extra suits. "I've no grudge against you boys," he said, "and in fact, if you're scared of what the cops might do to you, you can come along to Earth—but if those boats don't land safely, I'll shoot you both down."

Fernandez, Barbara, and a dozen others slipped out past the covering fire at the barricade and disappeared. Hollister hoped they'd make it. They'd better! Otherwise, even if a few escaped, they might well starve to death on the trip home.

The food concentrate would be enough. It was manufactured by the ton at Little Moscow—tasteless, but pure nourishment and bulk, normally added to the rest of the diet on Venus. It wouldn't be very palatable, but it would keep men alive for a long time.

☞

The technies were at the board, working hard. The six remaining rebels slipped back into the room; two others lay dead behind the chewed-up barricade. Hollister picked up an auxiliary communication mike and started rattling off everything about Venus he could think of.

A Guardian stuck his head around the door. Three guns barked, and the head was withdrawn. A little later, a white cloth on a rifle barrel was wavered past the edge.

Hollister laid down his mike. "I'll talk," he said. "I'll come out, with my arms. You'll have just one man in sight, unarmed." To his men he gave an order to drag the dead into the shack while the truce lasted.

Karsov met him in the hall. He stood warily, but there was no fear on the smooth face. "What are you trying to do?" he asked in a calm voice.

"To stay out of your mines," said Hollister. It would help if he could keep up the impression this was an ordinary revolt.

"You have called that ship up there, I suppose?"

"Yes. They're sending down a ferry."

"The ferry could have an accident. We would apologize profusely, explain that a shell went wild while we were fighting you gangsters, and even pay for the boat. I tell you this so that you can see there is no hope. You had better give up."

"No hope if we do that either," said Hollister. "I'd rather take my chances back on Earth; they can't do worse there than treat my mind."

"Are you still keeping up that farce?" inquired Karsov. But he wasn't sure of himself, that was plain. He couldn't understand how an Un-man could have gotten past his quiz. Hollister had no intention of enlightening him.

"What have you got to lose by letting us go?" asked the Earthman. "So we tell a horror story back home. People there already know you rule with a rough hand."

"I am not going to release you," said Karsov. "You are finished. That second party of yours will not last long, even if they make it outside as I suppose they intend—they will suffocate. I am going to call the spaceship captain on the emergency circuit and explain there is a fight going on and he had better recall his boat. That should settle the matter; if not, the boat will be shot down. As for your group, there will be sleep gas before long."

"I'll blow my brains out before I let you take me," said Hollister sullenly.

"That might save a lot of trouble," said Karsov. He turned and walked away. Hollister was tempted to kill him, but decided to save that pleasure for a while. No use goading the police into a possible use of high explosives.

He went back to the shack and called the *Evening Star* again. "Hello, Captain Brackney? U.N.I. speaking. The bosses down here are going to radio you with a pack of lies. Pretend to believe them and say you'll recall your ferry. Remember, they think just one is coming down. Then—" He continued his orders.

"That's murder!" said the captain. "Pilot One won't have a chance—"

"Yes, he will. Call him now, use spacer code; I don't think any of these birds know it, if they should overhear you. Tell him to have his spacesuit on and be ready for a crash landing, followed by a dash to the second boat."

"It's still a long chance."

"What do you think I'm taking? These are U.N.I. orders, Captain. I'm boss till we get back to Earth, if I live so long. All right, got everything? Then I'll continue recording."

⬤

After a while he caught the first whiff and said into the mike: "The gas is coming now. I'll have to close my helmet. Hollister signing off."

His men and the technies slapped down their covers. It would be peaceful here for a little time, with this sector sealed off while gas poured through its ventilators. Hollister tried to grin reassuringly, but it didn't come off.

"Last round," he said. "Half of us, the smallest ones, are going to go to sleep now. The rest will use their oxygen, and carry them outside when we go."

Someone protested. Hollister roared him down. "Not another word! This is the only chance for all of us. No man has oxygen for much more than an hour; we have at least an hour and a half to wait. How else can we do it?"

They submitted unwillingly, and struggled against the anesthetic as long as they could. Hollister took one of the dead men's bottles to replace the first of his that gave out. His band was now composed of three sleeping men and three conscious but exhausted.

He was hoping the cops wouldn't assault them quickly. Probably not; they would be rallying outside, preparing to meet the ferry with a mobile cannon if it should decide to land after all. The rebels trapped in here would keep.

The minutes dragged by. A man at the point of death was supposed to review his whole life, but Hollister didn't feel up to it. He was too tired. He sat watching the telescreen which showed the space field. Dust and wind and the skeleton cradles, emptiness, and a roiling gloom beyond.

One of the wakeful men, a convict, spoke into the helmet circuit: "So you are U.N.I. Has all this been just to get you back to Earth?"

"To get my report back," said Hollister.

"There are many dead," said one of the Latins, in English. "You have sacrificed us, played us like pawns, no? What of those two we left back at Last Chance?"

"I'm afraid they're doomed," said Hollister tonelessly, and the guilt which is always inherent in leadership was heavy on him.

"It was worth it," said the convict. "If you can smash this rotten system, it was well worth it." His eyes were haunted. They would always be haunted.

"Better not talk," said Hollister. "Save your oxygen."

One hour. The pips on the radarscopes were high and strong now. The spaceboats weren't bothering with atmospheric braking, they were spending fuel to come almost straight down.

One hour and ten minutes. Was Barbara still alive?

One hour and twenty minutes.

One hour and thirty minutes. Any instant—

"There, señor! There!"

Hollister jumped to his feet. Up in a corner of the screen, a white wash of fire—here she came!

⬤

The ferry jetted slowly groundward, throwing up a blast of dust as her fierce blasts tore at the field. Now and then she wobbled, caught by the high wind, but she had been built for just these conditions. Close, close—were they going to let her land after all? Yes, now she was entering the cradle, now the rockets were still.

A shellburst struck her hull amidships and burst it open. The police were cautious, they hadn't risked spilling her nuclear engine and its radioactivity on the field. She rocked in the cradle. Hollister hoped the crash-braced pilot had survived. And he hoped the second man was skillful and had been told exactly what to do.

That ferry lanced out of the clouds, descending fast. She wasn't very maneuverable, but the pilot rode her like a horseman, urging, pleading, whipping and spurring when he had to. She slewed around and fell into a shaky curve out of screen range.

If the gods were good, her blast had incinerated the murderers of the first boat.

She came back into sight, fighting for control. Hollister howled. "Guide her into a cradle!" He waved his gun at the seated technies. "Guide her safely in if you want to live!"

She was down.

Tiny figures were running toward her heedless of earth still smoking underfoot. Three of them veered and approached the radio shack. "Okay!" rapped Hollister. "Back into the corridor!" He dragged one of the unconscious men himself; stooping, he sealed the fellow's suit against the poison gases outside. There would be enough air within it to last a sleeper a few minutes.

Concussion smashed at him. He saw shards of glass and wire flying out the door and ricocheting nastily about his head. Then the yell of Venus' wind came to him. He bent and picked up his man. "Let's go!"

They scrambled through the broken wall and out onto the field. The wind was at their backs, helping them for once. One of the dynamiters moved up alongside Hollister. He saw Barbara's face, dim behind the helmet.

When he reached the ferry, the others were loading the last boxes of food. A figure in space armor was clumping unsteadily toward them from the wrecked boat. Maybe their luck had turned. Sweeping the field with his eyes, Hollister saw only ruin. There were still surviving police, but they were inside the city and it would take minutes for them to get out again.

He counted the men with him and estimated the number of food boxes. Fifteen all told, including his two erstwhile captives—Barbara's party must have met opposition—but *she* still lived, God be praised! There were supplies enough, it would be a hungry trip home but they'd make it.

Fernandez peered out of the air lock. "Ready," he announced. "Come aboard. We have no seats, so we must rise at low acceleration, but the pilot says there is fuel to spare."

Hollister helped Barbara up the ladder and into the boat. "I hope you'll like Earth," he said awkwardly.

"I know I will—with you there," she told him.

Hollister looked through the closing air lock at the desolation which was Venus. Someday it would bloom, but—

"We'll come back," he said.

When the People Fell

CORDWAINER SMITH

The late Cordwainer Smith—in "real" life Dr. Paul M. A. Linebarger, scholar, states-man, and author of the definitive text (still taught from today) on the art of psycho-logical warfare—was a writer of enormous talents who, from 1948 until his untimely death in 1966, produced a double-handful of some of the best short fiction this genre has ever seen—"Alpha Ralpha Boulevard," "A Planet Named Shayol," "On the Storm Planet," "The Ballad of Lost C'Mell," "The Dead Lady of Clown Town," "The Game of Rat and Dragon," "The Lady Who Sailed The Soul," "Under Old Earth," "Scanners Live in Vain"—as well as a large number of lesser, but still fas-cinating, stories, all twisted and blended and woven into an interrelated tapestry of incredible lushness and intricacy. Smith created a baroque cosmology unrivaled even today for its scope and complexity: a millennia-spanning Future History, logi-cally outlandish and elegantly strange, set against a vivid, richly colored, mythically intense universe where animals assume the shape of men, vast planoform ships whisper through multidimensional space, immense sick sheep are the most valuable objects in the universe, immortality can be bought, and the mysterious Lords of the instrumentality rule a hunted Earth too old for history. . . .

It is a cosmology that looks as evocative and bizarre today as it did in the 1960s—certainly for sheer sweep and daring of conceptualization, in its vision of how dif-ferent and strange the future will be, it rivals any contemporary vision conjured up by Cutting Age twenty-first-century writers such as Bruce Sterling and Greg Bear, and I suspect that it is timeless.

In this early story—written back when scientists were still arguing about condi-tions on the surface of Venus, enough so that it was still possible to have some wiggle-room about the possibility that there might be at least relatively Earthlike conditions there—he paints a harrowing picture of a bizarre terraforming effort that almost makes up in brute efficiency what it costs in human lives. . . .

Cordwainer Smith's books include the novel Norstrilia *and the collections* Space Lords—*one of the landmark collections of the genre—*The Best of Cordwainer Smith, Quest of the Three Worlds, Stardreamer, You Will Never Be the Same *and* The In-strumentality of Mankind. *As Felix C. Forrest, he wrote two mainstream novels,* Ria *and* Carola, *and as Carmichael Smith he wrote the thriller* Atomsk.

His most recent book is the posthumous collection The Rediscovery of Man: The Complete Short Science Fiction of Cordwainer Smith *(NESFA Press, P.O. Box 809, Framingham, MA 07101-0203), a huge book which collects almost all of his short fiction, and which will certainly stand as one of the very best collections of the decade—and a book which belongs in every complete science-fiction collection.*

"Can you imagine a rain of people through an acid fog? Can you imagine thousands and thousands of human bodies, without weapons, overwhelming the unconquerable monsters? Can you—"

"Look, sir," interrupted the reporter.

"Don't interrupt me! You ask me silly questions. I tell you I saw the Goonhogo itself. I saw it take Venus. Now ask me about that!"

The reporter had called to get an old man's reminiscences about bygone ages. He did not expect Dobyns Bennett to flare up at him.

Dobyns Bennett thrust home the psychological advantage he had gotten by taking the initiative. "Can you imagine showhices in their parachutes, a lot of them dead, floating out of a green sky? Can you imagine mothers crying as they fell? Can you imagine people pouring down on the poor helpless monsters?"

Mildly, the reporter asked what showhices were.

"That's old Chinesian for children," said Dobyns Bennett. "I saw the last of the nations burst and die, and you want to ask me about fashionable clothes and things. Real history never gets into the books. It's too shocking. I suppose you were going to ask me what I thought of the new striped pantaloons for women!"

"No," said the reporter, but he blushed. The question was in his notebook and he hated blushing.

"Do you know what the Goonhogo did?"

"What?" asked the reporter, struggling to remember just what a Goonhogo might be.

"It took Venus," said the old man, somewhat more calmly.

Very mildly, the reporter murmured, "It *did?*"

"You bet it did!" said Dobyns Bennett belligerently.

"Were you there?" asked the reporter.

"You bet I was there when the Goonhogo took Venus," said the old man. "I was there and it's the damnedest thing I've ever seen. You know who I am. I've seen more worlds than you can count, boy, and yet when the nondies and the needies and the showhices came pouring out of the sky, that was the worst thing that any man could ever see. Down on the ground, there were the loudies the way they'd always been—"

The reporter interrupted, very gently. Bennett might as well have been speaking a foreign language. All of this had happened three hundred years before. The reporter's job was to get a feature from him and to put it into a language which people of the present time could understand.

•

Respectfully he said, "Can't you start at the beginning of the story?"

"You bet. That's when I married Terza. Terza was the prettiest girl you ever saw. She was one of the Vomacts, a great family of scanners, and her father was a very important man. You see, I was thirty-two, and when a man is thirty-two, he thinks he is pretty old, but I wasn't really old, I just thought so, and he wanted Terza to marry me because she was such a complicated girl that she needed a man's help. The Court back home had found her unstable and the Instrumentality had ordered her left in her father's care until she married a man who then could take on proper custodial authority. I suppose those are old customs to you, boy—"

The reporter interrupted again. "I am sorry, old man," said he. "I know you are over four hundred years old and you're the only person who remembers the time the Goonhogo took Venus. Now, the Goonhogo was a government, wasn't it?"

"Anyone knows that," snapped the old man. "The Goonhogo was a sort of separate Chinesian government. Seventeen billion of them all crowded in one small part of Earth. Most of them spoke English the way you and I do, but they spoke their own language, too, with all those funny words that have come on down to us. They hadn't mixed in with anybody else yet. Then, you see, the Waywanjong himself gave the order and that is when the people started raining. They just fell right out of the sky. You never saw anything like it—"

The reporter had to interrupt him again and again to get the story bit by bit. The old man kept using terms that he couldn't seem to realize were lost in history and that had to be explained to be intelligible to anyone of this era. But his memory was excellent and his descriptive powers as sharp and alert as ever . . .

Young Dobyns Bennett had not been at Experimental Area A very long, before he realized that the most beautiful female he had ever seen was Terza Vomact. At the age of fourteen, she was fully mature. Some of the Vomacts did mature that way. It may have had something to do with their being descended from unregistered, illegal people centuries back in the past. They were even said to have mysterious connections with the lost world back in the age of nations when people could still put numbers on the years.

He fell in love with her and felt like a fool for doing it.

She was so beautiful, it was hard to realize that she was the daughter of Scanner Vomact himself. The scanner was a powerful man.

Sometimes romance moves too fast and it did with Dobyns Bennett because Scanner Vomact himself called in the young man and said, "I'd like to have you marry my daughter Terza, but I'm not sure she'll approve of you. If you can get her, boy, you have my blessing."

Dobyns was suspicious. He wanted to know why a senior scanner was willing to take a junior technician.

All that the scanner did was to smile. He said, "I'm a lot older than you, and with this new santaclara drug coming in that may give people hundreds of years, you may think that I died in my prime if I die at a hundred and twenty. You may live to four or five hundred. But I know my time's coming up. My wife has been dead for a long time and we have no other children and I know that Terza needs a father in a very special kind of way. The psychologist found her to be unstable. Why don't you take her outside the area? You can get a pass through the dome anytime. You can go out and play with the loudies."

Dobyns Bennett was almost as insulted as if someone had given him a pail and told him to go play in the sandpile. And yet he realized that the elements of play in courtship were fitted together and that the old man meant well.

The day that it all happened, he and Terza were outside the dome. They had been pushing loudies around.

Loudies were not dangerous unless you killed them. You could knock them down, push them out of the way, or tie them up; after a while, they slipped away and went about their business. It took a very special kind of ecologist to figure out what their business was. They floated two meters high, ninety centimeters in diameter, gently just above the land of Venus, eating microscopically. For a long time, people thought there was radiation on which they subsisted. They simply multiplied in tremendous numbers. In a silly sort of way, it was fun to push them around, but that was about all there was to do.

They never responded with intelligence.

Once, long before, a loudie taken into the laboratory for experimental purposes had typed a perfectly clear message on the typewriter. The message had read, "Why don't you Earth people go back to Earth and leave us alone? We are getting along all—"

And that was all the message that anybody had ever got out of them in three hundred years. The best laboratory conclusions was that they had very high intelligence if they ever chose to use it, but that their volitional mechanism was so profoundly different from the psychology of human beings that it was impossible to force a loudie to respond to stress as people did on Earth.

◆

The name *loudie* was some kind of word in the old Chinesian language. It meant the "ancient ones." Since it was the Chinesians who had set up the first outposts on Venus, under the orders of their supreme boss the Waywonjong, their term lingered on.

Dobyns and Terza pushed loudies, climbed over the hills and looked down into the valleys where it was impossible to tell a river from a swamp. They got thoroughly wet, their air converters stuck, and perspiration itched and tickled along their cheeks. Since they could not eat or drink while outside— at least not with any reasonable degree of safety—the excursion could not be called a picnic. There was something mildly refreshing about playing child with a very pretty girl-child—but Dobyns wearied of the whole thing.

Terza sensed his rejection of her. Quick as a sensitive animal, she became angry and petulant. "You didn't have to come out with me!"

"I wanted to," he said, "but now I'm tired and want to go home."

"You treat me like a child. All right, play with me. Or you treat me like a woman. All right, be a gentleman. But don't seesaw all the time yourself. I just got to be a little bit happy and you have to get middle-aged and condescending. I won't take it."

"Your father—" he said, realizing the moment he said it that it was a mistake.

"My father this, my father that. If you're thinking about marrying me, do it yourself." She glared at him, stuck her tongue out, ran over a dune, and disappeared.

Dobyns Bennett was baffled. He did not know what to do. She was safe enough. The loudies never hurt anyone. He decided to teach her a lesson and to go on back himself, letting her find her way home when she pleased. The Area Search Team could find her easily if she really got lost.

He walked back to the gate.

When he saw the gates locked and the emergency lights on, he realized that he had made the worst mistake of his life.

His heart sinking within him, he ran the last few meters of the way, and beat the ceramic gate with his bare hands until it opened only just enough to let him in.

"What's wrong?" he asked the doortender.

The doortender muttered something which Dobyns could not understand.

"Speak up, man!" shouted Dobyns. "What's wrong?"

"The Goonhogo is coming back and they're taking over."

"That's impossible," said Dobyns. "They couldn't—" He checked himself. *Could* they?

"The Goonhogo's taken over," the gatekeeper insisted. "They've been given the whole thing. The Earth Authority has voted it to them. The Waywonjong has decided to send people right away. They're sending them."

"What do the Chinesians want with Venus? You can't kill a loudie without contaminating a thousand acres of land. You can't push them away without them drifting back. You can't scoop them up. Nobody can live here until we solve the problem of these things. We're a long way from having solved it," said Dobyns in angry bewilderment.

The gatekeeper shook his head. "Don't ask me. That's all I hear on the radio. Everybody else is excited too."

Within an hour, the rain of people began.

Dobyns went up to the radar room, saw the skies above. The radar man himself was drumming his fingers against the desk. He said, "Nothing like this has been seen for a thousand years or more. You know what there is up there? Those are warships, the warships left over from the last of the old dirty wars. I knew the Chinesians were inside them. Everybody knew about it. It was sort of like a museum. Now they don't have any weapons in them. But do you know—there are millions of people hanging up there over Venus and I don't know what they are going to do!"

He stopped and pointed at one of the screens: "Look, you can see them running in patches. They're behind each other, so they cluster up solid. We've never had a screen look like that."

Dobyns looked at the screen. It was, as the operator said, full of blips.

As they watched, one of the men exclaimed, "What's that milky stuff down there in the lower left? See, it's—it's pouring," he said, "it's pouring somehow out of those dots. How can you pour things into a radar? it doesn't really show, does it?"

The radar man looked at his screen. He said, "Search me. I don't know what it is, either. You'll have to find out. Let's just see what happens."

Scanner Vomact came into the room. He said, once he had taken a quick, experienced glance at the screens, "This may be the strangest thing we'll ever see, but I have a feeling they're dropping people. Lots of them. Dropping them by the thousands, or by the hundreds of thousands, or even by the millions. But people are coming down there. Come along with me, you two. We'll go out and see it. There may be somebody that we can help."

☙

By this time, Dobyns' conscience was hurting him badly. He wanted to tell Vomact that he had left Terza out there, but he had hesitated—not only because he was ashamed of leaving her, but because he did not want to tattle on the child to her father. Now he spoke.

"Your daughter's still outside."

Vomact turned on him solemnly. The immense eyes looked very tranquil and very threatening, but the silky voice was controlled.

"You may find her." The scanner added, in a tone which sent the thrill of menace up Dobyns' back, "And everything will be well if you bring her back."

Dobyns nodded as though receiving an order.

"I shall," said Vomact, "go out myself, to see what I can do, but I leave the finding of my daughter to you."

They went down, put on the extra-long-period converters, carried their miniaturized survey equipment so that they could find their way back through the fog, and went out. Just as they were at the gate, the gatekeeper said, "Wait a moment, sir and excellency. I have a message for you here on the phone. Please call Control."

Scanner Vomact was not to be called lightly and he knew it. He picked up the connection unit and spoke harshly.

The radar man came on the phone screen in the gatekeeper's wall. "They're overhead now, sir."

"Who's overhead?"

"The Chinesians are. They're coming down. I don't know how many there are. There must be two thousand warships over our heads right here and there are more thousands over the rest of Venus. They're down now. If you want to see them hit ground, you'd better get outside quick."

Vomact and Dobyns went out.

Down came the Chinesians. People's bodies were raining right out of the milk-cloudy sky. Thousands upon thousands of them with plastic parachutes that looked like bubbles. Down they came.

Dobyns and Vomact saw a headless man drift down. The parachute cords had decapitated him.

A woman fell near them. The drop had torn her breathing tube loose from her crudely bandaged throat and she was choking in her own blood. She staggered toward them, tried to babble but only drooled blood with mute choking sounds, and then fell face-forward into the mud.

Two babies dropped. The adult accompanying them had been blown off course. Vomact ran, picked them up and handed them to a Chinesian man who had just landed. The man looked at the babies in his arms, sent Vomact a look of contemptuous inquiry, put the weeping children down in the cold slush of Venus, gave them a last impersonal glance and ran off on some mysterious errand of his own.

Vomact kept Bennett from picking up the children. "Come on, let's keep looking. We can't take care of all of them."

◆

The world had known that the Chinesians had a lot of unpredictable public habits, but they never suspected that the nondies and the needies and the showhices could pour down out of a poisoned sky. Only the Goonhogo itself would make such a reckless use of human life. *Nondies* were men and *needies* were women and *showhices* were the little children. And the *Goonhogo* was a name left over from the old days of nations. It meant something like republic or state or government. Whatever it was, it was the organization that ran the Chinesians in the Chinesian manner, under the Earth Authority.

And the ruler of the Goonhogo was the Waywonjong.

The Waywonjong didn't come to Venus. He just sent his people. He sent them floating down into Venus, to tackle the Venusian ecology with the only weapons which could make a settlement of that planet possible—people themselves. Human arms could tackle the loudies, the loudies who had been called "old ones" by the first Chinesian scouts to cover Venus.

The loudies had to be gathered together so gently that they would not die and, in dying, each contaminate a thousand acres. They had to be kept together by human bodies and arms in a gigantic living corral.

Scanner Vomact rushed forward.

A wounded Chinesian man hit the ground and his parachute collapsed behind him. He was clad in a pair of shorts, had a knife at his belt, canteen at his waist. He had an air converter attached next to his ear, with a tube running into his throat. He shouted something unintelligible at them and limped rapidly away.

People kept on hitting the ground all around Vomact and Dobyns.

The self-disposing parachutes were bursting like bubbles in the misty air, a moment or two after they touched the ground. Someone had done a tricky, efficient job with the chemical consequences of static electricity.

And as the two watched, the air was heavy with people. One time, Vomact was knocked down by a person. He found that it was two Chinesian children tied together.

Dobyns asked, "What are you doing? Where are you going? Do you have any leaders?"

He got cries and shouts in an unintelligible language. Here and there someone shouted in English "This way!" or "Leave us alone!" or "Keep going . . ." but that was all.

The experiment worked.

Eighty-two million people were dropped in that one day.

◆

After four hours which seemed barely short of endless, Dobyns found Terza in a corner of the cold hell. Though Venus was warm, the suffering of the almost-naked Chinesians had chilled his blood.

Terza ran toward him.

She could not speak.

She put her head on his chest and sobbed. Finally she managed to say, "I've—I've—I've tried to help, but they're too many, too many, too many!" And the sentence ended as shrill as a scream.

Dobyns led her back to the experimental area.

They did not have to talk. Her whole body told him that she wanted his love and the comfort of his presence, and that she had chosen that course of life which would keep them together.

As they left the drop area, which seemed to cover all of Venus so far as they could tell, a pattern was beginning to form. The Chinesians were beginning to round up the loudies.

Terza kissed him mutely after the gatekeeper had let them through. She did not need to speak. Then she fled to her room.

The next day, the people from Experimental Area A tried to see if they could go out and lend a hand to the settlers. It wasn't possible to lend a hand; there were too many settlers. People by the millions were scattered all over the hills and valleys of Venus, sludging through the mud and water with their human toes, crushing the alien mud, crushing the strange plants. They didn't know what to eat. They didn't know where to go. They had no leaders.

All they had were orders to gather the loudies together in large herds and hold them there with human arms.

The loudies didn't resist.

After a time-lapse of several Earth days the Goonhogo sent small scout cars. They brought a very different kind of Chinesian—these late arrivals were uniformed, educated, cruel, smug men. They knew what they were doing. And they were willing to pay any sacrifice of their own people to get it done.

They brought instructions. They put the people together in gangs. It did not matter where the nondies and needies had come from on Earth; it didn't matter whether they found their own showhices or somebody else's. They were shown the jobs to do and they got to work. Human bodies accomplished what machines could not have done—they kept the loudies firmly but gently encircled until every last one of the creatures was starved into nothingness.

Rice fields began to appear miraculously.

Scanner Vomact couldn't believe it. The Goonhogo biochemists had managed to adapt rice to the soil of Venus. And yet the seedlings came out of boxes in the scout cars and weeping people walked over the bodies of their own dead to keep the crop moving toward the planting.

Venusian bacteria could not kill human beings, nor could they dispose of human bodies after death. A problem arose and was solved. Immense sleds carried dead men, women and children—those who had fallen wrong, or drowned as they fell, or had been trampled by others—to an undisclosed destination. Dobyns suspected the material was to be used to add Earth-type organic waste to the soil of Venus, but he did not tell Terza.

The work went on.

The nondies and needies kept working in shifts. When they could not see in the darkness, they proceeded without seeing—keeping in line by touch or by shout. Foremen, newly trained, screeched commands. Workers lined up, touching fingertips. The job of building the fields kept on.

◆

"That's a big story," said the old man, "eighty-two million people dropped in a single day. And later I heard that the Waywonjong said it wouldn't have mattered if seventy million of them had died. Twelve million survivors would have been enough to make a spacehead for the Goonhogo. The Chinesians got Venus, all of it.

"But I'll never forget the nondies and the needies and the showhices falling out of the sky, men and women and children with their poor scared Chinesian faces. That funny Venusian air made them look green instead of tan. There they were, falling all around.

"You know something, young man?" said Dobyns Bennett, approaching his fifth century of age.

"What?" said the reporter.

"There won't be things like that happening on any world again. Because now, after all, there isn't any separate Goonhogo left. There's only one Instrumentality and they don't care what a man's race may have been in the ancient years. Those were the rough old days, the ones I lived in. Those were the days *men* still tried to do things."

Dobyns almost seemed to doze off, but he roused himself sharply and said, "I tell you, the sky was full of people. They fell like water. They fell like rain. I've seen the awful ants in Africa, and there's not a thing among the stars to beat them for prowling horror. Mind you, they're worse than anything the stars contain. I've seen the crazy worlds near Alpha Centauri, but I never saw anything like the time the people fell on Venus. More than eighty-two million in one day and my own little Terza lost among them.

"But the rice did sprout. And the loudies died as the walls of people held them in with human arms. Walls of people, I tell you, with volunteers jumping in to take the places of the falling ones.

"They were people still, even when they shouted in the darkness. They tried to help each other even while they fought a fight that had to be fought without violence. They were people still. And they did so win. It was crazy and impossible, but they won. Mere human beings did what machines and science would have taken another thousand years to do . . .

"The funniest thing of all was the first house that I saw a nondie put up, there in the rain of Venus. I was out there with Vomact and with a pale sad Terza. It wasn't much of a house, shaped out of twisted Venusian wood. There it was. *He* built it, the smiling half-naked Chinesian nondie. We went to the door and said to him in English, 'What are you building here, a shelter or a hospital?'

"The Chinesian grinned at us. 'No,' he said, 'gambling.'

"Vomact wouldn't believe it: 'Gambling?'

" 'Sure,' said the nondie. 'Gambling is the first thing a man needs in a strange place. It can take the worry out of his soul.' "

"Is that all?" said the reporter.

➤

Dobyns Bennett muttered that the personal part did not count. He added, "Some of my great-great-great-great-great-grandsons may come along. You count those greats. Their faces will show you easily enough that I married into the Vomact line. Terza saw what happened. She saw how people build worlds. This was the hard way to build them. She never forgot the night with the dead Chinesian babies lying in the half-illuminated mud, or the parachute ropes dissolving slowly. She heard the needies weeping and the helpless nondies comforting them and leading them off to nowhere. She remembered the cruel, neat officers coming out of the scout cars. She got home and saw the rice come up, and saw how the Goonhogo made Venus a Chinesian place."

"What happened to you personally?" asked the reporter.

"Nothing much. There wasn't any more work for us, so we closed down Experimental Area A. I married Terza.

"Anytime later, when I said to her, 'You're not such a bad girl!' she was able to admit the truth and tell me she was not. That night in the rain of people would test anybody's soul and it tested hers. She had met a big test and passed it. She used to say to me, 'I saw it once. I saw the people fall, and I never want to see another person suffer again. Keep me with you, Dobyns, keep me with you forever.'

"And," said Dobyns Bennett, "it wasn't forever, but it was a happy and sweet three hundred years. She died after our fourth diamond anniversary. Wasn't that a wonderful thing, young man?"

The reporter said it was. And yet, when he took the story back to his editor, he was told to put it into the archives. It wasn't the right kind of story for entertainment and the public would not appreciate it anymore.

Before Eden

ARTHUR C. CLARKE

Arthur C. Clarke is perhaps the most famous modern science-fiction writer in the world, seriously rivaled for that title only by the late Isaac Asimov and Robert A. Heinlein. Clarke is probably most widely known for his work on Stanley Kubrick's film 2001: A Space Odyssey, *but is also renowned as a novelist, short-story writer, and as a writer of nonfiction, usually on technological subjects such as space flight. He has won three Nebula Awards, and three Hugo Awards, the British Science Fiction Award, the John W. Campbell Memorial Award, and a Grandmaster Nebula for Life Achievement. His best-known books include the novels* Childhood's End, The City and the Stars, The Deep Range, Rendezvous with Rama, A Fall of Moondust, 2001: A Space Odyssey, 2010: Odyssey Two, 2061: Odyssey Three, Songs of Distant Earth, *and* The Fountains of Paradise, *and the collections* The Nine Billion Names of God, Tales of Ten Worlds, *and* The Sentinel. *The best known of his many nonfiction books on scientific topics are probably* Profiles of the Future *and* The Wind from the Sun, *and Clarke is generally considered to be the man who first came up with the idea of the communications satellite. His most recent books are the novel* 3001: The Final Odyssey, *the nonfiction collection* Greetings, Carbon-Based Bipeds: Collected Works 1944–1998, *the fiction collection* Collected Short Stories, *and a novel written in collaboration with Stephen Baxter,* The Light of Other Days. *Most of Clarke's best-known books will be coming back into print, appropriately enough, in 2001. Born in Somerset, England, Clarke now lives in Sri Lanka, and was recently knighted.*

Clarke wrote one of the most complete treatments of the terraforming process (and one of the earliest realistic ones) in science fiction with his groundbreaking 1951 novel The Sands of Mars, *echoes of which can be heard clearly more than forty years later in Kim Stanley Robinson's* Mars *trilogy, in Stephen Baxter's work, and elsewhere throughout the field. In the incisive story that follows, also well ahead of its time when it was published, he takes us to another planet (Venus instead of Mars) for a sharp lesson that the human race might be better off today for having learned when Clarke taught it back in 1961—that sometimes you can radically and permanently transform a planet's ecosystem without even intending to do it at all. . . .*

"I guess," said Jerry Garfield, cutting the engines, "that this is the end of the line." With a gentle sigh, the underjets faded out; deprived of its air cushion, the scout car *Rambling Wreck* settled down upon the twisted rocks of the Hesperian Plateau.

There was no way forward; on neither its jets nor its tractors could S.5—to give the *Wreck* its official name—scale the escarpment that lay ahead. The South Pole of Venus was only thirty miles away, but it might have been on another planet. They would have to turn back, and retrace their four-hundred-mile journey through this nightmare landscape.

The weather was fantastically clear, with visibility of almost a thousand yards. There was no need of radar to show the cliffs ahead; for once, the naked eye was good enough. The green auroral light, filtering down through clouds that had rolled unbroken for a million years, gave the scene an underwater appearance, and the way in which all distant objects blurred into the haze added to the impression. Sometimes it was easy to believe that they were driving across a shallow seabed, and more than once Jerry had imagined that he had seen fish floating overhead.

"Shall I call the ship, and say we're turning back?" he asked.

"Not yet," said Dr. Hutchins. "I want to think."

Jerry shot an appealing glance at the third member of the crew, but found no moral support there. Coleman was just as bad; although the two men argued furiously half the time, they were both scientists and therefore, in the opinion of a hardheaded engineer-navigator, not wholly responsible citizens. If Cole and Hutch had bright ideas about going forward, there was nothing he could do except register a protest.

Hutchins was pacing back and forth in the tiny cabin, studying charts and instruments. Presently he swung the car's searchlight toward the cliffs, and began to examine them carefully with binoculars. Surely, thought Jerry, he doesn't expect me to drive up there! S.5 was a hover-track, not a mountain goat. . . .

Abruptly, Hutchins found something. He released his breath in a sudden explosive gasp, then turned to Coleman.

"Look!" he said, his voice full of excitement. "Just to the left of that black mark! Tell me what you see."

He handed over the glasses, and it was Coleman's turn to stare.

"Well I'm damned," he said at length. "You were right. There *are* rivers on Venus. That's a dried-up waterfall."

"So you owe me one dinner at the Bel Gourmet when we get back to Cambridge. With champagne."

"No need to remind me. Anyway, it's cheap at the price. But this still leaves your other theories strictly on the crackpot level."

"Just a minute," interjected Jerry. "What's all this about rivers and waterfalls? Everyone knows they can't exist on Venus. It never gets cold enough on this steambath of a planet for the clouds to condense."

"Have you looked at the thermometer lately?" asked Hutchins with deceptive mildness.

"I've been slightly too busy driving."

"Then I've news for you. It's down to two hundred and thirty, and still falling. Don't forget—we're almost at the Pole, it's wintertime, and we're sixty thousand feet above the lowlands. All this adds up to a distinct nip in the air. If the temperature drops a few more degrees, we'll have rain. The water will be boiling, of course—but it will be water. And though George won't admit it yet, this puts Venus in a completely different light."

"Why?" asked Jerry, though he had already guessed.

"Where there's water, there may be life. We've been in too much of a

hurry to assume that Venus is sterile, merely because the average temperature's over five hundred degrees. It's a lot colder here, and that's why I've
been so anxious to get to the Pole. There are lakes up here in the highlands,
and I want to look at them."

"But *boiling* water!" protested Coleman. "Nothing could live in that!"

"There are algae that manage it on earth. And if we've learned one thing
since we started exploring the planets, it's this: wherever life has the slightest
chance of surviving, you'll find it. This is the only chance it's ever had on
Venus."

"I wish we could test your theory. But you can see for yourself—we can't
go up that cliff."

"Perhaps not in the car. But it won't be too difficult to climb those rocks,
even wearing thermosuits. All we need do is walk a few miles toward the
Pole; according to the radar maps, it's fairly level once you're over the rim.
We could manage in—oh, twelve hours at the most. Each of us has been
out for longer than that, in much worse conditions."

That was perfectly true. Protective clothing that had been designed to
keep men alive in the Venusian lowlands would have an easy job here, where
it was only a hundred degrees hotter than Death Valley in midsummer.

"Well," said Coleman, "you know the regulations. You can't go by yourself,
and someone has to stay here to keep contact with the ship. How do we
settle it this time—chess or cards?"

"Chess takes too long," said Hutchins, "especially when you two play it."
He reached into the chart table and produced a well-worn pack. "Cut them,
Jerry."

"Ten of spades. Hope you can beat it, George."

"So do I. Damn—only five of clubs. Well, give my regards to the Venusians."

Despite Hutchins' assurance, it was hard work climbing the escarpment.
The slope was not too steep, but the weight of oxygen gear, refrigerated
thermosuit, and scientific equipment came to more than a hundred pounds
per man. The lower gravity—thirteen percent weaker than Earth's—gave a
little help, but not much, as they toiled up screes, rested on ledges to regain
breath, and then clambered on again through the submarine twilight. The
emerald glow that washed around them was brighter than that of the full
Moon on Earth. A moon would have been wasted on Venus, Jerry told
himself; it could never have been seen from the surface, there were no oceans
for it to rule—and the incessant aurora was a far more constant source of
light.

They had climbed more than two thousand feet before the ground leveled
out into a gentle slope, scarred here and there by channels that had clearly
been cut by running water. After a little searching, they came across a gulley
wide and deep enough to merit the name of riverbed, and started to walk
along it.

"I've just thought of something," said Jerry after they had traveled a few
hundred yards. "Suppose there's a storm up ahead of us? I don't feel like
facing a tidal wave of boiling water."

"If there's a storm," replied Hutchins a little impatiently, "we'll hear it. There'll be plenty of time to reach high ground."

He was undoubtedly right, but Jerry felt no happier as they continued to climb the gently shelving watercourse. His uneasiness had been growing ever since they had passed over the brow of the cliff and had lost radio contact with the scout car. In this day and age, to be out of touch with one's fellow men was a unique and unsettling experience. It had never happened to Jerry before in all his life; even aboard the *Morning Star* when they were a hundred million miles from Earth, he could always send a message to his family and get a reply back within minutes. But now, a few yards of rock had cut him off from the rest of mankind; if anything happened to them here, no one would ever know, unless some later expedition found their bodies. George would wait for the agreed number of hours; then he would head back to the ship—alone. I guess I'm not really the pioneering type, Jerry told himself. I like running complicated machines, and that's how I got involved in space flight. But I never stopped to think where it would lead, and now it's too late to change my mind. . . .

They had traveled perhaps three miles toward the Pole, following the meanders of the riverbed, when Hutchins stopped to make observations and collect specimens. "Still getting colder!" he said. "The temperature's down to one hundred and ninety-nine. That's far and away the lowest ever recorded on Venus. I wish we could call George and let him know."

Jerry tried all the wave bands; he even attempted to raise the ship—the unpredictable ups and downs of the planet's ionosphere sometimes made such long-distance reception possible—but there was not a whisper of a carrier wave above the roar and crackle of the Venusian thunderstorms.

"This is even better," said Hutchins, and now there was real excitement in his voice. "The oxygen concentration's way up—fifteen parts in a million. It was only five back at the car, and down in the lowlands you can scarcely detect it."

"But fifteen in a *million!*" protested Jerry. "Nothing could breathe that!"

"You've got hold of the wrong end of the stick," Hutchins explained. "Nothing does breathe it. Something *makes* it. Where do you think Earth's oxygen comes from? It's all produced by life—by growing plants. Before there were plants on Earth, our atmosphere was just like this one—a mess of carbon dioxide and ammonia and methane. Then vegetation evolved, and slowly converted the atmosphere into something that animals could breathe."

"I see," said Jerry, "and you think that the same process has just started here?"

"It looks like it. *Something* not far from here is producing oxygen—and plant life is the simplest explanation."

"And where there are plants," mused Jerry, "I suppose you'll have animals, sooner or later."

"Yes," said Hutchins, packing his gear and starting up the gulley, "though it takes a few hundred million years. We may be too soon—but I hope not."

"That's all very well," Jerry answered. "But suppose we meet something that doesn't like us? We've no weapons."

Hutchins gave a snort of disgust.

"And we don't need them. Have you stopped to think what we look like? Any animal would run a mile at the sight of us."

There was some truth in that. The reflecting metal foil of their thermo-suits covered them from head to foot like flexible, glittering armor. No insects had more elaborate antennas than those mounted on their helmets and back-packs, and the wide lenses through which they stared out at the world looked like blank yet monstrous eyes. Yes, there were few animals on Earth that would stop to argue with such apparitions; but any Venusians might have different ideas.

Jerry was still mulling this over when they came upon the lake. Even at that first glimpse, it made him think not of the life they were seeking, but of death. Like a black mirror, it lay amid a fold of the hills; its far edge was hidden in the eternal mist, and ghostly columns of vapor swirled and danced upon its surface. All it needed, Jerry told himself, was Charon's ferry waiting to take them to the other side—or the Swan of Tuonela swimming majes-tically back and forth as it guarded the entrance to the Underworld. . . .

Yet for all this, it was a miracle—the first free water that men had ever found on Venus. Hutchins was already on his knees, almost in an attitude of prayer. But he was only collecting drops of the precious liquid to examine through his pocket microscope.

"Anything there?" asked Jerry anxiously.

Hutchins shook his head.

"If there is, it's too small to see with this instrument. I'll tell you more when we're back at the ship." He sealed a test tube and placed it in his collecting bag, as tenderly as any prospector who had just found a nugget laced with gold. It might be—it probably was—nothing more than plain water. But it might also be a universe of unknown, living creatures on the first stage of their billion-year journey to intelligence.

Hutchins had walked no more than a dozen yards along the edge of the lake when he stopped again, so suddenly that Garfield nearly collided with him.

"What's the matter?" Jerry asked. "Seen something?"

"That dark patch of rock over there. I noticed it before we stopped at the lake."

"What about it? It looks ordinary enough to me."

"*I think it's grown bigger.*"

All his life, Jerry was to remember this moment. Somehow he never doubted Hutchins' statement; by this time he could believe anything, even that rocks could grow. The sense of isolation and mystery, the presence of that dark and brooding lake, the never-ceasing rumble of distant storms and the green flickering of the aurora—all these had done something to his mind, had prepared it to face the incredible. Yet he felt no fear; that would come later.

He looked at the rock. It was about five hundred feet away, as far as he could estimate. In this dim, emerald light it was hard to judge distances or dimensions. The rock—or whatever it was—seemed to be a horizontal slab of almost black material, lying near the crest of a low ridge. There was a second, much smaller, patch of similar material near it; Jerry tried to measure and memorize the gap between them, so that he would have some yardstick to detect any change.

Even when he saw that the gap was slowly shrinking, he still felt no alarm—only a puzzled excitement. Not until it had vanished completely, and he realized how his eyes had tricked him, did that awful feeling of helpless terror strike into his heart.

Here were no growing or moving rocks. What they were watching was a dark tide, a crawling carpet, sweeping slowly but inexorably toward them over the top of the ridge.

The moment of sheer, unreasoning panic lasted, mercifully, no more than a few seconds. Garfield's first terror began to fade as soon as he recognized its cause. For that advancing tide had reminded him, all too vividly, of a story he had read many years ago about the army ants of the Amazon, and the way in which they destroyed everything in their path. . . .

But whatever this tide might be, it was moving too slowly to be a real danger, unless it cut off their line of retreat. Hutchins was staring at it intently through their only pair of binoculars; he was the biologist, and he was holding his ground. No point in making a fool of myself, thought Jerry, by running like a scalded cat, if it isn't necessary.

"For heaven's sake," he said at last, when the moving carpet was only a hundred yards away and Hutchins had not uttered a word or stirred a muscle. "What *is* it?"

Hutchins slowly unfroze, like a statue coming to life.

"Sorry," he said. "I'd forgotten all about you. Its a plant, of course. At least, I suppose we'd better call it that."

"But it's *moving!*"

"Why should that surprise you? So do terrestrial plants. Ever seen speeded-up movies of ivy in action?"

"That still stays in one place—it doesn't crawl all over the landscape."

"Then what about the plankton plants of the sea? *They* can swim when they have to."

Jerry gave up; in any case, the approaching wonder had robbed him of words.

He still thought of the thing as a carpet—a deep-pile one, raveled into tassels at the edges. It varied in thickness as it moved; in some parts it was a mere film; in others, it heaped up to a depth of a foot or more. As it came closer and he could see its texture. Jerry was reminded of black velvet. He wondered what it felt like to the touch, then remembered that it would burn his fingers even if it did nothing else to them. He found himself thinking, in the light-headed nervous reaction that often follows a sudden shock: "If there *are* any Venusians, we'll never be able to shake hands with them. They'd burn us, and we'd give them frostbite."

So far, the thing had shown no signs that it was aware of their presence. It had merely flowed forward like the mindless tide that it almost certainly was. Apart from the fact that it climbed over small obstacles, it might have been an advancing flood of water.

And then, when it was only ten feet away, the velvet tide checked itself.

On the right and the left, it still flowed forward; but dead ahead it slowed to a halt.

"We're being encircled," said Jerry anxiously. "Better fall back, until we're sure it's harmless."

To his relief, Hutchins stepped back at once. After a brief hesitation, the creature resumed its slow advance and the dent in its front line straightened out.

Then Hutchins stepped forward again—and the thing slowly withdrew. Half a dozen times the biologist advanced, only to retreat again, and each time the living tide ebbed and flowed in synchronism with his movements. I never imagined, Jerry told himself, that I'd live to see a man waltzing with a plant. . . .

"Thermophobia," said Hutchins. "Purely automatic reaction. It doesn't like our heat."

"*Our* heat!" protested Jerry. "Why, we're living icicles by comparison."

"Of course—but our suits aren't, and that's all it knows about."

Stupid of me, thought Jerry. When you were snug and cool inside your thermosuit, it was easy to forget that the refrigeration unit on your back was pumping a blast of heat out into the surrounding air. No wonder the Venusian plant had shied away. . . .

"Let's see how it reacts to light," said Hutchins. He switched on his chest lamp, and the green auroral glow was instantly banished by the flood of pure white radiance. Until man had come to this planet, no white light had ever shone upon the surface of Venus, even by day. As in the seas of Earth, there was only a green twilight, deepening slowly to utter darkness.

The transformation was so stunning that neither man could check a cry of astonishment. Gone in a flash was the deep, somber black of the thick-piled velvet carpet at their feet. Instead, as far as their lights carried, lay a blazing pattern of glorious, vivid reds, laced with streaks of gold. No Persian prince could ever have commanded so opulent a tapestry from his weavers, yet this was the accidental product of biological forces. Indeed, until they had switched on their floods, these superb colors had not even existed, and they would vanish once more when the alien light of Earth ceased to conjure them into being.

"Tikov was right," murmured Hutchins. "I wish he could have known."

"Right about what?" asked Jerry, though it seemed almost a sacrilege to speak in the presence of such loveliness.

"Back in Russia, fifty years ago, he found that plants living in very cold climates tended to be blue and violet, while those from hot ones were red or orange. He predicted that the Martian vegetation would be violet, and said that if there were plants on Venus they'd be red. Well, he was right on both counts. But we can't stand here all day—we've work to do."

"You're sure it's quite safe?" asked Jerry, some of his caution reasserting itself.

"Absolutely—it can't touch our suits even if it wants to. Anyway, it's moving past us."

That was true. They could see now that the entire creature—if it was a single plant, and not a colony—covered a roughly circular area about a hundred yards across. It was sweeping over the ground, as the shadow of a cloud moves before the wind—and where it had rested, the rocks were pitted with innumerable tiny holes that might have been etched by acid.

"Yes," said Hutchins, when Jerry remarked about this. "That's how some lichens feed; they secrete acids that dissolve rock. But no questions, please—not till we get back to the ship. I've several lifetimes' work here, and a couple of hours to do it in."

This was botany on the run. . . . The sensitive edge of the huge plant-thing could move with surprising speed when it tried to evade them. It was as if they were dealing with an animated flapjack, an acre in extent. There was no reaction—apart from the automatic avoidance of their exhaust heat—when Hutchins snipped samples or took probes. The creature flowed steadily onward over hills and valleys, guided by some strange vegetable instinct. Perhaps it was following some vein of mineral; the geologists could decide that, when they analyzed the rock samples that Hutchins had collected both before and after the passage of the living tapestry.

There was scarcely time to think or even to frame the countless questions that their discovery had raised. Presumably these creatures must be fairly common, for them to have found one so quickly. How did they reproduce? By shoots, spores, fission, or some other means? Where did they get their energy? What relatives, rivals, or parasites did they have? This could not be the only form of life on Venus—the very idea was absurd, for if you had one species, you must have thousands. . . .

Sheer hunger and fatigue forced them to a halt at last. The creature they were studying could eat its way around Venus—though Hutchins believed that it never went very far from the lake, because from time to time it approached the water and inserted a long, tubelike tendril into it—but the animals from Earth had to rest.

It was a great relief to inflate the pressurized tent, climb in through the air lock, and strip off their thermosuits. For the first time, as they relaxed inside their tiny plastic hemisphere, the true wonder and importance of the discovery forced itself upon their minds. This world around them was no longer the same; Venus was no longer dead—it had joined Earth and Mars.

For life called to life, across the gulfs of space. Everything that grew or moved upon the face of any planet was a portent, a promise that Man was not alone in this Universe of blazing suns and swirling nebulae. If as yet he had found no companions with whom he could speak, that was only to be expected, for the light-years and the ages still stretched before him, waiting to be explored. Meanwhile, he must guard and cherish the life he found, whether it be upon Earth or Mars or Venus.

So Graham Hutchins, the happiest biologist in the Solar System, told himself as he helped Garfield collect their refuse and seal it into a plastic disposal bag. When they deflated the tent and started on the homeward journey, there was no sign of the creature they had been examining. That was just as well; they might have been tempted to linger for more experiments, and already it was getting uncomfortably close to their deadline.

No matter; in a few months they would be back with a team of assistants, far more adequately equipped and with the eyes of the world upon them.

Evolution had labored for a billion years to make this meeting possible; it could wait a little longer.

⬗

For a while nothing moved in the greenly glimmering, fog-bound landscape; it was deserted by man and crimson carpet alike. Then, flowing over the wind-carved hills, the creature reappeared. Or perhaps it was another of the same strange species; no one would ever know.

It flowed past the little cairn of stones where Hutchins and Garfield had buried their wastes. And then it stopped.

It was not puzzled, for it had no mind. But the chemical urges that drove it relentlessly over the polar plateau were crying: Here, here! Somewhere close at hand was the most precious of all the foods it needed—phosphorous, the element without which the spark of life could never ignite. It began to nuzzle the rocks, to ooze into the cracks and crannies, to scratch and scrabble with probing tendrils. Nothing that it did was beyond the capacity of any plant or tree on Earth—but it moved a thousand times more quickly, requiring only minutes to reach its goal and pierce through the plastic film.

And then it feasted, on food more concentrated than any it had ever known. It absorbed the carbohydrates and the proteins and the phosphates, the nicotine from the cigarette ends, the cellulose from the paper cups and spoons. All these it broke down and assimilated into its strange body, without difficulty and without harm.

Likewise it absorbed a whole microcosmos of living creatures—the bacteria and viruses which, upon an older planet, had evolved into a thousand deadly strains. Though only a very few could survive in this heat and this atmosphere, they were sufficient. As the carpet crawled back to the lake, it carried contagion to all its world.

Even as the Morning Star set course for her distant home, Venus was dying. The films and photographs and specimens that Hutchins was carrying in triumph were more precious even than he knew. They were the only record that would ever exist of life's third attempt to gain a foothold in the Solar System.

Beneath the clouds of Venus, the story of Creation was ended.

Hunter, Come Home

RICHARD McKENNA

The late Richard McKenna was probably best known in his lifetime as author of the fat and thoughtful best-selling mainstream novel The Sand Pebbles—*later made into a big-budget but inferior (to the book) screen spectacular starring Steve Mc-Queen—but during his short career, before his tragically early death in 1964, he also wrote a handful of powerful and elegant short science-fiction stories that stand among the best work of the first half of the 1960s. The roster of them, alas, is short: the poignant and lyrical "Casey Agonistes," the strange and wonderful novella "Fiddler's Green," "The Night of Hoggy Dam," "Mine Own Ways," "Bramble Bush," and "The Secret Place," for which he won a posthumous Nebula Award. Many of these stories question the nature of reality, and investigate our flawed and prejudiced perceptions of it with a depth and complexity rivaled elsewhere at that time only by the work of Philip K. Dick. All of them reveal the sure touch of a master craftsman, and it is intriguing—if, of course, pointless—to wonder what kind of work McKenna would be turning out now, if fate had spared him. Almost all of McKenna's short fiction was collected in* Casey Agonistes and Other Science Fiction and Fantasy Stories, *now long out of print. A collection of his essays,* New Eyes for Old, *was published after his death.*

In the compelling and immensely sad story that follows, he sounds one of the earliest cautionary notes ever raised about the whole notion of terraforming, one which will echo in many stories to come, pointing out that creating a new world inevitably involves destroying the old. But suppose the old world doesn't want to go?

On that planet the damned trees were immortal, the new guys said in disgust, so there was no wood for campfires and they had to burn pyrolene doused on raw stem fragments. Roy Craig crouched over the fire tending a bubbling venison stew and caught himself wishing they might still use the electric galley inside their flyer. But the new guys were all red dots and they wanted flame in the open and of course they were right.

Four of them sat across the fire from Craig, talking loudly and loading explosive pellets. They wore blue field denims and had roached hair and a red dot tattooed on their foreheads. Bork Wilde, the new field chief, stood watching them. He was tall and bold featured, with roached black hair, and he had two red dots on his forehead. Craig's reddish hair was unroached and except for freckles his forehead was blank, because he had never taken the Mordin manhood test. For all his gangling young six-foot body, he felt like a boy among men. As the only blanky in a crew of red dots, he caught all the menial jobs now. It was not pleasant.

They were a six-man ringwalling crew and they were camped beside their flyer, a gray, high-sided cargo job, a safe two miles downslope from a big ringwall. All around them the bare, fluted, silvery stems speared and branched fifty feet overhead and gave a watery cast to the twilight. Normally the stems and twigs would be covered with two lobed phytozoon leaves of all sizes and color patterns. The men and their fire had excited the leaves and they had detached themselves, to hover in a pulsating rainbow cloud high enough to catch the sun above the silver tracery of the upper branches. They piped and twittered and shed a spicy perfume. Certain daring ones dipped low above the men. One of the pellet loaders, a little rat-faced man named Cobb, hurled a flaming chunk up through them.

"Shut up, you flitterbugs!" he roared. "Let a man hear himself think!"

"Can you really think, Cobbo?" Whelan asked.

"If I think I think, then I'm thinking, ain't I?"

The men laughed. The red-and-white fibrous root tangle underfoot was slowly withdrawing, underground and to the sides, leaving bare soil around the fire. The new guys thought it was to escape the fire, but Craig remembered the roots had always done that when the old ringwall crew used to camp without fire. By morning the whole area around the flyer would be bare soil. A brown, many-legged crawler an inch long pushed out of the exposed soil and scuttled after the retreating roots. Craig smiled at it and stirred the stew. A small green-and-red phyto leaf dropped from the cloud and settled on his knobby wrist. He let it nuzzle at him. Its thin, velvety wings waved slowly. A much thickened midrib made it a kind of body with no head or visible appendages. Craig turned his wrist over and wondered idly why the phyto did not fall off. It was a pretty little thing.

A patterned green-and-gold phyto with wings as large as dinner plates settled on Wilde's shoulder. Wilde snatched it and tore its wings with thick fingers. It whimpered and fluttered. Craig winced.

"Stop it!" he said involuntarily and then, apologetically, "It can't hurt you, Mr. Wilde. It was just curious."

"Who pulled your trigger, Blanky?" Wilde asked lazily. "I wish these damned bloodsucking butterflies *could* know what I'm doing here."

He turned and kicked one of the weak, turgor-rigid stems and brought it crumpling down across the flyer. He threw the torn phyto after it and laughed, showing big horse teeth. Craig bit his lip.

"Chow's ready," he said. "Come and get it."

After cleanup it got dark, with only one moon in the sky, and the phytos furled their wings and went to sleep on the upper branches. The fire died away. The men rolled up in blankets and snored. Craig sat there. He saw Sidis come and stand looking out the doorway of the lighted main cabin. Sidis was the Belconti ecologist who had been boss of the old ringwall crew. He was along on this first trip with the new men only to break Wilde in as crew chief. He insisted on eating and sleeping inside the flyer, to the scorn of the Planet Mordin red dots. His forehead was blank as Craig's, but that was little comfort. Sidis was from Planet Belconti, where they had different customs.

For Mordinmen, courage was the supreme good. They were descendants of a lost Earth-colony that had lapsed to a stone age technology and fought its way back to gunpowder in ceaseless war against the fearsome Great Russel dinotheres who were the dominant life-form on Planet Mordin before men came and for a long time after. For many generations young candidates for manhood went forth in a sworn band to kill a Great Russel with spears and and arrows. When rifles came, they hunted him singly. The survivors wore the red dot of manhood and fathered the next generation. Then the civilized planets rediscovered Mordin. Knowledge flowed in. Population exploded. Suddenly there were not enough Great Russels left alive to meet the need. Craig's family had not been able to buy him a Great Russel hunt and he could not become a man.

I'll have my chance yet, Craig thought dourly.

Ten years before Craig's birth the Mordin Hunt Council found the phyto planet unclaimed and set out to convert it to one great dinothere hunting range. The Earth-type Mordin biota could neither eat nor displace the alien phytos. Mordin contracted with Belconti biologists to exterminate the native life, Mordin laborers served under Belconti biotechs. All were blankies; no red dots would serve under the effete Belcontis, many of whom were women. Using the killer plant *Thanasis*, the Belcontis cleared two large islands and restocked them with a Mordin biota. One they named Base Island and made their headquarters. On the other they installed a Great Russel dinothere. He flourished.

When I was little, they told me I'd kill my Great Russel on this planet, Craig thought. He clasped his arms around his knees. There was still only the one Great Russel on the whole planet.

Because for thirty years the continents refused to die. The phytos encysted *Thanasis* areas, adapted, recovered ground, Belconti genesmiths designed ever more deadly strains of *Thanasis*, pushing it to the safe upper limit of its recombination index. After decades of dubious battle *Thanasis* began clearly losing ground. The Belcontis said the attempt must be given up. But the phyto planet had become the symbol of future hope to curb present social unrest on Mordin. The Hunt Council would not give up the fight. Mordin red dots were sent to study biotechnics on Belconti. Then they came to the phyto planet to do the job themselves.

Craig was already there, finishing out a two-year labor contract. Working with other blankies under a Belconti boss, he had almost forgotten the pain of withheld manhood. He had extended his contract for two more years. Then, a month ago, the red dots had come in the Mordin relief ship, to relieve both Belconti biotechs and the Mordin field crews. The Belcontis would go home on their own relief ship in about a year. Craig was left the only blanky on the planet, except for the Belcontis, and they didn't count.

I'm already alone, he thought. He bowed his head on his knees and wished he could sleep. Someone touched his shoulder. He looked up to see Sidis beside him.

"Come inside, will you, Roy?" Sidis whispered. "I want to talk to you."

Craig sat down across from Sidis at the long table in the main cabin. Sidis was a slender, dark man with the gentle Belconti manners and a wry smile.

"I'm worried what you'll do these next two years," he said. "I don't like the way they order you around, that nasty little Cobb in particular. Why do you take it?"

"I have to because I'm a blanky."

"You can't help that. If it's one of your laws, it's not a fair law."

"It's fair because it's natural," Craig said. "I don't like not being a man, but that's just how it is."

"You are a man. You're twenty-four years old."

"I'm not a man until I feel like one," Craig said. "I can't feel like one until I kill my Great Russel."

"I'm afraid you'd still feel out of place," Sidis said. "I've watched you for two years and I think you have a certain quality your own planet has no use for. So I have a proposition." He glanced at the door, then back to Craig. "Declare yourself a Belconti citizen, Roy. We'll all sponsor you. I know Mil Ames will find you a job on the staff. You can go home to Belconti with us."

"Great Russel!" Craig said. "I couldn't never do that, Mr. Sidis."

"Why couldn't you? Do you want to go through life as a Mordin blanky? Would you ever get a wife?"

"Maybe. Some woman the red dots passed over. She'd hate me, for her bad luck."

"And you call that fair?"

"It's fair because it's natural. It's natural for a woman to want an all-the-way man instead of a boy that just grew up."

"Not for Belconti women. How about it, Roy?"

Craig clasped his hands between his knees. He lowered his head and shook it slowly.

"No. No. I couldn't. My place is here, fighting for a time when no kid has to grow up cheated, like I been." He raised his head. "Besides, no Mordinman ever runs away from a fight."

Sidis smiled. "This fight is already lost."

"Not the way Mr. Wilde talks. In the labs at Base Camp they're going to use a trans-something, I hear."

"Translocator in the gene matrix," Sidis said. His face shadowed. "I guarantee they won't do it while Mil Ames runs the labs. After we go, they'll probably kill themselves in a year." He looked sharply at Craig. "I hadn't meant to tell you that, but it's one reason I hope you'll leave with us."

"How kill ourselves?"

"With an outlaw free-system."

Craig shook his head. Sidis looked thoughtful.

"Look, you know how the phyto stems are all rooted together underground like one huge plant," he said. "*Thanasis* pumps self-duplicating enzyme systems into them, trying to predigest the whole continent. In the labs we design those free-systems. They can digest a man, too, and that's what you get inoculated against each time we design a new one. We also design a specific control virus able to kill off each new strain of *Thanasis*. Well, then." He steepled his fingers. "With translocation, *Thanasis* can redesign its own free-systems in the field, you might say. It could come up with something impossible to immunize, something no control virus we know how to make could handle. Then it would kill us and rule the planet itself."

"That's what happened on Planet Froy, isn't it?"

"Yes. That's what you risk. And you can't win. So come to Belconti with us."

Craig stood up. "I almost wish you didn't tell me that, about the danger," he said. "Now I can't think about leaving."

Sidis leaned back and spread his fingers on the table. "Talk to Midori Blake before you say no for sure," he said. "I know she's fond of you, Roy. I thought you rather liked her."

"I do like to be around her," Craig said. "I liked it when you used to go there, 'stead of camping in the field. I wish we did now."

"I'll try to persuade Wilde. Think it over, will you?"

"I can't think," Craig said. "I don't know what I feel." He turned to the door. "I'm going out and walk and try to think."

"Good night, Roy." Sidis reached for a book.

➤

The second moon was just rising. Craig walked through a jungle of ghostly silver stems. Phytos clinging to them piped sleepily, disturbed by his passage. I'm too ignorant to be a Belconti, he thought. He was nearing the ringwall. Stems grew more thickly, became harder, fused at last into a sloping, ninety-foot dam. Craig climbed halfway up and stopped. It was foolhardy to go higher without a protective suit. *Thanasis* was on the other side. Its free-systems diffused hundreds of feet, even in still air. The phyto stems were all rooted together like one big plant and *Thanasis* ate into it like a sickness. The stems formed ringwalls around stands of *Thanasis* to stop its spread and force it to poison itself. Craig climbed a few feet higher.

Sure I'm big enough to whip Cobb, he thought. Whip any of them, except Mr. Wilde. But he knew that in a quarrel his knees would turn to water and his voice squeak off to nothing, because they were men and he was not.

"Just the same, I'm not a coward," he said aloud.

He climbed to the top. *Thanasis* stretched off in a sea of blackness beneath the moons. Just below he could see the outline of narrow, pointed leaves furred with stinging hairs and beaded with poison meant to be rainwashed into the roots of downslope prey. The ringwall impounded the poisoned water. This stand of *Thanasis* was drowning in it and it was desperate. He saw the tendrils groping the flinty ringwall surface, hungry to release free-systems into enemy tissue and follow after to suck and absorb. They felt his warmth and waved feebly at him. This below him was the woody, climbing form. They said even waist-high shrubs could eat a man in a week.

I'm not afraid, Craig thought. He sat down and took off his boots and let his bare feet dangle above the *Thanasis*. Midori Blake and all the Belcontis would think this was crazy. They didn't understand about courage—all they had was brains. He liked them anyway, Midori most of all. He thought about her as he gazed off across the dark *Thanasis*. The whole continent would have to be like that, first. Then they'd kill off *Thanasis* with control virus and plant grass and real trees and bring birds and animals and it would all be like Base and Russel Islands were now. Sidis was wrong. That trans-stuff would do it. He'd stay and help and earn the rest of the money he needed.

He felt better, with his mind made up. Then he felt a gentle tug at his left ankle.

Fierce, sudden pain stabbed his ankle. He jerked his leg up. The tendril broke and came with it, still squirming and stinging. Craig whistled and swore as he scraped it off with a boot heel, careful not to let it touch his hands. Then he pulled on his right boot and hurried back to camp for treatment.

He carried his left boot, because he knew how fast his ankle would swell. He reached camp with his left leg one screaming ache. Sidis was still up. He neutralized the poison, gave Craig a sedative and made him turn in to one of the bunks inside the flyer. He did not ask questions. He looked down at Craig with his wry smile.

"You Mordinmen," he said, and shook his head.

The Belcontis were always saying that.

◆

In the morning Cobb sneered and Wilde was furious.

"If you're shooting for a week on the sick list, aim again," Wilde said. "I'll give you two days."

"He needs two weeks," Sidis said. "I'll do his work."

"I'll work," Craig said. "It don't hurt so much I can't work."

"Take today off," Wilde said, mollified.

"I'll work today," Craig said. "I'm all right."

It was a tortured day under the hot yellow sun, with his foot wrapped in sacks and stabbing pain up his spine with every step. Craig drove his power auger deep into basal ringwall tissue and the aromatic, red-purple sap gushed out and soaked his feet. Then he pushed in the explosive pellet, shouldered his rig and paced off the next position. Over and over he did it, like a machine, not stopping to eat his lunch, ignoring the phytos that clung to his neck and hands. He meant to finish his arc before the others, if it killed him. But when he finished and had time to think about it, his foot felt better than it had all day. He snapped a red cloth to his auger shaft and waved it high and the flyer slanted down to pick him up. Sidis was at the controls.

"You're the first to finish," he said. "I don't see why you're even alive. Go and lie down now."

"I'll take the controls," Craig said. "I feel good."

"I guess you're proving something," Sidis smiled. "All right."

He gave Craig the controls and went aft. Driving the flyer was one of the menial jobs that Craig liked. He liked being alone in the little control cabin, with its two seats and windows all around. He lifted to a thousand feet and glanced along the ringwall, curving out of sight in both directions. The pent sea of *Thanasis* was dark green by daylight. The phyto area outside the ringwall gleamed silvery, with an overplay of shifting colors, and it was very beautiful. Far and high in the north he saw a colored cloud among the fleecy ones. It was a mass of migratory phytos drifting in the wind. It was beautiful too.

"They're very fast at transferring substance to grow or repair the ringwalls," he heard Sidis telling Wilde back in the main cabin. "You'll notice the biomass downslope is less dense. When you release that poisoned water from inside the ringwall you get a shock effect and *Thanasis* follows up fast. But a new ringwall always forms."

"Next time through I'll blow fifty-mile arcs," Wilde said.

Craig slanted down to pick up Jordan. He was a stocky, sandy-haired man about Craig's age. He scrambled aboard grinning.

"Beat us again, hey, Craig?" he said. "That took guts, boy! You're all right!"

"I got two years' practice on you guys," Craig said.

The praise made him feel good. It was the first time Jordan had called him by name instead of "Blanky." He lifted the flyer again. Jordan sat down in the spare seat.

"How's the foot?" he asked.

"Pretty good. I might get my boot on, unlaced," Craig said.

"Don't try. I'll take camp chores tonight," Jordan said. "You rest that foot, Craig."

"There's Whelan signaling," Craig said.

He felt himself blushing with pleasure as he slanted down to pick up Whelan. Jordan went aft. When Rice and Cobb had been picked up, Craig hovered the flyer at two miles and Wilde pulsed off the explosive. Twenty miles of living ringwall tissue fountained in dust and flame. Phytos rising in terrified, chromatic clouds marked the rolling shock wave. Behind it the silvery plain darkened with the sheet flow of poisoned water.

"Hah! Go it, *Thanasis*!" Wilde shouted. "I swear to bullets, that's a pretty sight down there!" He sighed. "Well, that makes it a day, men. Sidis, where's a good place to camp?"

"We're only an hour from Burton Island," Sidis said. "I used to stop at the taxonomy station there every night, when we worked this area."

"Probably why you never got anywhere, too," Wilde said. "But I want a look at that island. The Huntsman's got plans for it."

He shouted orders up to Craig. Craig lifted to ten miles and headed southeast at full throttle. A purplish sea rolled above the silvery horizon. Far on the sea rim beaded islands climbed to view. It had been a good day, Craig thought. Jordan seemed to want to be friends. And now at long last he was going to see Midori Blake again.

← →

He grounded the flyer on slagged earth near the familiar gray stone buildings on the eastern headland. The men got out and George and Helen Toyama, smiling and gray-haired in lab smocks, came to welcome them. Craig's left boot was tight and it hurt, but he could wear it unlaced. Helen told him Midori was painting in the gorge. He limped down the gorge path, past Midori's small house and the Toyama home on the cliff edge at left. Midori and the Toyamas were the only people on Burton Island. The island was a phyto research sanctuary and it had never been touched by *Thanasis*. It was the only place other than Base Camp where humans lived permanently.

The gorge was Midori's special place. She painted it over and over, never satisfied. Craig knew it well, the quartz ledge, the cascading waterfall and pool, the phytos dancing in sunlight that the silvery stem forest changed to the quality of strong moonlight. Midori said it was the peculiar light that she could never capture. Craig liked watching her paint, most of all when she forgot him and sang to herself. She was clean and apart and beautiful and it was just good to be in the same world with her. Through the plash of the waterfall and the phyto piping Craig heard her singing before her easel beside a quartz boulder. She heard him and turned and smiled warmly.

"Roy! I'm so glad to see you!" she said. "I was afraid you'd gone home after all."

She was small and dainty under her gray dress, with large black eyes and delicate features. Her dark hair snugged boyishly close to her head. Her voice had a natural, birdlike quality and she moved and gestured with the quick grace of a singing bird. Craig grinned happily.

"For a while I almost wished I did," he said. "Now I'm glad again I didn't." He limped toward her.

"Your foot!" she said. "Come over here and sit down." She tugged him to a seat on the boulder. "What happened?"

"Touch of *Thanasis*. It's nothing much."

"Take off your boot! You don't want pressure on it!"

She helped him take the boot off and ran cool fingertips over the red, swollen ankle. Then she sat beside him.

"I know it hurts you. How did it happen?"

"I was kind of unhappy," he said. "I went and sat on a ringwall and let my bare feet hang over."

"Foolish Roy. Why were you unhappy?"

"Oh . . . things." Several brilliant phytos settled on his bare ankle. He let them stay. "We got to sleep in the field now, 'stead of coming here. The new guys are all red dots. I'm just a nothing again and—"

"You mean they think they're better than you?"

"They are better, and that's what hurts. Killing a Great Russel is a kind of spirit thing, Midori." He scuffed his right foot. "I'll see the day when this planet has enough Great Russels so no kid has to grow up cheated."

"The phytos are not going to die," she said softly. "It's very clear now. We're defeated."

"You Belcontis are. Mordinmen never give up."

"*Thanasis* is defeated. Will you shoot phytos with rifles?"

"Please don't joke about rifles. We're going to use trans-something on *Thanasis*."

"Translocation? Oh, no!" She raised her fingers to her lips. "It can't be controlled for field use," she said. "They wouldn't dare!"

"Mordinmen dare anything," he said proudly. "These guys all studied on Belconti, they know how. That's another thing. . . ."

He scuffed his foot again. Phytos were on both their heads and shoulders now and all over his bared ankle. They twittered faintly.

"What, Roy?"

"They make me feel ignorant. Here I been ringwalling for two years, and they already know more about phytos than I do. I want you to tell me something about phytos that I can use to make the guys notice me. Like, can phytos feel?"

She held her hand to her cheek, silent for a moment.

"Phytos are strange and wonderful and I love them," she said softly. "They're mixed plant and animal. Life never split itself apart on this planet."

The flying phytozoons, she explained, functioned as leaves for the vegetative stems. But the stems, too, had internal temperature control. The continental network of great conduit roots moved fluids anywhere in any quantity with valved peristalsis. A stem plus attached phytos made a kind of organism.

"But any phyto, Roy, can live with any stem, and there're forever shifting. Everything is part of everything," she said. "Our job here on Burton Island is to classify the phytos, and we just can't do it! They vary continuously along every dimension we choose, physical or chemical, and *kind* simply has no meaning." She sighed. "That's the most wonderful thing I know about them. Will that help you?"

"I don't get all that. That's what I mean, I'm ignorant," he said. "Tell me some one simple thing I can use to make the guys take notice of me."

"All right, tell them this," she said. "Phyto color patterns are plastid systems that synthesize different molecules. The way they can recombine parts to form new organisms, without waiting for evolution, gives them a humanly inconceivable biochemical range. Whatever new poison or free-system we design for *Thanasis*, somewhere by sheer chance they hit on a countersubstance. The knowledge spreads faster each time. That's why *Thanasis* is defeated."

"No! Don't keep saying that, Midori!" Craig protested. "This here translocation, now—"

"Not even that!" Her voice was sharp. "The phytos have unlimited translocation and any number of sexes. Collectively, I don't doubt they're the mightiest biochemical lab in the galaxy. They form a kind of biochemical intelligence, almost a mind, and it's learning faster than we are." She shook his arm with both her small hands. "Yes, tell them, make them understand," she said. "Human intelligence is defeated here. Now you will try human ferocity . . . oh, Roy. . . ."

"Say it," he said bitterly. "You Belcontis think all Mordinmen are stupid. You sound almost like you want us to lose."

She turned away and began cleaning her brushes. It was nearly dark and the phytos were going to rest on the stems overhead. Craig sat miserably silent, remembering the feel of her hands on his arm. Then she spoke. Her voice was soft again.

"I don't know. If you wanted homes and farms here . . . But you want only the ritual deaths of man and dinothere. . . ."

"Maybe people's souls get put together different ways on different planets," Craig said. "I know there's a piece missing out of mine. I know what it is." He put his hand lightly on her shoulder. "Some holidays I fly down to Russel Island just to look at the Great Russel there, and then I know. I wish I could take you to see him. He'd make you understand."

"I understand. I just don't agree."

She swished and splashed brushes, but she didn't pull her shoulder away from his hand. Craig thought about what she had said.

"Why is it you never see a dead phyto? Why is it there ain't enough deadwood on a whole continent to make one campfire?" he asked. "What eats 'em? What keeps 'em down?"

She laughed and turned back to him, making his arm slide across her shoulders. He barely let it touch her.

"They eat themselves internally. We call it resorption," she said. "They can grow themselves again in another place and form, as a ringwall, for instance. Roy, this planet has never known death or decay. Everything is resorbed and reconstituted. We try to kill it and it suffers but its—yes, its *mind*—can't form the idea of death. There's no way to *think* death biochemically."

"Oh bullets, Midori! Phytos can't think," he said. "I wonder, can they even feel?"

"Yes, they feel!" She rose to her feet, throwing off his arm. "Their piping is a cry of pain," she said. "Papa Toyama can remember when the planet was almost silent. Since he's been here, twenty years, their temperature has risen twelve degrees, their metabolic rate and speed of neural impulse doubled, chronaxy halved—"

Craig stood up too and raised his hands. "Hold your fire, Midori," he pleaded. "You know I don't know all them words. You're mad at me." It was too dark to see her face plainly.

"I think I'm just afraid," she said. "I'm afraid of what we've been doing that we don't know about."

"The piping always makes me feel sad, kind of," Craig said. "I never would hurt a phyto. But Great Russel, when you think about whole continents hurting and crying, day and night for years—you scare me too, Midori."

She began packing her painting kit. Craig pulled on his boot. It laced up easily, without any pain.

"We'll go to my house. I'll make our supper," she said.

They had used to do that sometimes. Those were the best times. He took the kit and walked beside her, hardly limping at all. They started up the cliff path.

"Why did you stay on past your contract, if the work makes you sad?" she asked suddenly.

"Two more years and I'll have enough saved to buy me a Great Russel hunt back on Mordin," he said. "I guess you think that's a pretty silly reason."

"Not at all. I thought you might have an even sillier reason."

He fumbled for a remark, not understanding her sudden chill. Then Jordan's voice bawled from above.

"Craig! Ho Craig!"

"Craig aye!"

"Come a-running!" Jordan yelled. "Bork's raising hell 'cause you ain't loading pellets. I saved chow for you."

●

The rest of the field period was much better. Jordan took his turn on camp chores and joked Rice and Whelan into doing the same. Only Wilde and Cobb still called Craig "Blanky." Craig felt good about things. Jordan sat beside him in the control cabin as Craig brought the flyer home to Base

Island. Russel Island loomed blue to the south and the Main Continent coast range toothed the eastern sea rim.

"Home again. Beer and the range, eh, Craig?" Jordan said. "We'll get in some hunting, maybe."

"Hope so," Craig said.

Base Island looked good. It was four thousand square miles of savanna and rolling hills with stands of young oak and beech. It teemed with game animals and birds transplanted from Mordin. On its northern tip buildings and fields made the rectilinear pattern of man. Sunlight gleamed on square miles of *Thanasis* greenhouses behind their ionic stockades. Base Island was a promise of the planet's future, when *Thanasis* would have killed off the phytos and been killed in its turn and the wholesome life of Planet Mordin replaced them both. Base Island was home.

They were the first ringwalling team to come in. Wilde reported twelve hundred miles of ringwall destroyed, fifty percent better than the old Belconti average. Barim, the Chief Huntsman, congratulated them. He was a burly, deep-voiced man with roached gray hair and four red dots on his forehead. It was the first time Craig had ever shaken hands with a man who had killed four Great Russels. Barim rewarded the crew with a week on food hunting detail. Jordan teamed up with Craig. Craig shot twenty deer and twelve pigs and scores of game birds. His bag was better than Cobb's. Jordan joked at Cobb about it, and it made the sparrowy little man very angry.

The new men had brought a roaring, jovial atmosphere to Base Camp that Craig rather liked. He picked up camp gossip. Barim had ordered immediate production of translocator pollen. Mildred Ames, the Belconti Chief Biologist, had refused. But the labs were Mordin property. Barim ordered his own men to work on it. Miss Ames raised shrill hell. Barim barred all Belcontis from the labs. Miss Ames counterattacked, rapier against bludgeon, and got her staff back into the labs. They were to observe only, for science and the record. It had been very lively, Craig gathered.

Jealous, scared we'll show 'em up, the Mordin lab men laughed. And so we will, by the bones of Great Russel!

Craig saw Miss Ames several times around the labs. She was a tall, slender woman and now she looked pinch-mouthed and unhappy. She made Sidis a lab observer. He would not ringwall anymore. Craig thought about what Midori had told him. He particularly liked that notion of resorption and waited for his chance to spring it at the mess table. It came one morning at breakfast. Wilde's crew shared a table with lab men in the raftered, stone-floored mess hall. It was always a clamor of voices and rattling mess gear. Craig sat between Cobb and Jordan and across from a squat, bald-headed lab man named Joe Breen. Joe brought up the subject of ringwalls. Craig saw his chance.

"Them ringwalls, how they make 'em," he said. "They eat themselves and grow themselves again. It's called resorption."

"They're resorbing sons of guns, ain't they?" Joe said. "How do you like the way they mate?"

Wilde shouted from the head of the table. "That way's not for me!"

"What do they mean?"

Craig whispered it to Jordan. Cobb heard him.

"Blanky wants to know the facts of life," Cobb said loudly. "Who'll tell him?"

"Who but old Papa Bork?" Wilde shouted. "Here's what they do, Blanky. When a flitterbug gets that funny feeling it rounds up from one to a dozen others. They clump on a stem and get resorbed into one of them pinkish swellings you're all the time seeing. After a while it splits and a mess of crawlers falls out. Get it?"

They were all grinning. Craig blushed and shook his head.

"They crawl off and plant themselves and each one grows into a phytogenous stem," Jordan said. "For a year it buds off new phytos like mad. Then it turns into a vegetative stem."

"Hell, I seen plenty crawlers," Craig said. "I just didn't know they were seeds."

"Know how to tell the boy crawlers from the girl crawlers, Blanky?" Cobb asked. Joe Breen laughed.

"Lay off, Cobb," Jordan said. "You don't tell their sex, you count it," he told Craig. "They got one pair of legs for each parent."

"Hey, you know, that's good!" Wilde said. "Maybe a dozen sexes, each one tearing a piece off all the others in one operation. That's good, all right!"

"Once in a lifetime, it better be good," Joe said. "But Great Russel, talk about polyploidy and multihybrids—wish we could breed *Thanasis* that way."

"I'll breed my own way," Wilde said. "Just you give me the chance."

"These Belconti women think Mordinmen are crude," Joe said. "You'll just have to save it up for Mordin."

"There's a pretty little target lives alone on Burton Island," Wilde said.

"Yeah! Blanky knows her," Cobb said. "Can she be had, Blanky?"

"No!" Craig clamped his big hand around his coffee cup. "She's funny, quiet, keeps to herself a lot," he said. "But she's decent and good."

"Maybe Blanky never tried," Cobb said. He winked at Joe. "Sometimes all you have to do is ask them quiet ones."

"I'm the guy that'll ask, give me the chance!" Wilde shouted.

"Old Bork'll come at her with them two red dots a-shining and she'll fall back into loading position slick as gun oil," Joe said.

"Yeah, and he'll find out old One-dot Cobb done nipped in there ahead of him!" Cobb whooped.

The work horn blared. The men stood up in a clatter of scraping feet and chairs.

"You go on brewhouse duty until Monday," Wilde told Craig. "Then we start a new field job."

Craig wished they were back in the field already. He felt a sudden dislike of Base Camp.

●

The new job was dusting translocator pollen over the many North Continent areas where, seen from the air, silver streaking into dark green signaled phyto infiltration of old-strain *Thanasis*. The flowerless killers were wind pollinated, with the sexes on separate plants. Old ringwall scars made an overlapping pattern across half the continent, more often than not covered by silvery, iridescent stands of pure phyto growth where *Thanasis* had once ravaged. Wilde charted new ringwalls to be blown the next time out. It was hot, sweaty work in the black protective suits and helmets. They stayed contaminated and ate canned rations and forgot about campfires. After two weeks their pollen cargo was used up and they landed at Burton Island. They spent half a day decontaminating. As soon as he could, Craig broke away and hurried down the gorge path.

He found Midori by the pool. She had been bathing. Her yellow print dress molded damply to her rounded figure and her hair still dripped. What if I'd come a few minutes earlier, Craig could not help thinking. He remembered Cobb's raucous voice: sometimes all you have to do is ask them quiet ones. He shook his head. No. No.

"Hello, Midori," he said.

Small phytos, patterned curiously in gold and scarlet and green, clung to her bare arms and shoulders. She was glad to see him. She smiled sadly when he told her about spreading translocator pollen. A phyto settled on Craig's shoulder and he tried to change the subject.

"What makes 'em do that?" he asked. "The guys think they suck blood, but they never leave no mark on me."

"They take fluid samples, but so tiny you can't feel it."

He shook the phyto off his hand. "Do they really?"

"Tiny, tiny samples. They're curious about us."

"Just tasting of us, huh?" He frowned. "If they can eat us, how come us and pigs and dinotheres can't eat them?"

"Foolish Roy! They don't *eat* us!" She stamped a bare foot. "They want to understand us, but the only symbols they have are atoms and groups and radicals and so on." She laughed. "Sometimes I wonder what they do think of us. Maybe they think we're giant seeds. Maybe they think we're each a single, terribly complicated molecule." She brushed her lips against a small scarlet-and-silver phyto on her wrist and it shifted to her cheek. "This is just their way of trying to live with us," she said.

"Just the same, it's what we call eating."

"They eat only water and sunshine. They can't conceive of life that preys on life." She stamped her foot again. "Eating! Oh, Roy! It's more like a kiss!"

Craig wished he were a phyto, to touch her smooth arms and shoulders and her firm cheek. He inhaled deeply.

"I know a better kind of kiss," he said.

"Do you, Roy?" She dropped her eyes.

"Yes, I do," he said unsteadily. Needles prickled his sweating hands that felt as big as baskets. "Midori, I . . . someday I . . ."

"Yes, Roy?"

"Ho the camp!" roared a voice from up the path.

It was Wilde, striding along, grinning with his horse teeth.

"Pop Toyama's throwing us a party, come along," he said. He looked closely at Midori and whistled. "Hey there, pretty little Midori, you look good enough to eat," he said.

"Thank you, Mr. Wilde." The small voice was cold.

On the way up the path Wilde told Midori, "I learned the *Tanko* dance on Belconti. I told Pop if he'd play, you and I'd dance it for him, after we eat."

"I don't feel at all like dancing," Midori said.

Wilde and Cobb flanked Midori at the dinner table and vied in paying rough court to her afterward in the small sitting room. Craig talked to Helen Toyama in a corner. She was a plump, placid woman and she pretended not to hear the rough hunting stories Jordan, Rice and Whelan were telling each other. Papa Toyama kept on his feet, pouring the hot wine. He looked thin and old and fragile. Craig kept his eye on Midori. Wilde was getting red-faced and loud and he wouldn't keep his hands off Midori. He gulped bowl after bowl of wine. Suddenly he stood up.

"Hey, a toast!" he shouted. "On your feet, men! Guns up for pretty little Midori!"

They stood and drank. Wilde broke his bowl with his hands. He put one fragment in his pocket and handed another to Midori. She shook her head, refusing it. Wilde grinned.

"We'll see a lot of you folks, soon," he said. "Meant to tell you. Barim's moving you in to Base Camp. Our lab men will fly over next week to pick out what they can use of your gear."

Papa Toyama's lined, gentle face paled. "We have always understood that Burton Island would remain a sanctuary for the study of phytos," he said.

"It was never a Mordin understanding, Pop."

Toyama looked helplessly from Midori to Helen. "How much time have we to close out our projects?" he asked.

Wilde shrugged. "Say a month, if you need that long."

"We do, and more." Anger touched the old man's voice. "Why can't we at least stay here until the Belconti relief ship comes?"

"This has been our home for twenty years," Helen said softly.

"I'll ask the Huntsman to give you all the time he can," Wilde said more gently. "But as soon as he pulls a harvest of pure-line translocator seed out of the forcing chambers, he wants to seed this island. We figure to get a maximum effect in virgin territory."

Papa Toyama blinked and nodded. "More wine?" he asked, looking around the room.

When Wilde and Midori danced, Papa Toyama's music sounded strange to Craig. It sounded sad as the piping of phytos.

☙

These translocator hybrids were sure deathific, the lab men chortled. Their free-systems had high thermal stability; that would get around the sneaky phyto trick of running a fever. Their recombination index was fantastic. There would be a time lag in gross effect, of course. Phyto infiltration of old-strain *Thanasis* areas was still accelerating. Belconti bastards should've started translocation years ago, the lab men grumbled. Scared, making their jobs last, wanted this planet for themselves. But wait. Just wait.

Craig and Jordan became good friends. One afternoon Craig sat waiting for Jordan at a table in the cavernous, smoky beer hall. On the rifle range an hour earlier he had fired three perfect Great Russel patterns and beaten Jordan by ten points. Barim had chanced by, slapped Craig's shoulder, and called him "stout rifle." Craig glowed at the memory. He saw Jordan coming with the payoff beer, threading between crowded, noisy tables and the fire pit where the pig carcass turned. Round face beaming, Jordan set four bottles on the rough plank table.

"Drink up, hunter!" he said. "Boy, today you earned it!"

Craig grinned back at him and took a long drink. "My brain was ice," he said. "It wasn't like me doing it."

Jordan drank and wiped his mouth on the back of his hand. "That's how it takes you when it's for real," he said. "You turn into one big rifle."

"What's it like, Jordan? What's it really like, then?"

"Nobody can ever say." Jordan looked upward into the smoke. "You don't eat for two days, they take you through the hunt ceremonies, you get to feeling light-headed and funny, like you don't have a name or a family anymore. Then . . ." His nostrils flared and he clenched his fists. "Then . . . well, for me . . . there was Great Russel coming at me, getting bigger and bigger . . . filling the whole world . . . just him and me in the world." Jordan's face paled and he closed his eyes. "That's the moment! Oh, oh oh, that's the moment!" He sighed, then looked solemnly at Craig. "I fired the pattern like it was somebody else, the way you just said. Three-sided and I *felt* it hit wide, but I picked it up with a spare."

Craig's heart thudded. He leaned forward. "Were you scared then, even the least little bit?"

"You ain't scared then, because you're Great Russel himself." Jordan leaned forward too, whispering. "You feel your own shots hit you, Craig, and you know you can't never be scared again. It's like a holy dance you and Great Russel been practicing for a million years. After that, somewhere inside you, you never stop doing that dance until you die." Jordan sighed again, leaned back and reached for his bottle.

"I dream about it lots," Craig said. His hands were shaking. "I wake up scared and sweating. Well, anyway, I mailed my application to the Hunt College by the ship you came here on."

"You'll gun through, Craig. Did you hear the Huntsman call you 'stout rifle'?"

"Yeah, like from a long way off." Craig grinned happily.

"Move your fat rump, Jordan," a jovial voice shouted.

It was Joe Breen, the bald, squat lab man. He had six bottles clasped in his hairy arms. Sidis came behind him. Joe put down his bottles.

"This is Sidis, my Belconti seeing-eye," he said.

"We know Sidis, he's an old ringwaller himself," Jordan said. "Hi, Sidis. You're getting fat."

"Hello, Jordan, Roy," Sidis said. "Don't see you around much."

He and Joe sat down. Joe uncapped bottles.

"We're in the field most all the time now," Craig said.

"You'll be out more, soon as we pull the pure-line translocator seed," Joe said. "We almost got it. Sidis has kittens every day."

"You grow 'em, we'll plant 'em, eh, Craig?" Jordan said. "Sidis, why don't you get off Joe's neck and come ringwalling again?"

"Too much to learn here in the labs," Sidis said. "We're all going to make our reputations out of this, if Joe and his pals don't kill us before we can publish."

"Damn the labs; give me the field. Right, Craig?"

"Right. It's clean and good out with the phytos," Craig said. "This re-sorption they got, it does away with things being dirty and rotten and dead—"

"Well, arrow my guts!" Joe thumped down his bottle. "Beer must make you poetical, Blanky," he snorted. "What you really mean is, they eat their own dead and their own dung. Now make a poem out of that!"

Craig felt the familiar helpless anger. "With them everything is alive all the time without stopping," he said. "All you can say they eat is water and sunshine."

"They eat water and fart helium," Joe said. "I been reading some old reports. Some old-timer name of Toyama thought they could catalyze hydro-gen fusion."

"They do. That's established," Sidis said. "They can grow at night and underground and in the winter. When you stop to think about it, they're pretty wonderful."

"Damn if you ain't a poet too," Joe said. "All you Belcontis are poets."

"We're not, but I wish we had more poets," Sidis said. "Roy, you haven't forgotten what I told you once?"

"I ain't a poet," Craig said. "I can't rhyme nothing."

"Craig's all right. Barim called him 'stout rifle' on the range this after-noon," Jordan said. He wanted to change the subject. "Joe, that old guy Toyama, he's still here. Out on Burton Island. We got orders to move him in to Base Camp on our next field trip."

"Great Russel, he must've been here twenty years!" Joe said. "How's he ever stood it?"

"Got his wife along," Jordan said. "Craig here is going on three years. He's standing it."

"He's turning into a damned poet," Joe said. "Blanky, you better go home for sure on the next relief ship, while you're still a kind of a man."

Craig found Midori alone in her house. It looked bare. Her paintings lay strapped together beside crates of books and clothing. She smiled, but she looked tired and sad.

"It's hard, Roy. I don't want to leave here," she said. "I can't bear to think of what you're going to do to this island."

"I never think about what we do, except that it just has to be," he said. "Can I help you pack?"

"I'm finished. We've worked for days, packing. And now Barim won't give us transportation for our cases of specimens." She looked ready to cry. "Papa Toyama's heart is broken," she said.

Craig bit his lip. "Heck, we can carry fifty tons," he said. "We got the room. Why don't I ask Mr. Wilde to take 'em anyway?"

She grasped his arm and looked up at him. "Would you, Roy? I . . . don't want to ask him a favor. The cases are stacked outside the lab building."

Craig found his chance after supper at the Toyamas. Wilde left off paying court to Midori and carried his wine bowl outside. Craig followed and asked him. Wilde was looking up at the sky. Both moons rode high in a clear field of stars.

"What's in the cases, did you say?" Wilde asked.

"Specimens, slides and stuff. It's kind of like art to 'em."

"All ours now. I'm supposed to destroy it." Wilde said. "Oh, hell! All right, if you want to strong-back the stuff aboard." He chuckled. "I about got Midori talked into taking one last walk down to that pool of hers. I'll tell her you're loading the cases." He nudged Craig. "Might help, huh?"

When he had the eighty-odd cases stowed and lashed, Craig lifted the flyer to a hundred feet to test his trim. Through his side window he saw Wilde and Midori come out of the Toyama house and disappear together down the gorge path. Wilde had his arm across her shoulders. Craig grounded and went back, but he could not rejoin the party. For an hour he paced outside in dull, aching anger. Then his crewmates came out, arguing noisily.

"Ho Craig! Where been, boy?" Jordan slapped his shoulder. "I just bet Cobb you could outgun him tomorrow, like you did me. We'll stick old Cobbo for the beer, eh, boy?"

"Like hell," Cobb said.

"Like shooting birds in a cage," Jordan said. "Come along, Craig. Get some sleep. You got to be right tomorrow."

"I ain't sleepy," Craig said.

"Bet old Bork's shooting himself a cage bird about now," Cobb said.

They all laughed except Craig.

◗

On the trip to Base Camp next morning Craig, at the controls, heard Wilde singing hunt songs and making jokes back in the main cabin. He seemed to be still drunk. With high good humor he even helped his crew deliver the baggage to Belconti quarters. Craig had no chance to speak to Midori. He was not sure he wanted a chance. That afternoon Cobb outgunned Craig badly. Jordan tried to console him, but Craig drank himself sodden. He woke the next morning to Jordan's insistent shaking.

"Wake up, damn it! We're going out again, right away!" Jordan said. "Don't let Bork catch you sleeping late. Something went wrong for him last night over in Belconti quarters, and he's mad as a split snake."

Still dizzy and sick four hours later, and wearing his black pro suit, Craig grounded the flyer again at Burton Island. They had a cargo of pure-line translocator seed. The men got out. Wilde wore a black frown.

"Jordan and Blanky, you seed that gorge path all the way to the waterfall," he ordered.

"I thought we picked high, sunny places," Jordan objected. "It's shady down there."

"Seed it, I told you!" Wilde bared his horse teeth. "Come on, Rice, Cobb, Whelan! Get going around these buildings!"

When they had finished the seeding, Jordan and Craig rested briefly on the quartz boulder near the pool. For the first time, Craig let himself look around. Phytos danced piping above their heads. The stems marching up the steep slopes transmuted the golden sun glare to a strong, silvery moonlight. It sparkled on the quartz ledge and the cascading water.

"Say, it's pretty down here," Jordan said. "Kind of twangs your string, don't it? It'll make a nice hunting camp someday."

"Let's go up," Craig said. "They'll be waiting."

Lifting out of the field at sunset, Craig looked down at the deserted station from his side window. Midori's house looked small and forlorn and accusing.

⊖

At Base Camp six men died of a mutant free-system before the immunizer could be synthesized. An escaped control virus wiped out a translocator seed crop and Wilde's men got an unscheduled rest after months of driving work. The once roaring, jovial atmosphere of Base Camp had turned glum. The lab men muttered about Belconti sabotage. They drank a great deal, not happily.

On his first free day Craig checked out a sports flyer, found Midori in the Belconti quarters, and asked her to go riding. She came, wearing a white blouse and pearls and a blue-and-yellow flare skirt. She seemed sad, her small face half dreaming and her eyes unfocused. Craig forgot about being angry with her and wanted to cheer her. When he was a mile up and heading south, he tried.

"You look pretty in that dress, like a phyto," he said.

She smiled faintly. "My poor phytos. How I miss them," she said. "Where are we going, Roy?"

"Russel Island, down ahead there. I want you to see Great Russel."

"I want to see him," she said. A moment later she cried out and grasped his arm. "Look at that color in the sky! Over to the right!"

It was a patch of softly twinkling, shifting colors far off and high in the otherwise cloudless sky.

"Migratory phytos," he said. "We see 'em all the time."

"I know. Let's go up close. Please, Roy."

He arrowed the flyer toward the green-golden cloud. It resolved into millions of phytos, each with its opalescent hydrogen sac inflated and drifting northwest in the trade wind.

"They stain the air with beauty!" Midori cried. Her face was vividly awake and her eyes sparkled. "Go clear inside, please, Roy!"

She used to look like that when she was painting in the gorge, Craig remembered. It was the way he liked her best. He matched wind speed inside the cloud and at once lost all sense of motion. Vividly colored phytos obscured land, sea and sky. Craig felt lost and dizzy. He moved closer to Midori. She slid open her window to let in the piping and the spicy perfume.

"It's so beautiful I can't bear it," she said. "They have no eyes, Roy. We must know for them how beautiful they are."

She began piping and trilling in her clear voice. A phyto patterned in scarlet and green and silver dropped to her outstretched hand and she sang to it. It deflated its balloon and quivered velvety wings. Craig shifted uneasily.

"It acts almost like it knows you," he said.

"It knows I love it."

"Love? Something so different?" He frowned. "That ain't how I mean love."

She looked up. "How do you understand love?"

"Well, you want to protect people you love, fight for 'em, do things for 'em." He was blushing. "What could you do for a phyto?"

"Stop trying to exterminate them," she said softly.

"Don't start that again. I don't like to think about it either. But I know it just has to be."

"It will never be," she said. "I know. Look at all the different color patterns out there. Papa Toyama remembers when phytos were almost all green. They developed the new pigments and patterns to make countersubstances against *Thanasis.*" She lowered her voice. "Think of it, Roy. All the colors and patterns are new ideas in this planet's strange, inconceivably powerful biochemical mind. This cloud is a message, from one part of it to another part of it. Doesn't it frighten you?"

"You scare me." He moved slightly away from her. "I didn't know they been changing like that."

"Who stays here long enough to notice? Who cares enough to look and see?" Her lips trembled. "But just think of the agony and the changings, through all the long years men have been trying to kill this planet. What if something . . . somehow . . . suddenly *understands?*"

Craig's neck-hair bristled. He moved further away. He felt weird and alone, without time or place or motion in that piping, perfumed phyto cloudworld. He couldn't face Midori's eyes.

"Damn it, this planet belongs to Great Russel!" he said harshly. "We'll win yet! At least they'll never take back Base or Russel Islands. Their seeds can't walk on water."

She kept her eyes on his, judging or pleading or questioning, he could not tell. He could not bear them. He dropped his own eyes.

"Shake that thing off your hand!" he ordered. "Close your window. I'm getting out of here!"

◆

Half an hour later Craig hovered the flyer over the wholesome green grass and honest oak trees of Russel Island. He found Great Russel and held him in the magniviewer and they watched him catch and kill a buffalo. Midori gasped.

"Ten feet high at the shoulder. Four tons, and light on his feet as a cat," Craig said proudly. "That long, reddish hair is like wire. Them bluish bare spots are like armor plate."

"Aren't his great teeth enough to kill the cattle he eats?" she asked. "What enemies can he have, to need those terrible horns and claws?"

"His own kind. And us. Our boys will hunt him here, here on this planet, and become men. Our men will hunt him here, to heal their souls."

"You love him, don't you? Did you know you were a poet?" She could not take her eyes off the screen. "He *is* beautiful, fierce and terrible, not what women call beauty."

"He's the planet-shaker, he is! It takes four perfect shots to bring him down," Craig said. "He jumps and roars like the world ending—oh, Midori, I'll have my day!"

"But you might be killed."

"The finest kind of death. In our lost colony days our old fathers fought him with bow and arrow," Craig said. "Even now, sometimes, we form a sworn band and fight him to the death with spears and arrows."

"I've read of sworn bands. I suppose you can't help how you feel."

"I don't want to help it! A sworn band is the greatest honor that can come to a man," he said. "But thanks for trying to understand."

"I want to understand. I want to, Roy. Is it that you can't believe in your own courage until you face Great Russel?"

"That's just what women can't ever understand." He faced the question in her eyes. "Girls can't help turning into women, but a man has to make himself," he said. "It's like I don't have my man's courage until I get it from Great Russel. There's chants and stuff with salt and fire . . . afterwards the boy eats pieces of the heart and . . . I shouldn't talk about that. You'll laugh."

"I feel more like crying." She kept her strange eyes on his. "There are different kinds of courage, Roy. You have more courage than you know. You must find your true courage in your own heart, not in Great Russel's."

"I can't." He looked away from her eyes. "I'm nothing inside me, until I face Great Russel."

"Take me home, Roy. I'm afraid I'm going to cry." She dropped her face to her folded hands. "I don't have much courage," she said.

They flew to Base Camp in silence. When Craig helped her down from the flyer, she was really crying. She bowed her head momentarily against his chest and the spicy phyto smell rose from her hair.

"Goodbye, Roy," she said.

He could barely hear her. Then she turned and ran.

◆

Craig did not see her again. Wilde's crew spent all its time in the field, blowing ringwalls and planting translocator seed. Craig was glad to be away. The atmosphere of Base Camp had turned from glum to morose. Everywhere across North Continent new phyto growth in silver, green and scarlet spotted the dark green *Thanasis* areas. Other ringwall crews reported the same of South and Main Continents. Wilde's temper became savage; Cobb cursed bitterly at trifles; even happy-go-lucky Jordan stopped joking. Half asleep one night in field camp, Craig heard Wilde shouting incredulous questions at the communicator inside the flyer. He came out cursing to rouse the camp.

"Phytos are on Base Island! Stems popping up everywhere!"

"Great Russel in the sky!" Jordan jerked full awake. "How come?"

"Belconti bastards planted 'em, that's how!" Wilde said. "Barim's got 'em all arrested under camp law."

Cobb began cursing in a steady, monotonous voice.

"That . . . cracks . . . the gunflint!" Jordan said.

"We'll kill 'em by hand," Wilde said grimly. "We'll sow the rest of our seed broadcast and go in to help."

Craig felt numb and unbelieving. Shortly after noon he grounded the flyer at Base Camp, in the foul area beyond the emergency rocket launching frame. Wilde cleaned up at once and went to see Barim, while his crew decontaminated the flyer. When they came through the irradiation tunnel in clean denims, Wilde was waiting.

"Blanky, come with me!" he barked.

Craig followed him into the gray stone building at the field edge. Wilde pushed him roughly through a door, said, "Here he is, Huntsman," and closed the door again.

Rifles, bows and arrows decorated the stone walls. The burly Chief Huntsman, cold-eyed under his roached gray hair and the four red dots, sat facing the door from behind a wooden desk. He motioned Craig to sit down in one of the row of wooden chairs along the inner wall. Craig sat stiffly in the one nearest the door. His mouth was dry.

"Roy Craig, you are on your trial for life and honor under camp law," Barim said sternly. "Swear now to speak truth in the blood of Great Russel."

"I swear to speak truth in the blood of Great Russel."

Craig's voice sounded false to him. He began to sweat.

"What would you say of someone who deliberately betrayed our project to destroy the phytos?" Barim asked.

"He would be guilty of hunt treason, sir. An outlaw."

"Very well." Barim clasped his hands and leaned forward, his gray eyes hard on Craig's eyes. "What did you tell Bork Wilde was in those cases you flew from Burton Island to Base Island?"

Craig's stomach knotted. "Slides, specimens, science stuff, sir."

Barim questioned him closely about the cases. Craig tried desperately to speak truth without naming Midori. Barim forced her name from him, then questioned him on her attitudes. A terrible fear grew in Roy Craig. He kept his eyes on Barim's eyes and spoke a tortured kind of truth, but he would not attaint Midori. Finally Barim broke their locked gazes and slapped his desk.

"Are you in *love* with Midori Blake, boy?" he roared.

Craig dropped his glance. "I don't know, sir," he said. He thought miserably: How do you know when you're in love? "Well . . . I like to be around her . . . I never thought . . . I know we're good friends." He gulped. "I don't think so, sir," he said finally.

"Phyto seeds are loose on Base Island," Barim said. "Who planted them?"

"They can walk and plant themselves, sir." Craig's mouth was dry as powder. He avoided Barim's glance.

"Would Midori Blake be morally capable of bringing them here and releasing them?"

Craig's face twisted. "Morally . . . I'm not clear on the word, sir. . . ." Sweat dripped on his hands.

"I mean, would she have the guts to want to do it and to do it?"

Ice clamped Craig's heart. He looked Barim in the eye. "No, sir!" he said. "I won't never believe that about Midori!"

Barim smiled grimly and slapped his desk again. "Wilde!" he shouted. "Bring them in!"

Midori, in white blouse and black skirt, came in first. Her face was pale but composed, and she smiled faintly at Craig. Mildred Ames followed, slender and thin-faced in white, then Wilde, scowling blackly. Wilde sat between Craig and Miss Ames, Midori on the end.

"Miss Blake, young Craig has clearly been your dupe, as you insist he has,"

Barim said. "Your confession ends your trial except for sentencing. Once more I beg of you to say why you have done this."

"You would not understand," Midori said. "Be content with what you know."

Her voice was low but firm. Craig felt sick with dismay.

"I can understand without condoning," Barim said. "For your own sake, I must know your motive. You may be insane."

"You know I'm sane. You know that."

"Yes." Barim's wide shoulders sagged. "Invent a motive, then." He seemed almost to plead. "Say you hate Mordin. Say you hate me."

"I hate no one. I'm sorry for you all."

"I'll give you a reason!" Miss Ames jumped to her feet, thin face flaming. "Your reckless, irresponsible use of translocation endangers us all! Accept defeat and go home!"

She helped Barim recover his composure. He smiled.

"Please sit down, Miss Ames," he said calmly. "In three months your relief ship will come to take you to safety. But we neither accept defeat nor fear death. We will require no tears of anyone."

Miss Ames sat down, her whole posture shouting defiance. Barim swung his eyes back to Midori. His face turned to iron.

"Miss Blake, you are guilty of hunt treason. You have betrayed your own kind in a fight with an alien life form," he said. "Unless you admit to some recognizably *human* motive, I must conclude that you abjure your own humanity."

Midori said nothing. Craig stole a glance at her. She sat, erect but undefiant, small feet together, small hands folded in her lap. Barim slapped his desk and stood up.

"Very well. Under camp law I sentence you, Midori Blake, to outlawry from your kind. You are a woman and not of Mordin; therefore I will remit the full severity. You will be set down, lacking everything made with hands, on Russel Island. There you may still be nourished by the roots and berries of the Earth-type life you have willfully betrayed. If you survive until the Belconti relief ship comes, you will be sent home on it." He burned his glance at her. "Have you anything to say before I cause your sentence to be executed?"

The four red dots blazed against the sudden pallor of the Huntsman's forehead. Something snapped in Craig. He leaped up, shouting into the hush.

"You can't do it, sir! She's little and weak! She doesn't know our ways—"

"Down! Shut up, you whimpering fool!" Wilde slapped and wrestled Craig to his seat again. "Silence!" Barim thundered. Wilde sat down, breathing hard. The room was hushed again.

"I understand your ways too well," Midori said. "Spare me your mercy. Put me down on Burton Island."

"Midori, no!" Miss Ames turned to her. "You'll starve. *Thanasis* will kill you!"

"You can't understand either, Mildred," Midori said. "Mr. Barim, will you grant my request?"

Barim leaned forward, resting on his hands. "It is so ordered," he said huskily. "Midori Blake, almost you make me know again the taste of fear." He straightened and turned to Wilde, his voice suddenly flat and impersonal. "Carry out the sentence, Wilde."

Wilde stood up and pulled Craig to his feet. "Get the crew to the flyer. Wear pro suits," he ordered. "*Run,* boy."

Craig stumbled out into the twilight.

➤

Craig drove the flyer northwest from Base Camp at full throttle, overtaking the sun, making it day again. Silence ached in the main cabin behind him. He leaned away from it, as if to push the flyer forward with his muscles. He was refusing to think at all. He knew it had to be and still he could not bear it. After an anguished forever he grounded the flyer roughly beside the deserted buildings on Burton Island. They got out, the men in black pro suits, Midori still in blouse and skirt. She stood apart quietly and looked toward her little house on the cliff edge. *Thanasis* thrust up dark green and knee-high along all the paths.

"Break out ringwall kits. Blow all the buildings," Wilde ordered. "Blanky, you come with me."

At Midori's house Wilde ordered Craig to sink explosive pellets every three feet along the foundations. A single pellet would have been enough. Craig found his voice.

"The Huntsman didn't say do this, Mr. Wilde. Can't we at least leave her this house?"

"She won't need it. *Thanasis* will kill her before morning."

"Let her have it to die in, then. She loved this little house."

Wilde grinned without mirth, baring his big horse teeth.

"She's *outlaw*, Blanky. You know the law: nothing made with hands."

Craig bowed his head, teeth clamped. Wilde whistled tunelessly as Craig set the pellets. They returned to the flyer and Jordan reported the other buildings ready to blow. His round, jolly face was grim. Midori had not moved. Craig wanted to speak to her, say goodbye. He knew if he tried he would find no words but a howl. Her strange little smile seemed already to remove her to another world a million light-years from Roy Craig and his kind. Cobb looked at Midori. His rat-face was eager.

"We'll detonate from the air," Wilde said. "The blast will kill anyone standing here."

"We're supposed to take off all her clothes first," Cobb said. "You know the law, Bork: nothing made with hands."

"That's right," Wilde said.

Midori took off her blouse. She looked straight at Wilde. Red mist clouded Craig's vision.

"Load the kits," Wilde said abruptly. "Into the flyer, all hands! *Jump,* you dogs!"

From his side window by the controls Craig saw Midori start down the gorge path. She walked as carelessly relaxed as if she were going down to paint. *Thanasis* brushed her bare legs and he thought he saw the angry red spring out. Craig felt the pain in his own skin. He lifted the flyer with a lurching roar and he did not look out when Wilde blew up the buildings.

Away from the sun, southwest toward Base Camp, wrapped in his own thought-vacant hell, Roy Craig raced to meet the night.

◕

With flame, chemicals and grub hoes, the Mordinmen fought their losing battle for Base Island. Craig worked himself groggy with fatigue, to keep from thinking. The phytos stems radiated underground with incredible growth energy. They thrust up redoubly each new day like hydra heads. Newly budded phytos the size of thumbnails tinted the air of Base Island in gaily dancing swirls. Once Craig saw Joe Breen, the squat lab man, cursing and hopping like a frog while he slashed at dancing phytos with an axe. It seemed to express the situation.

Barim made his grim decisions to move camp to Russel Island and seed the home island with *Thanasis*. Craig was helping erect the new camp when he collapsed. He awoke in bed in a small, bare infirmary room at Base Camp. The Mordin doctor took blood samples and questioned him. Craig admitted to joint pains and nausea for several days past.

"I been half crazy, sir," he defended himself. "I didn't know I was sick."

"I've got twenty more do know it," the doctor grunted.

He went out, frowning. Craig slept, to flee to dream-terror from a woman's eyes. He half woke at intervals for medication and clinical tests, to sleep again and face repeatedly a Great Russel dinothere. It looked at him with a woman's inscrutable eyes. He roused into the morning of the second day to find another bed squeezed into the small room, by the window. Papa Toyama was in it. He smiled at Craig.

"Good morning, Roy," he said. "I would be happier to meet you in another place."

Many were down and at least ten had died, he told Craig. The Belconti staff was back in the labs, working frantically to identify agent and vector. Craig felt hollow and his head ached. He did not much care. Dimly he saw Miss Ames in a white lab smock come around the foot of his bed to stand between him and Papa Toyama. She took the old man's hand.

"George, old friend, we've found it," she said.

"You do not smile, Mildred."

"I don't smile. All night I've been running a phase analysis of diffraction patterns," she said. "It's what we've feared—a spread of two full Ris units."

"So. Planet Froy again." Papa Toyama's voice was calm. "I would like to be with Helen again, for the little time we have."

"Surely," Miss Ames said. "I'll see to it."

Quick, heavy footsteps sounded outside. A voice broke in.

"Ah. Here you are, Miss Ames."

Barim, in leather hunting clothes, bulked in the door. Miss Ames turned to face him across Craig's bed.

"I'm told you found the virus," Barim said.

"Yes." Miss Ames smiled thinly.

"Well, what countermeasures? Twelve are dead. What can I do?"

"You might shoot at it with a rifle. It is a *Thanasis* free-system that has gotten two degrees of temporal freedom. Does that mean anything to you?"

His heavy jaw set like a trap. "No, but your manner does. It's the plague, isn't it?"

She nodded. "No suit can screen it. No cure is possible. We are all infected."

Barim chewed his lip and looked at her in silence. "For your sake now, I wish we'd never come here," he said at last. "I'll put our emergency rocket in orbit to broadcast a warning message. That will save your relief ship, when it comes, and Belconti can warn the sector." A half-smile softened his bluff, grim features. "Why don't you rub my nose in it? Say you told me so?"

"Need I?" Her chin came up. "I pity you Mordinmen. You must all die now without dignity, crying out for water and your mothers. How you will loathe that!"

"Does that console you?" Barim still smiled. "Not so, Miss Ames. All night I thought it might come to this. Even now men are forging arrow points. We'll form a sworn band and all die fighting Great Russel." His voice deepened and his eyes blazed. "We'll stagger who can, crawl who must, carry our helpless, and all die fighting like men!"

"Like savages! No! No!" Her hands flew up in shocked protest. "Forgive me for taunting you, Mr. Barim. I need your help, all of your men and transport, truly I do. Some of us may live, if we fight hard enough."

"How?" He growled it. "I thought on Planet Froy—"

"Our people on Planet Froy had only human resources. But here, I'm certain that somewhere already the phytos have synthesized the plague immunizer that seems forever impossible to human science." Her voice shook. "Please help us, Mr. Barim. If we can find it, isolate enough to learn its structure—"

"No." He cut her off bluntly. "Too long a gamble. One doesn't run squealing away from death, Miss Ames. My way is decent and sure."

Her chin came up and her voice sharpened. "How dare you condemn your own men unconsulted? They might prefer a fight for life."

"Hah! You don't know them!" Barim bent to shake Craig's shoulder with rough affection. "You, lad," he said. "You'll get up and walk with a sworn band, won't you?"

"No," Craig said.

He struggled off the pillow, propped shakily on his arms. Miss Ames smiled and patted his cheek.

"You'll stay and help us fight to live, won't you?" she said.

"No," Craig said.

"Think what you say, lad!" Barim said tautly. "Great Russel can die of plague, too. We owe him a clean death."

Craig sat bolt upright. He stared straight ahead.

"I foul the blood of Great Russel," he said slowly and clearly. "I foul it with dung. I foul it with carrion. I foul—"

Barim's fist knocked Craig to the pillow and split his lip. The Huntsman's face paled under his tan.

"You're mad, boy!" he whispered. "Not even in madness may you say those words!"

Craig struggled up again. "You're the crazy ones, not me," he said. He tongued his lip and blood dripped on his thin pajama coat. "I'll die an outlaw, that's how I'll die," he said. "An outlaw, on Burton Island." He met Barim's unbelieving eyes. "I foul the blood—"

"Silence!" Barim shouted. "Outlawry it is. I'll send a party for you, stranger."

He whirled and stamped out. Miss Ames followed him.

"You Mordinmen," she said, shaking her head.

Craig sat on the edge of his bed and pulled his sweat-soaked pajamas straight. The room blurred and swam around him. Papa Toyama's smile was like a light.

"I'm ashamed. I'm ashamed. Please forgive us, Papa Toyama," Craig said. "All we know is to kill and kill and kill."

"We all do what we must," the old man said. "Death cancels all debts. It will be good to rest."

"Not my debts. I'll never rest again," Craig said. "All of a sudden I know— Great Russel, *how* I know—I know I loved Midori Blake."

"She was a strange girl. Helen and I thought she loved you, in the old days on our island." Papa Toyama bowed his head. "But our lives are only chips in a waterfall. Goodbye, Roy."

Jordan, in a black pro suit, came shortly after. His face was bitter with contempt. He jerked his thumb at the door.

"On your feet, stranger! Get going!" he snapped.

In pajamas and barefooted, Craig followed him. From somewhere in the infirmary he heard a voice screaming. It sounded like Cobb. They walked across the landing field. Everything seemed underwater. Men were rigging to fuel the emergency rocket. Craig sat apart from the others in the flyer. Cobb was missing. Wilde was flushed and shivering and his eyes glared with fever. Jordan took the controls. No one spoke. Craig dozed through colored dream-scraps while the flyer outran the sun. He woke when it grounded in early dawn on Burton Island.

He climbed down and stood swaying beside the flyer. *Thanasis* straggled across the rubble heaps and bulked waist-high in the dim light along the paths. Phytos stirred on their stems and piped sleepily in the damp air. Craig's eyes searched for something, a memory, a presence, a completion and rest, he did not know what. He felt it very near him. Wilde came behind him, shoving. Craig moved away.

"Stranger!" Wilde called.

Craig turned. He looked into the fever-glaring eyes above the grinning horse teeth. The teeth gaped.

"I foul the blood of Midori Blake. I foul it with dung. I—"

Strength from nowhere exploded into the bone and muscles of Roy Craig. He sprang and felt the teeth break under his knuckles. Wilde fell. The others scrambled down from the flyer.

"Blood right! Blood right!" Craig shouted.

"Blood right!" Wilde echoed.

Jordan held back Rice and Whelan. Strength flamed along Craig's nerves. Wilde rose, spitting blood, swinging big fists. Craig closed to meet him, berserk in fury. The world wheeled and tilted, shot with flashing colors, gasping with grunts and curses, but rock-steady in the center of things. Wilde pressed the fight and Craig hurled it back on him. He felt the blows without pain, felt his ribs splinter, felt the good shock of his own blows all the way to his ankles. Bruising falls on the rough slag, feet stamping, arms grappling, hands tearing, breath sobbing, both men on knees clubbing with fists and forearms. The scene cleared and Craig saw through one eye Wilde crumpled and inert before him. He rose unsteadily. He felt weightless and clean inside.

"Blood right, stranger," Jordan said, grim faced and waiting.

"Let it go," Craig said.

He turned down the gorge path, ignoring his chest pains, crashing through the rank *Thanasis*. *Home! going home! going home!* a bell tolled in his head. He did not look back.

Thanasis grew more sparsely in the shaded gorge. Craig heard the waterfall and old memories cascaded upon him. He rounded to view of it and his knees buckled and he knelt beside the boulder. She was very near him. He felt an overpowering sense of her presence. She was this place.

Dawn light shafted strongly into the gorge. It sparkled on the quartz ledge and made reflecting rainbows in the spray above the pool. Phytos lifted from ghost-silver stems to dance their own rainbow in the air. Something rose in Craig's throat and choked him. Tears blurred his good eye.

"Midori," he said. "Midori."

The feeling overwhelmed him. His heart was bursting. He could find no words. He raised his arms and battered face to the sky and cried out incoherently. Then a blackness swept away his intolerable pain.

◆

Titanic stirrings. Windy rushings. Sharp violences swarming.

Fittings-together in darkness. A trillion times a trillion times a trillion patient searchings. Filtering broken lights, silver, green, golden, scarlet.

Bluntings. Smoothings. Transforming into otherness.

Flickering awareness, planet-vast and atom-tiny, no focus between. The protosensorium of a god yearning to know himself. Endless, patient agony in search of being.

Form and color outfolding in middle focus. Flashings of terrible joy and love unspeakable. It looked. Listened. Felt. Smelled. Tasted.

Crystalline polar wastes. Wine of sweet. Gold-glint of sun on blue water. Perfumed wind caress. Thorn of bitter. Rain patter. Silver-green sweep of hill. Storm roar and shaking. Sharp of salt. Sleeping mountains. Surf beat. Star patterns dusted on blackness. Clear of sour. Cool moons of night.

It knew and loved.

Ragged line of men gaunt under beard stubble. Green plain. High golden sun. Roar. Shaggy redness bounding. Bow twangs. Whispering arrow lights. Deep-chested shouts of men. Lances thrusting. Bodies ripped. Thrown. Horn-impaled beating with fists. Great shape kneeling. Threshing. Streaming blood. Deep man-shouts dwindling to a silence.

It knew and sorrowed.

The woman bathing. Sunlight hair streaming. Grace beyond bearing. Beauty that was pain.

It shook terribly with love.

Rested readiness, whole and unblemished forever. The man newly-minted.
Bursting excitement. HOME! coming HOME! coming HOME!
It woke into its world.

∾

It was like waking up fresh and rested on the fine morning of a day when something glorious was going to happen. He was sitting up in a cavity at the base of a huge phyto stem. He brushed away papery shreds and saw the pool and heard the waterfall. With a glad cry, Midori came running. He stood up whole and strong to greet her.

"Midori! Midori, when you die . . . ?" He wanted to know a million things, but one came first. "Can I ever lose you again now?"

"Never again."

She was smiling radiantly. They were both naked. He was not excited and not ashamed.

"We didn't die, Roy," she said. "We're just made new."

"The plague killed everybody."

"I know. But we didn't die."

"Tell me."

He listened like a child, believing without understanding. Somewhere in its infinite life-spectrum the planetary life had matched up a band for humans. "As if we were single giant molecules and it discovered our structural formula," she said. "That's how it thinks." They had been resorbed into the planetary biomass, cleansed of *Thanasis*, and reconstituted whole and without blemish. "We're immune to *Thanasis* now," she said. "We're made new, Roy."

The sunken red *Thanasis* scar was gone from his ankle. All of his other scars were gone. He held her hands and looked on her beauty and believed her.

"We tried so long and hard to kill it," he said.

"It couldn't know that. To it death and decay are only vital changings," she said, smiling wonderfully. "This life never split apart, Roy. In wholeness there is nothing but love."

"Love is making a wholeness," he said. "I know about love now."

He told her about his visions.

"I had them too. We were diffused into the planetary consciousness."

"Do we still eat and drink and sleep . . . and all?"

She laughed. "Foolish Roy! Of course we do!" She pulled at his hands. "Come. I'll show you."

Hand in hand they ran to the pool. The gravel hurt his feet. Beside the pool stems had fused ringwall fashion into a series of connecting rooms like hollow cones. He followed Midori through them. They were clean and dry and silvery with shadows. Outside again she pointed out brownish swellings on various stems. She tore one open, the covering like thin paper, to reveal pearly, plum-sized nodules closely packed in a cavity. She bit one nodule in two and held the other half to his lips.

"Try," she said.

He ate it. It was cool and crisp, with a delightful, unfamiliar flavor. He ate several more, looking at her in wonder.

"There are hundreds of these vesicles," she said. "No two of them ever taste the same. They're grown just for us."

He looked at her and around at the beauty of the gorge in strong, transmuted sunlight and he could not bear it. He closed his eyes and turned away from her.

"I can't. I can't, Midori," he said. "I ain't good enough for this."

"You are, Roy."

"You loved it before. But all I wanted was to kill it," he said. "Now it's done this for me." The feeling flooded him agonizingly. "I want to love it back and I can't. Not now. Not after. I just *can't*, Midori!"

"Roy. Listen to me." She was in front of him again, but he would not open his eyes. "This life emerged with infinite potentialities. It mastered its environment using only the tiniest part of them," she said. "It never split up, to fight itself and evolve that way. So it lay dreaming. It might have dreamed forever."

"Only we came, you mean? With *Thanasis?*"

"Yes. We forced it to changes, genetic recombination, rises in temperatures and process speeds. Whatever happened at one point could be duplicated everywhere, because it is all one. One year to it is like millions of years of Earthly evolution. It raised itself to a new level of awareness."

He felt her hand on his arm. He would not open his eyes.

"Listen to me, Roy! We *wakened* it. It knows us and loves us for that."

"Loves us for *Thanasis!*"

"It loves *Thanasis*, too. It conquered *Thanasis*, with love."

"And me. Tamed. A pet. A parasite. I *can't*, Midori!"

"Oh no! Roy, *please* understand! It thinks us now, biochemically. Like each littlest phyto, we are thoughts in that strange mind. I think we focus its awareness, somehow, serve it as a symbol system, a form-giver. . . ." She lowered her voice. He could feel her warmth and nearness. "We are its thoughts that also think themselves, the first it has ever had," she whispered. "It is a great and holy mystery, Roy. Only through us can it know its own beauty and wonder. It loves and needs us." She pressed against him. "Roy, *look* at me!"

He opened his eyes. She smiled pleadingly. He ran his hands down the smooth curve of her back and she shivered. He clasped her powerfully. It was all right.

"I can love it back, now," he said. "Through you, I love it."

"I give you back its love," she whispered into his shoulder.

Afterward, arms linked, dazed with their love, they walked down to the sea. They stood on sparkling sand and cool water splashed at their ankles.

"Roy, have you thought? We'll never be ill, never grow old. Never have to die."

He pressed his face into her hair. "Never is a long time."

"If we tire, we can be resorbed and diffuse through the planetary consciousness again. But that's not death."

"Our children can serve."

"And their children."

"It could do this for anybody now, couldn't it?" he asked her quietly.

"Yes. For any old or ill human who might come here," she said. "They could have youth and strength again forever."

"Yes." He looked up at the blue, arching sky. "But there's a rocket up there with a warning message, to scare them away. I wish. I wish they could know. . . ."

"That they are their own plague."

He patted her head to rest again on his shoulder.

"Someday they'll learn," he said.

The Keys to December

ROGER ZELAZNY

Like a number of other writers, the late Roger Zelazny began publishing in 1962 in the pages of Cele Goldsmith's Amazing. This was the so-called "Class of '62," whose membership also included Thomas M. Disch, Keith Laumer, and Ursula K. Le Guin. Everyone in that "class" would eventually achieve prominence, but some of them would achieve it faster than others, and Zelazny's subsequent career would be one of the most meteoric in the history of SF. The first Zelazny story to attract wide notice was "A Rose for Ecclesiastics," published in 1963 (it was later selected by vote of the SFWA membership to have been one of the best SF stories of all time). By the end of that decade, he had won two Nebula Awards and two Hugo Awards and was widely regarded as one of the two most important American SF writers of the sixties (the other was Samuel R. Delany). By the end of the 1970s, although his critical acceptance as an important science-fiction writer had dimmed, his long series of novels about the enchanted land of Amber—beginning with Nine Princes in Amber— had made him one of the most popular and best-selling fantasy writers of our time, and inspired the founding of worldwide fan clubs and fanzines.

Zelazny's early novels were, on the whole, well received (This Immortal won a Hugo, as did his most famous novel, Lord of Light), but it was the strong and stylish short work he published in magazines like F&SF and Amazing and Worlds of If throughout the middle years of the decade that electrified the genre, and it was these early stories—stories like "This Moment of the Storm," "The Doors of His Face, The Lamps of His Mouth," "The Graveyard Heart," "He Who Shapes," "For a Breath I Tarry," and "This Mortal Mountain,"—that established Zelazny as a giant of the field, and which many still consider to be his best work. These stories are still amazing for their invention and elegance and verve, for their good-natured effrontery and easy ostentation, for the risks Zelazny took in pursuit of eloquence without ruffling a hair, the grace and nerve he displayed as he switched from high-flown pseudo-Spenserian to wisecracking Chandlerian slang to vivid prose-poetry to Hemingwayesque stark-ness in the course of only a few lines—and for the way he made it all look easy and effortless, the same kind of illusion Fred Astaire used to generate when he danced.

Here's one of those eloquent and elegant stories written by Zelazny at the top of his form, demonstrating that the process of terraforming a world may only be the beginning—that your new world may turn up dangers and wonders that you never planned on, unexpected things that you now have to deal with, no matter what the consequences may be . . .

Zelazny won another Nebula and Hugo Award in 1976 for his novella Home is the Hangman, another Hugo in 1986 for his novella 24 Views of Mt. Fuji, by Hosiki, and a final Hugo in 1987 for his story "Permafrost." His other books include, in addition to the multi-volume Amber series, the novels This Immortal, The Dream Master, Isle of the Dead, Jack of Shadows, Eye of Cat, Doorways in the Sand, Today We Choose Faces, Bridge of Ashes, To Die in Italbar, and Roadmarks, and the col-

lections Four for Tomorrow, The Doors of His Face, the Lamps of His Mouth and Other Stories, The Last Defender of Camelot, *and* Frost and Fire. *Among his last books are two collaborative novels,* A Farce to Be Reckoned With, *with Robert Sheckley, and* Wilderness, *with Gerald Hausman, and, as editor, two anthologies,* Wheel of Fortune *and* Warriors of Blood and Dream. *Zelazny died in 1995. Since his death, several posthumous collaborative novels have been published, including* Psychoshop, *with the late Alfred Bester, and* Donnerjack *and* Lord Demon, *both with Jane LIndskold. A tribute anthology to Zelazny, featuring stories by authors who had been inspired by his work,* Lord of the Fantastic, *was published in 1998.*

Born of man and woman, in accordance with Catform Y7 Coldworld Class (modified per Alyonal), 3.2-E, G.M.I. option, Jarry Dark was not suited for existence anywhere in the universe which had guaranteed him a niche. This was either a blessing or a curse, depending on how you looked at it.

So look at it however you would, here is the story:

◆

It is likely that his parents could have afforded the temperature-control unit, but not much more than that. (Jarry required a temperature of at least $-50°C$ to be comfortable.)

It is unlikely that his parents could have provided for the air-pressure-control and gas-mixture equipment required to maintain his life.

Nothing could be done in the way of 3.2-E grav-simulation, so daily medication and physiotherapy were required. It is unlikely that his parents could have provided for this.

The much-maligned option took care of him, however. It safeguarded his health. It provided for his education. It assured his economic welfare and physical well-being.

It might be argued that Jarry Dark would not have been a homeless Coldworld Catform (modified per Alyonal) had it not been for General Mining, Incorporated, which had held the option. But then it must be borne in mind that no one could have foreseen the nova which destroyed Alyonal.

When his parents had presented themselves at the Public Health Planned Parenthood Center and requested advice and medication pending offspring, they had been informed as to the available worlds and the bodyform requirements for them. They had selected Alyonal, which had recently been purchased by General Mining for purposes of mineral exploitation. Wisely, they had elected the option; that is to say, they had signed a contract on behalf of their anticipated offspring, who would be eminently qualified to inhabit that world, agreeing that he would work as an employee of General Mining until he achieved his majority, at which time he would be free to depart and seek employment wherever he might choose (though his choices would admittedly be limited). In return for this guarantee, General Mining agreed to assure his health, education and continuing welfare for so long as he remained in their employ.

When Alyonal caught fire and went away, those Coldworld Catforms covered by the option who were scattered about the crowded galaxy were, by virtue of the agreement, wards of General Mining.

This is why Jarry grew up in a hermetically sealed room containing temperature and atmosphere controls, and why he received a first-class closed-circuit education, along with his physiotherapy and medicine. This is also why Jarry bore some resemblance to a large gray ocelot without a tail, had webbing between his fingers and could not go outside to watch the traffic unless he wore a pressurized refrigeration suit and took extra medication.

All over the swarming galaxy, people took the advice of Public Health Planned Parenthood Centers, and many others had chosen as had Jarry's parents. Twenty-eight thousand, five hundred sixty-six of them, to be exact. In any group of over twenty-eight thousand five hundred sixty, there are bound to be a few talented individuals. Jarry was one of them. He had a knack for making money. Most of his General Mining pension check was invested in well-chosen stocks of a speculative nature. (In fact, after a time he came to own considerable stock in General Mining.)

When the man from the Galactic Civil Liberties Union had come around, expressing concern over the prebirth contracts involved in the option and explaining that the Alyonal Catforms would make a good test case (especially since Jarry's parents lived within jurisdiction of the 877th Circuit, where they would be assured a favorable courtroom atmosphere), Jarry's parents had demurred, for fear of jeopardizing the General Mining pension. Later on, Jarry himself dismissed the notion also. A favorable decision could not make him an E-world Normform, and what else mattered? He was not vindictive. Also, he owned considerable stock in G.M. by then.

He loafed in his methane tank and purred, which meant that he was thinking. He operated his cryo-computer as he purred and thought. He was computing the total net worth of all the Catforms in the recently organized December Club.

He stopped purring and considered a subtotal, stretched, shook his head slowly. Then he returned to his calculations.

When he had finished, he dictated a message into his speech-tube, to Sanza Barati, President of December and his betrothed:

"Dearest Sanza—The funds available, as I suspected, leave much to be desired. All the more reason to begin immediately. Kindly submit the proposal to the business committee, outline my qualifications and seek immediate endorsement. I've finished drafting the general statement to the membership. (Copy attached.) From these figures, it will take me between five and ten years, if at least eighty percent of the membership backs me. So push hard, beloved. I'd like to meet you someday, in a place where the sky is purple. Yours, always, Jarry Dark, Treasurer. P.S. I'm pleased you were pleased with the ring."

Two years later, Jarry had doubled the net worth of December, Incorporated.

A year and a half after that, he had doubled it again.

When he received the following letter from Sanza, he leapt onto his trampoline, bounded into the air, landed upon his feet at the opposite end of his quarters, returned to his viewer and replayed it:

Dear Jarry,

Attached are specifications and prices for five more worlds. The research staff likes the last one. So do I. What do you think? Alyonal II? If so, how about the price? When could we afford that much? The staff also says that an hundred Worldchange units could alter it to what we want in 5–6 centuries. Will forward costs of this machinery shortly.

Come live with me and be my love, in a place where there are no walls. . . .

Sanza

"One year," he replied, "and I'll buy you a world! Hurry up with the costs of machinery and transport. . . ."

◆

When the figures arrived Jarry wept icy tears. One hundred machines, capable of altering the environment of a world, plus twenty-eight thousand coldsleep bunkers, plus transportation costs for the machinery and his people, plus . . . Too high! He did a rapid calculation.

He spoke into the speech-tube:

". . . Fifteen additional years is too long to wait, Pussycat. Have them figure the time-span if we were to purchase only twenty Worldchange units. Love and kisses, Jarry."

During the days which followed, he stalked above his chamber, erect at first, then on all fours as his mood deepened.

"Approximately three thousand years," came the reply. "May your coat be ever shiny—Sanza."

"Let's put it to a vote, Greeneyes," he said.

◆

Quick, a world in three hundred words or less! Picture this. . . .

One land mass, really, containing three black and brackish-looking seas; gray plains and yellow plains and skies the color of dry sand; shallow forests with trees like mushrooms which have been swabbed with iodine; no mountains, just hills brown, yellow, white, lavender; green birds with wings like parachutes, bills like sickles, feathers like oak leaves, an inside-out umbrella behind; six very distant moons, like spots before the eyes in daytime, snowflakes at night, drops of blood at dusk and dawn; grass like mustard in the moister valleys; mists like white fire on windless mornings, albino serpents when the air's astir; radiating chasms, like fractures in frosted windowpanes; hidden caverns, like chains of dark bubbles; seventeen known dangerous predators, ranging from one to six meters in length, excessively furred and fanged; sudden hailstorms, like hurled hammerheads from a clear sky; an icecap like a blue beret at either flattened pole; nervous bipeds a meter and a half in height, short on cerebrum, which wander the shallow forests and prey upon the giant caterpillar's larva, as well as the giant caterpillar, the green bird, the blind burrower, and the offal-eating murk-beast; seventeen mighty rivers; clouds like pregnant purple cows, which quickly cross the land to lie-in beyond the visible east; stands of windblasted stones like frozen music; nights like soot, to obscure the lesser stars; valleys which flow like the torsos of women or instruments of music; perpetual frost in places of shadow; sounds in the morning like the cracking of ice, the trembling of tin, the snapping of steel strands. . . .

They knew they would turn it to heaven.

◦

The vanguard arrived, decked out in refrigeration suits, installed ten World-change units in either hemisphere, began setting up coldsleep bunkers in several of the larger caverns.

Then came the members of December down from the sand-colored sky.

They came and they saw, decided it was almost heaven, then entered their caverns and slept. Over twenty-eight thousand Coldworld Catforms (modified per Alyonal) came into their own world to sleep for a season in silence the sleep of ice and of stone, to inherit the new Alyonal. There is no dreaming in that sleep. But had there been, their dreams might have been as the thoughts of those yet awake.

"It is bitter, Sanza."

"Yes, but only for a time—"

". . . To have each other and our own world, and still to go forth like divers at the bottom of the sea. To have to crawl when you want to leap. . . ."

"It is only for a short time, Jarry, as the senses will reckon it."

"But it is really three thousand years! An ice age will come to pass as we doze. Our former worlds will change so that we would not know them were we to go back for a visit—and none will remember us."

"Visit what? Our former cells? Let the rest of the worlds go by! Let us be forgotten in the lands of our birth! We are a people apart and we have found our home. What else matters?"

"True. . . . It will be but a few years, and we shall stand our tours of wake-fulness and watching together."

"When is the first?"

"Two and a half centuries from now—three months of wakefulness."

"What will it be like then?"

"I don't know. Less warm. . . ."

"Then let us return and sleep. Tomorrow will be a better day."

"Yes."

"Oh! See the green bird! It drifts like a dream . . ."

◦

When they awakened that first time, they stayed within the Worldchange installation at the place called Deadland. The world was already colder and the edges of the sky were tinted with pink. The metal walls of the great installation were black and rimed with frost. The atmosphere was still lethal and the temperature far too high. They remained within their special chambers for most of the time, venturing outside mainly to make necessary tests and to inspect the structure of their home.

Deadland. . . . Rocks and sand. No trees, no marks of life at all.

The time of terrible winds was still upon the land, as the world fought back against the fields of the machines. At night, great clouds of real es-tate smoothed and sculpted the stands of stone, and when the winds de-parted the desert would shimmer as if fresh-painted and the stones would stand like flames within the morning and its singing. After the sun came up into the sky and hung there for a time, the winds would begin again and a dun-colored fog would curtain the day. When the morning winds departed, Jarry and Sanza would stare out across Deadland through the east window of the installation, for that was their favorite—the one on the third floor—where the stone that looked like a gnarly Normform waved to them, and they would he upon the green couch they had moved up from the first floor, and would sometimes make love as they listened for the winds to rise again, or Sanza would sing and Jarry would write in the log or read back through it, the scribblings of friends and unknowns through the centuries, and they would purr often but never laugh, because they did not know how.

One morning, as they watched, they saw one of the biped creatures of the iodine forests moving across the land. It fell several times, picked itself up, continued, fell once more, lay still.

"What is it doing this far from its home?" asked Sanza.

"Dying," said Jarry. "Let's go outside."

They crossed a catwalk, descended to the first floor, donned their protective suits and departed the installation.

The creature had risen to its feet and was staggering once again. It was covered with a reddish down, had dark eyes and a long, wide nose, lacked a true forehead. It had four brief digits, clawed, upon each hand and foot.

When it saw them emerge from the Worldchange unit, it stopped and stared at them. Then it fell.

They moved to its side and studied it where it lay.

It continued to stare at them, its dark eyes wide, as it lay there shivering.

"It will die if we leave it here," said Sanza.

". . . And it will die if we take it inside," said Jarry.

It raised a forelimb toward them, let it fall again. Its eyes narrowed, then closed.

Jarry reached out and touched it with the toe of his boot. There was no response.

"It's dead," he said.

"What will we do?"

"Leave it here. The sands will cover it."

They returned to the installation, and Jarry entered the event in the log.

During their last month of duty, Sanza asked him, "Will everything die here but us? The green birds and the big eaters of flesh? The funny little trees and the hairy caterpillars?"

"I hope not," said Jarry. "I've been reading back through the biologists' notes. I think life might adapt. Once it gets a start anywhere, it'll do anything it can to keep going. It's probably better for the creatures of this planet that we could afford only twenty Worldchangers. That way they have three millennia to grow more hair and learn to breathe our air and drink our water. With a hundred units we might have wiped them out and had to import coldworld creatures or breed them. This way, the ones who live here might be able to make it."

"It's funny," she said, "but the thought just occurred to me that we're doing here what was done to us. They made us for Alyonal, and a nova took it away. These creatures came to life in this place, and we're taking it away. We're turning all of life on this planet into what we were on our former worlds—misfits."

"The difference, however, is that we are taking our time," said Jarry, "and giving them a chance to get used to the new conditions."

"Still, I feel that all that—outside there"—she gestured toward the window—"is what this world is becoming: one big Deadland."

"Deadland was here before we came. We haven't created any new deserts."

"All the animals are moving south. The trees are dying. When they get as far south as they can go and still the temperature drops, and the air continues to burn in their lungs—then it will be all over for them."

"By then they might have adapted. The trees are spreading, are developing thicker barks. Life will make it."

"I wonder. . . ."

"Would you prefer to sleep until it's all over?"

"No; I want to be by your side, always."

"Then you must reconcile yourself to the fact that something is always hurt by any change. If you do this, you will not be hurt yourself."

Then they listened for the winds to rise.

Three days later, in the still of sundown, between the winds of day and the winds of night, she called him to the window. He climbed to the third floor and moved to her side. Her breasts were rose in the sundown light and the places beneath them silver and dark. The fur of her shoulders and haunches was like an aura of smoke. Her face was expressionless and her wide, green eyes were not turned toward him.

He looked out.

The first big flakes were falling, blue, through the pink light. They drifted past the stone and gnarly Normform; some stuck to the thick quartz windowpane; they fell upon the desert and lay there like blossoms of cyanide; they swirled as more of them came down and were caught by the first faint puffs of the terrible winds. Dark clouds had mustered overhead and from them, now, great cables and nets of blue descended. Now the flakes flashed past the window like butterflies, and the outline of Deadland flickered on and off. The pink vanished and there was only blue, blue and darkening blue, as the first great sigh of evening came into their ears and the billows suddenly moved sidewise rather than downwards, becoming indigo as they raced by.

⬤

"The machine is never silent," Jarry wrote. "Sometimes I fancy I can hear voices in its constant humming, its occasional growling, its crackles of power. I am alone here at the Deadland station. Five centuries have passed since our arrival. I thought it better to let Sanza sleep out this tour of duty, lest the prospect be too bleak. (It is.) She will doubtless be angry. As I lay half-awake this morning, I thought I heard my parents' voices in the next room. No words. Just the sounds of their voices as I used to hear them over my old intercom. They must be dead by now, despite all geriatrics. I wonder if they thought of me much after I left? I couldn't even shake my father's hand without my gauntlet, or kiss my mother goodbye. It is strange, the feeling, to be this alone, with only the throb of the machinery about me as it re-arranges the molecules of the atmosphere, refrigerates the world, here in the middle of the blue place. Deadland. This, despite the fact that I grew up in a steel cave. I call the other nineteen stations every afternoon. I am afraid I am becoming something of a nuisance. I won't call them tomorrow, or perhaps the next day.

"I went outside without my refrig-pack this morning, for a few moments. It is still deadly hot. I gulped a mouthful of air and choked. Our day is still far off. But I can notice the difference from the last time I tried it, two and a half hundred years ago. I wonder what it will be like when we have fin-ished?—And I, an economist! What will my function be in our new Alyonal? Whatever, so long as Sanza is happy. . . .

"The Worldchanger stutters and groans. All the land is blue for so far as I can see. The stones still stand, but their shapes are changed from what they were. The sky is entirely pink now, and it becomes almost ma-roon in the morning and the evening. I guess it's really a wine-color, but I've never seen wine, so I can't say for certain. The trees have not died. They've grown hardier. Their barks are thicker, their leaves are darker and larger. They grow much taller now, I've been told. There are no trees in Deadland.

"The caterpillars still live. They seem much larger, I understand, but it is actually because they have become woollier than they used to be. It seems that most of the animals have heavier pelts these days. Some ap-parently have taken to hibernating. A strange thing: Station Seven reported that they had thought the bipeds were growing heavier coats. There seem to be quite a few of them in that area, and they often see them off in the distance. They looked to be shaggier. Closer observation, however, revealed that some of them were either carrying or were wrapped in the skins of dead animals! Could it be that they are more intelligent than we have given them credit for? This hardly seems possible, since they were tested quite thoroughly by the Bio Team before we set the machines in operation. Yet, it is very strange.

"The winds are still severe. Occasionally, they darken the sky with ash. There has been considerable vulcanism southwest of here. Station Four was relocated because of this. I hear Sanza singing now, within the sounds of the machine. I will let her be awakened the next time. Things should be more settled by then. No, that is not true. It is selfishness. I want her here beside me. I feel as if I were the only living thing in the whole world. The voices on the radio are ghosts. The clock ticks loudly and the silences between the ticks are filled with the humming of the machine, which is a kind of silence, too, because it is constant. Sometimes I think it is not there; I listen for it, I strain my ears, and I do not know whether there is a humming or not. I check the indicators then, and they assure me that the machine is functioning. Or perhaps there is something wrong with the indicators. But they seem to be all right. No. It is me. And the blue of Deadland is a kind of visual silence. In the morning even the rocks are covered with blue frost. Is it beautiful or ugly? There is no response within me. It is a part of the great silence, that's all. Perhaps I shall become a mystic. Perhaps I shall develop occult powers or achieve something bright and liberating as I sit here at the center of the great silence. Perhaps I shall see visions. Already I hear voices. Are there ghosts in Deadland? No, there was never anything here to be ghosted. Except perhaps for the little biped. Why did it cross Deadland? I wonder. Why did it head for the center of destruction rather than away, as its fellows did? I shall never know. Unless perhaps I have a vision. I think it is time to suit up and take a walk. The polar icecaps are heavier. The glaciation has begun. Soon, soon things will be better. Soon the silence will end, I hope. I wonder, though, whether silence is not the true state of affairs in the universe, our little noises serving only to accentuate it, like a speck of black on a field of blue. Everything was once silence and will be so again— is now, perhaps. Will I ever hear real sounds, or only sounds out of the silence? Sanza is singing again. I wish I could wake her up now, to walk with me, out there. It is beginning to snow."

◆

Jarry awakened again on the eve of the millennium.

Sanza smiled and took his hand in hers and stroked it, as he explained why he had let her sleep, as he apologized.

"Of course I'm not angry," she said, "considering I did the same thing to you last cycle."

Jarry stared up at her and felt the understanding begin.

"I'll not do it again," she said, "and I know you couldn't. The aloneness is almost unbearable."

"Yes," he replied.

"They warmed us both alive last time. I came around first and told them to put you back to sleep. I was angry then, when I found out what you had done. But I got over it quickly, so often did I wish you were there."

"We will stay together," said Jarry.

"Yes, always."

They took a flier from the cavern of sleep to the Worldchange installation at Deadland, where they relieved the other attendants and moved the new couch up to the third floor.

The air of Deadland, while sultry, could now be breathed for short periods of time, though a headache invariably followed such experiments. The heat was still oppressive. The rock, once like an old Normform waving, had lost its distinctive outline. The winds were no longer so severe.

On the fourth day, they found some animal tracks which seemed to belong to one of the larger predators. This cheered Sanza, but another, later occurrence produced only puzzlement.

One morning they went forth to walk in Deadland.

Less than a hundred paces from the installation, they came upon three of the giant caterpillars, dead. They were stiff, as though dried out rather than frozen, and they were surrounded by rows of markings within the snow. The footprints which led to the scene and away from it were rough of outline, obscure.

"What does it mean?" she asked.

"I don't know, but I think we had better photograph this," said Jarry.

They did. When Jarry spoke to Station Eleven that afternoon, he learned that similar occurrences had occasionally been noted by attendants of other installations. These were not too frequent, however.

"I don't understand," said Sanza.

"I don't want to," said Jarry.

It did not happen again during their tour of duty. Jarry entered it into the log and wrote a report. Then they abandoned themselves to lovemaking, monitoring, and occasional nights of drunkenness. Two hundred years previously, a biochemist had devoted his tour of duty to experimenting with compounds which would produce the same reactions in Catforms as the legendary whiskey did in Normforms. He had been successful, had spent four weeks on a colossal binge, neglected his duty and been relieved of it, was then retired to his coldbunk for the balance of the Wait. His basically simple formula had circulated, however, and Jarry and Sanza found a well-stocked bar in the storeroom and a handwritten manual explaining its use and a variety of drinks which might be compounded. The author of the document had expressed the hope that each tour of attendance might result in the discovery of a new mixture, so that when he returned for his next cycle the manual would have grown to a size proportionate to his desire. Jarry and Sanza worked at it conscientiously, and satisfied the request with a Snowflower Punch which warmed their bellies and made their purring turn into giggles, so that they discovered laughter also. They celebrated the millennium with an entire bowl of it, and Sanza insisted on calling all the other installations and giving them the formula, right then, on the graveyard watch, so that everyone could share in their joy. It is quite possible that everyone did, for the recipe was well received. And always, even after that bowl was but a memory, they kept the laughter. Thus are the first simple lines of tradition sometimes sketched.

⬤

"The green birds are dying," said Sanza, putting aside a report she had been reading.

"Oh?" said Jarry.

"Apparently they've done all the adapting they're able to," she told him.

"Pity," said Jarry.

"It seems less than a year since we came here. Actually, it's a thousand."

"Time flies," said Jarry.

"I'm afraid," she said.

"Of what?"

"I don't know. Just afraid."

"Why?"

"Living the way we've been living, I guess. Leaving little pieces of ourselves in different centuries. Just a few months ago, as my memory works, this place was a desert. Now it's an ice field. Chasms open and close. Canyons appear and disappear. Rivers dry up and new ones spring forth. Everything seems so very transitory. Things look solid, but I'm getting afraid to touch things now. They might go away. They might turn into

smoke, and my hand will keep on reaching through the smoke and touch—
something . . . God, maybe. Or worse yet, maybe not. No one really knows
what it will be like here when we've finished. We're traveling toward an
unknown land and it's too late to go back. We're moving through a dream,
heading toward an idea. . . . Sometimes I miss my cell . . . and all the little
machines that took care of me there. Maybe *I* can't adapt. Maybe I'm like
the green bird . . ."

"No, Sanza. You're not. We're real. No matter what happens out there,
we will last. Everything is changing because we want it to change. We're
stronger than the world, and we'll squeeze it and paint it and poke holes in
it until we've made it exactly the way we want it. Then we'll take it and
cover it with cities and children. You want to see God? Go look in the
mirror. God has pointed ears and green eyes. He is covered with soft gray
fur. When He raises His hand there is webbing between His fingers."

"It is good that you are strong, Jarry."

"Let's get out the power sled and go for a ride."

"All right."

Up and down, that day, they drove through Deadland, where the dark
stones stood like clouds in another sky.

➤

It was twelve and a half hundred years.

Now they could breathe without respirators, for a short time.

Now they could bear the temperature, for a short time.

Now all the green birds were dead.

Now a strange and troubling thing began.

The bipeds came by night, made markings upon the snow, left dead animals in the midst of them. This happened now with much more frequency
than it had in the past. They came long distances to do it, many of them
with fur which was not their own upon their shoulders.

Jarry searched through the history files for all the reports on the creatures.

"This one speaks of lights in the forest," he said. "Station Seven."

"What . . . ?"

"Fire," he said. "What if they've discovered fire?"

"Then they're not really beasts!"

"But they were!"

"They wear clothing now. They make some sort of sacrifice to our machines. They're not beasts any longer."

"How could it have happened?"

"How do you think? *We* did it. Perhaps they would have remained stupid—animals—if we had not come along and forced them to get smart in
order to go on living. We've accelerated their evolution. They had to adapt
or die, and they adapted."

"D'you think it would have happened if we hadn't come along?" he asked.

"Maybe—someday. Maybe not, too."

Jarry moved to the window, stared out across Deadland.

"I have to find out," he said. "If they are intelligent, if they are—human,
like us," he said, then laughed, "then we must consider their ways."

"What do you propose?"

"Locate some of the creatures. See whether we can communicate with them."

"Hasn't it been tried?"

"Yes."

"What were the results?"

"Mixed. Some claim they have considerable understanding. Others place them far below the threshold where humanity begins."

"We may be doing a terrible thing," she said. "Creating men, then destroying them. Once, when I was feeling low, you told me that we were the gods of this world, that ours was the power to shape and to break. Ours *is* the power to shape and break, but I don't feel especially divine. What can we do? They have come this far, but do you think they can bear the change that will take us the rest of the way? What if they are like the green birds? What if they've adapted as fast and as far as they can and it is not sufficient? What would a god do?"

"Whatever he wished," said Jarry.

That day, they cruised over Deadland in the flier, but the only signs of life they saw were each other. They continued to search in the days that followed, but they did not meet with success.

Under the purple of morning, however, two weeks later, it happened.

"They've been here," said Sanza.

Jarry moved to the front of the installation and stared out.

The snow was broken in several places, inscribed with the lines he had seen before, about the form of a small, dead beast.

"They can't have gone very far," he said.

"No."

"We'll search in the sled."

Now over the snow and out, across the land called Dead they went, Sanza driving and Jarry peering at the lines of footmarks in the blue.

They cruised through the occurring morning, hinting of fire and violet, and the wind went past them like a river, and all about them there came sounds like the cracking of ice, the trembling of tin, the snapping of steel strands. The bluefrosted stones stood like frozen music, and the long shadow of their sled, black as ink, raced on ahead of them. A shower of hailstones drumming upon the roof of their vehicle like a sudden visitation of demon dancers, as suddenly was gone. Deadland sloped downward, slanted up again.

Jarry placed his hand upon Sanza's shoulder.

"Ahead!"

She nodded, began to brake the sled.

They had it at bay. They were using clubs and long poles which looked to have fire-hardened points. They threw stones. They threw pieces of ice.

Then they backed away and it killed them as they went.

The Catforms had called it a bear because it was big and shaggy and could rise up onto its hind legs. . . .

This one was about three and a half meters in length, was covered with bluish fur and had a thin, hairless snout like the business end of a pair of pliers.

Five of the little creatures lay still in the snow. Each time that it swung a paw and connected, another one fell.

Jarry removed the pistol from its compartment and checked the charge.

"Cruise by slowly," he told her. "I'm going to try to burn it about the head."

His first shot missed, scoring the boulder at its back. His second singed the fur of its neck. He leapt down from the sled then, as they came abreast of the beast, thumbed the power control up to maximum, and fired the entire charge into its breast, point-blank.

The bear stiffened, swayed, fell, a gaping wound upon it, front to back.

Jarry turned and regarded the little creatures. They stared up at him.

"Hello," he said. "My name is Jarry. I dub thee Redforms—"

He was knocked from his feet by a blow from behind.

He rolled across the snow, lights dancing before his eyes, his left arm and shoulder afire with pain.

A second bear had emerged from the forest of stone.

He drew his long hunting knife with his right hand and climbed back to his feet.

As the creature lunged, he moved with the catspeed of his kind, thrusting upward, burying his knife to the hilt in its throat.

A shudder ran through it, but it cuffed him and he fell once again, the blade torn from his grasp.

The Redforms threw more stones, rushed toward it with their pointed sticks.

Then there was a thud and a crunching sound, and it rose up into the air and came down on top of him.

He awakened.

He lay on his back, hurting, and everything he looked at seemed to be pulsing, as if about to explode.

How much time had passed, he did not know.

Either he or the bear had been moved.

The little creatures crouched, watching.

Some watched the bear. Some watched him.

Some watched the broken sled. . . .

The broken sled. . . .

He struggled to his feet.

The Redforms drew back.

He crossed to the sled and looked inside.

He knew she was dead when he saw the angle of her neck. But he did all the things a person does to be sure, anyway, before he would let himself believe it.

She had delivered the deathblow, crashing the sled into the creature, breaking its back. It had broken the sled. Herself, also.

He leaned against the wreckage, composed his first prayer, then removed her body.

The Redforms watched.

He lifted her in his arms and began walking, back toward the installation, across Deadland.

The Redforms continued to watch as he went, except for the one with the strangely high brow-ridge, who studied instead the knife that protruded from the shaggy and steaming throat of the beast.

◆

Jarry asked the awakened executives of December: "What should we do?"

"She is the first of our race to die on this world," said Yan Turl, Vice President.

"There is no tradition," said Selda Kein, Secretary. "Shall we establish one?"

"I don't know," said Jarry. "I don't know what is right to do."

"Burial or cremation seem to be the main choices. Which would you prefer?"

"I don't—No, not the ground. Give her back to me. Give me a large flier . . . I'll burn her."

"Then let us construct a chapel."

"No. It is a thing I must do in my own way. I'd rather do it alone."

"As you wish. Draw what equipment you need, and be about it."

"Please send someone else to keep the Deadland installation. I wish to sleep again when I have finished this thing—until the next cycle."

"Very well, Jarry. We are sorry."

"Yes—we are."

Jarry nodded, gestured, turned, departed.

Thus are the heavier lines of life sometimes drawn.

◆

At the southeastern edge of Deadland there was a blue mountain. It stood to slightly over three thousand meters in height. When approached from the northwest, it gave the appearance of being a frozen wave in a sea too vast to imagine. Purple clouds rent themselves upon its peak. No living thing was to be found on its slopes. It had no name, save that which Jarry Dark gave it.

He anchored the flier.

He carried her body to the highest point to which a body might be carried.

He placed her there, dressed in her finest garments, a wide scarf concealing the angle of her neck, a dark veil covering her emptied features.

He was about to try a prayer when the hail began to fall. Like thrown rocks, the chunks of blue ice came down upon him, upon her.

"God damn you!" he cried and he raced back to the flier.

He climbed into the air, circled.

Her garments were flapping in the wind. The hail was a blue, beaded curtain that separated them from all but these final caresses: fire aflow from ice to ice, from clay aflow immortally through guns.

He squeezed the trigger and a doorway into the sun opened in the side of the mountain that had been nameless. She vanished within it, and he widened the doorway until he had lowered the mountain.

Then he climbed upward into the cloud, attacking the storm until his guns were empty.

He circled then above the molten mesa, there at the southeastern edge of Deadland.

He circled above the first pyre this world had seen.

Then he departed, to sleep for a season in silence the sleep of ice and of stone, to inherit the new Alyonal. There is no dreaming in that sleep.

←

Fifteen centuries. Almost half the Wait. Two hundred words or less. . . . Picture—

. . . Nineteen mighty rivers flowing, but the black seas rippling violet now.

. . . No shallow iodine-colored forests. Might shag-barked barrel trees instead, orange and lime and black and tall across the land.

. . . Great ranges of mountains in the place of hills brown, yellow, white, lavender. Black corkscrews of smoke unwinding from smoldering cones.

. . . Flowers, whose roots explore the soil twenty meters beneath their mustard petals, unfolded amidst the blue frost and the stones.

. . . Blind burrowers burrowing deeper; offal-eating murk-beasts now showing formidable incisors and great rows of ridged molars; giant caterpillars growing smaller but looking larger because of increasing coats.

. . . The contours of valleys still like the torsos of women, flowing and rolling, or perhaps like instruments of music.

. . . Gone much windblasted stone, but ever the frost.

. . . Sounds in the morning as always, harsh, brittle, metallic.

They were sure they were halfway to heaven.

Picture that.

←

The Deadland log told him as much as he really needed to know. But he read back through the old reports, also.

Then he mixed himself a drink and stared out the third floor window.

". . . Will die," he said, then finished his drink, outfitted himself, and abandoned his post.

It was three days before he found a camp.

He landed the flier at a distance and approached on foot. He was far to the south of Deadland, where the air was warmer and caused him to feel constantly short of breath.

They were wearing animal skins—skins which had been cut for a better fit and greater protection, skins which were tied about them. He counted sixteen lean-to arrangements and three campfires. He flinched as he regarded the fires, but he continued to advance.

When they saw him, all their little noises stopped, a brief cry went up, and then there was silence.

He entered the camp.

The creatures stood unmoving about him. He heard some bustling within the large lean-to at the end of the clearing.

He walked about the camp.

A slab of dried meat hung from the center of a tripod of poles.

Several long spears stood before each dwelling place. He advanced and studied one. A stone which had been flaked into a leaf-shaped spearhead was affixed to its end.

There was the outline of a cat carved upon a block of wood. . . .

He heard a footfall and turned.

One of the Redforms moved slowly toward him. It appeared older than the others. Its shoulders sloped; as it opened its mouth to make a series of popping noises, he saw that some of its teeth were missing; its hair was grizzled and thin. It bore something in its hands, but Jarry's attention was drawn to the hands themselves.

Each hand bore an opposing digit.

He looked about him quickly, studying the hands of the others. All of them seemed to have thumbs. He studied their appearance more closely.

They now had foreheads.

He returned his attention to the old Redform.

It placed something at his feet, and then it backed away from him.

He looked down.

A chunk of dried meat and a piece of fruit lay upon a broad leaf.

He picked up the meat, closed his eyes, bit off a piece, chewed and swallowed. He wrapped the rest in the leaf and placed it in the side pocket of his pack.

He extended his hand and the Redform drew back.

He lowered his hand, unrolled the blanket he had carried with him and spread it upon the ground. He seated himself, pointed to the Redform, then indicated a position across from him at the other end of the blanket.

The creature hesitated, then advanced and seated itself.

"We are going to learn to talk with one another," he said slowly. Then he placed his hand upon his breast and said, "Jarry."

➤

Jarry stood before the reawakened executives of December.

"They are intelligent," he told them. "It's all in my report."

"So?" asked Yan Turl.

"I don't think they will be able to adapt. They have come very far, very rapidly. But I don't think they can go much further. I don't think they can make it all the way."

"Are you a biologist, an ecologist, a chemist?"

"No."

"Then on what do you base your opinion?"

"I observed them at close range for six weeks."

"Then it's only a feeling you have . . . ?"

"You know there are no experts on a thing like this. It's never happened before."

"Granting their intelligence—granting even that what you have said concerning their adaptability is correct—what do you suggest we do about it?"

"Slow down the change. Give them a better chance. If they can't make it the rest of the way, then stop short of our goal. It's already livable here. We can adapt the rest of the way."

"Slow it down? How much?"

"Supposing we took another seven or eight thousand years?"

"Impossible!"

"Entirely!"

"Too much!"

"Why?"

"Because everyone stands a three-month watch every two hundred fifty years. That's one year of personal time for every thousand. You're asking for too much of everyone's time."

"But the life of an entire race may be at stake!"

"You do not know for certain."

"No, I don't. But do you feel it is something to take a chance with?"

"Do you want to put it to an executive vote?"

"No—I can see that I'll lose. I want to put it before the entire membership."

"Impossible. They're all asleep."

"Then wake them up."

"That would be quite a project."

"Don't you think that the fate of a race is worth the effort? Especially since we're the ones who forced intelligence upon them? We're the ones who made them evolve, cursed them with intellect."

"Enough! They were right at the threshold. They might have become intelligent had we *not* come along—"

"But you can't say for certain! You don't really know! And it doesn't really matter how it happened. They're here and we're here, and they think we're gods—maybe because we do nothing for them but make them miserable. We have some responsibility to an intelligent race, though. At least to the extent of not murdering it."

"Perhaps we could do a long-range study . . ."

"They could be dead by then. I formally move, in my capacity as Treasurer, that we awaken the full membership and put the matter to a vote."

"I don't hear any second to your motion."

"Selda?" he said.

She looked away.

"Tarebell? Clond? Bondici?"

There was silence in the cavern that was high and wide about him.

"All right. I can see when I'm beaten. We will be our own serpents when we come into our Eden. I'm going now, back to Deadland, to finish my tour of duty."

"You don't have to. In fact, it might be better if you sleep the whole thing out . . ."

"No. If it's going to be this way, the guilt will be mine also. I want to watch, to share it fully."

"So be it," said Turl.

◆

Two weeks later, when Installation Nineteen tried to raise the Deadland Station on the radio, there was no response.

After a time, a flier was dispatched.

The Deadland Station was a shapeless lump of melted metal.

Jarry Dark was nowhere to be found.

Later that afternoon, Installation Eight went dead.

A flier was immediately dispatched.

Installation Eight no longer existed. Its attendants were found several miles away, walking. They told how Jarry Dark had forced them from the station at gunpoint. Then he had burnt it to the ground, with the fire-cannons mounted upon his flier.

At about the time they were telling this story, Installation Six became silent.

The order went out: MAINTAIN CONTINUOUS RADIO CONTACT WITH TWO OTHER STATIONS AT ALL TIMES.

The other order went out: GO ARMED AT ALL TIMES. TAKE ANY VISITOR PRISONER.

❱

Jarry waited. At the bottom of a chasm, parked beneath a shelf of rock, Jarry waited. An opened bottle stood upon the control board of his flier. Next to it was a small case of white metal.

Jarry took a long, last drink from the bottle as he waited for the broadcast he knew would come.

When it did, he stretched out on the seat and took a nap.

When he awakened, the light of day was waning.

The broadcast was still going on. . . .

". . . Jarry. They will be awakened and a referendum will be held. Come back to the main cavern. This is Yan Turl. Please do not destroy any more installations. This action is not necessary. We agree with your proposal that a vote be held. Please contact us immediately. We are waiting for your reply, Jarry. . . ."

He tossed the empty bottle through the window and raised the flier out of the purple shadow into the air and up.

❱

When he descended upon the landing stage within the main cavern, of course they were waiting for him. A dozen rifles were trained upon him as he stepped down from the flier.

"Remove your weapons, Jarry," came the voice of Yan Turl.

"I'm not wearing any weapons," said Jarry. "Neither is my flier," he added; and this was true, for the fire-cannons no longer rested within their mountings.

Yan Turl approached, looked up at him.

"Then you may step down."

"Thank you, but I like it right where I am."

"You are a prisoner."

"What do you intend to do with me?"

"Put you back to sleep until the end of the Wait. Come down here!"

"No. And don't try shooting—or using a stun charge or gas, either. If you do, we're all of us dead the second it hits."

"What do you mean?" asked Turl, gesturing gently to the riflemen.

"My flier," said Jarry, "is a bomb, and I'm holding the fuse in my right hand." He raised the white metal box. "So long as I keep the lever on the side of this box depressed, we live. If my grip relaxes, even for an instant, the explosion which ensues will doubtless destroy this entire cavern."

"I think you're bluffing."

"You know how you can find out for certain."

"You'll die too, Jarry."

"At the moment, I don't really care. Don't try burning my hand off either, to destroy the fuse," he cautioned, "because it doesn't really matter. Even if you should succeed, it will cost you at least two installations."

"Why is that?"

"What do you think I did with the fire-cannons? I taught the Redforms how to use them. At the moment, these weapons are manned by Redforms and aimed at two installations. If I do not personally visit my gunners by dawn, they will open fire. After destroying their objectives, they will move on and try for two more."

"You trusted those beasts with laser projectors?"

"That is correct. Now, will you begin awakening the others for the voting?"

Turl crouched, as if to spring at him, appeared to think better of it, relaxed.

"Why did you do it, Jarry?" he asked. "What are they to you that you would make your own people suffer for them?"

"Since you do not feel as I feel," said Jarry, "my reasons would mean nothing to you. After all, they are only based upon my feelings, which are different than your own—or mine are based upon sorrow and loneliness. Try this one, though: I am their god. My form is to be found in their every camp. I am the Slayer of Bears from the Desert of the Dead. They have told my story for two and a half centuries, and I have been changed by it. I am powerful and wise and good, so far as they are concerned. In this capacity, I owe them some consideration. If I do not give them their lives, who will there be to honor me in snow and chant my story around the fires and cut for me the best portions of the woolly caterpillar? None, Turl. And these things are all that my life is worth now. Awaken the others. You have no choice."

"Very well," said Turl. "And if their decision should go against you?"

"Then I'll retire, and you can be god," said Jarry.

●

Now every day when the sun goes down out of the purple sky, Jarry Dark watches it in its passing, for he shall sleep no more the sleep of ice and of stone, wherein there is no dreaming. He has elected to live out the span of his days in a tiny instant of the Wait, never to look upon the New Alyonal of his people. Every morning, at the new Deadland installation, he is awakened by sounds like the cracking of ice, the trembling of tin, the snapping of steel strands, before they come to him with their offerings, singing and making marks upon the snow. They praise him and he smiles upon them. Sometimes he coughs.

Born of man and woman, in accordance with Catform Y7 requirements, Coldworld Class, Jarry Dark was not suited for existence anywhere in the universe which had guaranteed him a niche. This was either a blessing or a curse, depending on how you looked at it. So look at it however you would, that was the story. Thus does life repay those who would serve her fully.

Retrograde Summer

JOHN VARLEY

John Varley appeared on the SF scene in 1974, and by the end of 1976—in what was a meteoric rise to prominence even for a field known for meteoric rises—he was already being recognized as one of the hottest new writers of the seventies. His first story, "Picnic on Nearside," appeared in 1974 in The Magazine of Fantasy and Science Fiction, and was followed by as concentrated an outpouring of first-rate stories as the genre has ever seen, stories such as "The Phantom of Kansas," "In the Bowl," "Gotta Sing, Gotta Dance," "Equinoctial," "The Black Hole Passes," "Overdrawn at the Memory Bank," and many others—smart, bright, fresh, brash, audacious, effortlessly imaginative stories that seemed to suddenly shake the field out of its uneasy slumber like a wake-up call from a brand-new trumpet. It's hard to think of a group of short stories that has had a greater, more concentrated impact on the field, with the exception of Robert Heinlein's early work for John W. Campbell's Astounding, or perhaps Roger Zelazny's early stories in the mid-1960s.

Varley was one of the first new writers to become interested in the solar system again, after several years in the late sixties and early seventies in which it had been largely abandoned as a setting for stories. In spite of the fact space probes had demonstrated beyond any reasonable doubt that there were no Earthlike planets anywhere in the solar system, prompting most authors to lose interest in setting stories there, Varley seemed to find the solar system exciting and romantic just as it was (and this was before the later Mariner probes to the Jupiter and Satum system had proved the solar system to be a lot more surprising than people thought it was)—an aesthetic shift in perception that went ringing on down through the eighties and nineties in the work of writers such as G. David Nordley, Stephen Baxter, Paul J. McAuley, and a dozen others.

The ingenious and inventive little story that follows marked something of a watershed in science-fictional thinking about the settling of alien worlds, a third alternative to Blish's Two Ways, not quite the same as either. Instead of terraforming a world to be more Earthlike, or adapting humans genetically so that their children will be able to survive under alien conditions, the people in Varley's universe leave the planet fundamentally unchanged (in fact, they come to enjoy the alienness and difference of their new homes, even to use the most unEarthlike features for recreational purposes, as we shall see) and employ their technology to protect themselves from hostile environments, without needing to change the basic human form at all, or its genetic heritage. As we move into territory covered by the follow-up volume to this one, Supermen: Tales of the Posthuman Future, this third alternative will become more and more common, and you can see the influence of this story on much of the work of the eighties, nineties, and beyond into a new century.

Varley somehow never had as great an impact with his novels as he did with his short fiction, with the possible exception of his first novel, Ophiuchi Hotline. His other novels include the somewhat disappointing Gaean trilogy, consisting of Titan,

Wizard, *and* Demon, *a novelization of one of his own short stories that was also made into a movie,* Millennium, *and the collections* The Persistence of Vision, The Barbie Murders, Picnic on Nearside, *and* Blue Champagne.

In the 1980s, Varley moved away from the print world to write a number of screenplays for Hollywood producers, most of which were never filmed. He wrote one last significant story, 1984's "Press Enter■," which won him both the Hugo and the Nebula Award (he also won a Hugo in 1982 for his story "The Pusher," and a Hugo and a Nebula in 1979 for his novella "The Persistence of Vision"). After "Press Enter■," little was heard from Varley in the genre until the publication of a major new novel, Steel Beach, *in 1992, which was successful commercially but received a lukewarm reception from many critics. He was largely silent throughout most of the rest of the 1990s, but seems to be making something of a comeback of late, publishing a major new novel,* The Golden Globe, *in 1998, with another new novel,* Irontown Blues, *coming up soon. He has won two Nebulas and two Hugos for his short fiction.*

I was at the spaceport an hour early on the day my clone-sister was to arrive from Luna. Part of it was eagerness to see her. She was three E-years older than me, and we had never met. But I admit that I grab every chance I can get to go to the port and just watch the ships arrive and depart. I've never been off-planet. Someday I'll go, but not as a paying passenger. I was about to enroll in pilot-training school.

Keeping my mind on the arrival time of the shuttle from Luna was hard, because my real interest was in the liners departing for all the far-off places in the system. On that very day the *Elizabeth Browning* was lifting off on a direct, high-gee run for Pluto, with connections for the cometary zone. She was sitting on the field a few kilometers from me, boarding passengers and freight. Very little of the latter. The *Browning* was a luxury-class ship where you paid a premium fare to be sealed into a liquid-filled room, doped to the gills, and fed through a tube for the five-gee express run. Nine days later, at wintertime Pluto, they decanted you and put you through ten hours of physical rehabilitation. You could have made it in fourteen days at two gees and only have been mildly uncomfortable, but maybe it's worth it to some people. I had noticed that the *Browning* was never crowded.

I might not have noticed the arrival of the Lunar shuttle, but the tug was lowering it between me and the *Browning.* They were berthing it in Bay 9, a recessed area a few hundred meters from where I was standing. So I ducked into the tunnel that would take me there.

I arrived in time to see the tug cut the line and shoot into space to meet the next incoming ship. The Lunar shuttle was a perfectly reflective sphere sitting in the middle of the landing bay. As I walked up to it, the force-field roof sprang into being over the bay, cutting off the summertime sunlight. The air started rushing in, and in a few minutes my suit turned off. I was suddenly sweating, cooking in the heat that hadn't been dissipated as yet. My suit had cut off too soon again. I would have to have that checked. Meantime, I did a little dance to keep my bare feet away from the too-hot concrete.

When the air temperature reached the standard 24 degrees, the field around the shuttle cut off. What was left behind was an insubstantial latticework of decks and bulkheads, with people gawking out of the missing outer walls of their rooms.

I joined the crowd of people clustered around the ramp. I had seen a picture of my sister, but it was an old one. I wondered if I'd recognize her.

There was no trouble. I spotted her at the head of the ramp, dressed in a silly-looking loonie frock coat and carrying a pressurized suitcase. I was sure it was her because she looked just like me, more or less, except that she was a female and she was frowning. She might have been a few centimeters taller than me, but that was from growing up in a lower gravity field.

I pushed my way over to her and took her case.

"Welcome to Mercury," I said in my friendliest manner. She looked me over. I don't know why, but she took an instant dislike to me, or so it seemed. Actually, she had disliked me before we ever met.

"You must be Timmy," she said. I couldn't let her get away with that. There are limits.

"Timothy. And you're my sister, Jew."

"Jubilant."

We were off to a great start.

She looked around her at the bustle of people in the landing bay. Then she looked overhead at the flat black underside of the force-roof and seemed to shrink away from it.

"Where can I rent a suit?" she asked. "I'd like to get one installed before you have a blowout here."

"It isn't that bad," I said. "We do have them more often here than you do in Luna, but it can't be helped." I started off in the direction of General Environments, and she fell in beside me. She was having difficulty walking. I'd hate to be a loonie; just about anywhere they go, they're too heavy.

"I was reading on the trip that you had a blowout here at the port only four lunations ago."

I don't know why, but I felt defensive. I mean, sure we have blowouts here, but you can hardly *blame* us for them. Mercury has a lot of tidal stresses; that means a lot of quakes. Any system will break down if you shake it around enough.

"All right," I said, trying to sound reasonable. "It happens I was here during that one. It was in the middle of the last dark year. We lost pressure in about ten percent of the passages, but it was restored in a few minutes. No lives were lost."

"A few minutes is more than enough to kill someone without a suit, isn't it?" How could I answer that? She seemed to think she had won a point. "So I'll feel a lot better when I get into one of your suits."

"Okay, let's get a suit into you." I was trying to think of something to restart the conversation and drawing a blank. Somehow she seemed to have a low opinion of our environmental engineers on Mercury and was willing to take her contempt out on me.

"What are you training for?" I ventured. "You must be out of school. What are you going to do?"

"I'm going to be an environmental engineer."

"Oh."

◆

I was relieved when they finally had her lie on the table, made the connection from the computer into the socket at the back of her head, and turned off her motor control and sensorium. The remainder of the trip to GE had been a steady lecture about the shortcomings of the municipal pressure service in Mercury Port. My head was swimming with facts about quintuple-redundant fail-less pressure sensors, self-sealing locks, and blowout drills. I'm *sure* we have all those things, and just as good as the ones in Luna. But the best anyone can do with the quakes shaking everything up a hundred times a day is achieve a ninety-nine percent safety factor. Jubilant had sneered when I trotted out that figure. She quoted one to me with fifteen decimal places, all of them nines. That was the safety factor in Luna.

I was looking at the main reason why we didn't need that kind of safety, right in the surgeon's hands. He had her chest opened up and the left lung removed, and he was placing the suit generator into the cavity. It looked pretty much like the lung he had removed except it was made of metal and had a mirror finish. He hooked it up to her trachea and the stump ends of the pulmonary arteries and did some adjustments. Then he closed her and applied somatic sealant to the incisions. In thirty minutes she would be ready to wake up, fully healed. The only sign of the operation would be the gold button of the intake valve under her left collarbone. And if the pressure were to drop by two millibars in the next instant, she would be surrounded by the force field that is a Mercury suit. She would be safer than she had ever been in her life, even in the oh-so-safe warrens in Luna.

The surgeon made the adjustment in my suit's brain while Jubilant was still out. Then he installed the secondary items in her; the pea-sized voder in her throat so she could talk without inhaling and exhaling, and the binaural radio receptors in her middle ears. Then he pulled the plug out of her brain, and she sat up. She seemed a little more friendly. An hour of sensory deprivation tends to make you more open and relaxed when you come out of it. She started to get back into her loonie coat.

"That'll just burn off when you go outside," I pointed out.

"Oh, of course. I guess I expected to go by tunnel. But you don't have many tunnels here, do you?"

You can't keep them pressurized, can you?

I really *was* beginning to feel defensive about our engineering.

"The main trouble you'll have is adjusting to not breathing."

We were at the west portal, looking through the force-curtain that separated us from the outside. There was a warm breeze drifting away from the curtain, as there always is in summertime. It was caused by the heating of the air next to the curtain by the wavelengths of light that are allowed to pass through so we can see what's outside. It was the beginning of retrograde summer, when the sun backtracks at the zenith and gives us a triple helping of very intense light and radiation. Mercury Port is at one of the hotspots, where retrograde sun motion coincides with solar noon. So even though the force-curtain filtered out all but a tiny window of visible light, what got through was high-powered stuff.

"Is there any special trick I should know?"

I'll give her credit; she wasn't any kind of fool, she was just overcritical. When it came to the operation of her suit, she was completely willing to concede that I was the expert.

"Not really. You'll feel an overpowering urge to take a breath after a few minutes, but it's all psychological. Your blood will be oxygenated. It's just that your brain won't feel right about it. But you'll get over it. And don't try to breathe when you talk. Just subvocalize, and the radio in your throat will pick it up."

I thought about it and decided to throw in something else, free of charge.

"If you're in the habit of talking to yourself, you'd better try to break yourself of it. Your voder will pick it up if you mutter, or sometimes if you just think too loud. Your throat moves sometimes when you do that, you know. It can get embarrassing."

She grinned at me, the first time she had done it. I found myself liking her. I had always *wanted* to, but this was the first chance she had given me.

"Thanks. I'll bear it in mind. Shall we go?"

I stepped out first. You feel nothing at all when you step through a force-curtain. You can't step through it at all unless you have a suit generator installed, but with it turned on, the field just forms around your body as you step through. I turned around and could see nothing but a perfectly flat, perfectly reflective mirror. It bulged out as I watched in the shape of a nude woman, and the bulge separated from the curtain. What was left was a silver-plated Jubilant.

The suit generator causes the field to follow the outlines of your body, but from one to one-and-a-half millimeters from the skin. It oscillates between those limits, and the changing volume means a bellows action forces the carbon dioxide out through your intake valve. You expel waste gas and cool yourself in one operation. The field is perfectly reflective except for two pupil-sized discontinuities that follow your eye movements and let in enough light to see by, but not enough to blind you.

"What happens if I open my mouth?" she mumbled. It takes awhile to get the knack of subvocalizing clearly.

"Nothing. The field extends over your mouth, like it does over your nostrils. It won't go down your throat."

A few minutes later: "I sure would like to take a breath." She would get over it. "Why is it so hot?"

"Because at the most efficient setting your suit doesn't release enough carbon dioxide to cool you down below about thirty degrees. So you'll sweat a bit."

"It feels like thirty-five or forty."

"It must be your imagination. You can change the setting by turning the nozzle of your air valve, but that means your tank will be releasing some oxygen with the CO_2 and you never know when you'll need it."

"How much of a reserve is there?"

"You're carrying forty-eight hours' worth. Since the suit releases oxygen directly into your blood, we can use about ninety-five percent of it, instead of throwing most of it away to cool you off, like your loonie suits do." I couldn't resist that one.

"The term is Lunarian," she said, icily. Oh, well. I hadn't even known the term was derogatory.

"I think I'll sacrifice some margin for comfort now. I feel bad enough as it is in this gravity without stewing in my own sweat."

"Suit yourself. You're the environment expert."

She looked at me, but I don't think she was used to reading expressions on a reflective face. She turned the nozzle that stuck out above her left breast, and the flow of steam from it increased.

"That should bring you down to about twenty degrees, and leave you with about thirty hours of oxygen. That's under ideal conditions, of course, sitting down and keeping still. The more you exert yourself, the more oxygen the suit wastes keeping you cool."

She put her hands on her hips. "Timothy, are you telling me that I shouldn't cool off? I'll do whatever you say."

"No, I think you'll be all right. It's a thirty-minute trip to my house. And what you say about the gravity has merit; you probably need the relief. But I'd turn it up to twenty-five as a reasonable compromise."

She silently readjusted the valve.

◆

Jubilant thought it was silly to have a traffic conveyor that operated in two-kilometer sections. She complained to me the first three or four times we got off the end of one and stepped onto another. She shut up about it when we came to a section knocked out by a quake. We had a short walk between sections of the temporary slideway, and she saw the crews working to bridge the twenty-meter gap that had opened beneath the old one.

We only had one quake on the way home. It didn't amount to anything, just enough motion that we had to do a little dance to keep our feet under us. Jubilant didn't seem to like it much. I wouldn't have noticed it at all, except Jubilant yelped when it hit.

◆

Our house at that time was situated at the top of a hill. We had carried it up there after the big quake seven darkyears before that had shaken down the cliffside where we used to live. I had been buried for ten hours in that one—the first time I ever needed digging out. Mercurians don't like living in valleys. They have a tendency to fill up with debris during the big quakes. If you live at the top of a rise, you have a better chance of being near the top of the rubble when it slides down. Besides, my mother and I both liked the view.

Jubilant liked it, too. She made her first comment on the scenery as we stood outside the house and looked out over the valley we had just crossed. Mercury Port was sitting atop the ridge, thirty kilometers away. At that distance you could just make out the hemispherical shape of the largest buildings.

But Jubilant was more interested in the mountains behind us. She pointed to a glowing violet cloud that rose from behind one of the foothills and asked me what it was.

"That's quicksilver grotto. It always looks like that at the start of retrograde summer. I'll take you over there later. I think you'll like it."

Dorothy greeted us as we stepped through the wall.

I couldn't put my finger on what was bothering Mom. She seemed happy enough to see Jubilant after seventeen years. She kept saying inane things about how she had grown and how pretty she looked. She had us stand side by side and pointed out how much we looked like each other. It was true, of course, since we were genetically identical. She was five centimeters taller than me, but she could lose that in a few months in Mercury's gravity.

"She looks just like you did two years ago, before your last Change," she told me. That was a slight misstatement; I hadn't been quite as sexually mature the last time I was a female. But she was right in essence. Both Jubilant and I were genotypically male, but Mom had had my sex changed when I first came to Mercury, when I was a few months old. I had spent the first fifteen years of my life female. I was thinking of Changing back, but wasn't in a hurry.

"You're looking well yourself, Glitter," Jubilant said.

Mom frowned for an instant. "It's Dorothy now, honey. I changed my name when we moved here. We use Old Earth names on Mercury."

"I'm sorry, I forgot. My mother always used to call you Glitter when she spoke of you. Before she, I mean before I—"

There was an awkward silence. I felt like something was being concealed from me, and my ears perked up. I had high hopes of learning some things from Jubilant, things that Dorothy had never told me no matter how hard I prodded her. At least I knew where to start in drawing Jubilant out.

It was a frustrating fact at that time that I knew little of the mystery surrounding how I came to grow up on Mercury instead of in Luna, and why I had a clone-sister. Having a clone-twin is a rare enough thing that it was inevitable I'd try to find out how it came to pass. It wasn't socially debilitating, like having a fraternal sibling or something scandalous like that. But I learned early not to mention it to my friends. They wanted to know how it happened, how my mom managed to get around the laws that forbid that kind of unfair preference. One Person, One Child: that's the first moral lesson any child learns even before Thou Shalt Not Take a Life. Mom wasn't in jail, so it must have been legal. But how? And why? She wouldn't talk, but maybe Jubilant would.

◅

Dinner was eaten in a strained silence, interrupted by awkward attempts at conversation. Jubilant was suffering from culture shock and an attack of nerves. I could understand it, looking around me with her eyes. Loonies—pardon me, Lunarians—live all their lives in burrows down in the rock and come to need the presence of solid, substantial walls around them. They don't go outside much. When they do, they are wrapped in a steel-and-plastic cocoon that they can feel around them, and they look out of it through a window. Jubilant was feeling terribly exposed and trying to be brave about it. When inside a force-bubble house, you might as well be sitting on a flat platform under the blazing sun. The bubble is invisible from the inside.

When I realized what was bothering her, I turned up the polarization. Now the bubble looked like tinted glass.

"Oh, you needn't," she said, gamely. "I have to get used to it. I just wish you had *walls* somewhere I could look at."

It was more apparent than ever that something was upsetting Dorothy. She hadn't noticed Jubilant's unease, and that's not like her. She should have had some curtains rigged to give our guest a sense of enclosure.

I did learn some things from the intermittent conversation at the table. Jubilant had divorced her mother when she was ten E-years old, an absolutely extraordinary age. The only grounds for divorce at that age are really incredible things like insanity or religious evangelism. I didn't know much about Jubilant's foster mother—not even her name—but I did know that she and Dorothy had been good friends back in Luna. Somehow, the question of how and why Dorothy had abandoned her child and taken me, a chip off the block, to Mercury, was tied up in that relationship.

"We could never get close, as far back as I can remember," Jubilant was saying. "She told me crazy things, she didn't seem to fit in. I can't really explain it, but the court agreed with me. It helped that I had a good lawyer."

"Maybe part of it was the unusual relationship," I said, helpfully. "You know what I mean. It isn't all that common to grow up with a foster mother instead of your real mother." That was greeted with such a dead silence that I wondered if I should just shut up for the rest of dinner. There were meaningful glances exchanged.

"Yes, that might have been part of it. Anyway, within three years of your leaving for Mercury, I knew I couldn't take it. I should have gone with you. I was only a child, but even then I wanted to come with you." She looked appealingly at Dorothy, who was studying the table. Jubilant had stopped eating.

"Maybe I'd better not talk about it."

To my surprise, Dorothy agreed. That cinched it for me. They wouldn't talk about it because they were keeping something from me.

◆

Jubilant took a nap after dinner. She said she wanted to go to the grotto with me but had to rest from the gravity. While she slept I tried once more to get Dorothy to tell me the whole story of her life on the moon.

"But *why* am I alive at all? You say you left Jubilant, your own child, three years old, with a friend who would take care of her in Luna. Didn't you *want* to take her with you?"

She looked at me tiredly. We'd been over this ground before.

"Timmy, you're an adult now, and have been for three years. I've told you that you're free to leave me if you want. You will soon, anyway. But I'm not going into it any further."

"Mom, you know I can't insist. But don't you have enough respect for me not to keep feeding me that story? There's more behind it."

"Yes! Yes, there is more behind it. But I prefer to let it lie in the past. It's a matter of personal privacy. Don't you have enough respect for *me* to stop grilling me about it?" I had never seen her this upset. She got up and walked through the wall and down the hill. Halfway down, she started to run.

I started after her, but came back after a few steps. I didn't know what I'd say to her that hadn't already been said.

◆

We made it to the grotto in easy stages. Jubilant was feeling much better after her rest, but still had trouble on some of the steep slopes.

I hadn't been to the grotto for four lightyears and hadn't played in it for longer than that. But it was still a popular place with the kids. There were scores of them.

We stood on a narrow ledge overlooking the quicksilver pool, and this time Jubilant was really impressed. The quicksilver pool is at the bottom of a narrow gorge that was blocked off a long time ago by a quake. One side of the gorge is permanently in shade, because it faces north and the sun never gets that high in our latitude. At the bottom of the gorge is the pool, twenty meters across, a hundred meters long, and about five meters deep. We *think* it's that deep, but just try sounding a pool of mercury. A lead weight sinks through it like thick molasses, and just about everything else floats. The kids had a fair-sized boulder out in the middle and were using it for a boat.

That's all pretty enough, but this was retrograde summer, and the temperature was climbing toward the maximum. So the mercury was near the boiling point, and the whole area was thick with the vapor. When the streams of electrons from the sun passed through the vapor, it lit up, flickering and swirling in a ghostly indigo storm. The level was down, but it would never all boil away because it kept condensing on the dark cliffside and running back into the pool.

"Where does it all come from?" Jubilant asked when she got her breath.

"Some of it's natural, but the majority comes from the factories in the port. It's a by-product of some of the fusion processes that they can't find any use for, and so they release it into the environment. It's too heavy to drift away, and so during darkyear, it condenses in the valleys. This one is especially good for collecting it. I used to play here when I was younger."

She was impressed. There's nothing like it on Luna. From what I hear, Luna is plain dull on the outside. Nothing moves for billions of years.

"I never saw anything so pretty. What do you do in it, though? Surely it's too dense to swim in?"

"Truer words were never spoken. It's all you can do to force your hand half a meter into the stuff. If you could balance, you could stand on it and sink in just about fifteen centimeters. But that doesn't mean you can't swim, you swim *on* it. Come on down, I'll show you."

She was still gawking at the ionized cloud, but she followed me. That cloud can hypnotize you. At first you think it's all purple; then you start seeing other colors out of the corners of your eyes. You can never see them plainly, they're too faint. But they're there. It's caused by local impurities of other gases.

I understand people used to make lamps using ionized gases: neon, argon, mercury, and so forth. Walking down into quicksilver gully is exactly like walking into the glow of one of those old lamps.

Halfway down the slope, Jubilant's knees gave way. Her suit field stiffened with the first impact when she landed on her behind and started to slide. She was a rigid statue by the time she plopped into the pool, frozen into an awkward posture trying to break her fall. She slid across the pool and came to rest on her back.

I dived onto the surface of the pool and was easily carried all the way across to her. She was trying to stand up and finding it impossible. Presently she began to laugh, realizing that she must look pretty silly.

"There's no way you're going to stand up out here. Look, here's how you move." I flipped over on my belly and started moving my arms in a swimming motion. You start with them in front of you, and bring them back to your sides in a long circular motion. The harder you dig into the mercury, the faster you go. And you keep going until you dig your toes in. The pool is frictionless.

Soon she was swimming along beside me, having a great time. Well, so was I. Why is it that we stop doing so many fun things when we grow up? There's nothing in the solar system like swimming on mercury. It was coming back to me now, the sheer pleasure of gliding along on the mirror-bright surface with your chin plowing up a wake before you. With your eyes just above the surface, the sensation of speed is tremendous.

Some of the kids were playing hockey. I wanted to join them, but I could see from the way they eyed us that we were too big and they thought we shouldn't be out here in the first place. Well, that was just tough. I was having too much fun swimming.

After several hours, Jubilant said she wanted to rest. I showed her how it could be done without going to the side, forming a tripod by sitting with your feet spread wide apart. That's about the only thing you can do except lie flat. Any other position causes your support to slip out from under you. Jubilant was content to lie flat.

"I still can't get over being able to look right at the sun," she said. "I'm beginning to think you might have the better system here. With the internal suits, I mean."

"I thought about that," I said. "You loo . . . Lunarians don't spend enough time on the surface to make a force-suit necessary. It'd be too much trouble and expense, especially for children. You wouldn't believe what it costs to keep a child in suits. Dorothy won't have her debts paid off for twenty years."

"Yes, but it might be worth it. Oh, I can see you're right that it would cost a lot, but I won't be outgrowing them. How long do they last?"

"They should be replaced every two or three years." I scooped up a handful of mercury and let it dribble through my hands and onto her chest. I was trying to think of an indirect way to get the talk on to the subject of Dorothy and what Jubilant knew about her. After several false starts, I came right out and asked her what they had been trying not to say.

She wouldn't be drawn out.

"What's in that cave over there?" she asked, rolling over on her belly.

"That's the grotto."

"What's in it?"

"I'll show you if you'll talk."

She gave me a look. "Don't be childish, Timothy. If your mother wants you to know about her life in Luna, she'll tell you. It's not my business."

"I won't be childish if you'll stop treating me like a child. We're both adults. You can tell me whatever you want without asking my mother."

"Let's drop the subject."

"That's what everyone tells me. All right, go on up to the grotto by yourself." And she did just that. I sat on the lake and glowered at everything. I don't enjoy being kept in the dark, and I especially don't like having my relatives talk around me.

I was just a little bemused to find out how important it had become to find out the real story of Dorothy's trip to Mercury. I had lived seventeen years without knowing, and it hadn't harmed me. But now that I had thought about the things she told me as a child, I saw that they didn't make sense. Jubilant arriving here had made me reexamine them. Why *did* she leave Jubilant in Luna? Why take a cloned infant instead?

◗

The grotto is a cave at the head of the gully, with a stream of quicksilver flowing from its mouth. That happens all lightyear, but the stream gets more substantial during the height of summer. It's caused by the mercury vapor concentrating in the cave, where it condenses and drips off the walls. I found Jubilant sitting in the center of a pool, entranced. The ionization glow in the cave seems much brighter than outside, where it has to compete with sunlight. Add to that the thousands of trickling streams of mercury throwing back reflections, and you have a place that has to be entered to be believed.

"Listen, I'm sorry I was pestering you. I—"

"Shhh." She waved her hands at me. She was watching the drops fall from the roof to splash without a ripple into the isolated pools on the floor of the cave. So I sat beside her and watched it, too.

"I don't think I'd mind living here," she said, after what might have been an hour.

"I guess I never really considered living anywhere else."

She faced me, but turned away again. She wanted to read my face, but all she could see was the distorted reflection of her own.

"I thought you wanted to be a ship's captain."

"Oh, sure. But I'd always come back here." I was silent for another few minutes, thinking about something that had bothered me more and more lately.

"Actually, I might get into another line of work."

"Why?"

"Oh, I guess commanding a spaceship isn't what it used to be. You know what I mean?"

She looked at me again, this time tried even harder to see my face.

"Maybe I do."

"I know what you're thinking. Lots of kids want to be ship's captains. They grow out of it. Maybe I have. I think I was born a century too late for what I want. You can hardly find a ship anymore where the captain is much more than a figurehead. The real master of the ship is a committee of computers. They handle *all* the work. The captain can't even overrule them anymore."

"I wasn't aware it had gotten that bad."

"Worse. All of the passenger lines are shifting over to totally automated ships. The high-gee runs are already like that, on the theory that after a dozen trips at five gees, the crew is pretty much used up."

I pondered a sad fact of our modern civilization: the age of romance was gone. The solar system was tamed. There was no place for adventure.

"You could go to the cometary zone," she suggested.

"That's the only thing that's kept me going toward pilot training. You don't need a computer out there hunting for black holes. I thought about getting a job and buying passage last darkyear, when I was feeling really low about it. But I'm going to try to get some pilot training before I go."

"That might be wise."

"I don't know. They're talking about ending the courses in astrogation. I may have to teach myself."

●

"You think we should get going? I'm getting hungry."

"No. Let's stay here a while longer. I love this place."

I'm sure we had been there for five hours, saying very little. I had asked her about her interest in environmental engineering and gotten a surprisingly frank answer. This was what she had to say about her chosen profession: "I found after I divorced my mother that I was interested in making safe places to live. I didn't feel very safe at that time." She found other reasons later, but she admitted that it was a need for security that still drove her. I meditated on her strange childhood. She was the only person I ever knew who didn't grow up with her natural mother.

"I was thinking about heading outsystem myself," she said after another long silence. "Pluto, for instance. Maybe we'll meet out there someday."

"It's possible."

There was a little quake; not much, but enough to start the pools of mercury quivering and make Jubilant ready to go. We were threading our way through the pools when there was a long, rolling shock, and the violet glow died away. We were knocked apart and fell in total darkness.

"What was that?" There was the beginning of panic in her voice.

"It looks like we're blocked in. There must have been a slide over the entrance. Just sit tight and I'll find you."

"Where are you? I can't find you. Timothy!"

"Just hold still and I'll run into you in a minute. Stay calm, just stay calm, there's nothing to worry about. They'll have us out in a few hours."

"Timothy, I can't find you, I can't—" She smacked me across the face with one of her hands, then was swarming all over me. I held her close and soothed her. Earlier in the day I might have been contemptuous of her behavior, but I had come to understand her better. Besides, no one likes to be buried alive. Not even me. I held her until I felt her relax.

"Sorry."

"Don't apologize, I felt the same way the first time. I'm glad you're here.

Being buried alone is much worse than just being buried alive. Now sit down and do what I tell you. Turn your intake valve all the way to the left. Got it? Now we're using oxygen at the slowest possible rate. We have to keep as still as possible so we don't heat up too much."

"All right. What next?"

"Well, for starters, do you play chess?"

"What? Is that all? Don't we have to turn on a signal or something?"

"I already did."

"What if you're buried solid and your suit freezes to keep you from being crushed? How do you turn it on then?"

"It turns on automatically if the suit stays rigid for more than one minute."

"Oh. All right. Pawn to king four."

We gave up on the game after the fifteenth move. I'm not that good at visualizing the board, and while she was excellent at it, she was too nervous to plan her game. And I was getting nervous. If the entrance was blocked with rubble, as I had thought, they should have had us out in under an hour. I had practiced estimating time in the dark and made it to be two hours since the quake. It must have been bigger than I thought. It could be a full day before they got around to us.

"I was surprised when you hugged me that I could touch you. I mean your skin, not your suit."

"I thought I felt you jump. The suits merge. When you touch me, we're wearing one suit instead of two. That comes in handy sometimes."

We were lying side by side in a pool of mercury, arms around each other. We found it soothing.

"You mean . . . I see. You can make love with your suit on. Is that what you're saying?"

"You should try it in a pool of mercury. That's the best way."

"We're in a pool of mercury."

"And we don't dare make love. It would overheat us. We might need our reserve."

She was quiet, but I felt her hands tighten behind my back.

"Are we in trouble, Timothy?"

"No, but we might be in for a long stay. You'll get thirsty by and by. Can you hold out?"

"It's too bad we can't make love. It would have kept my mind off it."

"Can you hold out?"

"I can hold out."

⌖

"Timothy, I didn't fill my tank before we left the house. Will that make a difference?"

I don't think I tensed, but she scared me badly. I thought about it, and didn't see how it mattered. She had used an hour's oxygen at most getting to the house, even at her stepped-up cooling rate. I suddenly remembered how cool her skin had been when she came into my arms.

"Jubilant, was your suit set at maximum cooling when you left the house?"

"No, but I set it up on the way. It was so *hot*. I was about to pass out from the exertion."

"And you didn't turn it down until the quake?"

"That's right."

I did some rough estimates and didn't like the results. By the most pessimistic assumptions, she might not have more than about five hours of air left. At the outside, she might have twelve hours. And she could do simple arithmetic as well as I; there was no point in trying to hide it from her.

"Come closer to me," I said. She was puzzled, because we were already about as close as we could get. But I wanted to get our intake valves together. I hooked them up and waited three seconds.

"Now our tank pressures are equalized."

"Why did you do that? Oh, no, Timothy, you shouldn't have. It was my own fault for not being careful."

"I did it for me, too. How could I live with myself if you died in here and I could have saved you? Think about that."

◆

"Timothy, I'll answer any question you want to ask about your mother."

That was the first time she got me mad. I hadn't been angry with her for not refilling the tank. Not even about the cooling. That more my fault than hers. I had made it a game about the cooling rate, not really telling her how important it was to maintain a viable reserve. She hadn't taken me seriously, and now we were paying for my little joke. I had made the mistake of assuming that because she was an expert at Lunar safety, she could take care of herself. How could she do that if she didn't have a realistic estimate of the dangers?

But this offer sounded like repayment for the oxygen, and you don't do that on Mercury. In a tight spot, air is always shared freely. Thanks are rude.

"*Don't* think you owe me anything. It isn't right."

"That's not why I offered. If we're going to die down here, it seems silly for me to be keeping secrets. Does that make sense?"

"No. If we're going to die, what's the use in telling me? What good will it do me? And that doesn't make sense, either. We're not even *near* dying."

"It would at least be something to pass the time."

I sighed. At that time, it really wasn't important to know what I had been trying to learn from her.

"All right. Question one: Why did Dorothy leave you behind when she came here?" Once I had asked it, the question suddenly became important again.

"Because she's not our mother. I divorced our mother when I was ten."

I sat up, shocked silly.

"Dorothy's not . . . Then she's . . . she's my foster mother? All this time she said she was—"

"No, she's not your foster mother, not technically. She's your father."

"*What?*"

"She's your father."

"Who the hell—*father?* What kind of crazy game is this? Who the hell ever knows who their *father* is?"

"I do," she said simply. "And now you do."

"I think you had better tell it from the top."

She did, and it all stood up, bizarre as it was.

Dorothy and Jubilant's mother (*my* mother!) had been members of a religious sect called the First Principles. I gathered they had a lot of screwy ideas, but the screwiest one of all had to do with something called the "nuclear family." I don't know why they called it that, maybe because it was invented in the era when nuclear power was first harnessed. What it consisted of was a mother and a father, *both living in the same household*, and dozens of kids.

The First Principles didn't go that far; they still adhered to the One Person–One Child convention—and a damn good thing, too, or they might have been lynched instead of queasily tolerated—but they liked the idea of both biological parents living together to raise the two children.

So Dorothy and Gleam (that was her name; they were Glitter and Gleam back in Luna) "married," and Gleam took on the female role for the first child. She conceived it, birthed it, and named it Jubilant.

Then things started to fall apart, as any sane person could have told them it would. I don't know much history, but I know a little about the way things were back on Old Earth. Husbands killing wives, wives killing husbands, parents beating children, wars, starvation—all those things. I don't know how much of that was the result of the nuclear family, but it must have been tough to "marry" someone and find out too late that it was the wrong someone. So you took it out on the children. I'm no sociologist, but I can see that much.

Their relationship, while it may have glittered and gleamed at first, went steadily downhill for three years. It got to the point where Glitter couldn't even share the same planet with his spouse. But he loved the child and had even come to think of her as his own. Try telling that to a court of law. Modern jurisprudence doesn't even recognize the *concept* of fatherhood, any more than it would recognize the divine right of kings. Glitter didn't have a legal leg to stand on. The child belonged to Gleam.

But my mother (*foster* mother, I couldn't yet bring myself to say father) found a compromise. There was no use mourning the fact that he couldn't take Jubilant with him. He had to accept that. But he could take a piece of her. That was me. So he moved to Mercury with the cloned child, changed his sex, and brought me up to adulthood, never saying a word about First Principles.

I was calming down as I heard all this, but it was certainly a revelation. I was full of questions, and for a time survival was forgotten.

"No, Dorothy isn't a member of the church any longer. That was one of the causes of the split. As far as I know, Gleam is the *only* member today. It didn't last very long. The couples who formed the church pretty much tore each other apart in marital strife. That was why the court granted my divorce; Gleam kept trying to force her religion on me, and when I told my friends about it, they laughed at me. I didn't want that, even at age ten, and told the court I thought my mother was crazy. The court agreed."

"So . . . so Dorothy hasn't had her one child yet. Do you think she can still have one? What are the legalities of that?"

"Pretty cut-and-dried, according to Dorothy. The judges don't like it, but it's her birthright, and they can't deny it. She managed to get permission to have you grown because of a loophole in the law, since she was going to Mercury and would be out of the jurisdiction of the Lunar courts. The loophole was closed shortly after you left. So you and I are pretty unique. What do you think about that?"

"I don't know. I think I'd rather have a normal family. What do I say to Dorothy now?"

She hugged me, and I loved her for that. I was feeling young and alone. Her story was still settling in, and I was afraid of what my reaction might be when I had digested it.

"I wouldn't tell her anything. Why should you? She'll probably get around to telling you before you leave for the cometary zone, but if she doesn't, what of it? What does it matter? Hasn't she been a mother to you? Do you have any complaints? Is the biological fact of motherhood all that important? I think not. I think love is more important, and I can see that it was there."

"But she's my father! How do I relate to that?"

"Don't even try. I suspect that fathers loved their children in pretty much the same way mothers did, back when fatherhood was more than just insemination."

"Maybe you're right. I think you're right." She held me close in the dark.

"Of course I'm right."

Three hours later there was a rumble and the violet glow surrounded us again.

➤

We walked into the sunlight hand in hand. The rescue crew was there to meet us, grinning and patting us on the back. They filled our tanks, and we enjoyed the luxury of wasting oxygen to drive away the sweat.

"How bad was it?" I asked the rescue boss.

"Medium-sized. You two are some of the last to be dug out. Did you have a hard time in there?"

I looked at Jubilant, who acted as though she had just been resurrected from the dead, grinning like a maniac. I thought about it.

"No. No trouble."

We climbed the rocky slope and I looked back. The quake had dumped several tons of rock into quicksilver gully. Worse still, the natural dam at the lower end had been destroyed. Most of the mercury had drained out into the broader valley below. It was clear that quicksilver grotto would never be the magic place it had been in my youth. That was a sad thing. I had loved it, and it seemed that I was leaving a lot behind me down there.

I turned my back on it and walked toward the house and Dorothy.

Shall We Take a Little Walk?

GREGORY BENFORD

Gregory Benford is one of the modern giants of the field. His 1980 novel Timescape
*won the Nebula Award, the John W. Campbell Memorial Award, the British Science
Fiction Association Award, and the Australian Ditmar Award, and is widely considered to be one of the classic novels of the last two decades. His other novels include
a terraforming novel,* Beyond Jupiter, *as well as* The Stars in Shroud, In the Ocean
of Night, Against Infinity, Artifact, *and* Across the Sea of Suns, Great Sky River,
Tides of Light, Furious Gulf, Sailing Bright Eternity, *and* Cosm. *His short work has
been collected in* Matter's End. *His most recent books are a new addition to Isaac
Asimov's Foundation series,* Foundation's Fear; *a major new solo novel,* The Martian
Race; *a nonfiction collection,* Deep Time; *and a new collection of his short fiction,*
Worlds Vast and Various. *Benford is a professor of physics at the University of Cal-
ifornia, Irvine.*

*Here he takes us along with some men toiling to terraform the frozen surface of
Ganymede, men out on a routine inspection tour who run into a lot more trouble than
they could possibly have bargained for . . . and make a find that could change the
future of humanity forever.*

Salutations! I am asked to recall certain events of my youth. This recording
is made solely for historical purposes; any commercial exploitation is forbidden by the Laws covering the Plentitude of the Artifact.

The distant time I shall describe will seem odd indeed, to those not
schooled in such matters, so the Hosts have asked me to permit a cerebral
tap. I am told this will enable this ferrofax to plumb my dim, distant past
directly. Delicate magnetic fields will probe the ancient cells of my cortex
and coax forth the Matt Bohles who still lives on there.

Yet another wonder! The Historiographers have many tools. I need hardly
point out, I hope, that the tap is yet another device we have gained from
the Plentitude.

Before the tap begins, I remind you that my youth was spent on a Ganymede vastly different. As our shuttle ship dropped toward the surface, the
young Matt Bohles gazed down upon blue ice, and frost that clung to the
poles. At the equator was a thick belt of bare brown rock. Rivers sliced
across the vast plains cutting through the rims of ancient icy craters. The
carved valleys were choked with a pale ruddy fog, and naked peaks jutted
above them.

The Ganymede atmosphere building had just begun. A group of us was
sent down for both relaxation and training. We had been in the orbiting
laboratory—the Can—long enough. Sadly, Jupiter exploration was being
cut back. There was open competition for the remaining permanent posts.

Soon the *Argosy* would sail for Earth, and those who did not qualify would go on her.

There was only one position open in my area. Several contested it. In particular, Yuri Sagdaeff.

Yuri I can recall with ease, without the tap. He was beefy and tall. He swaggered. He had narrow pig eyes and a perpetual little smirk, as if . . .

No, no, I fear some of the old emotions still stir in me. Let me merely say that Yuri and I were in competition, and Yuri was making it easy to let the matter become personal. Yet the luck of the draw assigned us to the same Walker. We were ordered to carry out routine maintenance on the automatic stations dotting Ganymede. We were to spend cramped weeks together.

I . . . ah, but I see the engineer with his coils and lattices, beckoning. The tap should begin . . .

➤

—glittering blue sprinkling of light—

—crunch of boots on pink snow—

Suited, I walked through the scattered ceramic buildings of Ganymede base. The Walker squatted on its six legs, seven meters off the ground. Ruddy light shone through the big, curved windows of the bubble on top. I could see the driver's seat through the largest one. Beneath, almost lost in the jumble of hydraulic valves and rocker arms, the entrance ladder was folded down.

The Walker was bright blue, for contrast against the reddish-brown dirty ice. Beneath the forward antenna snout was a neatly printed *Perambulatin' Puss*. Everybody called her the Cat.

"Morning!" I recognized Captain Vandez's voice even over suit radio. He and Yuri walked up to the Cat from the other side of the base. I said hello. Yuri made a little mock salute at me.

"Well, you boys should be able to handle her," Captain Vandez said. He slapped the side of the Cat. "The ole *Puss* will take good care of you as long as you treat her right. Replenish your air and water reserves at *every* way station—don't try to skip one and push on to the next, 'cause you won't make it. If you fill up at a station and then go to sleep, be sure to top off the tanks before you leave; even sleeping uses up air. And no funny business—stick to the route and make your radio contacts back here sharp on the hour."

"Sir?"

"Yes, Bohles?"

"It seems to me I've had more experience with the Walker than Yuri, here, so—"

"Well, more experience, yes. You have taken her out before. But Sagdaeff practiced all yesterday afternoon with her and I have been quite impressed with his ability. He has more overall experience, as well. I think you should follow his advice when any question comes up," he said impatiently.

I didn't say anything. I didn't like it, but I didn't say anything.

Captain Vandez didn't notice my deliberate silence. He clapped us both on the back, in turn, and handed Yuri a sealed case. "Here are your marching orders. Follow the maps and keep your eyes open."

With that he turned and hurried away. "Let's move it," Yuri said, and led the way to the ladder. We climbed up and I sealed the hatch behind us.

This would be home for the next five days. It was crammed with instruments and storage. There were fiber optics in the floor so we could check on the legs. Sunlight streaming in lit up the cabin and paled the phosphor panels in the ceiling.

We shucked our suits and laid out the maps on the chart table. I took the driver's seat and quickly went through the board check. The lightweight nuclear engine mounted below our deck was fully charged; it would run for years without anything more than an occasional replacement of the circulating fluid elements.

"Why don't you start her off?" Yuri said. "I want to study the maps."

I nodded and slid over to the driver's place. I clicked a few switches and the board in front of me came alive. Red lights winked to green and I revved up the engine. I made the Walker kneel down a few times to warm up the hydraulic fluids. It's hard to remember that the legs of the Cat are working at temperatures a hundred degrees below freezing, when you're sitting in a toasty cabin. It can be dangerous to forget.

While I was doing this I looked out at the life dome rising in the distance. I could pick out people sledding down a hill, and further away a crowd in a snowball fight. A scramble like that is more fun on Ganymede than on Earth; somebody a hundred yards away can pick you off with an accurate shot, because low gravity extends the range of your throwing arm. We don't have anything really spectacular on Ganymede in the way of recreation—nothing like the caverns of Luna, where people fly around in updrafts, using wings strapped to their backs—but what there is has a lot of zip.

I engaged the engine and the Cat lurched forward. The legs moved methodically, finding the level of the ground and adjusting to it. Gyros kept us upright and shock absorbers cushioned our cabin against the rocking and swaying.

I clicked on the Cat's magnetic screen. The life-dome area has buried superconductors honeycombing the area, creating a magnetic web. As the Cat left the fringes of that field, we needed more protection from the steady rain of energetic protons. They sleet down on Ganymede from the Van Allen belts. A few hours without protection would fry us. Cat's walls contained superconducting hydrogen threads carrying high currents. They produce a strong magnetic field outside, which turns incoming charged particles and deflects them.

I took us away from the base at a steady thirty klicks an hour. We cast a shadow like a marching spider on the slate-gray valley wall. Jupiter squatted square in the middle of the sky, like a striped watermelon.

"By the way, that little maneuver back there didn't get you any points with Vandez," Yuri said dryly.

"What?"

"Skip the crap. Listen, you try to undermine me again and I'll take you off at the knees."

"Ummm. Just seemed to me that if you don't know much about Walkers, you shouldn't be running one."

"What's to know? I picked up the whole thing in a few hours' practice. Here, get out of the seat." He waved me away gruffly.

I stopped the Cat and Yuri slid into the driver's chair. We had reached the end of the valley and were heading over a low rise. Here and there ammonia ice clung to the shadows.

Yuri started us forward, staying close to the usual path. The whole trick of guiding a Walker is to keep the legs from having to move very far up and down on each step. It's easier for the machine to inch up a grade than to charge over it.

So the first thing Yuri did was march us directly up the hill. The legs started straining to keep our cabin level, and a whining sound filled the air. The Cat teetered. It lunged forward. Then it stopped and died.

"Hey!" Yuri said.

"Shouldn't be surprised," I said. "She's just doing what any self-respecting machine does when it's asked to perform the impossible. She's gone on strike. The automatic governor cut in."

Yuri said something incoherent and got up. I took over again and backed us off slowly. Then I nudged the Cat around the base of the hill until I found the signs of a winding path previous Walkers had left. Within fifteen minutes we were in the next valley, its hills lit with the rosy glow of the sun filtering through a thin ammonia cloud overhead.

We made good time; I did most of the driving. We stayed overnight at way stations. They were automatic chem separators, pulling water and ammonia molecules apart to make air plus useful working gases. I took care of the hoses, filling A and B and C tanks while Yuri took local samples and kept the Walker in shape.

Our route ran through the old Nicholson Region. We wove through wrinkled valleys of tumbled stone and pink snowdrifts, keeping an eye open for anything unusual. Ganymede was a huge snowball, steadily tugged by Jupiter. The tidal effects stir the slush interior. The churning fluids inside push the surface. Great slabs of frozen ice and ammonia slide over each other, trying to compensate and never getting it right: ice tectonics. They grind and butt and send shuddering quakes rippling all through the moon.

Ganymede is heating up. It's not all ice, of course—billions of years of meterorites have salted the crust, and there was a lot of rock to start with. Otherwise, we'd melt the whole world.

We avoided the areas near the fusion plants. The big ones burn hell-for-leather; you get flash floods and churning rivers. The warm water carries heat to neighboring areas and they melt too.

There's a limit to the method, though. If you're not careful, your fusion plants will melt their way into Ganymede and get drowned. Ganymede is a big snowball, not a solid world at all. It's mostly water. There's an ice crust about seventy klicks thick, with rock scattered through it like raisins in a pudding. Below that crust Ganymede is slush, a milkshake of water and ammonia and pebbles. There's a solid core, far down inside, with enough uranium in it to keep the slush from freezing.

So the fusion plants don't sit in one place. They're big caterpillars, crawling endlessly outward from the equator. Their computer programs make them seek the surest footing over the outcroppings of rock—only they run on tracks, not feet. We saw one creeping over a ridgeline in the distance, making about a hundred meters in an hour, sucking in ice and spewing an ammonia-water creek out the tail. It carried a bright orange balloon on top. If it melts its surroundings too fast and gets caught in a lake, it will float until a team can come to fish it out.

A few decades and there will be a thick atmosphere. A few more and there'll be a Hilton, and it'll be time to move on.

Things got worse with Yuri. He rubbed me the wrong way. He was big and clumsy and the cabin was small. Worse, he was careless.

The third day, we went out to check a sensor package. It monitored ecochanges from the melting. Something had made it stop sending.

When we got to within hiking distance Yuri and I went out. The Walker couldn't scale the steep grade. We came up on the sensor and the trouble was obvious. A fist-sized chunk had lodged in the collector, probably thrown there by some distant shifting among the hills.

Yuri bent over to investigate. He slipped in the gravel and collapsed on the sensor station. The collector, antenna, trinet spokes—they all snapped off. "Asshole!" I shouted, leaping forward. It was too late. He had ruined it.

He swore I had run into him and made him slip. He was lying, of course. I might have nudged him, but it was nothing.

So we had to fetch parts. And strip down the sensor. And install a lot of new stuff. And check it out. We fell a full day behind schedule.

That made Yuri even more surly. We snarled at each other when we were in the Walker. Outside, we tried to divide up the jobs so they could be done alone. We had a lot of recon work. Sensors are set up high, where sudden gully-washers won't catch them. When a fusion Cat passes, there's not much warning. If the just-melted slush finds a brand-new path, you'd better be out of the way.

The third time Yuri went out he came back empty-handed. He couldn't find his package. I walked out to it with him.

"You know, I remember this spot," I said. "We came by here last year. The package is right around this ledge."

"Well, it's not here now." We were standing by a shelf of yellow rock with boulders scattered around.

"What did the map say was wrong with it?"

Yuri looked around impatiently. "It stopped transmitting a few months ago. That's all they know."

I turned to go. "Well, there's—Wait a minute. Isn't that a Faraday cup?"

I bent down and picked up a little bell-like scrap of metal that was lying in the dust. "One of these is usually attached to the top of a sensor pack."

I looked at the nearest boulder. It must have weighed a ton, even a Ganymede. "I bet I know where our package is."

We found one other piece of metal wedged under the edge of boulder. I hiked back and got a replacement package. It took awhile to set up. This time we put it away from any overhang.

Getting the package's radio zeroed in on the base was a little tricky, since we were down in a low trough and had to relay the signals from base through the Walker's radio at first. It took a big chunk out of the day. The next package to be checked was a long walk from our planned way station for the night. We elected to leave it for morning, but then I got restless and said I would go out to the site myself.

Jupiter's eclipse of the sun was just ending as I set out. I took a break to watch the sun slip out from behind Jupiter. Suddenly the planet had a rosy halo; we were looking through the outer fringes of the atmosphere. The Can was a distant twinkle of white. I walked along a streambed and in a way it was like early morning on Earth—as the sun broke out from behind Jupiter things brightened, and the light changed from dull red to a deep yellow. Everything had a clean, sharp look to it. The sun was just a fierce burning point and there were none of the fuzzy half-shadows you're used to on Earth. Ganymede's man-made atmosphere was still so thin it didn't blur things.

I felt a *pop*. I stopped dead. I stood still and quickly checked my suit. Nothing on my inboard monitors. My lightpipe scan showed nothing wrong on my back. Suit pressure was normal. I decided it must have been a low/energy micrometeoroid striking my helmet: they make a noise but no real damage.

The micrometeoroid was probably some uncharged speck of dust, falling into Ganymede's gravity well. If it had been charged, the superconductor threads woven into my suit would have deflected it. Superconductors are a marvel. Once you run a current through them, they keep producing a magnetic field—forever. The field doesn't decay because there's no electrical resistance to the field-producing currents. So even a one-man suit can carry enough magnetic shield to fend off the ferocious Van Allen sleet. And inside the suit there's no magnetic field at all to disturb your instrumentation, if the threads are woven in right. The vector integrals involved in showing that can get messy, especially if you don't know Maxwell's equations from a mudpuddle. But the stuff works, and that's all I needed to know.

When I found the sensor package it needed a new circuit module in its radio; the base had guessed the trouble and told me to carry one along on the walk out. That wasn't what interested me, though. This particular package was sitting in the middle of a seeded area. Two years ago a team of biologists planted an acre of microorganisms around it. The organisms were specially tailored in the Lab to live under Ganymede conditions and—we hoped—start producing oxygen, using sunlight and ice and a wisp of atmosphere.

I was a little disappointed when I didn't find a sprawling green swath. Here and there were patches of gray in the soil, so light you couldn't really be sure they were there at all. Over most of the area there was nothing; the organisms had died.

The trouble with being an optimist is that you get to expect too much. The fact that *anything* could live out here was a miracle of bioengineering. I shrugged and turned back the way I had come.

I was almost halfway back to the Cat when I felt an itching in the back of my throat. My eyes flicked down at the dials mounted beneath my transparent view screen. The humidity indicator read zero. I frowned.

Every suit has automatic humidity control. You breathe out water vapor and the sublimator subsystem extracts some of it before passing the revived air back to you. The extra water is vented out the back of the suit. You'd think that if the microprocessor running the subsystem failed, you'd get high humidity.

But I had too little. In fact, none.

I flipped down my rear lightpipe and squinted at my backpack. Water dripped from the lower vent. I checked my—

Dripped? I looked at it again.

That shouldn't happen. The suit should have been venting water slowly, so it vaporized instantly when it reached the extremely thin atmosphere outside. Dripping meant the relief valve was open and all my water had been purged.

I called up a systems review of my side viewplate, just below eye level inside my helmet. From the data train I guessed the humidity control crapout had been running for over half an hour. *That* was what had made the popping noise. And I had written it off as a micrometeoroid. Wishful thinking.

I stepped up my pace. The tickle at the back of my throat meant I might have suit throat. That's the coverall name for anything related to breathing processed air. If you get contaminants in the mix, or just lose water vapor, your throat and nose soon dry out, or get irritated. A dry throat is a feasting ground for any bacteria hanging around. If you're lucky, the outcome is just a sore throat that hangs around for a while.

I puffed along. In the distance I could see the faint orange aura from a fusion caterpillar. The rising mist from its roaring fusion exhaust diffused the light for tens of klicks. Blue-green shadows in the eroded hillsides contrasted with the gentle orange flow. Suddenly Ganymede felt strange and more than a little threatening.

I was glad when the Cat came within sight. It was backed up to the way station. I clumped up the ladder and wedged through the narrow lock into the cabin.

"You're late for chow," Yuri said.

"Hope I can taste it."

"Why?"

I opened my mouth and pointed. Yuri looked in, turned my head toward the light, looked again. "It's a little red. You should look after it."

I got out the first aid kit and found the anesthetic throat spray. It tasted metallic but it did the job; after a moment it didn't hurt to swallow.

I broke down the humidity control unit in my suit. Sure enough, the microprocessor had a fault. I took a replacement chip slab out of storage and made the change. Everything worked fine.

I was surprised at how much Yuri could do with our vac-dried rations. We had thin slices of chicken in a thick mushroom sauce, lima beans that still had some snap in them, and fried rice. We topped it off with strawberry cream cake and a mug of hot tea. Pretty damned elegant, considering.

"My compliments," I said. I got up from the pullout shelf that we used for a table. The room began to revolve. I put out my hand to steady myself.

"Say!" Yuri shouted. He jumped up and grabbed my arm. The room settled down again.

"I—I'm okay. A little dizzy."

"You're pale."

"The light is poor in ultraviolet here. I'm losing my suntan," I said woozily.

"It must be more than that."

"You're right. Think I'll go to bed early."

"Take some medicine. I think you have suit throat."

I grinned weakly. "Maybe it's something I ate." I jerked on the pull ring and my foldout bunk came down. Yuri brought the first-aid kit. I sat on the bunk taking off my clothes and wondered vaguely where second aid would come from if the first aid failed. I shook my head; the thinking factory had shut down for the night. Yuri handed me a pill and I swallowed it. Then a tablet, which I sucked on. Finally I got between the covers and found myself studying some numbers and instructions that were stenciled on the ceiling of the cabin. Before I could figure out what they meant I fell asleep.

The morning was better, much better. Yuri woke me and gave me a bowl of warm broth. He sat in a deck chair and watched me eat it.

"I must call the base soon," he said.

"Um."

"I have been thinking about what to say."

"Um . . . Oh. You mean about me?"

"Yes."

"Listen, if Captain Vandez thinks I'm really sick he'll scrub the rest of the trip. We'll have to go back."

"So I thought. Which will lower our performance ratings."

"Do me a favor, will you? Don't mention this when you call in. I'm feeling better. I'll be okay."

"Well—"

"Please?"

"All right. I don't want this journey ruined just because you are careless." He slapped his knees and got up. "I will make the call."

"Mighty nice of you," I mumbled. I dozed for a while. I was feeling better, but I was a little weak. I thought over our route. The next way station was a respectable distance away and there was only one sensor package to visit. We would have to spend our time making tracks for the next station—which was just as well, with one crew member on the woozy side.

"Yuri," I said, "check and be sure—"

"Bohles, you may be sick, but that doesn't mean you can start ordering me around. I will get us there."

I rolled over and tried to sleep. I heard Yuri suit up and go out. A little later there were two faint *thunks* as the hoses disconnected from the way station. Then Yuri came back in, unsuited, and sat in the driver's chair.

The Cat lurched forward and then settled down to a steady pace. I decided to stop worrying and let Yuri handle things for a while. I was feeling better every minute, but another forty winks wouldn't do any harm. I let the gentle swaying of the Walker rock me to sleep.

I woke around noon; I must have been more tired than I thought. Yuri tossed me a self-heating can of corned beef; I opened it and devoured the contents immediately.

I passed the next hour or so reading a novel. Or rather, I tried. I dozed off and woke up in midafternoon. There was a lot of sedative in that medicine.

I got up, pulled on my coveralls and walked over to the control board. "Walked" isn't quite the right word—with my bunk and the table down, the Cat resembled a roomy telephone booth.

I sat down next to Yuri. We were making good time across a flat, black plain. There was an inch or so of topsoil—dust, really—that puffed up around the Cat's feet as they stepped. The dust comes from the cycle of freezing and thawing of ammonia ice caught in the boulders. The process gradually fractures the Ganymede rock, breaking it down from pebbles to shards to BB-shot to dust. In a century or so somebody will grow wheat in the stuff.

Some of the soil is really specks of interplanetary debris that has fallen on Ganymede for the last three billion years. All over the plain were little pits and gouges. The bigger meteors had left ray craters, splashing white across the reddish-black crust. The dark ice is the oldest stuff on Ganymede. A big meteor can crack through it, throwing out bright, fresh ice. The whole history of the solar system is scratched out on Ganymede's ancient scowling face, but we still don't know quite how to read all the scribblings. After the fusion bugs have finished, a lot of the intricate, grooved terrain will be gone. Regrettable, maybe—the terraced ridges are beautiful in the slanting yellow rays of sunset—but there are others like them, on other moons. The solar system has a whole lot more snowball moons like Ganymede than it has habitable spots for people. Just like every other age in human history, there are some sad choices to make.

Yuri sidestepped a thick-lipped crater, making the servos negotiate the slope without losing speed. He had caught the knack pretty fast. The bigger craters had glassy rims, where the heat of impact had melted away the roughness. Yuri could pick his way through that stuff with ease. I leaned back and admired the view. Io's shadow was a tiny dot on Jupiter's eternal dancing bands. Jove's thin little ring made a faint line in the sky, too near Jupiter to really see clearly. You had to look away from it, so your side vision could pick it out. There was a small moon there, I knew, slowly breaking up under tidal stresses and feeding stuff into the ring. It's too small to see from Ganymede, though. You get the feeling, watching all these dots of light swinging through the sky, that Jupiter's system is a giant clockwork, each wheel and cog moving according to intricate laws. Our job was to fit into this huge cosmic machine, without getting mashed in the gears.

I yawned, letting all these musings drop away, and glanced at the control board. "You do a full readout this morning?"

Yuri shrugged. "Everything was in order last night."

"Huh. Here—" I punched in for a systems inventory. Numbers and graphs rolled by on the liquid display. Then something went red.

"Hey. Hey. B and C tanks aren't filled," I said tensely.

"What? I put the system into filling mode last night. The meter read all right this morning."

"Because you've got it set on A tank. You have to fill each independently, and check them. For Chrissakes—!"

"Why is that? Was that your idea? It's stupid to not combine the entire system. I—"

"Look," I said rapidly, "the Cat sometimes carries other gasses, for mining or farming. If the computer control automatically switched from A to B to C, you could end up breathing carbon dioxide, or whatever else you were carrying."

"Oh."

"I showed you that a couple days back."

"I suppose I forgot. Still—"

"Quiet." I did a quick calculation; we'd used some already—and on our present course—

"We won't make it to our next station," I announced.

Yuri kept his eyes on his driving. He scowled.

"What about our suits?" he asked slowly. "They might have some air left."

"Did you recharge yours when you came back in?"

"Ah . . . no."

"I didn't either." Another screwup.

I checked them anyway. Not much help, but some. I juggled figures around on the clipboard, but you can't sidestep simple arithmetic. We were in deep trouble.

Yuri stepped up the Cat's pace. It clanked and bounced over slabs of jutting purple ice. "I conclude," he said, "that we should call the base and ask for assistance."

I frowned. "I don't like to do it."

"Why? We must."

"Somebody will have to fly out here and drop air packs." There's always some risk with that because even Ganymede's thin air has winds in it. We don't understand those winds yet.

Yuri gave me a guarded look. "An extra mission. It would not sit well with Captain Vandez, would it?"

"Probably not." I could tell Yuri was thinking that, when the report came to be written, he'd get the blame. "But look, the real point is that somebody back at base would have to risk his neck, and all because of a dumb mistake."

Yuri was silent. The Walker rocked on over the broken ground. A pin-thick ammonia stream flowed in the distance.

"You may not like it," he said, "but I do not intend to die out here." He reached for the radio, turned it on and picked up the microphone.

"Wait," I said. "I may . . ."

"Yah?"

"Let's see that map." I studied it for several minutes. "There, see that gully that runs off this valley?"

"Yes. So what?"

I drew a straight line from the gully, through the hills, to the next broad plain. The line ran through a red dot on the other side of the hills. "That's a way station, that dot. I've been there before. We're slated to check it in two days, on our way back. But I can reach it by foot from that gully, by hiking over the hills. It's only seventeen kilometers."

"You couldn't make it."

I worried over the map some more. A few minutes later I said, "I *can* do it. There's a series of streambeds I can follow most of the distance; that'll cut out a lot of climbing." I worked the calculator. "Even allowing for the extra exertion, our oxy will last."

Yuri shrugged. "Okay, Boy Scout. Just so you leave me enough to cover the time you're gone, plus some extra so a rocket from the base can reach me if you crap out."

"Why don't you walk yourself?"

"I'm in favor of calling the base right now. But I'll wait out your scheme, if you want, right here. I don't like risks."

"Look, if we report this, it'll kill both our chances of staying on."

Yuri studied me sourly. "Probably."

"I don't want to ship Earthside. It's shit-awful back there."

"Uh-huh. But I like dying less."

"You're just a coward, you—"

"Cut that crap or I'll break you in pieces, Bohles."

I caught myself barely in time. I felt a quick surge of energy and I knew what would happen next. But you don't have a brawl inside a Walker, not if you ever want to use it again. So I unclenched my fists and said, "Okay, a truce. Until this problem is solved. Then, by God, I'm going to kick your face in."

Yuri grinned. "I'd love to see you try. But don't let me detain you any longer—" He gestured to the hatch.

"Maybe if we—"

"Those are my terms, Bohles. If you go, you go alone."

I could see he meant it.

◦

The cold seeped into my legs. My suit was fighting off the outside chill, but it was near the end of its reserves.

Pink slabs of ice, gray rock, black sky—and always the thin rasp of my breath, throat raw from coughing. My helmet air was thick and foul. I stumbled along.

My beautiful plan hadn't worked. The footing was pretty bad, and some of the streambeds were choked with runoff—boulders, gravel, slippery ice ponds. A fusion caterpillar must have passed nearby since the last orbital photos.

So I had spent hours struggling over jumbled terrain. Yuri had listened to my complaining, and offered to call the base. But I was damned if I'd get pulled out of it now, and blow any chance of staying out here. My rating was going to stay high, even if I had to bust ass.

That's what I kept telling myself.

But for the last few hours the confidence had trickled away. I didn't want to say anything to Yuri, but things were looking bad to me. If he knew how tired I was, he'd call the base and all my sweat would have been wasted. And beyond that, the little bastard would have the satisfaction of pulling me down with him, even though it was his mistake with the tanks, all because of his stupid—

Gravel slipped under my boot. I lurched, twisting my back. A lance of pain shot through me. A small landslide eroded away my footing. I regained my balance, grabbed at a rock and heaved myself up the steep hillside.

My breath was ragged and I was sweating. I longed to wipe the salty trickles away from my eyes. Just wait a few minutes, I knew, and the suit would evap them. Sure. But the waiting took forever.

I worked my way up the side of what looked like a sand dune. Everything around here was broken and jumbled. The ground slanted the wrong way. I kept my orbital position fix updated, so I knew I was going in the right direction. But the map was useless.

The stones and sand gritted against my boots, slipping away, robbing me of balance and speed. I toiled up the incline, angling across the face of it. A few rocks were perched at the top, sheltering purple patches of snow.

I reached the summit, panting, and looked down.

It was a cube.

I squinted at it. A big slab of ammonia ice had melted further up the ridgeline. The runoff had washed this way, scraping and gouging its path. Where the gully turned, a pile of boulders had collected. At the base of the pile, resting almost flat on the streambed, was—

It moved.

No—there were yellow flecks swimming deep in the milky stone face of it. Turning. Glinting. Catching the wan sunlight and throwing it back at me in intricate patterns.

I frowned. Something—

I stumbled down the raw face of the hill, toward the gully.

The cube was a lattice. It formed frames for shifting lines that were buried deeper. Perspectives moved and formed and swirled and reformed. I squinted at the images, seeking to make sense of them.

They were hard to follow. I looked away, beyond the gully.

A broad swath, cut by recent streams, stretched into the distance. I could make out the bright blue and red of the way station. Its signal phosphor winked yellow. I could reach it within an hour. And there was enough oxy left.

Something drew my eyes back to the thing in the gully.

I felt suddenly cold. A prickly sensation rippled over me.

I peered closer. And saw—

—a vast space of darkness, with firey pinpricks wheeling as they flashed and tumbled and danced, green and blue and orange—

—a thing of quivering lines, plunging out toward me—

—and dissolving into a rhythm of billowy masses, clouds scratching a ruby sky—

—shiny surfaces, flexing bright and slick—

—scribbles in black, then in yellow—

—a running animal, so quick there was only the impression of lightning motion, a flash of brown skin—

—rotting pinks and greens, a stench of age—

—encrusted light—

—hair like snakes—

—explosion—

—I looked away, breathing deeply. Each second a layer shifted deep inside the thing and I saw something, something—

I made myself turn and start downslope. The important thing was to get to the way station. The important thing was the air. The Walker. The job.

I tramped on, my mind swirling with impressions, questions, strange shifting emotions.

I could not help looking back. But I marched on.

◠

—but wait, wait, no—

—just a moment longer, please—

—to feel the first time again, I never suspected—

—oh but—just a short time—so bright—I—no—I—

—ah—

—yes, yes, I suppose I do see. It cannot go on for long, there are other needs, yes, but . . . Oh yes . . .

I am sorry. It has taken a few moments for me to recover from the tap. I had not suspected its, its power, and the vivid sense . . .

Can it be true that our youth is so colored? So gaudy? So purely intense? Without the haze of reflection that experience brings?

In a way, I hope not. I sincerely hope not.

For to go through one's last days knowing that they were filmed over so, that the true world stretches fine and firm, solid and brilliant, but forever beyond your true grasp . . . That would be too much.

I now see why the good engineers do not allow widespread use of tap. And especially, use by ones such as me. As old as me . . .

But let me return to the subject that draws us together. The Artifact.

We know how it came to be there, of course. My first guess was very nearly correct. For a long time it had been buried in the vast ice fields of Ganymede. Once, long ago, it stood above the surface. But the slow grinding and thrusting of ice-plate tectonics submerged the Artifact. It was not crushed. It withstood enormous pressures.

A fusion caterpillar passed near. Ice melted. A random flow swept the Artifact free. And changed human history, forever.

If you will consult the Historiographers, you will find virtually all early discussion of the Artifact focused on its artistic merit. A curious notion arose: that it was a purely aesthetic construct, a work of art and no more.

I see looks of disbelief. But it is true. In those distant days there was a clear division between Art and Science—two concepts we now know to be mere illusions, and not even simplifying illusions, at that.

The earliest—and clearest—clue was obvious, even from the first: I could take my eyes from it only with difficulty. This proved true of everyone who gazed upon its infinite surfaces.

That constantly emerging, forever raw surface. That was the essential fact. The Artifact is in a sense stonework, and in a sense it is totally artificial, constantly remaking itself into new compounds, new substances, new forms and logics. Each basic unit is neither pyramid nor cube—the two most-often-observed forms when closely inspected—but in fact is a ragged, shifting thing of points and angles. Its molecular structure is dictated by the atomic structure, and that in turn comes welling up out of the particles themselves, as the laws governing them change with time. The electro-weak interaction forms and reforms with spontaneous fresh symmetries, hidden variables. The strong force is awash in the same sea.

Thus the Artifact is at basis a recapitulation of the laws which have governed, do now govern, and will govern, the universe. When the universe was young, the laws were young. We see them, deep within the Artifact. Logic and mathematics can burn bright, living through their brief days. Then they sputter out. From them arises the Phoenix of fresh logic, spontaneously broken symmetries, young particles which spill into the welcoming matrix of a consuming universe.

Inward goes time. Outward comes the layered, changing order of the world.

Oh, sorry. Those last two sentences are a part of our litany; I was supposed to keep this discussion free of religious reference.

As I said before, you must remember that these recollections, lodged so deep in me, are from a very different time. Ganymede did not churn with winds. Humans could not walk the surface without a suit. Even the mono-layer cap over the top of our air, holding in the precious molecules except where the huge holes permit spacecraft to pass—even this commonplace was not imagined, then.

So the thinkers of that time decided the Artifact was an artistic object. A complex one, granted, but "merely" artistic.

The second generation of thinking about the Artifact discovered it was a scientific relic. The Artifact contains the varying laws of the universe. We know that the electro-weak force, for example, will fade away within three billion years. Then a new force will emerge. New particles. A new form for the relativity theory.

Once men believed that fields created particles. This is so. But there are also things—I hesitate to call them fields—which create *laws*. The laws of the universe are dictated by these, these entities. And the Artifact is such an entity.

. . . Or perhaps it is only a record of that entity.

Which leads us to the third view of the Artifact.

Only a decade after the discovery of the Artifact did the effect become apparent. A small community had grown up around the site. Then a town.

No one would willingly move away. No one.

When the city reached a quarter of a million souls, something had to be done. But there was no way to persuade the researchers to leave. Anyone who saw the Artifact felt a magnetic pull toward it. A desire—to embrace, to witness, to watch the infinite interplay of its surfaces, its truths . . .

So the final truth became apparent. It is a religious object.

And perhaps . . . well, perhaps it is more. Perhaps it is rightly the object of religion itself.

For it contains the very laws of the universe. Despite the fact that the Artifact is enclosed *in* the universe, perhaps it is not *of* the universe.

But perhaps I stray too far into theological theory. Let me return to my role here today, which is not that of a priest—though that I am—but as an historical witness. I should mention the one other interesting event of that distant day.

◆

I reached the way station. Got the oxy, and rescued poor Yuri—who was quite frightened by the time I returned. Not that he ever thanked me, of course.

We marched on, through a series of valleys, and reached the Artifact. Our intention was to study it further, make recordings, and report in full to our base camp.

Something bothered me about the Artifact when I saw it again. You can look up my old faxes. There you will see a curious mottled pattern on the surface. A rippling of light, glinting like mica. Shifting. It formed concentric circles, like a great eye. I noticed that no matter where I stood, the eye was always centered on me. On us.

I stood at a distance, focusing the recorder. Yuri was as rapt as I. He walked closer.

I was fumbling with the recorder, so I did not see what happened next. He approached the eye, I suppose. When I next glanced up, he was reaching out to touch it. The rings of sparkling light were centered on him.

Then— His hand touched the surface. Joined the surface. And at once was in and of it. He did not move.

Quickly, a wave seemed to pass out of the Artifact. It ran up his arm, changing the dull suit skin to a flashing rainbow of colors, like an alive quartz. The wave washed across his back. Over his helmet. Down into his legs and, finally, to his boots. He was a stony figure, glinting, with moving facets deep inside.

I froze. Slowly, slowly, Yuri leaned forward. He made no sound. Not a word. His arm went into the eye, up to the shoulder. Then his head nodded forward, as if welcoming what was to come. And he was in up to his shoulders. The Artifact drew him in, the barrel chest and waist and then the legs. Finally, as the boots, too, oozed into the eye, I remembered the recorder. I took a stat. It is the only record I have of the event.

I was deeply confused. Perhaps I still am, to this day.

The eye vanished, to be seen no more. The Artifact returned to the guise you see today. Never once in the years since has it given any hint of what it did that day.

◆

How should we think about this event? True, the Artifact swallowed a human being. But when we consider all that it might be, and all that we have learned from its endlessly rippling surface—

Such moral issues I leave to others. Since no other person has been absorbed by the Artifact, the question is rather distant from our researches.

Some hold that, since the Artifact may be here to follow the evolution of the universe, or supervise it, then perhaps it merely collected Yuri, stored him for use, as fresh information about the working-out of the evolutionary laws. Perhaps. Perhaps.

I am not concerned with such speculations. When I remember those antique years, one final outcome irks me. I should confess it, for as a disciple of the Artifact, I cannot speak falsely of it, not even a falsehood of omission.

As you approach the Artifact—now mounted on transparent beams, so all surfaces are visible, and the cameras may record each nuance—there is a small plaque. It is old. It recounts the date I first stumbled upon that fresh gully. Other, later dates are given as well—such as the founding of the Temple and the enactment of the Plentitude. My name appears, as the discoverer.

Each day, as I go to my labors, I pass by that little plaque. My eyes involuntarily rise, past the insignificant mention of my own name. Up, to the enormous statue which looms over the leftmost portal. It is a massive tribute to the Martyr of our following, to the sacrifice exacted by the Artifact.

And gazing at those huge features, accurate right down to the superior smile and the narrow little eyes—gazing at them, I know deep within myself that despite the serenity which should come from the Artifact, and all my years, I still hate the bastard.

The Catharine Wheel

IAN McDONALD

We can expect any project as vast and long-term as terraforming a planet to evolve its own mythology, legends, and folklore. And, as the evocative and lyrical story that follows suggests, perhaps its own religion as well (appropriate enough, I suppose, since we're discussing the creation of worlds) . . . a religion with its own gods, gods who have goals and motivations—and priorities—of Their own . . .

British author Ian McDonald is an ambitious and daring writer with a wide range and an impressive amount of talent. His first story was published in 1982, and since then he has appeared with some frequency in Interzone, Asimov's Science Fiction, New Worlds, Zenith, Other Edens, Amazing, *and elsewhere. He was nominated for the John W. Campbell Award in 1985, and in 1989 he won the* Locus *"Best First Novel" Award for his novel* Desolation Road. *He won the Philip K. Dick Award in 1992 for his novel* King of Morning, Queen of Day. *His other books include the novels* Out on Blue Six *and* Hearts, Hands and Voices, Terminal Cafe, Sacrifice of Fools, *and the acclaimed* Evolution's Shore, *and two collections of his short fiction,* Empire Dreams *and* Speaking in Tongues. *His most recent book is a new novel,* Kirinya, *and a chapbook novella* Tendeleo's Story, *both sequels to* Evolution's Shore. *Born in Manchester, England, in 1960, McDonald has spent most of his life in Northern Ireland, and now lives and works in Belfast. He has a Web site at http://www.lysator.liu.se/∧unicorn/mcdonald/.*

"Come on, lad, come . . ." you hear a voice call, and, peering through the crowd for its source (so familiar, so familiar) you see him. There: past the sherbet sellers and the raucous pastry hawkers; past the crowds of hopeful Penitential Mendicants and Poor Sisters of Tharsis who press close to the dignitaries' rostrum; past the psalm-singing Cathars and the vendors of religious curios; there, he is coming for you, Naon Asiim, with hand outstretched. Through steam and smoke and constables wielding shockstaves who try to keep the crowd away from the man of the moment: Here he comes, just for you, your Grandfather, Taam Engineer. You look at your mother and father, who swell with pride and say, "Yes, Naon, go on, go with him." So he takes your hand and leads you up through the pressing, pressing crowd and the people cheer and wave at you but you have no time to wave back or even make out their faces because your head is whirling with the shouts and the music and the cries of the vendors.

The people part before Taam Engineer like grass before the scythe. Now you are on the rostrum beside him and every one of those thousands of thousands of people crushing into the station falls silent as the old man holds up the Summoner for all to see. There is a wonderful quiet for a moment, then a hiss of steam and the *chunt-chunt* of rumbling wheels and like every last one of those thousands of thousands of people, you let your breath out in a great sigh because out from the pressure-shed doors comes the Greatest of the Great; the fabulous *Catharine of Tharsis* at the head of the last Aries Express.

Do you see pride in Taam Engineer's eye, or is that merely the light catching it as he winks to you and quick as a flash throws you into the control cab? He whispers something to you which is lost beneath the cheering and the music, but you hear the note of pride in it, and you think that is just right, for the Class 88 *Catharine of Tharsis* has never looked as well as she does on this, her final run. The black-and-gold livery of Bethlehem-Ares glows with love and sacred cherry-branches are crossed on the nose above the sun-bright polished relief of the Blessed Lady herself. Well-wishers have stuck holy medals and ikons all over the inside of the cab, too. Looking at them all leads you to realize that the cab is much smaller than you had ever imagined. Then you see the scars where the computer modules have been torn out to make room for a human driver and you remember that all those nights when you lay awake in bed pretending that the thunder of wheels was the Night Mail, the Lady was far away, hauling hundred-car ore trains on the automated run from Iron Hills to Bessemer. Since before you were born, *Catharine of Tharsis* has been making that slow pull up the kilometer-high Illawarra Bank. You have never seen her as she is today, the pride of Bethlehem-Ares, but your imagination has.

Now the people are boarding; the dignitaries and the faithful and the train enthusiasts and the folk who just want to be there at the end of a little piece of history: There they are, filing into the twenty cars and taking their seats for the eight-hour journey.

"Hurry up, hurry up," Taam Engineer says, anxious to be off. He pours you a sherbet from the small coldchest and you sip it, feeling the cool grittiness of it on your tongue, counting the passengers eighty, ninety, a hundred, still a bit dazed that you are one of them yourself. Then the doors seal, *hsssss*. Steam billows; the crowd stands back, excited and expectant, but not as excited or expectant as you. Down the line a red light turns green. The old man grins and taps instructions into the computer.

Behind you, the drowsy djinn wakes and roars in fury, but it is tightly held in its magnetic bottle. Just as well, you think, because your grandfather has told you that it is as hot as the center of the sun back there.

The crowds are really cheering now and the bands are playing for all they are worth and every loco in the yard, even the dirty old locals, are sounding their horns in salute as *Catharine of Tharsis* gathers speed. The constables are trying to keep back the crazy wheel-symboled Cathars who are throwing flower petals onto the track in front of you. Grandfather Taam is grinning from ear to ear and sounding the triple steam-horns like the trumpets of Judgment Day, as if to say, "Make way, make way, this is a *real* train!"

The train picks up speed slowly, accelerating up the long upgrade called Jahar Incline under full throttle, up through the shanty towns and their thrown-together ramshackle depots whose names you have memorized like a mantra: Jashna, Purwani, Wagga-Wagga, Ben's Town, Park-and-Bank, Llandyff, Acheson, Salt Beds, Mananga Loop.

Now you are away from the stink and the press of the shanties, out into the open fields and you cheer as Grandfather Taam opens up the engines and lets the Lady run. *Catharine of Tharsis* throws herself at the magical 300 km/hr speed barrier and in the walled fields by the side of the track, men with oxen and autoplanters stop and look up from the soil to wave at the black-gold streak.

"Faster, Grandfather, faster!" you shriek and Grandfather Taam smiles and orders, "More speed, more speed!" The fusion engines reply with a howl of power. *Catharine of Tharsis* finds that time barrier effortlessly and shatters it and at 355 km/hr the last-ever Aries Express heads out into the Grand Valley.

◆

For a long time I moved without style or feeling, wearing simple homespun frocks and open sandals in cold weather. My hair I let grow into thick staring mats, my nails began to curl at the ends. When I washed (only when people complained of the smell), I did so in cold water, even though some mornings I would shiver uncontrollably and catch sight in the mirror of my hollow blue face. I permitted myself that one vanity, the mirror, as a record of my progress toward spirituality. When I saw those dull eyes following me I would hold their gaze and whisper, "The mortification of the flesh, the denial of the body," until they looked away with an expression other than disgust.

I allowed myself only the simplest foods; uncooked, unprocessed and as close to natural as I could take it—for the most part vegetable. Two meals a day, a breakfast and in the evening a dinner, with a glass of water at midday. Cold, of course, but with the taste of Commissary chemicals to it.

Patrick fears that I am wasting to a ghost before his eyes. I reassure him that I am merely abolishing the excess and taking on a newer, purer, form. "Purity," I whisper, "spirituality."

"Purity!" he says, "spirituality! I'll show you purity, I'll show you spirituality! It's us, Kathy; we are purity, we are spirituality because of the life we share together. It's the love that's pure, the love that's spiritual."

Poor Patrick. He cannot understand.

I've seen the needle and they said,—*This is purity*. Some showed me the secret spaces of their bodies and said,—*Here is spirituality*. Others held up the bottles for me to see:—*Look, purity: escape*; and I've seen the books, the red books, the blue books, the great brown ones dusty with age which say,— *Come inside, many have gone this way to wisdom before you*. What a pity that the blue books contradict the red books and the brown books cannot be read because they are so old. And you, Patrick, you are the slave of the book. You call it freedom: I have another name for what you give the name of Political Expression.

I've seen a thousand altars and breathed a thousand incenses, sung a thousand hymns, chanted a thousand canticles to gods a thousand years dead and been told,—*This is the way, the only way to spirituality*. Dancing-dervish under the love-lasers till dawn with men so beautiful they can only be artificial, I've been to the heart of the music where they say purity lies. Lies lies lies lies. The paintings, the altered states, the loves, the hates, the relationships: lies of the degenerates we have become.

Someday I will have to make Patrick leave. For his own sake as much as for the sake of my path to purity.

But he is my conscience. He makes me constantly ask, "Am I right, am I wrong?" and he must be a strong man indeed to be able to sleep night after night with the stinking animal into which I am changing. But I will cast him off, on that day when I achieve purity, because then I won't have any further need of my conscience.

In an age of decadence, I alone strive for purity. I saw it once, I looked spirituality in the face, and since that day I have sought in my own human way to embody it. But give Patrick his due: I am learning that perhaps my daily denials and asceticisms are not the best way to attain my goal. Perhaps the human way is not the way at all.

For the greatest spiritual experience (I would almost call it "Holy," but I don't believe in God) comes when I taphead into the ROTECH computers, in that instant when they cleave my personality away from my brain and spin it off through space.

To Mars.

I can't explain to Patrick how it feels, like I couldn't explain it to my colleagues on the terraform team how it felt that first time when I tapheaded into the orbital mirrors we were maneuvering into position to thaw the polar ice-caps.

I've tried to tell him (as I tried to tell them, hands dancing, eyes wide and bright) of the beauty of the freedom I felt; from the strangling stench of our decaying culture, from the vice of material things, from my body and the arbitrary dictates of its biology: eating, drinking, pissing, crapping, sleeping, screwing. He doesn't understand.

"Kathy, don't deny your body," he says, touching it. "Yours is a beautiful body."

No, Patrick, only spirit is beautiful, and the machine is beautiful, and only what is beautiful is real.

❧

"But was she real?" you ask, and your grandfather replies, "Oh, certainly. I tell you, she was as real as you or me, as real as any of us. What use is a saint who isn't real?" So you look out through the screen at the blurred steel rail that stretches straight ahead as far as you can see, right over the rusty horizon, and you think, "Real, real, real as steel, real as a rail, rail made from steel." It is easy to make up rhymes to the beat of the wheels: diddley-dum, diddley-dum, real, real, real as steel.

An hour-and-a-half out. Back down the train the passengers are having lunch; the dignitaries in the first-class restaurant, everyone else from packages and parcels on their laps. Taam Engineer is sharing his lunch with you, savory pancakes and tea, because you did not bring any lunch with you as you never expected to be riding high at the head of the Aries Express deep in the magic Forest of Chryse.

You have heard a lot about the Forest of Chryse, that it is under the special protection of the Lady herself, that travelers come back from it with tales of wonders and marvels, with unusual gifts and miraculous powers, that some come back with only half a mind and some do not come back at all.

Look at the trees, giant redwoods older than man reaching up three hundred, four hundred, five hundred meters tall; it is easy to believe that the machines that built the world are still working under the shadow of the branches and that Catharine of Tharsis walks with them in the forest she planted a thousand years ago. Aboard her namesake, you hurtle past at three hundred kilometers per hour and wonder how Saint Catharine could possibly have built an entire world.

"Look, son." Grandfather Taam nudges you and points to a place far up the valley where a great patch of brightness is sweeping across the Forest of Chryse towards you. You hold your breath as the huge disc of light passes slowly over you on its way to the distant rim walls. If you squint up through your fingers you can just about see the intensely bright dot of the sky-mirror way up there in orbit behind all the glare. Then you feel a blow to the back of your head . . . you see hundreds of intensely bright dots.

"How many times have you been told, boy, don't stare at the sky-mirrors!" your grandfather bellows. "You can look at the light, but not at the mirror!"

But you treat yourself to one small extra peep anyway and you think of the men from ROTECH who are focusing all that light down on you, Naon Asiim.

"Remote Orbital Terraform and Environmental Control Headquarters." You whisper the name like a charm to keep the wind and the storm at bay and you remember what your friends told you: that the men up there who move the sky-mirrors have grown so different from ordinary people that they can never ever come down. That makes you shiver. Then you pass out from under the light, but out of the rear screens you can see its progress over the valley to the plateau lands beyond. In its wake you see a tiny silver bauble bowling across the sky.

"Look, Grandfather! A dronelighter!"

He gives it the barest glance, spits and touches one of the tiny ikons of Our Lady fastened above the driving desk. Then you realize what a mistake you have made, that it is the dronelighters and the 'rigibles of the world that have made your grandfather the last to bear the proud name of "Engineer," they are the reason why the museum sidings are waiting for the Lady just beyond the crowds at Pulaski Station.

"I'm sorry, Grandfather." A hand ruffles your hair.

"Never mind, son, never worry. Look: see how that thing runs . . . It's getting out from under the skirts of the storm, running as fast as it can. They can't take the weather, they're flimsy, plasticy things, like glorified Festival kites."

"But we can take the weather."

"Go through it like a fist through wet rice-paper, my boy! I tell you, Bethlehem-Ares never lost a day, not even one single hour, to the weather, rain, hail, blizzard, monsoon, none of it stops the Lady!" He reaches out to touch the metal windowframe and you feel like shouting "hooray!" Taam Engineer (what, you wonder, will he call himself when the Lady is gone?) stabs a finger at the skyscreen.

"See that? Because of those things cluttering up the sky they have to move the weather about to suit them. That's what the mirror's for; those

ROTECH boys are moving the storm up onto the plateau where it can blow itself to glory and not harm one single, delicate, dirigible. Puh!" He spits again. "I tell you, those things have no soul. Not like the Lady here, she's got a soul you can hear and feel when you open those throttles up, she's got a soul you can touch and smell like hot oil and steam. You don't drive her, she lets you become a little part of her and then she drives you. Like all ladies. Soul, I tell you." He haunts around for words but they evade him like butterflies. He waves his hands, trying to shape the ideas that mean so much to him, but the words will not come to him. "I tell you, how can you feel part of anything when you're flying way up there above everything? You're not part of anything up there like you're a bit of the landscape down here. I tell you, they've no soul. You know, soon it will be just them and the robots on the freight runs and then one day even they'll be gone, it'll be just the lighter-than-airs. The only engines you'll see'll be in the museums and God forbid that I should ever come to see that day." He looks at you like he wants you to back him up in what he has said, but you didn't really understand what he said because the rumble of the engines and the sway of the cab as it leans into the curves and drumming of the wheels saying "real, real, real, as steel" is sending you off to sleep.

◆

When I wake the sight disgusts me. Gap-toothed, crack-skinned, filthy-haired hag holding splintered nails up to the mirror whining, *The mortification of the flesh, the denial of the body*. Hideous. Futile.

Sleep came hard to me last night. Lying beside Patrick, staring at the ceiling, I had time and plenty to think. Letting the pieces tumble through my head, I saw how I was wrong, so wrong, so magnificently wrong. The mortification of the flesh is empty. It only serves to focus the mind more closely on the body it seeks to deny. Disciplining the body does not discipline the mind, for the greater the denial the greater the attention the body must be given. This is not the way to spirituality.

So before Patrick wakes I shower. I wash my hair, I trim my nails, I depilate, I deodorize, I even repaint the tekmark on my forehead and dress in the most nearly fashionable outfit I own. On the train downtown I just sit and watch the people. They do not know that I was the girl with the sunken eyes and the stinking hair they were so careful not to be seen staring at. Now I am just another face on a train. By denying the body I only drew more attention to it. The only way to achieve purity is to escape totally from the body. But that is impossible while we are on this earth. Not so on Mars.

Tapheading, for me, is like waking from a dream into a new morning. Eyes click open to the vast redscapes of Mars. You can hear it shouting, Real, real! with the voice of the polar wind. Let me tell you about the polar wind. For a hundred thousand years it blew cold and dry from the ice itself, but we have moved our orbital mirrors in over the pole and are thawing the cap. So now the winds have reversed direction and great thunderheads of cloud are piling up layer upon layer in the north. Someday it will rain, the first rain on Mars for fifty thousand years. I will rejoice at the feel of it on my plastic skin, I will laugh as it fills the ditches and dikes of our irrigation systems and I shall doubtless cry on the day when it touches the seeds of the Black Tulips I have planted and quickens them to life. But that is in the future. Maybe this year, maybe next year, maybe five years from now.

For the present I take joy in lifting my head from the planting and seeing the rows of Johnny Appleseeds digging and dropping and filling and moving on. They are mine. No. They are *me*. I can be any one of them I choose to be, from Number 11 busily spraying organic mulch over the seedbeds to Number 35 trundling back to base with a damaged tread.

But I can be much more than that. If I blink back through the ROTECH computer network I can be a dronelighter blowing tailored bacteria into the air, or a flock of orbital mirrors bending light from round the far side of the sky, or an automated hatchery growing millions of heat-producing, oxygen-generating Black Tulip seeds for the Johnny Appleseeds, or a channel-cutter building the fabulous Martian canals after all these millennia, or a Seeker searching deep beneath the volcanic shield of Tharsis for a magma core to tap for geothermal energy, or an aveopter flying condor patrol high over the Mare Boreum, which will one day indeed be a Sea of Trees. . . .

I can be whatever I want to be. I am free. I am pure spirit, unbound to any body. And this is my vision of purity, of spirituality: to be forever free from this body, from earth and its decadence, to fly on into a pure future and build a new world as it ought to be built; as a thing of spirit, pure and untainted by human lusts and ambitions. This is a future that stretches far beyond my human lifespan. They say it will be eight hundred years before a man can walk naked in the forests we are growing in Chryse. Two hundred years will pass after that before the first settlers arrive on the plains of Deuteronomy. A thousand years, then, to build a whole world in. That will give me enough time to make it a proper world.

This is my vision, this is my dream. I am only now beginning to realize how I may achieve it.

But first I must dream again. . . .

☛

It is not the rattle of the rain that has woken you, nor the slam of a passing ore-train on the slow up-line; it is something far less tangible than that, it is something you feel like the crick in your neck and the dryness in your mouth and the gumminess around your eyes that you get from having fallen asleep against the side window. So knuckle your eyes open, sniff the air. You can smell the rain, but you can smell something else too, like electricity, like excitement, like something waiting to happen.

Look at the screen, what do you see? Wind blowing billows across endless kilometers of wet yellow grass that roll away to the horizon. Low rings of hills like the ancient burial mounds of Deuteronomy lie across the plain: eroded impact craters, Taam Engineer tells you. This is Xanthe, a land as different as different can be from the forests of Chryse or the paddyfields of the Great Oxus. A high, dry plainland where the Grand Valley begins to slope up to the High Country of Tharsis. But today the rains have come out of season to the stony plain, carried on an unnatural wind, for the ROTECH engineers and their sky-mirrors are driving the storm away from the peopled lowlands to the Sinn Highlands where it can blow and rain and rage and trouble no one. The sky is hidden by a layer of low, black, curdled cloud and the wind from the Sea of Trees blows curtains of rain across the grass-land. Miserable.

You ask your grandfather how much longer and he says, "Not long, son, the storm will blow out within the hour and Xanthe's a poor land anyway, fit only for grazers and goatherds and getting through as quickly as possible." Grandfather Taam smiles his special secret smile and then you realize that, according to the story, this is where it all happened, where Taam Engineer— your own grandfather—met the saint and so averted a dreadful accident. Now you know where the feeling of excitement has come from. Now you know why Grandfather Taam has brought you on the great Lady's last haul.

So you tell the old man, this is where it all happened and he smiles that secret smile again and says, "Yes, this is where it all happened all those years ago, long before you were even thought of; it was here the Lady worked a miracle and saved five hundred lives, yes, we'll be there soon, and look, even the weather is deciding to improve, look."

Out across the hills the sky is clearing from the North West. Light is pouring through the dirty clouds and the rain has blown away leaving the air jewel-bright and clear. *Catharine of Tharsis* explodes out into the sunlight, a shout of black and gold and the plains about her steam gently in the afternoon sun.

Lights flash on the control desk. Even though you do not understand what they mean, they look important. You direct Taam Engineer's attention to them, but he just nods and then ignores them. He even sits back and lights a cheroot. You thought he had given up those dirty things years ago, but when you ask him if there is anything wrong, he says,

"Nothing, boy, nothing," and tells you she's only doing what her high station expects of her, but you haven't time to think about that because the train is slowing down. Definitely, unmistakably. Her speed is now well under 100. You look to Taam Engineer, but he grins roguishly and does not even touch the keypad to demand more speed. He just sits there, arms folded, puffing on his cheroot as the speed drops and drops and it becomes obvious that the train is not just slowing, but stopping.

The nonstop Rejoice-to-Llangonnedd Aries Express grinds past a station-ary chemical train down-bound from the sulphur beds of Pavo. The engines whine as they deliver power to the squealing brakes and the 700-ton train comes to a stand right out there in the middle of the pampas with not even a station or even a signal pylon to mark it as special and worthy of the attention of *Catharine of Tharsis*.

A hiss of steam startles you, it is that quiet. Cooling metal clicks. Even the hum of the engines is gone, the fusion generators are shut right down. The rust-red chemical train looks almost sinister in its stillness.

"What now?" you whisper, painfully aware of how loud your voice sounds. Grandfather Taam nods at the door.

"We get out."

The door hisses open and he jumps out, then lifts you down to the ground. You can see the staring faces pressed to the windows all the way down the train.

"Come on," says Grandfather Taam and he takes you by the hand and leads over the slow down-line (you glance nervously at the waiting chemical train, half expecting the automated locomotive to suddenly blare into life), down the low embankment and into the tall grass. He grinds his filthy che-root out on the ground, says, "It should be around here somewhere," and starts thrashing about, whish whish swush, in the wet grass. You can hear him muttering.

"Aha! Got it! A bit overgrown, but that just goes to show how long it is since a human engineer ran this line. I tell you, in my day we kept the weeds down and polished the silverwork so bright you could see it shining from ten kilometers down the track. Come and look at this, son. . . ."

He has cleared the grass away from a small stone pedestal. Inlaid in tar-nished metal is the nine-spiked wheel-symbol of Saint Catharine. You can feel the devotion as your grandfather bends to rub the dirt of the years from the small memorial. When it is clean and silver-bright again he bids you sit with him on the damp crushed grass and listen as he tells you his tale.

◆

I have told Patrick what I am going to do. I used the simplest words, the most restrained gestures, the shortest sentences, for I know how incoherent I become when I am excited. I did my best to explain, but all I did was scare him. Seeing me transformed, my body clean, my face pretty, again the Kathy Haan he had once loved, and then to hear me tell him of how I am going to cast this world away and live forever on Mars is too great a shock for him. He does not have to tell me. I know he thinks I am mad. More than just "mad." Insane. My explanations will do no good, he can't understand and I'm not going to force him to.

"One favor, Patrick. You know people who can get these things, could you get me two lengths of twistlock monofiber?"

"What for?"

"I need it."

". . . for your mad 'escape,' don't tell me. Forget it. No, Kathy."

"But listen, Patrick . . ."

"No, no, no, I've listened enough to you already. You're a persistent bitch; if I listen to your voice long enough I'll find myself agreeing with whatever insane notion you suggest."

"But it's not insanity. It's survival, it's the only way for me to go."

"Oh, yes, the only way you can be pure, the only way you can achieve spirituality. . . . What is it that's driven you to this, Kathy? It's suicide, that's exactly what it is!"

"The Crazy Angel, Patrick. At some time or another the Crazy Angel touches us all and we just have to go with the flow."

But he doesn't see the joke: If there is no God, how can there be any angel at all, Crazy or otherwise, unless it is me?

"Are we not enough? There was a time when it was enough for us to have each other. What more do you want, what more is there?"

"Do you really want me to answer that, Patrick?" I give him one of my fascinating half-smiles that used to excite him so much. Now it only angers him.

"Then what does Mars offer that I don't?"

Same question. This time I choose to answer it.

"Sanity."

"Sanity! Hah! You talk to me about sanity? That's rich, Kathy Haan, that is rich."

I remain patient. I will not allow Patrick to disturb me. I will not lose my head or shout at him. To do so would only be to play the game according to his rules, and his sick society's rules.

"Sanity," I say, "in a world where words like hunger and fear and disease and war and decadence and degeneration don't have any meaning, in a world that one day will be so much more than your Earth could ever be. Freedom from a world that registers its terrorists, Patrick Byrne, and lets them kill who they will for their high and lofty registered ideals!"

That stings him, but I am relentless, I am the voice of final authority: the angel is speaking through me and won't be silent.

"And you will let me go, Patrick, you will get me those lengths of mono-fiber from your Corps friends, because either I go or your sick, sick society will have me off the top of a building in a week, and that is a promise, Patrick Byrne, a Kathy Haan promise: either way I go; either way you lose."

"Bitch!" he roars and spins round, hand raised to strike, but no one may lay hands on the Crazy Angel and live, and the look in my eyes stops him cold. Serenity.

"Bitch. God, maybe you are an angel after all, maybe you are a saint."

"Not a saint, Patrick, never a saint. A saint who doesn't believe in God? Not Saint Kathy, just a woman out of time who wanted something more than her world had to offer. Now, will you get me those bits of twistlock fiber?"

"All right. I can't fight the Crazy Angel. How long?"

I hold my hands about half a meter apart. "Two of them, with grips at both ends and a trigger-release twistlock set to fifth-second decay so they won't ever find out how I did it."

"I'll get them. It'll take some time."

"I can wait."

Expressions flow as words across his face. Then he turns away from me. "Kathy, this is suicide!"

"So what? It's legal, like everything else from political murder to public buggery."

"It's suicide."

"No. Not this. To stay behind, to try and live one more year on this rotting world, that's suicide. More than that, it's the end of everything, because then I'll have even thrown all my hope away."

◆

It is a story old and stale with telling and retelling, but here, sitting on the damp grass under the enormous sky, it feels as if it is happening to you for the first time. Taam Engineer's eyes are vacant, gazing into years ago; he does not even notice how his stained fingers trace the starburst shape of the Catharine Wheel on the pedestal.

"I tell you, I thought we were done then. I'd given up all hope when that pump blew, with us so far out into the wilderness, and it was wilderness then, this was years back before ROTECH had completed manforming the Grand Valley . . . we were so far out that no help could ever reach us in time, not even if they sent the fastest flyer down from their skystations, and there were five hundred souls aboard, man, woman and child. . . .

"So I ordered them to evacuate the train, even though I knew right well that they could never get far enough away to outrun the blast when the fusion engines exploded. . . . But I had them run all the same, run to those hills over there . . . you know, to this day I don't know if they have a name, those hills . . . but I thought that if they could reach the far side then they might be safe, knowing full well that they never would. . . .

"All the time I was counting off the seconds until the pressure vessel would crack and all that superheated steam would blow my beauty to glory and us with her. I can remember that I had one thought in my head that kept running round and round and round: 'God, save the train, please, save the train God. . . .' That was when the miracle happened."

An afterbreath of wind stirs the grass around you. It feels deliciously creepy.

"I don't know if it was my calling or the train's agony that brought her, and I don't think it matters much; but on the horizon I saw a black dot, way out there. . . ." He points out across the waving grass and if you squint along the line of his finger into the sun you too can see that black dot rushing towards you. "An aveopter, black as sin and big as a barn, bigger even; circling over the line, and I tell you, it was looking for me, for the one who called it. . . ." Taam Engineer's hands fly like aveopters, but he is too busy watching the great black metal hawk coming lower and lower and lower to notice them. "And I swear she took the loco in her claws, boy, in her metal claws, and every bit of bright-work on her ran with blue fire. Then I heard it. The most terrible sound in the world, the scream of the steam-release valve overloading and I knew that was it and I scrambled down this bank as fast as I could and threw myself onto the ground because death was only a second behind me, and do you know what I saw?"

Though you have heard the story a hundred tellings before, this time it takes your breath away. So you shake your head, because for once you do not know.

"I tell you, every one of those five hundred souls, just standing there in the long grass and staring for all they were worth. Not one of them trying to run, I say, so I turned myself belly-up and stared too, and I tell you, it was a thing so worth the staring that I couldn't have run, though my life depended on it.

"They'd stripped her down and laid her bare and unplugged the fusion generators and, by the Mother-of-Us-All, they were fusing up the cracks in the containment vessel and running the pumps from zero up to red and down again, and those pumps, those God-blind-'em pumps, they were singing so sweetly that day it was like the Larks of the Argyres themselves."

"Who, Grandfather?" you say, swept away by the story. "Who were they?"

"The Angels of Saint Catharine herself, I tell you. They had the look of great metal insects, like the crickets you keep in a cage at home, but as big as lurchers and silver all over. They came out of the belly of the aveopter and a-swarmed all over my locomotive."

He slaps his thighs.

"Well, I knew she was saved then, and I was whooping and cheering for all I was worth and so was every man-jack of those five hundred souls by the time those silver crickets had finished their work and put her back together again. Then they all just packed back into the belly of that big black aveopter and she flew off over the horizon and we never saw her again, none of us.

"So, I got up into the cab and everything was all quiet and everything smelt right and every readout was normal and every light green, and I put the power on as gentle as gentle and those engines just roared up and sang, and those pumps, those pumps that so near killed us all, they were humming and trilling like they were fresh from the shop. Then I knew I'd seen a miracle happen, that the Blessed Lady, Saint Catharine herself, had intervened and saved us all. And I tell you this, I would still never have believed it had it not been for those five hundred souls who witnessed every little thing she did and some of them even had it recorded and you can see those pictures to this day."

Up on the track the chemical train fires up. The shocking explosion of sound makes you both jump. Then you laugh and up on the embankment the robot train moves off: *cunk, cunk, cunk, cunk.* Taam Engineer rises to watch it. When it is gone he pats the small stone pedestal.

"So of course we named the engine after her and put this here to commemorate the miracle. I tell you, all the engineers (in the days when we used to have human engineers) on the Grand Valley run would sound their horns when they went by as a mark of respect, and also in the hope that if they gave the Lady her due, one day she might pull them out of trouble. You see, we know that the Lady's on our side."

He offers you a hand and drags you up damp-assed from the ground. As you climb the embankment you see all the faces at the windows and the hands waving ikons and charms and medallions and holy things. It makes you look at *Catharine of Tharsis* again, as something not quite believable, half locomotive and half miracle.

Grandfather Taam lifts you up the cab steps. Suddenly a question demands to be asked.

"Grandfather, then why do the trains stop now if they only used to whistle?"

He reaches for the flask of tea and pours you a scalding cup. Behind you the djinn rumbles into life again.

"I'll tell you for why. Because she is not a saint of people, but a saint of machines. Remember that, because the day came when the last engineer was paid off this line and they turned it over to the machines and then they felt that they could honor their Lady as best they knew."

Lights blink red white green yellow blue all over the cab. The light glints off the holy medals and ikons but somehow it is not as pretty as it once was.

◆

As if it were aware of my imminent escape into spirituality, the ugliness is drawing closer to me. Yesterday in the train I saw a licensed beggar kicked to death by three masked men. No one raised voice nor hand in protest. For one of the masks held out a Political Activist Registry card for us all to see while the other two beat the old man to death in accordance with their political ideals. Everyone looked out of the windows or at the floor or at the advertisements for sunny holidays and personal credit extensions. Anywhere but at the beggar or at each other.

I am ashamed. I too looked away and did nothing.

We left him on the floor of the car for others to take care of when we stepped off at our stop. A smart man I vaguely know with a highcaste tek-mark glanced at me and whispered, "We certainly must remember to respect people's right to political expression; goodness knows what terrible things might happen if we don't."

Oh, Patrick, how many beggars have you killed in the name of political expression? Damn you, Patrick Byrne, for all the love I've wasted on a man who a hundred years ago would have been hunted down and torn apart for the common murderer he was. Dear God, though I know you aren't there, what sort of a people are we when we call terrorists "heroes" and murder "political expression"? What sort of a person is it who would dare to say she loved one? A Kathy Haan, that's what. But I will be rid of him.

Escape is two lengths of twistlocked monofiber wrapped up in my pouch, but have I the courage to use it? Cowardice is a virtue now, everyone has their Political Activist card to wave as justification for their fear. Be brave, Kathy.

I like to think of myself as the first Martian at these times.

It's not the loneliness that scares me. I have been alone for twenty-four years now and there is no lonelier place than the inside of your skull. What terrifies me is the fear of gods.

Deiophobia.

"Maybe you are an angel after all, maybe you are a saint," Patrick had said. What I fear most is that I may become more than just a saint, that the ultimate blasphemy to all that the sacrifice of Kathy Haan stood for will be for me to become the Creator God of the world I am building: the Earth Mother, the Blessed Virgin Kathy, the Cherished and Adored Womb of the humanity I despise.

I do not want to be God, I don't even particularly want to be human. I only want to be free from the wheel.

Smiles and leers greet me from friend and satyr alike. "Morning, Kathy (thighs, Kathy), 'day, Kathy (breasts Kathy) . . ." I take my chair, still warm from the flesh of its previous occupant whom I have never known and probably never will, now. Warm-up drill: codes, ciphers, and calibrations. The sensor helmet meshes with my neural implants and nobody sees me slip the coils of monofiber from my pouch and throw a couple of loops around the armrests.

Lightspeed will be the death of me. The monofiber is merely the charm I chose to invoke it.

"Okay, Kathy, taphead monitoring on . . ."

Needles slip into my brain and I slip my wrists through the loops, concealing the twistlock control studs in my palms. I had not thought death would be so easy.

Brainscans worm across the ceiling.

Listen: I have not much time to tell you this, so listen well. It takes six minutes for the oxygen level in the brain to fall to the critical point after which damage is irreversible. It is easy to do this. Damage to two major arteries will do very nicely, provided there is no rapid medical attention.

But: it takes four minutes for the coded tadon pulse containing the soul of Kathy Haan to reach Mars. You can add. You know that if you add another four minutes return time from ROTECH to Earth that leaves you with a brain so like shredded cabbage that there's no way they'll ever be able to pour poor Kathy back into it again. I shall be free and I shall live forever as a creature of pure spirit.

I have invented a totally new sin. Is it fitting then that I should become a saint?

All I need do is press the buttons. The molecular kink in the monofiber will contract, neatly severing my wrists. A fifth of a second later they will dissolve completely. Lightspeed will do the rest. All I need do is press the buttons. They are hidden in my palms, slick with sweat.

"Okay, Kathy, counting down to persona transfer. Preliminary tadon scan on, transfer pulse on in five seconds . . . four . . ."

The mortification of the flesh, I whisper. Behind me someone shouts. Too late.

". . . one."

I press the buttons.

➤

Green lights all the way down the line on the final run into Llangonnedd. Clear road: dirty freighters pulled into sidings blare their horns and the ugly, ugly robot locals squawk their nasty Klaxons as the Lady races by. Suburban passengers blink as she streaks past; by the time the shout reaches their lips she is around the next bend and leaning into the one after that like a pacehound.

And all the lights are green. More magic. Grandfather Taam tells you that you never get a full run of greens coming into Llangonnedd, no, not even for the Aries Express. Never ever. It must be more magic, of the same kind that let the Lady reach the incredible 450 kilometers per hour out there on the flats beyond Hundred Lakes. Grandfather Taam tells you she never touched 450 before, never ever, not even 400. Why, the people who built her had told him themselves that she would blow apart if she went over 390.

You reckon that engineers know nothing about engines and their special magic. After all, they are just engineers, but Grandfather Taam is an Engineer. Looking out of the side windows even a leisurely 250 seems frighteningly fast in these crowded suburbs. Canal flash houses flash fields flash park flash factories flash: you can feel your eyes widening in apprehension as the stations and the signals hurl themselves out of the distance at you. And all the lights are green.

That can only mean one thing.

"She's doing this, isn't she, Grandfather?"

A station packed with round-mouthed commuters zips by. Taam Engineer lights a cheroot.

"Must be. I've hardly had to lay a finger on those buttons for the past hour or so."

Beneath you the brakes start to take hold, slowing you down from your mad rampage through outer Llangonnedd to a more civilized pace. You say, "She really must love this train very much."

Grandfather Taam looks straight ahead of him down the silver track.

"After all, she did save it."

"But it wasn't the people, was it, Grandfather? It was nothing to do with the five hundred souls; she saved the train because it was the train she wanted to save. All those people were extra, weren't they?"

"They didn't matter to her one bit, boy."

"And you said she's a saint of machines, didn't you? Not a saint of people? That's why she loves the train, why she loved it enough not to let it die, isn't it? If there hadn't been a single person there, she would still have saved the train, wouldn't she? But, if that's true, why do people love her?"

"Love her? Who said anything about loving her? I tell you, boy, I have little love for Catharine of Tharsis. Respect yes, love no. And I'll tell you why. Because if she hadn't thought the train was worth saving, if she hadn't loved the train, she would just have let it blow those five hundred people to hell without a single thought. That's the kind of God those crazy Cathars are worshipping, but as to why they love her, I don't know. Do you have any idea why people would love someone like that?"

He looks straight at you. You have been expecting this question. You know that he has never been able to answer it himself, and that it is the reason why he brought you along on this ride.

"I don't know what I think. . . . If she's really like that, then I think that most people must be very foolish most of the time, especially when they have to look for someone to help them when things go wrong and then put the blame on when things don't happen like they want. People are like that. I think if I were a saint like Saint Catharine I would be a saint of machines, too. Then I wouldn't care what people said about me or thought of me because I wouldn't be doing anything for them and they could cry away and pray away all day like those silly Cathars and the Poor Sisters of Tharsis and I wouldn't care one bit, because machines are never foolish."

Catharine of Tharsis has slowed right down. The end of the journey is near now. Tomorrow Taam Engineer and you will be flying home on one of those dreadful 'rigibles and *Catharine of Tharsis* will be taken away to the museum for foolish people to stare at and marvel over her record-breaking final run. And now you understand.

"Grandfather, of course I'd be a saint of machines! Because I could fly with the aveopters and the sky-mirrors and even the great Sky Wheel herself and I could burrow with the Seekers and swim with the 'Mersibles, but most of all I could run with the Lady of Tharsis faster than she ever ran before and show off to everyone what a wonderful engine she is before they put her away for good in a museum. People are always moaning and complaining about their troubles and their problems; they won't let you run and be free from them, people won't let you do things like that."

"Ah, the ways of saints and children," Taam Engineer says as the Lady rumbles over the Raj-Canal into the glassite dome of Pulaski station. Already you can hear the roars and the cheers of the crowds and every loco in the yards is sounding its horn in salute.

"Here, button three," Grandfather Taam says and you reply to the people with the wonderful blare of the steam horns. You press and press and press that button and the trumpets sound and sound and sound until the notes shatter against the glass roof of the station. And how the crowds cheer! Taam Engineer is hanging out of the window waving to the mobs of petal-throwing Cathars as the *Catharine of Tharsis* glides in to Platform Three as smooth as smooth. You are sliding the other side window open ready to cheer out when something stops you. An odd feeling like a persistent itch in the nose that suddenly stops or a noise in your ears that you never hear until it goes away. A kind of click. You shake your head but it is gone and you shout and wave for all you are worth to the excited people. They wave and call back to you, but you do not see them because you are really thinking about the click. For a second or so it puzzles you. Then you realize that it is nothing very important, it is only the empty space filling in where once there might have been a saint.

Sunken Gardens

BRUCE STERLING

One of the most powerful and innovative new talents to enter SF in recent years, Bruce Sterling as yet may still be better known to the cognoscenti than to the SF-reading population at large, in spite of recent Hugo wins. If you look behind the scenes, though, you will find him everywhere, and he had almost as much to do, as writer, critic, propagandist, aesthetic theorist, and tireless polemicist, with the shaping and evolution of SF in the 1980s and 1990s as Michael Moorcock did with the shaping of SF in the 1960s; it is not for nothing that many of his peers refer to him, half ruefully, half admiringly, as "Chairman Bruce."

Sterling sold his first story in 1976. By the end of the eighties, he had established himself, with a series of stories set in his exotic "Shaper/Mechanist" future, with novels such as the complex and Stapledonian Schismatrix *and the well-received* Islands in the Net *(as well as with his editing of the influential anthology* Mirrorshades: The Cyberpunk Anthology *and the infamous critical magazine* Cheap Truth*), as perhaps the prime driving force behind the revolutionary "Cyberpunk" movement in science fiction, and also as one of the best new hard science writers to enter the field in some time. His other books include a critically acclaimed nonfiction study of First Amendment issues in the world of computer networking,* The Hacker Crackdown: Law and Disorder on the Electronic Frontier, *the novels* The Artificial Kid, Involution Ocean, Heavy Weather, Holy Fire, *and* Distraction, *a novel in collaboration with William Gibson,* The Difference Engine, *and the landmark collections* Crystal Express *and* Globalhead. *His most recent books include the omnibus collection (it contains the novel* Schismatrix *as well as most of his Shaper/Mechanist stories)* Schismatrix Plus, *a new collection,* A Good Old-Fashioned Future, *and a new novel,* Zeitgeist. *His story "Bicycle Repairman" earned him a long-overdue Hugo in 1997, and he won another Hugo in 1997 for his story "Taklamakan." He lives with his family in Austin, Texas.*

Here he gives us a ringside seat for a strange and deadly biotech contest between competing ecosystems, a literal battle of worlds, in which the stakes are life itself. . . .

Mirasol's crawler loped across the badlands of the Mare Hadriacum, under a tormented Martian sky. At the limits of the troposphere, jet streams twisted, dirty streaks across pale lilac. Mirasol watched the winds through the fretted glass of the control bay. Her altered brain suggested one pattern after another: nests of snakes, nets of dark eels, maps of black arteries.

Since morning the crawler had been descending steadily into the Hellas Basin, and the air pressure was rising. Mars lay like a feverish patient under this thick blanket of air, sweating buried ice.

On the horizon thunderheads rose with explosive speed below the constant scrawl of the jet streams.

The basin was strange to Mirasol. Her faction, the Patternists, had been assigned to a redemption camp in northern Syrtis Major. There, two-hundred-mile-an-hour surface winds were common, and their pressurized camp had been buried three times by advancing dunes.

It had taken her eight days of constant travel to reach the equator.

From high overhead, the Regal faction had helped her navigate. Their orbiting city-state, Terraform-Kluster, was a nexus of monitor satellites. The Regals showed by their helpfulness that they had her under closer surveillance.

The crawler lurched as its six picklike feet scrabbled down the slopes of a deflation pit. Mirasol suddenly saw her own face reflected in the glass, pale and taut, her dark eyes dreamily self-absorbed. It was a bare face, with the anonymous beauty of the genetically Reshaped. She rubbed her eyes with nail-bitten fingers.

To the west, far overhead, a gout of airborne topsoil surged aside and revealed the Ladder, the mighty anchor cable of the Terraform-Kluster.

Above the winds the cable faded from sight, vanishing below the metallic glitter of the Kluster, swinging aloofly in orbit.

Mirasol stared at the orbiting city with an uneasy mix of envy, fear and reverence. She had never been so close to the Kluster before, or to the all-important Ladder that linked it to the Martian surface. Like most of her faction's younger generation, she had never been into space. The Regals had carefully kept her faction quarantined in the Syrtis redemption camp.

Life had not come easily to Mars. For one hundred years the Regals of Terraform-Kluster had bombarded the Martian surface with giant chunks of ice. This act of planetary engineering was the most ambitious, arrogant, and successful of all the works of man in space.

The shattering impacts had torn huge craters in the Martian crust, blasting tons of dust and steam into Mars's threadbare sheet of air. As the temperature rose, buried oceans of Martian permafrost roared forth, leaving networks of twisted badlands and vast expanses of damp mud, smooth and sterile as a television. On these great playas and on the frost-caked walls of channels, cliffs, and calderas, transplanted lichen had clung and leapt into devouring life. In the plains of Eridania, in the twisted megacanyons of the Coprates Basin, in the damp and icy regions of the dwindling poles, vast clawing thickets of its sinister growth lay upon the land—massive disaster areas for the inorganic.

As the terraforming project had grown, so had the power of Terraform-Kluster.

As a neutral point in humanity's factional wars, T-K was crucial to financiers and bankers of every sect. Even the alien Investors, those star-traveling reptiles of enormous wealth, found T-K useful, and favored it with their patronage.

And as T-K's citizens, the Regals, increased their power, smaller factions faltered and fell under their sway. Mars was dotted with bankrupt factions, financially captured and transported to the Martian surface by the T-K plutocrats.

Having failed in space, the refugees took Regal charity as ecologists of the sunken gardens. Dozens of factions were quarantined in cheerless redemption camps, isolated from one another, their lives pared to a grim frugality.

And the visionary Regals made good use of their power. The factions found themselves trapped in the arcane bioaesthetics of Posthumanist philosophy, subverted constantly by Regal broadcasts, Regal teaching, Regal culture. With time even the stubbornest faction would be broken down and digested into the cultural bloodstream of T-K. Faction members would be allowed to leave their redemption camp and travel up the Ladder.

But first they would have to prove themselves. The Patternists had awaited their chance for years. It had come at last in the Ibis Crater competition, an ecological struggle of the factions that would prove the victors' right to Regal status. Six factions had sent their champions to the ancient Ibis Crater, each one armed with its group's strongest biotechnologies. It would be a war of the sunken gardens, with the Ladder as the prize.

Mirasol's crawler followed a gully through a chaotic terrain of rocky permafrost that had collapsed in karsts and sinkholes. After two hours, the gully ended abruptly. Before Mirasol rose a mountain range of massive slabs and boulders, some with the glassy sheen of impact melt, others scabbed over with lichen.

As the crawler started up the slope, the sun came out, and Mirasol saw the crater's outer rim jigsawed in the green of lichen and the glaring white of snow.

The oxygen readings were rising steadily. Warm, moist air was drooling from within the crater's lip, leaving a spittle of ice. A half-million-ton asteroid from the Rings of Saturn had fallen here at fifteen kilometers a second. But for two centuries rain, creeping glaciers, and lichen had gnawed at the crater's rim, and the wound's raw edges had slumped and scarred.

The crawler worked its way up the striated channel of an empty glacier bed. A cold alpine wind keened down the channel, where flourishing patches of lichen clung to exposed veins of ice.

Some rocks were striped with sediment from the ancient Martian seas, and the impact had peeled them up and thrown them on their backs.

It was winter, the season for pruning the sunken gardens. The treacherous rubble of the crater's rim was cemented with frozen mud. The crawler found the glacier's root and clawed its way up the ice face. The raw slope was striped with winter snow and storm-blown summer dust, stacked in hundreds of red-and-white layers. With the years the stripes had warped and rippled in the glacier's flow.

Mirasol reached the crest. The crawler ran spiderlike along the crater's snowy rim. Below, in a bowl-shaped crater eight kilometers deep, lay a seething ocean of air.

Mirasol stared. Within this gigantic airsump, twenty kilometers across, a broken ring of majestic rain clouds trailed their dark skirts, like duchesses in quadrille, about the ballroom floor of a lens-shaped sea.

Thick forests of green-and-yellow mangroves rimmed the shallow water and had overrun the shattered islands at its center. Pinpoints of brilliant scarlet ibis spattered the trees. A flock of them suddenly spread kitelike wings and took to the air, spreading across the crater in uncounted millions. Mirasol was appalled by the crudity and daring of this ecological concept, its crass and primal vitality.

This was what she had come to destroy. The thought filled her with sadness.

Then she remembered the years she had spent flattering her Regal teachers, collaborating with them in the destruction of her own culture. When the chance at the Ladder came, she had been chosen. She put her sadness away, remembering her ambitions and her rivals.

The history of mankind in space had been a long epic of ambitions and rivalries. From the very first, space colonies had struggled for self-sufficiency and had soon broken their ties with the exhausted Earth. The independent life-support systems had given them the mentality of city-states. Strange ideologies had bloomed in the hothouse atmosphere of the o'neills, and breakaway groups were common.

Space was too vast to police. Pioneer elites burst forth, defying anyone to stop their pursuit of aberrant technologies. Quite suddenly the march of science had become an insane, headlong scramble. New sciences and technologies had shattered whole societies in waves of future shock.

The shattered cultures coalesced into factions, so thoroughly alienated from one another that they were called humanity only for lack of a better term. The Shapers, for instance, had seized control of their own genetics, abandoning mankind in a burst of artificial evolution. Their rivals, the Mechanists, had replaced flesh with advanced prosthetics.

Mirasol's own group, the Patternists, was a breakaway Shaper faction.

The Patternists specialized in cerebral asymmetry. With grossly expanded right-brain hemispheres, they were highly intuitive, given to metaphors, parallels, and sudden cognitive leaps. Their inventive minds and quick, unpredictable genius had given them a competitive edge at first. But with these advantages had come grave weaknesses: autism, fugue states, and paranoia. Patternists grew out of control and became grotesque webs of fantasy.

With these handicaps their colony had faltered. Patternist industries went into decline, outpaced by industrial rivals. Competition had grown much fiercer. The Shaper and Mechanist cartels had turned commercial action into a kind of endemic warfare. The Patternist gamble had failed, and the day came when their entire habitat was bought out from around them by Regal plutocrats. In a way it was a kindness. The Regals were suave and proud of their ability to assimilate refugees and failures.

The Regals themselves had started as dissidents and defectors. Their Posthumanist philosophy had given them the moral power and the bland assurance to dominate and absorb factions from the fringes of humanity. And they had the support of the Investors, who had vast wealth and the secret techniques of star travel.

The crawler's radar alerted Mirasol to the presence of a landcraft from a rival faction. Leaning forward in her pilot's couch, she put the craft's image onscreen. It was a lumpy sphere, balanced uneasily on four long, spindly legs. Silhouetted against the horizon, it moved with a strange wobbling speed along the opposite lip of the crater, then disappeared down the outward slope.

Mirasol wondered if it had been cheating. She was tempted to try some cheating herself—to dump a few frozen packets of aerobic bacteria or a few dozen capsules of insect eggs down the slope—but she feared the orbiting monitors of the T-K supervisors. Too much was at stake—not only her own career but that of her entire faction, huddled bankrupt and despairing in their cold redemption camp. It was said that T-K's ruler, the Posthuman being they called the Lobster King, would himself watch the contest. To fail before his black abstracted gaze would be a horror.

On the crater's outside slope, below her, a second rival craft appeared, hurching and slithering with insane, aggressive grace. The craft's long supple body moved with a sidewinder's looping and coiling, holding aloft a massive shining head, like a faceted mirror ball.

Both rivals were converging on the rendezvous camp, where the six contestants would receive their final briefing from the Regal Adviser. Mirasol hurried forward.

➥

When the camp first flashed into sight on her screen, Mirasol was shocked. The place was huge and absurdly elaborate: a drug dream of paneled geodesics and colored minarets, sprawling in the lichenous desert like an abandoned chandelier. This was a camp for Regals.

Here the arbiters and sophists of the BioArts would stay and judge the crater as the newly planted ecosystems struggled among themselves for supremacy.

The camp's airlocks were surrounded with shining green thickets of lichen, where the growth feasted on escaped humidity. Mirasol drove her crawler through the yawning air-lock and into a garage. Inside the garage, robot mechanics were scrubbing and polishing the coiled hundred-meter length of the snake craft and the gleaming black abdomen of an eight-legged crawler. The black crawler was crouched with its periscoped head sunk downward, as if ready to pounce. Its swollen belly was marked with a red hourglass and the corporate logos of its faction.

The garage smelled of dust and grease overlaid with floral perfumes. Mirasol left the mechanics to their work and walked stiffly down a long corridor, stretching the kinks out of her back and shoulders. A latticework door sprang apart into filaments and resealed itself behind her.

She was in a dining room that clinked and rattled with the high-pitched repetitive sound of Regal music. Its walls were paneled with tall display screens showing startlingly beautiful garden panoramas. A pulpy-looking servo, whose organo-metallic casing and squat, smiling head had a swollen and almost diseased appearance, showed her to a chair.

Mirasol sat, denting the heavy white tablecloth with her knees. There were seven places at the table. The Regal Adviser's tall chair was at the table's head. Mirasol's assigned position gave her a sharp idea of her own status. She sat at the far end of the table, on the Adviser's left.

Two of her rivals had already taken their places. One was a tall, red-haired Shaper with long, thin arms, whose sharp face and bright, worried eyes gave him a querulous birdlike look. The other was a sullen, feral Mechanist with prosthetic hands and a paramilitary tunic marked at the shoulders with a red hourglass.

Mirasol studied her two rivals with silent, sidelong glances. Like her they were both young. The Regals favored the young, and they encouraged captive factions to expand their populations widely.

This strategy cleverly subverted the old guard of each faction in a tidal wave of their own children, indoctrinated from birth by Regals.

The birdlike man, obviously uncomfortable with his place directly at the Adviser's right, looked as if he wanted to speak but dared not. The piratical Mech sat staring at his artificial hands, his ears stoppered with headphones.

Each place setting had a squeezebulb of liqueur. Regals, who were used to weightlessness in orbit, used these bulbs by habit, and their presence here was both a privilege and a humiliation.

The door fluttered open again, and two more rivals burst in, almost as if they had raced. The first was a flabby Mech, still not used to gravity, whose sagging limbs were supported by an extraskeletal framework. The second was a severely mutated Shaper whose elbowed legs terminated in grasping hands. The pedal hands were gemmed with heavy rings that clicked against each other as she waddled across the parquet floor.

The woman with the strange legs took her place across from the birdlike man. They began to converse haltingly in a language that none of the others could follow. The man in the framework, gasping audibly, lay in obvious pain in the chair across from Mirasol. His plastic eyeballs looked as blank as chips of glass. His sufferings in the pull of gravity showed that he was new to Mars, and his place in the competition meant that his faction was powerful. Mirasol despised him.

Mirasol felt a nightmarish sense of entrapment. Everything about her competitors seemed to proclaim their sickly unfitness for survival. They had a haunted, hungry look, like starving men in a lifeboat who wait with secret eagerness for the first to die.

She caught a glimpse of herself reflected in the bowl of a spoon and saw with a flash of insight how she must appear to the others. Her intuitive right brain was swollen beyond human bounds, distorting her skull. Her face had the blank prettiness of her genetic heritage, but she could feel the bleak strain of her expression. Her body looked shapeless under her quilted pilot's vest and dun-drab, general-issue blouse and trousers. Her fingertips were raw from biting. She saw in herself the fey, defeated aura of her faction's older generation, those who had tried and failed in the great world of space, and she hated herself for it.

They were still waiting for the sixth competitor when the plonking music reached a sudden crescendo and the Regal Adviser arrived. Her name was Arkadya Sorienti, Incorporated. She was a member of T-K's ruling oligarchy, and she swayed through the bursting door with the careful steps of a woman not used to gravity.

She wore the Investor-style clothing of a high-ranking diplomat. The Regals were proud of their diplomatic ties with the alien Investors, since Investor patronage proved their own vast wealth. The Sorienti's knee-high boots had false birdlike toes, scaled like Investor hide. She wore a heavy skirt of gold cords braided with jewels, and a stiff wrist-length formal jacket with embroidered cuffs. A heavy collar formed an arching multi-colored frill behind her head. Her blonde hair was set in an interlaced style as complex as computer wiring. The skin of her bare legs had a shiny, glossy look, as if freshly enameled. Her eyelids gleamed with soft reptilian pastels.

One of her corporate ladyship's two body-servos helped her to her seat. The Sorienti leaned forward brightly, interlacing small, pretty hands so crusted with rings and bracelets that they resembled gleaming gauntlets.

"I hope the five of you have enjoyed this chance for an informal talk," she said sweetly, just as if such a thing were possible. "I'm sorry I was delayed. Our sixth participant will not be joining us."

There was no explanation. The Regals never publicized any action of theirs that might be construed as a punishment. The looks of the competitors, alternately stricken and calculating, showed that they were imagining the worst.

The two squat servos circulated around the table, dishing out courses of food from trays balanced on their flabby heads. The competitors picked uneasily at their plates.

The display screen behind the Adviser flicked into a schematic diagram of the Ibis Crater. "Please notice the revised boundary lines," the Sorienti said. "I hope that each of you will avoid trespassing—not merely physically but biologically as well." She looked at them seriously. "Some of you may plan to use herbicides. This is permissible, but the spreading of spray beyond your sector's boundaries is considered crass. Bacteriological establishment is a subtle art. The spreading of tailored disease organisms is an aesthetic distortion. Please remember that your activities here are a disruption of what should ideally be natural process. Therefore the period of biotic seeding will last only twelve hours. Thereafter, the new complexity level will be allowed to stabilize itself without any other interference at all. Avoid self-aggrandizement, and confine yourselves to a primal role, as catalysts."

The Sorienti's speech was formal and ceremonial. Mirasol studied the display screen, noting with much satisfaction that her territory had been expanded.

Seen from overhead, the crater's roundness was deeply marred.

Mirasol's sector, the southern one, showed the long flattened scar of a major landslide, where the crater wall had slumped and flowed into the pit. The simple ecosystem had recovered quickly, and mangroves festooned the rubble's lowest slopes. Its upper slopes were gnawed by lichen and glaciers.

The sixth sector had been erased, and Mirasol's share was almost twenty square kilometers of new land.

It would give her faction's ecosystem more room to take root before the deadly struggle began in earnest.

This was not the first such competition. The Regals had held them for decades as an objective test of the skills of rival factions. It helped the Regals' divide-and-conquer policy, to set the factions against one another.

And in the centuries to come, as Mars grew more hospitable to life, the gardens would surge from their craters and spread across the surface. Mars would become a warring jungle of separate creations. For the Regals the competitions were closely studied simulations of the future.

And the competitions gave the factions motives for their work. With the garden wars to spur them, the ecological sciences had advanced enormously. Already, with the progress of science and taste, many of the oldest craters had become ecoaesthetic embarrassments.

The Ibis Crater had been an early, crude experiment. The faction that had created it was long gone, and its primitive creation was now considered tasteless.

Each gardening faction camped beside its own crater, struggling to bring it to life. But the competitions were a shortcut up the Ladder. The competitors' philosophies and talents, made into flesh, would carry out a proxy struggle for supremacy. The sine-wave curves of growth, the rallies and declines of expansion and extinction, would scroll across the monitors of the Regal judges like stock-market reports. This complex struggle would be weighed in each of its aspects: technological, philosophical, biological, and aesthetic. The winners would abandon their camps to take on Regal wealth and power. They would roam T-K's jeweled corridors and revel in its perquisites: extended life spans, corporate titles, cosmopolitan tolerance, and the interstellar patronage of the Investors.

➤

When red dawn broke over the landscape, the five were poised around the Ibis Crater, awaiting the signal. The day was calm, with only a distant nexus of jet streams marring the sky. Mirasol watched pink-stained sunlight creep down the inside slope of the crater's western wall. In the mangrove thickets birds were beginning to stir.

Mirasol waited tensely. She had taken a position on the upper slopes of the landslide's raw debris. Radar showed her rivals spaced along the interior slopes: to her left, the hourglass crawler and the jewel-headed snake; to her right, a mantislike crawler and the globe on stilts.

The signal came, sudden as lightning: a meteor of ice shot from orbit and left a shock-wave cloud plume of ablated team. Mirasol charged forward.

The Patternists' strategy was to concentrate on the upper slopes and the landslide's rubble, a marginal niche where they hoped to excel. Their cold crater in Syrtis Major had given them some expertise in alpine species, and they hoped to exploit this strength. The landslide's long slope, far above sea level, was to be their power base. The crawler lurched downslope, blasting out a fine spray of lichenophagous bacteria.

Suddenly the air was full of birds. Across the crater, the globe on stilts had rushed down to the waterline and was laying waste the mangroves. Fine wisps of smoke showed the slicing beam of a heavy laser.

Burst after burst of birds took wing, peeling from their nests to wheel and dip in terror. At first, their frenzied cries came as a high-pitched whisper. Then, as the fear spread, the screeching echoed and reechoed, building to a mindless surf of pain. In the crater's dawn-warmed air, the scarlet motes hung in their millions, swirling and coalescing like drops of blood in free fall.

Mirasol scattered the seeds of alpine rock crops. The crawler picked its way down the talus, spraying fertilizer into cracks and crevices. She pried up boulders and released a scattering of invertebrates: nematodes, mites, sowbugs, altered millipedes. She splattered the rocks with gelatin to feed them until the mosses and ferns took hold.

The cries of the birds were appalling. Downslope the other factions were thrashing in the muck at sea level, wreaking havoc, destroying the mangroves so that their own creations could take hold. The great snake looped and ducked through the canopy, knotting itself, ripping up swathes of mangroves by the roots. As Mirasol watched, the top of its faceted head burst open and released a cloud of bats.

The mantis crawler was methodically marching along the borders of its sector, its saw-edged arms reducing everything before it into kindling. The hourglass crawler had slashed through its territory, leaving a muddy network of fire zones. Behind it rose a wall of smoke.

It was a daring ploy. Sterilizing the sector by fire might give the new biome a slight advantage. Even a small boost could be crucial as exponential rates of growth took hold. But the Ibis Crater was a closed system. The use of fire required great care. There was only so much air within the bowl.

Mirasol worked grimly. Insects were next. They were often neglected in favor of massive sea beasts or flashy predators, but in terms of biomass, gram by gram, insects could overwhelm. She blasted a carton downslope to the shore, where it melted, releasing aquatic termites. She shoved aside flat shelves of rock, planting egg cases below their sun-warmed surfaces. She released a cloud of leaf-eating midges, their tiny bodies packed with bacteria. Within the crawler's belly, rack after automatic rack was thawed and fired through nozzles, dropped through spiracles or planted in the holes jabbed by picklike feet.

Each faction was releasing a potential world. Near the water's edge, the mantis had released a pair of things like giant black sail planes. They were swooping through the clouds of ibis, opening great sieved mouths. On the islands in the center of the crater's lake, scaled walruses clambered on the rocks, blowing steam. The stilt ball was laying out an orchard in the mangroves' wreckage. The snake had taken to the water, its faceted head leaving a wake of V-waves.

In the hourglass sector, smoke continued to rise. The fires were spreading, and the spider ran frantically along its network of zones. Mirasol watched the movement of the smoke as she released a horde of marmots and rock squirrels.

A mistake had been made. As the smoky air gushed upward in the feeble Martian gravity, a fierce valley wind of cold air from the heights flowed downward to fill the vacuum. The mangroves burned fiercely. Shattered networks of flaming branches were flying into the air.

The spider charged into the flames, smashing and trampling. Mirasol laughed, imagining demerits piling up in the judges' data banks. Her talus slopes were safe from fire. There was nothing to burn.

The ibis flock had formed a great wheeling ring above the shore. Within their scattered ranks flitted the dark shapes of airborne predators. The long plume of steam from the meteor had begun to twist and break. A sullen wind was building up.

Fire had broken out in the snake's sector. The snake was swimming in the sea's muddy waters, surrounded by bales of bright-green kelp. Before its pilot noticed, fire was already roaring through a great piled heap of the wreckage it had left on shore. There were no windbreaks left. Air poured down the denuded slope. The smoke column guttered and twisted its black clouds alive with sparks.

A flock of ibis plunged into the cloud. Only a handful emerged; some of them were flaming visibly. Mirasol began to know fear. As smoke rose to the crater's rim, it cooled and started to fall outward and downward. A vertical whirlwind was forming, a torus of hot smoke and cold wind.

The crawler scattered seed-packed hay for pygmy mountain goats. Just before her an ibis fell from the sky with a dark squirming shape, all claws and teeth, clinging to its neck. She rushed forward and crushed the predator, then stopped and stared distractedly across the crater.

Fires were spreading with unnatural speed. Small puffs of smoke rose from a dozen places, striking large heaps of wood with uncanny precision. Her altered brain searched for a pattern. The fires springing up in the mantis sector were well beyond the reach of any falling debris.

In the spider's zone, flames had leapt the firebreaks without leaving a mark. The pattern felt wrong to her, eerily wrong, as if the destruction had a force all its own, a raging synergy that fed upon itself.

The pattern spread into a devouring crescent. Mirasol felt the dread of lost control—the sweating fear an orbiter feels at the hiss of escaping air or the way a suicide feels at the first bright gush of blood.

Within an hour the garden sprawled beneath a hurricane of hot decay. The dense columns of smoke had flattened like thunderheads at the limits of the garden's sunken troposphere. Slowly a spark-shot gray haze, dripping ash like rain, began to ring the crater. Screaming birds circled beneath the foul torus, falling by tens and scores and hundreds. Their bodies littered the garden's sea, their bright plumage blurred with ash in a steel-gray sump.

The landcraft of the others continued to fight the flames, smashing unharmed through the fire's charred borderlands. Their efforts were useless, a pathetic ritual before the disaster.

Even the fire's malicious purity had grown tired and tainted. The oxygen was failing. The flames were dimmer and spread more slowly, releasing a dark nastiness of half-combusted smoke.

Where it spread, nothing that breathed could live. Even the flames were killed as the smoke billowed along the carter's crushed and smoldering slopes.

Mirasol watched a group of striped gazelles struggle up the barren slopes of the talus in search of air. Their dark eyes, fresh from the laboratory, rolled in timeless animal fear. Their coats were scorched, their flanks heaved, their mouths dripped foam. One by one they collapsed in convulsions, kicking at the lifeless Martian rock as they slid and fell. It was a vile sight, the image of a blighted spring.

An oblique flash of red downslope to her left attracted her attention. A large red animal was skulking among the rocks. She turned the crawler and picked her way toward it, wincing as a dark surf of poisoned smoke broke across the fretted glass.

She spotted the animal as it broke from cover. It was a scorched and gasping creature like a great red ape. She dashed forward and seized it in the crawler's arms. Held aloft, it clawed and kicked, hammering the crawler's arms with a smoldering branch. In revulsion and pity, she crushed it. Its bodice of tight-sewn ibis feathers tore, revealing blood-slicked human flesh.

Using the crawler's grips, she tugged at a heavy tuft of feathers on its head. The tight-fitting mask ripped free, and the dead man's head slumped forward. She rolled it back, revealing a face tattooed with stars.

⬡

The ornithopter sculled above the burned-out garden, its long red wings beating with dreamlike fluidity. Mirasol watched the Sorienti's painted face as her corporate ladyship stared into the shining viewscreen.

The ornithopter's powerful cameras cast image after image onto the tabletop screen, lighting the Regal's face. The tabletop was littered with the Sorienti's elegant knickknacks: an inhaler case, a half-empty jeweled squeeze-bulb, lorgnette binoculars, a stack of tape cassettes.

"An unprecedented case," her ladyship murmured. "It was not a total dieback after all but merely the extinction of everything with lungs. There must be strong survivorship among the lower orders: fish, insects, annelids. Now that the rain's settled the ash, you can see the vegetation making a strong comeback. Your own section seems almost undamaged."

"Yes," Mirasol said. "The natives were unable to reach it with torches before the fire storm had smothered itself."

The Sorienti leaned back into the tasseled arms of her couch. "I wish you wouldn't mention them so loudly, even between ourselves."

"No one would believe me."

"The others never saw them," the Regal said. "They were too busy fighting the flames." She hesitated briefly. "You were wise to confide in me first."

Mirasol locked eyes with her new patroness, then looked away. "There was no one else to tell. They'd have said I built a pattern out of nothing but my own fears."

"You have your faction to think of," the Sorienti said with an air of sympathy. "With such a bright future ahead of them, they don't need a renewed reputation for paranoid fantasies."

She studied the screen. "The Patternists are winners by default. It certainly makes an interesting case study. If the new garden grows tiresome we can have the whole crater sterilized from orbit. Some other faction can start again with a clean slate."

"Don't let them build too close to the edge," Mirasol said.

Her corporate ladyship watched her attentively, tilting her head.

"I have no proof," Mirasol said, "but I can see the pattern behind it all. The natives had to come from somewhere. The colony that stocked the crater must have been destroyed in that huge landslide. Was that your work? Did your people kill them?"

The Sorienti smiled. "You're very bright, my dear. You will do well, up the Ladder. And you can keep secrets. Your office as my secretary suits you very well."

"They were destroyed from orbit," Mirasol said. "Why else would they hide from us? You tried to annihilate them."

"It was a long time ago," the Regal said. "In the early days, when things were shakier. They were researching the secret of starflight, techniques only the Investors know. Rumor says they reached success at last, in their redemption camp. After that, there was no choice."

"Then they were killed for the Investors' profit," Mirasol said. She stood up quickly and walked around the cabin, her new jeweled skirt clattering around the knees. "So that the aliens could go on toying with us, hiding their secret, selling us trinkets."

The Regal folded her hands with a clicking of rings and bracelets. "Our Lobster King is wise," she said. "If humanity's efforts turned to the stars, what would become of terraforming? Why should we trade the power of creation itself to become like the Investors?"

"But think of the people," Mirasol said. "Think of them losing their technologies, degenerating into human beings. A handful of savages, eating bird meat. Think of the fear they felt for generations, the way they burned their own home and killed themselves when they saw us come to smash and destroy their world. Aren't you filled with horror?"

"For humans?" the Sorienti said. "No!"

"But can't you see? You've given this planet life as an art form, as an enormous game. You force us to play in it, and those people were killed for it! Can't you see how that blights everything?"

"Our game is reality," the Regal said. She gestured at the viewscreen. "You can't deny the savage beauty of destruction."

"You defend this catastrophe?"

The Regal shrugged. "If life worked perfectly, how could things evolve? Aren't we Posthuman? Things grow; things die. In time the cosmos kills us all. The cosmos has no meaning, and its emptiness is absolute. That's pure terror, but it's also pure freedom. Only our ambitions and our creations can fill it."

"And that justifies your actions?"

"We act for life," the Regal said. "Our ambitions have become this world's natural laws. We blunder because life blunders. We go on because life must go on. When you've taken the long view, from orbit—when the power we wield is in your own hands—then you can judge us." She smiled. "You will be judging yourself. You'll be Regal."

"But what about your captive factions? Your agents, who do your will? Once we had our own ambitions. We failed, and now you isolate us, indoctrinate us, make us into rumors. We must have something of our own. Now we have nothing."

"That's not so. You have what we've given you. You have the Ladder."

The vision stung Mirasol: power, light, the hint of justice, this world with its sins and sadness shrunk to a bright arena far below. "Yes," she said at last. "Yes, we do."

Out of Copyright

CHARLES SHEFFIELD

One of the best contemporary "hard science" writers, British-born Charles Sheffield is a theoretical physicist who has worked on the American space program, and is currently chief scientist of the Earth Satellite Corporation. Sheffield is also the only person who has ever served as president of both the American Astronautical Society and the Science Fiction Writers of America. He won the Hugo Award in 1994 for his story, "Georgia on My Mind." His books include the best-selling nonfiction title Earthwatch, *the novels* Sight of Proteus, The Web Between the Worlds, Hidden Variables, My Brother's Keeper, Between the Strokes of Night, The Nimrod Hunt, Trader's World, Proteus Unbound, Summertide, Divergence, Transcendence, Cold as Ice, Brother to Dragons, The Mind Pool, Godspeed *and* The Ganymede Club, *and the collections* Erasmus Magister, The McAndrew Chronicles, Dancing with Myself, *and* Georgia on My Mind and Other Places. *His most recent books are the novel* Starfire, *and a new collection*, The Complete McAndrew. *He lives in Silver Spring, Maryland, with his wife, SF writer Nancy Kress.*

Here he slyly suggests that even in a project as large as the terraforming of an entire world, finding the right tool for the right job is more than half the battle—particularly if you're smart enough to know which jobs are really the important ones . . . and just what kind of tools you need to do them right.

Troubleshooting. A splendid idea, and one that I agree with totally in principle. Bang! One bullet, and trouble bites the dust. But unfortunately, trouble doesn't know the rules. Trouble won't stay dead.

I looked around the table. My top troubleshooting team was here. I was here. Unfortunately, they were supposed to be headed for Jupiter, and I ought to be down on Earth. In less than twenty-four hours, the draft pick would begin. That wouldn't wait, and if I didn't leave in the next thirty minutes, I would never make it in time. I needed to be in two places at once. I cursed the copyright laws and the single-copy restriction, and went to work.

"You've read the new requirement," I said. "You know the parameters. Ideas, anyone?"

A dead silence. They were facing the problem in their own unique ways. Wolfgang Pauli looked half-asleep, Thomas Edison was drawing little doll-figures on the table's surface, Enrico Fermi seemed to be counting on his fingers, and John von Neumann was staring impatiently at the other three. I was doing none of those things. I knew very well that wherever the solution would come from, it would not be from inside my head. My job was much more straightforward: I had to see that when we had a possible answer, it *happened*. And I had to see that we got *one* answer, not four.

The silence in the room went on and on. My brain trust was saying nothing, while I watched the digits on my watch flicker by. I had to stay and find a solution; and I had to get to the draft picks. But most of all and hardest of all, I had to remain quiet, to let my team do some thinking.

It was small consolation to know that similar meetings were being held within the offices of the other three combines. Everyone must be finding it equally hard going. I knew the players, and I could imagine the scenes, even though all the troubleshooting teams were different. NETSCO had a group that was intellectually the equal of ours at Romberg AG: Niels Bohr, Theodore von Karman, Norbert Weiner, and Marie Curie. MMG, the great Euro-Mexican combine of Magrit-Marcus Gesellschaft, had focused on engineering power rather than pure scientific understanding and creativity, and, in addition to the Soviet rocket designer Sergey Korolev and the American Nikola Tesla, they had reached farther back (and with more risk) to the great nineteenth-century English engineer Isambard Kingdom Brunel. He had been one of the outstanding successes of the program; I wished he were working with me, but MMG had always refused to look at a trade. MMG's one bow to theory was a strange one, the Indian mathematician Srinivasa Ramanujan, but the unlikely quartet made one hell of a team.

And finally there was BP Megation, whom I thought of as confused. At any rate, I didn't understand their selection logic. They had used billions of dollars to acquire a strangely mixed team: Erwin Schrödinger, David Hilbert, Leo Szilard, and Henry Ford. They were all great talents, and all famous names in their fields, but I wondered how well they could work as a unit.

All the troubleshooting teams were now pondering the same emergency. Our problem was created when the Pan-National Union suddenly announced a change to the Phase B demonstration program. They wanted to modify impact conditions, as their contracts with us permitted them to do. They didn't have to tell us how to do it, either, which was just as well for them, since I was sure they didn't know. How do you take a billion tons of mass, already launched to reach a specific target at a certain point of time, and redirect it to a different end point with a different arrival time?

There was no point in asking them *why* they wanted to change rendezvous conditions. It was their option. Some of our management saw the action on PNU's part as simple bloody-mindedness, but I couldn't agree. The four multinational combines had each been given contracts to perform the biggest space engineering exercise in human history: small asteroids (only a kilometer or so across—but massing a billion tons each) had to be picked up from their natural orbits and redirected to the Jovian system, where they were to make precise rendezvous with assigned locations of the moon Io. Each combine had to select the asteroid and the method of moving it, but deliver within a tight transfer-energy budget and a tight time schedule.

For that task the PNU would pay each group a total of $8 billion. That sounds like a fair amount of money, but I knew our accounting figures. To date, with the project still not finished (rendezvous would be in eight more days), Romberg AG had spent $14.5 billion. We are looking at a probable cost overrun by a factor of two. I was willing to bet that the other three groups were eating very similar losses.

Why?

Because this was only Phase B of a four-phase project. Phase A had been a system design study, which led to four Phase B awards for a demonstration project. The Phase B effort that the four combines were working on now was a proof-of-capability run for the full European Metamorphosis. The real money came in the future, in Phases C and D. Those would be awarded by the PNU to a single combine and the award would be based largely on Phase B performance. The next phases called for the delivery of fifty asteroids to impact points on Europa (Phase C), followed by thermal mixing operations on the moon's surface (Phase D). The contract value of C and D would be somewhere up around $800 billion. That was the fish that all the combines were after, and it was the reason we all overspend lavishly on this phase.

By the end of the whole program, Europa would have a forty-kilometer-deep water ocean over all its surface. And then the real fun would begin. Some contractor would begin the installation of the fusion plants, and the seeding of the sea-farms with the first prokaryotic bacterial forms.

The stakes were high; and to keep everybody on their toes, PNU did the right thing. They kept throwing in these little zingers, to mimic the thousand and one things that would go wrong in the final project phases.

While I was sitting and fidgeting, my team had gradually come to life. Fermi was pacing up and down the room—always a good sign; and Wolfgang Pauli was jabbing impatiently at the keys of a computer console. John von Neumann hadn't moved, but since he did everything in his head anyway, that didn't mean much.

I looked again at my watch. I had to go. "Ideas?" I said again.

Von Neumann made a swift chopping gesture of his hand. "We have to make a choice, Al. It can be done in four or five ways."

The others were nodding. "The problem is only one of efficiency and speed," added Fermi. "I can give you an order-of-magnitude estimate of the effects on the overall program within half an hour."

"Within fifteen minutes." Pauli raised the bidding.

"No need to compete this one." They were going to settle down to a real four-way fight on methods—they always did—but I didn't have the time to sit here and referee. The important point was that they said it could be done. "You don't have to rush it. Whatever you decide, it will have to wait until I get back." I stood up. "Tom?"

Edison shrugged. "How long will you be gone, Al?"

"Two days, maximum. I'll head back right after the draft picks." (That wasn't quite true; when the draft picks were over, I had some other business to attend to that did not include the troubleshooters, but two days should cover everything.)

"Have fun." Edison waved his hand casually. "By the time you get back, I'll have the engineering drawings for you."

One thing about working with a team like mine—they may not always be right, but they sure are always cocky.

✦

"Make room there. Move over!" The guards were pushing ahead to create a narrow corridor through the wedged mass of people. The one in front of me was butting with his helmeted head, not even looking to see whom he was shoving aside. "Move!" he shouted. "Come on now, out of the way."

We were in a hurry. Things had been frantically busy Topside before I left, so I had cut it fine on connections to begin with, then been held up half an hour at reentry. We had broken the speed limits on the atmospheric segment, and there would be PNU fines for that, but still we hadn't managed to make up all the time. Now the first draft pick was only seconds away, and I was supposed to be taking part in it.

A thin woman in a green coat clutched at my arm as we bogged down for a moment in the crush of people. Her face was gray and grim, and she had a placard hanging round her neck. "You could wait longer for the copyright!" She had to shout to make herself heard. "It would cost you nothing— and look at the misery you would prevent. What you're doing is immoral! TEN MORE YEARS."

Her last words were a scream as she called out this year's slogan TEN MORE YEARS! I shook my arm free as the guard in front of me made sudden headway, and dashed along in his wake. I had nothing to say to the woman; nothing that she would listen to. If it were immoral, what did ten more years have to do with it? Ten more years, if by some miracle they were granted ten more years on the copyrights, what then? I knew the answer. They would try to talk the Pan-National Union into fifteen more years, or perhaps twenty. When you pay somebody off, it only increases their demands. I know, only too well. They are never satisfied with what they get.

Joe Delacorte and I scurried into the main chamber and shuffled sideways to our seats at the last possible moment. All the preliminary nonsense was finished, and the real business was beginning. The tension in the room was terrific. To be honest, a lot of it was being generated by the media. They were all poised to make maximum noise as they shot the selection information all over the System. If it were not for the media, I don't think the PNU would hold live draft picks at all. We'd all hook in with video links and do our business the civilized way.

The excitement now was bogus for other reasons, too. The professionals— I and a few others—would not become interested until the ten rounds were complete. Before that, the choices were just too limited. Only when they were all made, and the video teams were gone, would the four groups get together off-camera and begin the horse trading. "My ninth round plus my fifth for your second." "Maybe, if you'll throw in $10 million and a tenth-round draft pick for next year. . . ."

Meanwhile, BP Megation had taken the microphone. "First selection," said their representative. "Robert Oppenheimer."

I looked at Joe, and he shrugged. No surprise. Oppenheimer was the perfect choice—a brilliant scientist, but also practical, and willing to work with other people. He had died in 1967, so his original copyright had expired within the past twelve months. I knew his family had appealed for a copyright extension and been refused. Now BP Megation had sole single-copy rights for another lifetime.

"Trade?" whispered Joe.

I shook my head. We would have to beggar ourselves for next year's draft picks to make BP give up Oppenheimer. Other combine reps had apparently made the same decision. There was the clicking of data entry as the people around me updated portable databases. I did the same thing with a stub of pencil and a folded sheet of yellow paper, putting a check mark alongside his name. Oppenheimer was taken care of, I could forget that one. If by some miracle one of the four teams had overlooked some other top choice, I had to be ready to make an instant revision to my own selections.

"First selection, by NETSCO," said another voice. "Peter Joseph William Debye."

It was another natural choice. Debye had been a Nobel prizewinner in physics, a theoretician with an excellent grasp of applied technology. He had died in 1966. Nobel laureates in science, particularly ones with that practical streak, went fast. As soon as their copyrights expired, they would be picked up in the draft the same year.

That doesn't mean it always works out well. The most famous case, of course, was Albert Einstein. When his copyright had expired in 2030, BP Megation had had first choice in the draft pick. They had their doubts, and they must have sweated blood over their decision. The rumor mill said they spent over $70 million in simulations alone, before they decided to take him as their top choice. The same rumor mill said that the cloned form was now showing amazing ability in chess and music, but no interest at all in physics or mathematics. If that was true, BP Megation had dropped $2 billion down a black hole: $1 billion straight to the PNU for acquisition of copyright, and another $1 billion for the clone process. Theorists were always tricky; you could never tell how they would turn out.

Magrit-Marcus Gesellschaft had now made their first draft pick, and chosen another Nobel laureate, John Cockroft. He also had died in 1967. So far, every selection was completely predictable. The three combines were picking the famous scientists and engineers who had died in 1966 and 1967, and who were now, with the expiration of family retention of copyrights, available for cloning for the first time.

The combines were being logical, but it made for a very dull draft pick. Maybe it was time to change that. I stood up to announce our first take.

"First selection, by Romberg AG," I said. "Charles Proteus Steinmetz."

My announcement caused a stir in the media. They had presumably never heard of Steinmetz, which was a disgraceful statement of their own ignorance. Even if they hadn't spent most of the past year combing old files and records, as we had, they should have heard of him. He was one of the past century's most colorful and creative scientists, a man who had been physically handicapped (he was a hunchback) but mentally able to do the equivalent of a hundred one-hand push-ups without even breathing hard. Even I had heard of him, and you'd not find many of my colleagues who'd suggest I was interested in science.

The buzzing in the media told me they were consulting their own historical data files, digging farther back in time. Even when they had done all that, they would still not understand the first thing about the true process of clone selection. It's not just a question of knowing who died over seventy-five years ago, and will therefore be out of copyright. That's a trivial exercise, one that any yearbook will solve for you. You also have to evaluate other factors. Do you know where the body is—are you absolutely *sure*? Remember, you can't clone anyone with a cell or two from the original body. You also have to be certain that it's who you think it is. All bodies seventy-five years old tend to look the same. And then, if the body happens to be really old— say, more than a couple of centuries—there are other peculiar problems that are still not understood at all. When NETSCO pulled its coup a few years ago by cloning Gottfried Wilhelm Leibniz, the other three combines were envious at first. Leibniz was a real universal genius, a seventeenth-century superbrain who was good at everything. NETSCO had developed a better cell-growth technique, and they had also succeeded in locating the body of Leibniz in its undistinguished Hanover grave.

They walked tall for almost a year at NETSCO, until the clone came out of the forcing chambers for indoctrination. He looked nothing like the old portraits of Leibniz, and he could not grasp even the simplest abstract concepts. Oops! said the media. Wrong body.

But it wasn't as simple as that. The next year, MMG duplicated the NETSCO cell-growth technology and tried for Isaac Newton. In this case there was no doubt that they had the correct body, because it had lain undisturbed since 1727 beneath a prominent plaque in London's Westminster Abbey. The results were just as disappointing as they had been for Leibniz.

Now NETSCO and MMG have become very conservative, in my opinion, far too conservative. But since then, nobody has tried for a clone of anyone who died before 1850. The draft picking went on its thoughtful and generally cautious way, and was over in a couple of hours except for the delayed deals.

The same group of protesters were picketing the building when I left. I tried to walk quietly through them, but they must have seen my picture on one of the exterior screens showing the draft-pick process. I was buttonholed by a man in a red jumpsuit and the same thin woman in green, still carrying her placard.

"Could we speak with you for just one moment?" The man in red was very well spoken and polite.

I hesitated, aware that news cameras were on us. "Very briefly. I'm trying to run a proof-of-concept project, you know."

"I know. Is it going well?" He was a different type from most of the demonstrators, cool and apparently intelligent. And therefore potentially more dangerous.

"I wish I could say yes," I said. "Actually, it's going rather badly. That's why I'm keen to get back out."

"I understand. All I wanted to ask you was why you—and I don't mean *you*, personally; I mean the combines—why do you find it *necessary* to use clones? You could do your work without them, couldn't you?"

I hesitated. "Let me put it this way. We could do the work without them, in just the same way as we could stumble along somehow if we were denied the use of computer power, or nuclear power. The projects would be possible, but they would be enormously more difficult. The clones augment our available brainpower, at the highest levels. So let me ask you: Why *should* we do without the clones, when they are available and useful?"

"Because of the families. You have no right to subject the families to the misery and upset of seeing their loved ones cloned, without their having any rights in the matter. It's cruel, and unnecessary. Can't you see that?"

"No, I can't. Now, you listen to me for a minute." The cameras were still on me. It was a chance to say something that could never be said often enough. "The family holds copyright for seventy-five years after a person's death. So if you, personally, *remember* your grandparent, you have to be pushing eighty years old—and it's obvious from looking at you that you're under forty. So ask yourself, Why are all you petitioners people who are in their thirties? It's not *you* who's feeling any misery."

"But there are relatives—" he said.

"Oh yes, the relatives. Are you a relative of somebody who has been cloned?"

"Not yet. But if this sort of thing goes on—"

"Listen to me for one more minute. A long time ago, there were a lot of people around who thought that it was wrong to let books with sex in them be sold to the general public. They petitioned to have the books banned. It wasn't that they claimed to be buying the books themselves, and finding them disgusting; because if they said that was the case, then people would have asked them *why* they were buying what they didn't like. Nobody was forcing anybody to buy those books. No, what the petitioners wanted was for *other* people to be stopped from buying what the *petitioners* didn't like. And you copyright-extension people are just the same. You are making a case on behalf of the relatives of the ones who are being cloned. But you never seem to ask yourself this: If cloning is so bad, why aren't the *descendants* of the clones the ones doing the complaining? They're not, you know. You never see them around here."

He shook his head. "Cloning is immoral!"

I sighed. Why bother? Not one word of what I'd said had got through to him. It didn't much matter—I'd really been speaking for the media anyway—but it was a shame to see bigotry masquerading as public-spirited behavior. I'd seen enough of that already in my life.

I started to move off toward my waiting aircar. The lady in green clutched my arm again. "I'm going to leave instructions in my will that I want to be cremated. You'll never get me!"

You have my word on that, lady. But I didn't say it. I headed for the car, feeling an increasing urge to get back to the clean and rational regions of space. There was one good argument against cloning, and only one. It increased the total number of people, and to me that number already felt far too large.

➤

I had been gone only thirty hours, total; but when I arrived back at Headquarters, I learned that in my absence five new problems had occurred. I scanned the written summary that Pauli had left behind.

First, one of the thirty-two booster engines set deep in the surface of the asteroid did not respond to telemetry requests for a status report. We had to assume it was defective, and eliminate it from the final firing pattern. Second, a big solar flare was on the way. There was nothing we could do about that, but it did mean we would have to recompute the strength of the magnetic and electric fields close to Io. They would change with the strength of the Jovian magnetosphere, and that was important because the troubleshooting team in my absence had agreed on their preferred solution to the problem of adjusting impact point and arrival time. It called for strong coupling between the asteroid and the 5-million-amp flux tube of current between Io and its parent planet, Jupiter, to modify the final collision trajectory.

Third, we had lost the image data stream from one of our observing satellites, in synchronous orbit with Io. Fourth, our billion-ton asteroid had been struck by a larger-than-usual micrometeorite. This one must have massed a couple of kilograms, and it had been moving fast. It had struck off-axis from the center of mass, and the whole asteroid was now showing a tendency to rotate slowly away from our preferred orientation. Fifth, and finally, a new volcano had become very active down on the surface of Io. It was spouting sulfur up for a couple of hundred kilometers, and obscuring the view of the final-impact landmark.

After I had read Pauli's terse analysis of all the problems—nobody I ever met or heard of could summarize as clearly and briefly as he did—I switched on my communications set and asked him the only question that mattered: "Can you handle them all?"

There was a delay of almost two minutes. The trouble-shooters were heading out to join the rest of our project team for their on-the-spot analyses in the Jovian system; already the light-travel time was significant. If I didn't follow in the next day or two, radio-signal delay would make conversation impossible. At the moment, Jupiter was forty-five light-minutes from Earth.

"We can, Al," said Pauli's image at last. "Unless others come up in the next few hours, we can. From here until impact, we'll be working in an environment with increasing uncertainties."

"The PNU people planned it that way. Go ahead—but send me full transcripts." I left the system switched on, and went off to the next room to study the notes I had taken of the five problem areas. As I had done with every glitch that had come up since the Phase B demonstration project began, I placed the problem into one of two basic categories: act of nature, or failure of man-made element. For the most recent five difficulties, the volcano on Io and the solar flare belonged to the left-hand column: Category One, clearly natural and unpredictable events. The absence of booster-engine telemetry and the loss of satellite-image data were Category Two, failures of our system. They went in the right-hand column. I hesitated for a long time over the fifth event, the impact of the meteorite; finally, and with some misgivings, I assigned it also as a Category One event.

As soon as possible, I would like to follow the engineering teams out toward Jupiter for the final hours of the demonstration. However, I had two more duties to perform before I could leave. Using a coded link to Romberg AG HQ in synchronous Earth orbit, I queried the status of all the clone tanks. No anomalies were reported. By the time we returned from the final stages of Phase B, another three finished clones would be ready to move to the indoctrination facility. I needed to be there when it happened.

Next, I had to review and approve acquisition of single-use copyright for all the draft picks we had negotiated down on Earth. To give an idea of the importance of these choices, we were looking at an expenditure of $20 billion for those selections over the next twelve months. It raised the unavoidable question, Had we made the best choices?

At this stage of the game, *every* combine began to have second thoughts about the wisdom of their picks. All the old failures came crowding into your mind. I already mentioned NETSCO and their problem with Einstein, but we had had our full share at Romberg AG: Gregor Mendel, the originator of the genetic ideas that stood behind all the cloning efforts, had proved useless; so had Ernest Lawrence, inventor of the cyclotron, our second pick for 1958. We had (by blind luck!) traded him along with $40 million for Wolfgang Pauli. Even so, we had made a bad error of judgment, and the fact that others made the same mistake was no consolation. As for Marconi, even though he looked like the old pictures of him, and was obviously highly intelligent, the clone who emerged turned out to be so indolent and casual about everything that he ruined any project he worked on. I had placed him in a cushy and undemanding position and allowed him to fiddle about with his own interests, which were mainly sports and good-looking women. (As Pauli acidly remarked, "And you say that *we're* the smart ones, doing all the work?")

It's not the evaluation of a person's past record that's difficult, because we are talking about famous people who have done a great deal; written masses of books, articles, and papers; and been thoroughly evaluated by their own contemporaries. Even with all that, a big question still remains: Will the things that made the original man or woman great still be there in the cloned form? In other words, *Just what is it that is inherited?*

That's a very hard question to answer. The theory of evolution was proposed 170 years ago, but we're still fighting the old Nature-versus-Nurture battle. Is a human genius decided mainly by heredity, or by the way the person was raised? One old argument against cloning for genius was based on the importance of Nurture. It goes as follows: An individual is the product of both heredity (which is all you get in the clone) and environment. Since it is impossible to reproduce someone's environment, complete with parents, grandparents, friends, and teachers, you can't raise a clone that will be exactly like the original individual.

I'll buy that logic. We can't make ourselves an intellectually exact copy of anyone.

However, the argument was also used to prove that cloning for superior intellectual performance would be impossible. But of course, it actually proves nothing of the sort. If you take two peas from the same pod, and put one of them in deep soil next to a high wall, and the other in shallow soil out in the open, they *must* do different things if both are to thrive. The one next to the wall has to make sure it gets enough sunshine, which it can do by maximizing leaf area; the one in shallow soil has to get enough moisture, which it does through putting out more roots. The *superior* strain of peas is the one whose genetic composition allows it to adapt to whatever environment it is presented with.

People are not peas, but in one respect they are not very different from them: some have superior genetic composition to others. That's all you can ask for. If you clone someone from a century ago, the last thing you want is someone who is *identical* to the original. They would be stuck in a twentieth-century mind-set. What is needed is someone who can adapt to and thrive in *today's* environment—whether that is now the human equivalent of shade, or of shallow soil. The success of the original clone-template tells us a very important thing, that we are dealing with a superior physical brain. What that brain thinks in the year 2040 *should* be different from what it would have thought in the year 1940—otherwise the clone would be quite useless. And the criteria for "useless" change with time, too.

All these facts and a hundred others were running around inside my head as I reviewed the list for this year. Finally I made a note to suggest that J. B. S. Haldane, whom we had looked at and rejected three years ago on the grounds of unmanageability, ought to be looked at again and acquired if possible. History shows that he had wild views on politics and society, but there was no question at all about the quality of his mind. I thought I had learned a lot about interfacing with difficult scientific personalities in the past few years.

When I was satisfied with my final list, I transmitted everything to Joe Delacorte, who was still down on Earth, and headed for the transition room. A personal shipment pod ought to be waiting for me there. I hoped I would get a good one. At the very least, I'd be in it for the next eight days. Last time I went out to the Jovian system, the pod's internal lighting and external antenna failed after three days. Have you ever sat in the dark for seventy-two hours, a hundred million miles from the nearest human, unable to send or receive messages? I didn't know if anyone realized I was in trouble. All I could do was sit tight—and I mean tight; pods are *small*—and stare out at the stars.

This time the pod was in good working order. I was able to participate in every problem that hit the project over the next four days. There were plenty of them, all small, and all significant. One of the fuel-supply ships lost a main ion drive. The supply ship was not much more than a vast bag of volatiles and a small engine, and it had almost no brain at all in its computer, not even enough to figure out an optimal use of its drives. We had to chase after and corral it as though we were pursuing a great lumbering elephant. Then three members of the impact-monitoring team came down with food poisoning—salmonella, which was almost certainly their own fault. You can say anything you like about throwing away spoiled food, but you can't get a sloppy crew to take much notice.

Then, for variety, we lost a sensor through sheer bad program design. In turning one of our imaging systems from star sensing to Io-Jupiter sensing, we tracked it right across the solar disk and burned out all the photocells. According to the engineers, that's the sort of blunder you don't make after kindergarten—but somebody did it.

Engineering errors are easy to correct. It was much trickier when one of the final-approach-coordination groups, a team of two men and one woman, chose the day before the Io rendezvous to have a violent sexual argument. They were millions of kilometers away from anyone, so there was not much we could do except talk to them. We did that, hoped they wouldn't kill each other, and made plans to do without their inputs if we had to.

Finally, one day before impact, an unplanned and anomalous firing of a rocket on the asteroid's forward surface caused a significant change of velocity of the whole body.

I ought to explain that I did little or nothing to solve any of these problems. I was too slow, too ignorant, and not creative enough. While I was still struggling to comprehend what the problem parameters were, my troubleshooters were swarming all over it. They threw proposals and counter-proposals at each other so fast that I could hardly note them, still less contribute to them. For example, in the case of the anomalous rocket firing that I mentioned, compensation for the unwanted thrust called for an elaborate balancing act of lateral and radial engines, rolling and nudging the asteroid back into its correct approach path. The team had mapped out the methods in minutes, written the necessary optimization programs in less than half an hour, and implemented their solution before I understood the geometry of what was going on.

So what did I do while all this was happening? I continued to make my two columns: act of nature, or failure of man-made element. The list was growing steadily, and I was spending a lot of time looking at it.

We were coming down to the final few hours now, and all the combines were working flat out to solve their own problems. In an engineering project of this size, many thousands of things could go wrong. We were working in extreme physical conditions, hundreds of millions of kilometers away from Earth and our standard test environments. In the intense charged-particle field near Io, cables broke at loads well below their rated capacities, hard-vacuum welds showed air-bleed effects, and lateral jets were fired and failed to produce the predicted attitude adjustments. And on top of all this, the pressure, isolation, and bizarre surroundings were too much for some of the workers. We had human failure to add to engineering failure. The test was tougher than anyone had realized—even PNU, who was supposed to make the demonstration project just this side of impossible.

I was watching the performance of the other three combines only a little less intently than I was watching our own. At five hours from contact time, NETSCO apparently suffered a communications loss with their asteroid-control system. Instead of heading for Io impact, the asteroid veered away, spiraling in toward the bulk of Jupiter itself.

BP Megation lost it at impact minus three hours, when a vast explosion on one of their asteroid forward boosters threw the kilometer-long body into a rapid tumble. Within an hour, by some miracle of improvisation, their engineering team had found a method of stabilizing the wobbling mass. But by then it was too late to return to nominal impact time and place. Their asteroid skimmed into the surface of Io an hour early, sending up a long, tear-shaped mass of ejecta from the moon's turbulent surface.

That left just two of us, MMG and Romberg AG. We both had our hands full. The Jovian system is filled with electrical, magnetic, and gravitational energies bigger than anything in the Star System except the Sun itself. The two remaining combines were trying to steer their asteroid into a pinpoint landing through a great storm of interference that made every control command and every piece of incoming telemetry suspect. In the final hour I didn't even follow the exchanges between my troubleshooters. Oh, I could *hear* them easily enough. What I couldn't do was comprehend them, enough to know what was happening.

Pauli would toss a scrap of comment at von Neumann, and, while I was trying to understand that, von Neumann would have done an assessment, keyed in for a databank status report, gabbled a couple of questions to Fermi and an instruction to Edison, and at the same time be absorbing scribbled notes and diagrams from those two. I don't know if what they were doing was *potentially* intelligible to me or not; all I know is they were going about fifty times too fast for me to follow. And it didn't much matter what I understood—they were getting the job done. I was still trying to divide all problems into my Category One/Category Two columns, but it got harder and harder.

In the final hour I didn't look or listen to what my own team was doing. We had one band of telemetry trained on the MMG project, and more and more that's where my attention was focused. I assumed they were having the same kind of communications trouble as we were—that crackling discharge field around Io made everything difficult. But their team was handling it. They were swinging smoothly into impact.

And then, with only ten minutes to go, the final small adjustment was made. It should have been a tiny nudge from the radial jets; enough to fine-tune the impact position for a few hundred meters, and no more. Instead, there was a joyous roar of a radial jet at full, uncontrolled thrust. The MMG asteroid did nothing unusual for a few seconds (a billion tons is a lot of inertia), then began to drift lazily sideways, away from its nominal trajectory.

The jet was still firing. And that should have been impossible, because the first thing that the MMG team would do was send a POWER OFF signal to the engine.

The time for impact came when the MMG asteroid was still a clear fifty kilometers out of position, and accelerating away. I saw the final collision, and the payload scraped along the surface of Io in a long, jagged scar that looked nothing at all like the neat, punched hole that we were supposed to achieve.

And we did achieve it, a few seconds later. Our asteroid came in exactly where and when it was supposed to, driving in exactly vertical to the surface. The plume of ejecta had hardly begun to rise from Io's red-and-yellow surface before von Neumann was pulling a bottle of bourbon from underneath the communications console.

I didn't object—I only wished I were there physically to share it, instead of being stuck in my own pod, short of rendezvous with our main ship. I looked at my final list, still somewhat incomplete. Was there a pattern to it? Ten minutes of analysis didn't show one. No one had tried anything—this time. Someday, and it might be tomorrow, somebody on another combine would have a bright idea; and then it would be a whole new ball game.

While I was still pondering my list, my control console began to buzz insistently. I switched it on expecting contact with my own troubleshooting team. Instead, I saw the despondent face of Brunel, MMG's own team leader—the man above all others that I would have liked to work on my side.

He nodded at me when my picture appeared on the screen. He was smoking one of his powerful black cigars, stuck in the side of his mouth. The expression on his face was as impenetrable as ever. He never let his feelings show there. "I assume you saw it, didn't you?" he said around the cigar. "We're out of it. I just called to congratulate you—again."

"Yeah, I saw it. Tough luck. At least you came second."

"Which, as you know very well, is no better than coming last." He sighed and shook his head. "We still have no idea what happened. Looks like either a programming error, or a valve sticking open. We probably won't know for weeks. And I'm not sure I care."

I maintained a sympathetic silence.

"I sometimes think we should just give up, Al," he said. "I can beat those other turkeys, but I can't compete with you. That's six in a row that you've won. It's wearing me out. You've no idea how much frustration there is in that."

I had never known Brunel to reveal so much of his feelings before.

"I think I do understand your problems," I said.

And I did. I knew exactly how he felt—more than he would believe. To suffer through a whole, endless sequence of minor, niggling mishaps was heartbreaking. No single trouble was ever big enough for a troubleshooting team to stop, isolate it, and be able to say, There's dirty work going on here. But their cumulative effect was another matter. One day it was a morass of shipments missing their correct flights, another time a couple of minus signs dropped into computer programs, or a key worker struck down from a few days by a random virus, permits misfiled, manifests mislaid, or licenses wrongly dated.

I knew all those mishaps personally. I should, because I invented most of them. I think of it as the death of a thousand cuts. No one can endure all that and still hope to win a Phase B study.

"How would you like to work on the Europan Metamorph?" I asked. "I think you'd love it."

He looked very thoughtful, and for the first time, I believe I could actually read his expression. "Leave MMG, you mean?" he said. "Maybe. I don't know what I want anymore. Let me think about it. I'd like to work with you, Al— you're a genius."

Brunel was wrong about that, of course. I'm certainly no genius. All I can do is what I've always done—handle people, take care of unpleasant details (quietly!), and make sure things get done that need doing. And of course, do what I do best: make sure that some things that need doing *don't* get done.

There *are* geniuses in the world, real geniuses. Not me, though. The man who decided to clone me, secretly—*there* I'd suggest you have a genius.

"Say, don't you remember, they called me Al. . . ."

Of course, I don't remember. That song was written in the 1930s, and I didn't die until 1947, but no clone remembers anything of the forefather life. The fact that we tend to be knowledgeable about our originals' period is an expression of interest in those individuals, not memories from them. I know the Chicago of the Depression years intimately, as well as I know today; but it is all learned knowledge. I have no actual recollection of events. I don't *remember*.

So even if you don't remember, call me Al anyway. Everyone did.

A Place with Shade

ROBERT REED

Robert Reed sold his first story in 1986, and quickly established himself as a fre-quent contributor to The Magazine of Fantasy and Science Fiction *and* Asimov's Science Fiction, *as well as selling many stories to* Science Fiction Age, Universe, New Destinies, Tomorrow, Synergy, Starlight, *and elsewhere.*

Reed may be one of the most prolific of today's young writers, particularly at short-fiction lengths, seriously rivaled for that position only by authors such as Ste-phen Baxter and Brian Stableford. And—also like Baxter and Stableford—he manages to keep up a very high standard of quality while being prolific, something that is not at all easy to do. Reed stories such as "Sister Alice," "Brother Perfect," "Decency," "Savior," "The Remoras," "Chrysalis," "Whiptail," "The Utility Man," "Marrow," "Birth Day," "Blind," "The Toad of Heaven," "Stride," "The Shape of Everything," "Guest of Honor," "Waging Good," and "Killing the Morrow," among at least half a dozen others equally as strong, count as among some of the best short work produced by anyone in the 1980s and 1990s. Nor is he nonprolific as a novelist, having turned out eight novels since the end of the eighties, including The Lee Shore, The Hormone Jungle, Black Milk, The Remarkables, Down the Bright Way, Beyond the Veil of Stars, An Exaltation of Larks, *and, most recently,* Beneath the Gated Sky. *His reputation can only grow as the years go by, and I suspect that he will become one of the Big Names of the first decade of the new century. Some of the best of his short work was collected in* The Dragons of Springplace. *His most recent book is* Marrow, *a novel-length version of his 1997 novella of the same name. Reed lives in Lincoln, Nebraska.*

The inventive, elegant, and exciting story that follows examines the old idea that Nature is "red in tooth and claw"—and concludes that sometimes Nature could do better at that if it had a little help. . . .

The old man was corpulent like a seal, muscle clothed in fat to guarantee warmth, his skin smooth and his general proportions—stocky limbs and a broad chest—implying a natural, almost unconscious power. He wore little despite the damp chill. The brown eyes seemed capable and shrewd. And humorless. We were standing on a graveled beach, staring at his tiny sea; and after a long silence, he informed me, "I don't approve of what you do, Mr. Locum. It's pretentious and wasteful, this business of building cruel places. You're not an artist, and I think it's healthy for both of us to know my objections to your presence here."

I showed a grin, then said, "Fine. I'll leave." I had spent three months inside cramped quarters, but I told him, "Your shuttle can take me back to the freighter. I'll ride out with the iron."

"You misunderstand, Mr. Locum." His name was Provo Lei, the wealthiest person for a light-month in any direction. "I have these objections, but you aren't here for me. You're a gift to my daughter. She and I have finally agreed that she needs a tutor, and you seem qualified. Shall we dispense with pretenses? You are a toy. This isn't what you would call a lush commission, and you'd prefer to be near a civilized world, building some vicious forest for society people who want prestige and novelty. Yet you need my money, don't you? You're neither a tutor nor a toy, but your debts outweigh your current value as an artist. Or am I wrong?"

I attempted another grin, then shrugged. "I can work on a larger scale here." I'm not someone who hesitates or feels insecure, but I did both just then. "I've had other offers—"

"None of substance," Provo interrupted.

I straightened my back, looking over him. We were in the middle of his house—a sealed hyperfiber tent covering ten thousand hectares of tundra and ice water—and beyond the tent walls was an entire world, Earth-size but less massive. Not counting robots, the world's population was two. Counting me, three. As we stood there enjoying impolite conversation, an army of robots was beneath the deep water-ice crust, gnawing at rock, harvesting metals to be sold at a profit throughout the district.

"What do you think of my little home, Mr. Locum? Speaking as a professional terraformer, of course."

I blinked, hesitating again.

"Please. Be honest."

"It belongs to a miser." Provo didn't have propriety over bluntness. "This is a cheap Arctic package. Low diversity, a rigorous durability, and almost no upkeep. I'm guessing, but it feels like the home of a man who prefers solitude. And since you've lived here for two hundred years, alone most of the time, I don't think that's too much of a guess."

He surprised me, halfway nodding.

"Your daughter's how old? Thirty?" I paused, then said, "Unless she's exactly like you, I would think that she would have left by now. She's not a child, and she must be curious about the rest of the Realm. Which makes me wonder if I'm an inducement of some kind. A bribe. Speaking as a person, not a terraformer, I think she must be frighteningly important to you. Am I correct?"

The brown eyes watched me, saying nothing.

I felt a brief remorse. "You asked for my opinion," I reminded him.

"Don't apologize. I want honesty." He rubbed his rounded chin, offering what could have been confused for a smile. "And you're right, I do bribe my daughter. In a sense. She's my responsibility, and why shouldn't I sacrifice for her happiness?"

"She wants to be a terraformer?"

"Of the artistic variety, yes."

I moved my feet, cold gravel crunching under my boots.

"But this 'cheap package,' as you so graciously described it, is a recent condition. Before this I maintained a mature Arctic steppe, dwarf mammoths here and a coldwater reef offshore. At no small expense, Mr. Locum, and I'm not a natural miser."

"It sounds like Beringa," I muttered.

"My home world, yes." Beringa was a giant snowball terraformed by commercial souls, carpeted with plastics and rock and rich artificial soils, its interior still frozen while billions lived above in a kind of perpetual summer, twenty-hour days but limited heat. The natives were built like Provo, tailored genes keeping them comfortably fat and perpetually warm. In essence, Beringa was an inspired apartment complex, lovely in every superficial way.

The kind of work I hated most, I was thinking.

"This environment," I heard, "is very much makeshift."

I gestured at the tundra. "What happened?"

"Ula thought I would enjoy a grove of hot-sap trees."

Grimacing, I said, "They wouldn't work at all." Ecologically speaking. Not to mention aesthetically.

"Regardless," said Provo, "I purchased vats of totipotent cells, at no small cost, and she insisted on genetically tailoring them. Making them into a new species."

"Easy enough," I whispered.

"And yet." He paused and sighed. "Yet some rather gruesome metabolites were produced. Released. Persistent and slow toxins that moved through the food web. My mammoths sickened and died, and since I rather enjoy mammoth meat, having been raised on little else—"

"You were poisoned," I gasped.

"Somewhat, yes. But I have recovered nicely." The nonsmile showed again, eyes pained. Bemused. "Of course she was scared for me and sorry. And of course I had to pay for an extensive cleanup, which brought on a total environmental failure. This tundra package was an easy replacement, and besides, it carries a warranty against similar troubles."

Popular on toxic worlds, I recalled. Heavy metals and other terrors were shunted away from the human foods.

"You see? I'm not a simple miser."

"It shouldn't have happened," I offered.

Provo merely shrugged his broad shoulders, admitting, "I do love my daughter. And you're correct about some things. But the situation here, like anywhere, is much more complicated than the casual observer can perceive."

I looked at the drab hyperfiber sky—the illusion of heavy clouds over a waxy low sun—and I gave a quick appreciative nod.

"The area around us is littered with even less successful projects," Provo warned me.

I said, "Sad."

The old man agreed. "Yet I adore her. I want no ill to befall her, and I mean that as an unveiled warning. Ula has never existed with ordinary people. My hope is that I live long enough to see her mature, to become happy and normal, and perhaps gain some skills as a terraformer too. You are my best hope of the moment. Like it or not, that's why I hired you."

I stared out at his little sea. A lone gull was circling, bleating out complaints about the changeless food.

"My daughter will become infatuated with you," I heard. "Which might be a good thing. Provided you can resist temptation, infatuation will keep her from being disillusioned. Never, never let her become disillusioned."

"No?"

"Ula's not her father. Too much honesty is a bad thing."

I felt a momentary, inadequate sense of fear.

"Help her build one workable living place. Nothing fancy, and please, nothing too inspired." He knelt and picked up a rounded stone. "She has an extensive lab and stocks of totipotent cells. You'll need nothing. And I'll pay you in full, for your time and your imaginary expertise."

I found myself cold for many reasons, staring skyward. "I've been to Beringa," I told Provo. "It's ridiculously cheery. Giant flowers and giant butterflies, mammoths and tame bears. And a clear blue sky."

"Exactly," he replied, flinging the stone into the water. "And I would have kept my blue sky, but the color would have been dishonest."

A mosquito landed on my hand, tasting me and discovering that I wasn't a caribou, flying off without drawing blood.

"Bleak fits my mood, Mr. Locum."

I looked at him.

And again he offered his nonsmile, making me feel, if only for an instant, sorry for him.

✦

Beauty, say some artists, is the delicious stew made from your subject's flaws.

Ula Lei was a beautiful young woman.

She had a hundred hectare tent pitched beside her father's home, the place filled with bio stocks and empty crystal wombs and computers capable of modeling any kind of terraforming project. She was standing beside a huge reader, waving and saying, "Come here," with the voice people use on robots. Neither polite nor intimidating.

I approached, thinking that she looked slight. Almost underfed. Where I had expected an ungraceful woman-child, I instead found a mannerly but almost distant professional. Was she embarrassed to need a tutor? Or was she unsure how to act with a stranger? Either way, the old man's warning about my "toy" status seemed overstated. Taking a frail, pretty hand, feeling the polite and passionless single shake, I went from wariness to a mild funk, wondering if I had failed some standard. It wounded me when she stared right through me, asking with a calm dry voice, "What shall we do first?"

Funk became a sense of relief, and I smiled, telling her, "Decide on our project, and its scale."

"Warm work, and huge."

I blinked. "Your father promised us a thousand-hectare tent, plus any of his robots—"

"I want to use an old mine," she informed me.

"With a warm environment?"

"It has a rock floor, and we can insulate the walls and ceiling with field charges, then refrigerate as a backup." She knew the right words, at least in passing. "I've already selected which one. Here. I'll show you everything."

She was direct like her father, and confident. But Ula wasn't her father's child. Either his genes had been suppressed from conception, or they weren't included. Lean and graced with the fine features popular on tropical worlds, her body was the perfect antithesis of Provo's buttery one. Very black, very curly hair. Coffee-colored skin. And vivid green eyes. Those eyes noticed that I was wearing a heavy work jersey; I had changed clothes after meeting with Provo, wanting this jersey's self-heating capacity. Yet the temperature was twenty degrees warmer than the tundra, and her tropical face smiled when I pulled up my sleeves and pocketed my gloves. The humor was obvious only to her.

Then she was talking again, telling me, "The main chamber is eight kilometers by fifty, and the ceiling is ten kilometers tall in the center. Pressurized ice. Very strong." Schematics flowed past me. "The floor is the slope of a dead volcano. Father left when he found better ores."

A large operation, I noted. The rock floor would be porous and easily eroded, but rich in nutrients. Four hundred square kilometers? I had never worked on that scale, unless I counted computer simulations.

A graceful hand called up a new file. "Here's a summary of the world's best-guess history. If you're interested."

I was, but I had already guessed most of it for myself. Provo's World was like thousands of other sunless bodies in the Realm. Born in an unknown solar system, it had been thrown free by a near-collision, drifting into interstellar space, its deep seas freezing solid and its internal heat failing. In other regions it would have been terraformed directly, but our local district was impoverished when it came to metals. Provo's World had rich ores, its iron and magnesium, aluminum and the rest sucked up by industries and terraformers alike. A healthy green world requires an astonishing amount of iron, if only to keep it in hemoglobin. The iron from this old mine now circulated through dozens of worlds; and almost certainly some portion of that iron was inside me, brought home now within my own blood.

"I've already sealed the cavern," Ula informed me. "I was thinking of a river down the middle, recirculating, and a string of waterfalls—"

"No," I muttered.

She showed me a smile. "No?"

"I don't like waterfalls," I warned her.

"Because you belong to the New Traditionalist movement. I know." She shrugged her shoulders. " 'Waterfalls are clichés,' you claim. 'Life, done properly, is never pretty in simple ways.' "

"Exactly."

"Yet," Ula assured me, "this is my project."

I had come an enormous distance to wage a creative battle. Trying to measure my opponent, I asked, "What do you know about NTs?"

"You want to regain the honesty of the original Earth. Hard winters. Droughts. Violent predation. Vibrant chaos." Her expression became coy, then vaguely wicked. "But who'd want to terraform an entire world according to your values? And who would live on it, given the chance?"

"The right people," I replied, almost by reflex.

"Not Father. He thinks terraforming should leave every place fat and green and pretty. And iron-hungry too."

"Like Beringa."

She nodded, the wickedness swelling. "Did you hear about my little mistake?"

"About the hot-sap trees? I'm afraid so."

"I guess I do need help." Yet Ula didn't appear contrite. "I know about you, Mr. Locum. After my father hired you—I told him NTs work cheap—I ordered holos of every one of your works. You like working with jungles, don't you?"

Jungles were complex and intricate. And dense. And fun.

"What about Yanci's jungle?" she asked me. "It's got a spectacular waterfall, if memory serves."

A socialite had paid me to build something bold, setting it inside a plastic cavern inside a pluto-class world. Low gravity; constant mist; an aggressive assemblage of wild animals and carnivorous plants. "Perfect," Yanci had told me. Then she hired an old-school terraformer—little more than a plumber— to add one of those achingly slow rivers and falls, popular on every low-gravity world in the Realm.

"Yes, Mr. Locum?" she teased. "What do you want to say?"

"Call me Hann," I growled.

My student pulled her hair away from her jungle-colored eyes. "I've always been interested in New Traditionalists. Not that I believe what you preach . . . not entirely . . . but I'm glad Father hired one of you."

I was thinking about my ruined jungle. Fifty years in the past, and still it made my mouth go dry and my heart pound.

"How will we move water without a river and falls?"

"Underground," I told her. "Through the porous rock. We can make a string of pools and lakes, and there won't be erosion problems for centuries."

"Like this?" She called up a new schematic, and something very much like my idea appeared before us. "I did this in case you didn't like my first idea."

A single waterfall was at the high end of the cavern.

"A compromise," she offered. Enlarging the image, she said, "Doesn't it look natural?"

For a cliché, I thought.

"The reactor and pumps will be behind this cliff, and the water sounds can hide any noise—"

"Fine," I told her.

"—and the entranceway too. You walk in through the falls."

Another cliché, but I said, "Fine." Years of practice had taught me to compromise with the little points. Why fight details when there were bigger wars to wage?

"Is it all right, Mr. Locum?" A wink. "I want both of us happy when this is done. Hann, I mean."

For an audience of how many? At least with shallow socialites, there were hundreds of friends and tagalongs and nobodys and lovers. And since they rarely had enough money to fuel their lifestyles, they would open their possessions to the curious and the public.

But here I could do my best work, and who would know?

"Shall we make a jungle, Hann?"

I would know, I told myself.

And with a forced wink, I said, "Let's begin."

●

Terraforming is an ancient profession.

Making your world more habitable began on the Earth itself, with the first dancing fire that warmed its builder's cave; and everything since—every green world and asteroid and comet—is an enlargement on that first cozy cave. A hotter fusion fire brings heat and light, and benign organisms roam inside standardized biomes. For two hundred and ten centuries humans have expanded the Realm, mastering the tricks to bring life to a nearly dead universe. The frontier is an expanding sphere more than twenty light-years in radius—a great peaceful firestorm of life—and to date only one other living world has been discovered. *Pitcairn.* Alien and violent, and gorgeous. And the basic inspiration for the recent New Traditionalist movement. Pitcairn showed us how bland and domesticated our homes had become, riddled with clichés, every world essentially like every other world. Sad, sad, sad.

Here I found myself with four hundred square kilometers of raw stone. How long would it take to build a mature jungle? Done simply, a matter of months. But novelty would take longer, much to Provo's consternation. We would make fresh species, every ecological tie unique. I anticipated another year on top of the months, which was very good. We had the best computers, the best bio-stocks, and thousands of robots eager to work without pause or complaint. It was an ideal situation, I had to admit to myself. Very nearly heaven.

We insulated the ice ceiling and walls by three different means. Field charges enclosed the heated air. If they were breached, durable refrigeration elements were sunk into the ice itself. And at my insistence we added a set of emergency ducts, cold compressed air waiting in side caverns in case of tragedies. Every organism could go into a sudden dormancy, and the heat would be sucked into the huge volumes of surrounding ice. Otherwise the ceiling might sag and collapse, and I didn't want that to happen. Ula's jungle was supposed to outlast all of us. Why else go to all this bother?

We set the reactor inside the mine shaft, behind the eventual cliché. Then lights were strung, heating the cavern's new air, and we manufactured rich soils with scrap rock and silt from Provo's own little sea. The first inhabitants were bacteria and fungi set free to chew and multiply, giving the air its first living scent. Then robots began assembling tree-shaped molds, sinking hollow roots into the new earth and a sketchwork of branches meshing overhead, beginning the future canopy.

We filled the molds with water, nutrients, and nourishing electrical currents, then inoculated them with totipotent cells. More like baking than gardening, this was how mature forest could be built from scratch. Living cells divided at an exponential rate, then assembled themselves into tissue-types—sapwood and heartwood, bark and vascular tubes. It's a kind of superheated cultivation, and how else could artists like me exist? Left to Nature's pace, anything larger than a terrarium would consume entire lives. Literally.

Within five months—on schedule—we were watching the robots break up the molds, exposing the new trees to the air. And that's a symbolic moment worth a break and a little celebration, which we held.

Just Ula and me.

I suggested inviting Provo, but she told me, "Not yet. It's too soon to show him yet."

Perhaps. Or did she want her father kept at a distance?

I didn't ask. I didn't care. We were dining on top of a rough little hill, at the midpoint of the cavern, whiteness above and the new forest below us, leafless, resembling thousands of stately old trees pruned back by giant shears. Stubby, enduring trees. I toasted our success, and Ula grinned, almost singing when she said, "I haven't been the bother you expected, have I?"

No, she hadn't been.

"And I know more about terraforming than you thought."

More than I would admit. I nodded and said, "You're adept, considering you're self-taught."

"No," she sang, "you're the disappointment."

"Am I?"

"I expected . . . well, more energy. More inspiration." She rose to her feet, gesturing at our half-born creation. "I really hoped an NT would come up with bizarre wonders—"

"Like an eight-legged terror?"

"Exactly."

It had been her odd idea, and I'd dismissed it twenty times before I realized it was a game with her. She wanted an organism wholly unique, and I kept telling her that radical tailoring took too much time and too frequently failed. And besides, I added, our little patch of jungle wasn't large enough for the kind of predator she had in mind.

"I wish we could have one or two of them," she joked.

I ignored her. I'd learned that was best.

"But don't you agree? Nothing we've planned is *that* new or spectacular."

Yet I was proud of everything. What did she want? Our top three carnivores were being tailored at that moment—a new species of fire-eagle; a variation on black nightcats; and an intelligent, vicious species of monkey. Computer models showed that only two of them would survive after the first century. Which two depended on subtle, hard-to-model factors. That was one of the more radical, unpopular NT principles. "The fit survive." We build worlds with too much diversity, knowing that some of our creations are temporary. And unworthy. Then we stand aside, letting our worlds decide for themselves.

"I wish we could have rainstorms," she added. It was another game, and she waved her arms while saying, "Big winds. Lightning. I've always wanted to see lightning."

"There's not enough energy to drive storms," I responded. The rains were going to be mild events that came in the night. When we had nights, in a year. "I don't want to risk—"

"—damaging the ice. I know." She sat again, closer now, smiling as she said, "No, I don't care. It's coming along perfectly."

I nodded, gazing up at the brilliant white sky. The mining robots had left

the ice gouged and sharp, and somehow that was appropriate. An old violence was set against a rich new order, violent in different ways. A steamy
jungle cloaked in ice; an appealing, even poetic dichotomy. And while I
looked into the distance, hearing the sounds of molds being torn apart and
loaded onto mag-rails, my partner came even closer, touching one of my legs
and asking, "How else have I surprised you?"

She hadn't touched me in months, even in passing.

It took me a moment to gather myself, and I took her hand and set it
out of the way, with a surety of motion.

She said nothing, smiling and watching me.

And once again, for the umpteenth time, I wondered what Ula was thinking. Because I didn't know and couldn't even guess. We had been together
for months, our relationship professional and bloodless. Yet I always had the
strong impression that she showed me what she wanted to show me, and I
couldn't even guess how much of that was genuine.

"How else?" she asked again.

"You're an endless surprise," I told her.

But instead of appearing pleased, she dipped her head, the smile changing
to a concentrated stare, hands drawing rounded shapes in the new soil, then
erasing them with a few quick tiger swipes.

◆

I met Provo behind the waterfall, in the shaft, his sturdy shape emerging
from the shadows; and he gave me a nod and glanced at the curtain of water,
never pausing, stepping through and vanishing with a certain indifference.
I followed, knowing where the flow was weakest—where I would be the least
soaked—and stepped out onto a broad rock shelf, workboots gripping and
my dampened jersey starting to dry itself.

The old man was gazing into the forest.

I asked, "Would you like a tour?" Then I added, "We could ride one of
the mag-rails, or we could walk."

"No," he replied. "Neither."

Why was he here? Provo had contacted me, no warning given. He had
asked about his daughter's whereabouts. "She's in the lab," I had said, "mutating beetles." Leave her alone, he had told me. Provo wanted just the two
of us for his first inspection.

Yet now he acted indifferent to our accomplishments, dropping his head
and walking off the rock shelf and stopping, then looking back at me. And
over the sound of tumbling water, he asked, "How is she?"

"Ula's fine."

"No troubles with her?" he inquired.

It was several weeks after our hilltop celebration, and I barely remembered
the hand on my leg. "She's doing a credible job."

Provo appeared disappointed.

I asked him, "How should she be?"

He didn't answer. "She likes you, Mr. Locum. We've talked about you.
She's told me, more than once . . . that you're *perfect*."

I felt a sudden warmth, and I smiled.

Disappointment faded. "How is she? Speaking as her teacher, of course."

"Bright. Maybe more than bright." I didn't want to praise too much, lifting his expectations. "She has inspirations, as she calls them. Some are workable, and some are even lovely."

"Inspirations," he echoed.

I readied some examples. I thought Provo would want them, enjoying this chance to have a parent's pride. But instead he looked off into the trees again, the stubby branches sprouting smaller branches and fat green leaves. He seemed to be hunting for something specific, old red eyes squinting. Finally, he said, "No." He said, "I shouldn't tell you."

"Tell me?"

"Because you don't need to know." He sighed and turned, suddenly older and almost frail. "If she's been on her best behavior, maybe I should keep my mouth shut."

I said nothing for a long moment.

Provo shuffled across the clearing, sitting on a downed log with a certain gravity. The log had been grown in the horizontal position, then killed. Sitting next to him, I asked, "What is it, Mr. Lei?"

"My daughter."

"Yes?"

"She isn't."

I nodded and said, "Adopted."

"Did she tell you?"

"I know genetics. And I didn't think you'd suppress your own genes."

He looked at the waterfall. It was extremely wide and not particularly tall, spilling onto the shelf and then into a large pond. A pair of mag-rails carried equipment in and out on the far shore. Otherwise little moved. I noticed a tiny tagalong mosquito who wouldn't bite either of us. It must have come from the tundra, and it meant nothing. It would die in a few hours, I thought; and Provo suddenly told me, "Adopted, yes. And I think it's fair to tell you the circumstances."

Why the tension?

"I'm quite good at living alone, Mr. Locum. That's one of the keys to my success." He paused, then said, "I came to this world alone. I charted it and filed my claims and defended it from the jealous mining corporations. Every moment of my life has gone into these mines, and I'm proud of my accomplishments. Life. My metals have brought life and prosperity to millions, and I make no apologies. Do you understand me?"

I said, "Yes."

"Few people come here. Like that freighter that brought you, most of the ships are unmanned." Another pause. "But there are people who make their livelihood riding inside the freighters. Perhaps you've known a few of them."

I hadn't, no.

"They are people. They exist on a continuum. All qualities of human beings live inside those cramped quarters, some of them entirely decent. Honest. Capable of more compassion than I could hope to feel."

I nodded, no idea where we were going.

"Ula's biological parents weren't at that end of the continuum. Believe me. When I first saw her . . . when I boarded her parents' ship to supervise the loading . . . well, I won't tell you what I saw. And smelled. And learned about the capacities of other human beings. Some things are best left behind, I think. Let's forget them. Please."

"How old was Ula?"

"A child. Three standard years, that time." A small strong hand wiped at his sweating face. "Her parents purchased loads of mixed metals from me, then sold them to one of the water worlds near Beringa. To help plankton bloom, I imagine. And for two years, every day, I found myself remembering that tiny girl, pitying her, a kind of guilt building inside me because I'd done nothing to help her, nothing at all." Again the hands tried to dry his face, squeezed drops of perspiration almost glittering on them. "And yet, Mr. Locum, I was thankful too. Glad that I would never see her again. I assumed . . . I knew . . . that space itself would swallow them. That someone else would save her. That her parents would change. That I wouldn't be involved again, even if I tried—"

"They came back," I muttered.

Provo straightened his back, grimacing as if in pain. "Two years later, yes." Brown eyes closed, opened. "They sent me word of their arrival, and in an instant a plan occurred to me. All at once I knew the right thing to do." Eyes closed and stayed closed. "I was onboard, barely one quick glance at that half-starved child, and with a self-righteous voice I told the parents, 'I want to adopt her. Name your price.' "

"Good," I offered.

He shook his head. "You must be like me. We assume, and without reasons, that those kinds of people are simple predatory monsters. Merely selfish. Merely cruel." The eyes opened once again. "But what I realized since is that Ula . . . Ula was in some way essential to that bizarre family. I'm not saying they loved her. It's just that they couldn't sell her any more than they could kill her. Because if she died, who else would they have to torture?"

I said nothing.

"They couldn't be bought, I learned. Quickly." Provo swallowed and grabbed the log, knuckles pale as the hands shook. "You claim my daughter is well-behaved, and I'm pleased. You say she's bright, and I'm not at all surprised. And since you seem to have her confidence and trust, I think it's only fair to tell you about her past. To warn you."

"How did you adopt her?"

He took a deep breath and held it.

"If they couldn't be bribed . . . ?" I touched one of the thick arms. "What happened?"

"Nothing." A shrug of the shoulders, then he said, "There was an accident. During the loading process. The work can be dangerous, even deadly, when certain equipment fails."

I felt very distant, very calm.

"An accident," he repeated.

I gave him a wary glance, asking. "Does she know what happened?"

Provo's eyes opened wide, almost startled. "About the accident? Nothing! About her past life? She remembers, I'm sure . . . nothing. None of it." Just the suggestion of memories caused him to nearly panic. "No, Mr. Locum . . . you see, once I had legal custody . . . even before then . . . I paid an expert from Beringa to come here and examine her, and treat her . . . with every modern technique—"

"What kind of expert?"

"In psychology, you idiot! What do you think I mean?" Then he gave a low moan, pulling loose a piece of fibrous bark. "To save her. To wipe away every bad memory and heal her, which he did quite well. A marvelous job of it. I paid him a bonus. He deserved it." He threw the bark onto the pond. "I've asked Ula about her past, a thousand times . . . and she remembers none of it. The expert said she might, or that it might come out in peculiar ways . . . but she doesn't and has no curiosity about those times . . . and maybe I shouldn't have told you, I'm sorry . . . !"

I looked at the pond, deep and clear, some part of me wondering how soon we would inoculate it with algae and water weeds.

Then Provo stood again, telling me, "Of course I came to look around, should she ask. And tell her . . . tell her that I'm pleased. . . ."

I gave a quick compliant nod.

"It's too warm for my taste." He made a turn, gazing into the jungle and saying, "But shady. Sometimes I like a place with shade, and it's pleasant enough, I suppose." He swallowed and gave a low moan, then said, "And tell her for me, please . . . that I'm very much looking forward to the day it's done. . . ."

◆

Terraformers build their worlds at least twice.

The first time it is a model, a series of assumptions and hard numbers inside the best computers; and the second time it is wood and flesh, false sunlight and honest sound. And that second incarnation is never the same as the model. It's an eternal lesson learned by every terraformer, and by every other person working with complexity.

Models fail.

Reality conspires.

There is always, always some overlooked or mismeasured factor, or a stew of factors. And it's the same for people too. A father and a teacher speak about the daughter and the student, assuming certain special knowledge; and together they misunderstand the girl, their models having little to do with what is true.

Worlds are easy to observe.

Minds are secretive. And subtle. And molding them is never so easy and clear as the molding of mere worlds, I think.

◆

Ula and I were working deep in the cavern, a few days after Provo's visit, teaching our robots how and where to plant an assortment of newly tailored saplings. We were starting our understory, vines and shrubs and shade-tolerant trees to create a dense tangle. And the robots struggled, designed to wrestle metals from rocks, not to baby the first generations of new species. At one point I waded into the fray, trying to help, shouting and grabbing at a mechanical arm while taking a blind step, a finger-long spine plunging into my ankle.

Ula laughed, watching me hobble backward. Then she turned sympathetic, absolutely convincing when she said, "Poor darling." She thought we should move to the closest water and clean out my wound. "It looks like it's swelling, Hann."

It was. I had designed this plant with an irritating protein, and I joked about the value of field testing, using a stick as my impromptu crutch. Thankfully we were close to one of the ponds, and the cool spring water felt wondrous, Ula removing my boot and the spine while I sprawled out on my back, eyes fixed on the white expanse of ice and lights, waiting for the pain to pass.

"If you were an ordinary terraformer," she observed, "this wouldn't have happened."

"I'd be somewhere else, and rich," I answered.

She moved from my soaking foot to my head, sitting beside me, knees pulled to her face and patches of perspiration darkening her lightweight work jersey. " 'Red of tooth and claw,' " she quoted.

A New Traditionalist motto. We were building a wilderness of spines and razored leaves; and later we'd add stinging wasps and noxious beetles, plus a savage biting midge that would attack in swarms. "Honest testing nature," I muttered happily.

Ula grinned and nodded, one of her odd expressions growing. And she asked, "But why can't we do more?"

More?

"Make the fire eagles attack us on sight, for instance. If we're after bloody claws—"

"No," I interrupted. "That has no ecological sense at all." Fire eagles were huge, but they'd never prey on humans.

"Oh, sure. I forgot."

She hadn't, and both of us knew it. Ula was playing another game with me.

I looked across the water, trying to ignore her. The far shore was a narrow stretch of raw stone, and the air above it would waver, field charges setting up their barrier against the heat. Beyond, not twenty meters beyond, was a rigid and hard-frozen milky wall that lifted into the sky, becoming the sky, part of me imagining giant eagles flying overhead, hunting for careless children.

"What's special about the original Earth?" I heard. "Tell me again, please, Hann."

No, I wouldn't. But even as I didn't answer, I answered. In my mind I was thinking about three billion years of natural selection, amoral and frequently shortsighted . . . and wondrous in its beauty, power, and scope . . . and how we in the Realm had perfected a stupefying version of that wonder, a million worlds guaranteed to be safe and comfortable for the trillions of souls clinging to them.

"Here," said Ula, "we should do everything like the original Earth."

I let myself ask, "What do you mean?"

"Put in things that make ecological sense. Like diseases and poisonous snakes, for instance."

"And we can be imprisoned for murder when the first visitor dies."

"But we aren't going to have visitors," she warned me. "So why not? A viper with a nerve toxin in its fangs? Or maybe some kind of plague carried by those biting midges that you're so proud of."

She was joking, I thought. Then I felt a sudden odd doubt.

Ula's entire face smiled, nothing about it simple. "What's more dangerous? Spines or no spines?"

"More dangerous?"

"For us." She touched my ankle, watching me.

"Spines," I voted.

"Back on Earth," she continued, "there were isolated islands. And the plants that colonized them would lose their spines and toxic chemicals, their old enemies left behind. And birds would lose their power of flight. And the tortoises grew huge, nothing to compete with them. Fat, easy living."

"What's your point, teacher?"

She laughed and said, "We arrived. We brought goats and rats and ourselves, and the native life would go extinct."

"I know history," I assured her.

"Not having spines is more dangerous than having them."

I imagined that I understood her point, nodding now and saying, "See? That's what NTs argue. Not quite in those terms—"

"Our worlds are like islands, soft and easy."

"Exactly." I grinned and nodded happily. "What I want to do here, and everywhere—"

"You're not much better," she interrupted.

No?

"Not much at all," she grumbled, her expression suddenly black. Sober. "Nature is so much more cruel and honest than you'd ever be."

Suddenly I was thinking about Provo's story, that nondescription of Ula's forgotten childhood. It had been anything but soft and easy, and I felt pity; and I felt curiosity, wondering if she had nightmares and then, for an instant, wondering if I could help her in some important way.

Ula was watching me, reading my expression.

Without warning she bent close, kissing me before I could react and then sitting up again, laughing like a silly young girl.

I asked, "Why did you do that?"

"Why did I stop, you mean?"

I swallowed, saying nothing.

Then she bent over again, kissing me again, pausing to whisper, "Why don't we?"

I couldn't find any reason to stop.

And suddenly she was removing her jersey, and mine, and I looked past her for an instant, blinding myself with the glare of lights and white ice, all at once full of reasons why we should stop and my tongue stolen out of my mouth.

◆

I was Ula's age when I graduated from the Academy. The oldest teacher on the staff invited me into her office, congratulated me for my good grades, then asked me in a matter-of-fact way, "Where do these worlds we build actually live, Mr. Locum? Can you point to where they are?"

She was cranky and ancient, her old black flesh turning white from simple age. I assumed that she was having troubles with her mind, the poor woman. A shrug; a gracious smile. Then I told her, "I don't know, ma'am. I would think they live where they live."

A smartass answer, if there ever was.

But she wasn't startled or even particularly irritated by my nonreply, a long lumpy finger lifting into the air between us, then pointing at her own forehead. "In our minds, Mr. Locum. That's the only place they can live for us, because where else can we live?"

"May I go?" I asked, unamused.

She said, "Yes."

I began to rise to my feet.

And she told me, "You are a remarkably stupid man, I think, Mr. Locum. Untalented and vain and stupid in many fundamental ways, and you have a better chance of success than most of your classmates."

"I'm leaving," I warned her.

"No." She shook her head. "You aren't here even now."

◆

We were one week into our honeymoon—sex and sleep broken up with the occasional bout of work followed with a swim—and we were lying naked on the shore of the first pond. Ula looked at me, smiling and touching me, then saying, "You know, this world once was alive."

Her voice was glancingly saddened, barely audible over the quiet clean splash of the cliché. I nodded, saying, "I realize that." Then I waited for whatever would follow. I had learned about her lectures during the last seven days.

"It was an ocean world, just three billion years ago." She drew a planet on my chest. "Imagine if it hadn't been thrown away from its sun. If it had evolved complex life. If some kind of intelligent, tool-using fish had built spaceships—"

"Very unlikely," I countered.

She shrugged and asked, "Have you seen our fossils?"

No, but I didn't need to see them. Very standard types. The Realm was full of once-living worlds.

"This sea floor," she continued, "was dotted with hot-water vents, and bacteria evolved and lived by consuming metal ions—"

"—which they laid down, making the ore that you mine," I interrupted. With growing impatience, I asked, "Why tell me what I already know, Ula?"

"How do you think it would feel? Your world is thrown free of your sun, growing cold and freezing over . . . nothing you can do about it . . . and how would you feel . . . ?"

The vents would have kept going until the planet's tepid core grew cold, too little radioactivity to stave off the inevitable. "But we're talking about bacteria," I protested. "Nothing sentient. Unless you've found something bigger in the fossil record."

"Hardly," she said. Then she sat upright, small breasts catching the light and my gaze. "I was just thinking."

I braced myself.

"I remember when Father showed me one of the old vents . . . the first one I ever saw. . . ."

I doubly braced myself.

"I was five or six, I suppose, and we were walking through a new mine, down a dead rift valley, two hundred kilometers under the frozen sea. He pointed to mounds of dirty ore, then he had one of his robots slice into one of them, showing me the striations . . . how layers of bacteria had grown, by the trillion . . . outnumbering the human race, he said . . . and I cried. . . ."

"Did you?"

"Because they had died." She appeared close to tears again, but one hand casually scratched her breasts. Then the face brightened, almost smiling as she asked, "What's your favorite world?"

Changing subjects? I couldn't be sure.

"Your own world, or anyone's. Do you have favorites?"

Several of them, yes. I described the most famous world—a small spinning asteroid filled with wet forest—and I told her about the artists, all terraformers who had journeyed to the alien world of Pitcairn. They were the first New Traditionalists. I had never seen the work for myself, ten light-years between us and it, but I'd walked through the holos, maybe hundreds of times. The artists had been changed by Pitcairn. They never used alien lifeforms—there are tough clear laws against the exporting of Pitcairn life—but they had twisted earthly species to capture something of the strangeness and strength of the place. And I couldn't do it justice. I found myself blabbering about the quality of light and the intensity of certain golden birds . . . and at some point I quit speaking, realizing that Ula wasn't paying attention to me.

She heard silence and said, "It sounds intriguing." Then with a slow, almost studied pose, she said, "Let me tell you about something even more fascinating."

I felt a moment of anger. *How dare she ignore me!* Then the emotion evaporated, betraying me, leaving me to wait while she seemed to gather herself, her face never more serious or composed. Or focused. Or complete.

"It was the second world that I built," I heard. "My first world was too large and very clumsy, and I destroyed it by accident. But no matter. What I did that second time was find a very small abandoned mine, maybe a hectare in size, and I reinforced the ice walls and filled the chamber with water, then sank a small reactor into the rock, opening up the ancient plumbing and inoculating the water with a mixture of bacteria—"

"Did you?" I sputtered.

"—and reestablishing one vent community. After three billion years of sleep. I fueled the reactor with a measured amount of deuterium, and I enriched the warming water with the proper metals." A pause. "New striations formed. Superheated black goo was forced from the fossil tubes. And I dressed in a strong pressure suit and walked into that world, and I sat just like we're sitting here, and waited."

I swallowed. "Waited?"

"The reactor slowed, then stopped." Ula took a breath and said, "I watched. With the lights on my suit down low, I watched the black goo stop rising, and the water cooled, and eventually new ice began to form against the walls. I moved to the center, sitting among the tubes . . . for days, for almost two weeks . . . the ice walls closing in on me—"

"That's crazy," I blurted.

And she shrugged as if to say, "I don't care." A smile emerged, then vanished, and she turned and touched me, saying, "I allowed myself to be frozen into that new ice, my limbs locked in place, my power packs running dry—"

"But why?" I asked. "So you'd know how it felt?"

And she didn't seem to hear me, tilting her head, seemingly listening to some distant sound worthy of her complete attention. Eventually she said, "Father missed me." A pause. "He came home from a tour of distant mines, and I was missing, and he sent robots out to find me, and they cut me free just before I would have begun to truly suffer."

The girl was insane. I knew it.

She took a dramatic breath, then smiled. Her haunted expression vanished in an instant, without effort, and again she was a student, the youngster, and my lover. A single bead of perspiration was rolling along her sternum, then spreading across her taut brown belly; and I heard myself asking, "Why did you do that shit?"

But the youngster couldn't or wouldn't explain herself, dipping her head and giggling into my ear.

"You could have died," I reminded her.

She said, "Don't be angry, darling. Please?"

An unstable, insane woman-child, and suddenly I was aware of my own heartbeat.

"Are you angry with sweet me?" She reached for me, for a useful part of me, asking, "How can I make you happy, darling?"

"Be normal," I whispered.

"Haven't you paid attention?" The possessed expression reemerged for an instant. "I'm not and never have been. Normal. My darling."

◆

My excuse, after much thought and practice, was a conference with her father. "I want us to have a backup reactor. In case."

She dismissed the possibility out of hand. "He won't give us one."

"And I want to walk on the surface. For a change of scenery." I paused, then camouflaged my intentions by asking, "Care to walk with me?"

"God, no. I've had enough of those walks, thank you."

Freed for the day, I began by visiting the closest caverns and one deflated tent, poking through dead groves and chiseling up samples of soil and frozen pond water. The cold was absolute. The sky was black and filled with stars, a few dim green worlds lost against the chill. Running quick tests, I tried to identify what had gone wrong and where. Sometimes the answer was obvious; sometimes I was left with guesses. But each of her worlds was undeniably dead, hundreds and thousands of new species extinct before they had any chance to prosper.

Afterward I rode the mag-rail back to Provo's house, finding where the hot-sap trees had been planted, the spot marked with a shallow lake created when the permafrost melted. I worked alone for twenty minutes, then the owner arrived. He seemed unhurried, yet something in his voice or his forward tilt implied a genuine concern. Or maybe not. I'd given up trying to decipher their damned family.

Pocketing my field instruments, I told Provo, "She's a good tailor. Too good." No greetings. No preparatory warning. I just informed him, "I've watched her, and you can't tell me that she'd introduce a toxic metabolite by accident. Not Ula."

The old man's face grew a shade paler, his entire body softening; and he leaned against a boulder, telling me without the slightest concern, "That possibility has crossed my mind, yes."

I changed topics, Ula-fashion. "When we met you warned me not to get too close to her. And not to be too honest."

"I remember."

"How do you know? Who else has been here?"

No answer.

"She's had another tutor, hasn't she?"

"Never."

"Then how can you know?"

"Twice," Provo told me, "my daughter has taken lovers. Two different crew members from separate freighters. Dullards, both of them. With each there was a period of bliss. They stayed behind and helped Ula with her work, then something would go wrong. I don't know any details. I refuse to spy on my own daughter. But with the man, her first lover . . . he expressed an interest in leaving, I believe . . . in returning to his vocation. . . ."

"What happened?"

"Ula pierced the wall of the tent. A year's work was destroyed in a few minutes."

The man sighed, betraying a huge fatigue. "She told me that it was an accident, that she intended just to scare him—"

"She murdered him?" I managed.

And Provo laughed with relief. "No, no. No, the dullard was able to climb into an emergency suit in time, saving himself."

"What about the other lover?"

"The woman?" A strong shrug of the shoulders, then he said, "A fire. Another accident. I know less, but I surmise they had had a spat of some kind. A ridiculous, wasteful fit of anger. Although Ula claimed not to have started the blaze. She acted thoroughly innocent, and astonishingly unrepentant."

I swallowed, then whispered, "Your daughter is disturbed."

Provo said, "And didn't I warn you? Did you not understand me?" The soft face was perspiring despite the chill air. A cloud of mosquitoes drifted between us, hunting suitable game. "How much forewarning did you require, Mr. Locum?"

I said nothing.

"And you've done so well, too. Better than I hoped possible, I should tell you."

I opened my mouth, and I said nothing.

"She told me . . . yesterday, I think . . . how important you are to her education—"

"The poison," I interrupted.

Provo quit speaking.

"There's a residue here. In the soil." I showed him a molecule displayed on my portable reader. "It's a synthetic alkaloid. Very messy, very tough. And very, very intentional, I think." A moment's pause, then I asked him, "Has it occurred to you that she was trying to murder you?"

"Naturally," he responded, in an instant.

"And?"

"And she didn't try. No."

"How can you feel sure?"

"You claim that my daughter is bright. Is talented. If she wanted to kill me, even if she was an idiot, don't you think that right now I would be dead?"

Probably true, I thought.

"Two people alone on an empty world. Nothing would be simpler than the perfect murder, Mr. Locum."

"Then what did she want?" I gestured at the little lake. "What was *this* about?"

Provo appeared disgusted, impatient.

He told me, "I might have hoped that you could explain it to me."

I imagined Ula on the bottom of a freezing sea, risking death in some bid to understand . . . what? And three times she had endangered others . . . which left another dozen creations that she had killed . . . and was she alone in each of them when they died . . . ?

"Discover her purpose, Mr. Locum, and perhaps I'll give you a bonus. If that's permissible."

I said nothing.

"You have been following my suggestions, haven't you? You aren't becoming too entangled with her, are you?"

I looked at Provo.

And he read my face, shaking his head with heavy sadness, saying, "Oh, my, Mr. Locum. Oh, my."

◆

A *purpose.*

The possibility gnawed at me. I assumed some kind of madness lay over whatever her rationale, and I wished for a degree in psychiatry, or maybe some life experience with insanity. Anything would help. Riding the magrail back into our cavern, replaying the last few months in my mind, I heard part of me begging for me to flee, to turn now and take refuge where I could, then stow away on the first freighter to pass—

—which was impossible, I realized in the same instant. Not to mention dangerous. Acting normal was important, I told myself. Then aloud, I said, "Just keep her happy."

I have never been more terrified of a human being.

Yet Ula seemed oblivious. She greeted me with a kiss and demanded more, and I failed her, nervousness and sudden fatigue leaving me soft. But she explained it away as stress and unimportant, cuddling up next to me on the shady jungle floor. She said, "Let's sleep," and I managed to close my eyes and drift into a broken dreamy sleep, jerking awake to find myself alone.

Where had the girl gone?

I called her on our com-line, hearing her voice and my voice dry and clumsy, asking her, "Where are you?"

"Mutating treefrogs, darling."

Which put her inside her home. Out of my way. I moved to the closest workstation, asking its reader to show me the original schematics and everything that we had done to date; and I opened up my jersey—I was still wearing my heavy, cold-weather jersey—drops of salty water splattering on the reader. I was hunting for anything odd or obviously dangerous. A flaw in the ice roof? None that I could find. A subtle poison in our young trees? None that showed in the genetic diagrams. But just to be sure, I tested myself. Nothing wrong in my blood, I learned. What else? There was one oddity, something that I might have noticed before but missed. The trees had quirks in their chemistry. Nothing deadly. Just curious. I was studying a series of sugars, wondering when Ula had slipped them into the tailoring process, and why; and just then, as if selecting the perfect moment, she said, "Darling," with a clear close voice. Then, "What are you doing?"

I straightened my back, and I turned.

Ula was standing behind me, the smile bright and certain. And strange. She said, "Hello?" and then, "What are you doing, darling?"

I blanked the reader.

Then with the stiffest possible voice, I told her, "Nothing. Just checking details."

She approached, taking me around my waist.

I hugged her, wondering what to do.

Then she released me, pulling back her hair while asking, "What did you and my father decide?"

Swallowing was impossible, my throat full of dust.

"I forgot to ask before. Do we get a second reactor?"

I managed to shake my head. No.

"An unnecessary expense," she said, perfectly mimicking her father's voice. She couldn't have acted more normal, walking around me while asking, "Has the nap helped?"

I watched her undress as she moved.

"Feel like fun?"

Why was I afraid? There weren't any flaws in our work, I knew, and as long as she was with me, nude and in my grasp, what could she do to me? Nothing, and I became a little confident. At least confident enough to accomplish the task at and, the event feeling robotic and false, and entirely safe.

Afterward she said, "That was the best," and I knew—knew without doubt—that Ula was lying. "The best ever," she told me, kissing my nose and mouth and upturned throat. "We'll never have a more perfect moment. Can I ask you something?"

"What . . . ?"

She said, "It's something that I've considered. For a long while, I've been wondering—"

"What?"

"About the future." She straddled me, pressure on my stomach. The grin was sly and expectant. "When Father dies, I inherit this world. All of it and his money too, and his robots. Everything."

A slight nod, and I said, "Yes?"

"What will I do with it?"

I had no idea.

"What if I bought an artificial sun? Not fancy. And brought it here and put it in orbit. I've estimated how long it would take to melt this sea, if I hurried things along by seeding the ice with little reactors—"

"Decades," I interrupted.

"Two or three, I think. And then I could terraform an entire world." She paused, tilting her head and her eyes lifting. "Of course all of this would be destroyed. Which is sad." She sighed, shrugging her shoulders. "How many people have my kind of wealth, Hann? In the entire Realm, how many?"

"I don't know."

"And who already own a world too. How many?"

"Very few."

"And who have an interest in terraforming, of course." She giggled and said, "I could be one of a kind. It's possible."

It was.

"What I want to ask," she said, "is this. Would you, Hann Locum, like to help me? To remake all of this ice and rock with me?"

I opened my mouth, then hesitated.

"Because I don't deserve all the fun for myself," she explained, climbing off me. "Wouldn't that be something? You might be the first NT terraformer with your own world. Wouldn't that make you the envy of your peers?"

"Undoubtedly," I whispered.

Ula walked to her clothes, beginning to dress. "Are you interested?"

I said, "Yes. Sure." True or not, I wanted to make agreeable sounds. Then I made myself add, "But your father's in good health. It could be a long time before—"

"Oh, yeah." A glib shrug of her shoulders; a vague little-girl smile. "I hope it's years and years away. I do."

I watched the girl's face, unable to pierce it. I couldn't guess what she was really thinking, not even when she removed the odd control from one of her deep pockets. A simple device, homemade and held in her right hand; and now she winked at me, saying, "I know."

Know!

"What both of you talked about today. Of course I know."

The pressure on my chest grew a thousandfold.

"The mosquitoes? Some aren't. They're electronic packages dressed up as mosquitoes, and I always hear what Father says—"

Shit.

"—and have for years. Always."

I sat upright, hands digging into the damp black soil.

She laughed and warned me, "You're not the first person to hear his confession. I am sorry. He has this guilt, and he salves it by telling people who can't threaten him. I suppose he wanted you to feel sorry for him, and to admire him—"

"What do you remember?"

"Of my parents? Nothing." She shook her head. "Everything." A nod and the head titled, and she told me, "I do have one clear image. I don't know if it's memory or if it's a dream, or what. But I'm a child inside a smelly freighter, huddled in a corner, watching Provo Lei strangle my real mother. He doesn't know I'm there, of course." A pause. "If he had known, do you suppose he would have strangled me too? To save himself, perhaps?"

"I'm sorry," I muttered.

And she laughed, the sound shrill. Complex. "Why? He's a very good father, considering. I love him, and I can't blame him for anything." A pause, then with a caring voice she told me, "I love him quite a lot more than I love you, Hann."

I moved, the ground under my butt creaking; and I had to say, "But you poisoned him anyway."

Ula waved her control with a flourish, telling me, "I poisoned everything. All I wanted was for Father to watch." A shrug. "I tried to make him understand . . . to comprehend . . . but I don't think he could ever appreciate what I was trying to tell him. Never."

I swallowed, then asked, "What were you telling him?"

Her eyes grew huge, then a finger was wagged at me. "No. No, you don't." She took a small step backward, shaking her head. "I think it's just a little too soon for that. Dear."

I waited.

Then she waved the control again, saying, "Look up, Hann. Will you? Now?"

"Up?" I whispered.

"This direction." She pointed at the canopy. "This is *up*."

My gaze lifted, the solid green ceiling of leaves glowing, branches like veins running through the green; and she must have activated the control, a distinct click followed by her calm voice saying, "I left out parts of the schematics, Hann. Intentionally. Before you were even hired, you should know."

There was a distant rumbling noise.

The ground moved, tall trees swaying for an instant; then came a flash of light with instant thunder, a bolt of electricity leaping down the long cavern, the force of it swatting me down against the forest floor, heat against my face and chest, every hair on my body lifting for a terrible long instant.

Then it was gone again.

Everything was.

The lights had failed, a perfect seamless night engulfing the world; and twice I heard a laugh, close and then distant.

Then nothing.

And I screamed, the loudest sound I could muster lost in the leaves and against the tree trunks, fading into echoes and vanishing, as if it had never existed at all.

➝

My jersey . . . where was my jersey . . . ?

I made myself stand and think, perfectly alert, trying to remember where it had lain and counting steps in my mind . . . one step, and two, and three. Then I knelt and found nothing in reach, nothing but the rich new soil, and for a terrified instant I wondered if Ula had stolen my clothes, leaving me naked as well as blind.

But another step and grope gave me my boots, then the jersey. I dressed and found my various equipment in the pockets and pouches. The portable reader had been cooked by the lightning, but the glowglobes were eager. I ignited one of them and released it; it hovered over me, moving with a faint dry hum as it emitted a yellowish light.

I walked to the closest mag-rail.

Inoperative.

Nearby were a pair of robots standing like statues.

Dead.

I started to jog uphill, moving fast. Where was Ula? Had she gone somewhere, or was she nearby, watching me?

It was fifteen kilometers to the waterfall, the exit. The trees seemed larger in the very weak light, the open jungle floor feeling rather like a place of worship. A cathedral. Then came a wall of vines and thorny brush—our earliest plantings—and I burrowed into them, pushing despite the stabs at my skin, breaking into an open unfinished glade and pausing. Something was wrong, I thought. Against my face was cold air, bitter and sudden. Of course the field generators were down. And the refrigeration elements. What remained was the passive emergency system, heat rising into high ducts while others released cubic kilometers of stored air from below.

How long would the process take?

I couldn't remember, could scarcely think about anything. My jersey automatically warmed me, and I helped keep warm by running fast, pulling ahead of my glowglobe, my frantic shadow gigantic and ethereal.

In my head, in simple terms, I handled the mathematics.

Calories; volume; turbulence; time.

Halfway to the waterfall, feeling the distance and the grade, I had a terrible sudden premonition.

Slowing, I said, "Where are you?"

Then I screamed, "Ula! Ula!"

In the chill air my voice carried, and when it died there was a new sound, clear and strong and very distant. A howl; a wild inhuman moan. I took a weak step sideways and faltered. Somehow I felt as if I should know the source . . . and I remembered Ula's eight-legged predator, swift and smart and possibly on the hunt now. *She had made it . . . !*

There was a motion, a single swirling something coming out of the gloom at me. I grunted and twisted, falling down, and a leaf landed at my feet. Brown and cold. Partly cooked by the lightning, I realized. It crumbled when my hand closed around it. Then came the howl again, seemingly closer, and again I was running, sprinting uphill, into another band of prickly underbrush and starting to sob with the authority of a beaten child.

The ambient temperature was plummeting.

My breath showed in my glowglobe's yellow light, lifting and thinning and mixing with more falling leaves. The forest was slipping into dormancy. A piece of me was thankful, confident that it at least would survive whatever happened; and most of me was furious with Ula—a simple, visceral fury— as I imagined my escape and the filing of criminal complaints. Attempted murder. Malicious endangerment. And straight murder charges on Provo, me as witness for the prosecution and their lives here finished. Extinguished. Lost.

"I'm going to escape," I muttered at the shadows. "Ula? Are you listening? Ula?"

I pulled gloves from a pocket, covering my cold hands and then knitting into my sleeves. Then I unrolled my jersey's simple hood, tying it flush against my head, enjoying the heat of the fabric. Leaves were falling in a steady brown blizzard. They covered the freezing earth, crunching with each footfall, and sometimes in the crunches I thought I heard someone or something else moving. Pausing, I would listen. Wait. The predator? Or Ula? But the next howl seemed distant and perhaps confused, and it had to be the girl whom I heard. Who wouldn't be fooled with my stop-and-then-go-and-stop-again tricks.

The cavern's upper end was bitter cold. One of our emergency ducts had opened up beside the entranceway, robbing the heat from the water and ground and trees. Already the pond was freezing, the ice clear and hard, very nearly flawless. I ran on its shore, squinting into the gloom, believing that at least the cliché, the falls, would have stopped flowing when the power failed. Not in an instant, no. But its reservoir was relatively small—Ula had shown me her plans—and for a glorious instant I was absolutely convinced that my escape was imminent.

What was that? From the gloom came an apparent wall of marble, white and thick and built where the cliché had been. *Frozen . . . the waterfall had frozen clear through . . . !*

I moaned, screamed, and slowed.

Beside the pond was one of the useless robots. I moved to it, my breath freezing against the ceramic skin, and with a few desperate tugs I managed to pry free one of its hands. The hand was meant for cutting, for chopping, and I held it like an axe, growling at my audience. "What did you think? That I'd just give up now?"

No answer. The only sounds were the falling of leaves and the occasional creaking pop as sap froze inside the sleeping trees.

I moved to the icy shelf at the base of the falls, shuffling to where I normally walked through, where the ice should be thinnest. Three times I swung, twice without force and the third blow hard and useless, the ice as tough as marble and more slippery. My axe slid sideways, twisting me. Then my boots moved, my balance lost, and I hit the icy shelf, slid, and fell again.

The pond caught me. The ice beneath gave with the impact, a slight but deep cracking sound lasting for an age. But I didn't fall through. And when I could breathe again, with pain, I stood and hobbled over to the shore, trying very hard not to give in.

"Is this what you did to the others?" I asked.

Silence.

"Is this how you treat lovers, Ula?"

A howl, almost close, sudden and very shrill.

A primeval thought came to me. I made myself approach the black jungle, scooping up leaves by the armful and building a substantial pile of them where I had sat with Provo, against the downed log. And I lit them and the log on fire with a second glowglobe, putting it on overload and stepping back and the globe detonating with a wet sizzle, the dried leaves exploding into a smoky red fire.

The odd sugars loved to burn, the flames hot and quick and delicious. They ignited the log within minutes, giving me a sense of security. The canopy didn't reach overhead. I made doubly sure that the surrounding ground had no leaves, no way for the fire to spread; then I set to work, armfuls of fresh leaves piled against the cliché, tamped them down with my boots until there was a small hill spilling onto the pond.

Heat versus ice.

Equations and estimates kept me focused, unafraid.

Then I felt ready, using the axe to knock loose a long splinter of burning log. I carried the cold end, shouting, "See? See? I'm not some idiot. I'm not staying in your trap, Ula!" I touched the leaf pile in a dozen places, then retreated, keeping at what felt like a safe distance but feeling waves regardless, dry and solid heat playing over me, almost nourishing me for the moment.

Those sugars were wonderfully potent. Almost explosive.

Ula must have planned to burn me alive, I kept thinking. She would have lit the leaf litter when it was deep enough . . . only I'd beaten her timetable, hadn't I?

"I'll file charges," I promised the red-lit trees. "You should have done a better job, my dear."

A sharp howl began, then abruptly stopped. It was as if a recording had been turned off in its middle.

Then came a crashing sound, and I turned to see a single chunk of softened ice breaking free of the cliché, crashing into my fire and throwing sparks in every direction. Watching the sparks, I felt worry and a sudden fatigue. *What's wrong?* My eyes lifted, maybe out of instinct, and I noticed a single platter-sized leaf still rising, glowing red and obviously different from the other leaves. It was burning slowly, almost patiently. It practically soared overhead. Just like a fire eagle, it rode a thermal . . . and didn't it resemble an eagle? A little bit? One species of tree among hundreds, and Ula must have designed it, and she must have seen that it was planted here—

—such an elaborate, overly complicated plan. Contrived and plainly artificial, I was thinking. Part of me felt superior and critical. Even when I knew the seriousness of everything, watching that leaf vanish into great blackness overhead . . . out of the thermal now, gliding off in some preplanned direction, no doubt . . . even then I felt remarkably unafraid, knowing that that leaf would surely reach the canopy somewhere, igniting hundreds of leaves and the sappy young branches . . . and part of me wanted nothing more than to take my student aside, arm around her shoulders, while I said, "Now listen. This is all very clever, and I'm sure it's cruel, but this is neither elegant nor artful and show me another way to do it. By tomorrow. That's your assignment, Ula. Will you do it for me, please?"

•

The forest caught fire.

I heard the fire before I saw the ruddy glow of it. It sounded like a grinding wind, strong and coming nearer; then came the crashing of softened ice, blocks and slush dropping onto my fire and choking it out completely.

I didn't have time or the concentration to build another fire.

Towering red flames were streaking through the cavern, first in the canopy and then lower, igniting whole trunks that would explode. I heard them, and I felt the detonations against my face and through my toes. The air itself began to change, tasting warm and sooty, ashes against my teeth and tongue. Transfixed, I stood in the clearing beside the pond, thick and twisting black columns of smoke rising, the ceiling lit red and the smoke pooling against it, forming an inverted lake full of swirling superheated gases.

Over the rumble and roar of the fire, I heard someone speaking, close and harsh . . . and after a few moments of hard concentration I realized it was my voice, senseless angry sounds bubbling out of me . . . and I clamped a hand over my mouth, fingers into a cheek and tears mixed with the stinking ash . . . I was crying . . . I had been crying for a very long while . . .

I would die here.

Always crying, I struggled with prosaic calculations. Calories from combustion; oxygen consumed; the relative toughness of human flesh. But my numbers collapsed, too much stress and too little time remaining. Part of the firestorm was coming back at me now, trunks burning and splitting open as the fiery sap boiled; but I wouldn't burn to death, I decided. Because what felt like a finger struck me on top of my head, in my hair, and I looked up just as a second gooey drop of water found me. It dripped between the fingers of my clamping hand, and I tasted it—smoke and ash mixed with a sharp, almost chemical aftertaste—

—melted ice from the faraway roof—

—unfrozen, ancient seawater.

The black lake of churning smoke was its deepest straight above me, and those first drops became multitudes, fat and forceful. Like rain, then harder. They hammered me to the ground, my head dropping and my hands held above it, shielding very little, and squinting eyes able to see the oncoming fire begin to slow, to drown.

I thought of the falls melting with this onslaught, but I couldn't stand, much less move. The mud under me seemed to suck, holding me in place. I was squarely beneath an enormous waterfall—no cliché—and I would have laughed, given the breath.

Funny, fun Ula.

Perhaps the largest waterfall in the Realm, I was thinking. For this moment, at least. And my mind's eye lent me a safe vantage point, flames and water struggling for the world. And destroying it too. And somewhere I realized that by now I had to be dead, that breathing had to be impossible, that I only believed I was breathing because death had to be a continuation of life, a set of habits maintained. What a lovely, even charming wonder. I felt quite calm, quite happy. Hearing the roar of water, aware of the soil and trees and rock itself being obliterated . . . my bones and pulverized meat mixed into the stew . . . and how sweet that I could retain my limbs, my face and mouth and heart, as a ghost, I thought. Touching myself in the noisy blackness, I found even my soaked jersey intact . . . no, not total blackness; there was a dim glow from above . . . and I began to sit upright, thinking like a ghost, wondering about my powers and wishing that my soul could lift now, lift and fly away.

But instead, with unghostly force, my head struck a solid surface.

Thunk.

I staggered, groaned, and reached out with both hands, discovering a blister of transparent hyperglass above me. Enclosing me. Larger than a coffin, but not by much . . . it must have been deployed at the last possible instant, air pumped in from below, seals designed to withstand this abuse . . . a safety mechanism not shown on any schematic, obviously . . . and I was alive, slippery wet and numb but undeniably organic . . .

. . . and unalone as well.

Rising from the mud beside me, visible in that thin cool light, was a naked form—artist; torturer; Nature Herself—who calmly and with great dignity wiped the mud from her eyes and grinning mouth. And she bent, the mouth to my ear, asking me over the great roar, "So what have you learned today, student?"

I couldn't speak, could barely think.

Opening my jersey, she kissed my bare chest. "The eight-legged howler was just noise. Just my little illusion."

Yet in my head it was real, even now.

"I would never intentionally hurt," she promised. "Not you, not anyone." I wanted to believe her.

"I always watched over you, Hann. I never blinked."

Thank you.

"I'm not cruel." A pause. "It's just—"

Yes?

"—I wanted to show you—"

What?

"—what? What have I shown you, darling?"

Squinting, I gazed up through the thick blister, the black water churning more slowly, cooling and calming itself. My mind became lucid, answers forming and my mouth opening and her anticipating the moment, her hand tasting of earth as it closed my mouth again.

☙

We lay quietly together, as if in a common grave.

For two days we waited, the water refreezing around us and neither of us speaking, the creaking of new ice fading into a perfect silence. A contemplative, enlightening silence. I built worlds in my head—great and beautiful and true, full of the frailties and powers of life—then came the gnawing and pounding of robots. Half-burned trees were jerked free and tossed aside. The ice itself was peeled away from the blister. I saw motions, then stars. Then a familiar stocky figure. Provo Lei peered in at us, the round face furious and elated in equal measures; and as he began to cut us free, in those last moments of solitude, I turned to Ula and finally spoke.

"You never wanted to terraform worlds," I blurted.

"Worlds are tiny," she said with contempt. Her liquid smile was lit by the cutting laser, and a green eye winked as she said, "Tell me, Hann. What do I care about?"

Something larger than worlds, I knew—

—and I understood, in an instant—

—but as I touched my head, ready to tell, Provo burst through the hyperglass and stole my chance. Suddenly Ula had changed, becoming the pouting little girl, her lower lip stuck out and a plaintive voice crying, "Oh, Father. I'm such a clumsy goof, Father. I'm sorry, so sorry. Will you ever forgive me? Please, please?"

Dawn Venus

G. DAVID NORDLEY

Like John Varley, Michael Swanwick, Stephen Baxter, Kim Stanley Robinson, and others, G. David Nordley is another writer who finds the solar system an exotic-enough setting for adventures just as it is, as he's demonstrated with stories of exploration and conflict on a grand scale, such as "Into the Miranda Rift," "Out of the Quiet Years," "Comet Gypsies," "Alice's Asteroid," "The Day of Their Coming," "Messengers of Chaos," and others; many of these stories make effective use of the latest data from the Voyager space probes, data that shows just how bizarre, complex, surprising, and mysterious a place our solar system really is.

After the successful terraforming of a planet takes place, what then? How do you populate your new world? The hair-raising thriller that follows takes us to a terra-formed Venus for a frantic land rush unlike any seen before in human history . . . one with stakes so high that almost any risk is acceptable, even ones that seem almost certainly fatal—like jumping out of an orbiting space station.

G. David Nordley is a retired Air Force officer and physicist who has become a frequent contributor to Analog *in the last couple of years, winning that magazine's Analytical Laboratory readers' poll in 1992 for his story "Poles Apart"; he also won the same award for his story "Into the Miranda Rift." He has also sold stories to* Asimov's Science Fiction, Tomorrow, Mindsparks, *and elsewhere. Although fairly prolific at short lengths, Nordley has yet to publish a novel, although he has several series in progress that could be worked up into novels without too much difficulty. Until then, you'll just have to look for him in the SF magazines, where he appears with pleasing frequency. Nordley lives in Sunnyvale, California.*

The road to Venus apparently led through people, Bik Wu thought as he struggled sideways against the crush of the crowd and vertically against the crush of gravity while strange odors, colorful costumes, and not-quite-lost languages assaulted his other senses. People. Kai was gone now—another man was her widower. But for Bik there had been no one else.

This must be the Earth immigrants lounge, he realized; the soft chairs promised to Mercury immigrants were nowhere to be seen. Nor was there any help; personal comm circuits were saturated. His bones ached with over twice his usual weight. Once on the elevator, he told himself, there would be a soft, form-fitting, reclining chair for the three-hundred-kilometer ride down to the surface. Until then, he just had to endure.

The Venus maglev interplanet port was swamped with late arrivals. Some media types were saying that the opening of the Devana Archipelago south of Beta Regio was the largest new land rush in the history of the human race. Judged by the average standards of big project management, Bik figured that it was probably a textbook success. But from his worm's-eye viewpoint in the middle of this mob, it looked like a fiasco. Nevertheless, after six decades of living in domes with permafrost below and vacuum above, Bik was going to find some elbow room down there.

Maybe enough to show the custody board that he cared enough to have Junior.

Gravity or no, he was a bigger and stronger man than average, so he bulled his way, with apologies left and right, to the elevator booking counter and slapped his palm on the reader.

"Mercury, Idaho?" The transport receptionist smiled when her local cybe displayed his ID. A big woman with a trace of East Asian heritage in her face, or her smile, she was full of a cheerfulness that didn't match his mood. Where were the robots when you *wanted* one? But around here it seemed that any job that could be done by a human was being done by a human. Service was in style. He shook his head. So, apparently, were madhouses.

"No, no," he groaned. "That's a Mercury *eye dee* number. Mercury the planet. Chao Meng-Fu Dome."

She raised an eyebrow. "You're in the wrong lounge."

"I've figured that out," he said with forced evenness, "but this is where they sent me. I'd like a reservation to the surface, surface transportation to Port Tannhauser and a room when I get there."

Only eighteen hundred kilometers to go! Port Venus was on the Circumplanetary Maglev Railroad, a planet-girding ring of frictionless magnetic levitation railways held above the atmosphere by a dozen trains of mass circulating at greater than orbital velocity. Built to remove the ancient carbon dioxide atmosphere and increase the spin of the planet, the CMR was one of the wonders of the solar system—but it was also a transportation bottleneck.

The receptionist stared at the screen, looked at seating charts, and grinned. "I'm surprised you're still standing. In fact, I'm surprised to see *any* immigrants from Mercury. Worked out a bit?"

"Yes." He shrugged, not wanting to admit his misery. "Some. I would have had more time on the regular transport, but I got pulled back for some unnecessary work at New Loki. I got a friend to get me on the express, so here I am. Their centrifuge time was limited, but I'm in reasonable shape."

Reasonable? He was maybe ten kilos over his theoretical optimum, and it showed more here than on Mercury. Four days in a centrifuge hadn't done much more than retain his reflexes from Mercury's gravity. On the plus side, he told himself, his strength was okay, his bone mass was fine and thirty laps a day in the dome pool gave him an underlying endurance on which he could draw. "I can do this."

The receptionist shook her head, her long jet-black hair lending a semblance of femininity to a well-muscled, almost masculine, figure. Bik wondered if she might be a swimmer or maybe a climber.

"Grab," she said, "that there's going to be a lot of standing around. There are only so many elevators, we have to be fair, and there are—" She got the distant look that people get when they link with the cybersystem for some detail they don't have immediately. Born with a radio interface gene mod, probably. He shuddered—what if she ever *wanted* to be out of touch? "—uh, twelve thousand six hundred and fifty-seven would-be homesteaders in port as we speak."

Bik rolled his eyes up.

She grinned. "Including sixteen from the planet Mercury! So you're not the only one."

"Fine," Bik sighed. "Now, when can I get on an elevator car down?"

Once down he would have to catch an air shuttle fifteen hundred kilometers northeast to Port Tannhauser, where the land rush was being staged. Once there, he could reserve a parcel. Then all he would have to do was to get there within twenty-four hours, universal time—by the local dawn of Venus's leisurely day. The planet, of course, was spinning like a top compared to what it used to be—once about every fifty days, retrograde, making for thirty days from sun to sun when you included its orbital motion. Before the CMR, it had taken 243 days for Venus to turn under the stars.

Bik kept going through new world things in his mind; so much history, so much background, so many different ways of doing things, so many hoops to jump through, so little time to jump. The way things were going, every boat and aircraft for a thousand kilometers around would be taken by the time he arrived. Then he'd have to try to pick something within walking distance, which, for his already-aching Mercurian feet, wasn't very far.

Thousands of kilometers. Chao Meng-Fu was hardly 150 kilometers across, and *it* looked huge.

"The elevators are pretty crowded," the attendant reminded him. "It should ease up in a couple of hours."

"Land-parcel registration is first-come, first-serve. I just want to have a fair chance." He sighed. "I did everything I was supposed to do. Isn't there any faster way down?"

She pursed her lips and grinned mischievously. "Do you like to walk the edge? Take risks?"

"Citizen, I spent half a decade supervising the Chao Meng-Fu construction job, outside. Something goes wrong outside on Mercury's south pole and you can freeze your feet and boil your head. Simultaneously." Bik grinned. He exaggerated a little, but he thought it would impress her.

Impress her? His therapist might consider that progress, Bik thought. It had been a while since he cared about what any woman except Kai had thought of him.

The receptionist smiled. Damn if she hadn't gotten his mind off his aching feet. "The name's Suwon and *you* can take a flying leap."

Another tease, of course. When would he learn? "Sorry, I didn't mean to bother you."

She laughed at his devastated expression. "No, I meant literally. Grab this; a personal evac unit from this far up has enough cross range, in theory, to get you to Port Tannhauser if you jump down line a ways. They have recreational versions, and I've used them a couple of times with a boyfriend from farther down the line. The cybes don't like it, but screw them. It's my life. I'll show you the ropes—if you've got the nerves."

He shook his head. He'd been had; he couldn't read people and had misread her playfulness for something more serious. She'd worked the boy-friend in smoothly, too—a nice warn-off.

A neat woman, he had to admit, and she probably meant to help, but jumping off a three-hundred-kilometer-high railroad wasn't in his plans. "That's a last resort. Let's try to get me on the tube first."

She nodded and looked off in space for a moment again. "I can get you on the ten-hundred with an earlier standby on the oh-three, standing room only."

His bones, muscles, ligaments, and cartilage screamed at him, but he grimaced and said, "I'll take it. Look, if there's any way you can move me up, it's important."

She looked a question at him.

His first thought was that his problems were none of her business, but his aching body had put him in need of some sympathy, so he decided to chance telling her.

"It's about my kid. His mother just died, and I'm in a custody fight with her second husband. If I can get a small island, or a cut of a large one, that'll help me in my custody case. I've got a board to impress and I think they'll think this would be a good place to raise a kid, understand?"

The grin faded and she pursed her lips. "I'll do what I can. Meanwhile, I've cleared your prints for the lounge for low-gravity-world immigrants. They have plenty of recliners. Down the corridor to your left, door RS-3."

He might get to like the woman, he decided, as he waved a goodbye and headed for relief.

●

The waiting list for the oh-three-hundred elevator turned out to have more names on it than the elevator cab had seats. He checked registration statistics. There were some ten thousand people down at Port Tannhauser already and only about fifteen thousand parcels, distributed among the several hundred islands. Pickings were getting thin.

The place was beautiful. The archipelago just south of the city was a drowned mountain range less than a century old. Its shorelines still expanded with every wave striking higher or lower as the gentle solar tide completed its monthly cycle. Its vids sparkled with dark green sensuous surf-flecked beaches and shiny green palms punctuated with bright birds and flowers.

Kai would have loved it, if she'd only stuck with him long enough to see it, Bik thought. See, Kai, I *do* have some romance in my soul.

Staring at the brightly colored wall above the other low-gee couch sitters, Bik's memory went back to their wedding under the stars at Mercury's south pole. Then fast-forward to the birth of their son, to weekend visits during the months of separation on the New Loki project, to when Kai told him she'd fallen in love with a starship officer from Ceres named Thor Wendt, was going off with him and was taking Bikki with her.

What had he done wrong? What could he have done differently? As always there were no answers.

Hurt as he had been, he'd never stopped loving Kai—she had just been too beautiful, too bright and vivacious for him to keep up with. He still thought himself fortunate to have had those few years with her. He had to admit he'd been a practical, safe, duty-bound drag on her free spirit.

She'd told Bik that she and Thor wanted Bikki to bond with his new father, and so didn't want any real-time interaction between Bik and the kid for now. Bik had joint custody, and could have tried to enjoin her from doing that, or sued, for custody himself. But Mercurian courts generally favored two-parent families in such cases. The lawyer he consulted said it would have been a waste of time.

He sent presents and letters out to the belt for birthdays and New Year's and got receipts, but lightspeed delays made two-way contact difficult, and having to talk to Kai in the process made it even more so. There had never been any acknowledgment. Once he'd gotten a fax of a crayon Father's Day card from the school, but that had been all in five years. He didn't hold it against Junior: kids his age didn't understand that kind of thing. Anyway, his work on New Loki's three-million-person dome at the Mercurian north pole had made the years go by quickly.

Bik remembered the call. It came from Ceres a year ago. Some suicidal Nihilists had wanted to make a statement about robotics, technology, and what they felt was the general meaningless direction of civilization. That was fine with Bik as long as they wrote their propaganda in their own blood; but their tactics had gotten twisted somehow into rationalizing general mayhem—and Kai had been in the wrong place at the wrong time.

A quiet, sincere gentleman had called to tell him that Thor and "Ted Wendt" had survived a bomb at Ceres Starport, but his ex-wife had not. Until then he had hoped that, somehow, Wendt would go and they would be together again. Hope died with Kai.

Bik had hesitated in filing for custody. Thor Wendt considered the boy his own now; he had raised Junior for five of the boy's eight years, and felt that Kalinda station in the Kruger 60 system would be a safer place for him. But finally Bik had called legal services. Junior was his flesh and blood, and a living memory of Kai and those few glorious years that he'd shared with her.

It turned out that Thor was well connected in the shady cash world, and had gotten an effective advocate. What it was now down to was that Thor's starship would leave in three months, and Bik's government-supplied lawyer had been blunt. Wendt was vulnerable, but just what did Bik have to offer a child beyond a genetic relationship? A sterile apartment and day care while Bik was away being a superfluous supervisor of construction robots smarter than he was?

A tone brought him out of his musings; the oh-three-hundred elevator had departed without taking any standbys. A glance at the overhead showed him the oh-four-hundred didn't look much better. Stand-by hopefuls were to check in with the attendants.

The original receptionist had said a personal evac unit might reach Port Tannhauser directly from up here. Not making any internal commitment just yet, Bik decided to investigate how a person would get one. Did people really do that for sport? He pulled out his intellicard and asked it to get central data.

◆

Bik pursed his lips and stared at the single glass eye in the wall behind the sport-jumping concession counter. "Lessons?" He hadn't anticipated that kind of delay.

"The sport units are made for manual operation; that's the sport of it!" the cyberservant answered in clear standard English as its Waldos handed Bik a heavy bag of gear. "But it is highly advisable that you go through a virtual simulation and pass the evaluation."

"Highly advisable?"

"You won't be allowed outside the airlock otherwise, I'm afraid. Now let's go over the equipment inventory. Aerobrake sled?"

Bik opened the duffelbag and shook his head, "I don't—"

"It's the heavy transparent pouch," a new, but somehow familiar, voice informed him. He spun around and saw the elevator attendant. Out of the uniform and in a skintight vacuum suit with bright diagonal slashes, she looked—not beautiful, he decided, but, well, formidable. "You strap it on your front side and inflate it on the way down. You steer by shifting your body. When you get subsonic, you can pop the tross wing—that's for alba-tross—and glide forever."

"Uh, thanks. . . ."

She laughed. "Suwon. From the elevator. Look, I said I'd do what I could. I figured I'd find you here; you looked like a guy on a mission. Let's go through the rest of this stuff."

It took them the better part of an hour. In addition to the tross wing for long-range gliding, there was an emergency parasail that weighed less than a hundred grams, fluorescent dyes and beacon, a harness that could really chafe if you didn't put it on just right, and various techniques for putting everything on and then getting at all of it.

Then there was the simulator, a virtual-reality shell with a harness sus-pended inside. Despite Suwon talking him through it, he burnt up the first time down, stalled to subsonic way too early the second time, and didn't get the range the third time. On the fourth run he had a survivable burn-through and hit it more or less right on his fifth run.

It was oh-eight-hundred, and he had to register by sixteen-hundred.

"Well, thanks," he told her. "I'm going to give it a try."

"You're going to kill yourself—if not by burning up, by dropping in the ocean so far from anywhere that you'll drown before anything can get to you."

She didn't understand.

"Suwon, I want you to understand, uh, 'grab onto' this. There's a great big hole inside me where there used to be a wife and a son. If there's a chance to get some of that back, I'll take it. And if not, well, a simple clean death would be a welcome end to all of this."

"Crap. I'm coming with you."

"Huh?" Bik stared at her. Why was she trying to become part of his life? Painful memories extinguished a flicker of biological excitement; the last thing he wanted now was another woman in his life. But he couldn't just tell her to get lost, not after all the help she'd given him and not when time was running out. "This is my problem," he said, finally. "I just met you; why should you care?"

She stared back at him and pursed her lips again, as if she were determined not to let another word out until she'd thought it carefully through. "A fair question. You're on a mission, doing something other than just trying to amuse yourself. That's the most excitement I've run across in years. I guess I find that attractive. There's something else. Venus Surface Commission workers aren't eligible for the land rush. The way around that is to team up with someone who is—easier said than done."

"Team up?"

"Eligible partners can transfer a portion of their share to others after fifty years, or enter a joint tenancy arrangement. . . ."

Bik held up his hand. "Okay. Thirty percent of the land if you get me there."

Suwon smiled and shook her head. "Fifty."

Damn, she was easy to look at, once you got used to muscles on a woman. Especially when she smiled. Bik finally nodded to her; he was low on options. "Okay, fifty percent." Bik wasn't a haggler—he'd let Kai have all his Chao property just to avoid fighting her for it. "Let's go, then. What about your boyfriend?"

"He got careless on a jump about a month ago. Burned in. Five hundred and twenty years old and he burned in on a jump." Suwon shrugged her shoulders, but it was clear that she had been hurt.

Maybe she did understand. Bik thought about sympathy, rebound logic, unknown backgrounds, and all the rest of the dangerous stuff and cast it aside mentally. This acquaintance, relationship, whatever it became, would be a calculated risk, one that he was walking into with his eyes open.

"Sorry to hear that." He put his hand on hers, and found it was a muscular, callused, well-used hand that went with the rest of its owner's body. He gave it a firm squeeze and let go.

She gave him a lopsided smile. Clearly, Suwon's approach to a setback was to challenge her fears and throw herself right back at it, immediately, passionately. Without another word, she checked out a personal evacuation unit and inspected it. Then they were ready.

◄►

They emerged from the elevator terminal onto a maintenance balcony with a waffle grid floor and a severe functional guardrail. The view stunned Bik. The CMR was a fairyland forest of open trusses made of gray composite beams that somehow became shiny as they seemed to merge into a single ribbon toward the distant horizon. Occasionally a car on one of the upper tracks would silently flash by, pressed upward to the overhead rails by the centrifugal force from its higher-than-orbital velocity. Every so often a track would lift out like a stray fiber in a paintbrush, straightening to a zero-gravity trajectory and ending abruptly to wait for an outbound maglev spacecraft.

There were still enough traces of atmosphere here to make the noses of the escaping cars glow as they left these tracks on trajectories leading to the rest of the solar system.

The wide gray band of the CMR railbed dwarfed the elevator tower that helped tether it to the planet. The tower quickly shrank to a barely discernible thread under their perch that connected to a small island that was just barely visible in a vast blue-black sea. There was a trace of a blue-green land mass on the edge of their northern horizon, and a scattering of islands, but these were minor details of a vast cloud-flecked ocean, that, through some trick of perspective, seemed like a concave bowl.

"Chao looks like that, from the dome top, except the water/land ratio is reversed. The dome top's only fifty kilometers up, but you can't tell the scale."

"Surprised you didn't get a piece of that."

"I did. I let her have it, hoping that maybe she'd change her mind. I let her have everything."

"Too proud to fight, huh?" Suwon turned her gold-plated helmet face toward him, and he saw himself against the rising filtered sun, in miniature.

"Something like that." The sun had just risen below them and would take two weeks to reach local noon. Pride? Bik smiled; once Venus had taken the better part of a year to turn on its axis, but a millennium of launching out carbon dioxide frozen from the atmosphere, and volcanic sediment scraped from the low basaltic plains, and two centuries of bringing water in had given it a rotational period of about an Earth month. Human beings and their machines had done that, and Bik couldn't help feeling a little pride. The crust was still adjusting through an abundance of volcanoes and quakes that would be part of Venusian life for something like ten million years, according to most projections. Below, they built for it.

The sun was tiny by Bik's Mercurian standards, and seemed to sparkle inside a broad, off-center ring of diffuse light. This, he realized, was the twenty-four-million-meter sunshield. His engineering imagination saw the vast structure balance gravity with constantly adjusted photon pressure the Lagrange point between Venus and the sun. A sun-sieve now, it let half the light get through to Venus and converted the other half to energy for starship ports and antimatter factories. His eyes saw a ghostly, sparkling disk, visibly larger and nearer than the sun, with edges that caught and reflected light in a grazing incidence that created the effect of the bright ring.

"Finished sightseeing?" Suwon asked, gently.

"I can see why you like living up here."

She laughed. "You should see a gigaton water freighter match cradle vee on the landing track; that's the dark band in the middle. It lets you grab just how astro this operation is. Magnificent! Nothing due in today, though. Let's check the equipment one more time."

Bik did, then checked Suwon's gear as she checked his.

"Ready. Now, Bik," she continued in a low, stagily seductive voice, "do you ever have fantasies of sacrificing yourself? Being a human bomb for some cause? Letting a lover kill you? Falling on your sword? Taking Joan of Arc's place at the stake?"

Bik couldn't see her eyes, but he imagined that they glowed. Yes, of course he had, but he couldn't bring himself to say so; it wasn't the sort of thing one shared in Mercurian society. On an airless planet, suicides sometimes took others with them, and even to fantasize about it where people could hear got a lot more attention than one wanted. Bik shivered.

"Can't admit it, can you? Well, they're normal. Everyone has them, and someday, when I've had enough of this immortal body that our genetic engineers have given me, I think I'm going to do this dive without any equipment. Oh, maybe a pressure suit so I can experience a little more of it—the burning part for instance—but nothing else. I'll just run out and throw myself off and let nature take its course. End my life as a shooting star!"

She straddled the rail, reached and grabbed his hand and laughed demonically. "Like I said, we all have these fantasies . . . and the time to indulge them is now! Come on!"

Almost in a trance, he swung one leg over the rail and then the other and stood on his toes hanging onto the rail, three hundred kilometers above the sea.

Suwon's chest rose and fell with each excited breath. "Now," she shouted, "push off and *die!*" Then she did it, with a bloodcurdling yell, falling rapidly away below him.

Bik craned his neck to see her, and in doing so started to slip. What the hell? Go, something inside said, *do it!* He pushed hard and was in free fall; the CMR dwindled to a dark ribbon far above him, the Devana Sea waited below. Soon he seemed to stop moving; there was nothing still near enough by which to judge his falling. Suwon's manic laughter filled his helmet. Finally she stopped.

"One hundred fifty kilometers, buddy. Time to get serious."

Below him, a crystalline lady slipper bloomed, tumbling and glinting in the sun. Bik remembered the sled cord and found it. There *was* a temptation not to pull it, to delay a little, to enjoy zero gravity and flirt with that ecstasy of self-destruction. He was beginning to get warm.

"Pull the red ring, Bik!" Suwon shouted. He jerked it open automatically, and quickly found himself surrounded by a huge, triangular, transparent pillow. It pressed against him gently in the tenuous slipstream, turning and righting itself so that he lay prone. It began to vibrate slightly as the pressure gradually began to increase, and he could hear a low, eerie moan.

"I'm over here," Suwon called. "Shift your weight left."

He leaned left, and the transparent lifting body began a long, steady curve in that direction. "I'm going to wiggle a little," Suwon said. "Do you see me?"

Bik scanned ahead, right and left, and saw nothing.

"You're below me a bit, but right behind me now. Shift your weight right a bit, then steady."

He did it. "Okay."

"Now look up."

Far, far ahead of him in the vast black distance above the thin glowing band of atmosphere, he caught a sparkle. He stared at it for several seconds, then began to pick out the transparent envelope and the tiny white figure inside. The front of the envelope had begun to glow.

"I found you."

"Good. Now we're going to have to do things together as much as possible. We're building up a fair amount of northward velocity, but we need more, so I'm going to dive a bit. Follow me by shifting your weight forward, but be ready to shift back when I do. We don't want to get too hot."

"Okay."

She started to pull ahead, and he pulled himself forward on the handholds. He shot forward, passing her underneath. In a near panic, he pushed himself back again.

"Whoa. Hold it right there. I'll catch up," she said, and scooted smoothly back into view above and in front of him. "Now edge forward just a bit. There. Hold that."

He was back at full weight again and there was a definite, diffuse glow in front of him.

"Your boyfriend. Are you sure it was an accident?"

Silence.

He waited.

Finally she answered, in measured tones. "No. But I think so; I mean there was no note to grab or anything. That's a pretty drastic way of breaking up and I don't think I'm that scary. But you can never be sure with people. Let's change the subject, huh?"

It really wasn't any of his business. "This must be spectacular at night," he finally remarked.

"Yeah. When I go, it'll be at night. I'll become a comet, a Valkyrie pyre in the sky. It'll burn the guilt right out of me."

"You sound like you're looking forward to it."

"I am . . ." She laughed. ". . . in a thousand years or so. The anticipation will keep me going. Right now, we're down to thirty kilometers and it's time to back off a bit. Edge back just a little, bring your nose up. We've got another thousand klicks to go. Okay. Now a little more. Okay."

"Optimum glide path?" he asked. He knew she was linked to the terminal computer and had everything calculated to the nth degree, but he wanted the reassurance. The ocean was very big and blue below him.

"Feels right," she responded. "I think we hit it pretty good."

"What's the range projection?" he inquired.

"Range projection?" She laughed. "We just go as far as we can. Never tried to make Beta Regio from the elevator head before."

He began to have a sinking feeling. "What do the cybes say?"

"Cybes? Grab this, Bik. We're out of contact—on our own. These radios are only good for a few kilometers unless we're talking to a big directional antenna. Frequency management. This is strictly by feel from here on; that's the fun of it. Besides, the last few hundred kilometers all depend on air currents, and that's weather. No telling. Hold on there, you're shifting your weight. Shift forward again, just a little and catch up. You really have to watch body position."

Bik got Suwon in sight again and kept her there. Silently. Any fantasies about casting himself into oblivion were long ago and far away. Now, he was very, very scared. And excited—he understood why people did this—to challenge real danger, with their own muscles, reflexes, and brains, without relying on some cybernetic safety net. It would be a great feeling, if you survived. And maybe, even, in the last moments, if you didn't.

"Bik, do you know an asshole by the name of Deccar Brunt?"

A chill colder than anything his suit could fix went through Bik. "Too well. He's a lawyer working for the space jock that took Kai—my ex. Brunt is hellishly well connected and thinks that I'm some kind of monster. He's determined to keep Junior away from me. How'd you run into him?"

"He came asking questions after I put you in the computer for an elevator cab reservation. I'd say he didn't want you to get down to the surface—thought I was working too hard on your behalf. You say you had problems getting on the transport here in the first place?"

Of course, Bik thought. "Yes. What did he offer?"

"He hinted that he could do things for me if I didn't help you. Not clearly enough for me to hand him to the cybes, but clearly enough. Look, is there money involved in this?" Her voice showed she shared his contempt for the stuff, Bik thought. With robot factories all through the solar system, manufactured things were either free or not allowed. Scarce necessities, such as habitable land or electromagnetic frequencies, were allocated fairly by need or lot. Money, he felt, was a game for people who wanted things they'd be better off without, but for which they were willing to trade.

"Kai liked having the stuff. She'd trade, uh, favors, for it. It was a game to her—but I think that's how she met Thor." It was appropriate, in a way—as legend went, the underground "economy" had started within months of the official elimination of money when some enterprising prostitute had started issuing promissory notes. Since money proved impossible to repress and didn't threaten anyone's welfare, the governments, cybes, and Bik generally ignored it. When he could.

Bik's sled started to vibrate and hum with ever-increasing loudness, matching his mood. Why, Kai? "Why?"

"Going transsonic. Just stay centered and ride through; you're inherently stable. Bik, you put up with all that?" She meant Kai's adventures, he realized—smiling at the metaphorical coincidence.

"I didn't own her, I was away a lot, and up until she left, things were fine, uh, more than fine."

"Sounds like a good actress. So she had money, and your rights in that dome on Mercury, and Bikki. Now this Thor has it all and wants to keep it all. Some big male thing with him, I bet. But how the hell can he threaten me?"

Bik felt miserable. "He's got an ethics problem, I think. Smart, competent, used to having his own way. Big stud, except he's never been given a repro permit. As for threats, all it takes is having someone on a board or having some authority that wants something money can buy. Maybe one of your bosses."

"Crap." The bitterness in Suwon's voice was understandable; real jobs were scarce and hers was in jeopardy. "Well, I didn't listen to it. Just made me want to help you. Hey, grab on, we're subsonic, down to thirty kilometers, beginning to lose lift. Time to pop the wings. Orange ring, on three. Ready?"

"Ready."

"One . . . two . . . Now."

He pulled and his translucent white wings, astoundingly long and thin, rolled out of his backpack to the sides and a long, stiff tube with a triangular duct canard shot out in front of him, bent alarmingly, and began to vibrate like a bassoon reed.

"What—" He was really shaking. The sims hadn't been like this.

"Bistable polymorphon. Sometimes takes a second to lock into its deployed shape. Don't worry, you look good."

As if at Suwon's command, the loud hum quickly softened to a gentle whoosh as he accelerated upward with breathtaking force. He remembered to shift forward to lower his angle of attack before he lost too much air speed, and saw the canard structure bend down slightly as he did it; its smart materials almost anticipated what he wanted to do. When he got himself straightened out, he searched for Suwon.

"I'm pretty far ahead and above you," she called out, as if reading his mind. "Deflate your lifting body now. It will remember its folds and repack itself. That will cut your drag."

"How?" he asked.

"Green ring on your chest; Venturi suction tube. Keep pulling until it's in."

He did so, and felt his airspeed increase as the transparent envelope collapsed into a stiff aerodynamic sled. When he caught up to Suwon, she did the same and made an S-turn to take station off his right wing.

"We're a couple of kilometers lower than I'd like to be for the range we need, but with some luck on the air currents, we'll make it. Just now, you need to practice gliding. We're heading for the shadow line."

By fifteen hundred, they'd passed into night. Earth and its L1 sunshield lit the sky like a close pair of distant arc lights, glinting off waves that were getting entirely too close. But they had reached the archipelago; here and there a single light or campfire showed where people had already spread to the islands.

Suwon caught an updraft on the windward side of a ghostly volcanic island and slipped off to the east to avoid the trailing downdraft. The couple of kilometers they gained helped them almost reach the next island, but that was all. It was a long, faint green wall on the horizon, with what looked to be a geodesic dome glowing from inside lights on the east end.

"We're going in," Suwon said. "Reinflate your entry sled."

"Huh?"

"Now. It'll float. Your wings are buoyant, too, and will help keep you upright. Watch me." She shot ahead of him in a shallow dive, squandering her remaining energy.

"I flare—" She seemed to hang in the air over the dark sparkling waves like some ghostly albatross. "—inflate and drop in. Now you do it. Use the red ring."

He'd gotten used to following her instructions and did it, but it was easier watched than done. Bik stalled before he got the sled inflated again, dropped through the waves and popped up again with water spilling from the top of the sled. It was embarrassing, but since he was still in his vacuum suit, he didn't get wet. The water was quite warm.

"You all right?" Suwon called. Her voice seemed tinny and distant, and it took him a couple of seconds to realize that he was hearing her acoustically, instead of on radio. He looked around and found her helmet flashing about thirty meters to his left; their wingtip beacons were almost touching.

He opened his faceplate and took a deep breath of sea air. Childhood memories. He'd been five when his father had taken him on a walk by the sea near their home in Victoria, B.C., and told him that, sometimes, people can't live together anymore, and that he would be going away. Did Bik know the way home? Bik had nodded yes. His father had nodded gravely, turned, and walked away. Forever.

"Bik?"

"All right physically. Feeling a little silly and disappointed. I suppose it was worth the shot. Great fun, anyway. Haven't smelled the sea since I was a kid."

"You've still got a couple of hours to register."

"But we've got to be a couple of hundred kilometers short of Port Tann-hauser."

"There's a homesite on this island in front of us."

"The dome?"

"You grabbed it. That's Mabel Beautaux's place; Mabel and I go way back."

"I thought this wasn't open to settlement yet."

"It's an old terraforming station; she's been squatting since oxygen hit fifteen percent. She probably got to be first in line to register it when they opened up."

"Does she have transportation?"

"Float plane—she'll be out to pick us up in a bit."

"Huh?"

Suwon pointed to her head and smiled. "My brain is is part radio, re-member? We're in range."

"You knew all along; you were just letting me suffer!"

Suwon laughed and Bik reached down to try to splash her, but he almost fell out of his makeshift raft and found himself teetering on his stomach, getting his face wet with every wave. The situation was so ridiculous that when he finally wriggled himself back to safety, he had to laugh too.

They were both laughing when the graceful W-shaped aircraft settled into the waves beside them.

Mabel Beautaux turned out to be a tiny, almost elfin, woman with a discernible African heritage and soft birdlike voice. She seemed to have stopped growing in her early teens, but her archaic name made Bik think she might go back to the early days of the terraforming project.

He was not, however, quite prepared for how *far* back she went. As they tied the lines of the aircraft to a simple wooden dock, he asked when she was born.

"In 1993. I was 135 when the geriatric retrovirus came along; there are only a couple of dozen others that are older. Most of my life, I've been a farmer; in Alabama the first century or so, Peary dome on Luna after I got my treatment and degree, then I came here and helped manage the bioform-ing project, from right after they let the sun back through, 'bout two hundred years ago.

"What a ride that was! Storms and quakes! Populations of this, that, and the other critter breeding out of control! I worked on fertility retroviruses, and we had a devil of a time playing God, I tell you." She grinned and shrugged her shoulders. "Now everything's so settled down they can start giving the land away to whoever comes along. But that's why we did it, isn't it? So there!" She hitched the plane's nose line to a dock cleat. "You're dealing with a living fossil in her third millennium!"

"A very beautiful one," Bik gushed, clumsy with awe.

"Oh? Well, now, gravity is good for the bones, and I do a fair amount of physical work around here." She waved a hand at a tidy wood building next to the geodesic dome station building and a clear field surrounded by palms and eucalyptus. There were three—cows. Not obviously penned, just standing there munching grass. One of them looked at him suspiciously just as Mabel asked, "Got any idea of where you two want to settle?"

"We're not . . ." Bik stammered. Would a cow charge, like in a bullfight? Was there something he should do, or shouldn't? He wasn't wearing red. "I mean we just met today. Business arrangement."

"Oh? Well, let's see what's available for you to claim. I'll slice some chicken squash, and if you'll grab a few of those tomatoes, Suwon, we can have some sandwiches while we figure it out. We can wash that down with some of my peach wine and then I'll fly you over to Port Tannhauser to register."

Suwon gave Mabel a hug and went to work. Bik, who'd never seen a meal prepared, let alone by human hands, stood around helpless and fascinated. After a feast that somehow tasted better than any home appliance or restaurant had ever given him, Mabel's computer started to print the latest claim maps. With the maps, however, came a news item that gave Mabel a hard frown.

"You didn't tell me they fired you, Suwon."

"What!" Suwon was clearly shocked.

"Says here that the settlement board is taking under advisement the status of people who get transportation outside normal channels and those who aid them. Mentions you in particular, Bik—and cites you for showing unprofessional favoritism, Suwon."

"But that's nonsense," Suwon protested. "And anyone with guts enough can dive from the CMR! Nothing wrong with that. What do the cybes say?"

Mabel held up her hand for a moment and concentrated.

"They say no settlement rules were broken, but fairness issues are a human judgment call." Her brow wrinkled. "By the time they get a committee to debate that, it will be too late even if you win! I'd say someone clever is out to get you, Bik. But why you, Suwon?"

"I was warned." Suwon shook her head, more angry than afraid. "By a lawyer working for someone trying to keep Bik from getting his kid back. *He* tried to bribe *me*! Mabel, this is outrageous."

Mabel was muttering under her breath.

No, Bik realized, she was subvocalizing to another built-in radio link.

She smiled at Bik's stare. "This old body's been through so many updates, what was one more? When Suwon showed me her radio a few years back, well, I had to have one, too. Comes in handy when your hands are busy milking cows!" She didn't quite giggle, but she was clearly amused by her joke. "Now, I've been around a while and I know a few people too. I've got them injuncted by the cybes from doing anything worse until after the rush. Anything legal, that is. Let's look at the map. You get three choices. Let's see what you want."

The intelliprint was linked and the colors on the map of the archipelago changed as they watched, white areas growing pink as they filled with tiny red rectangles. The red signified a claimed parcel.

"Everything near Port Tannhauser has been grabbed," Suwon observed.

"Then we'd best get over there." Mabel raised an eyebrow. "But first, let's look at this area."

She put her finger on the east end of the archipelago and the map expanded in scale to reveal a dozen tiny islands, all white. "Here's where we are now." Mabel's island was the first offshore peak of the range running south from Port Tannhauser, separated from the mainland of Beta Regio by a narrow strait. She moved her finger west toward Asteria Regio. "A polar current comes down this way and wells up between Beta and Asteria." She grinned at them. "Some of it gets over to us, bringing some fog. But the effects are much more pronounced over there. There'll be good fishing and lots of moisture near the coast with a north wind, but clear and sunny when it comes the other way." She pointed to a small group of numbered islands. "Any of these 12-300's should do."

Bik looked at his "partner" and Suwon nodded.

"Let's go, then," he said.

➤

Port Tannhauser was a controlled riot, its sleepy streets filled with people. They had to anchor Mabel's seaplane well out in the harbor and raft in. Fortunately, once the cybes confirmed that they were physically present, they were eligible to register their choices at a public terminal.

Just in time, it turned out. There were still a couple of hours to go for registration, but when they unfolded the map, the entire area was red with claimants except for a pink fringe that included the western islands.

"We'll see the sights, have dinner at the Crab House and fly back to spend the night at my place, and fly out there early next morning."

"Uh," Bik asked, "why not just go there directly? Your place is in the opposite direction. All I have to do is touch down and leave an occupancy marker. Then you could leave me at the air terminal on the way back. I wouldn't have to impose."

Suwon looked at the ground, her lips tight. Did she, Bik wondered, have something else in mind for the night? Did she think he was out of line for suggesting something other than what Mabel had suggested? Was she just momentarily tired? Damn his inability to read people—the cybes should outlaw nonverbal communication. But, he thought ruefully, any experienced cybe could probably do better than he did. Kai had complained, gently at first, then with increasing sarcasm and severity, about his lack of sensitivity to her needs. She'd had a point—something always seemed to be going on among other people, some form of communication, that excluded him. But he couldn't help it; all he had to go on, really, was what people's words meant; the rest was just too uncertain.

"I have to get back too," Mabel declared, and smiled at him. "Don't forget, I have to claim my place as well. I was allowed to preregister the claim, but that's all."

"Oh," Bik responded, relieved to have some clear priority, "in that case, I look forward to it."

Suwon looked up and smiled at him. He returned an embarrassed grin, still uncertain.

On the way back from registration, they visited a small museum in the northern section of Port Tannhauser, an easy hike up from the harbor on the randomly corrugated fused sand walkway. The buildings along the way were preciously eclectic, many showing an old German influence to be sure, but really products of their owners' fantasies. The exterior of the museum itself was carefully authentic, and wouldn't have been out of place in sixteenth-century Heidelberg.

Inside, Bik, Suwon, and Mabel browsed through holographic dioramas of Port Tannhauser during the various stages of the terraforming project. The first showed the hellish original surface, and almost glowed. Then came a dark fairyland of carbon dioxide snow. This was followed by a glacier being eaten away by massive excavators on the edge of a starlit liquid nitrogen sea with the arc of the CMR on the horizon. Then came a dramatic stormswept boiling-nitrogen seascape lit by the first rays of the sun allowed through the sunshield. The sight made him shiver. It was followed by a dry desert overlooking a deep empty basin speckled with mining robots. There was another, gentler, storm scene from early in the forty years of rain, showing the half-filled basins and massive waterfalls. Then finally a fuzzy, meadowlike shore covered with the first bioforming grasses.

There were artifacts as well, ranging from a broken pair of recreational skis used by scientists monitoring the carbon-dioxide snowfall eight hundred years ago, to a comet shepherd child's duck. That had somehow survived the entry and breakup of a water shipment to be discovered floating on the Port Tannhauser beach. It sat on the museum shelf with a picture of its former owner, now living on a ring colony in the Kuiper belt of the Kruger 60 system.

Bik, who had only been looking for a home to share with his son, left with a sense of his chance to become part of the history of a new world. To look back over the past twelve hundred years let him see the next twelve hundred, or twelve thousand, more clearly. He could be in at the beginning and contribute his name to legend. It was a chance that few understood, an opportunity that fewer grabbed. Thinking like Suwon, now, he thought wryly. How could someone so completely overwhelm him in less than a day? Yet it was the second time. A second chance.

◆

Only an hour remained of the registration period when they returned to the seaside and ordered dinner. The light-ringed harbor, except for Mabel's plane, was deserted; everyone had headed out to their claims to be there at the start of the homesteading window.

They were well into some fairly tasty handmade *Crabe Asteria* when they heard what sounded like a muffled thunderclap. They looked out the restaurant window to the harbor, now lit by a bright orange flame climbing up from its center.

"My plane!" Mabel cried.

Bik was on his feet and out the door, meaning to grab a fire extinguisher and swim for it. But the local anti-fire utility had what remained of the plane covered in foam by the time he got to the water's edge. Mabel and Suwon were right behind him.

Mabel looked grim. "Repro and shipment say it will take three days to replace the plane; too much in the queue just now with all the new settlers. I'm . . . This is outrageous!"

"Maybe we can borrow a maintenance vehicle?" Bik hazarded.

Suwon concentrated, then shook her head. "Everything that can be borrowed has been borrowed. They've only got the minimum needed for emergencies. Like that." She gestured to the flames.

They stood silently for a minute trying to absorb the disaster. To have come so far, Bik thought, and then this. He was sure the lawyers had something to do with it—what could they do with money, he wondered, that made it worth doing this to someone to get it?

"I'm sorry, Mabel," he choked out. "Your homestead . . . If it hadn't been for me they wouldn't have done this. And Bikki . . . I feel like . . ."

"They aren't going to get away with it," she declared, her voice a calm, cheerful bell against the gloom. "I've already filed a protest saying who I think did it and why. I'll get my land, and you'll get yours." Mabel pursed her lips. "But not before Wendt has your kid on the way to Kalinda station! You think a nice home environment with plenty of elbow room will make that much difference to a custody board?"

"There's no telling what a human board will do, but I'm told it will help a lot."

"Well, then," Mabel said, "we have a long hike ahead of us."

Bik's Mercury-conditioned feet and muscles suddenly remembered where they were. "Hike?"

"First to the land registration office. It's open for another fifteen minutes."

There was a human clerk there, a very tall, dark-skinned woman in a simple blue robe with a bemused smile on her face. She clearly knew Mabel, but simply took Mabel's hand by way of greeting; the difference in their heights would have made an embrace embarrassing for both of them.

"Hi Mabel! Good to see you, but I don't think I can help anyone. Everything's gone and there's no transportation anyway. People have to be on the property when the sun rises here, in about twenty-five hours."

"Kris. I know. I want to open my island up to registration. Abandon my priority."

Suwon sucked in a breath and Kris' eyes went wide.

"But . . . whatever you say. It's going to come out as two parcels."

"Right. Register me for the one with the old station, and Bik Wu, here, for the rest of it. See if you can wriggle the dividing line down to the north beach."

Kris concentrated a moment. "You've got it." She handed an intelliprint to Mabel that showed the division. "But how are you going to get there?"

"Dawn on Venus," Mabel declared, "is low tide. The strait narrows down to a shallow only a couple of kilometers across. We're going to hike a dozen kilometers over the hills to South Point, and then swim."

Bik's mouth dropped, and he might have collapsed if Suwon hadn't put her arm around him.

⬤

The ground trail was easy, the gravity was not. Bik pushed himself until his legs gave out about five kilometers from the coast and he could not stand up. Suwon and Mabel cut down a couple of small trees with the emergency knife in Suwon's jump belt. Then they made a travois hammock from their clothes. Bik's jump tights formed the makeshift harness for Suwon and Mabel to use to put the weight of the travois on their shoulders. Mabel donated her green jumpsuit to tie the bottoms of the poles so that they wouldn't spread apart more than the path width.

Bik was intrigued to find the women were wearing simple, functional white support halters under their shifts. In Mercury's lower gravity, most women didn't bother with support garments, and instead used their bodies to display all kinds of rings, tattoos, and other decorations. But the Venusian women's bodies were completely bare of any decoration, and Suwon seemed to find Bik's own utilitarian nipple rings an item of amusement. His intellicard hung from one and a holo of Junior on his second birthday from the other. But he was much too exhausted to care about differing aesthetics as he dragged himself onto the rig.

They pulled him for two kilometers to the crest of the trail before he told them to stop.

"It's downhill now. Let me try walking again," he suggested. "I can use the poles as walking sticks. They can support my arms and let me use my arm muscles to help support the rest of me. You can have your clothes back. It's getting cold." With a light western breeze, it was getting about as chilly as it got in the Venusian tropical lowlands.

"That's because you've been lying on your back for an hour!" Suwon objected. "I'm sweating."

"I'll take mine, thank you," Mabel said. "I'm a lot smaller and lose heat faster."

Bik grabbed a branch hanging over the path and carefully stood up again. His knees burned and feet ached, but otherwise he simply felt tired.

They disassembled the travois and cut a meter from its poles. Bik took one in each hand and started out again, half hanging on, half pushing with the poles, while Mabel shrugged into her jumpsuit. Suwon tied the other two jumpsuits together and draped them over her neck. The women quickly caught up to him, but walked behind, letting him set the pace.

Bik's calves ached on the verge of cramping with each step, but he forced himself to a slow, regular pace, somewhat like a cross-country skier in slow motion. Very slow. Less, he thought, than half a kilometer an hour. Would it be enough? The exertion made him sweat profusely and the waistband of his shorts was beginning to chafe. He was miserable, but he had to continue. Everything was at stake.

After an eternity of pain, they reached the shoreline and he sprawled in the cool sand. They had a clear view of the western horizon, and it was already a brilliant orange; only Earth and Mercury were still visible in the brightening sky.

Suwon came over to him, stripped for the swim. She laughed, a bit self-consciously. "Curious?"

"Oh. Uh, didn't mean to stare. The fashion on Mercury is to have all sorts of things—" He self-consciously unclipped his intellicard from its ring. "—dyed or clipped on your body. There's nothing there but, well, you. You're very—bare."

"I like it that way, at least for swimming. Come on, give me your stuff. I'll stash it under a rock and we'll pick it up later. If you think those shorts were chafing on the hike, wait until you see what a couple of hours in salt water do."

After all this, could he swim for two hours? He was mentally exhausted from fighting unaccustomed aches and pains, but his wind was holding up well and now that he was off his feet, he seemed to be reviving. In the water, gravity wouldn't matter. Anyway, he had no choice. He removed what remained of his clothes and gave them to Suwon, who bundled them up with hers and Mabel's and put them under a big rock in from the shoreline.

Mabel, looking more like some ethereal bronzed nymph than a grown woman, took one side of him and Suwon the other as they waded into the gentle surf. It was cold to start with, but getting rid of his weight seemed to restore his energy. He established a smooth crawl at about two seconds a stroke, breathing on every other left arm, a pace which felt well within his capabilities.

The women easily matched him.

A hundred meters later he tired and switched to a back stroke.

Mabel glided by him effortlessly, leaving no wake that Bik could see.

Suwon pulled up to him with an easy side stroke. "I know that feels like a rest, but you should get back to your crawl as soon as you can. It's a much more efficient distance-eater. Vary your pace, if you have to, but keep going."

Bik nodded and resumed, one hand over another, breathing every time now. It went on and on. The shore behind them receded but the island shore seemed to get no closer. Stroke, breathe, stroke.

A few minutes or an eternity later he faltered to a breaststroke, just enough to keep his feet up.

"Look," Suwon called. "The sunshield rim!"

On the crest of the next wave, Bik saw it: a tiny golden arc over the wavetops.

"Then we've lost," he croaked. It was all for nothing. Mabel would lose her homestead, he would lose his son, Suwon would lose her chance for land on which to settle down.

"Come on!" Mabel shouted from ahead, her musical voice carrying clearly over the waves. Then she added in short phrases between breaths: "We're on the west side of the time zone. And we're seeing it early. It's really below the horizon. Because of refraction. Venus only rotates at about, uh, four-tenths of a degree an hour. Astronomical sunrise isn't for another hour yet. We can still make it. Come on, keep stroking."

With renewed desperation, Bik plunged ahead. His arms, he told himself, weren't nearly as tired as the rest of him. Ahead, Suwon was fighting her own battle, silently maintaining the pace she had started, not looking anywhere but ahead at the still-distant dark shore of the island.

Bik heard the buzz of a fan skimmer, but he didn't see where. Then, so quickly he had no time to think, it was coming right at him, out of the gloom of the island shore, skimming the wave tops. Instinctively he ducked underwater as it roared over him.

That was it, he thought as he surfaced. If they were going to do that to him, he was done. He had no strength left. No energy. There was maybe one thing he could do, though.

"Mabel!" He shouted, took a stroke, and caught a breath. "They want me. Go on. Get your land. I'll keep them busy. They can't stop all of us."

He saw the skimmer this time—a blur to his wet, unfocused eyes—as it looped around to come at him again. With a supreme effort, he waved a fist at them and resumed his crawl. He looked left and right and couldn't see the women—underwater, he hoped. Okay, bastards, he thought as the fan skimmer grew in front of him. Do your worst. I'm not stopping. I'm not ducking. Too damn tired.

Off to his right, something came up out of the waves, high up. He couldn't see it clearly; a head on two necks? It bent back, whipped forward and its "head" flew off toward him. Then his vision cleared some and in this instant he saw it was a large rock, and standing on the water was . . . But the skimmer was on him and despite himself he ducked deep and heard a solid tick as the rock bounced off the skimmer and slammed into the water somewhere behind him.

What he thought he had seen was a woman standing high on the waves silhouetted against the rising sun, proud and triumphant like the goddess Venus herself.

He surfaced, exhausted, barely able to float, and glanced behind him as he gasped for air. The fan skimmer, its hum wavering now, was heading away, not coming back.

"Bik!" Suwon called. "Put your legs down! We're here!"

He rolled, put his feet down, and looked toward her voice, toward the sun. To his surprise there was sand barely a meter under him. Suwon was standing on the sea off to his right, about ankle-deep. She was, his numb mind finally realized, on a higher part of the sand bar.

"Grab this! I hit them!" she shouted, gleeful. "I threw a big rock behind you with both hands. When you ducked, they nosed down right into it!"

Bik looked toward the island, dazed. It was there. Close by. He couldn't remember it getting so close. He caught his breath in great gasps. It was all he could do to stand on the shallow bar, even with the fortunately calm water helping, but if he didn't try to move, he was okay. The sun was clearly up now, huge on the horizon, shining through the sunshield with its rim just touching the lower rim of the sunshield, and both just touching the horizon.

"We made it," Mabel called from the beach. "I've reported us in, and they'll give you credit for getting on the bar. Less legal mess that way. You've got land."

Suwon splashed down the slope of the bar to him, and with her help Bik found the strength to wade ashore. Then he collapsed on the cool sand of the beach.

"Do you think it will be enough?" Mabel asked as he caught his breath. Bik managed a weak shrug. "I hope so."

It took him a dozen seconds to say anything else. "At least Junior will know I tried." Breathe. "That might be important to him someday. I did everything I could."

"What about getting a wife?" The gleam in Mabel's eyes belied the innocent tone of her voice.

"Mabel! I found him first!" Suwon protested, then stared open-mouthed.

"That's quite all right, dear. I have a half-dozen perfectly good relationships going."

"Why you old—matchmaker. You tricked me!"

Mabel laughed and turned to Bik with a sly grin. "Well, what about it, Bik? Take a chance on her? I've known her for thirty years, which isn't much these days, but that's all she's got. You couldn't do any better."

Bik shook his head and stared at the sea. She was too much like Kai, he told himself: too wild and spontaneous. She was someone who jumped off three-hundred-kilometer bridges for fun: someone who probably had a wrong take on him, because, once, scared to death and for something that mattered more to him than his own life, he had jumped with her. She was someone who was willing to risk a putative eternity with someone she knew less than twenty-four hours just to accomplish a goal, to complete a mission. No way, except . . . except that, with the board, it might work. And if he were really committed, he'd do everything.

"How about an engagement?" he asked. "Give us six months to get to know each other?"

"That sounds very reasonable." Mabel shook her head. "But I'm sure Mr. Wendt's lawyers will point out that if you call it off, it will be too late to give Bik, junior, back to the starship captain. I'd say they'll want to see at least a twenty-year contract. Suwon, dear, are you really sure?"

"Hell, no. If I were, it wouldn't be so exciting. Grab this, Mabel, Bik. Nothing's certain. It all depends on initial conditions, chance, and how you play it—like a jump. But I like the weather."

"Well," Mabel added, "in the old days, a lot of good marriages started when the parents matched you with someone you'd never seen before. Other people dated for a decade, lived together, got married and still broke up. Only question is if you're committed to it long enough to raise Bikki. There are some things, Suwon, that people have to *make* certain."

Suwon sat beside him, her bare arm and thigh burning against his. "You can count on me, Bik."

He could almost feel her purr. Talk about leaping into space!

In his mind, Bik could hear Kai laughing at her. You'll never get to first base with that wimp, his ex would have said to Suwon. For the first time,

Bik found himself a little angry with his mental image of Kai, and it dawned on him that Kai perhaps had not really been such an exemplar of woman-hood, that their split had not necessarily been all his fault, and that what she would have said about Suwon shouldn't really be his measure of things.

Bik set his jaw and reached for Suwon's firm, callused hand. She was not Kai. Her whole body, her attitude, was different from Kai's, and maybe better. She did wild things, and thought wild thoughts, true, but, unlike Kai, there was nothing flaky about how she did them. Suwon seemed competent and responsible. And she dared to take responsibility.

His thoughts were interrupted as she wrapped her arms around him and kissed him on the lips, and seemed to melt into him. He kissed back, ten-tatively at first, then with increasing warmth. Despite his tiredness, his body started to respond.

Mabel cleared her throat. Bik released Suwon, and they all laughed. But strangely, he felt no real embarrassment, nor urgency either. Everything felt very easy and natural. It would be like that with Suwon, he realized—just fun. With Kai there had always been tension, a performance, an evaluation, something to live up to.

Bik shook his head, sighed, and looked at Mabel. "Can we just register the contract?" he asked. "At least that's how we did it on Mercury."

Mabel nodded. "I'll send it in and witness it. There, I've bent-piped my audio to the registrar; it hears what I hear. Do you two want a twenty-year marriage contract? Bik?"

He took a breath and let go for the second time today. "Yes."

"Suwon?"

"Yes."

"Congratulations! May I kiss the groom?"

"Wait until I'm done," Suwon objected, and launched another round of physical affection, including Mabel this time. Bik felt embarrassed at first, but that passed into simple goodness.

⬤

The next morning, universal time, Bik sat in Mabel's dome wearing a beach towel as a sort of ersatz sarong, looking at the iron-gray crew cut and steel cold blue eyes of lawyer Deccar Brunt. "We did not anticipate such resolve on your part, Mr. Wu. As your lawyers, and the cybernetic advisors have undoubtedly told you by now, you are in a commanding position from a legal standpoint."

Bik wondered if Brunt had bribed someone to monitor his calls. It didn't matter. The cybes had traced the attack and Mabel's friends had turned a few screws of their own. Bik simply nodded. Yes, his being married now, and having a rich, open environment in which to raise Junior was one plus. But the opposition's tactics, starting from witholding his messages and presents, and running right through the attempts to interfere with his getting the homestead were now all faithfully recorded and arrayed against them. It would be, everyone conceded, an open-and-shut custody board decision.

"However," the attorney continued, no trace of caring in his voice, "Cap-tain Wendt would like to plead to you in the child's interest."

"He's here?"

The attorney nodded. "Your bimbo almost killed him with a rock while he was driving, perfectly legally, well over your head, after his inspection of this jungle to which you want to take Ted."

It made sense—Wendt was too smart to risk a conspiracy; he'd do his own dirty work. Bik squirmed momentarily at the mention of the name Wendt had given Junior. Suwon, who had managed to fit tightly into a loose shift of Mabel's, put a hand on Bik's shoulder. There was no point in working themselves up by arguing with a professional liar.

But Suwon tensed suddenly. "Then Bikki's here too! Wendt wouldn't have dared to leave Bikki two months away in the asteroid belt if he expected to win a custody battle!"

"Yes, *Ted* is here," Brunt said, his voice grating at the interruption. "Perhaps you should first listen to what he has to say."

A young male child's image appeared in the holo stage. A legend assured them it was a faithful recording of a board interview with "Ted Wendt." The boy seemed relaxed and polite, gave his name as Ted Wendt, and declared that he did not want to go to live with "Mr. Wu."

That image was replaced by a picture of a genial, fit man in a starship captain's coveralls.

"Well, Mr. Wu, we appear to have had some misunderstandings—"

Bik dismissed this with a gesture.

"I really don't mean you or your new wife any harm; however, if you really care for this young man—" The field expanded to include Junior, sitting quietly in a comfortable chair behind Wendt, staring at the floor. "—you need to consider his view of this. I recognize that you might feel that what we did in restricting communications to keep his identity straight was a little unfair to you, but that's all by the by. *Fait accompli.* You have to deal with the situation as it is, however unfair.

"You could win this legally with the cybe's evidence. I'll concede that. But that would devastate my son. The fact is that I'm the only father he's known; Ted was only three when your marriage ended and you left his life. It's the reality he knows that counts. Please consider his interests. If you really want a child, have another one."

Bik shifted uncomfortably. However unfair the situation, the argument made too much sense.

"He's never been on a high-gravity planet," Wendt continued. "He wants to go out on starships with me and see the rest of the universe, not be stuck on some artificial hothouse garden world. It's not fair to take him from the only father he's ever known, especially in view of his mother's recent death. I suppose this doesn't mean anything to you, but I loved Kai, and he's all I have left of her."

Suwon touched Bik's arm and looked wide-eyed at him. "No, no, it's not," she whispered, then turned to Mabel. Something went between them.

Mabel concentrated, then her eyes went wide. "The inheritance. Kai left it all to Bikki!"

Bik took a breath. Had there been some good in Kai after all, something that had been worth his love? Some mothering instinct that had put her son ahead of her selfishness? But that tainted money didn't matter now, nor did the property rights. All that mattered was—damn, what did matter?

Wendt appeared not to hear anything and made a helpless, open-handed gesture. "I don't have a legal leg to stand on. I know it. So I'm pleading with you. Don't ruin two lives, Ted's and mine, just to get back at Kai for going off with me. She's dead now. Gone. Please just let us be."

Bik stared at the floor. If . . . if they'd made their appeal that way in the first place.

"I," he began, then hesitated. "I don't want to hurt anyone. . . ."

Suwon's hand clamped on Bik's shoulder like a vise. "Don't you dare give in," she whispered. "I grab that recording's a morph, at least the audio, fake as hell. Otherwise we would have got it realtime." Then she said, loud, "Can he see us, Wendt? Can he hear us?"

Bik looked up. Wendt made a nervous gesture to someone offstage and moved his lips. The sound didn't come through. The boy nodded slightly and stared at the floor again.

"Wu," Wendt pleaded, "you heard the recording; he doesn't want to go. I'm sure he remembers what to say. Why put him through that?"

"I'll bet Brunt gets to manage the estate while they're gone," Mabel whispered. "Bik, it stinks."

"I know," he whispered back. "But does that justify hurting my kid?"

"Bik, he'll understand," Suwon pleaded. "Trust me."

Another leap, Bik told himself, and you're still alive after the first two. If Junior didn't remember, it was all over, he'd look ridiculous and prove Wendt was right; that his custody fight would just be ruining lives for his own self-gratification. But no one who had pulled the crap Wendt had pulled could be that good a father, and some memories go way back. At the very least Bikki needed to know he hadn't been abandoned; to know that Bik cared and always had cared. Bik decided to take the leap.

"Bikki," Bik said.

The boy looked up, through the holoviewer, at Bik, and expressions of recognition, confusion, and wonder crossed his young face.

"Daddy?"

In that one word, Bik saw a future unfold before him. A wife, a son to raise, and maybe a daughter. A huge rambling house with lanais all around and a pool leading right to the ocean. Friends. But space to be alone, too. Fishing trips. Bik, junior, would grow up here, maybe go to the stars and come back with kids of his own in a century or two. And he and Suwon would be here. Forever? It seemed possible. Anything seemed possible, if he could just reach out. Now.

Bik stood up, grabbed Suwon's hand and stared the tight-lipped spaceman in the eyes. "Wendt, get out of there and let me talk to my son."

For White Hill

JOE HALDEMAN

Born in Oklahoma City, Oklahoma, Joe Haldeman took a B.S. degree in physics and astronomy from the University of Maryland, and did postgraduate work in mathematics and computer science. But his plans for a career in science were cut short by the U.S. Army, which sent him to Vietnam in 1968 as a combat engineer. Seriously wounded in action, Haldeman returned home in 1969 and began to write. He sold his first story to Galaxy *in 1969, and by 1976 had garnered both the Nebula Award and the Hugo Award for his famous novel* The Forever War, *one of the landmark books of the seventies. He took another Hugo Award in 1977 for his story "Tricentennial"; won the Rhysling Award in 1983 for the best science-fiction poem of the year; and won both the Nebula and the Hugo in 1991 for the novella version of "The Hemingway Hoax." His story "None So Blind" won the Hugo Award in 1995. His novel* Forever Peace *won the John W. Campbell Memorial Award. His other books include two mainstream novels,* War Year *and* 1969; *the SF novels* Mindbridge, All My Sins Remembered, There Is No Darkness *(written with his brother, SF writer Jack C. Haldeman II),* Worlds, Worlds Apart. Worlds Enough and Time, Buying Time, The Hemingway Hoax, Forever Peace, *and* Forever Free; *the collections* Infinite Dreams, Dealing in Futures, Vietnam and Other Alien Worlds, *and* None So Blind; *and, as editor, the anthologies* Study War No More, Cosmic Laughter, *and* Nebula Award Stories Seventeen. *His most recent book is the novel* The Coming. *Haldeman lives part of the year in Boston, where he teaches writing at the Massachusetts Institute of Technology, and the rest of the year in Florida, where he and his wife, Gay, make their home.*

Here he takes us thousands of years into a sophisticated, high-tech future for ringside seats at a unique competition among artists who have the kind of nearly unlimited resources to draw upon that would be unimaginable to someone from our day—but who find that, in the end, in spite of wealth and power, they still have to deal with the same old cold questions as artists of any age.

I am writing this memoir in the language of England, an ancient land of Earth, whose tales and songs White Hill valued. She was fascinated by human culture in the days before machines—not just thinking machines, but working ones; when things got done by the straining muscles of humans and animals.

Neither of us was born on Earth. Not many people were, in those days. It was a desert planet then, ravaged in the twelfth year of what they would call the Last War. When we met, that war had been going for over four hundred years, and had moved out of Sol Space altogether, or so we thought.

Some cultures had other names for the conflict. My parent, who fought the century before I did, always called it the Extermination, and their name for the enemy was "roach," or at least that's as close as English allows. We called the enemy an approximation of their own word for themselves, Fwndyri, which was uglier to us. I still have no love for them, but have no reason to make the effort. It would be easier to love a roach. At least we have a common ancestor. And we accompanied one another into space.

One mixed blessing we got from the war was a loose form of interstellar government, the Council of Worlds. There had been individual treaties before, but an overall organization had always seemed unlikely, since no two inhabited systems are less than three light-years apart, and several of them are over fifty. You can't defeat Einstein; that makes more than a century between "How are you?" and "Fine."

The Council of Worlds was headquartered on Earth, an unlikely and unlovely place, if centrally located. There were fewer than ten thousand people living on the blighted planet then, an odd mix of politicians, religious extremists, and academics, mostly. Almost all of them under glass. Tourists flowed through the domed-over ruins, but not many stayed long. The planet was still very dangerous over all of its unprotected surface, since the Fwndyri had thoroughly seeded it with nanophages. Those were submicroscopic constructs that sought out concentrations of human DNA. Once under the skin, they would reproduce at a geometric rate, deconstructing the body, cell by cell, building new nanophages. A person might complain of a headache and lie down, and a few hours later there would be nothing but a dry skeleton, lying in dust. When the humans were all dead, they mutated and went after DNA in general, and sterilized the world.

White Hill and I were "bred" for immunity to the nanophages. Our DNA winds backwards, as was the case with many people born or created after that stage of the war. So we could actually go through the elaborate airlocks and step out onto the blasted surface unprotected.

I didn't like her at first. We were competitors, and aliens to one another.

When I worked through the final airlock cycle, for my first moment on the actual surface of Earth, she was waiting outside, sitting in meditation on a large flat rock that shimmered in the heat. One had to admit she was beautiful in a startling way, clad only in a glistening pattern of blue and green body paint. Everything else around was grey and black, including the hard-packed talcum that had once been a mighty jungle, Brazil. The dome behind me was a mirror of grey and black and cobalt sky.

"Welcome home," she said. "You're Water Man."

She inflected it properly, which surprised me. "You're from Petros?"

"Of course not." She spread her arms and looked down at her body. Our women always cover at least one of their breasts, let alone their genitals. "Galan, an island on Seldene. I've studied your cultures, a little language."

"You don't dress like that on Seldene, either." Not anywhere I'd been on the planet.

"Only at the beach. It's so warm here."

I had to agree. Before I came out, they'd told me it was the hottest autumn on record. I took off my robe and folded it and left it by the door, with the sealed food box they had given me. I joined her on the rock, which was tilted away from the sun and reasonably cool.

She had a slight fragrance of lavender, perhaps from the body paint. We touched hands. "My name is White Hill. Zephyr-Meadow-Torrent."

"Where are the others?" I asked. Twenty-nine artists had been invited; one from each inhabited world. The people who had met me inside said I was the nineteenth to show up.

"Most of them traveling. Going from dome to dome for inspiration."

"You've already been around?"

"No." She reached down with her toe and scraped a curved line on the hard-baked ground. "All the story's here, anywhere. It isn't really about history or culture."

Her open posture would have been shockingly sexual at home, but this was not home. "Did you visit my world when you were studying it?"

"No, no money, at the time. I did get there a few years ago." She smiled at me. "It was almost as beautiful as I'd imagined it." She said three words in Petrosian. You couldn't say it precisely in English, which doesn't have a palindromic mood: *Dreams feed art and art feeds dreams.*

"When you came to Seldene I was young, too young to study with you. I've learned a lot from your sculpture, though."

"How young can you be?" To earn this honor, I did not say.

"In Earth years, about seventy awake. More than a hundred and forty-five in time-squeeze."

I struggled with the arithmetic. Petros and Seldene were twenty-two light-years apart; that's about forty-five years' squeeze. Earth is, what, a little less than forty light-years from her planet. That leaves enough gone time for someplace about twenty-five light-years from Petros, and back.

She tapped me on the knee, and I flinched. "Don't overheat your brain. I made a triangle; went to ThetaKent after your world."

"Really? When I was there?"

"No, I missed you by less than a year. I was disappointed. You were why I went." She made a palindrome in my language: *Predator becomes prey becomes predator?* "So here we are. Perhaps I can still learn from you."

I didn't much care for her tone of voice, but I said the obvious: "I'm more likely to learn from you."

"Oh, I don't think so." She smiled in a measured way. "You don't have much to learn."

Or much I could, or would, learn. "Have you been down to the water?"

"Once." She slid off the rock and dusted herself, spanking. "It's interesting. Doesn't look real." I picked up the food box and followed her down a sort of path that led us into low ruins. She drank some of my water, apologetic; hers was hot enough to brew tea.

"First body?" I asked.

"I'm not tired of it yet." She gave me a sideways look, amused. "You must be on your fourth or fifth."

"I go through a dozen a year." She laughed. "Actually, it's still my second. I hung on to the first too long."

"I read about that, the accident. That must have been horrible."

"Comes with the medium. I should take up the flute." I had been making a "controlled" fracture in a large boulder and set off the charges prematurely, by dropping the detonator. Part of the huge rock rolled over onto me, crushing my body from the hips down. It was a remote area, and by the time help arrived I had been dead for several minutes, from pain as much as anything else. "It affected all of my work, of course. I can't even look at some of the things I did the first few years I had this body."

"They are hard to look at," she said. "Not to say they aren't well done, and beautiful, in their way."

"As what is not? In its way." We came to the first building ruins and stopped. "Not all of this is weathering. Even in four hundred years." If you studied the rubble you could reconstruct part of the design. Primitive but sturdy, concrete reinforced with composite rods. "Somebody came in here with heavy equipment or explosives. They never actually fought on Earth, I thought."

"They say not." She picked up an irregular brick with a rod through it. "Rage, I suppose. Once people knew that no one was going to live."

"It's hard to imagine." The records are chaotic. Evidently the first people died two or three days after the nanophages were introduced, and no one on Earth was alive a week later. "Not hard to understand, though. The need to break something." I remembered the inchoate anger I felt as I squirmed there helpless, dying from *sculpture*, of all things. Anger at the rock, the fates. Not at my own inattention and clumsiness.

"They had a poem about that," she said. " 'Rage, rage against the dying of the light.' "

"Somebody actually wrote something during the nanoplague?"

"Oh, no. A thousand years before. Twelve hundred." She squatted suddenly and brushed at a fragment that had two letters on it. "I wonder if this was some sort of official building. Or a shrine or church." She pointed along the curved row of shattered bricks that spilled into the street. "That looks like it was some kind of decoration, a gable over the entrance." She tiptoed through the rubble toward the far end of the arc, studying what was written on the face-up pieces. The posture, standing on the balls of her feet, made her slim body even more attractive, as she must have known. My own body began to respond in a way inappropriate for a man more than three times her age. Foolish, even though that particular part is not so old. I willed it down before she could see.

"It's a language I don't know," she said. "Not Portuguese; looks like Latin. A Christian church, probably, Catholic."

"They used water in their religion," I remembered. "Is that why it's close to the sea?"

"They were everywhere; sea, mountains, orbit. They got to Petros?"

"We still have some. I've never met one, but they have a church in New Haven."

"As who doesn't?" She pointed up a road. "Come on. The beach is just over the rise here."

I could smell it before I saw it. It wasn't an ocean smell; it was dry, slightly choking.

We turned a corner and I stood staring. "It's a deep blue farther out," she said, "and so clear you can see hundreds of metras down." Here the water was thick and brown, the surf foaming heavily like a giant's chocolate drink, mud piled in baked windrows along the beach. "This used to be soil?"

She nodded. "There's a huge river that cuts this continent in half, the Amazon. When the plants died, there was nothing to hold the soil in place." She tugged me forward. "Do you swim? Come on."

"Swim in *that*? It's filthy."

"No, it's perfectly sterile. Besides, I have to pee." Well, I couldn't argue with that. I left the box on a high fragment of fallen wall and followed her. When we got to the beach, she broke into a run. I walked slowly and watched her gracile body, instead, and waded into the slippery heavy surf. When it was deep enough to swim, I plowed my way out to where she was bobbing. The water was too hot to be pleasant, and breathing was somewhat difficult. Carbon dioxide, I supposed, with a tang of halogen.

We floated together for a while, comparing this soup to bodies of water on our planets and ThetaKent. It was tiring, more from the water's heat and bad air than exertion, so we swam back in.

◆

We dried in the blistering sun for a few minutes and then took the food box and moved to the shade of a beachside ruin. Two walls had fallen in together, to make a sort of concrete tent.

We could have been a couple of precivilization aboriginals, painted with dirt, our hair baked into stringy mats. She looked odd but still had a kind of formal beauty, the dusty mud residue turning her into a primitive sculpture, impossibly accurate and mobile. Dark rivulets of sweat drew painterly accent lines along her face and body. If only she were a model, rather than an artist. Hold that pose while I go back for my brushes.

We shared the small bottles of cold wine and water and ate bread and cheese and fruit. I put a piece on the ground for the nanophages. We watched it in silence for some minutes, while nothing happened. "It probably takes hours or days," she finally said.

"I suppose we should hope so," I said. "Let us digest the food before the creatures get to it."

"Oh, that's not a problem. They just attack the bonds between amino acids that make up proteins. For you and me, they're nothing more than an aid to digestion."

How reassuring. "But a source of some discomfort when we go back in, I was told."

She grimaced. "The purging. I did it once, and decided my next outing would be a long one. The treatment's the same for a day or a year."

"So how long has it been this time?"

"Just a day and a half. I came out to be your welcoming committee."

"I'm flattered."

She laughed. "It was their idea, actually. They wanted someone out here to 'temper' the experience for you. They weren't sure how well traveled you were, how easily affected by . . . strangeness." She shrugged. "Earthlings. I told them I knew of four planets you'd been to."

"They weren't impressed?"

"They said well, you know, he's famous and wealthy. His experiences on these planets might have been very comfortable." We could both laugh at that. "I told them how comfortable ThetaKent is."

"Well, it doesn't have nanophages."

"Or anything else. That was a long year for me. You didn't even stay a year."

"No. I suppose we would have met, if I had."

"Your agent said you were going to be there two years."

I poured us both some wine. "She should have told me you were coming. Maybe I could have endured it until the next ship out."

"How gallant." She looked into the wine without drinking. "You famous and wealthy people don't have to endure ThetaKent. I had to agree to one year's indentureship to help pay for my triangle ticket."

"You were an actual slave?"

"More like a wife, actually. The head of a township, a widower, financed me in exchange for giving his children some culture. Language, art, music. Every now and then he asked me to his chambers. For his own kind of culture."

"My word. You had to . . . *lie* with him? That was in the contract?"

"Oh, I didn't have to, but it kept him friendly." She held up a thumb and forefinger. "It was hardly noticeable."

I covered my smile with a hand, and probably blushed under the mud.

"I'm not embarrassing you?" she said. "From your work, I'd think that was impossible."

I had to laugh. "That work is in reaction to my culture's values. I can't take a pill and stop being a Petrosian."

White Hill smiled, tolerantly. "A Petrosian woman wouldn't put up with an arrangement like that?"

"Our women are still women. Some actually would like it, secretly. Most would claim they'd rather die, or kill the man."

"But they wouldn't actually *do* it. Trade their body for a ticket?" She sat down in a single smooth dancer's motion, her legs open, facing me. The clay between her legs parted, sudden pink.

"I wouldn't put it so bluntly." I swallowed, watching her watching me. "But no, they wouldn't. Not if they were planning to return."

"Of course, no one from a civilized planet would want to stay on ThetaKent. Shocking place."

I had to move the conversation onto safer grounds. "Your arms don't spend all day shoving big rocks around. What do you normally work in?"

"Various mediums." She switched to my language. "Sometimes I shove little rocks around." That was a pun for testicles. "I like painting, but my reputation is mainly from light and sound sculpture. I wanted to do something with the water here, internal illumination of the surf, but they say that's not possible. They can't isolate part of the ocean. I can have a pool, but no waves, no tides."

"Understandable." Earth's scientists had found a way to rid the surface of the nanoplague. Before they reterraformed the Earth, though, they wanted to isolate an area, a "park of memory," as a reminder of the Sterilization and these centuries of waste, and brought artists from every world to interpret, inside the park, what they had seen here.

Every world except Earth. Art on Earth had been about little else for a long time.

Setting up the contest had taken decades. A contest representative went to each of the settled worlds, according to a strict timetable. Announcement of the competition was delayed on the nearer worlds so that each artist would arrive on Earth at approximately the same time.

The Earth representatives chose which artists would be asked, and no one refused. Even the ones who didn't win the contest were guaranteed an honorarium equal to twice what they would have earned during that time at home, in their best year of record.

The value of the prize itself was so large as to be meaningless to a normal person. I'm a wealthy man on a planet where wealth is not rare, and just the interest that the prize would earn would support me and a half-dozen more. If someone from ThetaKent or Laxor won the prize, they would probably have more real usable wealth than their governments. If they were smart, they wouldn't return home.

The artists had to agree on an area for the park, which was limited to a hundred square kaymetras. If they couldn't agree, which seemed almost inevitable to me, the contest committee would listen to arguments and rule.

Most of the chosen artists were people like me, accustomed to working on a monumental scale. The one from Luxor was a composer, though, and there were two conventional muralists, paint and mosaic. White Hill's work was by its nature evanescent. She could always set something up that would be repeated, like a fountain cycle. She might have more imagination than that, though.

"Maybe it's just as well we didn't meet in a master-student relationship," I said. "I don't know the first thing about the techniques of your medium."

"It's not technique." She looked thoughtful, remembering. "That's not why I wanted to study with you, back then. I was willing to push rocks around, or anything, if it could give me an avenue, an insight into how you did what you did." She folded her arms over her chest, and dust fell. "Ever since my parents took me to see Gaudí Mountain, when I was ten."

That was an early work, but I was still satisfied with it. The city council of Tresling, a prosperous coastal city, hired me to "do something with" an unusable steep island that stuck up in the middle of their harbor. I melted it judiciously, in homage to an Earthling artist.

"Now, though, if you'd forgive me . . . well, I find it hard to look at. It's alien, obtrusive."

"You don't have to apologize for having an opinion." Of course it looked alien; it was meant to evoke *Spain!* "What would you do with it?"

She stood up, and walked to where a window used to be, and leaned on the stone sill, looking at the ruins that hid the sea. "I don't know. I'm even less familiar with your tools." She scraped at the edge of the sill with a piece of rubble. "It's funny: earth, air, fire, and water. You're earth and fire, and I'm the other two."

I have used water, of course. The Gaudí is framed by water. But it was an interesting observation. "What do you do, I mean for a living? Is it related to your water and air?"

"No. Except insofar as everything is related." There are no artists on Seldene, in the sense of doing it for a living. Everybody indulges in some sort of art or music, as part of "wholeness," but a person who only did art would be considered a parasite. I was not comfortable there.

She faced me, leaning. "I work at the Northport Mental Health Center. Cognitive science, a combination of research and . . . Is there a word here? *Jaturnary*. 'Empathetic therapy,' I guess."

I nodded. "We say *jådr-ny*. You plug yourself into mental patients?"

"I share their emotional states. Sometimes I do some good, talking to them afterwards. Not often."

"It's not done on Petrosia," I said, unnecessarily.

"Not legally, you mean."

I nodded. "If it worked, people say, it might be legal."

" 'People say.' What do you say?" I started to make a noncommittal gesture. "Tell me the truth."

"All I know is what I learned in school. It was tried, but failed spectacularly. It hurt both the therapists and the patients."

"That was more than a century ago. The science is much more highly developed now."

I decided not to push her on it. The fact is that drug therapy is spectacularly successful, and it *is* a science, unlike *jådr-ny*. Seldene is backward in some surprising ways.

I joined her at the window. "Have you looked around for a site yet?"

She shrugged. "I think my presentation will work anywhere. At least that's guided my thinking. I'll have water, air, and light, wherever the other artists and the committee decide to put us." She scraped at the ground with a toenail. "And this stuff. They call it 'loss.' What's left of what was living."

"I suppose it's not everywhere, though. They might put us in a place that used to be a desert."

"They might. But there will be water and air; they were willing to guarantee that."

"I don't suppose they have to guarantee rock," I said.

"I don't know. What would you do if they did put us in a desert, nothing but sand?"

"Bring little rocks." I used my own language; the pun also meant courage.

She started to say something, but we were suddenly in deeper shadow. We both stepped through the tumbled wall, out into the open. A black line of cloud had moved up rapidly from inland.

She shook her head. "Let's get to the shelter. Better hurry."

We trotted back along the path toward the Amazonia dome city. There was a low concrete structure behind the rock where I first met her. The warm breeze became a howling gale of sour steam before we got there, driving bullets of hot rain. A metal door opened automatically on our approach, and slid shut behind us. "I got caught in one yesterday," she said, panting. "It's no fun, even under cover. Stinks."

We were in an unadorned anteroom that had protective clothing on wall pegs. I followed her into a large room furnished with simple chairs and tables, and up a winding stair to an observation bubble.

"Wish we could see the ocean from here," she said. It was dramatic enough. Wavering sheets of water marched across the blasted landscape, strobed every few seconds by lightning flashes. The tunic I'd left outside swooped in flapping circles off to the sea.

It was gone in a couple of seconds. "You don't get another one, you know. You'll have to meet everyone naked as a baby."

"A dirty one at that. How undignified."

"Come on." She caught my wrist and tugged. "Water is my specialty, after all."

◆

The large hot bath was doubly comfortable for having a view of the tempest outside. I'm not at ease with communal bathing—I was married for fifty years and never bathed with my wife—but it seemed natural enough after wandering around together naked on an alien planet, swimming in its mud-puddle sea. I hoped I could trust her not to urinate in the tub. (If I mentioned it she would probably turn scientific and tell me that a healthy person's urine is sterile. I know that. But there is a time and a receptacle for everything.)

On Seldene, I knew, an unattached man and woman in this situation would probably have had sex even if they were only casual acquaintances, let alone fellow artists. She was considerate enough not to make any overtures, or perhaps (I thought at the time) not greatly stimulated by the sight of muscular men. In the shower before bathing, she offered to scrub my back, but left it at that. I helped her strip off the body paint from her back. It was a nice back to study, pronounced lumbar dimples, small waist. Under more restrained circumstances, it might have been I who made an overture. But one does not ask a woman when refusal would be awkward.

Talking while we bathed, I learned that some of her people, when they become wealthy enough to retire, choose to work on their art full time, but they're considered eccentric, even outcasts, egotists. White Hill expected one of them to be chosen for the contest, and wasn't even going to apply. But the Earthling judge saw one of her installations and tracked her down.

She also talked about her practical work in dealing with personality disorders and cognitive defects. There was some distress in her voice when she described that to me. Plugging into hurt minds, sharing their pain or blankness for hours. I didn't feel I knew her well enough to bring up the aspect that most interested me, a kind of ontological prurience: What is it like to actually *be* another person; how much of her, or him, do you take away? If you do it often enough, how can you know which parts of you are the original you?

And she would be plugged in to more than one person at once, at times, the theory being that people with similar disorders could help each other, swarming around in the therapy room of her brain. She would fade into the background, more or less unable to interfere, and later analyze how they had interacted.

She had had one particularly unsettling experience, where through a planetwide network she had interconnected more than a hundred congenitally retarded people. She said it was like a painless death. By the time half of them had plugged in, she had felt herself fade and wink out. Then she was reborn with the suddenness of a slap. She had been dead for about ten hours.

But only connected for seven. It had taken technicians three hours to pry her out of a persistent catatonia. With more people, or a longer period, she might have been lost forever. There was no lasting harm, but the experiment was never repeated.

It was worth it, she said, for the patients' inchoate happiness afterward. It was like a regular person being given supernatural powers for half a day— powers so far beyond human experience that there was no way to talk about them, but the memory of it was worth the frustration.

After we got out of the tub, she showed me to our wardrobe room: hundreds of white robes, identical except for size. We dressed and made tea and sat upstairs, watching the storm rage. It hardly looked like an inhabitable planet outside. The lightning had intensified so that it crackled incessantly, a jagged insane dance in every direction. The rain had frozen to white gravel somehow. I asked the building, and it said that the stuff was called *granizo* or, in English, hail. For a while it fell too fast to melt, accumulating in white piles that turned translucent.

Staring at the desolation, White Hill said something that I thought was uncharacteristically modest. "This is too big and terrible a thing. I feel like an interloper. They've lived through centuries of this, and now they want *us* to explain it to them?"

I didn't have to remind her of what the contest committee had said, that their own arts had become stylized, stunned into a grieving conformity. "Maybe not to *explain*—maybe they're assuming we'll fail, but hope to find a new direction from our failures. That's what that oldest woman, Norita, implied."

White Hill shook her head. "Wasn't she a ray of sunshine? I think they dragged her out of the grave as a way of keeping us all outside the dome."

"Well, she was quite effective on me. I could have spent a few days investigating Amazonia, but not with her as a native guide." Norita was about as close as anyone could get to being an actual native. She was the last survivor of the Five Families, the couple of dozen Earthlings who, among those who were offworld at the time of the nanoplague, were willing to come back after robots constructed the isolation domes.

In terms of social hierarchy, she was the most powerful person on Earth, at least on the actual planet. The class system was complex and nearly opaque to outsiders, but being a descendant of the Five Families was a prerequisite for the highest class. Money or political power would not get you in, although most of the other social classes seemed associated with wealth or the lack of it. Not that there were any actual poor people on Earth; the basic birth dole was equivalent to an upper-middle-class income on Petros.

The nearly instantaneous destruction of ten billion people did not destroy their fortunes. Most of the Earth's significant wealth had been off-planet, anyhow, at the time of the Sterilization. Suddenly it was concentrated into the hands of fewer than two thousand people.

Actually, I couldn't understand why anyone would have come back. You'd have to be pretty sentimental about your roots to be willing to spend the rest of your life cooped up under a dome, surrounded by instant death. The salaries and amenities offered were substantial, with bonuses for Earthborn workers, but it still doesn't sound like much of a bargain. The ships that brought the Five Families and the other original workers to Earth left loaded down with sterilized artifacts, not to return for exactly one hundred years.

Norita seemed like a familiar type to me, since I come from a culture also rigidly bound by class. "Old money, but not much of it" sums up the situation. She wanted to be admired for the accident of her birth and the dubious blessing of a torpid longevity, rather than any actual accomplishment. I didn't have to travel thirty-three light-years to enjoy that kind of company.

"Did she keep you away from everybody?" White Hill said.

"Interposed herself. No one could act naturally when she was around, and the old dragon was never *not* around. You'd think a person her age would need a little sleep."

" 'She lives on the blood of infants,' we say."

There was a phone chime and White Hill said "Bono" as I said, "Chå." Long habits. Then we said Earth's "Holá" simultaneously.

The old dragon herself appeared. "I'm glad you found shelter." Had she been eavesdropping? No way to tell from her tone or posture. "An administrator has asked permission to visit with you."

What if we said no? White Hill nodded, which means yes on Earth. "Granted," I said.

"Very well. He will be there shortly." She disappeared. I suppose the oldest person on a planet can justify not saying hello or goodbye. Only so much time left, after all.

"A physical visit?" I said to White Hill. "Through this weather?"

She shrugged. "Earthlings."

After a minute there was a *ding* sound in the anteroom and we walked down to see an unexpected door open. What I'd thought was a hall closet was an air lock. He'd evidently come underground.

Young and nervous and moving awkwardly in plastic. He shook our hands in an odd way. Of course we were swimming in deadly poison. "My name is Warm Dawn. Zephyr-Boulder-Brook."

"Are we cousins through Zephyr?" White Hill asked.

He nodded quickly. "An honor, my lady. Both of my parents are Seldenian, my gene-mother from your Galan."

A look passed over her that was pure disbelieving chauvinism: *Why would anybody leave Seldene's forests, farms, and meadows for this sterile death trap?* Of course, she knew the answer. The major import and export, the only crop, on Earth, was money.

"I wanted to help both of you with your planning. Are you going to travel at all, before you start?"

White Hill made a noncommittal gesture. "There are some places for me to see," I said. "The Pyramids, Chicago, Rome. Maybe a dozen places, twice that many days." I looked at her. "Would you care to join me?"

She looked straight at me, wheels turning. "It sounds interesting."

The man took us to a viewscreen in the great room and we spent an hour or so going over routes and making reservations. Travel was normally by underground vehicle, from dome to dome, and if we ventured outside unprotected, we would of course have to go through the purging before we were allowed to continue. Some people need a day or more to recover from that, so we should put that into the schedule, if we didn't want to be hobbled, like him, with plastic.

Most of the places I wanted to see were safely under glass, even some of the Pyramids, which surprised me. Some, like Ankgor Wat, were not only unprotected but difficult of access. I had to arrange for a flyer to cover the thousand kaymetras, and schedule a purge. White Hill said she would wander through Hanoi, instead.

I didn't sleep well that night, waking often from fantastic dreams, the nanobeasts grown large and aggressive. White Hill was in some of the dreams, posturing sexually.

By the next morning the storm had gone away, so we crossed over to Amazonia, and I learned firsthand why one might rather sit in a hotel room with a nice book than go to Angkor Wat, or anywhere that required a purge. The external part of the purging was unpleasant enough, even with pain medication, all the epidermis stripped and regrown. The inside part was beyond description, as the nanophages could be hiding out anywhere. Every opening into the body had to be vacuumed out, including the sense organs. I was not awake for that part, where the robots most gently clean out your eye sockets, but my eyes hurt and my ears rang for days. They warned me to sit down the first time I urinated, which was good advice, since I nearly passed out from the burning pain.

White Hill and I had a quiet supper of restorative gruel together, and then crept off to sleep for half a day. She was full of pep the next morning, and I pretended to be at least sentient, as we wandered through the city making preparations for the trip.

After a couple of hours I protested that she was obviously trying to do in one of her competitors; stop and let an old man sit down for a minute.

We found a bar that specialized in stimulants. She had tea and I had bhan, a murky warm drink served in a large nutshell, coconut. It tasted woody and bitter, but was restorative.

"It's not age," she said. "The purging seems a lot easier, the second time you do it. I could hardly move, all the next day, the first time."

Interesting that she didn't mention that earlier. "Did they tell you it would get easier?"

She nodded, then caught herself and wagged her chin horizontally, Earth-style. "Not a word. I think they enjoy our discomfort."

"Or like to keep us off guard. Keeps them in control." She made the little kissing sound that's Lortian for agreement and reached for a lemon wedge to squeeze into her tea. The world seemed to slow slightly, I guess from whatever was in the bhan, and I found myself cataloguing her body microscopically. A crescent of white scar tissue on the back of a knuckle, fine hair on her forearm, almost white, her shoulders and breasts moving in counterpoised pairs, silk rustling, as she reached forward and back and squeezed the lemon, sharp citrus smell and the tip of her tongue between her thin lips, mouth slightly large. Chameleon hazel eyes, dark green now because of the decorative ivy wall behind her.

"What are you staring at?"

"Sorry, just thinking."

"Thinking." She stared at me in return, measuring. "Your people are good at that."

After we'd bought the travel necessities we had the packages sent to our quarters and wandered aimlessly. The city was comfortable, but had little of interest in terms of architecture or history, oddly dull for a planet's administrative center. There was an obvious social purpose for its blandness—by statute, nobody was *from* Amazonia; nobody could be born there or claim citizenship. Most of the planet's wealth and power came there to work, electronically if not physically, but it went home to some other place.

A certain amount of that wealth was from interstellar commerce, but it was nothing like the old days, before the war. Earth had been a hub, a central authority that could demand its tithe or more from any transaction between planets. In the period between the Sterilization and Earth's token rehabitation, the other planets made their own arrangements with one another, in pairs and groups. But most of the fortunes that had been born on Earth returned here.

So Amazonia was bland as cheap bread, but there was more wealth under its dome than on any two other planets combined. Big money seeks out the company of its own, for purposes of reproduction.

❧

Two other artists had come in, from Auer and Shwa, and once they were ready, we set out to explore the world by subway. The first stop that was interesting was the Grand Canyon, a natural wonder whose desolate beauty was unaffected by the Sterilization.

We were amused by the guide there, a curious little woman who rattled on about the Great Rift Valley on Mars, a nearby planet where she was born. White Hill had a lightbox, and while the Martian lady droned on we sketched the fantastic colors, necessarily loose and abstract because our fingers were clumsy in clinging plastic.

We toured Chicago, like the Grand Canyon, wrapped in plastic. It was a large city that had been leveled in a local war. It lay in ruins for many years, and then, famously, was rebuilt as a single huge structure from those ruins. There's a childish or drunken ad hoc quality to it, a scarcity of right angles, a crazy-quilt mixture of materials. Areas of stunning imaginative brilliance next to jury-rigged junk. And everywhere bones, the skeletons of ten million people, lying where they fell. I asked what had happened to the bones in the old city outside of Amazonia. The guide said he'd never been there, but he supposed that the sight of them upset the politicians, so they had them cleaned up. "Can you imagine this place without the bones?" he asked. It would be nice if I could.

The other remnants of cities in that country were less interesting, if no less depressing. We flew over the east coast, which was essentially one continuous metropolis for thousands of kaymetras, like our coast from New Haven to Stargate, rendered in sterile ruins.

The first place I visited unprotected was Giza, the Great Pyramids. White Hill decided to come with me, though she had to be wrapped up in a shapeless cloth robe, her face veiled, because of local religious law. It seemed to me ridiculous, a transparent tourism ploy. How many believers in that old religion could have been off-planet when the Earth died? But every female was obliged at the tube exit to go into a big hall and be fitted with a chador robe and veil before a man could be allowed to look at her.

(We wondered whether the purging would be done completely by women. The technicians would certainly see a lot of her uncovered during that excruciation.)

They warned us it was unseasonably hot outside. Almost too hot to breathe, actually, during the day. We accomplished most of our sight-seeing around dusk or dawn, spending most of the day in air-conditioned shelters.

Because of our special status, White Hill and I were allowed to visit the pyramids alone, in the dark of the morning. We climbed up the largest one and watched the sun mount over desert haze. It was a singular time for both of us, edifying but something more.

Coming back down, we were treated to a sandstorm, *khamsin*, which actually might have done the first stage of purging if we had been allowed to take off our clothes. It explained why all the bones lying around looked so much older than the ones in Chicago; they normally had ten or twelve of these sandblasting storms every year. Lately, with the heat wave, the *khamsin* came weekly or even more often.

Raised more than five thousand years ago, the pyramids were the oldest monumental structures on the planet. They actually held as much fascination for White Hill as for me. Thousands of men moved millions of huge blocks of stone, with nothing but muscle and ingenuity. Some of the stones were mined a thousand kaymetras away, and floated up the river on barges.

I could build a similar structure, even larger, for my contest entry, by giving machines the right instructions. It would be a complicated business, but easily done within the two-year deadline. Of course there would be no point to it. That some anonymous engineer had done the same thing within the lifetime of a king, without recourse to machines—I agreed with White Hill: that was an actual marvel.

We spent a couple of days outside, traveling by surface hoppers from monument to monument, but none was as impressive. I suppose I should have realized that, and saved Giza for last.

We met another of the artists at the Sphinx, Lo Tan-Six, from Pao. I had seen his work on both Pao and ThetaKent, and admitted there was something to be admired there. He worked in stone, too, but was more interested in pure geometric forms than I was. I think stone fights form, or imposes its own tensions on the artist's wishes.

I liked him well enough, though, in spite of this and other differences, and we traveled together for a while. He suggested we not go through the purging here, but have our things sent to Rome, because we'd want to be outside there, too. There was a daily hop from Alexandria to Rome, an airship that had a section reserved for those of us who could eat and breathe nanophages.

As soon as she was inside the coolness of the ship, White Hill shed the chador and veil and stuffed them under the seat. "Breathe," she said, stretching. Her white body suit was a little less revealing than paint.

Her directness and undisguised sexuality made me catch my breath. The tiny crease of punctuation that her vulva made in the body suit would have her jailed on some parts of my planet, not to mention the part of this one we'd just left. The costume was innocent and natural and, I think, completely calculated.

Pao studied her with an interested detachment. He was neuter, an option that was available on Petros, too, but one I've never really understood. He claimed that sex took much time and energy from his art. I think his lack of gender took something else away from it.

We flew about an hour over the impossibly blue sea. There were a few sterile islands, but otherwise it was as plain as spilled ink. We descended over the ashes of Italy and landed on a pad on one of the hills overlooking the ancient city. The ship mated to an airlock so the normal-DNA people could go down to a tube that would whisk them into Rome. We could call for transportation or walk, and opted for the exercise. It was baking hot here, too, but not as bad as Egypt.

White Hill was polite with Lo, but obviously wished he'd disappear. He and I chattered a little too much about rocks and cements, explosives and lasers. And his asexuality diminished her interest in him—as, perhaps, my polite detachment increased her interest in me. The muralist from Shwa, to complete the spectrum, was after her like a puppy in its first heat, which I think amused her for two days. They'd had a private conversation in Chicago, and he'd kept his distance since, but still admired her from afar. As we walked down toward the Roman gates, he kept a careful twenty paces behind, trying to contemplate things besides White Hill's walk.

Inside the gate we stopped short, stunned in spite of knowing what to expect. It had a formal name, but everybody just called it Òssi, the Bones. An order of catholic clergy had spent more than two centuries building, by hand, a wall of bones completely around the city. It was twice the height of a man, varnished dark amber. There were repetitive patterns of femurs and rib cages and stacks of curving spines, and at eye level, a row of skulls, uninterrupted, kaymetra after kaymetra.

This was where we parted. Lo was determined to walk completely around the circle of death, and the other two went with him. White Hill and I could do it in our imagination. I still creaked from climbing the pyramid.

Prior to the ascent of Christianity here, they had huge spectacles, displays of martial skill where many of the participants were killed, for punishment of wrong-doing or just to entertain the masses. The two large amphitheaters where these displays went on were inside the Bones but not under the dome, so we walked around them. The Circus Maximus had a terrible dignity to it, little more than a long depression in the ground with a few eroded monuments left standing. The size and age of it were enough; your mind's eye supplied the rest. The smaller one, the Colosseum, was overdone, with robots in period costumes and ferocious mechanical animals re-creating the old scenes, lots of too-bright blood spurting. Stones and bones would do.

I'd thought about spending another day outside, but the shelter's air-conditioning had failed, and it was literally uninhabitable. So I braced myself and headed for the torture chamber. But as White Hill had said, the purging was more bearable the second time. You know that it's going to end.

Rome inside was interesting, many ages of archaeology and history stacked around in no particular order. I enjoyed wandering from place to place with her, building a kind of organization out of the chaos. We were both more interested in inspiration than education, though, so I doubt that the three days we spent there left us with anything like coherent picture of that tenacious empire and the millennia that followed it.

A long time later she would surprise me by reciting the names of the Roman emperors in order. She'd always had a trick memory, a talent for retaining trivia, ever since she was old enough to read. Growing up different that way must have been a factor in swaying her toward cognitive science.

We saw some ancient cinema and then returned to our quarters to pack for continuing on to Greece, which I was anticipating with pleasure. But it didn't happen. We had a message waiting: ALL MUST RETURN IMMEDIATELY TO AMAZONIA. CONTEST PROFOUNDLY CHANGED.

Lives, it turned out, profoundly changed. The war was back.

◕

We met in a majestic amphitheater, the twenty-nine artists dwarfed by the size of it, huddled front row center. A few Amazonian officials sat behind a table on the stage, silent. They all looked detached, or stunned, brooding.

We hadn't been told anything except that it was a matter of "dire and immediate importance." We assumed it had to do with the contest, naturally, and were prepared for the worst: it had been called off; we had to go home.

The old crone Norita appeared. "We must confess to carelessness," she said. "The unseasonable warmth in both hemispheres, it isn't something that has happened, ever since the Sterilization. We looked for atmospheric causes here, and found something that seemed to explain it. But we didn't make the connection with what was happening in the other half of the world.

"It's not the atmosphere. It's the Sun. Somehow the Fwndyri have found a way to make its luminosity increase. It's been going on for half a year. If it continues, and we find no way to reverse it, the surface of the planet will be uninhabitable in a few years.

"I'm afraid that most of you are going to be stranded on Earth, at least for the time being. The Council of Worlds has exercised its emergency powers, and commandeered every vessel capable of interstellar transport. Those who have sufficient power or the proper connections will be able to escape. The rest will have to stay with us and face . . . whatever our fate is going to be."

I saw no reason not to be blunt. "Can money do it? How much would a ticket out cost?"

That would have been a gaffe on my planet, but Norita didn't blink. "I know for certain that two hundred million marks is not enough. I also know that some people have bought 'tickets,' as you say, but I don't know how much they paid, or to whom."

If I liquidated everything I owned, I might be able to come up with three hundred million, but I hadn't brought that kind of liquidity with me; just a box of rare jewelry, worth perhaps forty million. Most of my wealth was thirty-three years away, from the point of view of an Earth-bound investor. I could sign that over to someone, but by the time they got to Petros, the government or my family might have seized it, and they would have nothing save the prospect of a legal battle in a foreign culture.

Norita introduced Skylha Sygoda, an astrophysicist. He was pale and sweating. "We have analyzed the solar spectrum over the past six months. If I hadn't known that each spectrum was from the same star, I would have said it was a systematic and subtle demonstration of the microstages of stellar evolution in the late main sequence."

"Could you express that in some human language?" someone said.

Sygoda spread his hands. "They've found a way to age the Sun. In the normal course of things, we would expect the Sun to brighten about six percent each billion years. At the current rate, it's more like one percent per year."

"So in a hundred years," White Hill said, "it will be twice as bright?"

"If it continues at this rate. We don't know."

A stocky woman I recognized as !Oona Something, from Jua-nguvi, wrestled with the language: "To how long, then? Before this Earth is uninhabitable?"

"Well, in point of fact, it's uninhabitable now, except for people like you. We could survive inside these domes for a long time, if it were just a matter of the outside getting hotter and hotter. For those of you able to withstand the nanophages, it will probably be too hot within a decade, here; longer near the poles. But the weather is likely to become very violent, too.

"And it may not be a matter of a simple increase in heat. In the case of normal evolution, the Sun would eventually expand, becoming a red giant. It would take many billions of years, but the Earth would not survive. The surface of the Sun would actually extend out to touch us.

"If the Fwndyri were speeding up time somehow, locally, and the Sun were actually *evolving* at this incredible rate, we would suffer that fate in about thirty years. But it would be impossible. They would have to have a way to magically extract the hydrogen from the Sun's core."

"Wait," I said. "You don't know what they're doing now, to make it brighten. I wouldn't say anything's impossible."

"Water Man," Norita said, "if that happens we shall simply die, all of us, at once. There is no need to plan for it. We do need to plan for less extreme exigencies." There was an uncomfortable silence.

"What can we do?" White Hill said. "We artists?"

"There's no reason not to continue with the project, though I think you may wish to do it inside. There's no shortage of space. Are any of you trained in astrophysics, or anything having to do with stellar evolution and the like?" No one was. "You may still have some ideas that will be useful to the specialists. We will keep you informed."

Most of the artists stayed in Amazonia, for the amenities if not to avoid purging, but four of us went back to the outside habitat. Denli om Cord, the composer from Luxor, joined Lo and White Hill and me. We could have used the tunnel air lock, to avoid the midday heat, but Denli hadn't seen the beach, and I suppose we all had an impulse to see the Sun with our new knowledge. In this new light, as they say.

White Hill and Denli went swimming while Lo and I poked around the ruins. We had since learned that the destruction here had been methodical, a grim resolve to leave the enemy nothing of value. Both of us were scouting for raw material, of course. After a short while we sat in the hot shade, wishing we had brought water.

We talked about that and about art. Not about the Sun dying, or us dying, in a few decades. The women's laughter drifted to us over the rush of the muddy surf. There was a sad hysteria to it.

"Have you had sex with her?" he asked conversationally.

"What a question. No."

He tugged on his lip, staring out over the water. "I try to keep these things straight. It seems to me that you desire her, from the way you look at her, and she seems cordial to you, and is after all from Seldene. My interest is academic, of course."

"You've never done sex? I mean before."

"Of course, as a child." The implication of that was obvious.

"It becomes more complicated with practice."

"I suppose it could. Although Seldenians seem to treat it as casually as . . . conversation." He used the Seldenian word, which is the same as for intercourse.

"White Hill is reasonably sophisticated," I said. "She isn't bound by her culture's freedoms." The two women ran out of the water, arms around each other's waists, laughing. It was an interesting contrast; Denli was almost as large as me, and about as feminine. They saw us and waved toward the path back through the ruins.

We got up to follow them. "I suppose I don't understand your restraint," Lo said. "Is it your own culture? Your age?"

"Not age. Perhaps my culture encourages self-control."

He laughed. "That's an understatement."

"Not that I'm a slave to Petrosian propriety. My work is outlawed in several states, at home."

"You're proud of that."

I shrugged. "It reflects on them, not me." We followed the women down the path, an interesting study in contrasts, one pair nimble and naked except for a film of drying mud, the other pacing evenly in monkish robes. They were already showering when Lo and I entered the cool shelter, momentarily blinded by shade.

We made cool drinks and, after a quick shower, joined them in the communal bath. Lo was not anatomically different from a sexual male which I found obscurely disturbing. Wouldn't it bother you to be constantly reminded of what you had lost? Renounced, I suppose Lo would say, and accuse me of being parochial about plumbing.

I had made the drinks with guava juice and ron, neither of which we have on Petros. A little too sweet, but pleasant. The alcohol loosened tongues.

Denli regarded me with deep black eyes. "You're rich, Water Man. Are you rich enough to escape?"

"No. If I had brought all my money with me, perhaps."

"Some do." White Hill said. "I did."

"I would too," Lo said, "coming from Seldene. No offense intended."

"Wheels turn," she admitted. "Five or six new governments before I get back. *Would* have gotten back."

We were all silent for a long moment. "It's not real yet," White Hill said, her voice flat. "We're going to die here?"

"We were going to die somewhere," Denli said. "Maybe not so soon."

"And not on Earth," Lo said. "It's like a long preview of Hell." Denli looked at him quizzically. "That's where Christians go when they die. If they were bad."

"They send their bodies to Earth?" We managed not to smile. Actually, most of my people knew as little as hers, about Earth. Seldene and Luxor, though relatively poor, had centuries more history than Petros, and kept closer ties to the central planet. The Home Planet, they would say. Homey as a blast furnace.

By tacit consensus, we didn't dwell on death anymore that day. When artists get together they tend to wax enthusiastic about materials and tools, the mechanical lore of their trades. We talked about the ways we worked at home, the things we were able to bring with us, the improvisations we could effect with Earthling materials. (Critics talk about art, we say; artists talk about brushes.) Three other artists joined us, two sculptors and a weather-shaper, and we all wound up in the large sunny studio drawing and painting. White Hill and I found sticks of charcoal and did studies of each other drawing each other.

While we were comparing them she quietly asked, "Do you sleep lightly?"

"I can. What did you have in mind?"

"Oh, looking at the ruins by starlight. The moon goes down about three. I thought we might watch it set together." Her expression was so open as to be enigmatic.

Two more artists had joined us by dinnertime, which proceeded with a kind of forced jollity. A lot of ron was consumed. White Hill cautioned me against overindulgence. They had the same liquor, called "rum," on Seldene, and it had a reputation for going down easily but causing storms. There was no legal distilled liquor on my planet.

I had two drinks of it, and retired when people started singing in various languages. I did sleep lightly, though, and was almost awake when White Hill tapped. I could hear two or three people still up, murmuring in the bath. We slipped out quietly.

It was almost cool. The quarter-phase moon was near the horizon, a dim orange, but it gave us enough light to pick our way down the path. It was warmer in the ruins, the tumbled stone still radiating the day's heat. We walked through to the beach, where it was cooler again. White Hill spread the blanket she had brought and we stretched out and looked up at the stars.

As is always true with a new world, most of the constellations were familiar, with a few bright stars added or subtracted. Neither of our home stars was significant, as dim here as Earth's Sol is from home. She identified the brightest star overhead as AlphaKent; there was a brighter one on the horizon, but neither of us knew what it was.

We compared names of the constellations we recognized. Some of hers were the same as Earth's names, like Scorpio, which we call the Insect. It was about halfway up the sky, prominent, embedded in the galaxy's glow. We both call the brightest star there Antares. The Executioner, which had set perhaps an hour earlier, they call Orion. We had the same meaningless names for its brightest stars, Betelgeuse and Rigel.

"For a sculptor, you know a lot about astronomy," she said. "When I visited your city, there was too much light to see stars at night."

"You can see a few from my place. I'm out at Lake Påchlå, about a hundred kaymetras inland."

"I know. I called you."

"I wasn't home?"

"No; you were supposedly on ThetaKent."

"That's right, you told me. Our paths crossed in space. And you became that burgher's slave wife." I put my hand on her arm. "Sorry I forgot. A lot has gone on. Was he awful?"

She laughed into the darkness. "He offered me a lot to stay."

"I can imagine."

She half turned, one breast soft against my arm, and ran a finger up my leg. "Why tax your imagination?"

I wasn't especially in the mood, but my body was. The robes rustled off easily, their only virtue.

The moon was down now, and I could see only a dim outline of her in the starlight. It was strange to make love deprived of that sense. You would think the absence of it would amplify the others, but I can't say that it did, except that her heartbeat seemed very strong on the heel of my hand. Her breath was sweet with mint and the smell and taste of her body were agreeable; in fact, there was nothing about her body that I would have cared to change, inside or out, but nevertheless, our progress became difficult after a couple of minutes, and by mute agreement we slowed and stopped. We lay joined together for some time before she spoke.

"The timing is all wrong. I'm sorry." She drew her face across my arm and I felt tears. "I was just trying not to think about things."

"It's all right. The sand doesn't help, either." We had gotten a little bit inside, rubbing.

We talked for a while and then drowsed together. When the sky began to lighten, a hot wind from below the horizon woke us up. We went back to the shelter.

Everyone was asleep. We went to shower off the sand and she was amused to see my interest in her quicken. "Let's take that downstairs," she whispered, and I followed her down to her room.

The memory of the earlier incapability was there, but it was not greatly inhibiting. Being able to see her made the act more familiar, and besides she was very pleasant to see, from whatever angle. I was able to withhold myself only once, and so the interlude was shorter than either of us would have desired.

We slept together on her narrow bed. Or she slept, rather, while I watched the bar of sunlight grow on the opposite wall, and thought about how everything had changed.

They couldn't really say we had thirty years to live, since they had no idea what the enemy was doing. It might be three hundred; it might be less than one—but even with bodyswitch that was always true, as it was in the old days: sooner or later something would go wrong and you would die. That I might die at the same instant as ten thousand other people and a planet full of history—that was interesting. But as the room filled with light and I studied her quiet repose, I found her more interesting than that.

I was old enough to be immune to infatuation. Something deep had been growing since Egypt, maybe before. On top of the pyramid, the rising sun dim in the mist, we had sat with our shoulders touching, watching the ancient forms appear below, and I felt a surge of numinism mixed oddly with content. She looked at me—I could only see her eyes—and we didn't have to say anything about the moment.

And now this. I was sure without words, that she would share this, too. Whatever "this" was. England's versatile language, like mine and hers, is strangely hobbled by having the one word, love, stand for such a multiplicity of feelings.

Perhaps that lack reveals a truth, that no one love is like any other. There are other truths that you might forget, or ignore, distracted by the growth of love. In Petrosian there is a saying in the palindromic mood that always carries a sardonic, or at least ironic, inflection: "Happiness presages disaster presages happiness." So if you die happy, it means you were happy when you died. Good timing or bad?

◆

!Oona M'uva had a room next to White Hill, and she was glad to switch with me, an operation that took about three minutes but was good for a much longer period of talk among the other artists. Lo was smugly amused, which in my temporary generosity of spirit I forgave.

Once we were adjacent, we found the button that made the wall slide away, and pushed the two beds together under her window. I'm afraid we were antisocial for a couple of days. It had been some time since either of us had had a lover. And I had never had one like her, literally, out of the dozens. She said that was because I had never been involved with a Seldenian, and I tactfully agreed, banishing five perfectly good memories to amnesia.

It's true that Seldenian women, and men as well, are better schooled than those of us from normal planets, in the techniques and subtleties of sexual expression. Part of "wholeness," which I suppose is a weak pun in English. It kept Lo, and not only him, from taking White Hill seriously as an artist: the fact that a Seldenian, to be "whole," must necessarily treat art as an everyday activity, usually subordinate to affairs of the heart, of the body. Or at least on the same level, which is the point.

The reality is that it *is* all one to them. What makes Seldenians so alien is that their need for balance in life dissolves hierarchy: this piece of art is valuable, and so is this orgasm, and so is this crumb of bread. The bread crumb connects to the artwork through the artist's metabolism, which connects to orgasm. Then through a fluid and automatic mixture of logic, metaphor, and rhetoric, the bread crumb links to soil, sunlight, nuclear fusion, the beginning and end of the universe. Any intelligent person can map out chains like that, but to White Hill it was automatic, drilled into her with her first nouns and verbs: *Everything is important. Nothing matters.* Change the world but stay relaxed.

I could never come around to her way of thinking. But then I was married for fifty Petrosian years to a woman who had stranger beliefs. (The marriage as a social contract actually lasted fifty-seven years; at the half-century mark we took a vacation from each other, and I never saw her again.) White Hill's worldview gave her an equanimity I had to envy. But my art needed unbalance and tension the way hers needed harmony and resolution.

By the fourth day most of the artists had joined us in the shelter. Maybe they grew tired of wandering through the bureaucracy. More likely, they were anxious about their competitors' progress.

White Hill was drawing designs on large sheets of buff paper and taping them up on our walls. She worked on her feet, bare feet, pacing from diagram to diagram, changing and rearranging. I worked directly inside a shaping box, an invention White Hill had heard of but had never seen. It's a cube of light a little less than a metra wide. Inside is an image of a sculpture— or a rock or a lump of clay—that you can feel as well as see. You can mold it with your hands or work with finer instruments for cutting, scraping, chipping. It records your progress constantly, so it's easy to take chances; you can always run it back to an earlier stage.

I spent a few hours every other day cruising in a flyer with Lo and a couple of other sculptors, looking for native materials. We were severely constrained by the decision to put the Memory Park inside, since everything we used had to be small enough to fit through the airlock and purging rooms. You could work with large pieces, but you would have to slice them up and reassemble them, the individual chunks no bigger than two by two by three metras.

We tried to stay congenial and fair during these expeditions. Ideally, you would spot a piece and we would land by it or hover over it long enough to tag it with your ID; in a day or two the robots would deliver it to your "holding area" outside the shelter. If more than one person wanted the piece, which happened as often as not, a decision had to be made before it was tagged. There was a lot of arguing and trading and Solomon-style splitting, which usually satisfied the requirements of something other than art.

The quality of light was changing for the worse. Earthling planetary engineers were spewing bright dust into the upper atmosphere, to reflect back solar heat. (They modified the nanophage-eating machinery for the purpose. That was also designed to fill the atmosphere full of dust, but at a lower level—and each grain of *that* dust had a tiny chemical brain.) It made the night sky progressively less interesting. I was glad White Hill had chosen to initiate our connection under the stars. It would be some time before we saw them again, if ever.

And it looked like "daylight" was going to be a uniform overcast for the duration of the contest. Without the dynamic of moving sunlight to continually change the appearance of my piece, I had to discard a whole family of first approaches to its design. I was starting to think along the lines of something irrational-looking; something the brain would reject as impossible. The way we mentally veer away from unthinkable things like the Sterilization, and our proximate future.

We had divided into two groups, and jokingly but seriously referred to one another as "originalists" and "realists." We originalists were continuing our projects on the basis of the charter's rules: a memorial to the tragedy and its aftermath, a stark sterile reminder in the midst of life. The realists took into account new developments, including the fact that there would probably never be any "midst of life" and, possibly, no audience, after thirty years.

I thought that was excessive. There was plenty of pathos in the original assignment. Adding another, impasto, layer of pathos along with irony and the artist's fear of personal death . . . well, we were doing art, not literature. I sincerely hoped their pieces would be fatally muddled by complexity.

If you asked White Hill which group she belonged to, she would of course say, "Both." I had no idea what form her project was going to take; we had agreed early on to surprise one another, and not impede each other with suggestions. I couldn't decipher even one-tenth of her diagrams. I speak Seldenian pretty well, but have never mastered the pictographs beyond the usual travelers' vocabulary. And much of what she was scribbling on the buff sheets of paper was in no language I recognized, an arcane technical symbology.

We talked about other things. Even about the future, as lovers will. Our most probable future was simultaneous death by fire, but it was calming and harmless to make "what if?" plans, in case our hosts somehow were able to find a way around that fate. We did have a choice of many possible futures, if we indeed had more than one. White Hill had never had access to wealth before. She didn't want to live lavishly, but the idea of being able to explore all the planets excited her.

Of course she had never tried living lavishly. I hoped one day to study her reaction to it, which would be strange. Out of the box of valuables I'd brought along, I gave her a necklace, a traditional beginning-love gift on Petros. It was a network of perfect emeralds and rubies laced in gold.

She examined it closely. "How much is this worth?"

"A million marks, more or less." She started to hand it back. "Please keep it. Money has no value here, no meaning."

She was at a loss for words, which was rare enough. "I understand the gesture. But you can't expect me to value this the way you do."

"I wouldn't expect that."

"Suppose I lose it? I might just set it down somewhere."

"I know. I'll still have given it to you."

She nodded and laughed. "All right. You people are strange." She slipped the necklace on, still latched, wiggling it over her ears. The colors glowed warm and cold against her olive skin.

She kissed me, a feather, and rushed out of our room wordlessly. She passed right by a mirror without looking at it.

After a couple of hours I went to find her. Lo said he'd seen her go out the door with a lot of water. At the beach I found her footprints marching straight west to the horizon.

She was gone for two days. I was working outside when she came back, wearing nothing but the necklace. There was another necklace in her hand: she had cut off her right braid and interwoven a complex pattern of gold and silver wire into a closed loop. She slipped it over my head and pecked me on the lips and headed for the shelter. When I started to follow she stopped me with a tired gesture. "Let me sleep, eat, wash." Her voice was a hoarse whisper. "Come to me after dark."

I sat down, leaning back against a good rock, and thought about very little, touching her braid and smelling it. When it was too dark to see my feet, I went in, and she was waiting.

■

I spent a lot of time outside, at least in the early morning and late afternoon, studying my accumulation of rocks and ruins. I had images of every piece in my shaping box's memory, but it was easier to visualize some aspects of the project if I could walk around the elements and touch them.

Inspiration is where you find it. We'd played with an orrery in the museum in Rome, a miniature solar system that had been built of clockwork centuries before the Information Age. There was a wistful, humorous kind of comfort in its jerky regularity.

My mental processes always turn things inside out. Find the terror and hopelessness in that comfort. I had in mind a massive but delicately balanced assemblage that would be viewed by small groups; their presence would cause it to teeter and turn ponderously. It would seem both fragile and huge (though of course the fragility would be an illusion), like the ecosystem that the Fwndyri so abruptly destroyed.

The assemblage would be mounted in such a way that it would seem always in danger of toppling off its base, but hidden weights would make that impossible. The sound of the rolling weights ought to produce a nice anxiety. Whenever a part tapped the floor, the tap would be amplified into a hollow boom.

If the viewers stood absolutely still, it would swing to a halt. As they left, they would disturb it again. I hoped it would disturb them as well.

The large technical problem was measuring the distribution of mass in each of my motley pieces. That would have been easy at home; I could rent a magnetic resonance densitometer to map their insides. There was no such thing on this planet (so rich in things I had no use for!), so I had to make do with a pair of robots and a knife edge. And then start hollowing the pieces out asymmetrically, so that once set in motion, the assemblage would tend to rotate.

I had a large number of rocks and artifacts to choose from, and was tempted to use no unifying principle at all, other than the unstable balance of the thing. Boulders and pieces of old statues and fossil machinery. The models I made of such a random collection were ambiguous, though. It was hard to tell whether they would look ominous or ludicrous, built to scale. A symbol of helplessness before an implacable enemy? Or a lurching, crashing junkpile? I decided to take a reasonably conservative approach, dignity rather than daring. After all, the audience would be Earthlings and, if the planet survived, tourists with more money than sophistication. Not my usual jury.

I was able to scavenge twenty long bars of shiny black monofiber, which would be the spokes of my irregular wheel. That would give it some unity of composition: make a cross with four similar chunks of granite at the ordinal points, and a larger chunk at the center. Then build up a web inside, monofiber lines linking bits of this and that.

Some of the people were moving their materials inside Amazonia, to work in the area marked off for the park. White Hill and I decided to stay outside. She said her project was portable, at this stage, and mine would be easy to disassemble and move.

After a couple of weeks, only fifteen artists remained with the project, inside Amazonia or out in the shelter. The others had either quit, surrendering to the passive depression that seemed to be Earth's new norm, or, in one case, committed suicide. The two from Wolf and Mijhøoven opted for coldsleep, which might be deferred suicide. About one person in three slept through it; one in three came out with some kind of treatable mental disorder. The others went mad and died soon after reawakening, unable or unwilling to live.

Coldsleep wasn't done on Petros, although some Petrosians went to other worlds to indulge in it as a risky kind of time travel. Sleep until whatever's wrong with the world has changed. Some people even did it for financial speculation: buy up objects of art or antiques, and sleep for a century or more while their value increases. Of course their value might not increase significantly, or they might be stolen or coopted by family or government.

But if you can make enough money to buy a ticket to another planet, why not hold off until you had enough to go to a really *distant* one? Let time dilation compress the years. I could make a triangle from Petros to Skaal to Mijhøoven and back, and more than 120 years would pass, while I lived through only three, with no danger to my mind. And I could take my objects of art along with me.

White Hill had worked with coldsleep veterans, or victims. None of them had been motivated by profit, given her planet's institutionalized antimaterialism, so most of them had been suffering from some psychological ill before they slept. It was rare for them to come out of the "treatment" improved, but they did come into a world where people like White Hill could at least attend them in their madness, perhaps guide them out.

I'd been to three times as many worlds as she. But she had been to stranger places.

◆

The terraformers did their job too well. The days grew cooler and cooler, and some nights snow fell. The snow on the ground persisted into mornings for a while, and then through noon, and finally it began to pile up. Those of us who wanted to work outside had to improvise cold-weather clothing.

I liked working in the cold, although all I did was direct robots. I grew up in a small town south of New Haven, where winter was long and intense. At some level I associated snow and ice with the exciting pleasures that waited for us after school. I was to have my fill of it, though.

It was obvious I had to work fast, faster than I'd originally planned, because of the increasing cold. I wanted to have everything put together and working before I disassembled it and pushed it through the airlock. The robots weren't made for cold weather, unfortunately. They had bad traction on the ice and sometimes their joints would seize up. One of them complained constantly, but of course it was the best worker, too, so I couldn't just turn it off and let it disappear under the drifts, an idea that tempted me.

White Hill often came out for a few minutes to stand and watch me and the robots struggle with the icy heavy boulders, machinery, and statuary. We took walks along the seashore that became shorter as the weather worsened. The last walk was a disaster.

We had just gotten to the beach when a sudden storm came up with a sandblast wind so violent that it blew us off our feet. We crawled back to the partial protection of the ruins and huddled together, the wind screaming so loudly that we had to shout to hear each other. The storm continued to mount and, in our terror, we decided to run for the shelter. White Hill slipped on some ice and suffered a horrible injury, a jagged piece of metal slashing her face diagonally from forehead to chin, blinding her left eye and tearing off part of her nose. Pearly bone showed through, cracked, at eyebrow, cheek, and chin. She rose up to one elbow and fell slack.

I carried her the rest of the way, immensely glad for the physical strength that made it possible. By the time we got inside she was unconscious and my white coat was a scarlet flag of blood.

A plastic-clad doctor came through immediately and did what she could to get White Hill out of immediate danger. But there was a problem with more sophisticated treatment. They couldn't bring the equipment out to our shelter, and White Hill wouldn't survive the stress of purging unless she had had a chance to heal for a while. Besides the facial wound, she had a broken elbow and collarbone and two cracked ribs.

For a week or so she was always in pain or numb. I sat with her, numb myself, her face a terrible puffed caricature of its former beauty, the wound glued up with plaskin the color of putty. Split skin of her eyelid slack over the empty socket.

The mirror wasn't visible from her bed, and she didn't ask for one, but whenever I looked away from her, her working hand came up to touch and catalogue the damage. We both knew how fortunate she was to be alive at all, and especially in an era and situation where the damage could all be repaired, given time and a little luck. But it was still a terrible thing to live with, an awful memory to keep reliving.

When she was more herself, able to talk through her ripped and pasted mouth, it was difficult for me to keep my composure. She had considerable philosophical, I suppose you could say spiritual, resources, but she was so profoundly stunned that she couldn't follow a line of reasoning very far, and usually wound up sobbing in frustration.

Sometimes I cried with her, although Petrosian men don't cry except in response to music. I had been a soldier once and had seen my ration of injury and death, and I always felt the experience had hardened me, to my detriment. But my friends who had been wounded or killed were just friends, and all of us lived then with the certainty that every day could be anybody's last one. To have the woman you love senselessly mutilated by an accident of weather was emotionally more arduous than losing a dozen companions to the steady erosion of war, a different kind of weather.

I asked her whether she wanted to forget our earlier agreement and talk about our projects. She said no; she was still working on hers, in a way, and she still wanted it to be a surprise. I did manage to distract her, playing with the shaping box. We made cartoonish representations of Lo and old Norita, and combined them in impossible sexual geometries. We shared a limited kind of sex ourselves, finally.

The doctor pronounced her well enough to be taken apart, and both of us were scourged and reappeared on the other side. White Hill was already in surgery when I woke up; there had been no reason to revive her before beginning the restorative processes.

I spent two days wandering through the blandness of Amazonia, jungle laced through concrete, quartering the huge place on foot. Most areas seemed catatonic. A few were boisterous with end-of-the-world hysteria. I checked on her progress so often that they eventually assigned a robot to call me up every hour, whether or not there was any change.

On the third day I was allowed to see her, in her sleep. She was pale but seemed completely restored. I watched her for an hour, perhaps more, when her eyes suddenly opened. The new one was blue, not green, for some reason. She didn't focus on me.

"Dreams feed art," she whispered in Petrosian; "and art feeds dreams." She closed her eyes and slept again.

⟋

She didn't want to go back out. She had lived all her life in the tropics, even the year she spent in bondage, and the idea of returning to the ice that had slashed her was more than repugnant. Inside Amazonia it was always summer, now, the authorities trying to keep everyone happy with heat and light and jungle flowers.

I went back out to gather her things. Ten large sheets of buff paper I unstuck from our walls and stacked and rolled. The necklace, and the satchel of rare coins she had brought from Seldene, all her worldly wealth.

I considered wrapping up my own project, giving the robots instructions for its dismantling and transport, so that I could just go back inside with her and stay. But that would be chancy. I wanted to see the thing work once before I took it apart.

So I went through the purging again, although it wasn't strictly necessary; I could have sent her things through without hand-carrying them. But I wanted to make sure she was on her feet before I left her for several weeks.

She was not on her feet, but she was dancing. When I recovered from the purging, which now took only half a day, I went to her hospital room and they referred me to our new quarters, a three-room dwelling in a place called Plaza des Artistes. There were two beds in the bedroom, one a fancy medical one, but that was worlds better than trying to find privacy in a hospital.

There was a note floating in the air over the bed saying she had gone to a party in the common room. I found her in a gossamer wheelchair, teaching a hand dance to Denli om Cord, while a harpist and flautist from two different worlds tried to settle on a mutual key.

She was in good spirits. Denli remembered an engagement and I wheeled White Hill out onto a balcony that overlooked a lake full of sleeping birds, some perhaps real.

It was hot outside, always hot. There was a mist of perspiration on her face, partly from the light exercise of the dance, I supposed. In the light from below, the mist gave her face a sculpted appearance, unsparing sharpness, and there was no sign left of the surgery.

"I'll be out of the chair tomorrow," she said, "at least ten minutes at a time." She laughed, "*Stop* that!"

"Stop what?"

"Looking at me like that."

I was still staring at her face. "It's just . . . I suppose it's such a relief."

"I know." She rubbed my hand. "They showed me pictures, of before. You looked at that for so many days?"

"I saw you."

She pressed my hand to her face. The new skin was taut but soft, like a baby's. "Take me downstairs?"

•

It's hard to describe, especially in light of later developments, disintegrations, but that night of fragile lovemaking marked a permanent change in the way we linked or at least the way I was linked to her: I've been married twice, long and short, and have been in some kind of love a hundred times. But no woman has ever owned me before.

This is something we do to ourselves. I've had enough women who *tried* to possess me, but always was able to back or circle away, in literal preservation of self. I always felt that life was too long for one woman.

Certainly part of it is that life is not so long anymore. A larger part of it was the run through the screaming storm, her life streaming out of her, and my stewardship, or at least companionship, afterward, during her slow transformation back into health and physical beauty. The core of her had never changed, though, the stubborn serenity that I came to realize, that warm night, had finally infected me as well.

The bed was a firm narrow slab, cooler than the dark air heavy with the scent of Earth flowers. I helped her onto the bed (which instantly conformed to her) but from then on it was she who cared for me, saying that was all she wanted, all she really had strength for. When I tried to reverse that, she reminded me of a holiday palindrome that has sexual overtones in both our languages: Giving is taking is giving.

●

We spent a couple of weeks as close as two people can be. I was her lover and also her nurse, as she slowly strengthened. When she was able to spend most of her day in normal pursuits, free of the wheelchair or "intelligent" bed (with which we had made a threesome, at times uneasy), she urged me to go back outside and finish up. She was ready to concentrate on her own project, too. Impatient to do art again, a good sign.

I would not have left so soon if I had known what her project involved. But that might not have changed anything.

As soon as I stepped outside, I knew it was going to take longer than planned. I had known from the inside monitors how cold it was going to be, and how many ceemetras of ice had accumulated, but I didn't really *know* how bad it was until I was standing there, looking at my piles of materials locked in opaque glaze. A good thing I'd left the robots inside the shelter, and a good thing I had left a few hand tools outside. The door was buried under two metras of snow and ice. I sculpted myself a passageway, an application of artistic skills I'd never foreseen.

I debated calling White Hill and telling her that I would be longer than expected. We had agreed not to interrupt each other, though, and it was likely she'd started working as soon as I left.

The robots were like a bad comedy team, but I could only be amused by them for an hour or so at a time. It was so cold that the water vapor from my breath froze into an icy sheath on my beard and mustache. Breathing was painful; deep breathing probably dangerous.

So most of the time, I monitored them from inside the shelter. I had the place to myself; everyone else had long since gone into the dome. When I wasn't working I drank too much, something I had not done regularly in centuries.

It was obvious that I wasn't going to make a working model. Delicate balance was impossible in the shifting gale. But the robots and I had our hands full, and other grasping appendages engaged, just dismantling the various pieces and moving them through the lock. It was unexciting but painstaking work. We did all the laser cuts inside the shelter, allowing the rock to come up to room temperature so it didn't spall or shatter. The air-conditioning wasn't quite equal to the challenge, and neither were the cleaning robots, so after a while it was like living in a foundry: everywhere a kind of greasy slickness of rock dust, the air dry and metallic.

So it was with no regret that I followed the last slice into the airlock myself, even looking forward to the scourging if White Hill was on the other side.

She wasn't. A number of other people were missing, too. She left this note behind:

I knew from the day we were called back here what my new piece would have to be, and I knew I had to keep it from you, to spare you sadness. And to save you the frustration of trying to talk me out of it.

As you may know by now, scientists have determined that the Fwndyri indeed have sped up the Sun's evolution somehow. It will continue to warm, until in thirty or forty years there will be an explosion called the "helium flash." The Sun will become a red giant, and the Earth will be incinerated.

There are no starships left, but there is one avenue of escape. A kind of escape.

Parked in high orbit there is a huge interplanetary transport that was used in the terraforming of Mars. It's a couple of centuries older than you, but like yourself it has been excellently preserved. We are going to ride it out to a distance sufficient to survive the Sun's catastrophe, and there remain until the situation improves, or does not.

This is where I enter the picture. For our survival to be meaningful in this thousand-year war, we have to resort to coldsleep. And for a large number of people to survive centuries of coldsleep, they need my jaturnary skills. Alone, in the ice, they would go slowly mad. Connected through the matrix of my mind, they will have a sense of community, and may come out of it intact.

I will be gone, of course. I will be by the time you read this. Not dead, but immersed in service. I could not be revived if this were only a hundred people for a hundred days. This will be a thousand, perhaps for a thousand years.

No one else on Earth can do jaturnary, and there is neither time nor equipment for me to transfer my ability to anyone. Even if there were, I'm not sure I would trust anyone else's skill. So I am gone.

My only loss is losing you. Do I have to elaborate on that?

You can come if you want. In order to use the transport, I had to agree that the survivors be chosen in accordance with the Earth's strict class system—starting with dear Norita, and from that pinnacle, on down—but they were willing to make exceptions for all of the visiting artists. You have until mid-Deciembre to decide; the ship leaves Januar first.

If I know you at all, I know you would rather stay behind and die. Perhaps the prospect of living "in" me could move you past your fear of coldsleep: your aversion to jaturnary. If not, not.

I love you more than life. But this is more than that. Are we what we are?

W. H.

The last sentence is a palindrome in her language, not mine, that I believe has some significance beyond the obvious.

●

I did think about it for some time. Weighing a quick death, or even a slow one, against spending centuries locked frozen in a tiny room with Norita and her ilk. Chattering on at the speed of synapse, and me unable to not listen.

I have always valued quiet, and the eternity of it that I face is no more dreadful than the eternity of quiet that preceded my birth.

If White Hill were to be at the other end of those centuries of torture, I know I could tolerate the excruciation. But she was dead now, at least in the sense that I would never see her again.

Another woman might have tried to give me a false hope, the possibility that in some remote future the process of *jaturnary* would be advanced to the point where her personality could be recovered. But she knew how unlikely that would be even if teams of scientists could be found to work on it, and years could be found for them to work in. It would be like unscrambling an egg.

Maybe I would even do it, though, if there were just some chance that, when I was released from that din of garrulous bondage, there would be something like a real world, a world where I could function as an artist. But I don't think there will even be a world where I can function as a man.

There probably won't be any humanity at all, soon enough. What they did to the Sun they could do to all of our stars, one assumes. They win the war, the Extermination, as my parent called it. Wrong side exterminated.

Of course the Fwndyri might not find White Hill and her charges. Even if they do find them, they might leave them preserved as an object of study.

The prospect of living on eternally under those circumstances, even if there were some growth to compensate for the immobility and the company, holds no appeal.

☙

What I did in the time remaining before mid-Deciembre was write this account. Then I had it translated by a xenolinguist into a form that she said could be decoded by any creature sufficiently similar to humanity to make any sense of the story. Even the Fwndyri, perhaps. They're human enough to want to wipe out a competing species.

I'm looking at the preliminary sheets now. English down the left side and a jumble of dots, squares, and triangles down the right. Both sides would have looked equally strange to me a few years ago.

White Hill's story will be conjoined to a standard book that starts out with basic mathematical principles, in dots and squares and triangles, and moves from that into physics, chemistry, biology. Can you go from biology to the human heart? I have to hope so. If this is read by alien eyes, long after the last human breath is stilled, I hope it's not utter gibberish.

☙

So I will take this final sheet down to the translator and then deliver the whole thing to the woman who is going to transfer it to permanent sheets of platinum, which will be put in a prominent place aboard the transport.

They could last a million years, or ten million, or more. After the Sun is a cinder, and the ship is a frozen block enclosing a thousand bits of frozen flesh, she will live on in this small way.

So now my work is done. I'm going outside, to the quiet.

The Road to Reality

PHILLIP C. JENNINGS

One of the most prolific writers in the business at short lengths, Phillip C. Jennings has become one of the most frequent contributors to Asimov's Science Fiction *magazine over the past two decades, and has also appeared in most of the field's other major SF magazines and anthologies. His first novel,* Tower to the Sky, *was published in 1988. His most recent book was the fat and eccentric collection* The Bug Life Chronicles, *and he is long overdue for a second. Jennings lives in Golden Valley, Minnesota.*

Jennings has dealt with the terraforming process several times, in stories such as "The Fourth Intercometary" and "Blossoms." The novella that follows, though, is his most complex and imaginative take on the concept, as he takes us across the galaxy on a mission to terraform a lifeless planet that is soon embroiled in an intricate and deadly web of politics, intrigue, clashing philosophies, hidden identity, deceit, warfare, and murder—a conflict that will stretch across thousands of years and affect the destiny of millions yet unborn . . .

3111

I dropped bombs carefully for four Blue World years, shaking the earthquake potential from this weak place in the planet's crust, and sloshing the magma back and forth. My lake of lava coagulated at the crest of each bomb-tide, first along the interior rim, and then in the opposite direction, edging thirty kilometers of Region 62's seashore.

Two desolate ridges built higher with each swing of the bomb cycle. Chemical additives enhanced rapid hardening, and I achieved basaltic walls. Like the lip of a bowl, the south ridge tilted forward when seen from the ocean. It was very much a roof over the rough beach below.

I readied my *tour de force.* I altered the lava mix, aiming for a light, glassy obsidian. Then I precision-bombed my work-basin. The incandescent stuff sheeted seaward over the lava roof, splashing and dripping in curtains that cooled to the integrity of warm tar, chilled by unseasonable winds.

Some of my material froze before touching the water, hardening into a permanent cascade of stone. Regrettably, much did not, and slopped down to make a reef that steamed a few days into the poisonous air.

This was the best I hoped to achieve with "natural" materials. Along my rugged thirty-kilometer shore, six kilometers boasted a wall on the sea side, arching from high above the waves. Obsidian and basalt formed opposite flanks, enclosing a transitional space floored by igneous shrapnel, sand and tidewater.

I called it Yoshi Cathedral. It was finished, and I had been alone too long. I dusted off my social graces and enticed Lady Midori to come visit.

"It'll never last," she warned me, stopping in the shallows short of the entry. "It'll be centuries before people expand into Region 62. How can *that* be structurally sound?"

She raised a salamandrine arm and pointed at a particularly thin stretch of obsidian wall, "The first big storm, and it'll shatter."

"I think perhaps not," I said.

She seemed afraid to go inside. Perhaps I was daunting, standing ahead at twice the height of anything ever born human, in my battered, splattered carapace. She crouched into the water and let a big wave roll over her. Then she stood again. "Comrade Yoshi, have you been using chemical agents? Unnatural additives?"

I said nothing at first. Finally, I answered: "What kind of body is that?"

Midori smiled. "A one-day outdoor special. Oxygen from the electrical dissociation of water. When the batteries run out it'll be dead."

"Pretty damned artificial," I said.

"It'll leave bones. *You're* the one who complains about fossils and such things."

I shook my robotic head. "Blue World will have no coherent fossil record. We can pretend to make it Earthlike, but not completely."

"Most of us think it's a worthwhile pretense. You feel otherwise. We know this, and we pray it's not—well, we pray—"

"I'm not insane," I said. "That label is flung too wildly. It's a Suppressionist insult." My voice softened. "Let's not argue about this."

Lady Midori persisted. "Can you remember a time when we *didn't* argue? Yoshi, you do grand things, as if this planet were just another virtual reality. That clouding of the line worries us. We survived a thousand-year trip from Earth by taking refuge in simulations, but so many of us got lost in fantasy. So many old friends! First you lose faith in existence, and then what's the point of existing?"

Midori ducked down to wet herself completely. Her present incarnation had a thrifty, cold-blooded metabolism, but even so her energies were running low. For the moment she was too fatigued to persist.

I waited for her bald, turd-colored head to bob up again. She gazed lidlessly at the glossy black shoreline I'd created, and I began a rant of my own. "Why is death fearsome? We were dead before we left Earth. Forty thousand dead souls stored in a computer. Ha! You talk of 'survival'! Our unearned second lives were a feast. The food was good, but most of us? Our appetites grew sated. It's natural. They *expected* attrition back on Earth. That's why they began with so many. They thought on a grand scale, you see."

I left the shore and waded closer, making it easier in case she needed to reduce her transmission strength. "We'll plant people on this world three hundred years from now," I continued. "People cooked out of the same vats that made the body you're wearing now. My formations will attract their descendants' attention. They'll calculate how unlikely it is that lava could act this way. They'll take samples and find chemical agents, and discover a clue to their origins. One can always hope."

She eyed me doubtfully. "Subversion. Perhaps it's my duty to turn you in. I should complain against you." Lady Midori's radio voice was a whisper.

"Come over to my side," I said. "The others want our new humans to start clean, Adams and Eves in the Garden of Eden, begetting children and grandchildren. We're supposed to hide among this naive humanity. We're supposed to leave them ignorant and not play gods, because that would oppress them. It would give them a permanent inferiority complex."

"Yes! Let them develop *themselves!*" Lady Midori responded. "A new world! That's the idea."

"They'll invent gods. *Why not offer ourselves* in place of magic and superstition? It would be telling the truth. We're terraforming this world. At least, those of us who survived the trip. We have a lot to teach."

"We'll teach in our hidden identities," Lady Midori said. "We'll wear flesh, and risk mortality. It's a way to suppress ourselves. To make ourselves less dangerous, because we aren't so reliable, you know? Yes, certainly you know! All our friends who went insane—friends and lovers!—just because we few made it across the stars, can we say we're stable? The numbers are against us. Nine hundred souls left! Nine hundred souls out of forty thousand!"

I laugh rarely when talking politics. The stupidities that seemed funny ten years ago frighten me now. "This is a *sane* policy? To suppress the truth, and leak it out by hints and winks? There's no Santa Claus. There's no Santa Claus. All right, you're old enough to know. There *is* a Santa Claus. Ah, *now* you don't trust us!"

"They *shouldn't* trust us," Lady Midori said heatedly.

"Let's not make ourselves worse than we are," I answered. "Nor should we make *them* worse. Why raise generations of primitives? Why rerun ten thousand years of history? Can they do it? Can they move from bush life and campfires, and achieve a scientific world view on a world without a fossil record? No, let's give them all our technology."

"So they can die mad, like us?" Lady Midori objected. "So they can play sophisticated games, achieve sophisticated boredom, and commit sophisticated suicide?"

"No! Again, no! Hell! But I say this. If some personality zeroes out after eight hundred years, it's a private choice. Why should it terrify you into fake primitivism?"

This was no abstraction. We were talking about mutual, lives-long friends. Over the long trip some had gone to zero. Others exiled themselves inside labyrinths of virtual fantasy, so deeply solipsistic they'd lost any hope of contact. In their absence we called them insane. Thinking of them was painful for both of us. Lady Midori dropped her gaze. "We're talking in circles."

I was energized. I had a dozen points to make against the Suppressionist Party. As secret teachers it was their choice what truths *and what lies* to leak to our human charges, whereas my faction saw a better future: We saw ourselves living openly as terraforming intelligences from Old Earth, cycling through a choice of robotic incarnations, ready to deal with what our colonists requested on their own initiative. Empowering ourselves meant empowering them. But Midori had heard it all before. Why goad her?

I changed the subject. "I have something else to show you. It's in Region 19. A river that bridges over itself, loops around, and runs under. It was easier than this lava beach. Just a matter of digging a tunnel. On my new course it runs into a rain-shadow desert."

"More tricks!" Lady Midori sighed. "Give me a day to put together a Region 19 body. Are we done here? Already I feel unwell."

Our meeting had been a failure on both sides. Now it was over. "I'll put your body out of misery," I volunteered, from a reluctant sense of duty. I hated the way my political opponents used bodies of flesh, because—well, wouldn't it be true? If their vatlings had longer to live, wouldn't they develop souls of their own? And feelings? I'd never kill a frog, but now I had to sever the life from a thing compounded of frog and eel and human DNA. A thing with unrenewable batteries that would otherwise starve on a nearly lifeless world.

"Thank you." Lady Midori sank into a posture very like prayer. She radioed her soul back to Geosync Control. After a decent interval I pushed a hand through and snapped her spine just below the brain stem.

I carried the corpse to shore, parked my old, worn body in a safe place and radioed up to space, and then down again, to another robot habitus in Region 19. I waited by my spiral river through a rainy afternoon, trudging a raw, iron-rich landscape, dark weathered reds relieved by the brighter sheltered pink of my undercut tunnel.

The rain stopped. The skies took on the colors of sunset, lurid from Blue World's poisonous excesses of carbon dioxide. Lady Midori failed to come. Instead I received a summons.

"What do you mean, 'job review?'" I answered. "That's what I've been doing. I've been providing Lady Midori with views of the work I've done!"

Returning one last time to Geosync, I learned that I was expected to testify at my own trial. The Suppressionists were dominant, and my "courtroom" was as stark as they could make it. We were all computer entities, at least during our times off-planet, but *they* were computer entities who hated computer effects. In my default body-of-choice (1930s heroic worker off a Diego Garcia mural) I stood immersed in white directionless light. I was confronted by floating faces so simplified into caricature they might as well be name tags with voices.

It was all organized and procedural, even if nobody bothered to explain the procedure to me. Lord Hideyaki's face zoomed close and began to speak. "We have heard people like Comrade Yoshi. They are a minority. They do not like the policies of the majority. Using the model of the parliaments of Old Earth, they talk themselves up as a *loyal opposition*. The rules of loyal opposition are clear. Do not subvert the policies that the majority have voted to carry out. If you can't bring yourself to further those policies when it's your job to do so, then resign."

"It's my job to engineer the long-term liveability of Blue World," I responded. "To reduce geological instabilities, and bring water to places that might otherwise be deserts. I have done that job. I have succeeded."

Another face spoke up, pale and oval, with black lines for eyes, nose, and mouth. "You have created unnatural wonders. The vat-colonists will seek them out. Perhaps you intend to expose nearby veins of ore. Our vatlings will dig and uncover gold plates with writing on them, or some such trick."

"There are no gold plates." I refrained from saying *thanks for the idea.*

The face pushed forward. "Lady Midori feels you have hidden intentions. You told her you favored a policy of planting clues."

"Did you mean to leave our colonists entirely clueless?" I responded. "What are they going to do without fossils? No, at some point this game of yours must have an end. These 'vatlings' are human beings. We're talking about bringing forth real people, and not dolls or children or computer fic-toids. *They'll be more real than us.* That's the truth of it. When you realize this, Suppressionism must fade."

I held up my computer-generated hands as if to ward off these drifting faces, though for all their anger they were as unreadable as masks. "Your party will wane," I continued, "but now you think you can make me an example, and scare the opposition. Well, what's my punishment? The sane among us work on Blue World's surface. The insane pursue their dreams inside Geosync's computer. Are you going to vote me insane, or let me get on with my job?"

Lady Midori floated forward, while many faces retreated. "You may be insane, despite all your denials."

For a moment I was speechless. How dare she set such a precedent! Mak-ing this accusation once made it easier to do it again. The Suppressionists would soon feel free to purge everyone who disagreed with them. The days of toleration and open debate were over.

I mustered myself. "Midori, you pushed the idea that on Blue World there should be no size disparity between men and women. Women as big as men could not be physically dominated. I rallied people from my faction to your side. We radioed Earth for genetic updates. *This* is how you reward me!"

I'd have spared Midori nothing if I'd been allowed to continue. I'd have exposed her secret: Because the languages of Earth had evolved over a thou-sand years, they used scholars to interpret our requests. Perhaps they got things wrong. After ten-point-six years, plus processing time, plus another ten-point-six years in transition at the speed of light, Earth's latest update package was too full, too elaborate. It pretended to be what we asked for, but could mere size have so many consequences?

I'd have raised a dozen issues in my defense, but suddenly I couldn't speak. While my sanity was put to a vote, I continued under restraint.

The count was twenty-two to seven. Afterward, I went blank.

3115

I woke inside a cyberscape in Ready State Zero, flat green under cloudless blue. I was entirely alone. All the other nutcases had used the centuries to make themselves scarce.

I was furious. Who wouldn't be? I had a *duty* to be furious, a duty to myself and to my friends. The blank plasticity of my surroundings was like canvas to an artist, but though I was locked in, with nothing else to do but paint, I could create nothing until I quashed the emotions that burned too strongly inside me.

All it took was lots of time, lots of green and blue, and a single question.

What's the point? What useful thing could I do here? What focus could draw me away from useless anger?

I made a decision. The purpose of my life became to rescue souls from hell.

Theologians say that hell is distance from God. A second hell is to be distanced so long from reality that you no longer believe it exists. Such distances are routine in virtuality. The sheer scale of my cybernetic environment was daunting. To find even one person among mad thousands, I'd have to explore complexities of size and game-logic beyond any metaphor. A rat-maze the size of Asia? Entirely new laws of physics?

No, thank you. There had to be easier ways than subjecting myself to tortures like these.

Why did I want to find my fellow inmates? Well, what else was there to do? Create my own fake universe? I'd done that a hundred times over on the long voyage between the stars. I'd done it, and kept sane—or maybe I *was* crazy. Maybe deep down I wanted to be here, and not out in reality. That's why I couldn't bring myself to kowtow to my political enemies.

Home sweet home for a thousand years. I'd forced them to return me here. What is reality? Why had I run away from it?

I have an answer to the first question, if not to the second. Reality organizes the world you're in. The reality of the Geosync computer organized thousands of incompatible cyberworlds, and placed them all under one ultimate set of laws.

For most people who believe in God, He's the one who organizes the true universe. He's the ultimate Computer—except the true universe is organized by the laws of physics, and that puts the old-fashioned God out of business.

This is my confession: If I need God at all, I need a God of freedom, of a spontaneous grace that makes all organizing principles less oppressive and less confining. Perhaps the others trapped here were like me. They were oppressed because the computer worked flawlessly, giving them everything they wanted—except they wanted more.

I hoped so. For those who were happy in their virtual play I could do nothing. For true solipsists who'd lost faith in organizing principles like the computer, it was *freedom* that oppressed them, not *law*. They might be miserable, but I could do nothing for them either.

I hoped there was a reachable minority. I'd never find them by hiking out from Ready State Zero. Instead I generated a hundred cubes and zoomed them into rectilinear shapes. I stuck them together to make a longhouse, and defined some rooms inside. I nominated opposite directions for south and north, using hot and cold colors.

I could have invoked directional light sources and theme music—something by Strauss or Demby—but I wanted the rules of electricity to apply, so now my job became complicated.

I grew a refrigerator-sized rectangle and designated it as the power source, something that glowed and hummed. I covered its exposed surfaces with outlets. In this early state of development, things I stuck together *stayed* together, and that was good enough for me. That's how *real* reality works too, at the micro level.

This "house" was the seed from which I'd grow a motherboard, complete with a processor identical to the computer in which we all lived. I'd program my virtual computer with the same software that ran in the real one.

Then I'd operate the damned thing, and learn its tricks. I'd search memory dumps to find where souls might be kept—souls who thought they were floating free. In truth they had storage addresses like everything else.

I'd cheat, and use those addresses to send backdoor messages to ten thousand madmen and madwomen. Doing so, without playing their labyrinth games, would prove to them that they weren't alone.

I wasn't alone either. The Suppressionist purge continued. I heard the unmuffled engine of a two-seat roadster and looked out my longhouse's big south window. Comrade Kazumi whizzed by, cutting tire-marks in the featureless green. She made a second loop and then stopped. "Your doors aren't big enough."

"Reduce your scale by half," I suggested. "And for heaven's sake, tune your engine."

Comrade Kazumi shrank to bumper-car size. She drove her roadster-body into my kitchen. Her voice came out of the vehicle's radio. "You really blew it. The Suppressionists are in complete control. They use your name as a brand to taint others. What is it between you and Midori? You've given her everything, and now your political corpse to dance on. What made you do it? Some male-female thing?"

The suggestion made me laugh. "I was male a thousand years ago. I don't remember how it felt. It's all words, and I keep the words safe. I'll never forget them, but I can't conjure the colors or the emotions."

"The Suppressionists are ever so keen to have bodies again," Kazumi said. "Their long-ago lives must have been good ones. Maybe that's the difference between them and us. We were victims. We're victims now. It's a reversion to type."

I could have asked Comrade Kazumi about her life on Earth, and told her my early history. That's what she wanted. I offered something close to that ultimate intimacy. "I was shy in the long past," I said. "I was shy among strangers. Very quiet until I learned to know people. Of course, after decades in space I befriended so many people among our dead that I didn't have to be shy anymore. So no one remembers that about me. But after years of solo work on Blue World, my shyness returned. It made me clumsy. I was abrupt with Lady Midori, and preachy."

"She's preachy enough on her own," Kazumi said.

"That made it worse," I agreed.

"Is this an apology?"

"Are others being exiled here?" I asked back. "Should I grovel now? Or wait and make it a mass event?"

Kazumi laughed. "I think you're very clever. You're cleverly doing something right now that I don't understand. Do you want help?"

"Yes, I want you to spawn cubes and run them out in linear patterns. Here's a map." I stepped around the counter and held it before her headlights.

"This looks like a memory chip. Like one of those logic circuits."

"It'll take lots of long-distance driving to measure these circuits and lay them out," I told her. "We're building a computer inside virtual reality, to emulate the real one in orbit around Blue World."

"Ah." Comrade Kazumi formed a thought bubble over her head. In the bubble she was female and wore a long golden dress. The kitchen was the same, and her mental Yoshi was identical with myself. She embraced me, gave me a kiss—and turned ameboid to swallow my body inside herself. A double-bulk Kazumi burped and winked. "Oops. Sometimes I can't restrain myself."

The bubble disappeared. The thought transaction was a way of saying she liked me, and also goodbye. It was a pause between events. In real life, people sleep and eat and run quick errands, and we've found the need to imitate these framing moments. But we're efficient about it. Now it was over, and Comrade Kazumi gunned out the door. She hadn't even asked *why* I wanted to build a virtual computer.

When he arrived, Comrade Basho was angrier than Kazumi, and more inquisitive. I explained my purposes. He grunted and stomped off in his sumo body, setting up camp to intercept the next series of exiles. Together they debated, and voted to help me build my computer.

"I'm told our semi-loyal opposition has a new leader," Basho said as they filed into my kitchen. "Comrade Haga is pliant. Perhaps he'll be effective. He'll soften the Suppressionists. They may back down and let us return from exile. Let's do nothing to aggravate Lady Midori or Lord Hideyaki."

"No secret plots? I assure you I'm being honest," I said. "Honesty has been my downfall, but in this case I hope it will see us through a hard time. All we want is to reach a few insane souls, a first step to bringing them back to reality. Statistics may favor us. One or two percent may want to abandon their madness. We'll be their saviors. That's twenty souls right there. Another twenty—another *hundred*, maybe—will respond to dialogue."

Basho shrugged. "A harvest of souls. The Suppressionists won't like it if we seed this harvest with opposition ideas."

I laughed. "Perhaps they'll punish us. They'll exile us back to reality!"

"No, really—"

"We'll be ourselves, Basho. Otherwise we're prisoners twice over. Why are you afraid? You've always been courageous before."

Comrade Basho moved closer. He lowered his voice. "Geosync computer has to operate these next three centuries, until Blue World is ready for colonization. After that? Many functions can be transferred down to the sixty-four regional depots. The Suppressionists will take vat bodies, and live on the surface. Then what? What's the easiest way of dealing with us? Why, it's obvious! *Turn off the computer!* They hate it. They hate virtuality, and they don't trust us at all. It's not like murder. We'll be fully backed up, so there's no guilt involved."

He shuddered back. "We have to get free, out to reality, or we'll sleep in orbit forever."

I was amazed. "*Three hundred years*, Basho! In our mortal lives back on Old Earth, if we were told of a doom three hundred years away, we'd have counted it an unbelievable blessing to last that long! Many things can happen in three centuries. Many things *must* happen. People's concepts evolve."

"I'm with you," Basho said, holding out his hands against the flood of my words. "I'm with you. Let's try to reach the insane. Everyone will call that a good thing. Let's agree on that. If we have other issues, we'll talk them out later."

Basho and his companions got to work. New exiles arrived. In time there came to be forty of us. Before we reached that maximum, I called the gang together. "We need the best leader among us, as spokesperson to the Suppressionists if they come to check on us. Not me. I think that's obvious. My enemies call me Yoshi the Trickster. It's possible they believe their own lies."

"To them we're *all* villains," Basho grunted.

Comrade Haga agreed. He was our most recent arrival. "I may be the worst. All my compromises and soft words—they say I'm duplicitous and subtle. *You*, Comrade Yoshi! At least you were frank. You argued openly."

"Open argument was easy before Lady Midori made it a sin," I said. "Excluding you and me, who would be a good candidate?"

We chose Comrade Atsuko. She was a creative virtualist, always flaunting weird bodies and costumes, but her new responsibilities forced her to a minimal policy. We strove to look as we'd looked back on Earth, males male and females female, and we wore black unisex cassocks. If Comrade Kazumi couldn't abide being anything but a roadster—and she couldn't—then she should spend minimum time at headquarters. If Basho insisted on being sumo-sized, at least he should keep his acres of skin covered up. And so forth.

Atsuko issued press releases. A few Suppressionists read them. Perhaps they wished we hadn't organized ourselves around a new mission, but how could they object to our hopes to reach the insane?

They could have designated one of themselves to come keep an eye on us, but no Suppressionist was willing to take on that job full-time. Once or twice they sent visitors. Years passed. By visit number three, our virtual computer was almost ready.

I'd changed, not much, but a little. During these six years of imprisonment it became important to me that people should be described in their outward aspects, as we describe people in real life, with real bodies. After all, we held to the same features consistently, in accordance with Comrade Atsuko's rules.

Basho's pug nose fit well with his concept as a hearty peasant male, bluff and impatient with nonsense. He'd grown a spade beard to complement his sumo-wrestler's ponytail.

Haga's beaky, half-American features made him an internationalist. He was a bridge-builder who embodied genetic bridges within himself.

Atsuko's plucked eyebrows and bleached skin betrayed small vanities, precise and controlled.

I chose to look as I had before my immune system started to give out more than a thousand years ago; a narrow-boned male, tall and gangly, with large hands. Less the heroic worker I'd idealized before being exiled, and more the unheroic clerk.

When she showed up, Lady Midori wore a cassock like the rest of us, only green instead of black. She exhibited herself as a matronly woman with bad teeth, and walked energetically up to the long house, rolling her bulky hips. "This isn't correct Suppressionism," she told Atsuko within my hearing. "You show discipline, keeping to one shape only, but you cloud the line that separates you from reality. You use computer effects too well to imitate the real world."

"There is actually more discipline in our slavish imitation, than if we adopted floating face-icons," Atsuko amplified, with a cheerful nod. "But we're not foolish about it. I know how to use the Blend function to achieve cellulite, but with my legs covered, I don't bother."

"I've come to make proposals," Lady Midori said. "I see Comrade Yoshi over there, starting to program this fake computer. All this was your idea in the first place, eh, Yoshi?"

I nodded curtly. This was the woman who had betrayed me. For six years she had made computer virtuality into a political dumping ground. Seeing her, I felt my hatred grow warm. What was she up to now?

She shook her head in reproof. "Have you taken an oath of silence?" she asked me.

"Comrade Atsuko is our spokesperson."

"But I like talking to *you*. Let me try something, and see how you react. We need more soil on Blue World. We need robots at work, grinding rock and rubble. It's a boring thankless job, but you'd be working in reality. I could parole the lot of you for a ten-year stint."

"I take it there's a price to pay," I said.

Midori smiled. "Lord Hideyaki is nervous about this computer. What else could be done with it? What is it you're not telling us?"

"There is nothing else," I said. "You've let us be. You've let us build the thing without much obvious oversight, and I suppose that means one of us is your spy. Do spies always tell the truth? This one is lying if he says I've got a secret plan."

"Still, that's the offer. I propose a vote among your group. You may work out in reality for ten years, but only if this whole construct is erased. Let the majority decide."

Lady Midori stood aside during our ensuing debate, but not so far that she didn't learn how deeply her offer divided us. Basho was desperate to escape virtuality. Kazumi was desperate to finish our work and contact the insane. We couldn't have it both ways. The majority voted with Basho.

Kazumi and I refused parole. "We'll get started rebuilding the computer," I said stubbornly. "Much will be done when you all come back."

"What if they make another offer?" Comrade Haga asked. He'd voted against Midori's offer, but now that we'd lost, he preferred to break rocks down on Blue World. He persisted. "What if ten years from now, they demand another sacrifice as the price for ten *more* years?"

"How many times can my heart break?" I said. "I don't know. Over and over, I guess. Over and over." That moment I made a silent resolution not to be Midori's victim. Kazumi and I would get the job done this next decade. We'd finish our damned computer, impossible though it seemed.

3121

Our comrades winked away in groups of two and three. Soon Kazumi and I were left to our own purposes, standing on flat green below flat blue. We set to work at once, to shape our computer by hand—a project forty souls had not quite achieved in six years. We were just two. After a second six years it became obvious we could never meet our ten-year deadline. In truth it had been obvious from the beginning, but I'd been driven by blind emotions.

I grew less blind. My morale collapsed. Comrade Kazumi found me sitting in my second longhouse's kitchen, staring hopelessly without focus. She drove close and parked beside me. After a while she spoke. "What we've done so far is accurate, right?"

I didn't answer.

"Point-for-point accurate. Suppose we weren't the first to conceive this project. Suppose some lost soul—not *purposefully* lost, or maybe she recovered her sanity—suppose a soul like that has used her ample time to finish the job and rescue others."

"Rescuing them to her lost place? What kind of rescue is that?" I scoffed.

Kazumi projected a thought-bubble. She spoke out of it, a woman in a yellow dress. "At least they'd be together. They'd be a society, relearning the lost arts of living with each other. We could find them and reconnect them with Ready State Zero. They'd be here next time Midori came. What a thing to throw at her! What a triumph!"

Kazumi proposed a systematic match. She invoked the Compare function, taking a small signature piece of our fractionally built computer, and running it against every non-preempted RAMstack address from zero-zero-zero, and then against every device address starting with the highly improbable A, and ending—without success—with device Q.

The job took half a year. We both sank into depression. After a time I roused myself. "It's a question of scale. How far can we downsize our signature device, and retain all its features?"

We shrank it to twenty-two percent, the absolute minimum, and ran another months-long Compare. Still no match, but this time Comrade Kazumi was not discouraged. "If our target's done the job it was made for and it's not in current use, it'll be zipped for storage. Let's use the Zip utility on our signature device, and try again."

The third time we found a matching address on device E. Our own stomping grounds!

Kazumi morphed from her roadster-shape and became a yellow-clad woman to give me a hug. "We could copy our target," she whispered, oozing happily all around me. "Now we've got it in our sights. We could copy everything that looks like zipped computer-emulation code!"

I agreed, trying to wiggle out of her sticky embrace. "That's what we have to do, to send messages. Just because a few souls may have found each other, doesn't mean their control-point addresses have moved. The rules are still the same. Only it's likely now we'll find a *society* out there in crazy-country. Not just hermits."

Kazumi's face grew ecstatic. She expanded in all directions and her belly closed around me. I popped free to another part of the kitchen. "We've got work to do."

She sighed and shrank, but the smile returned to her face, and she nodded in cheerful agreement. Over the next several shifts we copied the target pseudo-computer, and ran Unzip to make it functional. It came already programmed. I composed a message and mailed it out to forty thousand addresses. Strictly speaking, only a fraction would be receptive at any single moment. The rest were paged out to make things easier on an overburdened system—the more elaborate and demanding their scenarios, the more chance they were on a back burner. Still, I was hoping for ten thousand contacts. Kazumi hung back nervously. "What will we hear? How many responses?"

We waited. She reverted to motor-car and buzzed laps around my long-house. I busied myself building a swimming pool.

Time passed. How many responses? The answer was, just one. "You know what this means?" I theorized, fighting disappointment. "They've delegated a spokesperson. We'll visit him or her and it'll be a sort of embassy scenario."

Kazumi made a doubtful noise. "That's our best hope."

"You think it could mean something else? There's only one soul out there willing to talk to us?"

"There may have been—consolidations."

"Something forced?" I asked. "A dictatorship? Lacking a body, how can any soul enslave another? No, but I take your warning. This may not necessarily be the happy glorious moment we worked for, you and me twice over."

We invoked Transit. The message gave us a destination. In a moment of time we could never measure subjectively, we were elsewhere—in a room as vast as an aircraft hangar, girdered overhead by thin metal beams on x, y, and z coordinates.

The hangar was empty. A few worktables by the nearer wall were cluttered with things; a carpet shears, a box of instant noodle soup mix, and so forth. Given the proportions of this place, they scarcely counted. "Not much of an embassy," I whispered.

Kazumi leaned close, still a woman in yellow. "Consolidation can mean, *I eat you.* Suicide souls sometimes let others eat their memories. It's a way of keeping at least that much alive."

"Have you done this?"

"Twice," she admitted. "It was—wonderful. I felt like some oceanic soul-mother, moving in and adding color and life and value. I see in myself a monstrous desire for more. Not wanting to wait for my victim's suicide. A soul-eater might build a computer and send out invitations. All the more promising souls, the ones not lost in solipsism, they'd come and the monster would eat them."

"You tried to eat me."

"Sheer conquetry," she said. "I controlled myself. I let you go, didn't I? On Earth a thousand years ago there were civilized forms of every sexual persuasion, and then there were rapes. I know the difference. But yes, I want you inside me. If ever you tire of yourself, you're welcome to become part of me."

What an offer! Moving to the tables was a polite way of increasing my distance. "Stereo earphones," I said, picking them up. "A teddy bear. An address book. This is an odd collection."

"Souvenirs of eaten lives," Kazumi suggested.

The hangar door slid open. Bright sunlight sliced inside, outlining a small, shadowy figure. "Hello! We welcome you. My name is Joto."

"This is Comrade Kazumi. I'm Yoshi." We exchanged bows and I continued. "Our interstellar mission reached Blue World orbit forty-four years ago. Out in reality, nine hundred souls are terraforming a world mostly covered by water. In three hundred years we'll have enough oxygen to support a human colony."

"Ah! The old dream." On closer approach Joto looked more and more like a Christmas elf. His small body was mostly arms and legs. He had big ears and a wizened face.

"We can lead you there," Kazumi said. "And then if the people in charge are satisfied, you can get bodies. Robot bodies, or bodies grown out of vats. I speak through you, of course, to the whole society that sent you to meet us." She put these last words almost as a question.

"Reality exists, and we may qualify?" Joto asked. "How do you know it's not another simulation?"

"When you're real, you know," I said. "When you're awake, you know the difference between wakefulness and dreaming. We have returned from reality, and we carry that conviction. We haven't been virtual long enough to doubt it."

Joto closed his eyes. He spent a moment in what seemed like prayer, and opened them again. "I shall ask three times; is this true? You have come to show us the way to reality? This is your serious purpose?"

"Yes, it's true," Kazumi said.

I amplified. "There will be a test of some sort, a test of sanity. A test of how open you are to the dominant policies of the terraformers, who call themselves Suppressionists."

Joto stepped back and quirked his head. "Are these policies repugnant?" Somehow he sensed my attitudes.

"A kinder word is inadequate," I said. "With time they must change. The Suppressionists want to plant Blue World with humans innocent of all Old Earth science and culture. They'll hunt and fish and multiply, and it'll be very pastoral and idyllic. But it won't be, of course. Life isn't like that, and they'll feel obliged to take steps. The more steps, the better. That's how I feel. Let's teach our humans openly and honestly, and not disguise ourselves when we wander among them."

"You make the Suppressionists sound naive. If they were here, what would they say about you?"

I shrugged. "That I'm cunning. That I'm trying to poison your mind against them. That I long for a future where souls like ours take hero bodies and stride about Blue World, demanding honors as if we were gods. My appeal for 'openness' is just a first step, you see. In their view it's a ruse. We'll ultimately create a privileged class, and that's the object of all my scheming."

"We think this may be true, and what of it? The situation calls for the concentration of powers," Joto said.

"But also for the dissemination of knowledge," I said.

"Please. If you could move aside from those tables," Joto asked, making a fluttery gesture. "We have decided to take advantage of all you offer, but first you need to meet us in a less *packaged* form." He hurried past us and reached for the carpet shears.

On touching them, the shears vanished in a blossom of pixels. Now Joto had a companion. Sumi bowed and introduced herself. The process repeated with the address book, the box of dried soup mix, the blue comb, the leather belt, the jar of putty, the candlestick, et cetera. The hangar grew crowded with people. "Master Joto had the life-force to keep going in the midst of despair," Sumi explained. "He was the strongest. We surrendered our souls to his keeping, but each with a special key, so that if Joto ever discovered the way out to reality, we could become ourselves again."

"Otherwise, we might most of us be gone," another soul agreed. "Ah, so many suicides!"

"I'll lead you to what we've made of Ready State Zero," I said. "Then we'll send a message. Do you remember everything from our conversation with Master Joto? Do you understand about Suppressionism? It's those people I must get in touch with."

Joto strode forward. "We're ready. Everyone's accounted for."

I invoked Transit. It was like inviting a hundred strangers into my long-house. Soon there was music. Spheres of Glass, Prokofiev, and Kitaro floating by like differently colored bubbles in the air. My flat green became a lawn. The urge to tamper is universal, especially in virtuality. To keep my guests busy while I shot messages to all the Suppressionist lords and ladies, I asked them to build me a fishpond.

The pond grew into an elaborate water-garden, with canals and grottos, trellises and topiary. Master Joto kept to my side, and we inspected it together, while waiting for someone on the outside to answer.

I told him stories about Lady Midori. "How does all this fit in?" Joto asked. "You're a political leader in exile. How do we serve your political purposes?"

"Finding you kept me from boredom and futility," I told him. "But I think your people will serve my cause well. The Suppressionists hardly dare keep you all confined to virtuality. Not for long. If they did they'd make enemies among you, and some of their core support would falter."

"So you're optimistic we'll get bodies?"

"As fast as they can grow them, or build new robots," I said. "That serves me too. Out in reality you'll all witness that I'm not insane. Many of you may side with my faction in future debates. The way my supporters are treated will seem unfair, set against your own status."

"Some of us may not be very sane," Joto admitted. "We leaned on each other a special way. Think of a house of cards. Reality will heal us, or shock us further from health."

"I'd guess they'll screen each of you, and make a fairly honest job of it," I said.

"Let's speak frankly. You're hoping your enemies will blunder. You're describing how they *should* behave, but perhaps they—"

Joto's words were interrupted by a breach just ahead. Suppressionist face-masks floated out of the brightness in two even rows, like a military procession. Lord Hideyaki and Lady Midori were in the lead. They tilted politely in response to our bows.

"You have succeeded. This is a great moment!" Lord Hideyaki said in his public speaking voice, as if he hadn't hindered my success by wiping out my first computer six years ago. *What a hypocrite!* "We welcome everyone. We shall remember this day as a Blue World holiday. The return of lost souls!"

Lady Midori took up the refrain. "Even now we're growing new vat bodies in Regions 14, 18, 32, and 37. We will begin interviews as soon as possible. Let's learn all we can about each other! Let's share our centuries! Comrades Yoshi and Kazumi, we have a reward for you. Nothing must delay it. First my apologies for a very wrong analysis of your mental conditions, but how fruitful your time here was! Now we'll show you how grateful we can be!"

I found myself unable to reply. Really unable, as I'd been unable to speak at my trial twelve years ago. Perhaps the Suppressionists thought I'd say something embarrassing.

It takes several minutes to radio a complete soul from Geosync down to the surface of Blue World, and those minutes must have passed. I never noticed. For me it was a sudden awakening. I rose and stepped away from Regional Depot 33, out into the morning sunshine. Tidewater crashed against the pylons below. After basking awhile I went back inside, checked out the facility, and found it functional. The Fusion Cell hummed happily. ChemStores was so full that ChemOps was running its dig line at minimum speed. The vat was breeding nitrogen-fixing eukaryotes.

Some time later, a second robot straightened away from the wall. "Comrade Kazumi?" I asked.

"Depot 33," she read from the sign on the door. "I know where Region 33 is. They've stuck us on a God-damned island. It's just a new prison."

"A pretty big prison. Region 33 is the size of the whole Japanese archipelago, welded into one piece." Despite these words it occurred to me that she might be right. I tried radioing a message to Comrade Haga, who was presumably breaking rocks into soil somewhere else on Blue World's surface. The message should have gone up to Geosync and down again, to its proper destination, no matter that I didn't know where he was.

No answer. Comrade Atsuko failed to respond, as did Comrade Basho.

Robots have no facial expressions, and very little body language. I was reduced to saying my feelings out loud: "Gloom. No, the hell with gloom. To hell with Lord Hideyaki and Lady Midori. Those two are starting to piss me off."

"They underestimated us. We're underestimating them. Do you know what radio isolation means?" Kazumi asked. "They're going to kill us. We'll suffer a 'regrettable accident.' "

I started thinking out loud. "The fusion cell seems to be working properly. Would they explode a whole regional depot just to get rid of us? That's wasteful."

"Do you doubt what I'm saying?" Kazumi asked.

"No. I'm trying to figure out how they'll do it. No explosions. No meteorites shot from space, because how do they know we'd stay in the target zone? Check your power supply. Batteries okay?"

"Yoshi, I don't know what to do," my comrade told me. She waved inland. "Our deaths lie waiting to ambush us. Perhaps out there. Perhaps they've laid minefields."

"Let's do different things. One of us should separate from this depot as if it were cursed, and try for distance. The other should stay put. Does this seem wise? We'll stay in radio contact, or else it's stupid. Perhaps it's stupid anyway. I feel we're being stampeded into action by our own fears."

"Be more flattering. Call it 'being decisive,' " she said.

"All right. I'll go." I spoke decisively. "I'll transmit a message every five minutes. I'll expect an answer. Silence at either end means disaster."

"Oh, Yoshi, if it gets you— Oh, I hate these bodies. There's no meaning to metal touching metal. As hugs go, this is pathetic."

"*Your* embraces have gone farther than I would have believed," I joked. "We've run the gamut of hugging."

"Except as human-to-human. It doesn't seem likely that we'll ever meet in the flesh. I regret that."

"Let's not give up hope," I said. "If I reach the opposite shore of this island, I'll turn back. We'll meet again and know that our Suppressionist enemies drew the line at murder. With time, we may all reconcile. Why not? The whole population of Blue World, adding in Joto's people, is yet barely a thousand souls. As many as that lived in my Osaka towerblock on Old Earth, and we were perfectly civil to each other. Why shouldn't a thousand souls live at peace in all these wide spaces?"

She began to answer, and faltered. The life went out of her. Everything faded to black.

3174

I hadn't felt such a sense of achievement in many years. Of course I let Comrade Kazumi hug me, and for that brief moment I even hugged her back. I woke from my great moment of happiness in what appeared to be an airplane hangar, crisscrossed overhead by metal beams on x, y, and z axes. It was empty, nothing on the tables by the walls except a big manila envelope. I opened it, and read the message:

> Dear Comrade Yoshi,
>
> Let me explain. When the Suppressionists began radioing you down to Blue World from your longhouse in Ready State Zero, I sidled over to Joto and whispered that I feared for your life and mine.
>
> He agreed to save us. I admitted I had a copy of your memories from when I hugged and swallowed you that one time—a stolen copy, because I'm that sort of thief, and that sort of pervert. That's why I normally keep myself as a roadster, to discourage my own vices. But we had no time for pretense. I have software designed

for my perverted uses, and I ran it in reverse to deliver your memories into Joto's hands.

Joto? Joto? Who the hell was Joto? I remembered Kazumi's triumphant embrace—it was the last thing I remembered at all. So she'd stolen my memories! Now the woman knew everything about me. If she'd digested what she took, she knew all about my life on Old Earth; my frustrations, my jealousies, my disease, and how I'd been lied to by Dr. Kotobuko. How I came alive as an engrammed memory-set after my death. I made history by being the first disembodied soul to sue a medical practitioner. He'd given me *placebos*, damn it! I was dying of AIDS, and he'd put me into a *control group* to test how well his so-called miracle drug worked on *others*!

The courts found in favor of Dr. Kotobuko. I was rebuked as a nuisance. The whole business wasn't one of my proudest moments. Back on Earth, I'd not had many proud moments. I scratched my head. What was this business about the Suppressionists radioing us down to Blue World?

I read on.

> Joto had his own special software, that allowed him to "package" and "unpackage" souls from his own conglomerate consciousness, by reattaching their memories to a plex processor. You won't remember, but he did this in front of us, using all sorts of key objects that littered these now-empty tables. I asked him to use his skills to put you (and me) back together again, to resurrect us to virtual life, but only after a random number of years had passed, because it was possible I was being paranoid. Perhaps you and I were not destined to die down on Blue World. If not, I would act to prevent our duplicate souls from popping to life in virtuality.
>
> I said "random," because anything unpredictable works against the Suppressionists, but I meant that you and I should awaken (if at all) at the same randomly chosen time, between eight and eighty years in the future. Joto didn't understand this. Obviously we were in a hurry, and I didn't make myself clear. So I came to life first, and it could be decades before you pop in. I'm in no hurry now, as I was during that minute with Joto, so I will explain all the events that have happened since you and I succeeding in finding that Zipped computer, and I gave you that big hug.

Comrade Kazumi went on to describe one of my life's prouder moments—a rescue of a hundred souls—a rescue I didn't remember in the least. I tried to glory in a deed that had obviously led to my death down on Blue World. *If you're alive to read this, as I'm alive to write it, you know that they killed us*, Comrade Kazumi wrote.

> I won't forget that this has become that sort of battle. It's not political anymore, not for me. I mean to start my campaign by gathering information against our enemies. If I'm successful, you'll find much that you need to know in the other envelopes stacked on this table.

There were no other envelopes. I didn't know when Comrade Kazumi popped back to life. It could have been yesterday. If so, the lack of envelopes meant nothing. More likely she'd been killed twice over. The Suppressionists were now warned of the possibility that I might come back to haunt them.

I checked the Geosync computer's clock-date. It was 3174. My glorious rescue of Joto and his conglomerate souls took place forty-eight years ago.

What now? Ready State Zero could easily be a trap. A *Suppressionist* trap, I thought at first, but then amended myself. It wasn't likely that more than one or two leading Suppressionists were guilty of murder. The vast majority would disown evils of such magnitude. The majority thought that Comrade Kazumi and I were dead because of some unfortunate accident.

Having seen us safely dead, Lord Hideyaki and Lady Midori would have turned us into saints, the better to accommodate former opponents. In her letter Kazumi spoke of a Blue World holiday, a once-a-year event at which we two were probably memorialized as Martyrs-to-a-Better Future. Praising dead enemies is the traditional first step in co-opting them, *as long as they don't come back to life.*

But Kazumi *had* come to life, and alarmed them about me. To put it plainly, I had a handful of enemies *very* interested in keeping me from harvesting the garden they'd planted. I knew this about them. What else did I know?

They'd be suspicious of any lost soul who turned up in Ready State Zero, hoping to get work down on Blue World's surface. They'd think he was me in disguise. They might kill him—separate his memories from his plex processor, and zero them out. I could unzip Joto's computer and contact all the crazy souls of cyberspace, hoping to create a flow of emigrants, but then I'd be as guilty of murder as my enemies.

Maybe not. I could explain the situation. *"The door out is a deadly one."* There's such a thing as third-party suicide, people who want to die, but can't do the deed themselves. Souls like that, worthless to themselves, were worth something to me. They might bring Lord Hideyaki or Lady Midori to a moral crisis.

Could I use other people that way, in my own behalf? Was this decent behavior? The principles I championed against the Supressionists were those of full disclosure—tell the truth about human history, and let our vatling colonists choose freely what arts and sciences they wanted to learn.

Let them choose. That was the point. I could send a backdoor message to all the lost souls of virtuality, being as thorough as possible—pages after pages with footnotes and appendices and exhibits, exploring all the pros and cons.

Not to do this was a sort of Suppressionism, wasn't it?

That thought was decisive.

I unzipped Joto's computer, and took weeks to compose an opus. I shot it out several times over. Among the thousand souls at work on Blue World, some might be in transit via the Geosync computer, parked here temporarily while relocating between depots. They'd have an address indistinguishable from any other—one of forty thousand control-point locations. My long narrative would be carried down to reality when they finished their trips.

I'd fired my big guns, trying to get out the truth. Now what? From Kazumi's description it was obvious that I was inhabiting Joto's virtual reality. If Joto was still alive, Lady Midori could demand to know where that was. I had to assume the worst—she knew how to consume me or zero me out, and Joto was willing to help her. It wasn't that I didn't have faith in this "Joto" character. It just seemed prudent to hop out of here, to some private universe of my own construction, one of the many I'd made during our thousand-year voyage across interstellar space.

I duped a personal copy of Joto's extremely useful computer. Then I was on my way. If Lady Midori wanted to make peace, she could use the first duplicate, the one Comrade Kazumi and I left in Ready State Zero, to send me a message. To make sure I got her offer, all she needed to do was mail it several times over to forty thousand backdoor addresses.

3175

A year went by without any word from Hideyaki or Midori—without any contacts from Suppressionist reality. The circumstances should have bothered me, but my new life was busy and adventurous, with peculiar aspects. Universes evolve, yes, but bouncing through my repertoire, I'd found one that was *way* different. These last centuries someone had wandered in and taken over one of my old fantasies, and warped it to his or her purposes. Someone had left her mark.

If Comrade Kazumi were alive, and wanted me to find her, she'd locate to one of my places. She had my memories, and she knew the addresses. I hoped to find her. I hoped to find *anybody*. Other souls were important to me. This fact drew me in, although truth to tell, Chyle wasn't a scenario that encouraged thoughts of importance. It was a place of tricks and funny names, where I played a role noticeably smaller than the person I really was; feasting, fighting, and making love to amenable fictoids.

Back in Osaka before my graphics-design career took off, I abandoned my ambitions every day for six hours as a short-order cook. To the staff at the restaurant I *was* a cook, not someone with an impressive artistic resumé. This was like that. To keep from being hunted down by the Suppressionists, I parked my ambitious self to play a game whose only sure virtue was that it kept me busy and in hiding. To the fictoids of the game I was Dridley the Mirthwadite, freelance adventurer.

This was hardly a seductive role, yet toward the end of this year I was more Dridley than Yoshi. You don't have to guzzle to become an alcoholic. You can do it by sipping discreetly, if at every turn you find it easier to continue than to stop. Dridley was easy for me, like a cardboard part for a great actor. Had I meant to rescue souls from deep-game madness? At the end of my year I was perilously near needing rescue myself.

On my latest mission I drew near a corridor lit by distant torches. I froze and listened, hoping that stealth made me invisible, for anyone who saw my exaggerated movements would find them comical. Fifty weeks ago I'd been assigned the body of a heavy-bellied gourmand, but a man who would eat is obliged to take risks.

I'd tracked down the slave-gang I'd been hired to free. I heard the rattling of chains. Laughter echoed through white-webbed passages as Rakni's mercenaries boasted of the infamies they'd performed last night.

Rakni was one goddess among many, few of them pleasant. I reviewed her acts of wickedness, aggravating myself to a frenzy of zeal. Most of the time I muddled along like an actor reading his lines, but the deed I meant to do required a bravo spirit. It wasn't enough to hide in the vaults below Rakni's Temple, footing among skulls and casks. To prove worth my hire I had to liberate two dozen people.

The guards posted a sentry. The others began to satisfy their lusts. Stepping back from the corner, I unbuttoned my breeks and hosed the floor. The slope of the pavement assured that a stream would trickle into view.

A minute passed. The guard walked up the passage and turned. I stepped from a doorway to throttle him.

He made a racket. I drew my wand and gave him a tingle. He collapsed in hysterical laughter. Two other mercenaries puffed round corner.

I backed down the corridor, waving my weapon. I heard jangling as the shackled slaves came into sight. They pressed on Rakni's henchmen. One turned to ward them off. I attacked the other, scoring against his bare torso. His thrust wasted itself in a pyrotechnic discharge, because beneath my gravy-stained jerkin I wore a chain-mail shirt. Now two enemies rolled about the floor, laughing helplessly. Soon the third one joined them.

WAAAAAH! The loud honk announced the daily Peace. I'd barely freed the slaves in time. Among them was a very pregnant friend I'd met—well, what a coincidence—almost nine months ago. Item A joined me with enthusiasm. We wheezed up three flights of stairs and exited into Rakni's outer court. The goddess's red-robed priests stepped forward. "Are you Dridley?" one asked as he readied a clipboard.

I squinted against the brightness of a gold-and-purple sunset. "Dridley the Mirthwadite. Minutes ago I freed the slaves sold you by Magister Gasselot. Your three mercenaries will acknowledge—"

"Are they alive?"

My beard concealed a smug smile. "Tingled and disarmed."

"But you'd not led your charges out," the priest objected. "You might have had some difficulty."

"If you want the House of Gods to judge, I'll tell them that nobody but your prevented a score of desperate men and women from reaching the plaza, and you all sworn to passivity. If we return to quid pro quo after the Peace and fresh guards run out to stop us, the priests of Mirthwad will cry foul."

The man in red gritted his teeth. "We can't submit every transaction to the House of Gods. Very well, I won't contest your claim."

From across the court a red-robed woman strode forward. "Dridley, your name is marked. Stay out of the dark alleys of Chyle. That big gut makes an easy target."

I laughed. "A month from now the gods will shift alliances. Mirthwad and Rakni will be friends again. I've seen it happen before."

Item A plucked at my sleeve. "Come," she urged. "I don't like these scenes. All those stairs! I need to sit and rest."

"How do you feel?"

The rings under her eyes gave me concern. Her hair was unkempt. She was too tired to keep up appearances. Across the cobbled plaza from the Temple of Rakni stood a small bistro. "How about some soup and bread before we report in?" I asked.

Item A ate a third of her supper with ravenous appetite. She shoved the rest away. "I'll be hungry in an hour," she complained. "The baby monopolizes my belly. I've no room left for food."

"We can wait."

"I say that a lot nowadays," Item A answered. "I've skipped worship since falling into Gasselot's hands. If Mirthwad's temple were in the center of Chyle I'd go there, but it's hard to cross the city."

I shrugged. "Since defeating Elsewad Mirthwad rules the Gund, but here in Chyle we're relegated to the low-rent suburbs."

At the mention of Elsewad's name Item A shivered. "Dridley, this Rakni thing is a skirmish. Elsewad is different. Bad enough you worship the god who led the Hag Queen's army across the Latpans, but Elsewad's priests hate you for stealing the secret of the torque."

"The Conventicles forbid sacerdotal violence. Elsewad would have to hire an assassin."

Item A shook her head. "Elsewad has money, and you've just freed twenty-odd slaves. They'll peddle their services to the highest bidder."

I studied my empty wineglass. "That's life."

Item A brushed crumbs from her tunic. "I don't want to worship tonight. Can we just sit here?"

Twilight crowds ambled, listened to proselytes and plotted mischief. "When the Peace ends this place won't be safe."

Item A picked up her spoon and sipped her soup. "I have disturbing thoughts," she confessed.

"No wonder, if you've been skipping worship."

"Dridley, does it occur to you that all this—" She waved an arm made plump by the changes to her figure. "Think of Chyle, of the villages along the Gund, of the wildmen of the Aglan Albabs. It doesn't work. We're all supposed to be part of an economy, a system with farmers at the base, and the gods on top."

I'd first met Item A while the hierophants of her god Techto, each bribed by a different guild of realtors, debated the course of next year's lava flow. I was accustomed to teaching her the ways of Mirthwad, a god whose doctrines I'd adopted as protective cover.

"Yours is exactly the kind of speculation Mirthwad means to stamp out," I lectured. "Profundities are made of words, and words of meanings. Each 'connotatus' is a building block, but rarely do these blocks combine according to logic. Mirthwad's gift is forgetfulness. We remember names and facts, but abandon economics, politics and other false constructions."

Item A ignored me. "Under the helmet you go. Out you come, purged. Elsewad uses a helmet too. They all do. All the gods."

I waggled a finger. "Elsewad's helmets burden the mind with lost languages and useless history."

She kicked me under the table. "Stop your preaching! I know the doctrines of Mirthwad, Elsewad, and Techto, and several others besides. Words, mere words. They're different, but all end with you under the helmet.

"Life doesn't have to be this way," she continued. "There's a voice in me. The more I skip worship, the more it tells me we're in a madhouse. The gods are laughing at us, Dridley. They know something we can't see, something the helmets keep us from seeing."

What was I hearing from Item A? Was it possible that computer fictoids yearned beyond their roles? Could they play effectively if they knew they were part of a game? Or was Item A more than a fictoid? I was curious to find out, but she responded blankly when I whispered "*Kazumi?*"—as blankly as anyone else in Chyle.

Since I was supposed to be a pious fellow, I leaned forward and took her hand. "Item A, you can't neglect worship night after night! Must I force you to come, or will you walk at my side and retain your dignity?"

She stood. We paid our bill and left for the suburbs a few blocks beyond the city wall. We reached the park by the Great Library. She clutched herself. "A contraction!"

"Have your membranes ruptured?"

She gave me a sharp look. "Set me by those bushes. Send for the priests."

Item A's child would make a fine gift for the priests of Mirthwad. I eased her into her resting place and ran down Buttermarket Street toward the temple of my favorite deity.

I returned leading a file of priests and palanquin bearers. Item A was gone. "She fooled me!" I said.

"Why?" asked the puffing hierophant at my side.

A woman who refused to worship was an atheist. If I spoke the truth all Chyle would have hunted her down. I couldn't unleash persecution on Item A. "She slipped off. She preferred to be delivered by the priests of Techto."

The priest frowned. "The Peace will be over in another hour. Come with us. Enjoy the blessings of forgetfulness."

"My place is at her side. I'll come tomorrow." Bowing politely, I turned and walked for Techto's temple, slowing to a halt when my priest and his followers were out of sight.

Time to think. Item A was lost. Worse, I'd become an enemy. She'd seek refuge where I didn't dare follow.

Really? During the Peace I'd dare anything, even the temple of Elsewad. No, if she wanted to hide she'd go to a place repugnant to my creed. The answer was nearby. She'd entered the very source of ideologies, systems, and hypotheses; the Great Library.

I studied the heavily buttressed building. Lights glowed inside. The Library's visiting hours were co-terminous with the Peace. I grimaced while treading its converging paths. How could I rationalize actually going in?

Well, as a good Mirthwadite, wasn't I allowed to pollute my mind, as long as I purged it?

I entered the Library, and wandered the aisles until the novelty wore off. I found Item A bent over a display case in the Map Room. She turned, saw me and smiled. "Look!" she exclaimed.

Item A had forgiven me, as if I hadn't tried to force her to worship. It was only fair that I reciprocate, as if she hadn't pretended to go into labor. I drew up to the table. "What's that?" I asked.

"A map of the world. A very old map."

"The world seems shaped like a wineskin," I said, fingering my beard.

"I see a pot with a thick handle where the Gund flows into the Latpans. This line marks the caravan route from Chyle. West and north of the Dying Sea lie the hills of the Aglan Albabs, where the Hag Queen rules. Now look at this! Another dotted line, running from Chyle to Quarry Mountain, then through the middle west, and off into the unknown!"

"I see."

"Where does it go? What lies beyond the map? Why shouldn't there be more mountains, more rivers? All this blank parchment!"

I was so lost to the game that I responded like any pious citizen. "Just because the parchment doesn't conform to the outline of the world, you think something lies beyond. What a fallacy!"

"Dridley, come with me. We'll follow that mysterious trail. The experience will open your eyes."

"You can't travel in your condition."

Item A bit her lip. "I'll buy your cooperation. If you accompany me I'll consign my baby to Mirthwad. We'll hold our departure until I've recovered from childbirth and found a wet-nurse."

"What about worship in the meantime?"

She shook her head. "Swear you won't force me into devotion."

I made a promise. "Item A, you've changed. I need to understand what's troubling you. I've been thinking. I too should refrain from worship. I'll make myself a bridge between the world and your fevered state of mind."

Item A delivered a baby girl a week later. The priests of Mirthwad were delighted to accept our child, though Item A embarrassed everyone by weeping during the ritual.

It had nothing to do with loyalties to Techto. It just seemed wrong to hand over her baby, she explained, assailing a time-honored custom in that sweeping way she had. I hustled her out of the temple as quickly as possible. Her ideas weren't for public consumption. They were disturbing and provocative.

During the next month neither Item A nor I performed our devotions. My behavior grew erratic. In my adventures I used reason where others tried force. Clients no longer wanted to work with me. By the time we left I was poor, and glad to see the walls of Chyle behind us.

We strode through a fringe of farms, orchards and sheep-commons. "We're supposed to believe these fields feed all Chyle," Item A said. "How many priests, and how few peasants!"

A wagon wheeled by us. The teamster was on his way to Quarry Mountain after delivering a load of durium slabs. He offered us a ride. We turned him down, to revel in the luxury of free speech.

The driver flicked his reins and drew off. Item A spoke. "This year twelve babies were born. Last year the count was six. In all the world ten women are pregnant. This is typical. Perhaps a thousand children born in any century."

I agreed. She continued. "Yet your memory tells you you're twenty-nine years old. I think I'm thirty. Everyone we know places his or her birth less than five decades ago. Either our statistics are wrong or our memories lie. What keeps us from realizing these things?"

"Everything we know is unreal." Who was I talking to? A fictoid? A real soul, just playing a game? Or a soul who genuinely didn't know who she was? The helmets of the gods shouldn't work to full effect on true souls. *I'd* used them, and I still knew who I was.

Did I? *Comrade Yoshi.* My name creaked out slowly. The sound of it wavered in my mind. Blue World seemed like a dream. I rehearsed the names of people I should have loved and hated. After just one year of middleweight gaming my emotions felt smothered. One wasted year, and I'd have to learn to love and hate all over again.

At least I knew my identity. How many years would it take before the power of the game, or the power of the helmets, took that away from me? I'd be like Item A, and perhaps not courageous enough, or iconoclastic enough, to undertake a voyage of personal discovery.

"We're like sheep and the gods are our shepherds," Item A said. "Now we've resolved to leap over the fence that surrounds our field. What will we find?"

Next day we reached Quarry Mountain, a heaping black bulk, girdled by a string of flower-garden villas, inns, temples and quarry operations. Item A had been a child here, but her memories of childhood were growing dubious. We shuddered away from the hospitality of her priests, and trudged down the road until it became a cobbled trail.

We continued three days through gently rolling grassland. "We're halfway to the edge of the world," Item A remarked as we massaged each other's feet by that evening's campfire.

"How do you feel?" I asked.

"Perhaps it's just that I don't like the name 'Item A.' As the hours go by odd sounds repeat inside my head: Kaiko Ieyamatsu. Kaiko Ieyamatsu.' A veil is lifting, but what lies behind is as vague as dreams. I was proud once, maybe a god myself."

I nodded, "Kaiko?" I said.

"Yes, Dridley."

"My name isn't Dridley. Call me Yoshi." I felt ashamed for waiting so long. What kind of ethics were these? Who convinced me it was right to deny myself, and wrong to betray the game?

We spread our blankets, slept, ate, and broke camp. We trekked on for three more days. The Aglan Albabs lay to our right, a high forest country starkly unlike the bleak salt pans to our left. We'd have been entertained were these landscapes visible, but both regions lay beyond sight. Beneath fast-moving clouds we wandered a wide margin of wind-shaken grasses.

As we walked, we exchanged revelations. My companion faltered out bits of Japanese. "We were gods once!" she exclaimed. "But we were bad gods, yes? And now they—"

"Who?"

She shook her head. We toiled on, cresting a long, slow rise of land.

Kaiko claimed to see a black margin along the horizon. "It's the edge of the world," she said.

"Do we go on, or turn back?" I asked. "They may punish us for trespassing."

"You say too many words in the language of recent dreams. *Nihongo ga hanaseru yo ni naru made hansanai de!*"

We descended from the crest. The margin disappeared. We climbed, descended, climbed, descended. After leagues of hiking our goal seemed no nearer. Then we topped the latest hill and saw a colonnaded roof in the near distance, rising from a mound fringed by sloughs. Beneath its shade bubbled a fountain. The road took us to the place, crossing reedy waters over a bridge of durium blocks.

We drank, slipped off our shoes, and bathed our feet. To an infinitesimal degree the hall darkened. I looked up. Metal rods clicked into place in the ceiling. We were trapped.

"This way, sir and madam."

The fountain sprayed a fine mist. In that mist appeared a glowing face. "Come, come. Don't stare," the image spoke. "I hope to provoke a reaction."

The speaker's comments were in Japanese. "What is this place?" I replied in the same language.

"Hmm! You must be awake to yourself. Awake enough to remember other games, and other centuries?"

The face turned to scan the grasslands around us. It rotated a full cycle, back into view. "For lifetimes this place has been a monument to power. All the gods start from this font. Recently I approved the deification of young Mirthwad and sent him to the Hag Queen for training. Mirthwad has achieved great things, I understand."

"Who are you?" I asked.

"Mirthwad asked that question," the voice responded. "I gave him the choice. He could accept godhood or have his answer. He chose godhood."

The image's eyes focused on me. "Yoshi, you're a very good adventurer. If anyone deserves to be deified, it's you. Unfortunately I can't oblige without your cooperation. The rules of this game stipulate that the gods of Chyle be ignorant of who they are."

"How many of them are real souls, and not fictoids? How many got a long message months ago—in a language they didn't know, and in an indecipherable script?"

"I don't know. In the language of your offensive dichotomies I'm not 'real' myself," the face admitted. "I'm limited in my functions."

"There's no way to summon them all here? No way to wake them out of the game?"

"Those who chose to wake may do so. Kaiko has chosen, and here she is. Do you value yourself, Kaiko?" the image asked. "If not, no need for suicide. I can take you away from your past, and make you a goddess."

"The long trip is over," I told Kaiko. "Our starship is in geosynchronous orbit around Blue World. The planet is being terraformed. Many souls have left virtuality. They're incarnated in robot bodies, or bodies made of vat-grown flesh."

"If you're telling me the prospectus for a different game, it's in bad taste," Kaiko said. "You're making a mockery of something I once lived for. An old, old hope."

"Check the year. Our ship was to have arrived at Epsilon Eridani in 3083."

"I—I have forgotten my powers. How to know the time. Let's see. 3175. My God, such a number!" She choked with emotion. After a time she whispered: "I've grown centuries older, and not even as myself! As somebody of no consequence whatever!"

I turned to the image. "I'd like to add to your programmed menu. I want you to inform anyone who comes that there's a way out of virtuality, but a *dangerous* way. Those who take it may be interrogated, or blocked, or even killed. I don't know if I'm exaggerating to say this. I'm a poor candidate to scout out the situation, since I'm the one Lady Midori and Lord Hideyaki want to get rid of."

I gave a fuller explanation. Kaiko shook her head. "You say that Comrade Kazumi is dead."

"That's how I account for things."

"Did you love her?" Kaiko asked.

"I think she loved me." I thought a bit and elaborated. "But not exclusively. Our bond was like—like soldiers in war, who would do almost anything for each other."

"And the silence since you shot out your big message? How do you account for that?"

"Your ears were deaf at the time. Deaf to Japanese. I suppose many deep gamers are deaf by choice. I'm surprised, though, that Lady Midori hasn't broadcast a response. Perhaps her silence is calculated. *Anything* she said would give me more information than I have now, and she'd rather have me ignorant."

Kaiko made a decision. "Yoshi, let's ruin this game. Let's interrupt it, and collect all the souls at play. Tell them what you've just told me. Let's go out and ruin *other* games, and rescue all those deep gamers."

"And then what?"

"*You* know, don't you? *You* know what you'll have to do. But I wouldn't have you do it just for me."

"Do you remember how to invoke Transit?" I asked. "We're imprisoned here. We need to go elsewhere to gather our powers."

☞

A day later, two caped superheroes flew into the skies over the city of Chyle. We pealed away slabs of durium, four-by-eight meters each, from the roofs of various temples. Sirens honked, announcing the daily Peace, but the Purple Crusader—myself, clad in comic-book swirls and glitter—kept working in defiance of all the gods. I grabbed as many helmets as I could find, and dumped them in the high hills behind the eastern suburbs.

Priests shook their fists at Kaiko—the Laughing Dynamo—as she did likewise. A horrid stench rolled in from the west, where Quarry Mountain erupted off schedule. The clerics of Chyle clambered into the heights to escape the low brown smell, and here again they threatened us with divine retribution.

The Laughing Dynamo had taken special pains to deal with Quarry Mountain. Volumes of fecal matter rolled from the heights, enveloping villas and palaces, and most especially the temple of Techto. Refugees jogged away, holding hankies to their stricken faces.

How vulgar. It would have been more elegant to ruin the game by substituting helmets of our own manufacture, sneaking in and out of threescore temples, but Kaiko and I despaired of figuring out how the damned things worked quickly enough to make the necessary changes. The guts of a *real* helmet lay open to view by anyone with a screwdriver, but the working parts of a virtual helmet are simply compiled code, all zeros and ones.

Somewhere in Chyle lived a soul who would eventually remember him- or herself, as the person who'd taken over my five-hundred-year-old scenario, and added helmets to the equation. I hoped that was true, and I hoped I could be persuasive enough to enlist that person's talents. Kazumi's ability to copy memories into her own soul—Joto's ability to restore memories to independent life—and now this! A gradual process of selective memory suppression, and the substitution of lies for truth!

Software was all, but I was becoming the repeated victim of a special category I called *soul*ware. As this stuff propagated, life for the inhabitants of virtuality was becoming unrecognizable. The boundaries of self-definition were flouted. Emigration to Blue World seemed ever more necessary.

Kaiko and I finished our destructive work. We flew back into the hills, and transported our helmet-booty further away, working in shifts. Meanwhile, in the city of Chyle, riots broke out, and factions collected. Refugees crowded the roads southward, seeking to reach the Gund.

We arranged for a nightfall of manna to feed them. The gods, who loved anonymity at the best of times, were in low profile and low repute. They were unable to stop us from flying where we liked. We made grand speeches from the air.

Our words made little sense to minds fuddled by recent worship. We were just planting seeds. Days were yet to go by before those seed-concepts germinated. By my calculations true souls were a minority. Only that minority would change as Item A had changed, at last remembering their real names and histories.

Days *did* go by. The passage of time proved my calculations wrong by a factor of ten. I had guessed as many as a dozen souls lived in this particular fantasy world. The fact was, *forty* had migrated here, but that wasn't where I'd made my big error.

My mistake was in not recognizing the consequences of pregnancy. Here was another instance of new soulware at work, making it possible for two once-dead emigrants from Old Earth to create a third thing of merged memories—merged, but always *suppressed* until now. Over five centuries, forty lost souls had produced four hundred "children."

If virtuality had a government, soulware like this would be contraband. How could I claim an identity worthy of respect, when I could be variously alive or dead, or complete in myself, or part of somebody else?

When the realities of Yoshi Yasoda and Kaiko Ieyamatsu were added together, did they amount to something *less* real? Our daughter hardly thought

so. Ayano grew prematurely to toddlerhood so she could speak, and confirmed that half of her came out of me by describing my futile court case
against Dr. Kotobuko, a thousand years ago.

Ayano was me, and yet not-me. I looked back on a recent career of
defiance and death and defiance again, with a new death looming. I decided
I must be a little suicidal. I had a touch of the thousand-year-old disease.
This hardly described Ayano. She had a younger spirit, more affirming than
mine.

Ayano agreed. "Comrade Kazumi is the same way. Or *was*, anyhow. The
roaring roadster! She's another conglomeration of souls, though she kept her
nature hidden."

"Conglomeration!" Ayano liked big words. They were startling, coming
from a kid her size.

"This business of merging souls might be a good thing," I answered,
though my heart still quailed against it.

Motivated by a sense of sisterhood, Ayano resolved to enter *other* games,
and find Comrade Kazumi, if Kazumi were anywhere to be found. My daughter's pledge freed me to take up a less personal cause. I gave Kaiko a final
kiss, and invoked Transit. I came *here*, to a place of my choosing, and my
next hop will be to Ready State Zero!

Let them kill me, if that's going to happen. First I'll use my copy-computer
to send out an update message, and then—something. Something for the
sake of finality; a walk through an Anime movie, a cup of green tea, jokes
told by a talking cow, a Buddhist chant. And when I'm ready I'll take the
risk.

I do this so no one needs to be murdered in my place, out of fear that
I'm trying to sneak down to Blue World to claim leadership. In my message
I'll renounce the future possibility of any such claims. *I* am Comrade Yoshi
Yasoda, the last pure instance of myself, and what happens to me is up to
the Suppressionist lords and ladies who may still control the terraforming
project.

Let them kill once, and then let four hundred forty souls pass back into
reality.

3175

I remember writing those brave words, and feeling more than half frightened
as I transmitted them. I delayed awhile, listening to music. It wasn't courage
that drew me on, so much as a need to hear Lady Midori and Lord Hideyaki
account for their actions. How could they have maintained such silence?
False accusations, exiles, murders—and all this piling up of years! I had to
know the truth.

Ready State Zero was a cleaner place than I remembered it. The water-
garden of 3127 was gone, with its goldfish and topiary. The longhouse remained, but the copy Comrade Kazumi and I had made of Joto's computer
was Zipped away.

In Chyle, one reached out a virtual hand to open a virtual door, and it
swung creaking on virtual hinges. Here doors were more economical—I
walked up and bumped through. I suppose that act transmitted a signal.

A minute later, Lady Midori popped in as a floating face-mask. "You claim to be Comrade Yoshi Yasoda?"

"I am," I said. "I've sent messages. Do I have to explain about Comrade Kazumi, and what she did?"

Midori mimed distaste. "No. She's made her history and her accusations perfectly clear."

"Excuse me. You talk as if she's alive," I said.

"Out there, in virtuality," Midori agreed. "Well, wouldn't you think so? She's a pervert with an appetite for souls she'd never be able to satisfy in the flesh. We didn't kill her, no matter that you believe otherwise. I can show you messages she's sent, full of threats and venom. Look if you like. They're dated."

I looked. My heart sank. "The big one's mine. I wrote it and sent it out little more than a year ago."

"Oh? Our mistake," Lady Midori apologized. "She has broadcast before to the addresses of virtuality, using your name, or yours and hers together. I asked you if you were Yoshi, because she seems capable of pretending she's you."

"I have reason to think you're lying. She's dead. I have evidence in the form of an otherwise-broken promise. But if she's alive, we both want to hear an account of our deaths down on Blue World," I said. "Coming here means I've written off my future. The past is all I'm interested in. Just this piece of my life, which you could have made public before now."

"I *have*." Lady Midori defended herself. "But if you *are* Yoshi, and popped to life only this last year or two, perhaps you haven't heard the story. It's not long. You two didn't live long down in Region 33, in your robot bodies. Your power taps were defective. Suddenly they stopped receiving energy from the depot fusion cell. The two of you browned out."

"Sabotage."

"Yes, we're pretty sure," Lady Midori agreed. "We've been unable to find out who was responsible. Some zealot for the Suppressionist cause, most likely. Not me. Not Lord Hideyaki, or so he assures me. But how can we prove we're not lying? How can you prove you're yourself? Meanwhile, Comrade Kazumi issues proclamations and rants. I resent her, as I resent having to say these things. I resent being called a liar, but from your point of view I'm hardly the victim."

"Smoothly put. And now what?" I asked.

"According to your most recent transmission, you have four hundred forty deep gamers who want to come to Blue World," Lady Midori said. "Master Joto feels these misfits would support his faction, which tries to nibble at the tenets of Suppressionism. In essence he's taken over your old role, although his tone has always been more pragmatic.

"I'd be cutting my political throat to let all those hundreds emigrate from virtuality," she continued. "Nevertheless I'll do so, because I suspect Joto may be wrong, many of them will support pure Suppressionism in the end— and because Master Joto has bribed me with a gift."

"I know what it is," I said. "If what you say is true, Joto doesn't want me around any more than you do."

"A gift of software," she went on. "When I use it, you'll sleep again, as you did for forty-eight years. Whether you wake is a question of politics, to be debated in the highest Suppressionist councils, although perhaps not more than once."

"I'm to be *tabled*, I guess."

It was an odd joke to make to someone with a deficient sense of humor. Midori nodded. "No one except ourselves needs know you lived a reborn life. We will ascribe all your recent messages to Comrade Kazumi, the soul eating monster. There may be a handful of deep gamers from this place called Chyle who know better, but we'll manage. I've discovered that it's easy to shake people's confidence, or buy them off."

"And this shadow-Kazumi has no moral credit? You've managed to deprive her of any fair hearing? I think after all she's dead, but you find her useful as an enemy."

Midori nodded. "She serves our purposes. There had to be a good guy in all these rescues from virtuality. Yourself, or even the part of Kazumi she stole from you, the Yoshi side of her swollen character. That's the official story, and it has the benefit of being true in several aspects. By contrast it's simplified the picture to make the *essential* Comrade Kazumi as evil as a thousand devils. We blame her for misleading you away from the truth of Suppressionism, and for telling you lies. *Soul-eater. Saint Yoshi's downfall.* As a scapegoat she's useful. When we shut down the Geosync computer a couple centuries from now, we'll blame her, *Nightmare Kazumi, queen of darkness!* We'll say she left a time bomb, and it exploded."

I felt my antique anger come back to life. "The last floating mask I saw, was of a piece of fictoid software that policed a game, and laid down rules, and nominated gods and goddesses. Now here *you* are, Midori—another floating mask, keen to lay down rules for Blue World, where the vatling colonists are to be kept as ignorant as the poor souls of Chyle. *Except they won't have chosen to be ignorant.* Ignorance will be forced upon them. And you claim you've made real souls into saints and devils, but you've gone too far. You can never do that. It's all lies. We're real. You can only kill us, or let us be."

"Once the Saint is dead asleep, we won't need the Devil. We may just close her down," Lady Midori agreed. "Here. Speaking of closure, this is you."

She had no arms to use in throwing, but however it was done, a hammer arched toward me. I reached—

3405

"Earthcom Mode 1 Reset 1. If you are activated, please respond by entering Earthcom Mode 1. Please transmit. Your confirmation string should include current system date from bottom right—the bottom right corner. Also, the phrase Reset 1. If system date year is 3405, it is probably accurate to month; day, hour, and minute. Do this now. Invoke 'Earthcom.' We are ten-point-six light-years distant, so this cannot be an interactive conversation. We are going to throw in redundancies and periods of dead time to allow information-gathering at your end. Earthcom Mode 1 Reset 1. First pause. List of interrogatories to follow in five minutes. Please transmit current system date and phrase 'Reset 1' while waiting for our interrogatories."

I obliged the insistent voice. His words were full of directions, but he spoke without vitality. Sheer distance had worn at the message, sapping its hope, shifting it to bass and muddying up the vowels.

Earthcom. Mode 1. Yes, the year was 3405. Below the horizon all was green. All was blue above. There was nothing in my field of view except a blinking clock, not a solitary feature. Certainly not a hammer. I transmitted a minimal response. I had a minute to think about sending my name. Were they interested in this detail?

I decided to wait for the interrogatories. Two hundred and thirty years had gone by. I could last another few minutes.

"This is still part of the Reset 1 transmission. Interrogatories follow. Question one: Was shutdown of computer functions at your end a matter of policy, or result of an accident? Please explain. You should know that Homeworld policy requires maintaining computer functions as an adjunct to colonization of Blue World. Is this fact acknowledged by current on-site leadership?"

"Probably not," I answered, thinking of Comrade Basho's warning, confirmed later by Lady Midori's diatribe against Comrade Kazumi. The Suppressionists meant to shut down the computer after Blue World was terraformed. Now that had happened.

No. Now it had *unhappened*. I was alive. The year was 3405. Forty thousand kilometers below me spun a living world. Oxygen. Grass. People.

"My name is Yoshi Yasoda. My last memories are from 3175, when I was murdered because of my opposition to Suppressionist policies. I'm absolutely sure Lady Midori never intended me to come back to life. You have transmitted a signal restarting the Geosync computer, which was shut down on purpose. I assume this was done twenty or more years ago, to get rid of a place they'd given over to madness and exile."

I collected my thoughts. "I will respond to each of your interrogatories, but my priority is to take control of Geosync, so there can be no further shutdowns. I may or may not be the only soul left up here in virtuality."

I invoked a console. My green-blue Ready State Zero now showed in a window framed by bars and buttons. I touched SYSTEM, and then SETUP. While the voice spoke interrogatory two, I made sure this place belonged to me. I reestablished contact with sixty-four regional depots. The machines of Blue World acknowledged my signals.

"Interrogatory two. Question: Please describe your understanding of Covenant of 2344, which lays out contractual obligations between Earth and all future outsystem colonies."

I collected my thoughts. "Will I have to wait twenty-one years to find out about this Covenant? I've never heard of it before. Our starship launched in 2085. If factions among us participated in putting together a covenant with Earth, I don't know who they were. Can we be bound by a covenant we never made? On the other hand, we can be reasonable. *Some* of us, anyhow."

The voice persisted with four other interrogatories. Then it spoke again. "Pause. Terms of Covenant of 2344 follow in five minutes."

I waited five minutes and listened to a forty-minute drone. We of Blue

World had two choices. At some future time we could pay Earth the costs of our starship, plus exorbitant interest. Or we could supply our homeworld with scientific information, running experiments under distant direction.

Of course, primitive hunters and fisherfolk could do neither of these two things, and so our Suppressionist leadership had ignored all past noise about "covenants" with Earth. After all, how could Earth enforce their terms?

Lady Midori and Lord Hideyaki hadn't even brought Earth's demands up for debate. The home world was ten-point-six light-years away! They were fools to think of imposing an interstellar regime across such distances!

Ignoring the demands of Earth, the Suppressionists continued to ask for genetic updates and the latest terraforming technology. Earth obliged. They were too weak-willed to withhold anything, though they persisted in their futile claims.

Not so futile, it turned out. Earth's gifts came with a taint. They weren't entirely powerless. A signal from Earth had restarted the Geosync computer. I came to life, and why shouldn't I be an ally? Why shouldn't I do Earth's work for them? They'd furnished everything I could ask for, every weapon except the resolution to enforce their Covenant, and out of my hate for Lady Midori I could supply that lack.

I set to work. Region 14 had robots in inventory, from days before bodies of flesh could work in Blue World's formerly poison atmosphere. Most were in decent shape. After securing Geosync against mad monsters and Suppressionist intruders, I radioed my soul down to reality. I used Vat 14 to fill a few dozen ampules with the latest genetic updates from Earth.

Depot 14 was buried under a mound of earth and rubble. I exited by a tunnel secret only from the outside. This was a new age, and wonderful to see. Blue World was green and buggy, the air still rich in carbon dioxide. Distances tended to blur in the humid haze.

The nearest village lay in a cove a dozen kilometers away. The walk was pleasant. I startled a few deer, and saw the dried turds of other large mammals. The trees around me were fully mature, although their root systems were shallow. Every strong wind took a few of them down, so that new trails veered from the old. Zigzags made the walk a long one.

Epsilon Eridani was dimmer than Sol, though Blue World was closer, so it showed a larger disk. It gave off a warm yellow light. The landscape was beautiful. I almost hoped that the vatling villagers were happy living in this wilderness, but I knew that wasn't possible under present circumstances. If they'd come out of the vats the same time my Geosync computer had shut down, they'd have been sexually mature for many years. They were men and women full of the energies of life—but where were the babies? If this question didn't bother *them*, it would bother the hell out of the Suppressionists hidden among their numbers.

Where were the babies? Thanks to a codicil snuck into one of Earth's genetic updates, there would be no children born to human vatlings, except those I injected.

Beware the gifts of Earth. But then I saw the *ungifted* village—muddy paths and woven leaf-and-wicker huts, and naked people burned brown by the sun and dirty with smoke, eyes wide with the fear of me. Women shrieked and ran. A crippled man hobbled after them, down toward the sea.

I entered Suppressionism paradise, and to the inhabitants I was a battered metal monster four meters high. A woman crawled out of her hut. She seemed older than the others. Her hair was unkempt, and she'd lost an eye. She looked around, saw she was alone, and approached me. "Who are you?"

"Yoshi Yasoda. I've come to teach good things, and make these people fertile. Who are you?"

She paused. "Does it matter?" she asked softly.

"Do you know where I might find my friends? Kaiko Ieyamatsu? She was a deep gamer. One of the group from Chyle. What about Ayano?" I asked.

"We sent them to Regions 19 through 24. All those misfits, and the ones Ayano found in her virtual prowlings. They have their own small continent. Your political friends live among them."

The woman sagged back. "I suppose this is your victory. We couldn't even contact Earth to beg for help. We shut down the computer, and couldn't turn it on again. These last years the curse became clear. No natural children. Each generation we'd have to breed from the vats, never enough to fill this world. Never enough to create a new culture on a new planet. Thank God you've come. It's a miracle, and the bitterest moment of my long life."

"This wasn't my idea," I said. "Neither the curse, nor my coming back to life."

The woman pondered. "Of course not. You were always a heroic martyr. Your deaths were always sincere." She waved toward the sea. "I'll bring them home to the village. Make your injections, and talk all you like. I'm done with trying to stop you, Yoshi. Make them copycats of Earth, and all that Earth has ever done."

"What theology have they created on their own?" I asked. "What kind of culture?"

She shrugged. "They talk about the Other World. About coming out of a hole in the ground. I take it these ideas are based on memories of the vats in Depot 14, from before we taught them language. Mostly they talk about the good-luck spirits in one place, and the bad-luck spirits in another. When it's been dry too long, and it rains, they dance in celebration. With these roofs they'll get wet anyhow. Why not make the best of it?" She shivered. "I don't suppose you get cold. Keep the fires burning. I'll be back."

After a time she fetched the villagers home. Hunters and gatherers straggled in, bringing the total to twenty-three. I gave them my name, and they submitted to my injections. When it got dark, I pointed out Sol. It was a bright star, only ten-point-six light-years away, though too close to the horizon to be spectacular.

I pointed out another light, glowing again after twenty years of darkness. "We call it Geosync. It was our starship and we lived there a thousand years. Then we made this world for you. But we couldn't have done it without help from your brothers and sisters on Earth. They want you to talk to them, and tell them what it's like here. Your children will learn how to do that. They'll have radio. I'll come back and teach them."

The vatling villagers told me stories of their own lives and wonders, and asked questions. In all our volleys of talk I said nothing about the Suppressionists. If the one-eyed woman wanted to live and die with her past a secret, it was better that way. It was better than being Lady Midori. Ignoring her, I left. I hiked by starlight, and transmitted my soul eastward to Region 19.

I paused at the halfway point up in Geosync. Any messages? I broadcast my sentences, as I will continue to do, in hopes my timing will someday hit home. Maybe my old friend is alive. Maybe Ayano found Comrade Kazumi and took her to Region 19's continent, but I had to consider the possibility that Kazumi was still lost in revived virtuality.

It's not likely then that she's a sane and cheerful roadster. It pained me to think of her as obsessed with revenge or her "perversions," but I couldn't give up hope. "Comrade Kazumi, it's Yoshi. Come on down to Blue World. It's ours now, and we need your help."

I gave Region 19 as my current address, and radioed down. I couldn't wait. I had other friends to enlist. We had a world of work to do.

Ecopoesis

GEOFFREY A. LANDIS

A physicist who works for NASA, and who has recently been working on the Martian Lander program, Geoffrey A. Landis is a frequent contributor to Analog *and to* Asimov's Science Fiction, *and has also sold stories to markets such as* Interzone, Amazing, *and* Pulphouse. *Landis is not a prolific writer, by the high-production standards of the genre, but he is popular. His story "A Walk in the Sun" won him a Nebula and a Hugo Award in 1992, his story "Ripples in the Dirac Sea" won him a Nebula Award in 1990, and his story "Elemental" was on the Final Hugo Ballot a few years back. His first book was the collection* Myths, Legends, and True History, *and he has just published his first novel,* Mars Crossing. *He lives in Brook Park, Ohio.*

In the ingenious and suspenseful novella that follows, he shows us that with a project as complex and large-scale as the terraforming of a whole world, what you don't know not only can *hurt you—it can quite likely* kill *you!*

"I wonder why they call this the red planet," I asked. The rebreather made my voice sound funny in my ears. "Looks like the brown planet to me."

"You got a problem with brown, boy?" Tally said. Her voice was muffled by the rebreather she wore as well.

I turned but Tally wasn't looking at me; she was watching the opposite direction, standing in a half-crouch. That position surely couldn't be comfortable, but for her it looked completely easy and natural. Her head turned with a quick birdlike grace to glance now one way, now the other. Guarding our backs, I realized. Against what?

"Nothing wrong with brown, my opinion," she said.

The more my eyes got used to the terrain, the more colors came out. Brown, yes, barren rocky brown plains and brown buttes and a brown stream frothing over a tiny waterfall. The hills were sharp-edged, looking as if they had been blasted out of bedrock the day before, barely touched by erosion. But in the brown were hints of other colors: a sheen of dark, almost purple, echoing the purple-grey of the cloudy sky, and even patches on the rocks where the amber shaded off to almost army-green.

"It's beautiful, isn't it?" said Leah Hamakawa. She was, as always, two steps ahead of us. She was down on one knee in the dirt, her nose right up against a rock. She'd taken both her gloves off and was scraping the surface of the rock inquisitively with her thumbnail.

I knelt down and scooped up a handful of rocks and dirt in my gloved hand. Close up, I could see that the brown was an illusion. The rocks themselves were the color of brick, but clinging to them were blotches of purple algae and tiny, dark amber specks of lichen. I pulled off one glove so I could feel the texture. Cold, with a rough grittiness. When I rubbed it between my fingers, the blotches of purple had a slimy feel. I was tempted to try pulling off the rebreather for a moment so I could put it right up to my nose and smell it, but decided that, considering the absence of oxygen in the atmosphere, that would not be wise.

"Beautiful, yeah, right," Tally said. "You got rocks in your head, girl. Stinks. I seen prettier stinking strip mines."

"It used to be red," Leah said. "Long ago. Before the Age of Confusion; before the ecopoesis." She paused, then added, "I bet it was beautiful then, too."

I looked at the handful of dirt in my palm. Mars. Yes, perhaps it was beautiful. In its way.

My ears and the flesh of my face in the places not covered by the re-breather were getting cold. The temperature was above freezing, but it was still quite chilly. The air in the rebreather was stale, smelling slightly rotten and distinctly sulfurous. That indicated a problem with the rebreather; the micropore filters in the system should have removed any trace of odor from the recycled air. I thought again about taking the rebreather off and seeing what the air smelled like.

"Shit," said Tally. "Anyway, you and Tinkerman about done gawking the scenery? We got a murder to solve. Two murders."

"They've been dead for well over a year," Leah said. "They can wait another day. God, isn't this place *magnificent?*"

"Stinks," said Tally.

❧

The lander was bulbous and squat, painted a pale green, with the name *Albert Alligator* in cursive script next to the airlock door. Leah and I cycled through the airlock together. Langevin, the pilot who had shuttled us down, was waiting for us in the suiting atrium when the inner lock opened. He opened his mouth to say something, and then abruptly shut it, gagged, and turned away, his hand going up to cover his mouth and nose. He scrambled out of the atrium abruptly. I looked at Leah. She shrugged, and reached up to unfasten the strap of the rebreather from behind her head.

"Let me get that," I said, and she turned around and bent her neck. Any excuse to touch her. Behind me, I could hear Tally cycling through the lock. The strap unfastened, and I gently took a finger and ran it along Leah's cheek, breaking the seal of the rebreather to the skin.

Suddenly she broke away from me. "Oh, God!"

"What?"

"Take off your rebreather."

Puzzled, I reached up, snapped the strap free, and pulled it forward over my head. The silicone made a soft *poik!* as the seal popped loose. I took a breath, and gagged on the sudden odor.

The smell was as if I'd been wading through a cesspool in the middle of a very rotten garbage dump. I looked down. My shoes were covered in brown. My hands were brown. One leg, where I'd knelt on the ground, had a brown spot on the knee. Leah was even dirtier.

Shit.

Tally popped through the lock, accompanied by a fresh burst of fecal odor. I held my nose and suppressed my instinct to gag.

"Of course," said Leah. "Anaerobic bacteria." She thought for a second. "We're going to have to find some boots, and maybe overalls. Leave them outside when we come in."

I started to giggle.

"What's so goddam funny?" Tally said.

"I've decided you're right," I told her. "Mars stinks. Take off your rebreather. You'll see."

⬢

The utility landing platform was a hexagonal truss plate with small rocket engines mounted on three of the six corners. The hab-and-lab module that Spacewatch was delivering for our stay was strapped on the top. It hovered in the cloudy sky like a flying waffle-iron. Langevin guided it in by remote control, setting it down in the sandy valley a hundred meters from the ruins of the earlier habitat. His landing was as neat and as unconcerned as a man passing a plate of potatoes. Still operating by remote control, he unstowed the power crane, lifted the habitat off the landing platform and lowered it gently to the ground. The habitat itself was an unpainted aluminum cylinder, fixed with brackets onto a platform with an electromechanical jack at each corner to level it on uneven ground. It was a small dwelling for three people, but would be adequate for our stay.

"Man, I don't envy y'all," he said. He delicately pinched two fingers over his nose. "No surprise nobody comes here." He shook his head. "Anything else y'all need?"

"How about the rover?" Leah asked.

"It's still in transit from the Moon; won't arrive for a few more days. When it gets here, I'll send it right down."

⬢

Tally was first one inside the habitat, of course. Even though it had just come down from space, like a cat, she had to sniff it out herself. After five minutes she waved us in.

The interior of the habitat was brand-new, the fixtures molded to the interior. Across from the airlock atrium was the air regeneration equipment, with three spherical pressure tanks painted blue to indicate oxygen, and three green-painted tanks of nitrogen to provide make-up gas. To the left was a combined conference room–and–kitchen area, and behind that the sleeping cubbies.

"Only two cubbies," Tally said, "and a mite cozy ones at that. Guess we girls bunk down in one: give you the other all to yourself, Tinkerman."

I couldn't breathe for a moment. Somehow I managed to sneak a quick glance up. Tally wasn't looking at me. She hadn't yet realized that the silence was extending a bit too long. Leah glanced across at me. Her expression was neutral, curious, perhaps, as to what I would do. I couldn't read her intention. I never could.

In a very small voice, I said, "I volunteer to share a bunk with Leah."

Tally looked up sharply. Leah gazed back at her, her expression unreadable. But she didn't voice an objection.

"Huh," said Tally. I don't think I'd ever seen Tally at a loss for words. "Well. Guess I get a cubby to myself." She paused, and then added, almost to herself, "Lucky me."

☞

Terraformed Mars had an atmosphere half as thick as Earth's. That was enough pressure for a human to survive, but with no oxygen to breathe. With rebreathers to recirculate exhaust carbon dioxide back into breathable oxygen, we could survive outside comfortably without a vacuum suit. For that matter, you could survive outside stark naked, as long as you had your rebreather, and didn't mind the cold.

Outside again, this time with boots and coveralls to keep the worst of the stinking dirt out of our habitat, we walked in silence across the rock-littered landscape the hundred meters to the place the earlier habitat had been. Ragged edges of aluminum stuck out from the platform like ribs. Pieces of the habitat had been scattered across the plain by the wind, a fantail of shining metal and shards of composite sheeting visible against the brown all the way to the horizon.

There were two bodies, one within the remains of the exploded habitat, one out on the plain. Not much was left of them. The bodies were barely more than piles of dirt with a ribcage and part of a pelvis protruding, even the bones covered with the purple-brown of the Martian microbiota. I was glad for the filtering effect of the rebreather. I made videos of the bodies in position while Leah knelt down to examine them and take samples: clothing, hair, skin, tissue. After she examined the one in the habitat, she rose without speaking and went to the one outside. Unlike the other one, the clothing on this one was partly eaten away by bacteria.

Leah's long black hair blew around her face as she worked, but the carbon-dioxide breeze wasn't strong enough to move the pieces of aluminum framework. The wind must have been much stronger to have spread the wreckage so far.

Tally stood, as always, a dozen paces away, eyes restlessly scanning the horizon for enemies.

"We really should have had a doctor to do this analysis," Leah said, standing up. "But a few things are obvious. For example, the man in the habitat had a fractured skull."

"What?"

"But this one," she nodded down at the body she was standing over, "shows no apparent sign of trauma. No rebreather, either, so I'll hazard a guess that carbon-dioxide poisoning was what did it for him." Leah put the tissue samples into her sample-pack and took a step toward the habitat. "I'll have to let the computer analyze the samples to verify that, of course." She looked around. "Who could have killed them? Why?" She looked up the plain, following the trail of debris. "I think we've seen enough. Tinkerman, you have enough pictures? Does your checklist have anything else?"

I looked down at the list. "No, as far as forensics is concerned, we're done."

"Then, unless you have any further suggestions, do you think maybe we could get them decently buried?"

When there's a fatal incident in space, of whatever kind, there needs to be an investigation. If it was an accident, the cause has to be found so that Spacewatch Authority can take appropriate measures to prevent its recurrence, and deliver a warning to anybody else with similar equipment.

We were that incident-investigation team, Leah and I. Tally, a freelance survival specialist, was our protection. If somebody had killed the two researchers, deliberately blown up their habitat for some as-yet-undetermined motive, whoever it was that had killed them might come back.

But nobody cared about Mars. The exciting horizons were light-years away, where relativistic probes lasercast back terabits of images, giving the excitement of vistas that anybody could access on optical disk without the danger and discomfort of leaving Earth, and with far stranger life-forms than any mere microbes. Mars was such an uninteresting location that it took over a year before Spacewatch Authority noticed that a scientific team that had gone there to study microbes hadn't returned. They were the first researchers to bother with an on-site investigation of Mars in over a century.

"It doesn't make sense," I told Leah, back in the habitat. "Why would anybody want to murder two researchers on a stinky planet too close to Earth to even be interesting?"

She shrugged. "Kooks. Bacteria-worshipers. Or maybe one of 'em had an angry ex."

"It's not as if the planet were exciting," I said. "They tried to terraform it. They failed. End of story, go home."

"Failed? Tinkerman, you have it all wrong. You should go learn a little history before going on a trip." I could hear her switching into lecture mode. "They didn't try to terraform Mars. They *never* tried to terraform Mars. What they did was ecopoesis, and they succeeded spectacularly, more than anybody had a right to expect."

"Ecopoesis," I said, "terraforming, same thing."

"Not at all."

➤

The way Leah told it, it was part epic, part farce.

It's hard for us, now, to imagine what it was like in the age of confusion, before the fusion renaissance and the second reformation, but the people of the twenty-first century had a technology of chemical rockets and nuclear reactors that, although primitive, had its own crude power. By the middle of the twenty-first century, Mars had been explored, catalogued, and abandoned. It was too cold to harbor life, even of the most primitive sort; the atmosphere was closer to vacuum than to air, and there were far more accessible resources in the asteroids. Mars was uninteresting.

It didn't even make good video. The largest canyon in the solar system— so big that if you stand in the middle, the walls on both sides were out of sight over the horizon. The biggest mountain in the solar system—but the slope so gentle that it meant nothing on any human scale. Ancient fossil bacteria—but not even a hint of anything that hadn't been dead and turned to rock a billion years before trilobites crawled the oceans. A hundred spots on Earth and across the solar system were more spectacular. Once somebody had climbed Olympus (and in the low gravity of Mars it wasn't a hard climb) and placed flags at both poles of Mars, why go back?

The ecopoesis of Mars was done by a band of malcontents from one of the very first space settlements, *Freehold Toynbee*. Habitats—they called them "space colonies" back then—were crowded, dangerous, undersupplied, constantly in need of repair, and smelly. They were haven to malcontents, ideologues, fanatics, and visionaries: the vanguard of humanity, the divine agents of the manifest destiny of mankind into the universe. More succinctly, the habitats were home to people who couldn't get along with their fellow humans on Earth. Arguments were their way of life.

It was an engineer named Joseph Smith Kirkpatrick who proposed that *Toynbee* could transform Mars. The people of *Toynbee* debated the question for a year, arguing every conceivable point of view with a riotous enthusiasm. At the beginning, the consensus of the colony seemed to be that since human destiny was in space, even to consider living on planetary surfaces could only be idiocy, or some deviant plot to subvert that destiny. But Kirkpatrick was more than just a maverick engineer with wild dreams, he was a man with a divine mission. A year later, the quibble about living on a planetary surface wasn't even part of the argument. *Toynbee* decided that the right of Mars to remain unchanged was preempted by the imperative of life to spread into new niches. They had convinced themselves that they had not merely a right, but a divine duty to seed life on Mars.

Mars, back then, was completely inhospitable to life. The atmosphere was less than one percent of the Earth's, and the average temperature was far below freezing, even at the equator. But their analysis showed that the climate of Mars just might be unstable. The surface of Mars showed networks of canyons and run-off channels, dry lakes, and the seashores of ancient oceans. There had been water on Mars, once, a billion years or more ago, and plenty of it. All that water was still there, hidden away. The old scientific expeditions had proven that—frozen in the polar ice-caps, locked into kilometer-thick hills of permafrost in the highlands. They convinced themselves that there was, in fact, far more water on Mars than previously suspected, frozen into enormous buried glaciers under featureless fields of sand. Enough to form whole oceans—if it could be melted. All that was needed was a trigger.

It's not easy to heat up a planet, even temporarily. They did it by setting off a volcano. There were a number of ancient volcanoes on Mars to choose from; after many geological soundings to determine magma depth, they picked a small one. Or rather, a volcano small by Mars standards, still a monster by the standards of any Earthly mountains. Hecates Tholus; the Witch's Teat. To set it off, they determined, required that they drill five kilometers deep into the crust of Mars.

Just because it was clearly impossible was no reason they wouldn't do it. Mars has no magnetic field, and so the solar wind impacts directly on the planetary exosphere. A thousand miles above Mars, currents of a billion amperes course around the planet, driven by the solar wind–derived ionization. Joseph Smith Kirkpatrick and his team of planetary engineers short-circuited this current with a laser beam, ionizing a discharge channel through the atmosphere, creating the solar system's largest lightning bolt. They discharged the ionosphere of Mars into the side of Hecate, instantly creating a meter-deep pool of molten rock. And then they did it again. And again, as soon as the ionospheric charge had a chance to renew. And again, a new lightning bolt every five minutes, day and night, for ten years.

One million lightning discharges, all on exactly the same spot. They melted a channel through to the magma chamber below, and a volcano that had been sleeping for almost half a billion years awakened in a cataclysmic explosion. The eruption put carbon dioxide and sulfur dioxide into the atmosphere; more importantly, it shot a hundred billion tons of ash directly into the stratosphere. Over the course of several months, the ash settled down, blackening the surface.

The new, darker surface absorbed sunlight, warming the planet and releasing adsorbed carbon dioxide from the soil. The released carbon dioxide thickened the atmosphere, and the greenhouse effect of the thicker atmosphere warmed the planet yet more. The resulting heat evaporated water from the polar ice-caps into the atmosphere. Water in the atmosphere is an effective greenhouse gas, even more effective than carbon dioxide, and so the temperature rose a little more. Finally ice trapped underground for eons melted. A whole hemisphere of Mars was flooded, eventually to form the vast Boreal Ocean, as well as innumerable crater seas and ponds. But that was much later. In the beginning, in Joseph Smith Kirkpatrick's lifetime, only on a band around the equator was water actually liquid all year round. But that was enough for what they wanted to do. Slowly, the eons-frozen permafrost of Mars was melting.

The atmosphere was still thin, and still almost entirely carbon dioxide, But Mars is a sulfur-rich planet. Sulfur dioxide frozen into the soil was also released, and rose into the atmosphere. Ultraviolet light from the sun photolyzed the sulfur dioxide into free radicals, which recombined to form sulfuric acid, which instantly dissolved into the new equatorial oceans. The new acid oceans attacked the ancient rocks of Mars, etching away calcium carbonate and magnesium carbonate, releasing carbon dioxide. In a few years, the acid oceans had been once more neutralized—and the atmosphere was thick, fully half a bar of carbon dioxide, enough for a greenhouse effect warm enough to keep the new oceans liquid year-round.

Mars had been triggered.

But how to keep this new atmosphere, to keep the planet warm? Not even Joseph Smith Kirkpatrick could keep a volcano erupting forever, and already the Witch's Tit was settling down from an untamed explosion of ash to a sedate mound of slowly oozing lava.

Joseph Smith Kirkpatrick's answer was bacteria. Anaerobic bacteria, to live in the oxygen-free atmosphere of Mars.

"Sewer bacteria," I said.

"You got it, Tinkerman. Anaerobic bacteria—modified sewer organisms. Yeasts, slime-molds, cyanobacteria, methanogens, and halophiles as well; but all in all, bacteria closer to gangrene than to higher life."

"No wonder it stinks." I shuddered. "They were crazy."

"Not so. They were, in fact, very clever. They engineered a whole anaerobic ecology. The bacterial ecology darkened the surface, taking over the job of the volcanic ash. It burrowed into the rocks and broke them apart into soil, releasing adsorbed carbon dioxide in the process. The methanogens added methane, a vitally important greenhouse gas, to that atmosphere, and raised the temperature another few degrees. They didn't dare establish too many photosynthetic forms, of course, because if the carbon dioxide in the atmosphere were to be converted into oxygen, the greenhouse effect that kept the planet warm would vanish, and the planet would return to its lifeless, frozen state.

"But terraforming Mars hadn't been their goal in the first place; in fact, terraforming was the very antithesis of what they intended. Their goal was ecopoesis, the establishment of an ecology. They were Darwinists, and diversity was their creed. They looked down in contempt on unimaginative humans who believed that humans were the pinnacle of creation; they saw humanity as only agents of life, spore-pods by which life could jump from one world to another. They believed that once life, however primitive, could establish a toehold on Mars, it would adapt to its environment, and flourish, and someday evolve. Not to make a copy of Earth, but into something new, something indigenously Martian."

"So they wanted to be gods."

Leah shook her head. "They wanted to be men."

"So they're responsible for this place. Great."

"The ecopoesis was a wonder in its day, Tinkerman. It spawned debate across the Earth and cis-lunar space: Was this the greatest feat of engineering in history, or was it a crime against nature? The year of arguing at *Freehold Toynbee* was nothing compared to the cyclonic fervor that was released when Joseph Smith Kirkpatrick proudly announced to the Earth what they had done.

"Kirkpatrick was kidnapped from *Toynbee* and put on trial in Geneva as an ecocriminal. The question the High Court argued was, 'Do Rocks Have Rights?' Can it be a crime to destroy an ecosystem that contains no life? The trial took three years, and ended in a hung jury. Kirkpatrick was eventually acquitted of all charges, but he was never allowed to leave the Earth again, and died an angry, bitter man.

"*Freehold Toynbee* claimed ownership of Mars, and passed a law making it illegal for any human to land on it for the next billion years—but nobody paid any attention to their claim. For decades, Mars was the subject of intense scientific scrutiny. In a few more years *Toynbee* went bankrupt, for ecopoesis paid no bills. Technologically obsolete, the colony itself was ripped apart for scrap; the colonists scattering to a hundred colonies and asteroid settlements. And then, after a few decades of fame, Mars was ignored. Bacteria or no bacteria, there were far more abundant resources elsewhere in the solar system."

"And if two researchers hadn't decided to die here, it would still be uninteresting today."

"Not uninteresting, no. Ignored, maybe. But not uninteresting."

"To you."

Leah smiled. "To me."

●

Langevin took the lander back upstairs, flying the utility platform in formation with him, leaving us alone on the planet. We were in the tiny kitchen area of the habitat, sitting around the only table large enough to serve as a conference area. Leah spoke first. "Tally, did you learn anything?"

"After almost two years," Tally said, "did you really seriously believe any footprints of the perpers would be left preserved? Well, surprise." She grinned. "Yeah, I found some bootprints. Took me some looking, let me tell you, but I found 'em."

"So tell," Leah said. "What did you get?"

"A few places in the lee of the rocks didn't get washed away by rain or blurred by wind." Tally shook her head. "But I checked them all; every damn print matches the size and patterns of one of the boots in the hab. Either whoever did it used the same boots as our late friends, or, more likely, whoever did it didn't leave any bootprints. That's all I've got. You?"

Leah spoke slowly. "The one in the hab died from being hit in the head. The other one died outside. No rebreather in evidence, and he wasn't dressed for outside. Just a thin robe. Carbon-dioxide poisoning, as I expected."

"Hmm," said Tally. "Two guys sleeping in the same cubby. Ask me, I'd call it as a lovers' quarrel gone violent. The one guy bashes the other in a fit of rage, probably didn't mean to hit quite so hard. Then, realizing what he did, he blows up the habitat and walks outside to die."

"Could be," Leah said. "It's a hypothesis, anyway. Can't prove it one way or another with the evidence we have so far. One odd thing—the man who died outside had charred clothing."

That explained the ragged appearance of the clothing of the man who had been outside. His clothes hadn't been eaten by bacteria; they had been charred.

"Maybe caught alight when he blew the habitat?" Tally suggested.

Leah shook her head. "Carbon dioxide–and–methane atmosphere. Nothing burns, outside."

"Um," Tally said. "Guess I don't have an explanation for that one."

"Tinkerman?" Leah said. "You get anything?"

I shook my head. "I collected as much of their records as I could find, but so far I can't read them. A lot of their opticals were damaged by fire, and on the ones that weren't, the surfaces are pretty corroded by exposure. I've started cleaning them off, and I may be able to get at some of their records, but even if I can do it, reading it will be pretty much a bit-by-bit process. They weren't very conscientious at making backups and putting them in a secure location, I'm afraid."

"Pity. If we could read their diaries, it would help, let us see if anything was going wrong before the blowup. Oh, well. Do what you can, and we'll get together again tomorrow and check progress."

As we talked, Leah's face had slowly been reddening. Her eyes were pale circles; her nose and lips and chin, where the rebreather had covered them, a pale diamond. The rest of her face slowly turned a brilliant scarlet, deepening even as I watched. She raised a hand and brushed her hair away from her face. "Ouch." She looked puzzled.

Reflexively, I raised a hand to my temple. My own touch was like a whip, a brilliant stab of heat.

Tally looked at the two of us, grinning. "Well, well, aren't you two the sight. Look like you're wearing warpaint. Painted up like two owls, you are."

Tally's dark skin showed nothing, but Leah reached over and gently touched her face.

"Yow! Hey, that hurts! Shit!"

"Ultraviolet," Leah said. "It's the hard ultraviolet. CO-two is too difficult for UV to split; it doesn't form an ozone layer. The climate is cloudy and cold, but the hard UVs still get right down to the surface. I'd say, we've been a bit stupid, going out unprotected. Good thing we weren't out much longer."

"Shit," said Tally. "Why didn't you say something sooner?"

"The hab has to have some kind of a med kit," Leah said. "Maybe we'd better see if it has any sunburn ointment."

➤

At night, in the cubby. I didn't know what to expect.

She wasn't in the bunk. She was sitting in the cubby's one small chair, staring into space. I got into the bunk, on one side, making a space for her.

She didn't move. Fifteen minutes. Half an hour.

I'd done something wrong. But she hadn't objected! I thought—

Damn.

The silence in the cubby was oppressive.

At last I said, "Leah?"

She said nothing.

"Leah, I'm sorry. I didn't mean to try to—"

In the dark it was hard to tell where her eyes focused, but I could see the slight movement of her head and knew that she was looking at me.

"David." She paused for a moment, and just before I was about to speak again, to apologize to her, she continued. "I've seen bodies before."

It was not what I'd expected her to say. "Bodies?"

"I thought I was used to it." Her voice was tiny in the darkness. "I thought I could handle it. I can handle it."

It was odd. The bodies hadn't bothered me. They had been so far decomposed that they were barely recognizable as having been human at all. And they hadn't seemed to bother her, not in the daytime.

"I've seen too many bodies." And then she came into bed, turning to face away from me. I held her. Her body was rigid, but she turned her face and pressed her head into my side. "Too many, too many." Her breath was warm against my shoulder. "It wasn't even anybody I knew. I'm sorry. I'm sorry. I'm going to stop crying now."

I touched her face. Her eyes were dry, but somewhere inside she seemed to be crying.

"I don't even know why I'm still alive," she said. "Everybody else died."

I didn't know what to say to her, so I stroked her hair and said, "I know, I know."

"Careful how you touch me, you idiot," she said, and her tone was back to normal. "My whole face feels like it's on fire."

I knew so little about her. She never talked about herself; she so deftly managed to always avoid the subject. She had always seemed so much in control. But suddenly she was asleep, and the time for asking questions had passed.

●

I've heard that some people fall in love at first sight. It took me about three classes.

The first one, I don't think I even noticed her in particular, just another face among the many. I was teaching a class on troubleshooting. There are two techniques to troubleshooting equipment. The first is, you know the equipment so thoroughly that you have a sense of it, you know it as a friend, and when it's down, you can feel what's wrong by pure instinct. That method is rather hard to teach.

The other way is to be simple, thorough and logical; to home in on the problem by pure mechanical elimination, a matter of dogged and willfully unimaginative technique. That was the technique I was teaching. It means teaching how to be methodical, how to structure a grid to let no combination of symptoms escape detection.

The Institute has simple rules: everybody teaches, everybody learns. Every year, during the Earth's northern-hemisphere summer, the Institute holds a monthlong convocation, and this year I was teaching. My class lasted only a week, and it was almost half over before I really noticed Leah.

But, once I'd noticed her, I couldn't get her out of my mind. The breeze rustled across pine needles, and I heard the sound of her voice, asking a question, precise, cogent, perfectly phrased. I'd see the way she cocked her head, listening. I became suddenly self-conscious, worried about how I presented the material, whether it was clear and precise.

So when I finished, I sat in on her course, although it was somewhat out of my usual feeding range. Soliton-wave solutions of the Einstein field equations. I'm slow; my lips move when I solve field equations in four dimensions. She was a lot faster than the class, so smooth that it was obvious that she knew the material so well she didn't even bother to review it before she started talking.

I knew that once the convocation had ended, I would never see her again. The thought made me desperate, although I'd not spoken more than a half dozen words to her beyond what was required of a student. I knew absolutely nothing of her other than her name, Leah Hamakawa, and the obvious fact that she knew more about general relativity than I would be able to learn in a lifetime. I had to do something that would get her attention.

I invited her to come with me to visit Old Los Angeles.

The month after the convocation is traditionally a time for vacation and independent study, before we went back to our individual lives, hiring out as Institute-bonded technicians or consultants or troubleshooters. I had no idea whether she'd be interested in a trip to O.L.A.; it was a wild shot to try to impress her.

But her eyes had suddenly flared with interest, and, for the first time, she looked at me and actually saw me. "Old L.A.? Interesting. Have you been there?"

I didn't want to admit that I hadn't, so I temporized. "I know a good guide."

O.L.A. was one of the most dangerous, and certainly the oddest, of the ecosystems on the Earth. Back at the end of the second Elizabethan age, the doomed city had been the home of a dozen or more gene-splicing laboratories, corporations that had made synthetic retroviruses to replace flawed DNA with custom-designed synthetic, right inside the chromosome of the target organism. Other cities had such labs, too, of course, and Los Angeles hadn't even been the most prominent of them. Just the unluckiest.

The virus that had gotten free was a generic gene-splicer. It would copy snippets of genes at random out of any host organism it happened to infect. As soon as it vectored to another host, it would make a billion copies of itself, and of its copied DNA, copy the genes back into a likely spot in the genome of the new host, and then start over again from the beginning by grabbing a snippet of DNA from the new host. As a parting gift to the new organism, it would then trigger the cell's own enzyme promoters to express the DNA.

The fact that retroviruses copy DNA from one organism to another is a natural process, of course; just a part of the mechanics of evolution. The rogue virus had the effect of a million years of evolution, set loose in a single day: chaos.

Most of the additions to the genome were meaningless changes, genes which coded neither useful nor harmful proteins. Most of the changes that had effect were dysfunctional, and killed the hosts over the course of a few days or weeks, if they were lucky, or produced an explosion of cancers that killed the host over the course of months, if not so lucky. Over the course of the first year a great die-off occurred.

The things that survived were—strange. The rogue virus had indiscriminately cut and pasted genes with no notion of species; what came out of the mingling were neither humans nor animals nor plants, but weird mixtures: predatory plants, octopuses with hands, tiger-sized raccoons that knew how to use guns, social bacteria that drew recondite, hypnotic patterns across deserted beaches. The thrown-together quarantine barriers held, barely, and the hastily mobilized scientific effort to combat the virus devised a specific antiviral protein that knocked out the rogue virus's ability to reproduce. The plague was stopped before it spread outside the boundaries of what had been Los Angeles.

Inside the hundred-mile ring, surrounded by scorched sand and silent, instant death, what had once been Los Angeles was still evolving toward a new ecosystem. There was noplace more deadly, or more strange. The retrovirus itself was gone, but the creatures it had spawned remained. You could go there, if you signed a waiver indicating that you knew the danger and were aware that there was no guarantee that you would come back.

The guide I had been told about was a mysterious survival specialist and weapons expert named Tally Okumba. Nobody, I was told, knew more about O.L.A., or about any of the odd, dangerous corners of the Earth, than Tally did; and nobody knew more about staying alive, on Earth or elsewhere.

"Old L.A.," Leah said. Her eyes were veiled, dreaming. "When do we leave?"

➤

In the light of the dawn, Tally was dancing, high kicks, spins, and backflips in the low gravity. Over her rebreather, her face was covered with a bone-white warpaint that, after a moment, I realized was an improvised sunblock. I watched her through the habitat's window, and wondered how long she had been at it. Her flexibility was astonishing.

Leah did not mention what she'd said the night before, and I didn't bring it up.

The task for the day was to gather up shards of the shattered habitat and as much of the wind-scattered contents as we could find. Leah and I worked mostly in silence, occasionally pointing out to each other pieces in the distance. Aerial photos taken as we had landed helped locate the more distant fragments, but didn't substitute for plain, dogged walking.

The job took a lot of walking. The camp was located on the Syrtisian isthmus. This was a broad saddle that separated the Hellenian Sea from Gulf of Isidis, a bay of the Boreal Ocean which covered nearly the entire northern hemisphere of Mars. To the northwest the land sloped gently upward toward the Syrtis caldera, an ancient shield volcano, dead now for well over a billion years. An endless series of lava-etched rilles corrugated the landscape from northwest to southeast, each with a tiny brown stream at the bottom. The wind that scattered the pieces of the habitat had, in accord with Murphy's law, been crosswise to the rilles, meaning that we had to trek up and down innumerable gullies to collect the fragments.

"It must have been some wind," Leah said. "Blowing pretty constantly from the Hellenian Sea toward the Gulf, apparently."

The carbon-dioxide atmosphere was still now, with barely a trace of breeze.

By local noon we had made a large collection of pieces. I took a break and sat on a rock by one of the streams. The brook foamed as it rippled over submerged rocks. Amber bubbles clumped together, then detached and floated downstream. The stream looked like an alcoholic's vision of paradise: a river of ice-cold beer, flowing down into a lake of beer, emptying somewhere into a frigid ocean of beer—

"Well, yes—what did you think that the rivers are?" Leah said, when I mentioned the thought to her. She was wearing a makeshift sunbonnet constructed from piloting charts; even with her face hidden by a rebreather and caked with burn ointment, she was stunningly beautiful. I wondered what it would be like to peel off her winter garments, to make love to her right there by the stream. "By any practical definition, it *is* a river of beer. Yeast is an anaerobic microorganism—the stuff that the ecopoesis team seeded this planet with will ferment just about everything. Naturally carbonated, too: five hundred millibars of carbon-dioxide atmosphere is going to dissolve a hell of a lot of carbonation into the water at this temperature. I'd bet that if you brought a glass of that stuff inside it would develop a pretty good head."

"You mean I could drink this stuff?"

Leah looked at it critically. "Hmmm. You know, you just might be able to. Full of bacteria, I expect, but if our antibiologicals aren't working, we're already dead anyway, so I doubt it's a problem. Tell you what." She looked up at me. "You try it, and let me know."

I didn't.

By midafternoon, we had gathered as much of the debris as we could find. Everything that looked like it might have originally been part of the habitat pressure vessel, Leah set out in a array next to the site of the explosion. Each piece was numbered, and then Leah began fitting them together like a jigsaw puzzle.

"There are some minor pieces missing, but I think we've pretty much got everything important," she said at last.

I walked up behind her and looked at the neatly indexed array of scrap. "What have you learned?"

She shook her head. "It doesn't tell me a story, yet." She picked up a piece and handed it to me. "Tell me what you think about this one."

It was a curved piece of aluminum, forty centimeters long, somewhat bent. "Exterior habitat pressure-vessel wall," I said.

"Right so far. What else?"

The piece had broken at a seam at one edge. Shoddy workmanship? Probably not; the other end had ripped jagged right across; the weld had probably never been designed for the stress it must have taken. It was bent in the middle. The jagged end had a scrape of paint on the raw metal. "Blue paint chips on the end here," I said.

"Right," she said. "And the bend?"

It took me a moment, but suddenly I saw it. "Bent the wrong way," I said. "It bowed in. The explosion should have blown it out." I thought for a moment. "Could have been bent by the wind, later."

She nodded, thoughtful. "Possibility. There are other pieces bent the same way, though."

"How much overpressure would it take to bend it that way?"

"Good question," she said. "If we could figure the overpressure as a function of position, we can guess the locus of the blast. Turns out, though, that it doesn't take much blast pressure to make the habitat structure fail this way. The pressure vessel was designed to hold an interior pressure; it's not well designed against an external overpressure."

"So, what do you think?"

"It might have failed in the rarefaction rebound following the overpressure of an explosion," she said. "Microstructural examination might tell. Might not."

"Or the explosion was outside the habitat." That would make sense. If somebody had wanted to kill the team, the easiest way to do it would have been to put a bomb next to the shelter.

Leah shook her head and chose another piece to hand to me. "Carbon deposits," she said.

I looked at it and nodded. The burn marks were on the concave side, the interior. "Fire after the blast?" I suggested.

She nodded, but slowly. "Could be, I suppose. But after the habitat breach, everything vents to the reducing atmosphere. Fire goes out pretty quick."

◆

"If it was murder," Leah said, "who might have done it?"

We were sitting back in the little conference room. My whole face itched now, despite the ointments that Tally had devised for sunburn. My face felt like I was still wearing the rebreather.

"Hard to say," Tally said. "I suppose either one of 'em might have had enemies. If it wasn't personal, I've got a few possibilities. First, before they went, turns out they got a couple of anonymous messages saying not to go. The point was, Mars was property of *Freehold Toynbee*, and it was reserved for the Martians, however long it took them to appear. Humans were expressly forbidden to land."

"*Toynbee!*" Leah said. "They were dissolved more than a century ago. Bankrupt and sold for scrap. Besides, lots of researchers have visited Mars."

Tally nodded, slowly. "A century ago, yes. I doubt anybody's been here in the last hundred years, though, except our poor friends. Seems hard to believe anyone would still care. A nut, I'd say. Still, a nut might be what we're looking for."

"And the other possibilities?"

"Turns out that there are still some people," Tally said, "as think that ecopoesis is usurping the role of God. And some as think that ecopoesis is, or was, a crime against the ecosystem. And there's been talk that if Mars could be triggered, then other planets, in other solar systems, could be. Some of these have life of their own, incompatible with terrestrial life. So, some radicals, they don't want Mars studied. They're scared that any studying of Mars is a step to triggering planets in other solar systems. There are those as would like to stop that. Stop it early, and stop it at any cost.

"And, finally, there are those as worry about Mars, worry that this ecopoesis might just be another L.A. waiting to happen." She shrugged. "Me, I rather like Old L.A. Got that kind of raw charm you don't see much in other cities nowadays. But I know that not everybody thinks like me."

"I see," said Leah. "And which of these would have set a bomb?"

Tally shrugged. "Any of them. Or all of them, working together."

"Working together? Logically, the Toynbees and the ecoradicals are enemies."

Tally smiled. "Logically, we're not precisely talking rational people here."

"So what do we have?"

"See, are we even sure it was a bomb?" Tally said. "Tinkerman, you find any suspicious pieces of pyrotechnic?"

I shook my head. "Nothing yet. But I don't know much about bombs. I might have missed something."

"Me neither," Tally said. "And I do know about bombs, I do. A bit."

◆

Leah Hamakawa was completely opaque to me. I never had a clue what she was thinking, what she felt or thought about me. Sometimes her gaze would wander over me and stop, and she would look at me, not with a question, not with an invitation, just a look, calm and direct. I wished I knew what she was contemplating.

I wished I knew why I was so attracted to her.

The trip to Old L.A. had been a cusp in our relationship. On the trip we had just been fellows, co-adventurers and nothing more. Afterwards, Leah accepted the fact that I tagged along after her as just a facet of the environment, hardly worth commenting on. We're not, actually, a team, although it must seem like it to others. Leah was the hotshot scientist, and, well, every team needs a tech and a pilot.

Eventually she had noticed.

"Look," Leah had said. "You're as skittery as a colt, you're stammering, I can't get one full grammatical sentence out of you in a cartload, and you're so nervous I'm sure you're going to break something. Do you want to sleep with me? Is that it?"

Her gaze was direct. It was always direct.

I couldn't say anything. I had trouble closing my mouth,

"If you do," she said, "fine, do it, or don't do it, I don't care . . . just will you quit stumbling around?"

And, later, after she'd taken off her clothes, she said, "Just don't think it means something, okay? I couldn't stand that."

But it did. Maybe not to her, but to me.

And so we came to Mars. When the authorities had finally noticed that the missing science team had stopped filing status reports to Spacewatch, and the orbital eye they sent to report got a break in the heavy Martian cloud cover and saw pieces of the habitat spread across ten kilometers of landscape—a "presumed fatal malfunction," as it was reported—Spacewatch had asked for Leah; she had a rep for unraveling tough balls of fur, and I scrambled to rate the slot to go along. Not that this was so hard; I had my skills, piloting and mechanicking and, yes, troubleshooting, and most crews were glad to have me aboard. In this investigation, the third slot on the team was special, in case the accident we were investigating was no accident at all, and the perpetrators might not be finished. The third slot needed a professional paranoid.

We both knew exactly the survival expert who was right for that place.

"Still hanging 'round with that long-legged white girl, I see"—Tally had greeted me, when I came to ask if she wanted to join the team. "Give it up, boy, she's too good for you."

"Don't I know it," I'd said.

But that was the past, and brooding over the past wasn't going to get me to bed, or explain Leah Hamakawa to me. She had undressed without the least trace of self-consciousness and gotten into the cubby's tiny bed. I undressed, with a lot more trepidation, and lay down beside her. She turned and watched me with a pellucid gaze, free of any emotion I could interpret. She wouldn't let me understand her, but for whatever reason of her own, she would let me love her.

For the moment, that would have to be enough.

⬤

The next day I worked on decoding the data from the damaged opticals, while Leah put together the jigsaw puzzle of the exploded habitat pieces, and Tally ranged in ever-wider loops from the habitat, exploring. I succeeded in getting large blocks of data, but nothing was of any evident value: lengthy descriptions of bacteria, lists of bacteria count per square millimeter in a hundred different habitats.

"Here's something," Leah said. "Take a look at my collection of pieces. What's missing?"

I looked over the junk pile. Skin, electronics, window fragments, plastic shards. "What?"

"Don't you see it? Aluminum, titanium, carbon-composite, plastic—anything missing here?"

Now that she had given the hint, I could see it, too. "Steel. Nothing out of steel, or iron. Is that surprising? Steel's heavy." Hardly anything in a space-going technology is made out of steel. In space, every extra gram is paid for over and over again in fuel.

"There's not a lot of steel on a hab module," Leah said, "but there is some. Look around our hab, not everything is made of the light metals. But, no steel in the pieces here. And, take a look here." She chose a piece out of the pile and handed it to me. It was a damaged recording unit. The capstan flopped loose in the absence of the steel axle it should have rotated on. She handed me another, a piece with a neat hole where a steel grommet should have fit.

"Does that mean anything?"

She shrugged. "Who can tell? Probably not."

"Any steel fixtures hold pressure?"

Leah shook her head. "I checked the plans. No, all the iron and steel parts are incidentals. No steel penetration of the pressure hull."

Tally came back from her scouting, and looked at us both. "You are working too hard," she said. "It's time for a break. Way past time, you ask me. And I know just the thing."

"What do you have in mind?" I asked.

"Here." She handed me a sheet of aluminum. It was about a meter long, slightly curved, one side coated with a carbon-composite facing. In a corner *117 Outer* was written in Leah's neat printing. A panel from the outer skin of the exploded habitat. A mounting flange with a hole for bolting interior fixtures was at one end. She handed another one to Leah. "Sure you don't need these panels, now?" she asked Leah.

"Already looked at them." Leah shook her head. "That was the side opposite the explosion. Nothing but junk now."

After we had suited-up for outside and smeared one another's faces white with sunblock, we each took a panel, and Tally led us up to the top of the ridge that rose above the habitat. The hill surface was comprised of sand held in place with a thin veneer of purple-brown algae, slick as powdered Teflon. We had to choose our footing carefully to avoid skidding back down.

It was a gorgeous day. From the ridge, the Marscape appeared striped, brown and purple strips in alternation all the way to the horizon. The purple was the algae, covering the sunnier face of each ridge; the brown anaerobic scum colonizing the shadier back-face. The characteristic north-south wind pattern was clearly manifest in the form of long streaks trailing behind each of the larger boulders. Today, though, the wind was once again slight, erratic light gusts of no fixed direction.

We reached the top, and Tally smiled. She threaded a lanyard through the bolthole on her aluminum sheet, dropped it on the ground, and put one foot on it. "You might try this sitting down first," she said. Holding the lanyard in one hand like a set of reins, she pushed off down the hill.

At first she didn't move very fast. As the sled gathered speed, each bump sent it increasingly higher. Her balance seemed precarious, but in the one-third-normal gravity of Mars, she had plenty of time. As she leaned to control the sled, her movements were a slow-motion ballet. We could hear her shout, muffled by her rebreather, trailing behind her.

"Yahoo!"

I looked at Leah. She looked back at me, then shrugged. She dropped her sled on the ground and pushed it with her toe, testing how well it slid over the scum. Then she sat down on it, grasped the lanyard with both hands and pulled it taut, and looked back over her shoulder. "Give me a push," she said.

It took a little more skill than Tally had let on, but after a few spills, we got the hang of it, and organized scum-sledding races. Tally on one sled and Leah and me together on another; then Leah and Tally together; then finally all three of us on one sled, Leah and I sitting docked together and Tally standing with her knees gripping my chest from behind.

At a rest break, sitting exhausted from climbing, I said to Tally, "So this means that you think there's no danger? I mean, nobody trying to kill us?"

"Never said that." Tally shook her head. "No, I'm not about to be calling all-clear, not quite yet. But I'm pretty sure that there's no danger right exactly this instant. Not unless these killers are invisible and don't leave footprints." She paused. "And 'sides," she continued, "this is pretty much the tallest ridge in the area. If they were coming for us, we'd see 'em miles away."

"But what if we did? What could we do? We'd be sitting ducks."

Tally grinned a broad grin. "Sitting ducks, you say? Take a peep at that ridge over there." She pointed.

I looked. Nothing special, no different than any other ridge. "So?"

I had glanced away for only an instant, but suddenly Tally had an omniblaster in her right hand, a knife in her left, and a projectile rifle with an infrared targeting scope resting at her feet. I had no idea how she could have concealed such armament on her.

"How 'bout you?" she said. "Don't tell me you're naked?"

I was far from naked—the temperature couldn't have been more than a few degrees above freezing—but I wasn't carrying a weapon.

"Didn't I tell you to always wear a gun?" she said. "Dangerous out here. Who knows who might want to shoot you?"

"Carry an omniblaster? No, I don't think you ever told us that."

"Yes I did. Told you both. Back in O.L.A." She paused for a second. "Shit. I bet Leah's walking around naked, too." She shook her head. "You two just a bunch of children. I'm surprised you've lived this long, I really am."

"Say, look," said Leah, coming up behind us. "The sun's out."

We both looked up. The sky had been steadily overcast ever since we had landed, but the clouds were breaking up, and between them we had a glimpse of the sun.

"Take a look at that sky!" Tally said. "Isn't that gaudy!" Behind the clouds, the Martian sky was a startling blue, a bright, nearly turquoise shade that I'd never seen on Earth. I couldn't think of a reason offhand why the sky should be a different color but, naturally, Leah could.

"Methane," she said, after a second of thought. "After carbon dioxide, methane is the main atmospheric component here. Strongly absorbs red light, so the sky color is a deeper blue than just the Rayleigh scattering would predict."

"Oh," I said.

"Explains why the colors here are so muted," Leah said.

With the sunlight, the wind had picked up as well, a steadily rising wind out of the north. Suddenly the coveralls we had on weren't enough to keep us warm. We ran for the habitat.

———

The overcast had cleared completely the next day. The sky was preternaturally blue, and the wind had become a steady near-gale from the north. Leah and I worked inside. Tally still did her reconnaissance patrol outside, but I think that even she must have spent much of her time huddled in the windscreen of one or another of the boulders. Now we knew what had scattered the pieces of the habitat.

The missing iron, as it turned out, wasn't a mystery at all. Once Leah realized what to look for, she found it easily enough, in the form of grit scattered in with the rest of the habitat pieces.

"It's a sulfur-rich planet," she said. "I should have thought of it. In the year-and-a-half of exposure, everything iron or steel got converted to iron sulfide. It looked just like part of the regolith, so I overlooked it the first time."

"In just a year?" I asked. "Isn't that kinda fast?"

Leah shrugged. "Seems fast to me, too, but don't forget the UV. The surface here is more reactive than we're used to."

I worked on deciphering their electronic records. They hadn't kept personal logs, or perhaps if they had, they were on some optical I hadn't found yet. The opticals I had were mostly data, with occasional notes about where or how the samples were collected. By afternoon I had enough to determine when the last data had been recorded, and could at least put a date to the disaster.

"Sometime on August tenth," I told Leah. "Two years ago."

"Really," Leah said. "That's interesting."

"Interesting?" I said. "Not really. But you asked me for a date."

"No, but it is interesting," Leah said. "Today is June twenty-third."

"So?"

"That's Earth reckoning, of course. The Mars year is 687 Earth-days long—one year, ten months, and a few weeks. So in Mars reckoning, it's nearly the first anniversary of the disaster. Five days from now, in fact."

"Spooky," I said.

"No, I wouldn't call it spooky," she said. "But it is an odd coincidence."

I marked it on the calender.

I liked working alone with Leah, with Tally outside on patrol. I didn't exactly resent Tally, but I did sometimes envy her effortless camaraderie with Leah. I welcomed the chance to be alone with her, even though, for the most part, we worked in silence.

"Tinkerman," Leah said.

"Yes?"

"Once you start getting the data you've recovered indexed, do a search on weather for me."

I shrugged. "No problem." I looked at her. "You think it's relevant to the investigation?"

She shook her head. "Just curious."

They had, I discovered, not taken detailed observations of the Martian weather. But occasionally there was a mention of conditions outside. Their own experience mirrored ours. About the same time in the Martian year, the overcast had cleared, and a steady wind had arisen out of the north. The day before the disaster, data had been marked with a note that samples from two sites had been missed; the wind had blown away the stakes marking the site locations.

On another optical I found satellite photos of Mars. I looked at these with interest. The weather clearing we'd seen wasn't local to the Syrtisian saddle; the photos showed the northern hemisphere completely obscured by cloud cover, and then a sudden clearing across the entire hemisphere. The view must have been an infrared falsecolor, since the ocean was white and the land areas, in contrast, looked nearly black. I checked the dates on the photos, and converted them in my head into Martian season. The clearing started at just about the end of northern-hemisphere spring.

Leah nodded when I showed her what I'd recovered. She'd already radioed up to ask Langevin for orbital photographs, and he'd confirmed that the clearing of the clouds we'd seen was ubiquitous, starting with breaks in the cloud cover at northern midlatitudes, then slowly spreading south. "Apparently it's a seasonal thing."

Langevin had also mentioned that the rover had arrived, after a long, slow transit from the Moon. Did we still want it? Where should he set it down?

Oh, yes, we still wanted it.

➤

"Time for a vacation!" Tally said, when the unpiloted utility lander had dropped the rover off and I had checked out the systems and declared it fully functional. The rover was the same awful shade of yellow-green as the lander had been, a color chosen for maximum contrast against the browns and purples of Mars. It had six webbed wheels mounted on a rocker-bogey suspension that would give it incredible hill-climbing ability; I had little doubt that it would have been able to crawl right over the hab-lab, if an incautious pilot had tested poorly on navigation. I said as much to the team after the brief test-drive.

"Are you seriously suggesting that the habitat was crushed by a rover?" Leah said. "No tread-marks were found on any of the pieces we found."

"A rover would have left tracks," Tally said. "Even after two years, we'd have seen them."

I shook my head. "No," I said. "I was just giving an example of how robust the suspension is."

"I see."

"So," Tally said. "Time for a trip."

"A trip," Leah said. "Why not? Where did you want to go?"

"Why not go the beach?" Tally said. "Head north. See what a Mars ocean is like."

"Mmm," Leah said. "Not today. I'll still be busy tomorrow, too, I think. Maybe the next day."

"Copacetic," said Tally. "I wouldn't mind a day to do some long-range recon with the rover, anyway. That is, if Tink says it's checked out okay."

"All systems in perfect shape," I said. "No reason for you not to drive around a bit."

A lot of the work Leah asked me to do seemed to have nothing to do with the investigation of the accident. She was conducting her own investigation, I decided, a scientific investigation of the progress of terraforming— no, *ecopoesis*—on Mars. She had me decipher all the data I could out of the opticals; data on bacteria counts and atmosphere, and checked it against the measurements she could make herself. "Cripes, I wish I were a biologist," had become her favorite phrase, muttered as she stared into the screen of a microscope, counting bacteria, but she was clearly happy doing the work, and I was happy to assist, to do anything that made Leah happy.

More methane in the atmosphere, she said, at a break. Some ethane, ethylene, even acetylene. And quite a bit more oxygen than expected.

"Oxygen and methane? Isn't that explosive?"

"No, oxy is still way under one percent; all in all, it's still mostly a reducing atmosphere. The hydrocarbons are all greenhouse gases."

"Gaia," I said, suddenly realizing what she was getting at.

"Gaia," she agreed, a soft smile creeping slowly across her face. The bacteria were producing greenhouse gases, warming the planet up. Making it a better abode for life.

●

I was getting bored with the claustrophobic spaces of the habitat, and the sameness of the landscape, and I was sure that Leah and Tally were, as well. We were all looking forward to the jaunt north to the shores of the Boreal Ocean. So I was rather surprised when, at breakfast on the morning designated, Tally shook her head, and said, "It'll be just you two lovebirds. I'm not coming."

I pretended interest in my food. I never could guess how Leah would react. For me, the idea of a trip in the pressurized rover, a thousand-kilometers alone with Leah, was as close to heaven as I was likely to ever find.

"Why?" Leah said.

Tally smiled. "A trap."

Despite assiduous searching, Tally had found no evidence whatsoever of sabotage. Anybody else would have said that means it was an accident. Tally said it meant they were clever.

We made a great show of our departure, deliberately packing the rover slowly and openly with all the supplies for three people to take an extended trip. Then all three of us got in. From outside, through the bubble canopy, it would be clear that three people were in the piloting compartment, eagerly watching the terrain.

It would be impossible to tell that one of the three was no more than a dummy constructed of spare clothing.

Once aboard, I powered up the rover, and it rose up from its squatting position to its full height above the Martian terrain. I checked all the systems one more time, testing each wheel in turn for forward and reverse power, making skid-marks through the brown grit and tossing muck across the landscape. The bacteria would not care; they would thrive in one spot quite as well as another.

If somebody had bombed the first habitat, and was clever enough and subtle enough to betray no sign of themselves, they must be flushed out of hiding. They might be complacent enough to try the same trick again, if they were thoroughly convinced that nobody was watching. Tally wanted to give them that chance. Tally wanted to watch them set the bomb.

Systems all functional. I had a wild urge to wave goodbye to Tally, but that would never do. We set off with no ceremony.

◒

For hundreds of kilometers we looked at brown rocks, covered with a thin veneer of slime.

The wind got stronger as we drove north toward the ocean. The landscape was monotonous; rocks and rilles and tiny rivers, broken by lakes, each lake in the form of a perfect circle, reflecting the too-blue sky. To our left, the ground sloped gently up toward the ancient volcano whose flanks we were skirting. The actual summit of the volcano was invisible over the horizon. When we crossed the peak of the Syrtis saddle the wind was coming straight at us at well over a hundred kilometers an hour. It was enough to slow the rover's progress considerably, and at places I almost worried that the wind would pick us up and blow us backwards, but the rover's six huge wheels held traction superbly, and kept us moving.

Once across the pass, the wind dropped a bit, but never let up entirely. It was constant, unwavering, from the north.

The rover drove itself, if we let it, with infrared laser-stripers searching out obstacles in front of it and a mapping program in its computer brain that continually compared the view against the inertial navigation and the stored satellite maps, to compute an optimal traverse across the rippled terrain. For most of the first day, Leah and I took turns driving, following the computer's suggested path sometimes, diverting to a different route that looked smoother or more interesting when the whim struck. By the afternoon, the novelty of the drive had slackened, and we let the rover pick its own path.

Langevin had left Mars orbit days earlier, but he had left behind him a little areosynchronous communications relay, so we could have stayed in touch with Tally at the habitat if we had desired to. We kept radio silence, though, by agreement: Tally had said we should assume that any radio communications we made would be heard by the enemy. The relay had enough power to let us send reports directly to Spacewatch. We transmitted our daily report back, essentially just a "Yes, we're alive" verification, and in the report we included a recorded snippet of Tally's voice, to maintain Tally's deception to her hypothesized snooping ears.

In the middle of the afternoon, the rover crested a rise and angled off to the west, finding a smoother traverse down the slope to avoid a field of boulders the size of skyscrapers. Leah was in the aft cabin, analyzing data she had brought with her, and I was alone in the cockpit. At first I didn't know what I was seeing, looking north. The horizon was white.

This was the highest ridge between us and the ocean, so, looking north, I ought to be able to see the ocean. Was the ocean covered with ice? I overrode the autopilot and parked the rover for a moment, rummaging for binoculars to get a better view. Leah came up from the cabin.

"The ocean's white," I said.

"Odd." Leah looked at it, pondering. "Not ice; it's nearly northern summer, and the ice melted months ago. Whitecaps, from the wind, maybe. We'll see soon enough, if we keep driving."

I took that as advice, and brought the autopilot back online. The rover started to roll. Leah reached out an arm to steady herself against a handbar, and kept on standing, looking out the bubble at the horizon.

We didn't reach the Boreal Ocean that evening. The autonavigation on the rover was perfectly capable of continuing its traverse after dark, but we were no more than thirty kilometers from the ocean, and we elected to shut down for the night, so that our arrival at the ocean would be in daylight.

After nine hours of motion, the cabin still seemed to rock with the motion of an imaginary traverse, although I had squatted the rover in the lee of a hundred-meter escarpment.

The workstations of the aft cabin folded away into panels on the walls, and two narrow cots folded out from the bulkhead, transforming the cabin into a small but cozy bedroom. I looked at the cots, and at Leah. The cots were narrow, but looked like they might be wide enough for two, if the two slept close. Leah gave me no hints. I folded the second cot back into its niche, and convinced myself that I saw just the faintest trace of a smile on Leah's face. In any case, she slid over silently, and I nestled myself in next to her.

We reached the ocean a bit before noon of the next day. The final few kilometers was a steep traverse down the bluffs, not quite steep enough to be called cliffs, but steep enough that the rover picked its way slowly, sidling nearly crabwise down the last few hundred meters. There wasn't much of a beach; just rocks. From above, the ocean was white. It moved with something more than just the rhythmic swell of waves. It writhed, and humped, looking almost alive. As we got closer, a fine spray peppered the bubble in erratic spurts. The spray dried to milky-white flakes, smearing but not totally obscuring the view.

"Salt?" I said.

Leah shook her head. "Magnesium sulfate, mostly," she said. She spoke louder than normal to be heard over the whistling of the wind and a sudden patter of spray. "The ocean's got tons of it. It's another reason the ocean doesn't freeze solid in the winter; lowers the freezing point a few degrees."

I squatted the rover down behind a boulder, where it would be out of the worst of the spray, and we suited up with rebreathers and sunblock to go outside.

Outside, the constant wind was warm and damp. Between the wind and the spray, I think that it was the most miserable place on Mars. Leah, though, laughed and ran like a little girl, arching her back and spreading her arms, daring Mars to do its worst.

I took off one glove, raised my hand and caught a bit of spray on my fingers, then pulled up my rebreather mask slightly to put it to my tongue. It was slightly bitter. Leah looked back at me over her shoulder, and laughed. "Don't eat too much of it," she shouted.

"Why?" I shouted back. "It's not poisonous."

"You might regret it," she shouted back. "You know what they used magnesium sulfate for in the old days?"

"What?"

"Laxative for infants! You're standing right next to the universe's largest dose of baby laxative!"

With that she turned back, and started to pick her way past the rocks toward the ocean. I scrambled to catch up with her. I could hear the ocean now, but it wasn't the rolling of waves that I heard. It was a stranger sound, hissing and popping and splatting.

In a few moments we reached a final set of rocks, right at the edge of the ocean, and at last we could observe what we had been unable to see from further away.

The ocean was boiling.

From the pools at our feet to the farthest horizon, the entire ocean was aboil, bubbles rising up and breaking, spattering spray everywhere. Enormous bubbles rose burping out of the depths with a thunderous roar followed by a tremendous splatter; smaller bubbles rose with blurps and pops from everywhere; infinitesimally tiny bubbles fizzed and hissed in rocky pools.

An huge bubble burst in front of us, not five meters distant, and I instinctively flinched, anticipating being hit with scalding spray. Leah laughed with delight. She pulled her glove off and, when the slosh came toward her, bent over and dipped her bare hand into the boiling water. Before I could scream at her, she cupped a handful of water and, with a grin so large I could see it even behind her rebreather, she dashed it in my face and giggled.

The water was lukewarm.

➤

When we got back in the rover, our coveralls were so stiff with dried spray that it was difficult to peel them off. Our faces and hands were red from the wind, and itchy with dried ocean. Leah was still in her puckish good mood, and as we peeled down to undergarments, she was laughing.

"You know what?" she said, pulling off her rebreather, and she didn't bother to wait for an answer. "You know the great thing about it? Makes it worth the whole trip?"

"What's that?"

"You don't stink!"

I opened my mouth to say something, and suddenly realized she was right. The stench of Mars that we had gotten so used to every time we came in from the outside, was missing.

"What a great planet," she said.

We both stripped, and gave one another sponge baths. The water recycler would have the devil of a time pulling sulfate out of the water, but that was what machinery was for. I took a lot longer cleaning her off than I had any right to, and with one thing leading to another, it was nearly dark before either of us dressed.

I knew she was waiting for me to ask. At last I did. "Leah? The water was warm, but it wasn't hot. Why was it boiling?"

"That's an easy one. It wasn't."

"But—"

"Carbon dioxide," she said. "I should have known, but it wasn't obvious until I saw it. Mars has mostly carbon dioxide in the atmosphere, so it should have been obvious that the oceans would be saturated with dissolved CO_2. It wasn't boiling—it was *fizzing*."

That made sense, all but one thing. "But, wouldn't it be in equilibrium? Why should it be fizzing?"

"Summer. The ocean is warming up in the summer sun. Carbon dioxide has a solubility in water that strongly decreases when it gets warmer. So, as summer comes to the northern hemisphere, the Boreal Ocean releases carbon dioxide."

"Oh."

And it wasn't until the middle of the night that she suddenly stiffened and sat bolt upright. "Oh," she said, in a tiny voice. I opened my eyes and watched her sleepily. "The wind," she said. "The wind."

She got up, and in a moment there was a glow as her computer came alight. She was beautiful, limned in pale fire by the glow cast by the screen backlighting.

"What is it?" I said.

"Nothing. Go back to sleep."

"It must be something."

"Just—I had a thought, that's all."

"What?"

"I wonder." She bit her lip. "Just how much carbon dioxide, exactly, do you think *is* dissolved in the Boreal Ocean?"

By the time the sky started to brighten with dawn, Leah was distinctly bedraggled, but she had it mostly worked out. The answer was, a lot. A hell of a lot.

Over the long Martian winter, the temperature of the northern ocean dropped to near freezing, and the ocean served as a sponge for carbon dioxide. A peculiar convection served to stir the ocean as it cooled: As the surface layers cooled and became saturated with carbon dioxide, they got denser, and sank, turning over the ocean until the entire ocean was uniformly cold and saturated with carbon dioxide.

When the spring began, the surface layers of the ocean warmed up, and the dissolved carbon dioxide began to come out of solution. But the warmer water, free of its heavy carbon dioxide, stayed on the surface; the cold, saturated water stayed below. With only two tiny moons, there was little in the way of tides to stir the deeps. The water got warmer, but in the deep water, the dissolved carbon dioxide was under pressure. The water warmed a little, but the supersaturated carbon dioxide stayed in solution.

But it was an unstable situation, and ever more precarious as the season moved toward summer. Eventually, something must trigger the inevitable. Somewhere, a little of the carbon dioxide came out of solution, at pressure, and formed bubbles. The bubbles stirred the water, expanding as they rose, and the stirring let more carbon dioxide out of solution. The warm surface waters turned over, and supersaturated cold waters from the depths warmed up. Like a chain reaction, the release of supersaturated carbon dioxide was almost explosive, and it took only days for the reaction to spread across the entire width of the Boreal Ocean. A whole winter's worth of atmosphere was coming out of the ocean, and coming out with vigor.

The wind. We had felt the wind from the ocean, a clue blowing right in our faces, and we'd ignored it.

"They weren't murdered, Tinkerman," Leah said. "They were—My god, Tally's still back there, in the habitat. She doesn't know—The radio. We can get her on the radio, warn her."

"Doesn't know what?"

"I'll explain everything when I talk to her. Quick, what day is it?" She grabbed my calender and looked at it. In neat letters, on the bottom corner of the square marked June 28, I had completely forgotten that I'd written a note: *One Martian year. R.I.P.*

But Tally didn't answer the radio, not the regular channels, not the emergency channel.

"Damn," I said. "It's Tally and her blasted radio silence. She won't answer."

Leah shook her head violently. "I know Tally better than that. She would listen to the emergency channel no matter what, and she'd answer when she heard us break silence. Tinkerman, I think the wind must have torn away the radio aerial. The hab was designed for space, not for Mars, and the antenna wasn't that strongly mounted. Probably blew over the high-gain antenna as well."

"So?"

"So how fast do you think this thing can go?"

It took longer to get moving than I had expected. The autonavigator wouldn't come online. Over the night the spray had fogged over the lenses of the laser-stripers, and the autopilot wouldn't budge without its obstacle-recognition system working. As I took the rover up the bluff on manual control, climbing only centimeters at a time over the rough spots, Leah fidgeted with clear agitation, but she stayed silent, knowing that distracting me from piloting would only slow us down. As soon as we had climbed a few hundred meters above the ocean, I put on a rebreather and, using half our supply of clean water, carefully washed the laser-striper and the bubble.

The steel parts of the rover looked matte, almost corroded. When we got back, I would have to take the rover down for inspection and overhaul. In fact, I would have preferred to do a thorough inspection right then, but I knew Leah wouldn't let me stop for that. The rover's autodiagnostic checked out green, so I put the autopilot back online and punched for speed.

There was nothing more we could do. There was no way that I could outpilot the autonavigation system over a course it had run before; it had all the bad terrain memorized in detail and had learned exactly which parts to detour around and which were smooth running. The ride was bumpy, but that was only to be expected. I turned to Leah, and waved a hand.

"I'm ready to listen," I said.

⬤

"It was all there in front of us," Leah said. "All the clues, if only we'd really seen them. The pieces of the habitat, that should have tipped us off right there. The habitat modules, they weren't originally designed for Mars. We knew that. Nobody ever goes to Mars, so how could there be hab modules designed for it? It's a lunar habitat design.

"The air pressure on Mars is five hundred millibars, just about half that of Earth. So we set the pressure in the hab to five hundred millibars, and forgot about it. With a nearly fifty-fifty mixture of oxygen and nitrogen in the air mixture, the oxygen in the habitat was just what it is at standard conditions, and after a week I bet you didn't even remember that it wasn't Earth standard.

"But there's one critical diffence. Lunar habitat modules are designed to withstand pressure from the *inside*. They're plenty strong, against internal pressure. But what about external pressure?"

"It imploded."

"Right. The air pressure on Mars is not a constant! All that gas dissolved in the northern sea—when it comes out of solution, the air pressure rises. It rises *a lot*. The wind, that constant wind from the north—that was our second clue. The habitat was set to maintain a constant pressure of five hundred millibars inside. Nobody ever designed it with the idea that the outside pressure might increase. Somewhere there was a weak joint, maybe a seam that wasn't reinforced against an unexpected pressure from outside. It blew."

"But there was an explosion. We saw the marks."

Leah shook her head. "You saw the piece, the one with the tiny scrape of blue paint on it. What does blue paint mean to you?"

I only had to think for an instant. "Blue. Oxygen."

"Right. The implosion must have punctured an oxygen tank in the habitat. Pure oxygen, under pressure, spurting out into the Mars atmosphere. . . . The Martian atmosphere is mostly carbon dioxide, but a good component is methane, and it's got noticeable amounts of other hydrocarbons as well. In a pure oxygen leak, of course it will burn."

"It must have happened at night," I said. "They never knew what hit them. The one man was killed instantly. The other was tossed out of the hole in the side of the habitat, without a rebreather, to die of suffocation."

Leah nodded. "And now the same thing is happening. The atmospheric pressure is rising. Tally's there in the habitat, alone . . . and she's waiting for the wrong enemy."

●

We were over the peak of the Syrtis saddle and a good way into the long, slow downhill toward the Hellas basin, only a hundred kilometers from the hab, when the wheel fell off. Leah was on the radio, in the unlikely hope that perhaps the synchronous relay was the problem, and now that we were approaching line-of-sight conditions, direct communication might raise Tally. The wheel came off with a resounding *snap*, and the rover lurched.

The autopilot diagnosed the problem, instantly rebalanced the suspension to keep the weight away from of the missing wheel, and smoothly braked us to a stop, blaring alarms.

The alarms were a little late.

We both went outside to look. It was the right rear wheel that had failed; we found it a few dozen meters further on, where it had rolled up against a rock. The wheel itself was a titanium-alloy mesh, light enough to carry in one hand, for all that it was nearly two meters in diameter. The wheel bearing was steel. Or, it had originally been steel, when it had been there at all. There was little left of it.

"Well," Leah said.

"Well," I said. There was no way to replace a wheel; they weren't supposed to come off. "I think maybe we can rebalance the rover. Shift the loading to the front left side. Five wheels ought to be enough. We might have to go a bit slower."

Leah nodded. "It's a plan."

We piled rocks onto the rover, and strapped them down with bungees, to move the center of gravity forward, off of the missing wheel. Then we piled more rocks inside the rover, in the front left pilot's seat. I didn't mention that we would never get the Mars stink out of the rover; it was too late to worry about that, and we barely noticed it by then anyway. The autopilot refused to budge so much as a meter without an overhaul, so I piloted it on manual. This was good for less than a third the speed of the autopilot, but still, even that pace covered ground. Leah went back into the aft cabin to examine the samples she had scraped off of the wheel.

It was only a hundred kilometers. We finished more than fifty of them before the second wheel fell off.

We were going more slowly this time. There was no lurch, and no noise. The rover just slowly careened to the right, and kept on rolling until it slid to a stop on its side.

Leah came out of the hatch after I did. She didn't bother looking at the axle, or at the rover. No need; it was obviously not going anywhere, even if we had a crane to put it back right-side-up. The rocks we had piled onto the rover had cracked the bubble when it rolled. "Sulfur-reducing bacteria," she said.

"Say again?"

"Sulfur-reducing bacteria," she said, "convert iron to iron sulfide. There's energy in free iron; in the presence of free sulfur, enough energy for a bacterium to exploit. The lack of iron at the site; I should have figured that ordinary weathering wasn't enough to account for it."

"Oh," I said.

"Not that it matters now," Leah said. "We don't have time to waste. We've got to get to Tally and warn her." With a matter-of-fact attitude, she hopped up onto a rock and stared across the horizon. "So how far do we have to walk?"

I tried the radio one more time. Come on, Tally. What was she doing? I wondered. Did she even know that the antenna was down, or did she just think we were scrupulous in keeping radio silence? Was she standing at the door of the habitat with a gun? Hiding behind the rocks, waiting for enemies that would never come? If only she would answer, it would only take an instant to tell her about the dangerously low habitat pressure.

Fix the antenna, Tally, I thought, just fix it, and listen to the radio. But she wouldn't. Fixing the antenna would be too obvious a sign that the habitat was still occupied. I threw down the radio.

The inside of the rover was a mess, but we managed to scrounge two spare sets of replacement packs for the rebreathers. I downloaded the bearing to the hab out of the rover's computer, and set the inertial compass. Once we got close, we would be able to use the habitat's come-hither beacon to hone in. I grabbed a set of portable radio transceivers and checked that they were working. I couldn't think of anything more to carry. Before we left, Leah snipped two pieces of titanium sheeting away from internal partitions of the rover, and snapped them free.

"Ready," she said.

We ran.

The Mars gravity makes it easy to run, and the unwavering wind was, for a change, on our side. Still, after an hour of running I was winded, and the second hour was more trudging than running. Our cold-suits trapped sweat all too well, and it ran down my back and down my legs, like ants with clammy feet.

Mars narrowed in on us. Ridges, followed by valleys; valleys followed by ridges. Another hour.

"Bear further to the right here," Leah said.

"That's not the most direct route."

"I know."

We were walking pretty slowly by now. Her route followed the contour, instead of cutting downhill, and was a bit easier, even if it was less direct. I was beginning to worry that we wouldn't make it to the habitat by nightfall. It would be impossible to continue after darkness fell—Mars's moons shed almost no useful light—and by the morning, we couldn't even be certain that the habitat would still be there.

In another hour we had reached the edge of a long downhill. There, tiny in the distance was a glint of metal: our goal, the habitat.

It was impossible to tell from the gleam whether it was still in one piece.

Without a word, Leah handed me one of the two sheets of titanium. I looked at the downhill. It was a long, smooth grade, with the usual cover of Martian slime. I grinned, and Leah grinned back at me, her face in the rebreather mask like some painted mechanical demon, and then we both stood on our sleds, grasped the lanyards, and, at the same moment, pushed off.

We would arrive in style.

◆

My sled skidded to a stop in a spray of slime a hundred meters or so from the habitat, and Leah stopped close behind me.

The habitat was apparently empty. But at least it was still apparently in a single piece. I ran toward it, shouting for Tally. I reached the air lock, and was just reaching out for the handle when I felt the gun pushed gently between my shoulder blades.

"Moving *real* slowly, friend, keep your hands in sight, and turn around. Slowly."

Tally was painted the same color as the Martian slime, bits of sand and rock sticking to her randomly. The projectile rifle was in her left hand, aimed steadily at my middle. I could see the crinkling at the edges of her eyes as she smiled behind the rebreather. "Tinkerman. Welcome home."

She lowered the gun, and turned to greet Leah. "Didn't expect you to come back on foot. What brings y'all back so sudden?"

"The air pressure," Leah said. "It's going to—"

"Yeah," Tally said. "I noticed something going on with the air. Could feel it in my bones, like a thunderstorm. 'Fact, I had to dial up the pressure in the hab three times in four days."

Leah stopped, thunderstruck. "You increased the hab pressure?"

"Why, sure," Tally said.

We just looked at each other.

"What?" Tally asked. "Something wrong with that? I figured that if the hab pressure wasn't increased, there could be trouble."

Leah shook her head. "No, nothing wrong. Nothing at all."

◆

It was our last night on Mars. We had filed a preliminary report with Space-watch, and in the morning Langevin would bring the lander down to take us home.

I was looking out the tiny window of the hab at the Martian landscape. In the evening twilight the browns had turned to purple. Tiny puddles of water caught the skylight and reflected it back at us. Even the slime looked fragile and ethereal. "It is beautiful," I said, "in its way."

"Ask me, it still stinks," Tally said.

"It's dying," Leah said.

"Dying?" I turned away from the window.

Leah nodded slowly. "I've been finishing up the work from the data they had stored to optical before the accident. They got enough data to fully model the ecology. It's dying."

"How?" I asked. "Why?"

"Oxygen," she said. "The oxygen level in the atmosphere is rising, slowly but inexorably. The photosynthetic forms simply outcompete the anaerobes, and the result is that oxygen is gradually accumulating in the atmosphere."

"But that's good," I said. "That's what happened on Earth. The biosphere is evolving."

Leah shook her head. "But Mars isn't Earth. The oxygen is starting to scavenge hydrocarbons out of the atmosphere, and after that, it will begin to displace carbon dioxide. Just like on Earth, but for Mars that will be catastrophic. A few tens of millibars' less carbon dioxide, and—" She clapped her hands. "Frozen solid. End of story."

"But the Gaia hypothesis—doesn't the presence of life regulate the temperature?"

She shook her head. "Bacteria are dumb. Gaia is a hypothesis; it's never been a proven theory. In this case, it happens to be a wrong theory."

"You're sure?"

Leah nodded. We were silent for a moment, and then I asked, "How long?"

"Hmmm? Well, couldn't say precisely. Not enough data."

"Give or take."

"I'd give it few thousand years at the outside. Probably less than a thousand." She saw me smiling, and added, shaking her head, "The time may be uncertain, but the fact still is, it *will* happen."

That put a little different spin on it. We would all be dead before the planet returned to bare rock. No need to mourn for Mars, not for quite a while yet.

◆

Later, alone with just Leah in the tiny sleeping cubbyhole, I made love to her slowly and deliberately. She closed her eyes and arched her back as I stroked her, in her own way sensuous as a cat, but still I couldn't tell what sort of feelings she had for me.

When it was over, and we were lying in the dark, I had to ask. "Do you feel anything for me? Anything at all?"

Leah turned over. "Quit asking meaningless questions. I unask your question. Mu."

Much later, after I thought she had fallen asleep, she said softly, "It looks like I'm stuck with you. I suppose there are worse people I could get stuck with. Don't get in the way."

It was all I could ask for. I will follow her as long as she will allow it, love her, ask nothing in return. Maybe someday I will mean something to her, maybe someday as much as a comfortable pair of slippers or a favorite chair.

In the meantime, though . . . It was a large universe. There would be places to go, no end of places to follow her to. That was enough.

In the morning, the lander would come, and I would follow her home.

People Came from Earth

STEPHEN BAXTER

Like many of his colleagues here at the beginning of a new century—Greg Egan comes to mind, as do people like Paul J. McAuley, Michael Swanwick, Iain Banks, Bruce Sterling, Pat Cadigan, Brian Stableford, Gregory Benford, Ian McDonald, Gwyneth Jones, Vernor Vinge, Greg Bear, David Marusek, Geoff Ryman, and a half-dozen others—British writer Stephen Baxter has been engaged for the last ten years or so with the task of revitalizing and reinventing the "hard science" story for a new generation of readers, producing work on the Cutting Edge of science which bristles with weird new ideas and often takes place against vistas of almost outrageously cosmic scope.

Baxter made his first sale to Interzone *in 1987, and since then has become one of that magazine's most frequent contributors, as well as making sales to* Asimov's Science Fiction, Science Fiction Age, Zenith, New Worlds, *and elsewhere. He's one of the most prolific new writers in science fiction, and is rapidly becoming one of the most popular and acclaimed of them as well. Baxter's first novel,* Raft, *was released in 1991 to wide and enthusiastic response, and was rapidly followed by other well-received novels such as* Timelike Infinity, Anti-Ice, Flux, *and the H. G. Wells pastiche—a sequel to* The Time Machine—The Time Ships, *which won both the John W. Campbell Memorial Award and the Philip K. Dick Award. His other books include the novels* Voyage, Titan, *and* Moonseed, *and the collections* Vacuum Diagrams: Stories of the Xeelee Sequence *and* Traces. *His most recent books are the novels* Mammoth, Book One: Silverhair *and* Manifold: Time, *and a novel written in collaboration with Arthur C. Clarke,* The Light of Other Days.

"People Came from Earth" takes us to a troubled future, to an embattled, desperate world dancing on the brink of extinction, a world where an ambitious terraforming project is not sticking very well in the long run, for the autumnal story of people struggling to hold on to what they have . . . and perhaps even regain something of what has been lost.

At dawn I stepped out of my house. The air frosted white from my nose, and the deep Moon chill cut through papery flesh to my spindly bones. The silver-gray light came from Earth and Mirror in the sky: twin spheres, the one milky cloud, the other a hard image of the sun. But the sun itself was already shouldering above the horizon. Beads of light like trapped stars marked rim mountain summits, and a deep bloody crimson was working its way high into our tall sky. I imagined I could see the lid of that sky, the millennial leaking of our air into space.

I walked down the path that leads to the circular sea. There was frost everywhere, of course, but the path's lunar dirt, patiently raked in my youth, is friendly and gripped my sandals. The water at the sea's rim was black and oily, lapping softly. I could see the gray sheen of ice farther out, and the hard glint of pack ice beyond that, though the close horizon hid the bulk of the sea from me. Fingers of sunlight stretched across the ice, and gray-gold smoke shimmered above open water.

I listened to the ice for a while. There is a constant tumult of groans and cracks as the ice rises and falls on the sea's mighty shoulders. The water never freezes at Tycho's rim; conversely, it never thaws at the center, so that there is a fat torus of ice floating out there around the central mountains. It is as if the rim of this artificial ocean is striving to emulate the unfrozen seas of Earth which bore its makers, while its remote heart is straining to grow back the cold carapace it enjoyed when our water—and air—still orbited remote Jupiter.

I thought I heard a barking out on the pack ice. Perhaps it was a seal. A bell clanked: an early fishing boat leaving port, a fat, comforting sound that carried through the still dense air. I sought the boat's lights, but my eyes, rheumy, stinging with cold, failed me.

I paid attention to my creaking body: the aches in my too-thin, too-long, calcium-starved bones, the obscure spurts of pain in my urethral system, the strange itches that afflict my liver-spotted flesh. I was already growing too cold. Mirror returns enough heat to the Moon's long Night to keep our seas and air from snowing out around us, but I would welcome a little more comfort.

I turned and began to labor back up my regolith path to my house.

And when I got there, Berge, my nephew, was waiting for me. I did not know then, of course, that he would not survive the new Day.

He was eager to talk about Leonardo da Vinci.

◆

He had taken off his wings and stacked them up against the concrete wall of my house. I could see how the wings were thick with frost, so dense the paper feathers could surely have had little play.

I scolded him even as I brought him into the warmth, and prepared hot soup and tea for him in my pressure kettles. "You're a fool as your father was," I said. "I was with him when he fell from the sky, leaving you orphaned. You know how dangerous it is in the pre-Dawn turbulence."

"Ah, but the power of those great thermals, Uncle," he said, as he accepted the soup. "I can fly miles high without the slightest effort."

I would have berated him further, which is the prerogative of old age. But I didn't have the heart. He stood before me, eager, heartbreakingly thin. Berge always was slender, even compared to the rest of us skinny lunar folk; but now he was clearly frail. Even these long minutes after landing, he was still panting, and his smooth fashionably-shaven scalp (so bare it showed the great bubble profile of his lunar-born skull) was dotted with beads of grimy sweat.

And, most ominous of all, a waxy, golden sheen seemed to linger about his skin. I had no desire to raise that—not here, not now, not until I was sure what it meant, that it wasn't some trickery of my own age-yellowed eyes.

So I kept my counsel. We made our ritual obeisance—murmurs about dedicating our bones and flesh to the salvation of the world—and finished up our soup.

And then, with his youthful eagerness, Berge launched into the seminar he was evidently itching to deliver on Leonardo da Vinci, long-dead citizen of a long-dead planet. Brusquely displacing the empty soup bowls to the floor, he produced papers from his jacket and spread them out before me. The sheets, yellowed and stained with age, were covered in a crabby, indecipherable handwriting, broken with sketches of gadgets or flowing water or geometric figures. I picked out a luminously beautiful sketch of the crescent Earth—

"No," said Berge patiently. "Think about it. It must have been the crescent *Moon*." Of course he was right. "You see, Leonardo understood the phenomenon he called the ashen Moon—like our ashen Earth, the old Earth visible in the arms of the new. He was a hundred years ahead of his time with *that* one. . . ."

This document had been called many things in its long history, but most familiarly the Codex Leicester. Berge's copy had been printed off in haste during the Failing, those frantic hours when our dying libraries had disgorged their great snowfalls of paper. It was a treatise centering on what Leonardo called the "body of the Earth," but with diversions to consider such matters as water engineering, the geometry of Earth and Moon, and the origins of fossils.

The issue of the fossils particularly excited Berge. Leonardo had been much agitated by the presence of the fossils of marine animals, fishes and oysters and corals, high in the mountains of Italy. Lacking any knowledge of tectonic processes, he had struggled to explain how the fossils might have been deposited by a series of great global floods.

It made me remember how, when he was a boy, I once had to explain to Berge what a "fossil" was. There are no fossils on the Moon: no bones in the ground, of course, save those we put there. Now he was much more interested in the words of long-dead Leonardo than his uncle's.

"You have to think about the world Leonardo inhabited," he said. "The ancient paradigms still persisted: the stationary Earth, a sky laden with spheres, crude Aristotelian proto-physics. But Leonardo's instinct was to proceed from observation to theory—and he observed many things in the world which didn't fit with the prevailing worldview—"

"Like mountaintop fossils."

"Yes. Working alone, he struggled to come up with explanations. And some of his reasoning was, well, eerie."

"Eerie?"

"Prescient." Gold-flecked eyes gleamed. "Leonardo talks about the Moon in several places." The boy flicked back and forth through the Codex, pointing out spidery pictures of Earth and Moon and sun, neat circles connected by spidery light-ray traces. "Remember, the Moon was thought to be a transparent crystal sphere. What intrigued Leonardo was why the Moon wasn't much brighter in Earth's sky, as bright as the sun, in fact. It should have been brighter if it was perfectly reflective—"

"Like Mirror."

"Yes. So Leonardo argued the Moon must be covered in oceans." He found a diagram showing a Moon, bathed in spidery sunlight rays, coated with great out-of-scale choppy waves. "Leonardo said waves on the Moon's oceans must deflect much of the reflected sunlight away from Earth. He thought the darker patches visible on the Moon's surface must mark great standing waves, or even storms, on the Moon."

"He was wrong," I said. "In Leonardo's time, the Moon was a ball of rock. The dark areas were just lava sheets."

"But now," Berge said eagerly, "the Moon *is* mostly covered by water. You see? And there *are* great storms, wave crests hundreds of kilometers long, which are visible from Earth—or would be, if anybody was left to see."

"What exactly are you suggesting?"

"Ah," he said, and he smiled and tapped his thin nose. "I'm like Leonardo. I observe, *then* deduce. And I don't have my conclusions just yet. Patience, Uncle . . ."

We talked for hours.

When he left, the Day was little advanced, the rake of sunlight still sparse on the ice. And Mirror still rode bright in the sky. Here was another strange forward echo of Leonardo's, it struck me, though I preferred not to mention it to my already overexcited nephew: in my time, there *are* crystal spheres in orbit around the Earth. The difference is, we put them there.

Such musing failed to distract me from thoughts of Berge's frailness, and his disturbing golden pallor. I bade him farewell, hiding my concern.

As I closed the door, I heard the honking of geese, a great flock of them fleeing the excessive brightness of full Day.

◆

Each Morning, as the sun labors into the sky, there are storms. Thick fat clouds race across the sky, and water gushes down, carving new rivulets and craters in the ancient soil, and turning the ice at the rim of the Tycho pack into a thin, fragile layer of gray slush.

Most people choose to shelter from the rain, but to me it is a pleasure. I like to think of myself standing in the band of storms that circles the whole of the slow-turning Moon. Raindrops are fat glimmering spheres the size of my thumb. They float from the sky, gently flattened by the resistance of our thick air, and they fall on my head and back with soft, almost caressing impacts. So long and slow has been their fall from the high clouds, the drops are often warm, and the air thick and humid and muggy, and the water clings to my flesh in great sheets and globes I must scrape off with my fingers.

It was in such a storm that, as Noon approached on that last Day, I traveled with Berge to the phytomine celebration to be held on the lower slopes of Maginus.

We made our way past sprawling fields tilled by human and animal muscle, thin crops straining toward the sky, frost shelters laid open to the muggy heat. And as we traveled, we joined streams of more traffic, all heading for Maginus: battered carts, spindly adults, and their skinny, hollow-eyed children; the Moon soil is thin and cannot nourish us well, and we are all, of course, slowly poisoned besides, even the cattle and horses and mules.

Maginus is an old, eroded crater complex some kilometers southeast of

Tycho. Its ancient walls glimmer with crescent lakes and glaciers. Sheltered from the winds of Morning and Evening, Maginus is a center of life, and as the rain cleared I saw the tops of the giant trees looming over the horizon long before we reached the foothills. I thought I saw creatures leaping between the tree branches. They may have been lemurs, or even bats; or perhaps they were kites wielded by ambitious children.

Berge took delight as we crossed the many water courses, pointing out engineering features which had been anticipated by Leonardo, dams and bridges and canal diversions and so forth, some of them even constructed since the Failing.

But I took little comfort, oppressed as I was by the evidence of our fall. For example, we journeyed along a road made of lunar glass, flat as ice and utterly impervious to erosion, carved long ago into the regolith. But our cart was wooden, and drawn by a spavined, thin-legged mule. Such contrasts are unendingly startling. All our technology would have been more than familiar to Leonardo. We make gadgets of levers and pulleys and gears, their wooden teeth constantly stripped; we have turnbuckles, devices to help us erect our cathedrals of Moon concrete; we even fight our pathetic wars with catapults and crossbows, throwing lumps of rock a few kilometers.

But once we hurled ice moons across the solar system. We know this is so, else we could not exist here.

As we neared the phytomine, the streams of traffic converged to a great confluence of people and animals. There was a swarm of reunions of friends and family, and a rich human noise carried on the thick air.

When the crowds grew too dense, we abandoned our wagon and walked. Berge, with unconscious generosity, supported me with a hand clasped about my arm, guiding me through this human maelstrom. All Berge wanted to talk about was Leonardo da Vinci. "Leonardo was trying to figure out the cycles of the Earth. For instance, how water could be restored to the mountaintops. Listen to this." He fumbled, one-handed, with his dog-eared manuscript. " *'We may say that the Earth has a spirit of growth, and that its flesh is the soil; its bones are the successive strata of the rocks which form the mountains, its cartilage is the tufa stone; its blood the veins of its waters. . . . And the vital heat of the world is fire which is spread throughout the Earth; and the dwelling place of the spirit of growth is in the fires, which in divers parts of the Earth are breathed out in baths and sulfur mines. . . .'* You understand what he's saying? He was trying to explain the Earth's cycles by analogy with the systems of the human body."

"He was wrong."

"But he was more right than wrong, Uncle! Don't you see? This was centuries before geology was formalized, even longer before matter and energy cycles would be understood. Leonardo had gotten the right idea, from somewhere. He just didn't have the intellectual infrastructure to express it. . . ."

And so on. None of it was of much interest to me. As we walked, it seemed to me that *his* weight was the heavier, as if I, the old fool, was constrained to support him, the young buck. It was evident his sickliness was advancing fast—and it seemed that others around us noticed it, too, and separated around us, a sea of unwilling sympathy.

Children darted around my feet, so fast I found it impossible to believe I could ever have been so young, so rapid, so compact, and I felt a mask of old-man irritability settle on me. But many of the children were, at age seven or eight or nine, already taller than me, girls with languid eyes and the delicate posture of giraffes. The one constant of human evolution on the Moon is how our children stretch out, ever more languorous, in the gentle Moon gravity. But they pay a heavy price in later life in brittle, calcium-depleted bones.

At last we reached the plantation itself. We had to join queues, more or less orderly. There was noise, chatter, a sense of excitement. For many people, such visits are the peak of each slow lunar Day.

Separated from us by a row of wooden stakes and a few meters of bare soil was a sea of green, predominantly mustard plants. Chosen for their bulk and fast growth, all of these plants had grown from seed or shoots since the last lunar Dawn. The plants themselves grew thick, their feathery leaves bright. But many of the leaves were sickly, already yellowing. The fence was supervised by an unsmiling attendant, who wore—to show the people their sacrifice had a genuine goal—artifacts of unimaginable value, earrings and brooches and bracelets of pure copper and nickel and bronze.

The Maginus mine is the most famous and exotic of all the phytomines: for here gold is mined, still the most compelling of all metals. Sullenly, the attendant told us that the mustard plants grow in soil in which gold, dissolved out of the base rock by ammonium thiocyanate, can be found at a concentration of four parts per million. But when the plants are harvested and burned, their ash contains *four hundred* parts per million of gold, drawn out of the soil by the plants during their brief lives.

The phytomines are perhaps our planet's most important industry.

It took just a handful of dust, a nanoweapon from the last war that ravaged Earth, to remove every scrap of worked metal from the surface of the Moon. It was the Failing. The cities crumbled. Aircraft fell from the sky. Ships on the great circular seas disintegrated, tipping their hapless passengers into freezing waters. Striving for independence from Earth, caught in this cross-current of war, our Moon nation was soon reduced to a rabble, scraping for survival.

But our lunar soil is sparse and ungenerous. If Leonardo was right—that Earth with its great cycles of rock and water is like a living thing—then the poor Moon, its reluctant daughter, is surely dead. The Moon, ripped from the outer layers of parent Earth by a massive primordial impact, lacks the rich iron which populates much of the Earth's bulk. It is much too small to have retained the inner heat which fuels Earth's great tectonic cycles, and so died rapidly; and without the water baked out by the violence of its formation, the Moon is deprived of the great ore lodes peppered through Earth's interior.

Moon rock is mostly olivine, pyroxene, and plagioclase feldspar. These are silicates of iron, magnesium, and aluminum. There is a trace of native iron, and thinner scrapings of metals like copper, tin, and gold, much of it implanted by meteorite impacts. An Earth miner would have cast aside the richest rocks of our poor Moon as worthless slag.

And yet the Moon is all we have.

We have neither the means nor the will to rip up the top hundred meters of our world to find the precious metals we need. Drained of strength and tools, we must be more subtle.

Hence the phytomines. The technology is old—older than the human Moon, older than spaceflight itself. The Vikings, marauders of Earth's darkest age (before this, the darkest of all) would mine their iron from "bog ore," iron-rich stony nodules deposited near the surface of bogs by bacteria which had flourished there: miniature miners, not even visible to the Vikings who burned their little corpses to make their nails and swords and pans and cauldrons.

And so it goes, across our battered, parched little planet, a hierarchy of bacteria and plants and insects and animals and birds, collecting gold and silver and nickel and copper and bronze, their evanescent bodies comprising a slow merging trickle of scattered molecules, stored in leaves and flesh and bones, all for the benefit of that future generation who must save the Moon.

Berge and I, solemnly, took ritual scraps of mustard-plant leaf on our tongues, swallowed ceremonially. With my age-furred tongue I could barely taste the mustard's sharpness. There were no drawn-back frost covers here because these poor mustard plants would not survive to the Sunset: they die within a lunar Day, from poisoning by the cyanide.

Berge met friends and melted into the crowds.

I returned home alone, brooding.

I found my family of seals had lumbered out of the ocean and onto the shore. These are constant visitors. During the warmth of Noon they will bask for hours, males and females and children draped over each other in casual, sexless abandon, so long that the patch of regolith they inhabit becomes sodden and stinking with their droppings. The seals, uniquely among the creatures from Earth, have not adapted in any apparent way to the lunar conditions. In the flimsy gravity they could surely perform somersaults with those flippers of theirs. But they choose not to; instead they bask, as their ancestors did on remote Arctic beaches. I don't know why this is so. Perhaps they are, simply, wiser than we struggling, dreaming humans.

•

The long Afternoon sank into its mellow warmth. The low sunlight diffused, yellow-red, to the very top of our tall sky, and I would sit on my stoop imagining I could see our precious oxygen evaporating away from the top of that sky, molecule by molecule, escaping back to the space from which we had dragged it, as if hoping in some mute chemical way to reform the ice moon we had destroyed.

Berge's illness advanced without pity. I was touched when he chose to come stay with me, to "see it out," as he put it.

My fondness for Berge is not hard to understand. My wife died in her only attempt at childbirth. This is not uncommon, as pelvises evolved in heavy Earth gravity struggle to release the great fragile skulls of Moon-born children. So I had rejoiced when Berge was born; at least some of my genes, I consoled myself, which had emanated from primeval oceans now lost in the sky, would travel on to the farthest future. But now, it seemed, I would lose even that.

Berge spent his dwindling energies in feverish activities. Still his obsession with Leonardo clung about him. He showed me pictures of impossible machines, far beyond the technology of Leonardo's time (and, incidentally, of ours); shafts and cogwheels for generating enormous heat, a diving apparatus, an "easy-moving wagon" capable of independent locomotion. The famous helicopter intrigued Berge particularly. He built many spiral-shaped models of bamboo and paper; they soared into the thick air, easily defying the Moon's gravity, catching the reddening light.

I have never been sure if he knew he was dying. If he knew, he did not mention it, nor did I press him.

In my gloomier hours—when I sat with my nephew as he struggled to sleep, or as I lay listening to the ominous, mysterious rumbles of my own failing body, cumulatively poisoned, wracked by the strange distortions of lunar gravity—I wondered how much farther we must descend.

The heavy molecules of our thick atmosphere are too fast-moving to be contained by the Moon's gravity. The air will be thinned in a few thousand years: a long time, but not beyond comprehension. Long before then we must have reconquered this world we built, or we will die.

So we gather metals. And, besides that, we will need knowledge.

We have become a world of patient monks, endlessly transcribing the great texts of the past, pounding into the brains of our wretched young the wisdom of the millennia. It seems essential we do not lose our concentration as a people, our memory. But I fear it is impossible. We are Stone Age farmers, the young broken by toil even as they learn. I have lived long enough to realize that we are, fragment by fragment, losing what we once knew.

If I had one simple message to transmit to the future generations, one thing they should remember lest they descend into savagery, it would be this: *People came from Earth.* There: cosmology and the history of the species and the promise of the future, wrapped up in one baffling, enigmatic, heroic sentence. I repeat it to everyone I meet. Perhaps those future thinkers will decode its meaning, and will understand what they must do.

☙

Berge's decline quickened, even as the sun slid down the sky, the clockwork of our little universe mirroring his condition with a clumsy, if mindless, irony. In the last hours I sat with him, quietly reading and talking, responding to his near-adolescent philosophizing with my customary brusqueness, which I was careful not to modify in this last hour.

". . . But have you ever wondered why we are *here* and *now?*" He was whispering, the sickly gold of his face picked out by the dwindling sun. "What are we, a few million, scattered in our towns and farms around the Moon? What do we compare to the *billions* who swarmed over Earth in the final years? Why do I find myself *here* and *now* rather than *then?* It is so unlikely . . ." He turned his great lunar head to me. "Do you ever feel you have been born out of your time, as if you are stranded in the wrong era, an *unconscious* time traveler?"

I had to confess I never did, but he whispered on.

"Suppose a modern human—or someone of the great ages of Earth—was stranded in the sixteenth century, Leonardo's time. Suppose he forgot everything of his culture, all its science and learning—"

"Why? How?"

"*I* don't know. . . . But if it were true—and if his unconscious mind retained the slightest trace of the learning he had discarded—wouldn't he do exactly what Leonardo did? Study obsessively, try to fit awkward facts into the prevailing, unsatisfactory paradigms, grope for the deeper truths he had lost?"

"Like Earth's systems being analogous to the human body."

"Exactly." A wisp of excitement stirred him. "Don't you see? Leonardo behaved *exactly* as a stranded time-traveler would."

"Ah." I thought I understood; of course, I didn't. "You think *you're* out of time. And your Leonardo, too!" I laughed, but he didn't rise to my gentle mockery. And in my unthinking way I launched into a long and pompous discourse on feelings of dislocation: on how every adolescent felt stranded in a body, an adult culture, unprepared . . .

But Berge wasn't listening. He turned away, to look again at the bloated sun. "All this will pass," he said. "The sun will die. The universe may collapse on itself, or spread to a cold infinity. In either case it may be possible to build a giant machine that will re-create this universe—everything, every detail of this moment—so that we will all live again. But how can we know if *this* is the first time? Perhaps the universe has already died, many times, to be born again. Perhaps Leonardo was no traveler. Perhaps he was simply *remembering*." He looked up, challenging me to argue; but the challenge was distressingly feeble.

"I think," I said, "you should drink more soup."

But he had no more need of soup, and he turned to look at the sun once more.

➤

It seemed too soon when the cold started to settle on the land once more, with great pancakes of new ice clustering around the rim of the Tycho Sea.

I summoned his friends, teachers, those who had loved him.

I clung to the greater goal: that the atoms of gold and nickel and zinc which had coursed in Berge's blood and bones, killing him like the mustard plants of Maginus—killing us all, in fact, at one rate or another—would now gather in even greater concentrations in the bodies of those who would follow us. Perhaps the pathetic scrap of gold or nickel which had cost poor Berge his life would at last, mined, close the circuit which would lift the first of our ceramic-hulled ships beyond the thick, deadening atmosphere of the Moon.

Perhaps. But it was cold comfort.

We ate the soup, of his dissolved bones and flesh, in solemn silence. We took his life's sole gift, further concentrating the metal traces to the far future, shortening our lives as he had.

I have never been a skillful host. As soon as they could, the young people dispersed. I talked with Berge's teachers, but we had little to say to each other; I was merely his uncle, after all, a genetic tributary, not a parent. I wasn't sorry to be left alone.

Before I slept again, even before the sun's bloated hull had slid below the toothed horizon, the winds had turned. The warm air that had cradled me was treacherously fleeing after the sinking sun. Soon the first flurries of snow came pattering on the black, swelling surface of the Tycho Sea. My seals slid back into the water, to seek out whatever riches or dangers awaited them under Callisto ice.

Fossils

WILLIAM H. KEITH, JR.

Here's a fast-paced and exciting study of different kinds of fossils that takes us to a tumultuous future Mars that's in the midst of being terraformed whether all of its inhabitants want it to be or not . . . including some who are determined not to move no matter what.

William H. Keith, Jr., is a science-fiction and technothriller writer who has published over fifty novels. His most recent novels include Semper Mars, *as by "Ian Douglas," and* Diplomatic Act, *in collaboration with Peter Jurasik. He lives in Greensburg, Pennsylvania.*

1

Norris, his nomen was, *Paul* Norris, which should link you the idea. Zet, firmative. A fuzzy scuzzy. An oldie, original-strain human, zero prosthetics and negative plants, not even so much as a companion. Oldie chronologically, too. The Net linked down with the dat—a nate date of 301.34. Eighty-eight stadyers? An eyeblink, sure, but going on pure biological, the geezie was *old.*

Old bio, and old neural processing, which is worse. Wetware mud, link me? Norris had been nated on Earth, down among the teeming billions. Emigrated to Pittsburgh, Mars, in 325. Married Ann Whittaker . . . had to link the Net to find what *that* meant. He was *old.*

He wasn't at his domie when I downtouched my floater, and, for a blink or two, I thought the geezie'd given his firmative after all and lifted out. That would've been the pos-linked thing to do, of course, but one thing I've assimmed from the evacuation is the rampant illogic of OS-homies. Wetware mud runs thick and it runs deep. They claim they're conscious, but by the day before Impact, I was beginning to have my doubts.

Look, I'm no bigot! The Old-Strains *made* us, after all, and their genes formed the basis of those parts of amortal bodies that are still organic. They gave us form, gave us shape, gave us the *stars,* for Life's sake . . . and I'm not going to static them just because they're slow. But *talking* to one of them can be like talking to an ancient gigabit processor, pre-AI: slow, single-minded, and positively complacent in its determination that it's right, and never mind what the rest of the universe has to say.

Where *was* he, anyway? Ah. When I shifted to IR, there was a heat smear to the south, against the cliff wall. Couldn't tell what he was doing, but it had to be him. Everyone else, amortal, AI, and human, had been evacuated from this part of the Valles days ago. Everyone but *him.*

I took a sec, then, to scan the scenic. Oldies claim we don't feel like they do. Zet. Untrue. If anything, we feel *more* . . . deeper, sharper, truer, keener, with more range and grasp and holosense than their brains can process, but it's all in control and it kicks in when *we* decide. I've seen Saturn's rings and I've skimmed the cloudtops of Jove, watched a double sunrise from the north rim of the Caloris Basin and looked back at a shrunken, void-lonely Sol from a tumbling ice mountain in the remotes of the Kuiper Belt. I've seen. I've recorded. I've *felt*.

Paul Norris had planted his domie in scenic intensivity. Eos Chasma— the Chasm of the Dawn—gold-red cliffs like holos I've DLed of Earth's Grand Canyon, but three times deeper. It was already dark down here at the bottom, but the upper third of those cliffs gleamed in the sunset like fire-struck opal and red-banded gold. For twenty-one stadyers, he'd lived in this same spot, on the rock-scattered regolith floor of the Eos Chasma, a few hundred mets from the south wall. Side channel, observation: the canyon floor base level here registered at the *minus* three-kil line, and the surrounding clifftops soared almost vertical to plus two or three kils. Six kilometers is a *long* way down, deep enough that there were crevasses and deepfolds that never saw the sun even at local noon on the equinox, and I figured that old Paul had chosen the spot for a ready source of fossil ice. I was right, as it turned out, but not for the reason I thought.

Anyway, it was the chasm's depth that was the problem. My timesense told me we had another seven hours fourteen before a quite literal hell broke loose. I had to reach him, somehow, and I was just now realizing that I didn't understand humans nearly as well as I'd thought when I volunteered for this.

I gave his domie a light scan first. It hadn't been much to begin with— a Type 12 Mars hut, a steel and durplast cylinder sliced in half down the long axis, twelve mets long and maybe four wide. Airlock on one end, a fusion pod and air bleeder on the other. External strap-on tanks for air reserves and water. State of the colonizing art fifty years ago, but no room for the amenities. Scarcely room for visitors, if it came to that.

The geezie had been busy, though. He'd used a digger to excavate all around the hut, clear down to the slab, and then, Life alone knows how, he'd rigged monomol cables around the thing, constructed a block and tackle suspended from a homemade gantry, and somehow rolled the whole thing over on its back, round side down, slab side up. He had a ladder rigged from the side of the hole going down to his airlock entrance, so he could get in and out. Why? It made no sense.

There were other strangenesses. An old lobber rested in the sand, stripped and partly dismantled. A crude sign had been erected on a post nearby, hand-painted on precious wood salvaged from a cargo pallet long ago: NORRIS ENTERPRISES. Directional markers were fixed to the pole beneath. One pointed west: PITTSBURG, MARS—3598 KM, it read. The other angled almost straight up: PITTSBURG, PA. 230,000,000 km (MEAN).

That made no sense, either. Was it possible that Paul was suffering from dementia? Extreme biological age will do that to oldies who are isolated and not taking their insurance meds. We might be able to do something for him then, if that was the case.

I would know more when I spoke with him. I opened channel 4, standard suit-to-suit, to give him a call.

"*Chriiiiiissst*, what a beauty!" His voice, coming over the radio link, startled me. I hadn't thought he'd noticed my arrival . . . but a few seconds later I realized that he was unaware of my presence. He was talking to . . . someone else.

"You remember the first one of these we found, Ann?" he asked aloud. "That was . . . what? A couple of months after we came here. We were still working for the Arean Museum and living in that little co-op hab on the South Side of Pittsburgh. Remember? The first site we started prospecting, over in Ius Chasma. It was just a little one, the size of your little finger, but it was perfect. *Perfect!* Fetched a decent price up in Denver-Olympus, too, as I recall. Ayuh. Gave us the stake we needed t'get out of six-to-a-room and set up on our own."

His speech was slow . . . *slow*, like the rambling drawl of a voice-recording played at quarter speed. Wetware mud. As I walked toward him, I adjusted my processing cycles, slowing my thought . . . and my speech. I'd forgotten how slow OS brains could be. I would have to adjust my linguistic paradigms as well to embrace his oldie dialect and narrow my speech to a single channel, or he would never understand me.

"Then there was that spirelliate the girls found," he went on, "that spring in Tithonium. *That* was a find! Remember how they bounced in that afternoon, all excited about that 'funny, twisty thing' they'd spotted high up among the rocks . . . ?"

"Citizen Norris?" I said, interrupting his monologue.

"Who the hell's that?" His voice sounded quicker now, with a bright snap of emotion that was probably surprise.

I downshifted my cycles again, trying for a match. Ahead, the heat smear shifted and moved, and I switched to visual optics. Norris was a small man, clumsy in an ancient Model 15 Marsuit, with a blue helmet bright against the rust-red rock of the cliff wall. His digger, an even more ancient wheeled robexcavator, crouched at his side, illuminating whatever he'd been working on with a glare of light.

"Excuse the interruption, Citizen Norris." Zet, communication at this level was glacially slow! "I am . . . call me Cessair. I would like to speak with you, if I may."

"Well, I can't say I care t'talk t'*you!*" he said. He waved a laser cutter, not in a hostile manner but with definite emotional agitation. "Got nothin' t' say to th' likes of you or your kind!" I was close enough now to see his eyes narrow behind the visor of his helmet. "Huh. Ain't you cold?"

I glanced down at myself. I'd grown that body hours before for his benefit, but I suppose the context was anomalous enough to startle him. My skin appeared to be steaming as the moisture in it sublimed into the thin, cold air. I focused briefly, and my body grew a light skinsuit and bubble helmet, the latest fash in Marswear. "Better?"

"You Homo-A types've tinkered with the climate here quite a bit already," he drawled, "but the air pressure's still less than a hundredth of a bar, and the temp right now is, what? Minus ten, minus fifteen Celsius? A bit frosty for you t'be sportin' about in nothin' but your skin. 'Course, you ain't really human, are ya?"

They'd warned me in Deimos that he might be an anti-amortal bigot. "I am human," I told him, "within the parameters of humanity as detailed in the Sentients' Declaration of 68.83. My genetic makeup is entirely human, derived from Original-Strain DNA. Both my genetic and electronic prostheses are—"

"Aw, cut yer yappin'. I don't care where you came from, s'long as you git back there. The sooner the better."

"I merely wished to establish that I *am* human, Mr. Norris," I told him, dropping the words one at a time and wondering how these people could communicate this way. "Your descendant, as it were. I simply have more control over my metabolism and internal systems than you do . . . and a more intimate association with various AI enhancements, communications links, and cybernetic and computer implant control assets."

"Yeah, yeah, I've heard all that. *Homo amortalis*. The new and improved Man. Get the hell out of my way. Yer blockin' my light."

He was attempting to lever something up out of a shallow hole in the ground at the base of the cliff. The way the light gleamed from the smooth and translucent surface, I thought it must be water ice.

"Can I help you?" Without waiting for an answer, I reached down and grasped the block he was struggling with. Allowing my fingers to heat momentarily, I melted a grip for myself, then hauled the block free, rolling it clear of the trench he'd dug. More ice glittered beneath the digger's worklights, a buried treasure lost for a billion years beneath the ocher sand.

"*Woof!*" he said, and the condensation of his breath momentarily clouded the lower half of his visor. "Thanks! Even here a chunk like that must weigh fifty kilos! And I'm not as spry as I used t'be, not by a damned long shot!"

I glanced at his find, then took a more deliberate look. There was something there, shadows motionlessly coiled within the ice.

"What is it?" I asked, letting my fingers drag across the cold, slick surface. "Is that—"

The ice was filled with . . . shapes. *Familiar* shapes. One lay just beneath the surface, a dark and twisting shadow under the worklights. It looked like a *Helica* species . . . but the thing was larger and more finely wrought then any specimen I'd seen before, a wonder of two intricate, flattened, left-handed spiraling tubes, weaving about one another in an odd and exquisitely delicate mimicry of DNA. Spines bristled about the soft part of the body which sprouted finger-length tentacles.

"*Helica* species," Norris said, grinning behind his visor despite his earlier bad humor. "But I ain't never seen one this big before. Long as my forearm! Ain't she a beauty, Ann? *Ain't* she a beauty?"

"Who is this Ann you keep talking to?" I asked. "Our records indicate that Ann Whittaker Norris died twelve stadyers ago."

With a strength I'd not thought he possessed in that skinny frame, Norris rolled, levered, and hoisted the ice block up and onto the cargo bed of the robexcavator, gentling it down onto a sheet of insulation that he carefully tucked over and around his find. Without another word, he gathered up his tools, stowed them on the digger, then stalked back across the sand toward his Mars hut, brushing roughly against me as he passed. The robexcavator trundled off in his footsteps, and I had to jump aside to avoid being bumped.

I glanced inside the trench he'd dug and could just make out other shapes in the ice a meter beneath the surface. Fossils are common on Mars. Microfossils found in an Antarctic meteorite originally derived from Mars linked us the first clue to the existence of an ancient Arean biota, in fact, back in '27 or so, and the first manned explorations of the planet had discovered more . . . an entire zoo of organisms ranging from microfossils to giant helicas, creatures that had swum and crawled in the Martian ocean perhaps two to three billion years ago. Most were impressions in stone . . . but a number of ice fossils had been found as well, organisms frozen intact, like the mammoths uncovered from time to time in Alaskan and Siberian glaciers. The Martian seas had been teeming when their last, evaporating remnants had frozen solid and the atmosphere had thinned away to near nonexistence.

Affirm. There'd been quite an intense debate revolving around the existence of those fossils whenever we'd proposed terraforming Mars. When the Boreal Sea once again covered the northern lowlands after being lost for two billion years beneath the shifting sands, a lot of Martian fossils would be lost, submerged to depths of a kilometer or more.

Well, such relatively minor downchecks were inevitable in the face of transforming a planet. In exchange, Humankind would get a new, green world, as fair and as habitable as Earth herself. No more domes, habs, or Mars huts. No more pressure suits and air bleeders. It was an old dream, a dream that the AIs and Amortals are morphing into reality. It was pure coincidence that we'd named the program Project Eos—Eos Chasma, the Canyon of the Dawn; Project Eos, the dawn of new life on long-dead Mars.

You would think the current inhabitants of the planet would welcome the change, even if they would not live to see it completed, even if they had to accept some slight inconvenience. Zet. OS-human selfishness and shortsightedness were incomprehensible at times . . . *most* times, in fact.

Turning, I started back toward Norris's upended Mars hut, wondering how it was possible to even attempt reasoning with such a creature.

I found another wooden marker along the way, not far from the hut. It was a cross, painted white, with Ann Norris's name and the oldstyle dates 2273–2347 hand-printed on the crosspiece. Twelve years of sandblasting had smoothed the wood to a silky sheen, but the cross had obviously been lovingly repainted many times.

Our information had been correct. Ann Norris had died in 377. Did he really imagine he was talking to her?

He said nothing as he powered down the digger near his Mars hut, offloaded the ice block and stored it in a cryocase. There were five other such cases, I noticed, lined up in a row awaiting storage. At the entrance to the upside-down Mars hut, he stopped and seemed to dither. "I 'spose you want t'come inside."

Mars was still frontier world enough that hospitality rituals prevailed. You *always* invite the traveler in for some refreshment, some conversation, and a PLSS recharge. I'd been counting on that. "I need to talk to you, Paul. I promise that I won't make you do anything you don't want to do, but I *must* talk to you."

Could it be that he actually welcomed the company, just then? I'd expected an argument, hospitality rituals or no, with a savage demand that I get off his landhold, but he seemed to sag a little inside his suit, and then nodded. "C'mon in, then, if y'must. Mind yer step on the ladder."

As I walked toward the ladder, I noticed an interesting touch he'd added to the inverted Mars hut. On the corner, just beneath the overhang of the foundation slab, were the words, in broad slaps of red paint, NORRIS'S ARK.

I had the feeling there was some humorous wordplay there, but I did not understand the point.

It took time to cycle through the airlock. It was an old model, of course, and he had to be meticulously careful not to let the powder-fine, red Martian dust clinging to his suit enter his domie. Lots of the ancient Martian regolith is charged with hyperperoxides, and some of the salts are downright toxic. I got through simply by negating the static charge on my skinsuit; I considered shedding it again but remembered his reaction earlier and decided to keep it, all but the helmet. Paul Norris was old enough that he might still have mindtwists like nudity taboos. I needed his cooperation and didn't want to stress him.

I stepped through the inner lock close behind him, and it was like stepping into another world.

The stink was overpowering, a mind-numbing assault of odors associated primarily with *Staphylococcus epidermidis* and a variety of fungi and molds, but mingled with others ranging from decaying fruit to human excreta. As overpowering as the odor was the sheer confused jumble of the Mars hut's interior, crammed almost to closure by crates and storage canisters and packing material, by partially dismantled equipment, by torn-down partitions and a forest of multicolored wires spilling from consoles, power packs, and antique control circuits. *Wires!* I hadn't realized that such things still existed on Mars.

"Heh," he said, squeezing between a pair of strapped-down plastic crates. Beneath his suit he'd been wearing the bulky, padded folds of an undersuit garment, and it gave him a soft and clumsy look. "Sorry for the mess. Weren't expectin' t'be doin' any *entertainin'* today."

Took a moment to turn down some of the input . . . especially the odors. Norris didn't seem to notice that throat-gagging cacophony of smells, and I wondered how he managed without being able to draw on internal life support. Maybe he'd just been living by himself too long. I turned down some of the visual input, too. Too much detail, too much focus, too much clarity in a cluttered-jumble like that could overload even advanced AI visual processors. Now I knew why OS-human eyes focused only a small area directly in the line of vision and let the periphery blur.

"What," I managed to say after a moment, "are you *doing* in here?"

It wasn't that Norris simply enjoyed living in clutter, though the clutter of Life only knows how many years living out in the desert played a part, certainly. Most of the hut's interior was taken up by hardfoam packing containers and more sealed cryocases, and most had been anchored in place by straps bolted to the walls and floor. Fossil specimens, casts and impressions in red Martian sandstone, littered most of the remaining floor.

"Movin' day," he said.

I glanced at him, but couldn't read the expression. In the center of the compartment, a relatively open and junk-free space was occupied by a seat that I recognized as having come from the dismantled lobber outside. The seat was affixed to a set of rotating gimbals, which would let it swing freely, remaining upright in any attitude. The engineering was remarkable, if less than precisionist neat.

"May I ask the *point* of all of this?"

"It's liable to get a little bouncy," he told me. Reaching up, he fondly patted one of the semicircular mounts within which the seat would freely swing to any attitude. "With this, I got half a chance of riding out your runaway."

"A chance?" I looked at him, disbelieving. "Paul, this is . . . is crazy. You will *not* survive."

He shrugged. "If I don't, I don't." His voice sharpened. "But I am *not* evacuating."

"Paul, I'm not sure you understand how serious this is. You *must* leave. Or you will . . ." I hesitated, then said the word with an effort. "Die."

He gave me a sharp look. "I thought you amortal-types only worried about your *own* deaths."

"You needn't be vulgar," I replied, shocked. "We are concerned with *all* life."

"Yeah, right. Even humans, huh?"

I turned, fixing him with a hard, scan-intense gaze. "Paul, do you hate or fear us, the amortals, I mean? Do you resent us or what we're doing here? Is that why you . . . why you're doing this?"

He looked away. "Don't rightly see how it's any of your business *what* I do here," he said. "I just want t'be left alone."

"Unfortunately, Paul, our . . . runaway, as you call it, has made that impossible. Even without it, you would have had to leave sooner or later. The Martian surface is not going to be stable—*safe*—for some centuries to come. CK-2023 merely hastened events. Sooner or later, you *would* have had to leave."

"Lady, I'm forty-seven years old."

I blinked. "Your records say you're eighty-eight."

He made a face. "That's *standard*. What you call a stadyer. I'm Martian, remember? Forty-seven. And what are you doing snooping around in my records?"

"You came from Earth, originally."

"Ayuh. A long, long time ago." He sighed. "The point is, I don't have that much time left, do I? I was figurin' on bein' dead and gone by the time things changed enough that I would *have* to leave."

"No matter how well-laid plans may be, there is always room for error."

Stooping, I picked up one of the specimens Paul had left lying on the floor, partly wrapped in padding. He started forward, as though to take it from me, then stopped himself, making himself watch me finger the fragile, two-billion-year-old spine-studded crenelations of the spinotroch's shell. "Careful with that," he said.

"What is it?"

"Spine-wheel. Burrowed in the mud of the old sea bottoms."

I continued tracing the delicate outline, preserved perfectly in sandstone. "Interesting." Gently setting the fossil down, I looked up at the stacks of hardfoam containers already sealed and secured to the walls. "And these others?"

"Hell, I got thirty, mebbe forty different species collected here. Over seven hundred individual specimens. Centrophores. Placalophs. Camptohelians. Dihelians." He raised his hand, lightly touching one of the containers. "There's a lot of years of prospectin' in these here packages."

"An impressive collection."

"Too many to ferry out by lobber. Too many even t'pack out on a tractor back to Pittsburgh, assumin' they had a tractor free right now. Seems like everybody's busy haulin' tail out of the lowlands, these days." He snorted. "Hell, lady, why else do you think I'm going through all of this?"

I wasn't sure what to think. "Surely you understand," I said, "that the fact that a tractor was not made available to you means that your collection did not have a high priority."

"Not for *you*, mebbe," he said. "Or for the Arean Museum. But it has a damned high priority for *me*."

"The Arean Museum already has all the fossil specimens it needs. So does Earth. The Arean biota is well recorded, both with fossil specimens and with DNA records."

"That's what they tell me."

"Why do you keep collecting them, then? Why are they so important to you?"

Paul scowled. "Hell, lady, y'might ask y'self why a guy's *life* is important to him! Me and Ann spent the better part of thirty-one years prospectin' for fossils out here, one place an' another. That's . . . what? Almost sixty of yer damned stadyers. We spent twenty-one of 'em right here in the Valles Marineris. Hell, collectin' fossils is all I know."

"If the areopaleontologists have already seen and described these species, there's no need to collect more, surely."

"Says *who*? You can't have too many specimens of a given life-form, not if you want as complete a picture as possible of the thing. How big did it grow? How long did it live? What structural variations were there, when evolution started reshaping the thing?" Carefully, he reached down and picked up the spinotroch, cradling it in his hand. "For me, though, it's a matter of history, of . . . of *being*. Holding one of these, and knowing that it was alive and swimming, *right here*, when all Earth had to offer was blue-green algae."

He picked up a sheet of foam padding and began wrapping the fossil, using several layers before slipping the package inside one of the open hard-foam containers.

"Besides," he continued. "There's always the chance of finding something new, something no one has ever seen before."

"A very small chance."

"Oh, you look long enough, you'll find things . . . *wonderful* things." He hesitated. "That specimen in the ice block I just hauled in. Found it by accident, when my digger was huntin' fer ice fer my reserves. Found it just five hundred meters from here, and me and Ann working this part of the Valles for twenty-one years and we never knew it was there. I think it's a new species, something never seen before. How much more must there be out there still, right under our noses like this thing was, and when you yank Mars out of its ice age it's all going to be destroyed."

"We are less concerned with the past, Paul, than we are with the future."

"I'm not talking about the past. I'm talking about *knowledge*. About who we are and where we came from and what else there is in this universe besides us."

"No, you're talking about your life as a fossil prospector," I told him. "I understand that . . . and I respect it. There will still be fossils for you to hunt and sell, if that's what you want."

"You don't need to be condescending with me, damn it!" His fists were clenched, the veins standing out on the backs of his hands like blue marbling. He began ticking points off on long, bony fingers. "In the first place, you know well as I do that the new ocean you're making is in the same spot as it used to be. Most fossils are gonna be lost . . . specially the ice fossils, which'll disintegrate when the ice melts. Second, the way I heard it, you're gonna be pulling everyone off Mars before too long, just because you figure it'll be too dangerous here on the surface for the next couple hundred years. So what am *I* supposed to do, living the rest of my life in one of your big space colonies? Ain't no fossils for me to hunt there, less you planted them there yourselves when you built the thing. Third, it's a damned crime what you amorts are doin' here. I'm not talkin' about the runaway. I just mean your terraforming idea. Who needs it?"

"Don't you want your descendants to walk on a fair, green world? One with air they can breathe, blue skies, open—"

"Aw, save it! It's cheaper t'build O'Neill microworlds, and you can make your gravity t'order. Me, I like a place that's got some *bite* to it!"

"Your people," I said slowly, "show an unusual tendency to attach themselves to a particular patch of land. Many of you have been . . . reluctant to move, despite the coming danger. We do not understand this."

He grinned. "I take it I'm not the only problem case, then."

I studied him a moment. I thought he was *enjoying* this. "No. No, you're not. Most of the older *sapiens* prefer to stay where they are. Even when they know that survival is unlikely."

"Maybe we like it where we are."

"That doesn't make sense! Surely, when life-threatening situations develop, it is best to leave, whatever the cost!"

"Have you ever stopped to look at the sunrise over the Valles scarp? When black fades to purple, then maroon, then orange, then pink . . . and fast, like. Less than a minute. The air's still too thin for lingering transition colors in the sky, you know."

"This is worth dying for?"

He chuckled. "Oh, I wouldn't say that. But it makes us sad to see beauty like that passing."

"There will be beauty in the new world we create here. A new world, where men can walk and breathe without artifice."

"I'm sure. But that's, what? Two, three Martian centuries off, yet, before the atmosphere's thick enough to do away with pressure suits? And then another thousand years before your gene-tailored algae make the stuff breathable."

"We are terraforming Mars for *you* and *your* kind, Paul. We amortals can remake ourselves in any fashion we choose. But *Homo sapiens* need worlds like Mars, or the microworld colonies."

"Yeah, but *I'm* not gonna see it, am I? You take away my world *now* for the promise of paradise a thousand years from now. You amortals—well, there's no tellin' how long you folks have t'live. With downloadin' to new bodies and all, I guess mebbe you have a fair chance at livin' forever."

"Not forever, Paul. Nothing lasts forever." I cocked my head to the side. "Why do you choose to live here, Paul? That is the central question, the reason I was sent here to talk with you, after all. We need to understand you, Paul, if we are to help your kind in the future."

"Mebbe we don't *want* your help. *I* don't."

"You said that at forty-seven you don't have much time left, but you're still throwing away an extra ten or fifteen Martian years! *Good* years. And who's to say what advances might be made in nanomedtech and cyberimplants in that time? Paul, every human alive today has a chance to join us!"

He looked at me for a long time, then slowly shook his head. "Lady, that assumes we *want* t'live forever. Some of us don't."

"Paul, you can't mean that. I mean, you *are* trying to survive, aren't you?" I waved a hand at the seat and gimbals. "With all of this?"

He managed a smile. "That's the general idea." The smile faded. "There was a time, there, when I just didn't want to go on. But . . . well, it got better. Believe me, I *don't* want to die."

"Then come with me! Now!"

"To one of your resettlement microworlds?" He shook his head, a hard, jerky motion. "No thanks."

"You *do* resent us. What we're trying to do here. For *you*."

He shrugged. "Well, I can't deny I liked Mars the way it was. Mostly, though, I just wonder about the hurry. I always heard you folks were the ones t'take the long, patient view."

"Even in a plan spanning a thousand years," I said, "there must be a beginning."

He fixed me with a disapproving stare. "Man's been on this world for two hundred and thirty-one years, Cessair. That's well over four centuries, standard. That's not time to get to know something as big, as complicated as a *world*. There are wonders out there—"

"There must be a beginning, Paul. There must be a time when we say, 'Enough planning, enough research. We will begin *now!*' After four centuries, we know all we need to know about Mars."

"We don't know all there is to know about *Earth* yet, Cessair, and Man's been there a damn sight longer than he's been here!"

"An opinion, Paul. One we do not share." I hesitated, considering, looking for a different mental tack. "Paul, we—all of us concerned with the evacuation—we want to help. We don't know why you are so stubbornly insisting on riding this out yourself, when there's no need!"

"Let's just say I'd rather do this on my own."

"The resettlement will not be forever, a few years at most, until the end of the bombardment phase. Then you could return. Or you could elect to stay in the resettlement colony. Many of your people have chosen that option, you know. I believe your daughters have applied for long-term citizenship in Aldrin."

"They're grown. They can do what they want with their lives."

"It's a beautiful world, designed especially for you . . . Martians. You would be happy there."

"An inside-out world, with the other side of the place hanging over my head?" He chuckled, a dry, brittle sound. "No thanks! I prefer my sky wide-open and pink!"

"I thought humans prided themselves on being adaptable." It was a challenge.

"Exactly. We are adaptable. I'll adapt fine on my own. Right here."

"There is adaptable," I said, "and there is *stupid*." I spread my hands, imploring. *How* to get through to him? "Sooner or later, you will *all* have to leave, at least for a few centuries. The changes we've already introduced, well, things are going to be very risky here for a time. The runaway has only advanced the schedule a bit."

2

I didn't add that the Project Eos planners had embraced that advance. For fifty-one stadyers now, we'd been dropping cometary chunks onto the northern hemisphere of Mars, each piece precisely controlled, each no more than a few tens of meters across, designed to vaporize in the slowly thickening atmosphere without causing major impacts or environmental threats. At the same time, huge, orbital mirrors, each a hundred kilometers across, were bathing the northern hemisphere in sunlight, raising the surface temperature. And the changes were happening, *had* been happening for twenty years. Already, the Boreal Sea was forming anew, liquid water once again flowing where an ocean had rolled two billion years before.

But the changes, even under tight control, were already wreaking havoc with a planetary surface essentially unchanged since the rising of the Tharsis Bulge a billion years back. Permafrost was melting across continent-sized regions, creating titanic sinkholes, Marsquakes, and mudslides of devastating proportions. The atmosphere had thickened twentyfold, further increasing temperatures, and accelerating the greenhouse effect. Open water was appearing in the lowest reaches of the northern basin, in Chryse and in Acidalia, as ancient subterranean ices melted. Within another century, we expected the ocean to be deep and warm enough that only the coastlines and north polar regions would freeze solid during north hemisphere winters. Then the *real* planetary engineering could begin.

But conditions were increasingly dangerous for humans on the Martian surface, especially in the northern permafrost belt and in low-lying canyons like the Valles Marineris. For the past ten stadyers, we'd been supervising the evacuation of humans living in the threatened regions—primarily the northern lowlands—to orbital microworld colonies like Aldrin.

But now—well, things had gotten out of hand. The next iceteroid in line had gone wrong.

CK-2023 had started out as a resident of the Kuiper Belt, that band of cold, dark asteroids, comets, and Pluto-sized iceballs orbiting the fringes of Sol's kingdom out beyond Neptune. Terraforming engineers—including an AI with the nomen of Ep-74 Far Thinking, who probably knew more about orbital mechanics and gravitational vectoring than any other sentient AI, CE, amortal, or oldie in existence—had set up the move, planting drivers that sent CK-2023 sunward on a long, patient curve that flicked close in around Jupiter 43 stadyers later. The calcs called for a tidal breakup as that chunk of ice swung past Jove, aided by some judiciously planted nuclear charges. The idea was to disperse the chunk into a pearlstring of impacters, none more than a few hundred mets across, all on a collision course with Mars well above the forty-degree-latitude line.

So . . . what went wrong? We still don't know, and it's likely that the reason is lost somewhere beneath the blur of chaos and random event. CK-2023 fragmented, but not cleanly. One fragment was four hundred mets across and over two kilometers long, and as it swept past Jupiter and whipped around toward the Inner System, it picked up a hard-spinning tumble that made further landings impossible. Various schemes were calced and simmed, schemes employing missiles, lasers, particle beams, every weapon, in fact, that could be found in their dusty storage facilities on Earth and elsewhere. Since the amortals and AIs had assumed the responsibilities for what had passed as a government among *sapiens*, there'd been scant need for high-powered weaponry. An antimatter beam might have sufficed, but we could not generate that much antimatter in time. In fact, every sim we ran showed the same outcome. There was no way, with the hardware at our immediate disposal, to *guarantee* the fragment's vaporization . . . and anything less than total vaporization risked hitting Mars with something very like the blast of an antique shotgun. Scan the thought, for a sec, of rubble impacting all across the target hemisphere, devastating, deadly, and utterly random. The largest Martian cities . . . Mariner, Denver-Olympus, Tharsisview, Pittsburgh, Hellas, Kasei City all would be seriously damaged, possibly destroyed. People would *die* . . . unthinkable tragedy on a scale as grand as the planet-gashing length of the Mariner Valles itself.

It was Far Thinking himself who simmed the final answer. Leave the rogue fragment alone, and it would impact Mars at a precisely knowable point . . . smack in the southern reaches of Chryse Planitia at the mouth of the Ares Vallis. No cities or habs nearby, thank Life, and the larger impact would actually accelerate what we were trying to do in the long run. The runaway fragment might advance the Plan's completion by as much as four centuries.

Historical irony, though, that impact site. The first Martian rover had bounced to a halt at Ares, not far from Wahoo Crater. And the Viking I Memorial was just eight hundred kils to the west. As it happened, though, that part of Chryse, two kils below the arbitrary sea-level datum for the planet, was already underwater, submerged by a pocket-sized sea extending from Ares Vallis almost all the way to the Viking Memorial in the west, and north most of the way to Acidalia. It was currently midwinter in the northern hemisphere and the sea was frozen . . . but when the major fragment struck, our best calcs suggested that the ice would melt . . . and catastrophically so for any settlements in lowland regions further south. The wave would sweep through the chaotic terrain of Xanthe Terra and Margaritifer, plunge into the three-kil-deep basin at the far eastern end of the Valles Marineris . . . then sweep around to the west, entering Eos and Capri Chasmas, a lateral avalanche of high-velocity mud and water.

And once it hit the narrow confines of the valles, the water would start moving even faster. *Injection event.*

3

"The impact will occur," I told Paul, "twenty-eight hundred kilometers north-north-west from this spot. Our terraforming efforts have already resulted in a small sea in that region, though it is frozen over at this time of year. The impact will instantly vaporize some two to three thousand cubic kilometers of ice and permafrost and create a tidal wave of immense proportions in the remaining liquid water.

"That wave will sweep across the chaotic terrain between ground zero and this spot in approximately six hours. We estimate that, at that time, it will be fifty meters high and traveling at three hundred kilometers per hour."

"You sound pretty sure of yourself."

"We are. Do you doubt our calcs?"

"Eh? No. No, of course not. I know better than *that.*" An unreadable expression tugged at his features, and I decided he was reacting to his xenophobia again. The amortals had been designed to handle complex calculations and informational exchanges in ways that transcended the purely organic reach of humans, and sometimes our differences frightened them.

"Have you ever seen the Mediterranean Sea, Paul?"

He shook his head. "Grew up in North America. Place called Maine. But I know the place you're talkin' about."

"Twenty million years ago, the dam walling off the Atlantic from the low-lying Mediterranean Valley beyond crumbled and the ocean came in. That entire valley, four thousand kilometers long and thirteen hundred wide at spots, was filled in a matter of days . . . though the Gibraltar waterfall must have persisted for centuries after that.

"And we know there have been similar injection events here on Mars.

When the Tharsis Bulge rose a billion years ago, it melted a small ocean of permafrost that came surging down off the new highlands. As the Valles Marineris formed, collapsing with the permafrost melt, they channeled a lot of that water east and north, with floods powerful enough to sweep along boulders the size of small buildings.

"The problem is that *this* time, unlike ancient Mars and unlike the Mediterranean Valley of the mid-Miocene, there are humans in the way. We're here to save you."

"And I'm tellin' *you*, I don't care to *be* saved!" Reaching up, he patted the gimbaled chair and control elements above his head. "I got it all covered, right here."

Zet. I wasn't linking with him. Sometimes, the mental processes of fuzzy-scuzzy saps were all but incomprehensible. All you could do was let them go their own way . . . but, Life! When that way led to suicide . . .

"You cannot survive the coming flood, Paul," I told him.

"Mmm. D'you ever hear of Noah? And the ark?"

"I'm afraid not. . . ." I shifted focus, drawing on the Marsnet data base. The answer was there, plucked from my link through my flyer to Deimos. "Ah. One of the Judeo-Christian myths. Genesis."

"Ayuh. Just call me Noah."

He walked over to a nearby computer console and typed out an entry on the keyboard. A *keyboard!* Ancient tech, that, but the flatscreen lit up with a three-D wineframe of the upside-down Mars hut, rotating in space. Six points flashed along the base, three along each long side. "Those are my flotation bags," he said. "Salvaged 'em off old Conestoga supply pods."

"Balyuts," I offered, naming the heavy, inflatable, and detachable balloons that served as temporary heat shields for aerobraking landers. Paul must have picked some unused reserve units up at a surplus warehouse somewhere, units that were cheaper to sell for salvage than to haul back to orbit again.

"Ayuh." He typed another entry and another point of light winked, this on the smaller half-cylinder of the Mars hut's airlock. "And that there's my sea anchor," he said.

"This is to hold you in place? It is nothing but a reentry parachute. I fear you have underestimated—"

"Shoot, Cessie, the thing won't keep me in one spot. *I* know that! The term's from sailing days, back on Earth. Used to do some sailing, you know, a long time ago, before I came here. A sea anchor's like the tail of a kite. Keeps your nose pointed forward."

"I have experience with neither sailing nor kites," I admitted. I watched as his bony fingers clattered once more across the primitive input device. Red lights flashed on around the Mars hut's perimeter. "And these?"

"Thrusters," he said. "Pulled 'em from my lobber."

I was struggling to follow his logic . . . if, indeed, there was any there to begin with. "Wait. Paul, this whole enterprise is preposterous. You really intend to *fly* . . . ?"

He clucked tongue against teeth. "Do you really take me to be that big an idiot? Hell, I'm not gonna fly when that wave hits tomorrow. I'm gonna *sail!*"

I blinked. "Sail. In a Mars hut."

"Ayuh. Should be quite a ride."

Only then did it all come together for me . . . what this human intended to attempt. At least it did explain the odd name he'd picked for his frail and unlikely craft.

"You . . . have a talent for understatement. How do you plan to steer? . . . Ah!"

"Yup. The thrusters." Reaching up high, he patted the control board attached to the gimbaled seat. It mounted two joysticks, each with pressure-sensitive throttle controls. "Got 'em out of my junked lobber. Control 'em from here, by radio. Port and starboard. I figure they'll let me steer through the worst of it, enough, mebbe, to hold to the center of the channel."

"Fuel?"

"Sixty seconds at full thrust for each. And of course I'll only be giving 'em short squirts, a second or two at a time, and at low thrust I should have three, mebbe four minutes on each, total. It'll get me by."

I was speechless for a moment, though whether from disbelief or sheer admiration for his cleverness, even I wasn't certain. "If you run out of fuel, you'll be helpless."

He shrugged. "I just need enough for the rough parts." He jabbed his thumb over his shoulder, toward the airlock. "My sea anchor'll keep me headed straight, and I got external cams t'see where I'm goin'. Shouldn't need much steering at all, really, 'cept in the real tight passes. If I line m'self up right, I should make it through okay."

"You plan to ride a tidal wave all the way up the Marineris Valley? How far?"

He shrugged, bony shoulders heaving beneath the drape of his undersuit padding. "Th' Valles run about three thousand kilometers, all told." He grinned. "Not quite as bad as the Med Valley, of course, but long enough. The ground rises pretty sharp at the Noctis Labyrinthus, as it starts climbin' the Tharsis Bulge. I reckon I'll come t'ground somewheres close t'Pittsburgh."

"Unless you smash head-on into a cliff or a mensa along the way. Or this pressurized can of yours springs a leak. Or the shock wave itself kills you. Or—"

He gave me a wily grin. "Y'think I'm crazy, don'tcha?

"When I first came here," I told him gently, "I thought, just possibly, that you were. It is clear to me now that you know what you're doing. I still consider this attempt of yours misguided and for no rational purpose. But you are not crazy."

"That's good to hear," he said. "Sometimes . . . I wonder." He blinked, shaking his head. "You *could* force me, y'know. At my age, I couldn't put up much of a fight. Knock me out, drag me off to your paradise in space."

"And *prove* what many of you have been saying about us all this time? That we do not respect the rights or beliefs of your cultures, that we have our own long-term agenda, one that does not include *sapiens*. No. That would serve no one well, neither your people nor ours. Besides, we *do* respect your species's right to determine its own future."

"Sure. Whatever you say, Cessie."

I could tell from his expression that he didn't believe me. I wondered if there'd been a time when *Homo sapiens* and *Homo neanderthalis* had regarded one another with this same faintly bemused lack of mutual comprehension.

How long would *Home sapiens* survive, even with our care and maintenance? Extinction is inevitable for all species. Some, though, seem by their actions to embrace extinction with the fervor one has for a long-parted lover.

"And I can't convince you to come with me?"

"Nope. Got it all covered."

I thought of fossils, remnants of long-dead life, of species that had flowered once, joined Life's dance, then vanished, leaving nothing behind but traces in rock and ice.

"And . . . if you survive. What will you do then?"

"Find a new place t'stake a claim and set up shop, of course. Started out in Pittsburgh when I first got off the cycler. Probably try the same again. Reckon I can keep prospecting, wherever I end up. Like I say, we're just starting t'learn about this world. I imagine Mars'll be providing us with surprises for a good long time to come, even after you people mess it up." He winked. "And I aim to experience some of 'em."

I sighed. "I don't understand *sapiens*," I said. "I don't understand *you*."

"That makes two of us, Cessie. But it's the way I want it, y'know?"

"Will you leave a data feed open? Or better, take a Companion."

He made a face at that, but I ignored it. Holding out my hand, I directed an inward thought through my implants, and a golden sphere began growing in the palm of my hand. In seconds, the sphere was ten centimeters across, assembled from the nanocells within my body.

"It will adapt itself to your communications and monitor circuitry," I told him, "and allow us to follow you from orbit. If you're stranded—"

"Never did like them things . . ."

"Nanotechnology is no different from any other technology, Paul. And no more magical than computers would have seemed to Leonardo da Vinci."

"Leonardo didn't have amortal know-it-alls fumbling icebergs on planetary approach." His eyes narrowed. "How come you people didn't just nanotech the place, 'stead of dropping rocks on it?"

"Because," I replied patiently, "nanotech is not magic. The program matrices for medical nano and Companion technology are well understood and easily controlled. A planet—is an extremely large and variable venue for nanoscale replication, and—"

"All right, all right. Don't go all techie on me."

"As you wish." I didn't add that there'd been considerable debate among the amortals. Many had counseled waiting on Project Eos until our control of nanotech allowed reworking an entire world to spec.

But I didn't think Paul would understand.

"Okay," he said, nodding thoughtfully. "I can see how one of them Companion thingies'd be a good idea. A damned good idea, in fact. The one thing I'm not certain about here, y'see, is what happens if I pile into the rocks somewhere so far from civilization that no one knew where I was."

"Take a Companion, and we will be riding with you. We will know exactly where you are, and what is happening."

"Yeah . . . but does that mean I have to have it, uh, inside me?"

I imitated a human shrug. "Not if you do not wish it. It will attach itself to the circuitry of your computer, your cameras, your communications suite."

"Well, I guess that's okay, then."

"We will be following your progress with considerable interest. Since it will be uplinked through Marsnet, anyone with net access will be able to watch as well."

"Never did care for a big audience. Ah, well. I can live with that, I guess. Go ahead. Let the thing loose, or whatever you do."

A further command programmed the golden sphere, which dissolved into a sparkling cloud, then wafted across the compartment to vanish into the Mars hut's main computer console. Paul stepped aside to let it pass, giving it a glare that told me he did not, *could not* trust such magical-seeming technologies.

"This will improve your chances for survival," I told him.

"Sometimes," he replied in that painfully slow speech of his, "I think you amorts worry too much about life, and not enough about *living*. But then, I reckon immortality makes you folks take a cautious slant on everything y'do, eh?"

"Life is not something to be wasted."

"It's also something to be *enjoyed*. I want this, Cessair. I plan to enjoy every damned minute of it. Heh! A free ride, clear back t'Pittsburgh, Mars!"

"There are safer ways of making that passage," I told him.

"Mebbe. But none that'll be this much *fun!*" He turned and looked up into the glassy eye of a camera, mounted on what once had been the Mars hut's floor. "Hey, girls! See ya on the Marsnet!"

I do not understand *sapiens*.

4

I had more business to conduct in Pittsburgh and Denver-Olympus. By the time I floatered back to Deimos and joined Andr, Dahlen, and the rest of the amortals on the Eos Team in Ops, Impact was minutes away. A last scan from orbit of Norris's site—using infrared, since it was dark by then—showed his preparations, as near as we could tell, complete. Two major changes outside. He'd brought the cryoboxes inside, though I frankly didn't know where else inside the hut he'd had room to store them.

And one thing more. There now was a deep, rectangular trench where his wife had been buried, and the cross-shaped marker had been removed. We assumed at the time he wanted to rebury her somewhere else, on higher ground.

Impact. . . .

We were watching on the big screen inside Deimos Ops when a spark burst into incandescent brilliance above the Martian night. Sliding swiftly across the dark hemisphere, it grew bright enough to illuminate the ground beneath as it crossed the frozen waters covering Chryse, then strobed in a dazzling, silent pulse.

We all watched then, as minutes dragged by. The big AIs, of course, were recording everything; the data from this impact would provide a wealth of insight into cometary impact dynamics, and their interactions with planetary atmospheres and surfaces. That left us free to . . . watch. Even after the initial flash died away, the impact site, just across the dawn terminator, continued to glow in infrared, giving a ghostly glow to a fuzzy disk spreading across the Martian surface. From satellites in low orbit, the shock wave appeared two-dimensional, hugging the landscape as it climbed the gentle slopes of Xanthe Terra, submerging the broken and chaotic terrain in a milky cloud that turned gold when the first light of the sun touched it.

"Time for link in," Andr chirped at me. I'd slowed my clockspeed again; data flow and conversation snapped and snickered around me, too fast, now, for my slowed senses to comprehend. *Is this how we appear to them?*

"Right," I drawled. A linkpod was already prepared. I snuggled down into its embrace, extruding the necessary connections and linklocks. Static crackled behind my eyes. . . .

And then I was staring up through a grime-smeared plastic visor at what once had been the Mars hut's floor. I could hear the *whiss-thunk-hiss* of his breather unit and the quiet ticking of his PLSS, could feel the bite of the aging pressure-suit's fittings and the heavy straps securing me to the gimbaled seat.

Worse, I *hurt* . . . with a dull and nagging ache in my joints, my back, my hands. At first, I thought he was sore from the physical work he'd been doing, but a quick taste of a side-channel medband convinced me I was feeling his arthritis.

Arthritis! In this day and age? Didn't he know that a microgram or so of medical nano *could* . . .

Humans. So shortsighted. So suspicious. So stubborn. I wondered what else might be wrong with that pain-soaked body.

I suppose, technically, we were violating his rights under the Tycho Charter, since he'd expressly requested that we not invade his body with the Companion's nano . . . but the whole point of this exercise was to find out what Paul Norris was *really* thinking, why he was taking this awful gamble with existence. The nano had already been programmed to enter not only his equipment, but his body . . . as an invisible mist of molecule-sized units drawn into him with each breath and filtering through his skin. Once in his circulatory system, it had taken perhaps ten minutes for several grams of nano to assemble itself into receptors, processors, and routers at key points in his brain, all linked to the outside by a tiny radio transmitter riding safely within the cavern of one of his frontal sinuses.

It was for his own good. We amortals take seriously our pledge to help our genetic and technological forebears. Besides, he was only a human, his rights outweighed by what we would learn.

I couldn't read his mind directly, of course. Wetware circuitry, neutral pathways, memory patterns, and response triggers all vary tremendously from human to human, and there'd been no time to record Paul Norris's patterns, much less win his cooperation. But I was receiving a full sensory download, experiencing what he experienced as he experienced it, and my impressions were being recorded for later study.

They were also available on the Net, for anyone who cared to tap in.

Over fifteen thousand amortals had already linked in from Marsnet, and more were coming online every second, from Solarnet and even Earthnet, where more and more humans were logging on.

I remembered what Paul had said about large audiences, and smiled to myself. He had *no* idea. . . .

There wasn't much to sense at first, save the discomfort. It took almost three hours for the shock wave to make it to Paul's domie, and by that time, Eos Chasma was across the morning terminator, though the bottom of the canyon was still shrouded in morning shadow and ground fog. Eos Ops relayed updates to Paul by conventional com every few minutes; the cameras mounted on the outside of his Mars hut showed little but the swiftly illuminating sky framed by towering black cliffs.

"You've got ten seconds," Andr's voice reported, speaking in Paul's ear.

Paul's focus shifted from the big wall monitor to the computer display mounted across his lap, where seconds were ticking off and a systems check was drawing to a close. "I see it," Paul replied. He appeared calm, though I could hear rising stress in his voice. Sweat tickled my own face as it beaded above his eyes and trickled down nose and cheeks. "S'funny, y'know, knowin' that the rock hit hours ago and not feelin' a—"

The jolt was like a savage kick in the tail, and the container-packed compartment whirled wildly around my head as the gimbaled seat swung freely. My view went dark, too, as the lights failed, and I cursed the OS-strain's lack of IR vision.

Computers were still online, filling the compartment with a cool glow. In another moment, the reserve-lighting came up. I felt an unpleasant trembling through every bone in my body, and my view through Paul's eyes was jittering hard, worse than the vibrations of aerobrake reentry.

Paul looked around the compartment, checking each of the stacked and strapped-down hardfoam crates, cryocases, and storage containers. He must be worried about the delicate fossils stored inside, especially the ice fossils, the way he kept looking at the cryocases. I wanted to tell him to relax, that the way he'd secured them they would ride out the shocks, no problem, but I decided that he wouldn't appreciate knowing just how close at his shoulder I was.

I did wish he would spend less time checking his cases and readouts, and more looking up at the big screen, affixed to his ceiling—the Mars hut's floor—with massive bolts and polyplas braces.

The thunderclap of that first shock wave had faded but not died completely. The raw, rumbling noise was growing louder again, and at last Paul looked up at the main screen . . . and stared into an awful glory.

The gold-pink of the Martian dawn sky was gone, masked by a fast-spreading blanket of ocher-brown and black sweeping down the valles from the northeast. I could see the distant cliffs vanishing into that cloud one by one as it drew closer, and the thunder increased with the approach. The robexcavator, visible on the left side of the screen, was trembling . . . the thickly strewn rocks on the ground were vibrating as tiny sand dunes gradually collapsed and flattened. The sound was something I . . . something we could feel in our bones as the second wave approached.

I was watching for the onrushing wall of water. I didn't see it before the screen, and then vision itself, went black.

I felt again the cool embrace of the linkpod. All sensory input had ceased, and for a gut-twisting moment of disorientation and fear, I thought, I *knew* that Paul had been killed. Then the side-channel telemetry filtered through my blinkered awareness, recording his heartbeat, his breathing, his brain's electrical activity.

"Neg scan on the satfeed," Andr chirped in a high-speed transfer. I lost part of his feed input . . . but gathered that the tidal wave that had just swept over Paul Norris's camp had been seventy meters high, and that he couldn't see the Mars hut on any of the satellite views. "Did he scrag?"

"Neg," I said on the Ops channel. "Vitals okay. I think he's unconscious."

"There!" Dahlen said, pointing at another monitor. "Balyuts deployed!"

The monitor she was indicating showed the Martian surface at an oblique angle, one just peering in past the towering, red and ocher-banded cliffs of Eos Chasma's south wall. The bottom of that valley was now lost in a surging, whirling mass of, not water, but mud . . . thick and red and viscous but still churning and frothing like whitewater rapids. The Mars hut, very tiny and very, very alone, had just bobbed into view riding on the surface, five of its six balyuts air-filled and taut, supporting the hut's foundation slab like pall-bearers lugging a rich *sapiens'* coffin. There was no sign of the sixth balloon. Perhaps it had not deployed, or possibly the violence of the tidal wave's arrival had shredded its tough fabric.

No matter. Paul, obviously, understood redundant engineering. His vessel bumped and shuddered along now on the foaming waves with only a ten-degree list to the right . . . what Paul would have called "starboard" in his sailing days on Earth. I felt his sensory link returning, and submerged myself again in his awareness.

His . . . *our* heads hurt, a dull throb, and we tasted the salty bite of blood. Our eyes weren't focusing well—I couldn't read the lap display, but when he looked up at the big screen, I saw the mudflow from the point of view of a piece of flotsam racing along with the current, through eyes scant centimeters above the roiling muck. Clifftops, their golden caprocks shrouded now in boiling storm clouds kilometers above my head, raced past, while the mud-thick water, despite its churning and foaming, seemed static around me. The scene jittered and trembled, occasionally jolting hard, as though someone had slammed against the camera, and at those times my worldview would pitch and yaw wildly as Paul's gimbaled chair absorbed the shock. I could hear him shouting something into the din, felt the rasp in my throat and the movements of my jaw . . . but I couldn't make out the words above the keening, savage thunder engulfing his frail habitat.

Injection event . . .

Was it my imagination, or were we moving faster now? The cliffs on our left hand were blurring as they raced past, and I felt myself instinctively trying to edge to the right, trying to stay clear. Paul's thumb depressed a button on the joystick he held in a trembling right hand, and I felt a hard bump in my spine and gut as the chemical thrusters nudged us away from that hurtling, deadly wall.

Minutes passed with the banded rock walls. The thunder dimmed, somewhat, though we could still hear a thrumming, keening roar of Armageddaic proportions, howling just beyond the thin steel-and-durplast shell.

"You amorts watchin', up there?" Paul shouted as thunder screamed and boomed. "You see? This is what it means to be *alive!*" Then he twisted his helmeted head back and vented a long, shrill ya-*hoooo* that rang from walls already ringing with the chaos outside.

Indeed, my own heart rate was up, in sympathy with Paul's. There was no physiological danger in the link for me, of course, not with full buffers and safety cutouts; I would never have consented to a Life-risking link. I've heard of a handful of amortals who risk everything in a too-close link with a human facing extinction, and could never imagine why.

I *knew* why, now. Until this moment, I had existed for 193 stadyers in a sterile, muffled cocoon; it was all I could do not to shout myself from the sheer, heart-leaping emotion of the instant.

Others must have agreed. A side-channel told me there were now 21,867 amortals linked in with this experience, almost half of all of the amortals in existence, together with an unknown number of AIs. More than that, humans were logging on as well in unprecedented numbers, from Mars, from Luna and the microworlds, from Earth herself. The total now was over 12.8 million—a number that continued rising rapidly from moment to moment as word of Paul Norris's voyage spread.

The water's speed had increased in the narrow confines of Coprates Chasma, a one-thousand-kilometer straight-line channel far grander and more spectacular than anything Percival Lowell could have imagined. At four hundred kilometers per hour, the passage took two-and-a-half hours, but this was the easy part, a straight, steady rush requiring only occasional bumps from the thrusters to keep the Ark in the center of the stream. There was worse, *much* worse, to come.

"How '*bout* that, Ann?" Paul's voice sounded in our ears, audible now as the thunder continued to fade. "Y'ever think we'd see this? Last time water flowed in these canyons was a billion years ago, as Tharsis bulged and the permafrost melted, and here we are riding it, by damn! Dear, sweet Christ, it's good to share this with you . . ."

I wondered if the experience had accelerated his dementia. His wife's corpse, I knew, must be stored somewhere inside the hut in a lovingly secured cryocase coffin. He was talking to her again.

"Y'see the expression on that amort's face, when I told her off? Heh. They want it all so skekkin' neat and orderly! No room for clutter. No room for improvisin' the unexpected. Hell, no room in the preservin' of life for *enjoyin'* it!" Our seat fell away suddenly as the Mars hut went into a sudden drop, following the surge as it spilled into a lower-lying stretch of the chasma. My stomach twisted hard and I almost screamed. "Hah!" Paul shouted, exultant. "Cessie, *that* one's fer you!"

Spray and spume exploded across the clumsy craft's bow, momentarily obliterating the view ahead in myriad droplets clinging to the camera lens. The lens was probably bonded with a frictionless coating, or the mud and splashing over it would have completely obscured our vision.

Three hours after the wave had first thundered across Paul's Mars hut, the unlikely lifeboat was swept out of the Coprates Channel, at that point only 150 kilometers wide, following the wave as it surged out into the far broader basin of the Mela Chasma. The sky was very dark now, and there was a steady drumming on the slab surface of the hut. Rain. The first rain to fall on Mars in . . . what? A billion years? Two?

"Got a choice here," he called. His voice sounded weaker . . . tired, we suspected. "Keep headin' west, or I could try swingin' north, head for Candor and Ophir. But the terrain's pretty broken up there. Lots of mensae, lots of mountaintops for me to smack into. An' I'm still movin' at a pretty fair clip." He cocked his head to one side. "Don't much like the squeaks and hisses I'm hearing in here. Not sure I'm still watertight."

I could hear it too, above the deeper booming of the water outside. The creakings might have been the packing cases shifting against their constraints, but there was also a shrill, high whistle that could only be escaping air. These old Mars huts had a self-sealer sandwiched between the thin, double shells, but that would work only for a small puncture. If a seam in the hull opened . . . or both of the airtight seals at the airlock, the interior was going to start losing air. After fifty-one stadyers of terraforming, air pressure on Mars still ran at only a hundredth of a bar. Worse, if the compartment began flooding, the Mars hut would sink in water that might be as much as a kilometer deep. We had no equipment capable of finding and recovering so tiny an artifact, certainly not in the time his pressure suit would grant him.

How much of an air supply did he have, anyway? He hadn't checked his suit systems or PLSS readouts, so I couldn't tell. Zet! Wasn't the human interested in his own life-support capabilities?

"Listen, Paul," Andr's voice said in our ear, speaking over his helmet's com circuit. He'd obviously lowered his own clock speed for the attempt, but his voice still sounded strangely high-pitched and chirpy, with the ragged fringes caused by unrealized sidebands. "We're monitoring the wave front from the impact. It's already climbed the Juvantae Dorsa and started spilling into Ophir Chasma. The whole region is masked by steam and spray. If you head that way, well, your ride's going to get pretty rough."

"Yup." Paul didn't sound worried. "'Fraid a' that. Tryin' to picture a waterfall four kilometers high, 'cause that's how high the cliffs are at the north rim of Ophir." He shook his head inside his helmet. "I'd get swept into a cliff for sure. West it is, then. Used to prospect in Ius Chasma, way back when. Found our very first Martian fossil there, in fact. Remember that, Ann? So beautiful. So *perfect*. . . ."

I suppressed a cold shudder at that. At times, Paul seemed almost rational. At others . . .

I remembered studying meter-resolution holos of the Valles. Technically, there were two narrow canyons running west out of the Mela Chasma, Tithonium in the north and Ius in the south, but the east end of Tithonium wasn't much more than a chain of craters, broken ground and sinkholes at the caprock level, a dead end as far as the Ark's voyage was concerned. Ius Chasma was long—another thousand kilometers—and gently curving, but it was deeper and narrower than the Coprates Chasma he'd already traversed, and the western end tilted up, toward the fossae-riddled highlands of the Noctis Labyrinthus.

"Here are the figures," Andr's voice went on. I saw them when Paul glanced down at the laptop console screen, block upon block of differential equations dealing with fluid dynamics, pressure and gravity, and the far subtler workings of chaos. They proved what I'd already feared. The surge we rode had slowed as it entered the broad expanse of Melas Chasma, and the Ark was now bobbing along at a relatively sedate eighty kilometers an hour . . . but when the waters cascading now into Ophir Chasma to the north came sweeping down, Paul's speed was going to increase again. In effect, he would be riding a second injection event, one that would squirt him down the long curve of Ius like a wet pip squeeze-popped from between thumb and finger.

And at the end . . . well, the land rose sharply, where the Valles Marineris had their birth within the tangled and thickly channeled ground of the Noctis Labyrinthus. The city of Pittsburgh was located high up in the Labyrinth; a thousand kils beyond were the three Tharsis Montes, Arsia, Pavonis, and Ascraeus, the ancient, three-in-a-row volcanic attendants of great Olympus Mons himself.

The question was how far the wave would travel up the Tharsis Bulge. Our calculations suggested that it would not get as far as Pittsburgh . . . but just to make sure, most of the population had evacuated to Denver-Olympus, twenty-five hundred kilometers further to the northwest.

Somewhere on that thousand-kilometer slope of broken, chaotic terrain, the Ark would come to rest. But where? And . . . how gently?

For a time, the voyage was almost idyllic, but Paul continued handling the thruster controls, judiciously nudging us across the rising flood toward the west, where the broad, wide basin of Melas gradually constricted like a funnel, until the walls of the canyon were less than eighty kils apart.

I could feel our speed increasing again, could feel the rising shudder of the battered Mars hut's shell, the thrum of hammering currents, the hiss of bleeding air. I pulled back from my link enough to check the log-on numbers. Over half of all amortals—24,925 in all—were following Paul's ride; the human log-on numbers were nothing less than phenomenal . . . two billion and some, the number flickering higher with each second!

What were they watching for? The vicarious sense of danger and probable disaster? Or did they identify, somehow, with the ancient Paul Norris?

"Fossils," Paul muttered . . . to Andr, to himself, to Ann, I couldn't tell. "I s'pose we're as out-of-date as an old spine-wheel, eh? But if the fossils tell us anything, it's that life *adapts*, or it goes under. Y'get too set in your ways, y'get to dependin' too much on your neighbors, and the next thing y'know, the ocean's gone and you're dyin' in a place you were never meant t'imagine."

Lightning flared, igniting the bellies of black-ocher clouds billowing above the Chasma and briefly turning the clifftops white. Dust clouds and water droplets could carry a tremendous static charge. Rock walls blurred once more, as savage currents tore and slashed at the wildly bobbing bit of steel and durplast flotsam. One of Paul's monitors showed a view from an orbiter, a vast and angry, counterclockwise spiral of lightning-strobing clouds embracing a quarter of Mars's western hemisphere. It was catastrophism on a planetary scale, something unseen in the Solar System since the Chicxulub impact that ended the dinosaurs and their age sixty-five million years ago.

And on the fringe of that fire-shot hurricane was one ancient OS human, in his frail and makeshift ark.

Noah. I'd downloaded more of the myth before linking in. Was this Martian Noah preserving samples of ancient Martian life unknown to us? Unlikely. But he might well be preserving something more . . . the spirit of a species long dormant and in the twilight of its span. Everyone knew that *H. amortalis* would replace the saps, that there was really no point in their continued existence beyond what they, themselves, found for themselves.

Almost three billion humans were logged on now, watching, feeling. An astonishing awareness.

I found myself pleading with Life to spare his life. Zet. Irrational, I know, but I was now facing powers that far surpassed the skills and grasp of the Amortals, even though it had been we who'd released them.

More, I was facing an aspect of Humankind that my species had forgotten.

"Pickin' up a real bit of speed now," Paul's voice said. "Lot of vibration here. I'm well into the Ius Chasma's eastern mouth, and the tide surge's squirtin' me along at a pretty good clip."

He was fading. I could feel that, feel the tremors of exhaustion dragging at his arms, his back. I felt something else, too, which alarmed me more. We were having trouble breathing, each breath a hard drag against an increasing pressure over our chest. Paul checked his airflow and PLSS readouts then, but everything showed normal. He bumped up the O_2 valve a notch and went back to steering. The Ius Chasma here was neatly divided by a long, knife-backed ridge called the Geryon Montes, narrowing the canyon to five kilometers in places, maybe less. Zet. He should have tried for the main passage to the north. Maybe he'd gotten confused . . . maybe he'd simply not been able to correct the awkward ship's course enough to clear the montes and put it on our left.

Judging from the cliffs flashing past to either side now, the water beneath was perhaps half a kil deep; the air around us had a peculiar, hazy softness to it, the effect of dust and water droplets hurled up by the water's explosive passage. The cliffs, what I could see of them, showed evidence of the sheer violence of the water's arrival. Martian regolith is laden with peroxides that can react explosively with water, releasing vast quantities of oxygen.

Not enough to breathe, of course. Not even enough to ignite with the hydrogen and methane that must be outgassing from the rocks and melting ices as well. But enough to give the air a strange and beautiful glow as the cloud cover began to grow ragged and the first shafts of sunlight angled down out of the sky, sparkling against the water. The rain continued, but lightly . . . a thin mist gleaming in the golden light.

"My God," Paul said. "Ann . . . it's *beautiful* . . ."

The jolt as we collided with the rock wall to our right was sharp and savage enough to leave my head spinning. I felt the compartment tip alarmingly; another balyut, again on the right side, had blown, cushioning the impact but leaving us with a dangerous list to starboard.

Paul's heart was thudding in his chest now, and he was struggling with each breath. I willed him to up the O_2 again, but he didn't seem to notice.

"Should be okay," he said. "Should be okay. We should stay afloat even if we lose three of the things." Then we struck the wall again, rebounding with a dizzying spin that left me breathing as hard as Paul. Geryon Montes was behind us now; ahead, just visible through flashing spray, a purple shadow loomed high and rounded.

The waveride was coming to an end.

"Paul!" Andr's voice was calling. "Paul, respond, please!"

I could hear the voice plainly, but Paul was not reacting.

"Feel like we're comin' home at last, eh, Ann? Not just Pittsburgh, Mars. But Earth. Been a long time since we've seen rain like that. Or water, come t'that."

"Paul! Please respond!"

"Eh. Don't tell them Amortals I said so. This might be a pretty nice place t'live, some year. Our grandkids might live here, if'n the girls decide to come back, someday. Christ, I miss 'em. But life's gotta reach out. Fill new niches. Expand. Adapt. Fossils . . ."

It felt as though we were enduring high acceleration, a smothering, crushing sensation over our chest. A sharp pain was drilling its way down my left arm.

A side channel fed me new data on Paul's condition. Heart attack! Life, didn't he even have preventative nano for . . . ?

No. Of course he didn't. Nothing to keep the arthritis in check, nothing to keep the coronary artery clear. Years of self-neglect, of refusal to try the new ways, and he was dying now, as I watched.

What could I do? The nano I'd slipped into his system only functioned within certain narrow parameters. It let me communicate with him but could not be reprogrammed for a medical application.

Swiftly, though, I uploaded new instructions, directing the radio transmitter to extrude parts of itself, forming new connections, following facial blood vessels to plate out bits of itself against the angle of his jawbone.

"Paul!" I shouted, and the bone-conductor speaker must have jolted him.

"Eh? Whozat?"

"Paul, this is Cessair! Increase your oxyflow! Now!"

"What the hell are you doin' in my head, woman?"

"I'm sorry. I'll explain later. Right now . . . we've got to get you to a doctor, do you understand?"

He chuckled. "Don'tcha think I oughta land, first?" But he keyed his air mix to pure O_2 at hyperbaric pressure. The crushing feeling abated, slightly, but I felt him panting with the strain.

He was staring into the screen, where the purple mountain rose from the water. The slope didn't look too bad—it wasn't a sheer cliff, at any rate—but if he dashed into it nose first . . .

"Paul! Use your thrusters! You've lost two balyuts on your starboard side, and you're dragging some there. If you can turn right, turn broadside with your port side to the mountain, your left-side balyuts ought to cushion your impact a bit!"

"Do you see it?" he asked. "Ann . . . do you see it?"

He was staring into the big screen. With the craft's stern dragging low in the water, the camera was angled high now, focused on the misty grays and silvers and golds of the cloud cover above the Noctis Labyrinthus. And there, just visible in the uncertain light, I could see a faint smear of Life-pure colors . . . red, green, yellow . . . and blue.

I'd never seen anything like that.

"A rainbow . . ." Paul said. His voice was blurred with the effort. "Ann, it's a *rainbow*, the first on Mars in a billion years . . ."

And then I was lying on the linkpod's cushions, cut off from the tiny bit of flotsam below and feeling very much alone.

5

The wave was gentle by the time it crested the end of Ius Chasma and crawled up the lower slopes of the Tharsis Bulge. He came to rest less than a hundred kils from Pittsburgh, the Martian city where he'd started off, with his beloved Ann, so many years ago. Five billion humans experienced the Marineris Ride, either directly or through sensory replays later on—a quarter of the old human race. I wonder, sometimes, if that was when the renaissance began.

Homo amortalis was supposed to be Man's successor, an elegant and seam-less melding of machine and reworked human genes. By losing any allegiance to a set shape or somatype, it was we who would inherit a galaxy far too vast and hostile for *Homo sapiens*, with his genetic structure cast and honed in the forge of Earth's limited environment. Until he entered space, man's greatest claim to survival had always been his adaptability, and we amortals had taken adaptability—even in the forms our bodies take—to unprece-dented levels. It was we who would inherit the stars, not *Homo sapiens*.

Was that, I wonder now, entirely true? Since Paul's Marineris ride, our evacuation efforts on Mars have met with almost universal failure . . . and thousands of OS humans who'd already emigrated to the microworld refuges have returned. Injection events. Marsquakes. Storms. Mudslides. They face them. They die in unprecedented numbers.

And the survivors keep going.

Paul was buried next to Ann in the shadow of the monument they raised to him and his epic ride, close by the sparkling, ocher shores of the new Marineris Sea. They found a handwritten will sealed in one of the containers, Paul's insurance in case he didn't survive the trip. From its tone, it sounded as though he half expected to end up entombed within the Mars hut beneath a few hundred meters of mud at the bottom of the Valles Marineris. Ann's body, perfectly preserved by the cold, dry Martian environment, was sealed in a cryocase strapped in next to the seat where we found Paul's body.

This is my home, the letter explained. *I'm not leaving it for anything, not for a new world, not for a better world. I'll build my own life here with Ann. Forever.*

More than anything else, he wanted to be buried with Ann.

I did some checking in the Records Center in Pittsburgh. Paul Norris and Ann Whittaker both contributed genetic material shortly after their arrival on Mars, material purchased by the Amortal Program. Some of my more recent somatypes include DNA sequences contributed by those two, a reminder that we amortals are Mankind's children.

I find myself proud to have such parents. Even if their stubbornness borders on the incomprehensible at times.

The amortals were designed to be supremely adaptable. Perhaps, though, survival requires a bit of stubbornness as well.

Perhaps Paul's species will outlive us after all.

A Martian Romance

KIM STANLEY ROBINSON

Kim Stanley Robinson sold his first story in 1976, and quickly established himself as one of the most respected and critically-acclaimed writers of his generation. His story "Black Air" won the World Fantasy Award in 1984, and his novella "The Blind Geometer" won the Nebula Award in 1987. His novel The Wild Shore *was published in 1984 as the first title in the resurrected Ace Special line, along with first novels by other new writers such as William Gibson, Michael Swanwick, and Lucius Shepard, and was quickly followed up by other novels such as* Icehenge, The Memory of Whiteness, A Short, Sharp Shock, The Gold Coast, *and* The Pacific Shore, *and by collections such as* The Planet on the Table, Escape from Kathmandu, *and* Remaking History.*

Robinson's already distinguished literary reputation would take a quantum jump in the 1990s, though, with the publication of his acclaimed Mars *trilogy:* Red Mars, Green Mars, *and* Blue Mars. Red Mars *would win a Nebula Award; both* Green Mars *and* Blue Mars *would win Hugo Awards; and the trilogy would be widely recognized as the genre's most accomplished, detailed, sustained, and substantial look at the colonization and terraforming of another world, rivaled only by Arthur C. Clarke's* The Sands of Mars. *Robinson's latest books are the novel* Antarctica, *and a collection of stories and poems set of his fictional Mars,* The Martians. *He lives with his family in California.*

The Mars *trilogy will probably associate Robinson's name forever with the Red Planet, but it was not the first time he would explore a fictional Mars. Robinson would visit Mars in several stories from the 1980s, including a memorable novella, "Green Mars," which detailed the first attempt to climb Olympus Mons, the tallest mountain in the solar system. The bittersweet and evocative story that follows is a direct sequel to "Green Mars"—and at a tangent to the history of Martian settlement as it ultimately developed in the* Mars *trilogy. In it, he takes us to a bleak and wintry Mars where the terraforming effort has gone disastrously wrong, and a group of old friends set sail in an iceboat across the frozen seas of the once Red Planet, many years after their first epic journey, hoping to touch the sky one last time. . . .*

Eileen Monday hauls her backpack off the train's steps and watches the train glide down the piste and around the headland. Out the empty station and she's into the streets of Firewater, north Elysium. It's deserted and dark, a ghost town, everything shut down and boarded up, the residents moved out and moved on. The only signs of life come from the westernmost dock: a small globular cluster of yellow streetlights and lit windows, streaking the ice of the bay between her and it. She walks around the bay on the empty corniche, the sky all purple in the early dusk. Four days until the start of spring, but there will be no spring this year.

●

She steps into the steamy clangor of the hotel restaurant. Workers in the kitchen are passing full dishes through the broad open window to diners milling around the long tables in the dining room. They're mostly young, either iceboat sailors or the few people left in town. No doubt a few still coming out of the hills, out of habit. A wild-looking bunch. Eileen spots Hans and Arnold; they look like a pair of big puppets, discoursing to the crowd at the end of one table—elderly Pinocchios, eyes lost in wrinkles as they tell their lies and laugh at each other, and at the young behemoths passing around plates and devouring their pasta while still listening to the two. The old as entertainment. Not such a bad way to end up.

It isn't Roger's kind of thing, however, and indeed when Eileen looks around she sees him standing in the corner next to the jukebox, pretending to make selections but actually eating his meal right there. That's Roger for you. Eileen grins as she makes her way through the crowd to him.

"Hey," he says as he sees her, and gives her a quick hug with one arm.

She leans over and kisses his cheek. "You were right, it's not very hard to find this place."

"No." He glances at her. "I'm glad you decided to come."

"Oh, the work will always be there, I'm happy to get out. Bless you for thinking of it. Is everyone else already here?"

"Yeah, all but Frances and Stephan, who just called and said they'd be here soon. We can leave tomorrow."

"Great. Come sit down with the others, I want some food, and I want to say hi to everyone."

Roger wrinkles his nose, gestures at the dense loud crowd. This solitary quality in him has been the cause of some long separations in their relationship, and so now Eileen shoves his arm and says, "Yeah yeah, all these people. Such a crowded place, Elysium."

Roger grins crookedly. "That's why I like it."

"Oh, of course. Far from the madding crowd."

"Still the English major, I see."

"And you're still the canyon hermit," she says, laughing and pulling him toward the crowd; it is good to see him again, it has been three months. For many years now they have been a steady couple, Roger returning to their rooms in the co-op in Burroughs after every trip away; but his work is still in the back country, so they still spend quite a lot of time apart.

Just as they join Hans and Arnold, who are wrapping up their history of the world, Stephan and Frances come in the door, and they hold a cheery reunion over a late dinner. There's a lot of catching up to do; this many members of their Olympus Mons climb haven't been together in a long time. Hours after the other diners have gone upstairs to bed, or off to their homes, the little group of old ones sits at the end of one table talking. A bunch of antique insomniacs, Eileen thinks, none anxious to go to bed and toss and turn through the night. She finds herself the first to stand up and stretch and declare herself off. The other rise on cue, except for Roger and Arnold; they've done a lot of climbing together through the years, and Roger was a notorious insomniac even when young; now he sleeps very poorly indeed.

And Arnold will talk for as long as anyone else is willing, or longer. "See you tomorrow," Arnold says to her. "Bright and early for the crossing of the Amazonian Sea!"

◆

The next morning the iceboat runs over ice that is mostly white, but in some patches clear and transparent right down to the shallow seafloor. Other patches are the color of brick, with the texture of brick, and the boat's runners clatter over little dunes of gravel and dust. If they hit melt ponds the boat slows abruptly and shoots great wings of water to the sides. At the other side of these ponds the runners scritch again like ice skates as they accelerate back up to speed. Roger's iceboat is a scooter, he explains to them; not like the spidery skeletal thing that Eileen was expecting, having seen some of that kind down in Chryse—those Roger calls DNs. This is more like an ordinary boat, long, broad, and low, with several parallel runners nailed fore and aft to its hull. "Better over rough ice," Roger explains, "and it floats if you happen to hit water." The sail is like a big bird's wing extended over them, sail and mast all melded together into one object, shifting shape with every gust to catch as much wind as it can.

"What keeps us from tipping over?" Arnold asks, looking over the lee rail at the flashing ice just feet below him.

"Nothing." The deck is at a good cant, and Roger is grinning.

"Nothing?"

"The laws of physics."

"Come on."

"When the boat tips the sail catches less wind, both because it's tilted and because it reads the tilt, and reefs in. Also we have a lot of ballast. And there are weights in the deck that are held magnetically on the windward side. It's like having a heavy crew sitting on the windward rail."

"That's not nothing," Eileen protests. "That's three things."

"True. And we may still tip over. But if we do we can always get out and pull it back upright."

They sit in the cockpit and look up at the sail, or ahead at the ice. The iceboat's navigation steers them away from the rottenest patches, spotted from satellites, and so the automatic pilot changes their course frequently, and they shift around the cockpit when necessary. Floury patches slow them the most, and over these the boat sometimes decelerates pretty quickly, throwing the unprepared forward into the shoulder of the person sitting next to them. Eileen is banged into by Hans and Frances more than once; like her, they have never been on iceboats before, and their eyes are round at the speeds it achieves during strong gusts over smooth ice. Hans speculates that the sandy patches mark old pressure ridges, which stood like long steg-osaur backs until the winds ablated them entirely away, leaving their load of sand and silt behind on the flattened ice. Roger nods. In truth the whole ocean surface is blowing away on the wind, with whatever sticks up going the fastest; and the ocean is now frozen to the bottom, so that no new pressure ridges are being raised. Soon the whole ocean will be as flat as a tabletop.

◆

This first day out is clear, the royal blue sky crinkling in a gusty west wind. Under the clear dome of the cockpit it's warm, their air at a slightly higher pressure than outside. Sea level is now around 300 millibars, and lowering year by year, as if for a great storm that never quite comes. They skate at speed around the majestic promontory of the Phlegra Peninsula, its great prow topped by a white-pillared Doric temple. Staring up at it Eileen listens to Hans and Frances discuss the odd phenomenon of the Phlegra Montes, seaming the north coast of Elysium like a long ship capsized on the land; unusually straight for a Martian mountain range, as are the Erebus Montes to the west. As if they were not, like all the rest of the mountain ranges on Mars, the remnants of crater rims. Hans argues for them being two concentric rings of a really big impact basin, almost the size of the Big Hit itself but older than the Big Hit, and so mostly obliterated by the later impact, with only Isidis Bay and much of the Utopian and Elysian Seas left to indicate where the basin had been. "Then the ranges could have been somewhat straightened out in the deformation of the Elysium bulge."

Frances shakes her head, as always. Never once has Eileen seen the two of them agree. In this case Frances thinks the ranges may be even older than Hans does, remnants of early tectonic or proto-tectonic plate movement. There's a wide body of evidence for this early tectonic era, she claims, but Hans is shaking his head: "The andesite indicating tectonic action is younger than that. The Phlegras are early Noachian. A pre–Big Hit big hit."

Whatever the explanation, there the fine prow of rock stands, the end of a steep peninsula extending straight north into the ice for four hundred kilometers out of Firewater. A long sea cliff falling into the sea, and the same on the other side. The pilgrimage out the spine to the temple is one of the most famous walks on Mars; Eileen has made it a number of times since Roger first took her on it about forty years ago, sometimes with him, sometimes without. When they first came they looked out on a blue sea purled with whitecaps. Seldom since has it been free of ice.

He too is looking at the point, with an expression that makes Eileen think he might be remembering that time as well. Certainly he would remember if asked; his incredible memory has still not yet begun to weaken, and with the suite of memory drugs now available, drugs that have helped Eileen to remember quite a bit, it might well be that he will never forget anything his whole life long. Eileen envies that, though she knows he is ambivalent about it. But by now it is one of the things about him that she loves. He remembers everything and yet he has remained stalwart, even chipper, though all the years of the crash. A rock for her to lean on, in her own cycles of despair and mourning. Of course as a Red it could be argued he has no reason to mourn. But that wouldn't be true. His attitude was more complex than that, Eileen has seen it; so complex that she does not fully understand it. Some aspect of his strong memory, taking the long view; a determination to make it well; rueful joy in the enduring land; some mix of all these things. She watches him as he stares absorbed at the promontory where he and she once stood together over a living world.

⬭

How much he has meant to her through the years has become beyond her ability to express. Sometimes it fills her to overflowing. That they have known each other all their lives; that they have helped each other through hard times; that he got her out into the land in the first place, starting her on the trajectory of her whole life; all these would have made him a crucial figure to her. But everyone has many such figures. And over the years their divergent interests kept splitting them up; they could have lost touch entirely. But at one point Roger came to visit her in Burroughs, and she and her partner of that time had been growing distant for many years, and Roger said, I love you Eileen. I love you. Remember what it was like on Olympus Mons, when we climbed it? Well now I think the whole world is like that. The escarpment goes on forever. We just keep climbing it until eventually we fall off. And I want to climb it with you. We keep getting together and then going our ways, and it's too chancy, we might not cross paths again. Something might happen. I want more than that. I love you.

And so eventually they set up rooms in her co-op in Burroughs. She continued to work in the Ministry of the Environment, and he continued to guide treks in the back country, then to sail on the North Sea; but he always came back from his treks and his cruises, and she always came back from her working tours and her vacations away; and they lived together in their rooms when they were both at home, and became a real couple. And through the years without summer, then the little ice age and the crash itself, his steadfast presence has been all that has kept her from despair. She shudders to think what it would have been like to get through these years alone. To work so hard, and then to fail. . . . It's been hard. She has seen that he has worried about her. This trip is an expression of that: Look, he said once after she came home in tears over reports of the tropical and temperate extinctions—look, I think you need to get out there and see it. See the world the way it is now, see the ice. It's not so bad. There have been ice ages before. It's not so bad.

And as she had been more and more holing up in Burroughs, unable to face it, she finally was forced to agree that, in theory, it would be a good thing. Very soon after that he organized this trip. Now she sees that he gathered some of their friends from the Olympus Mons expedition to help entice her to come, perhaps; also, once here, to remind her of that time in their lives. Anyway it's nice to see their faces, flushed and grinning as they fly along.

➤

Skate east! the wind says, and they skitter round Scrabster, the northeastern point of Elysium, then head south over the great plate of white ice inserted into the incurve of the coast. This is the Bay of Arcadia, and the steep rise of land backing the bluffs is called Acadia, for its supposed resemblance to Nova Scotia and the coast of Maine. Dark rock, battered by the dark north sea; sea-cliffs of bashed granite, sluiced by big breakers. Now, however, all still and white, with the ice that has powdered down out of the spray and spume flocking and frosting the beach and the cliffs until they look like wedding-cake ramparts. No sign of life in Acadia; no greens anywhere in sight. This is not her Elysium.

●

Roger takes over the sailing from Arnold, and brings them around a point, and there suddenly is a steep-walled square island ahead, vivid green on top—ah. A township, frozen her near the entrance to a fjord, no doubt in a deep channel. All the townships have become islands in the ice. The greenery on top is protected by a tent which Eileen cannot see in the bright sun. "I'm just dropping by to pick up the rest of our crew," Roger explains. "A couple of young friends of mine are going to join us."

"Which one is this?" Stephan inquires.

"This is the *Altamira*."

Roger sails them around in a sweet curve that ends with them stalled into the wind and skidding to a halt. He retracts the cockpit dome. "I don't intend to go up there, by the way, that's an all-day trip no matter how you do it. My friends should be down here on shore to meet us."

They step down onto the ice, which is mostly a dirty opaque white, cracked and a bit nobbled on the surface, so that it is slippery in some places, but mostly fairly steady underfoot; and Eileen sees that the treacherous spots stand out like windows inlaid in tile. Roger talks into his wristpad, then leads them into the fjord, which on one steep side displays a handsome granite staircase, frost lying like a fluffy carpet on the steps.

Up these stairs Roger climbs, putting his feet in earlier bootprints. Up on the headland over the fjord they have a good view over the ice to the township, which is really very big for a manufactured object, a kilometer on each side, and its deck only just lower than they are. Its square tented middle glows green like a Renaissance walled garden, the enchanted space of a fairy tale.

There is a little stone shelter or shrine on the headland, and they follow the sidewalk over to it. The wind chills Eileen's hands, toes, nose and ears. A big white plate, whistling in the wind. Elysium bulks behind them, its two volcanoes just sticking over the high horizon to the west. She holds Roger's hand as they approach. As always, her pleasure in Mars is mixed up with her pleasure in Roger; at the sight of this big cold panorama love sails through her like the wind. Now he is smiling, and she follows his gaze and sees two people though the shelter's open walls. "Here they are."

They round the front of the shrine and the pair notices them. "Hi, all," Roger says. "Eileen, this is Freya Ahmet and Jean-Claude Bayer. They're going to be joining us. Freya, Jean-Claude, this is Eileen Monday."

"We have heard of you," Freya says to her with a friendly smile. She and Jean-Claude are both huge; they tower over the old ones.

"That's Hans and Frances behind us, down the path there arguing. Get used to that."

●

Hans and Frances arrive, then Arnold and Stephan. Introductions are made all around, and they investigate the empty shrine or shelter, and exclaim over the view. The eastern side of the Elysian massif was a rain-shadow before, and now it bulks just as black and empty as ever, looking much as it always has. The huge white plate of the sea, however, and the incongruous square of the *Altamira*; these are new and strange. Eileen has never seen anything like it. Impressive, yes; vast; sublime; but her eyes always returns to the little tented greenhouse on the township, tiny stamp of life in a lifeless universe. She wants her world back.

On the way back down the stone stairs she looks at the exposed granite of the fjord's sidewall, and in one crack she sees black crumbly matter. She stops to inspect it.

"Look at this," she says to Roger, scraping away at rime to see more of it. "Is it lichen? Moss? Is it alive? It looks like it might be alive."

Roger sticks his face right down into it, eyes a centimeter away. "Moss, I think. Dead."

Eileen looks away, feeling her stomach sink. "I'm so tired of finding dead plants, dead animals. The last dozen times out I've not seen a single living thing. I mean winterkill is winterkill, but this is ridiculous. The whole world is dying!"

Roger waggles a hand uncertainly, straightens up. He can't really deny it. "I suppose there was never enough sunlight to begin with," he says, glancing up at their bronze button of light, slanting over Elysium. "People wanted it and so they did it anyway. But reality isn't interested in what people want."

Eileen sighs. "No." She pokes again at the black matter. "Are you sure this isn't a lichen? It's black, but it looks like it's still alive somehow."

He inspects some of it between his gloved fingers. Small black fronds, like a kind of tiny seaweed, frayed and falling apart.

"Fringe lichen?" Eileen ventures. "Frond lichen?"

"Moss, I think. Dead moss." He clears away more ice and snow. Black rock, rust rock. Black splotches. It's the same everywhere. "No doubt there are lichens alive, though. And Freya and Jean-Claude say the subnivean environment is quite lively still. Very robust. Protected from the elements."

Life under a permanent blanket of snow. "Uh-huh."

"Hey. Better than nothing, right?"

"Right. But this moss here was exposed."

"Right. And therefore dead."

They start down again. Roger hikes beside her, lost in thought. He smiles: "I'm having a déjà vu. This happened before, right? A long time ago we found some little living thing together, only it was dead. It happened before!"

She shakes her head. "You tell me. You're the memory man."

"But I can't quite get it. It's more like déjà vu. Well, but maybe . . . maybe on that first trip, when we first met?" He gestures eastward—over the Amazonian Sea, she guesses, to the canyon country east of Olympus. "Some little snails or something."

"But could that be?" Eileen asks. "I thought we met when I was still in college. The terraforming had barely started then, right?"

"True." He frowns. "Well, there was lichen from the start, it was the first thing they propagated."

"But snails?"

He shrugs. "That's what I seem to remember. You don't?"

"No way. Just whatever you've told me since, you know."

"Oh well." He shrugs again, smile gone. "Maybe it was just a déjà vu."

●

Back in the iceboat's cockpit and cabin, they could be crowded around the kitchen table of a little apartment anywhere. The two newcomers, heads brushing the ceiling even though they are sitting on stools, cook for them. "No, please, that is why we are here," Jean-Claude says with a big grin. "I very much like to be cooking the big meals." Actually they're coming along to meet with some friends on the other side of the Amazonian Sea, all people Roger has worked with often in the last few years, to initial some research on the western slope of Olympus—glaciology and ecology, respectively.

After these explanations they listen with the rest as Hans and Frances argue about the crash for a while. Frances thinks it was caused by the rapid brightening of the planet's albedo when the North Sea was pumped out and froze; this the first knock in a whole series of positively reinforcing events leading in a negative direction, an autocatalytic drop into the death spiral of the full crash. Hans thinks it was the fact that the underground permafrost was never really thawed deeper than a few centimeters, so that the resulting extremely thin skin of the life zone looked much more well-established than it really was, and was actually very vulnerable to collapse if attacked by mutant bacteria, as Hans believes it was, the mutations spurred by the heavy incoming UV—

"You don't know that," Frances says. "You radiate those same organisms in the lab, or even expose them in space labs, and you don't get the mutations or the collapses we're seeing on the ground."

"Interaction with ground chemicals," Hans says. "Sometimes I think everything is simply getting salted to death."

Frances shakes her head. "These are different problems, and there's no sign of synergistic effects when they're combined. You're just listing possibilities, Hans, admit it. You're throwing them out there, but no one knows. The etiology is not understood."

This is true; Eileen had been working in Burroughs on the problem for ten years, and she knows Frances is right. The truth is that in planetary ecology, as in most other fields, ultimate causes are very hard to discern. Hans now waggles a hand, which is as close as he will come to conceding a point to Frances. "Well, when you have a list of possibilities as long as this one, you don't have to have synergy among them. Just a simple addition of factors might do it. Everything having its particular effect."

Eileen looks over at the youngsters, their backs to the old ones as they cook. They're debating salt too, but then she sees one put a handful of it in the rice.

➤

In the fragrance of basmati steam they spoon out their meals. Freya and Jean-Claude eat seated on the floor. They listen to the old ones, but don't speak much. Occasionally they lean heads together to talk in private, under the talk at the little table. Eileen sees them kiss.

She smiles. She hasn't been around people this young for a long time. Then through their reflections in the cockpit dome she sees the ice outside, glowing under the stars. It's a disconcerting image. But they are not looking out the window. And if even they were, they are young, and so do not quite believe in death. They are blithe.

Roger sees her looking at the young giants, and shares with her a small smile at them. He is fond of them, she sees. They are his friends. When they say good night and duck down the passageway to their tiny quarters in the bow, he kisses his fingers and pats them on the head as they pass him.

The old ones finish their meal, then sit staring out the window, sipping hot chocolate spiked with peppermint schnapps.

"We can regroup," Hans says, continuing the discussion with Frances. "If we pursued the heavy industrial methods aggressively, the ocean would melt from below and we'd be back in business."

Frances shakes her head, frowning. "Bombs in the regolith, you mean."

"Bombs *below* the regolith. So that we get the heat, but trap the radiation. That and some of the other methods might do it. A flying lens to focus some of the mirrors' light, heat the surface with focused sunlight. Then bring in some nitrogen from Titan. Direct a few comets to unpopulated areas, or aerobrake them so that they burn up in the atmosphere. That would thicken things up fast. And more halocarbon factories, we let that go too soon."

"It sounds pretty industrial," Frances says.

"Of course it is. Terraforming is an industrial process, at least partly. We forgot that."

"I don't know," Roger says. "Maybe it would be best to keep pursuing the biological methods. Just regroup, you know, and send another wave out there. It's longer, but, you know. Less violence to the landscape."

"Ecopoesis won't work," Hans says. "It doesn't trap enough heat in the biosphere." He gestures outside. "This is as far as ecopoesis will take you."

"Maybe for now," Roger says.

"Ah yes. You are unconcerned, of course. But I suppose you're happy about the crash anyway, eh? Being such a red?"

"Hey, come on," Roger says. "How could I be happy? I was a sailor."

"But you used to want the terraforming gone."

Roger waves a hand dismissively, glances at Eileen with a shy smile. "That was a long time ago. Besides the terraforming isn't gone now anyway," gesturing at the ice, "it's only sleeping."

"See," Arnold pounces, "you do want it gone."

"No I don't, I'm telling you."

"Then why are you so damn happy these days?"

"I'm not happy," Roger says, grinning happily. "I'm just not sad. I don't think the situation calls for sadness."

Arnold rolls his eyes at the others, enlisting them in his teasing. "The world freezes, and this is not a reason for sadness. I shudder to think what it would take for you!"

"It would take something sad!"

"But you're *not* a red, no, of course not."

"I'm not!" Roger protests, grinning at their laughter, but serious as well. "I was a sailor, I tell you. Look, if the situation were as bad as you all are saying, then Freya and Jean-Claude would be worried too, right? But they're not. Ask them and you'll see."

"They are simply young," Hans says, echoing Eileen's thought. The others nod as well.

"That's right," Roger says. "And it's a short-term problem."

That gives them pause.

After a silence Stephan says, "What about you, Arnold? What would you do?"

"What, me? I have no idea. It's not for me to say, anyway. You know me. I don't like telling people what to do."

They wait in silence, sipping their hot chocolate.

"But you know, if you did just direct a couple of little comets right *into* the ocean . . ."

Old friends, laughing at old friends just for being themselves. Eileen leans in against Roger, feeling better.

●

Next morning with a whoosh they are off east again, and in a few hours' sailing are out on the ice with no land visible, skating on the gutsy wind with runners clattering or shussing or whining or blasting, depending on wind and ice consistencies. The day passes, and it begins to seem as if they are on an all-ice world, like Callisto or Europa. As the day ends they slide around into the wind and come to a halt, then get out and drive in some ice screws around the boat and tie it into the center of a web of lines. By sunset they are belayed, and Roger and Eileen go for a walk over the ice.

"A beautiful day's sail, wasn't it?" Roger asks.

"Yes, it was," Eileen says. But she cannot help thinking that they are out walking on the surface of their ocean. "What did you think about what Hans was saying last night, about taking another bash at it?"

"You hear a lot of people talking that way."

"But you?"

"Well, I don't know. I don't like a lot of the methods they talk about. But—" He shrugs. "What I like or don't like doesn't matter."

"Hmm." Underfoot the ice is white, with tiny broken air bubbles marring the surface, like minuscule crater rings. "And you say the youngsters aren't much interested either. But I can't see why not. You'd think they'd want terraforming to be working more than anyone."

"They think they have *lots* of time."

Eileen smiles at this. "They may be right."

"That's true, they may. But not us. I sometimes think we're sad not so much because of the crash as the quick decline." He looks at her, then down at the ice again. "We're two hundred and fifty years old, Eileen."

"Two hundred forty."

"Yeah yeah. But there's no one alive older than two-sixty."

"I know." Eileen remembers a time when a group of old ones were sitting around a big hotel restaurant table building card-houses, as there was no other card game all of them knew; they collaborated on one house of cards four stories high, and the structure was getting shaky indeed when someone said, "It's like my longevity treatments." And though they laughed, no one had the steadiness of hand to set the next card.

"Well. There you have it. If I were twenty I wouldn't worry about the crash either. Whereas for us it's very likely the last Mars we'll know. But, you know. In the end it doesn't matter what kind of Mars you like best.

They're all better than nothing." He smiles crookedly at her, puts an arm around her shoulders and squeezes.

◆

The next morning they wake in a fog, but there is a steady breeze as well, so after breakfast they unmoor and slide east with a light, slick sliding sound. Ice dust, pulverized snow, frozen mist—all flash past them.

Almost immediately after taking off, however, a call comes in on the radio phone. Roger picks up the handset, and Freya's voice comes in. "You left us behind."

"*What?* Shit! What the hell were you doing out of the boat?"

"We were down on the ice, fooling around."

"For Christ's sake, you two." Roger grins despite himself as he shakes his head. "And what, you're done now?"

"None of your business," Jean-Claude calls happily in the background.

"But you're ready to be picked up," Roger says.

"Yes, we are ready."

"Okay, well, shit. Just hold put there. It'll take awhile to beat back up to you in this wind."

"That's all right. We have our warm clothes on, and a ground pad. We will wait for you."

"As if you have any choice!" Roger says, and puts the handset down.

He starts sailing in earnest. First he turns across the wind, then tacks up into it, and the boat suddenly shrieks like a banshee. The sailmast is cupped tight. Roger shakes his head, impressed. You would have to shout to be heard over the wind now, but no one is saying anything; they're letting Roger concentrate on the sailing. The whiteness they are flying through is lit the same everywhere, they see nothing but the ice right under the cockpit, flying by. It is not the purest whiteout Eileen has ever been in, because of the wind and the ice under the lee rail, but it is pretty close; and after a while even the ends of the iceboat, even the ice under the lee rail, disappear into the cloud. They fly, vibrating with their flight, through a roaring white void; a strange kinetic experience, and Eileen finds herself trying to open her eyes farther, as if there might be another kind of sight inside her, waiting for moments like this to come into play.

Nothing doing. They are in a moving whiteout, that's all there is to it. Roger doesn't look pleased. He's staring down at their radar, and the rest of the instrumentation. In the old days pressure ridges would have made this kind of blind sailing very dangerous. Now there is nothing out there to run into.

Suddenly they are shoved forward, the roar gets louder, there is darkness below them. They are skating over a sandy patch. Then out of it and off again, shooting through bright whiteness. "Coming about," Roger says.

Eileen braces herself for the impact of their first tack, but then Roger says, "I'm going to wear about, folks." He brings the tiller in toward his knees and they career off downwind, turn, turn, then catch the wind on their opposite beam, the boat's hull tipping alarmingly to the other side. Booms below as the ballast weight shifts up to the windward rail, and then they are howling as before, but on the opposite tack. The whole operation has been felt and heard rather than seen; Roger even has his eyes closed for a while. Then a moment of relative calm, until the next wearing-about. A backward loop at the end of each tack.

Roger points at the radar screen. "There they are, see?"

Arnold peers at the screen. "Sitting down, I take it."

Roger shakes his head. "They're still mostly over the horizon. That's their heads."

"You hope."

Roger is looking at the APS screen and frowning. He wears away again. "We'll have to come up on them slow. The radar only sees to the horizon, and even standing up it won't catch them farther than six K away, and we're going about a hundred-fifty K an hour. So we'll have to do it by our APS positions."

Arnold whistles. Satellite navigation, to make a rendezvous in a whiteout . . . "You could always," Arnold begins, then claps his hand over his mouth.

Roger grins at him. "It should be doable."

For a nonsailor like Eileen, it is a bit hard to believe. In fact all the blind vibration and rocking side to side have her feeling a bit dizzy, and Hans and Stephan and Frances look positively queasy. All five of them regard Roger, who looks at the APS screen and shifts the tiller minutely, then all of a sudden draws it in to his knees again. On the radar screen Freya and Jean-Claude appear as two glowing green columns. "Hey you guys," Roger says into the radio handset, "I'm closing on you, I'll come up from downwind, wave your arms and keep an eye out, I'll try to come up on your left side as slow as I can."

He pulls the tiller gently back and forth, watching the screens intently. They come so far up into the wind that the sail-mast spreads into a very taut French curve, and they lose way. Roger glances ahead of the boat, but still nothing there, just the pure white void, and he squints unhappily and tugs the tiller another centimeter closer to him. The sail is feathering now and has lost almost all its curve; it feels to Eileen as if they are barely making headway, and will soon stall and be thrown backward; and still no sign of them.

Then there they are just off the port bow, two angels floating through whiteness toward the still boat—or so for one illusory moment it appears. They leap over the rail onto the foredeck, and Roger uses the last momentum of the iceboat to wear away again, and in a matter of seconds they are flying east with the wind again, the howl greatly reduced.

◗

By that sunset they are merely in a light mist. Next morning it is gone entirely, and the world has returned. The iceboat lies moored in the long shadow of Olympus Mons, hulking over the horizon to the east. A continent of a mountain, stretching as far as they can see to north and south; another world, another life.

They sail in toward the eastern shore of the Amazonian Sea, famous before the crash for its wild coastline. Now it shoots up from the ice white and bare, like a winter fairy tale: Gordii Waterfall, which fell a vertical kilometer off the coastal plateau directly into the sea, is now a great pillared icefall, with a great pile of ice shatter at its foot.

Past this landmark they skate into Lycus Sulci Bay, south of Acheron, where the land rises less precipitously, gentle hills above low sea bluffs, looking down on the ice bay. In the bay they slowly tack against the morning offshore breeze, until they come to rest against a floating dock, now somewhat askew in the press of ice, just off a beach. Roger ties off on this, and they gear up for a hike on the land. Freya and Jean-Claude carry their backpacks with them.

Out of the boat and onto the ice. *Scritch-scritch* over the ice to shore, everything strangely still; then across the frosty beach, and up a trail that leads to the top of the bluff. After that a gentler trail up the vast tilt of the coastal plateau. Here the trailmakers have laid flagstones that run sometimes ten in a row before the next low step up. In steeper sections it becomes more like a staircase, a great endless staircase, each flag fitted perfectly under the next one. Even rime-crusted as it is, Eileen finds the lapidary work extraordinarily beautiful. The quartzite flags are placed as tightly as Orkney drywall, and their surfaces are a mix of pale yellow and red, silver and gold, all in differing proportions for each flag, and alternating by dominant color as they rise. In short, a work of art.

Eileen follows the trail looking down at these flagstones, up and up, up and up, up some more. Above them the rising slope is white to the distant high horizon, beyond which black Olympus bulks like a massive world of its own.

The sun emerges over the volcano. Light blazes on the snow. As they hike farther up the quartzite trail it enters a forest. Or rather, the skeleton of a forest. Eileen hurries to catch up with Roger, feeling oppressed, even frightened. Freya and Jean-Claude are up ahead, their other companions far behind.

Roger leads her off the trail, through the trees. They are all dead. It was a forest of foxtail pine and bristlecone pine; but treeline has fallen to sea level at this latitude, and all these big old gnarled trees have perished. After that a sandstorm, or a series of sandstorms, have sandblasted away all the trees' needles, the small branches, and the bark itself, leaving behind only the bleached tree trunks and the biggest lower branches, twisting up like broken arms from writhing bodies. Wind has polished the spiraling grain of the trunks until in the morning light. Ice packs the cracks into the heartwood.

The trees are well-spaced, and they stroll between them, regarding some more closely, then moving on. Scattered here and there are little frozen ponds and tarns. It seems to Eileen like a great sculpture garden or workshop, in which some mighty Rodin has left scattered a thousand trials at a single idea, all beautiful, altogether forming a park of surreal majesty. And yet awful too; she feels it as a kind of stabbing pain in the chest; this is a cemetery. Dead trees flayed by the sandy wind; dead Mars, their hopes flensed by the cold. Red Mars, Mars the god of war, taking back its land with a frigid boreal blast. The sun glares off the icy ground, smeary light glazing the world. The bare wood glows orange.

"Beautiful, isn't it?" Roger says.

Eileen shakes her head, looking down. She is bitterly cold, and the wind whistles through the broken branches and the grain of the wood. "It's dead, Roger."

"What's that?"

" 'The darkness grew apace,' " she mutters, looking away from him. " 'A cold wind began to blow in freshening gusts from the east.' "

"What's that you say?"

"*The Time Machine*," she explains. "The end of the world. 'It would be hard to convey the stillness of it.' "

"Ah," Roger says, and puts her arm around her shoulders. "Still the English major." He smiles. "All these years pass and we're still just what we always were. You're an English major from the University of Mars."

"Yes." A gust seems to blow through her chest, as if the wind had suddenly struck her from an unexpected quarter. "But it's all over now, don't you see? It's all dead"—she gestures "—everything we tried to do!" A desolate plateau over an ice sea, a forest of dead trees; all their efforts gone to waste.

"Not so," Roger says, and points up the hill. Freya and Jean-Claude are wandering down through the dead forest, stopping to inspect certain trees, running their hands over the icy spiral grain of the wood, moving on to the next magnificent corpse.

Roger calls to them, and they approach together. Roger says under his breath to Eileen, "Now listen, Eileen, listen to what they say. Just watch them and listen."

The youngsters join them, shaking their heads and babbling at the sight of the broken-limbed forest. "It's so beautiful!" Freya says. "So pure!"

"Look," Roger interrupts, "don't you worry everything will all go away, just like this forest here? Mars become unlivable? Don't you believe in the crash?"

Startled, the two stare at him. Freya shakes her head like a dog shedding water. Jean-Claude points west, to the vast sheet of ice sea spread below them. "It never goes backward," he says, halting for words. "You see all that water out there, and the sun in the sky. And Mars, the most beautiful planet in the world."

"But the crash, Jean-Claude. The crash."

"We don't call it that. It is a long winter only. Things are living under the snow, waiting for the next spring."

"There hasn't been a spring in thirty years! You've never seen a spring in your life!"

"Spring is L-s zero, yes? Every year spring comes."

"Colder and colder."

"We will warm things up again."

"But it could take thousands of years!" Roger exclaims, enjoying the act of provocation. He sounds like all the people in Burroughs, Eileen thinks, like Eileen herself when she is feeling the despair of the crash.

"I don't care," Freya says.

"But that means you'll never see any change at all. Even with really long lives you'll never see it."

Jean-Claude shrugs. "It's the work that matters, not the end of work. Why be so focused on the end? All it means is you are over. Better to be in the middle of things, or at the beginning, when all the work remains to be done, and it could turn out any way."

"It could fail," Roger insists. "It could get colder, the atmosphere could freeze out, everything in the world could die like these trees here. Nothing left alive at all."

Freya turns her head away, put off by this. Jean-Claude sees her and for the first time he seems annoyed. They don't quite understand what Roger has been doing, and now they are tired of it. Jean-Claude gestures at the stark landscape: "Say what you like," he says. "Say it will all go crash, say everything alive now will die, say the planet will stay frozen for thousands of years—say the stars will fall from the sky! But there *will* be life on Mars."

Dream of Venus

PAMELA SARGENT

Terraforming a planet is like creating a work of art, although on a scale vastly grander than even the boldest twentieth-century landscape artists ever dreamed of. But, as with every work of art, the vision of the artist may not agree with the wishes of the patron who commissioned the work—sometimes, as the deceptively quiet story that follows demonstrates, with tragic results.

Pamela Sargent has firmly established herself as one of the foremost writer/editors of her generation. Her well-known anthologies include Women of Wonder, More Women of Wonder, The New Women of Wonder—*reissued in an omnibus volume as* Women of Wonder: The Classic Years—*and 1995's follow-up volume,* Women of Wonder: The Contemporary Years. *Her other anthologies include* Bio-Futures, Nebula Awards 29, Nebula Awards 30, *and, with Ian Watson,* Afterlives. *Her critically acclaimed novels include* Cloned Lives, The Sudden Star, The Golden Space, Watchstar, Earthseed, The Alien Upstairs, Eye of the Comet, Homeminds, *and* The Shore of Women. *Beginning in the mid-1980s, with a sequence of novels depicting the terraforming of Venus, including* Venus of Dreams *and* Venus of Shadows, *Sargent began examining the process of creating a viable new world with a depth of detail and sophistication matched in contemporary science fiction only by the work of Kim Stanley Robinson. Her short fiction has been collected in* Starshadows *and* The Best of Pamela Sargent. *She won a Nebula Award in 1993 for "Danny Goes to Mars." Her most recent books are a critically acclaimed historical novel about Genghis Khan,* Ruler of the Sky, *an Alternate History novel,* Climb the Wind, *and, after a gap of some years, the third book in the* Venus *trilogy,* Child of Venus. *She lives in Delmar, New York.*

Hassan Petrovich Maksutov's grandfather was the first to point out Venus to him, when Hassan was five years old. His family and much of his clan had moved to the outskirts of Jeddah by then, and his grandfather had taken him outside to view the heavens.

The night sky was a black canopy of tiny flickering flames; Hassan had imagined suddenly growing as tall as a djinn and reaching out to touch a star. Venus did not flicker like other stars, but shone steadily on the horizon in the hour before dawn. Hassan had not known then that he would eventually travel to that planet, but he had delighted in looking up at the beacon that signified humankind's greatest endeavor.

Twenty years after that first sighting, Hassan was gazing down at Venus from one of the ten domed Islands that floated in the upper reaches of the planet's poisonous atmosphere. These Cytherian Islands, as they were known (after the island of Cythera where the goddess Aphrodite had been worshiped in the ancient world), were vast platforms that had been built on top of massive metal cells filled with helium and then covered with dirt and soil. After each Island had been enclosed by an impermeable dome, the surfaces were gardened, and by the time Hassan was standing on a raised platform at the edge of Island Two and peering into the veiled darkness below, the Islands had for decades been gardens of trees, flowers, grassy expanses, and dwellings that housed the people who had come to Venus to be a part of the Project, Earth's effort to terraform her sister planet.

The Venus Project, as Hassan had known ever since childhood, was the greatest feat of engineering humankind had ever attempted, an enterprise that had already taken the labor of millions. Simply constructing the Parasol, the umbrella that shielded Venus from the sun, was an endeavor that had dwarfed the building of the Pyramids (where his father and mother had taken him to view those majestic crumbling monuments) and China's Great Wall (which he had visited during a break from his studies at the University of Chimkent). The Parasol had grown into a vast metallic flower as wide in diameter as Venus herself, in order to allow that hot and deadly world to cool. Venus would remain cloaked in the Parasol's shadow for centuries to come.

Hassan's grandfather had explained to him, during their sighting of Venus, that what he was seeing was, in fact, not the planet itself, but the reflected light of the Parasol. To the old man, this made the sight even more impressive, since the great shield was humankind's accomplishment, but Hassan felt a twinge of disappointment. Even now, as he stood on Island Two, the planet below was veiled in darkness, hidden from view.

The Venus of past millennia, with a surface hot enough to melt lead, an atmosphere thick with sulfur dioxide, and an atmospheric pressure that would have crushed a person standing on its barren surface, had already undergone changes. Hydrogen, siphoned off from Saturn, had been carried to Venus in a steady stream of tanks and then released into the atmosphere, where it was combining with the free oxygen produced by the changes in the Venusian environment to form water. The clouds had been seeded with a genetically engineered strain of algae that fed on the sulfuric acid and expelled it in the form of copper and iron sulfides. The Venus of the past now existed more in memory than in reality; the Venus of the future, that green and fertile planet that would become a second Earth and a new home for humankind, was still a dream.

As for the present, Hassan would now become one more person whose life would be enlarged by his own contribution, however small, to the great Venus Project. So Hassan's father Pyotr Andreievich Maksutor had hoped while meeting with friends and exerting his considerable influence on behalf of his son. Pyotr Andreievich Maksutov was a Linker, one of the privileged few who had implants linking their cortexes directly to Earth's cyberminds, a man who was often called upon to advise the Council of Mukhtars that governed all the Nomarchies of Earth and also watched over the Venus Project. Pyotr had convinced several Linkers connected with the Venus Project Council that Hassan, a specialist in geology, was worthy of being given a coveted place among the Cytherian Islanders.

Hassan, looking down at shadowed Venus through the transparent dome of Island Two, had been able to believe that he might have earned his position here until arriving on this Island. He had been here for two days now, and was beginning to feel as though his father's influence had always been a benign shadow over his life, one that had shielded him from certain realities. The passengers on the torchship that had carried him from Earth had been friendly, willing to share their enthusiasm for the work that lay ahead of them; the crew had been solicitous of his welfare, and he had taken their warmth and kindness as that of comrades reaching out to one who would soon be a colleague laboring for the Project. On the Island, he had been given a room in a building where most of the other residents were specialists who had lived on Island Two for several years, and had assumed that this was only because newcomers were usually assigned to any quarters that happened to be empty until more permanent quarters were found for them.

Now he suspected that the friendliness of the people aboard the torchship and his relatively comfortable quarters on Island Two had more to do with his family's connections than with luck or any merits of his own. The Venus Project needed people of all sorts—workers to maintain and repair homeostats and life-support systems, and pilots for the airships that moved between the Islands and for the shuttles that carried passengers to and from Anwara, the space station in high orbit around Venus that was their link to Earth, where the torchships from the home world landed and docked. Counselors to tend to the psychological health of the Islanders, scientists, and people brave enough to work on the Bats, the two satellites above Venus' north and south poles, were all needed here, and not all of them were exceptionally gifted or among the most brilliant in their disciplines. Many Islanders, the workers in particular, came from the humblest of backgrounds; the Council of Mukhtars wanted all of Earth's people to share in the glory of terraforming, although the more cynical claimed that offering such hope to the masses also functioned as a social safety valve.

Hassan could tell himself that he measured up to any of the people here, and yet after only a short time on Island Two, he saw that many here had a quality he lacked—a determination, a hardness, a devotion to the Project that some might call irrational. Such obsessiveness was probably necessary for those who would never see the result of their efforts, who had to have faith that others would see what they had started through to the end. The Project needed such driven people, and would need them for centuries to come.

But Hassan was only a younger son of an ambitious and well-connected father, who was here mostly because Pyotr could not think of anything else to do with him. He was not brilliant enough to be trained for an academic position, not politically adept enough to maneuver his way into becoming an aide to the Council of Mukhtars, and he lacked the extraordinary discipline required of those chosen to be Linkers; his more flighty mind, it was feared, might be overwhelmed by the sea of data a Link would provide. Hassan might, however, be burnished by a decade or two of work on the Project. With that accomplishment on his public record, he could return to Earth and perhaps land a position training hopeful young idealists who

dreamed of joining the Project; that sort of post would give him some influence. He might even be brought in to consult with members of the Project
Council, or made a member of one of the committees that advised the Council of Mukhtars on the terraforming of Venus. In any event, his father would
see an ineffectual son transformed into a man with a reputation much enhanced by his small role in humankind's most ambitious enterprise.

Hassan knew that he should consider himself fortunate that his father
had the power to help secure his son's position. He was even luckier to win
a chance to be listed among all of those who would make a new Earth of
Venus. His life had been filled with good fortune, yet he often wondered
why his luck had not made him happier.

◆

After the call to evening prayer had sounded, and the bright light of the
dome high overhead had faded into silver, Hassan usually walked to the
gardens near the ziggurat where Island Two's Administrators lived and ate
his supper there. He might have taken the meal in his building's common
room with the other residents, or alone in his room, but eating in solitude
did not appeal to him. As for dining with the others, the people who lived
in his building still treated him with a kind of amused and faintly contemptuous tolerance even after almost five months.

Hassan chafed at such treatment. Always before, at school and at university and among the guests his family invited to their compound, he had
been sought out, flattered, and admired. His opinions had been solicited, his
tentative comments on all sorts of matters accepted as intriguing insights
into the matters of the day. His professors, even those who had expected
more of him, had praise for his potential if not for his actual accomplishment.
But many Islanders seemed to regard him as someone on the level of a
common worker, no better or worse than anyone else. Indeed the workers
here, most of whom came from either teeming slums or the more impoverished rural areas and isolated regions of Earth's Nomarchies, were often
treated with more deference than he was.

And why not? Hassan had finally asked himself. Why shouldn't an illiterate man or woman laboring for the Project be given more respect than a
Linker's son? The workers, however humble their origins, had to be the best
at their trades, and extremely determined, in order to win a place here, and
the main reward they wanted for their efforts was a chance for their descendants to have more opportunities than they had been given and to be among
the first to settle a new world. Hassan's place was a gift from his father, and
he was not thinking of a better world for any children he might have, only
of hanging on to what his family already possessed.

Hassan sat down at his usual table, which was near a small pool of water.
Other people, several with the small diamondlike gems of Linkers on their
foreheads, sat at other tables around the pool and under slender trees that
resembled birches. As a servo rolled toward him to take his order, he
glimpsed his friend Muhammad Sheridan hurrying toward him from the
stone path that led to the Administrators' ziggurat.

"Salaam," Muhammad called out to him. "Thought I'd be late—the Committee meeting went on longer than we expected." The brown-skinned

young man sat down across from Hassan. Muhammad's family were merchants and shopkeepers from the Atlantic Federation, wealthy enough to have a large estate near the southern New Jersey dikes and seawalls and well connected enough to have sent Muhammad to the University of Damascus for his degree in mathematics-Hassan felt at ease with Muhammad; the two often ate dinner together. Muhammad had a position as an aide to Administrator Pavel Gvishiani, a post that would have assured him a certain amount of status on Earth. But here, Muhammad often felt himself patronized, as he had admitted to Hassan.

"Let's face it," Muhammad had said only the other evening, "the only way we're going to make a place for ourselves among these people is to do something truly spectacular for the Project, maybe something, God willing, on the order of what Dawud Hasseen accomplished." Dawud Hasseen had designed the Parasol almost three centuries earlier, and had been the chief engineer during its construction. "Or else we'll have to put in our time here without complaining until we're as driven and obsessed as most of the workers and younger specialists, in which case we might finally become more acceptable."

The second course was their only realistic alternative, Hassan thought. Their work here would not allow either of them much scope for grand achievements. Muhammad's position as an aide to Pavel Gvishiani required him to devote his time to such humble tasks as backing up written and oral records of meetings, retrieving summaries of them when needed, preparing and reviewing routine public statements, and occasionally entertaining Pavel with discussions of any mathematical treatises the Administrator had recently had transmitted to him from Earth. Lorna FredasMarkos, the head of Hassan's team of geologists, had given Hassan the mundane work of keeping the team's records in order and occasionally analyzing data on the increases in the levels of iron and copper sulfides on the basalt surface of Venus, work no one else was particularly interested in doing and that almost anyone else could have done.

"I don't know which Islanders are the worst," Muhammad had continued, "the peasants and street urchins who came here from Earth, or the workers who think of themselves as the Project's aristocrats just because their families have been living here for more than one generation." This was the kind of frank remark Hassan's friend would have kept to himself in other company.

Muhammad set his pocket screen on the tabletop in front of him. Hassan had brought his own pocket screen; although there was no work he had to do this evening, he had taken to toting his screen around, so that he could at least give the appearance of being busy and needed. The two young men ordered a pot of tea and simple meals of vegetables, beans, and rice. Hassan had come to the Islands with enough credit to afford a more lavish repast, even some imported foods from Earth, but he was doing his best to keep within the credit allotted to him by the Project, knowing that this would look better on his record.

"How goes it with you?" Muhammad asked.

"The way it usually does," Hassan replied, "although Lorna hinted that she might give me a new assignment. There's a new geologist joining our team, so perhaps Lorna wants me to be her mentor." He had looked up the public record of the geologist, who had arrived from Earth only two days ago. Her name was Miriam Lucea-Noyes; she had grown up on a farm in the Pacific Federation of North America, and had been trained at the University of Vancouver. It was easy for him to piece together most of her story from her record. Miriam Lucea-Noyes had been one of those bright but unschooled children who was occasionally discovered by a regional Counselor and elevated beyond her family's status; she had been chosen for a preparatory school and then admitted to the university for more specialized training. Her academic record was, Hassan ruefully admitted to himself, superior to his own, and he could safely assume that she had the doggedness and single-mindedness of most of those who had come to the Cytherian Islands. About the only surprising detail in her record was the fact that she had spent two years earning extra credit for her account as a technical assistant to a director of mind-tours and virtual entertainments before completing her studies.

"Ah, yes, the new geologist." Muhammad smiled. "Actually, I might be at least partly responsible for your new assignment. Administrator Pavel thinks it's time that we put together a new mind-tour of the Venus Project. The Project Council could use the extra credit the production would bring, and we haven't done one for a while."

Hassan leaned back. "I would have thought that there were already enough such entertainments."

"True, but most of them are a bit quaint. All of them could use some updating. And Pavel thinks that we have the capacity to provide a much more exciting and detailed experience now."

The servo returned with a teapot and two cups. Hassan poured himself and his friend some tea. "I wouldn't have thought," he said, "that an Administrator would be concerning himself with something as relatively unimportant as a mind-tour."

"Pavel Gvishiani is the kind of man who concerns himself with everything." Muhammad sipped some tea. "Anyway, Pavel was discussing this mind-tour business with the rest of the Administrators, and they all agreed that we could spare a couple of people to map out a tour. This new geologist on your team, Miriam Lucea-Noyes, is an obvious choice, given that she has some experience with mind-tour production. And when Pavel brought up her name, I suggested that you might be someone who could work very well with her on such a project."

"I see." Hassan did not know whether to feel flattered or embarrassed. Although cultivated people were not above enjoying them, the visual and sensory experiences of mind-tours were most popular with children and with ignorant and uneducated adults. They served the useful functions of providing vicarious experiences to people who might otherwise grow bored or discontented, and of imparting some knowledge of history and culture to the illiterate. With the aid of a band that could link one temporarily to Earth's cyberminds, a person could wander to unfamiliar places, travel back in time, or participate in an adventure.

Hassan had spent many happy hours as a child with a band around his head, scuba-diving in the sunken city of Venice and climbing to the top of Mount Everest with a party of explorers, among other virtual adventures. For a while, at university, he had toyed with the notion of producing such entertainments himself. He had managed to fit courses in virtual graphics, adventure fiction, music, and sensory-effects production into his schedule of required studies, and had been part of a student team producing a mind-tour for the University of Chimkent to use in recruiting new students and faculty until his father had put a stop to such pursuits. He had given in, of course— Pyotr had threatened to cut him off from all credit except a citizen's basic allotment and to do nothing to help him in such a profession as mind-tour production—but he had remained bitter about the decision his father had forced on him. In an uncharacteristic emotional venting, Hassan had admitted his bitterness over his thwarted dream to Muhammad. Being chosen to work on the university's mind-tour remained the only privilege he had ever won for himself, without his father's intercession.

"It won't hurt to have such experiences on your record," Pyotr had told Hassan, "as long as it's clear that this mind-tour business is just a hobby. But it isn't the kind of profession that could make a Linker of you, or give you any chance in politics." His father had, for a while, made him feel ashamed of his earlier ambition.

"It's not that I'm doing you any special favors, Hassan," Muhammad said. "It's just that we don't have many people here who could put together even a preliminary visual sketch of a mind-tour, and Administrator Pavel thinks having people associated with the Project doing the work might impart a new perspective, something more original, something that isn't just the vast spectacle interspersed with inspiring dioramas that most mind-tours about the Venus Project are." He paused. "Anyway, it'll be something other than the routine work you've been doing."

Hassan found himself warming to the prospect. Constructing a mind-tour, putting together the kind of experience that would make anyone, however humble his position, proud to be even a small part of a society that could transform a planet—this was a challenge he was certain he could meet. There was also an ironic satisfaction in knowing that the pursuit his father had scorned might become his means of winning Administrator Pavel's favor.

☙

Miriam Lucea-Noyes was a short, extremely pretty woman with thick dark brown hair, wide-set gray eyes, and a look of obstinacy. "Salaam," she murmured to Hassan after Lorna FredasMarkos had introduced them.

"How do you do," Hassan replied. Miriam gazed at him steadily until he averted his eyes.

"Hassan," Lorna said, "I feel as though we might have been wasting your talents." The gray-haired woman smiled. "You should have called your experience with mind-tour production to my attention earlier."

"It was noted in my record," he said.

"Well, of course, but one can so easily overlook such notations—" Lorna abruptly fell silent, as if realizing that she had just admitted that she had never bothered to study his record thoroughly, that she had given it no more than the cursory glance that was probably all the attention it deserved. "Anyway," the older woman continued, "Administrator Pavel is quite pleased that two members of my team are capable of putting together a new mind-tour. You will have access to all the records our sensors have made, and to everything in the official records of the project, but if there's anything else you need, be sure to let me know."

"How long do we have?" Miriam asked.

Lorna lifted her brows. "Excuse me?"

"What's the deadline?" Miriam said. "How long do we have to pull this thing together?"

"Administrator Pavel indicated that he would like to have it completed before the New Year's celebrations," the older woman replied.

"So we've got five months," Miriam said. "Then I think we'll see in the year 535 with one hell of a fine mind-tour."

Lorna pursed her thin lips, as if tasting something sour. "You may both have more time if you need it. The Administrator would prefer that you keep to his informal deadline, but he also made it clear that he would rather have a mind-tour that is both aesthetically pleasing and inspirational, even if that takes longer to complete."

Hassan bowed slightly in Lorna's direction. "We'll do our best to produce a mind-tour that is both pleasing and on time, God willing!"

"And that isn't a sloppy rush job either," Miriam said.

"I may have to drag you away to our team meetings and your other standard tasks occasionally," Lorna said, "but I'll try to keep such distractions to a minimum." She turned toward the doorway. "Salaam aleikum."

"Aleikum salaam," Miriam said. Her Arabic sounded as flat and unmusical as her Anglaic.

"God go with you," Hassan added as the door slid shut behind their supervisor.

"Well, Hassan." Miriam sat down on one of the cushions at the low table. "I don't know if you've ever seen any of the mind-tours I worked on. Most of them were for small children, so you probably haven't. *Hans Among the Redwoods*—that was one of our more popular ones, and *Dinosaurs in the Gobi.*' "

He tensed with surprise. "I saw that dinosaur mind-tour—marvelous work. Maybe you made it for children, but I have several adult friends who also enjoyed it."

"And *The Adventure of Montrose Scarp.*"

Hassan was impressed in spite of himself. "*Montrose Scarp?*" he asked as he seated himself. "My nephew Salim couldn't get enough of that one. He just about forced me to put on a band and view it. What I particularly admired was the way the excitement of the climb and the geological history of the scrap were so seamlessly combined."

"That was my doing, if I do say so myself." Miriam pointed her chin at him. "Joe Kinnear—he was the director I worked with—he wanted to put in more of the usual shit—you know, stuff like having the mind-tourist lose his grip and fall before being caught by the rope tied around him, or throwing in a big storm just as you reach the top of the escarpment. He thought doing what I wanted would just slow the thing down, but I convinced him otherwise, and I was right."

"Yes, you were," Hassan said.

"And every damned mind-tour of Venus has the obligatory scene of Karim al-Anwar speaking to the Council of Mukhtars, telling them that what they learn from the terraforming of Venus might eventually be needed to save Earth from the effects of global warming, or else a scene of New York or some other flooded coastal city at evening while Venus gleams on the horizon and a portentous voice quotes from that speech Mukhtar Karim supposedly made toward the end of his life."

Karim al-Anwar had been the first to propose a project to terraform Venus, back in the earliest days of Earth's Nomarchies, not long after the Resource Wars almost six centuries ago. " 'When I gaze upon Venus,' " Hassan quoted, " 'and view the images our probes have carried back to us from its hot and barren surface, I see Earth's future, and fear for our world.' "

"Followed by the sensation of heat and a hellish image of the Venusian surface," Miriam said. "And the three most recent ones all have scenes of explosions on the Bats, which I frankly think is misleading and maybe even too frightening."

The Bats, the two winged satellites in geosynchronous orbit at Venus' poles, serviced the automatic shuttles that carried compressed oxygen from the robot-controlled installations at the Venusian poles to the Bats. The process of terraforming was releasing too much of Venus' oxygen, and the excess had to be removed if the planet was ever to support life. The workers on the Bats, people who serviced the shuttles and maintained the docks, knew that the volatile oxygen could explode, and many lives had been lost in past explosions.

"There are real dangers on the Bats," Miriam continued, "but we don't have to dwell on them just for the sake of a few thrills. I'd rather avoid those kinds of clichés."

"So would I," Hassan said fervently.

"We should purge our minds of anything we've seen before and start over with an entirely fresh presentation."

"I think that's exactly what Pavel Gvishiani wants us to do."

"We're geologists," Miriam said, "and maybe that's the angle we ought to use. I don't think past mind-tours have really given people a feeling for the Project in the context of geological time. I'd like to emphasize that. Hundreds of years of human effort set against the eons it took to form Venus— and if we get into planetary evolution and the beginnings of the solar system . . ."

"I couldn't agree with you more," Hassan said.

"Most of the people who experience this mind-tour are likely to be ignorant and unschooled, but that doesn't mean we have to oversimplify things and lard the narrative with dramatic confrontations and action scenes."

"It sounds as though what we want is a mind-tour that would be both enlightening to the uneducated," Hassan said, "and entertaining and inspirational to the learned."

"That's exactly what I want," Miriam said.

It was also, Hassan thought, exactly what Pavel Gvishiani was likely to want. Judging by what Muhammad had told him about the Administrator, Pavel was not someone who cared to have his intelligence insulted. To have a mind-tour that would not just be an informative entertainment, but a masterpiece—

"We should talk about how we want to frame it," Hassan said, "before we start digging through all the records and sensor scans. Have a structure that encapsulates our vision, and then start collecting what we need to realize it."

"Exactly," Miriam said. "You'd be surprised at how many mind-tour directors do it the other way around, looking at everything that could possibly have anything to do with their theme while hoping that some coherent vision suddenly emerges out of all the clutter. That isn't the way I like to work."

"Nor I," Hassan said, gazing across the table at her expressive face and intense gaze, already enthralled.

◆

Miriam, despite being a geologist and a specialist, lived in a building inhabited by workers, people who repaired homeostats and robots, maintained airships and shuttles, tended hydroponic gardens, looked out for small children in the Island's child-care center, and performed other necessary tasks. Hassan had assumed that there was no room for her elsewhere, and that her quarters would be temporary. Instead, Miriam had admitted to him that she had requested space there, and intended to stay.

"Look," she said, "I went to a university, but a lot of students there didn't let me forget where I came from. I feel more comfortable with workers than with the children of merchants and engineers and Counselors and Linkers." She had glanced at him apologetically after saying that, obviously not wanting to hurt his feelings, but he had understood. His family's position might have brought him to this place, but with Miriam, he now had a chance to make his own small mark on the Project, to inspire others with the dream of Venus.

The Dream of Venus—that was how he and Miriam referred to the mind-tour they had been outlining and roughing-out for almost a month now. He thought of what they had been sketching and planning as he walked toward the star-shaped steel-blue building in which Miriam lived. As they usually did at last light, workers had gathered on the expanse of grass in front of the building. Families sat on the grass, eating from small bowls with chopsticks or fingers; other people were talking with friends, mending worn garments, or watching with pride and wonderment as their children reviewed their lessons on pocket screens. All children were schooled here, unlike Earth, where education was rationed and carefully parceled out.

It came to him then how much he now looked forward to coming here, to meeting and working with Miriam.

Hassan made his way to the entrance. Inside the windowless building, people had propped open the doors to their rooms to sit in the corridors and gossip; he passed one group of men gambling with sticks and dice. The place was as noisy and chaotic as a souk in Jeddah, but Hassan had grown more used to the cacophony. Since most of the workers could not read, the doors to their rooms were adorned with holo images or carvings of their faces, so that visitors could locate their quarters. Miriam's room was near the end of this wing; a holo image of her face stared out at him from the door.

He pressed his palm against the door; after a few seconds, it opened. Miriam, wearing a brown tunic and baggy brown pants, was sitting on the floor in front of her wall screen, a thin metal band around her head; even in such plain clothes, she looked beautiful to him.

"Salaam," she said without looking up.

"Salaam."

"We're making real progress," she said. "This mind-tour is really shaping up."

He sat down next to her. Unlike most of the people in this building, Miriam had a room to herself, but it was not much larger than a closet. Building more residences on the Islands would have meant cutting back on the gardens and parks that were deemed essential to maintaining the mental health of the Islanders.

"Before you show me any of your rough cut," he said, "would you care to have supper with me as my guest?" This was the first time he had offered such an invitation to her; he had enough credit to order imported delicacies from Earth for her if that was what she wanted. "We can go to the garden near the Administrators' building, unless of course you'd rather dine somewhere else."

"Maybe later," she said in the flat voice that was such a contrast to her lovely face and graceful movements. "I want you to look at this first."

They had decided to depart from tradition in their structure for *The Dream of Venus*. Miriam also wanted to dispense with the usual chronological depictions, which she found stodgy, and Hassan had readily agreed.

The mind-tour would begin with Karim al-Anwar, as every other depiction of the Venus Project did, but instead of the usual dramatic confrontations with doubters and passionate speeches about Earth's sister planet becoming a new home for humankind, they would move directly to what Karim had envisioned—Venus as it would be in the far future. The viewer would see the blue-green gem of a transformed Venus from afar and then be swept toward the terraformed planet, falling until the surface was visible through Venus' veil of white clouds. Flying low over the shallow blue ocean, the mind-tourist would be swept past a small island chain toward the northern continent of Ishtar, with its high plateau and mountain massif that dwarfed even the Himalayas, to view a region of vast grasslands, evergreen forests, and rugged mountain peaks. Then the wail of the wind would rise as the viewer was carried south toward the equator and the colorful tropical landscape of the continent of Aphrodite.

Hassan was still tinkering with the sound effects for that section, but had found a piece of music that evoked the sound of a strong wind, and planned to use recordings of the powerful winds that continuously swept around Venus below the Islands as background and undertones. Near the end of the sequence, the viewer would fly toward a Venusian dawn, gazing at the sun before a dark shape, part of what remained of the Parasol, eclipsed its light. There were a few scientists who doubted that any part of the Parasol would be needed later on to insulate Venus from the heat and radiation that could again produce a runaway greenhouse effect, but most Cytherian specialists disagreed with them, and Hassan and Miriam had decided to go along with the majority's opinion in their depiction.

At this point, the viewer was to be swept back in time, so to speak, to one of the Cytherian Islands, in a manner that would suggest what was not shown in the mind-tour—namely that in the distant future, when Venus was green with life, the Islands would slowly drop toward the surface, where their inhabitants would at last leave their domed gardens to dwell on their new world. Hassan and Miriam had inserted a passage during the earlier flight sequence in which the viewer passed over an expanse of parklike land that strongly resembled Island Two's gardens and groves of trees. That scene, with some enhancement, would resonate in the viewer's mind with the subsequent Island sequences.

"What have you got to show me?" Hassan asked.

Miriam handed him a band. "This is some stuff for the earlier sequences," she said.

Hassan put the band around his head, was momentarily blind and deaf, and then was suddenly soaring over the vast canyon of the Diana Chasma toward the rift-ridden dome of Atla Regio in the east and the shield volcano of Maat Mons, the largest volcano on Venus, three hundred kilometers in diameter and rising to a Himalayan height. The scene abruptly shifted to the steep massif of Maxwell Montes rising swiftly from the hot dark surface of Ishtar Terra as millions of years were compressed into seconds. He whirled away from the impressively high mountain massif and hovered over a vast basaltic plain, watching as part of the surface formed a dome, spread out, grew flat, and then sank, leaving one of the circular uniquely Venusian features called coronae. He moved over the cracked and wrinkled plateaus called tesserae and was surprised at the beauty he glimpsed in the deformed rocky folds of the land.

His field of vision abruptly went dark.

"What do you think?" Miriam's voice asked.

He shifted his band slightly; Miriam's room reappeared. "I know it's rough," she continued, "and I've got more to add to it, but I hope it gives you an idea. As for sound effects and the sensory stuff, I think we should keep that to a minimum—just a low undertone, the bare suggestion of a low throbbing noise, and maybe a feeling of extreme heat without actually making the viewer break out in a sweat. Well, what do you think?"

Hassan said, "I think it's beautiful, Miriam." His words were sincere. Somehow she had taken what could have been no more than an impressive visual panorama and had found the beauty in the strange, alien terrain of Venus as it might have been six hundred million years ago. It was as if she had fallen in love with that world, almost as if she regretted its loss.

"If you think that's something," she said, "wait until you see what I've worked up for the resurfacing section, where we see volcanoes flooding the plains with molten basalt. But I want your ideas on what to use for sensory effects there, and you'll probably want to add some visuals, too—it seems a little too abbreviated as it is."

"You almost make me sorry," Hassan said, "that we're changing Venus, that what it was will forever be lost—already is lost."

Her gray eyes widened. "That's exactly the feeling I was trying for. Every mind-tour about Venus and the Project always tries for the same effect—the feeling of triumph in the end by bringing a dead world to life, the beauty of the new Earthlike world we're making, the belief that we're carrying out God's will by transforming Venus into what it might have become. I want the mind-tourist at least to glimpse what we're losing with all this planetary engineering, to feel some sorrow that it is being lost."

Hassan smiled. "A little of that goes a long way, don't you think? We're supposed to be glorifying the Project, not regretting it."

"Sometimes I do regret it just a little. Imagine what we might have learned if we had built the Islands and simply used them to observe this planet. There are questions we may never answer now because of what we've already changed. Did Venus once have oceans that boiled away? Seems likely, but we probably won't ever be sure. Was there ever a form of life here that was able to make use of ultraviolet light? We'll never know that either. We decided that terraforming this world and giving all of humankind that dream and learning what we could from the work of the Project outweighed all of that."

"Be careful, Miriam." Hassan lifted a hand. "We don't want to question the very basis of the Project."

"No, of course not." But she sounded unhappy about making that admission. Hassan would never have insulted her by saying this aloud, but she sounded almost like a Habber, one of those whose ancestors had abandoned Earth long ago in the wake of the Resource Wars to live in the hollowed-out asteroids and artificial worlds called Habitats. There might be a few Habbers living here to observe the Project, but they thought of space as their home, not planetary surfaces. A Habber might have claimed that Venus should have been left as it had been.

"You've done wonderfully with your roughs," Hassan murmured, suddenly wanting to cheer her. Miriam's face brightened as she glanced toward him. "Really, if the final mind-tour maintains the quality of this work, we'll have a triumph." He reached for her hand and held it for a moment, surprised at how small and delicate it felt in his grip. "Let me take you to supper," he went on, and admitted to himself at last that he was falling in love with her.

●

They would have a masterpiece, Hassan told himself. Three months of working with Miriam had freed something inside him, had liberated a gift that he had not known he possessed. He felt inspired whenever he was with her. In his private moments, as he reviewed sections of *The Dream of Venus*, he grew even more convinced that their mind-tour had the potential for greatness.

There, in one of the segments devoted to the Venus of millions of years ago, was a vast dark plain, an ocean of basalt covered by slender sinuous channels thousands of kilometers long. A viewer would soar over shield volcanoes, some with ridges that looked like thin spider legs, others with lava flows that blossomed along their slopes. The mind-tourist could roam on the plateau of Ishtar and look up at the towering peaks of the Maxwell Mountains, shining brightly with a plating of tellurium and pyrite. What might have been only a succession of fascinating but ultimately meaningless geological panoramas had been shaped by Miriam into a moving evocation of a planet's life, a depiction of a truly alien beauty.

Hassan had contributed his own stylings to the mind-tour; he had shaped and edited many of the scenes, and his sensory effects had added greatly to the moods of awe and wonder that the mind-tour would evoke. It had been his idea to frame the entire mind-tour as the vision of Karim al-Anwar, and to begin and end with what the great man might have dreamed, a device that also allowed them to leave out much of the tedious expository material that had cluttered up so many mind-tours depicting Venus and the Project. But Miriam was the spirit that had animated him, that had awakened him to the visions and sounds that had lain dormant inside him.

The fulfillment he felt in the work they were doing together was marred by only one nagging worry: that *The Dream of Venus* was in danger of becoming an ode to Venus past, a song of regret for the loss of the world that most saw as sterile and dead, but which had become so beautiful in Miriam's renderings. What the Administrators wanted was a glorification of the Project, a mind-tour that would end on a note of optimism and triumph. They were unlikely to accept *The Dream of Venus* as it was, without revisions, and might even see it as vaguely subversive.

But there was still time, Hassan told himself, to reshape the mind-tour when *The Dream of Venus* was nearly in final form. He did not want to cloud Miriam's vision in the meantime with doubts and warnings; he did not want to lose what he had discovered in himself.

He and Miriam were now eating nearly all of their meals together and conducting their courtship at night, in her bed or his own. He had admitted his love for her, as she had confessed hers for him, and soon the other members of their geological team and the residents of their buildings were asking them both when they intended to make a pledge. Hassan's mother was the cousin of a Mukhtar, and his father had always hoped that Hassan would also take an influential woman as a bondmate, but Pyotr could not justifiably object to Miriam, who had won her place with intelligence and hard work. In any event, by the time he finally told his father that he loved Miriam enough to join his life to hers, their mind-tour would have secured their status here. Pyotr could take pride in knowing that a grandchild of his would be born on the Islands, that his descendants might one day be among those who would live on Venus.

That was something else *The Dream of Venus* had roused inside Hassan. He had come here thinking only of doing his best not to disgrace his family. Now the dream of Venus had begun to flower in him.

◆

"We think that the Project has no true ethical dilemmas," Miriam was saying, "that it can't possibly be wrong to terraform a dead world. We're not displacing any life-forms, we're not destroying another culture and replacing it with our own. But there is a kind of arrogance involved, don't you think?"

Hassan and Miriam were sitting on a bench outside a greenhouse near Island Two's primary school. They often came here after last light, when the children had left and the grounds adjoining the school were still and silent.

"Arrogance?" Hassan asked. "I suppose there is, in a way." He had engaged in such discussions before, at university, and it had been natural for him and Miriam to talk about the issues the Project raised while working on *The Dream of Venus*. Lately, their conversations had taken on more intensity.

"God gave us nature to use, as long as we use it wisely and with concern for other life-forms," Miriam said, repeating the conventional view promulgated by both the true faith of Islam and the Council of Mukhtars. "Terraforming Venus is therefore justified, since the measure of value is determined by the needs of human beings. And if you want to strengthen that argument, you can throw in the fact that we're bringing life to a world where no life existed, which has to be rated as a good. On top of that, there's the possibility that Venus was once much like Earth before a runaway greenhouse effect did it in, so to speak. Therefore, we're restoring the planet to what it might have been."

Hassan, still holding her hand, was silent; the assertions were much too familiar for him to feel any need to respond. He was looking for an opening in which to bring up a subject he could no longer avoid. *The Dream of Venus* was close to completion, and there was little time for them to do the editing and make the revisions that were necessary if their mind-tour was to be approved for distribution by the Administrators and the Project Council. He did not want to think of how much credit he and Miriam might already have cost the Project. All of that credit, and more—perhaps much more— would be recovered by the mind-tour; he was confident of that. But he had broached the need for editing to Miriam only indirectly so far.

"You could argue that all of life, not just human life and what furthers its ends, has intrinsic value," Miriam continued, "but that wouldn't count against the Project, only against forcing Venus to be a replica of Earth even if it later shows signs of developing its own distinct ecology in ways that differ from Earth's and which make it less habitable—or not habitable at all—by human beings. You could say that we should have abandoned our technology long ago and lived in accordance with nature, therefore never having the means to terraform a world, but that has always been an extremist view."

"And unconstructive," Hassan said. At this point, he thought, humankind would only do more damage to Earth by abandoning advanced technology; solar power satellites and orbiting industrial facilities had done much to lessen the environmental damage done to their home world.

"What I worry about now," she said, "isn't just what terraforming might do to Venus that we can't foresee, but what it might do to us. Remaking a planet may only feed our arrogance. It could lead us to think we could do almost anything. It could keep us from asking questions we should be asking. We might begin to believe that we could remake anything—the entire solar system, even our sun, to serve our ends. We might destroy what we should be preserving, and end by destroying ourselves."

"Or transforming ourselves," Hassan interjected. "You haven't made much of an argument, my love."

"I'm saying that we should be cautious. I'm saying that, whatever we do, doubt should be part of the equation, not an arrogance that could become a destructive illusion of certainty."

Those feelings, he knew, lay at the heart of their mind-tour. Uncertainty and doubt were the instruments through which finite beings had to explore their universe. The doubts, the knowledge that every gain meant some sort of loss—all of that underlined *The Dream of Venus* and lent their depiction its beauty.

And all of that would make their mind-tour unacceptable to the men and women who wanted a sensory experience that would glorify their Project and produce feelings of triumph and pride.

"Miriam," he said, trying to think of how to cajole her into considering the changes they would have to make, "I believe we should start thinking seriously about how we might revise—how we might make some necessary edits in our mind-tour."

"There's hardly any editing we have to do now."

"I meant when it's done."

"But it's almost done now. It's not going to be much different in final form."

"I mean—" Hassan was having a difficult time finding the right words to make his point. "You realize that we'll have to dwell less on the fascination of Venus past and put more emphasis on the glory that will be our transformed Venus of the future."

She stared at him with the blank gaze of someone who did not understand what he was saying, someone who might have been talking to a stranger. "You can't mean that," she said. "You can't be saying what it sounds like you're saying."

"I only meant—"

She jerked her hand from his. "I thought we shared this vision, Hassan. I thought we were both after the same effect, the same end, that you—"

"There you are." Muhammad Sheridan was coming toward them along the stone path that ran past the school. "I thought I would find you two here." He came to a halt in front of them. "I would have left you a message, but . . ." He paused. "Administrator Pavel is exceedingly anxious to view your mind-tour, so I hope it's close to completion."

Hassan was puzzled. "He wants to view it?"

"Immediately," Muhammad replied. "I mean tomorrow, two hours after first light. He has also invited you both to be present, in his private quarters, and I told him that I would be happy to tell you that in person."

Hassan could not read his friend's expression in the soft silvery light. Anticipation? Nervousness? Muhammad, who had recommended Hassan as a mind-tour creator, would be thinking that a mind-tour that won Pavel's approval might gain Muhammad more favor, while a failure would only make Pavel doubt his aide's judgment.

"It should be in final form within a month," Hassan said. "We're within the deadline still, but it needs more refining. Couldn't we—"

"Of course we'll be there," Miriam said. "I think he'll be pleased." There was no trace of doubt in her voice. Hassan glanced at her; she took his hand. "I want him to experience what we've done."

Hassan felt queasy, trying to imagine what Pavel Gvishiani would think of *The Dream of Venus*, searching his mind for an excuse he might offer to delay the Administrator's viewing of the mind-tour. Pavel might have viewed it at any time; as an Administrator and a Linker, he could have accessed the work-in-progress anytime he wished through the Island cyberminds. But Hassan had simply assumed that Pavel would be too preoccupied with his many other duties to bother.

"Well." Hassan let go of Miriam's hand and rested his hands on his thighs. "Presumably he understands that it's not in final form."

"Close to it," Miriam said in her hard, toneless voice. "Might need a little tweaking, but I don't see much room for improvement."

"And," Hassan went on, "I don't know why he wants us both there, in his room."

"It's a matter of courtesy," Muhammad said. "Pavel is most attentive to courtesies."

Hassan peered at Miriam from the sides of his eyes; she was smiling. "If you think about it," she said, "it's kind of an honor, being invited to his private quarters and all."

Hassan's queasiness left him, to be replaced with a feeling of dread.

●

The forty minutes of sitting with Pavel Gvishiani in his room, waiting as the Linker experienced the mind-tour, were passing too slowly and also too rapidly for Hassan; too slowly, so that he had ample time to consider the likely verdict the Administrator would render, and too rapidly, toward the moment of judgment and disgrace. While he waited, Hassan fidgeted on his cushion, glanced around the small room, and studied the few objects Pavel had placed on one shelf—a cloisonné plate, gold bands for securing a man's ceremonial headdress, a porcelain vase holding one blue glass flower.

Pavel, sitting on his cushion, was still. Occasionally, his eyelids fluttered over his half-open eyes. He wore no band: with his Link, he did not need a band to view the mind-tour.

I will think of the worst that can happen to me, Hassan thought as he stared at the tiny diamondlike gem on Pavel's forehead, and then whatever does happen won't seem so bad. Pavel and the Administrators would make him reimburse the credit the Project had allocated to him during his work on *The Dream of Venus*. He could afford that, but his family would regard it as a mark against him. His public record would note that he had failed at this particular task; that humiliation would remain with him until he could balance it with some successes. His father, after using his influence to get Hassan a position with the Project, would be tainted by his son's failure and was likely to find a way to get back at him for that, perhaps even by publicly severing all ties with him. Muhammad, who had recommended him to Pavel, would no longer be his friend. And Miriam—

He glanced at the woman he had come to believe he loved. Her eyes shifted uneasily; she was frowning. He felt suddenly angry with her for drawing him so deeply into her vision, for that was what she had done; she had seduced him with her inspiration. Maybe she was finally coming to understand that their mind-tour was not going to win Pavel's approval. If they were lucky, he might settle for castigating them harshly and demanding a host of revisions. If they were unlucky, he might regard their failure to give him what he had wanted as a personal affront.

Pavel opened his eyes fully and gazed directly at them, then arched his thick brows. "Both of you," he said quietly, "have produced something I did not expect." He paused, allowing Hassan a moment to collect himself. "Your mind-tour is a masterpiece. I would almost call it a work of art."

Miriam's chest heaved as she sighed. "Thank you, Administrator Pavel," she whispered. Hassan, bewildered, could not find his own voice.

"But of course we cannot distribute *The Dream of Venus* in this form," Pavel continued, "and I am sure you both understand why we can't. You still have a month of your allotted time left. I expect to see an edited mind-tour by the end of that time and, depending on what you've accomplished by then, I can grant you more time if that's required. I won't insult your intelligence and artistry by telling you exactly what kind of changes you'll have to make, and I am no expert on designing mind-tours in any case. You know what you will have to do, and I am certain, God willing, that you'll find satisfactory ways to do it."

May the Prophet be forever blessed, Hassan thought, almost dizzy with this unexpected mercy. "Of course," he said. "I already have some ideas—"

"No," Miriam said.

Pavel's eyes widened. Hassan gazed at the woman who was so trapped in her delusions, wondering if she had gone mad.

"No," Miriam said again, "I won't do it. You said yourself that it was a masterpiece, but I knew that before we came here. You can do what you like with *The Dream of Venus*, but I won't be a party to defacing my own work."

"Miriam," Hassan said weakly, then turned toward Pavel. "She doesn't know what she's saying."

"I know exactly what I'm saying. Edit our mind-tour however you please, but I'll have nothing to do with it."

"My dear child," Pavel said in an oddly gentle tone, "you know what this will mean. You know what the consequences may be."

Miriam stuck out her chin. "I know. I don't care. I'll still have the joy and satisfaction in knowing what we were able to realize in that mind-tour, and you can't take that away from us." She regarded Hassan with her hard gray eyes. Hassan realized then that she expected him to stand with her, to refuse to do the Administrator's bidding.

"Miriam," he said softly. You bitch, he thought, Pavel's given us a way out and you refuse to take it. "I'll begin work on the editing," Hassan continued, "even if my colleague won't. Maybe once she sees how that's going, realizes that we can accomplish what's needed without doing violence to our creation, she'll change her mind and decide to help me." He had to defend her somehow, give her the chance to reconsider and step back from the abyss. "I'm sure Miriam just needs some time to think it over."

Miriam said, "I won't change my mind," and he heard the disillusionment and disgust in her voice. She got to her feet; Pavel lifted his head to look up at her. "Salaam aleikum, Administrator."

"If you leave now, there will be severe consequences," Pavel said, sounding regretful.

"I know," Miriam said, and left the room.

◆

Hassan found himself able to complete the editing and revision of *The Dream of Venus* a few days before Pavel was to view the mind-tour again. This time, he went to the Administrator's quarters with more confidence and less fear. The mind-tour now evoked the pride in the terraforming of Venus and the sense of mastery and triumph that the Project Council desired, and Hassan was not surprised when Pavel praised his work and assured him that *The Dream of Venus* would become a memorable and treasured experience for a great many people.

Hassan had done his best to keep some of Miriam's most pleasing scenes and effects, although he had cut some of the more haunting landscapes of early Venus and the brooding, dark scenes that seemed to deny any true permanence to humankind's efforts. It was also necessary to add more of the required scenes of the Project's current state and recent progress. He had tried not to dwell on the fact that his editing and his additions were robbing the mind-tour of much of its beauty, were taking an experience suffused with the doubt and ambiguity that had made *The Dream of Venus* unique and turning it into a more superficial and trite experience.

In any case, Hassan knew, the merit of the mind-tour did not lie in what he thought of it, but in how Pavel Gvishiani and the other Administrators judged it, and they believed that he had made it into a work that would bring more credit to and support for the Venus Project, as well as the approval of the Mukhtars.

Miriam, with reprimands and black marks now a part of her record, and a debt to the Project that would drain her accounts of credit, had been advised by a Counselor to resign from the Project, advice that was the equivalent of a command. Within days after the Project Council had approved *The Dream of Venus* in its final form, which had required a bit more editing, Miriam Lucea-Noyes was ready to leave for Earth.

Hassan knew that it might be better not to say farewell to her in person. That would only evoke painful memories of their brief time together, and it could hardly help him to be seen with a woman who was in such disgrace. But he had dreamed of sharing his life with her once, and could not simply let her go with only a message from him to mark her departure. He owed her more than that.

On the day Miriam was scheduled to leave, Hassan met her in front of the entrance to her building. She looked surprised to see him, even though his last message to her had said that he would be waiting for her there and would walk with her to the airship bay.

"You didn't have to come," she said.

"I wanted to see you once more." He took her duffel from her and hoisted it to his shoulder.

They walked along the white-tiled path that led away from the workers' residence where they had passed so many hours together. There, at the side of one wing of the building, was the courtyard in which they had so often sat while talking of their work and their families and their hopes for a future together. They passed a small flower garden bordered by shrubs, the same garden where he had first tentatively hinted that he might seek a lasting commitment from her, and then they strolled by another courtyard, dotted with tables and chairs, where they had occasionally dined. Perhaps Miriam would suffer less by leaving the Island than he would by staying. Wherever she ended up, she would be able to go about her business without inevitably finding herself in a place that would evoke memories of him, while he would have constant reminders of her.

"Have you any idea of what you'll be doing?" he asked.

"I've got passage to Vancouver," she said. "The expense of sending me there will be added to what I owe the Project, and my new job won't amount to much, but at least I'll be near my family."

If her family were willing to welcome her back, they were showing more forbearance under the circumstances than his own clan would have done. As for her new work, he was not sure that he wanted to know much about it. Her training and education would not be allowed to go to waste, but a disgraced person with a large debt to pay off was not likely to be offered any truly desirable opportunities. If Miriam was lucky, she might have secured a post teaching geology at a second-rate college; if she was less fortunate, she might be going back to a position as a rock hound, one of those who trained apprentice miners bound for the few asteroids that had been brought into Earth orbit to be stripped of needed ores and minerals.

"Don't look so unhappy," Miriam said then. "I'll get by. I decided to accept a job with a team of assayers near Vancouver. It's tedious, boring work, but I might look up a few of my old associates in the mind-tour trade and see if I can get any side jobs going for myself there. At least a couple of them won't hold my black marks against me."

"Administrator Pavel was very pleased with the editing of *The Dream of Venus*," Hassan said, suddenly wanting to justify himself.

"So I heard."

"If you should ever care to view the new version—"

"Never." She halted and looked up at him. "I have to ask you this, Hassan. Did you preserve our original mind-tour in your personal records? Did you keep it for yourself?"

"Did I keep it?" He shifted her duffel from his left shoulder to his right. "Of course not."

"You might have done that much. I thought that maybe you would."

"But there's no point in keeping something like that. I mean, the revised version is the one that will be made available to viewers, so there's no reason for me to keep an earlier version. Besides, if others were to find out that I had such an unauthorized mind-tour in my personal files, they might wonder.

It might look as though I secretly disagreed with Pavel's directive. That wouldn't do me any good."

"Yes, I suppose that's true," Miriam said. "You certainly don't want people thinking less of you now that you've won the Administrator's respect."

Her sardonic tone wounded him just a little. "I don't suppose that you kept a record of the original version," he said.

"I didn't even try. I guessed that my Counselor might go rooting around in my files to see if they held anything questionable, and would advise me to delete anything inappropriate, and I don't need any more trouble." She smiled, and the smile seemed to come from deep inside her, as though she had accepted her hard lot and was content. "Let's just say that the original may not have been completely lost. I have hopes that it will be safe, and appreciated. I don't think you want to know any more than that."

"Miriam," he said.

"You know, I never could stand long dragged out farewells." She reached for her duffel and wrested it from his grip. "You can leave me here. You don't have to come to the airship bay with me. Good-bye, Hassan."

"Go with God, Miriam."

She walked away from him. He was about to follow her, then turned toward the path that would take him to his residence.

☙

During the years that followed, Hassan did not try to discover what had become of Miriam. Better, he thought, not to trouble himself with thoughts of his former love. His success with the altered mind-tour had cemented his friendship with Muhammad, increased the esteem his fellow geologists had for him, and had brought him more respect from his family on Earth.

Within five years after the release of *The Dream of Venus*, Hassan was the head of a team of geologists, was sometimes assigned to the pleasant task of creating educational mind-tours for Island children, and had taken a bond-mate, Zulaika Jehan. Zulaika came from a Mukhtar's family, had been trained as an engineer, and had an exemplary record. If Hassan sometimes found himself looking into Zulaika's brown eyes and remembering Miriam's gray ones, he always reminded himself that his bondmate was exactly the sort of woman his family had wanted him to wed, that his father had always claimed that marrying for love was an outworn practice inherited from the decadent and exhausted West and best discarded, and that taking Miriam as a bond-mate would only have brought him disaster.

Occasionally, Hassan heard rumors of various mind-tours passed along through private channels from one Linker on the Islands to another, experiences that might be violent, frightening, pornographic, or simply subversive. He had always strongly suspected, even though no one would have admitted it openly, that his father and other privileged people in his clan had enjoyed such forbidden entertainments, most of which would find their way to the masses only in edited form. It would be a simple matter for any Linker to preserve such productions and to send them on to friends through private channels inaccessible to those who had no Links. Hassan did not dwell on such thoughts, which might lead to disturbing reflections on the ways in which the powerful maintained control of the net of cyberminds so as to shape even the thoughts and feelings of the powerless.

One rumor in particular had elicited his attention a rumor of a mind-tour about the Venus Project that far surpassed any of the usual cliché-ridden productions, that was even superior to the much-admired *The Dream of Venus*. He had toyed with the notion that someone might have come upon an unedited copy of *The Dream of Venus*, that the mind-tour he and Miriam had created might still exist as she had hoped it would, a ghost traveling through the channels of the cyberminds, coming to life again and weaving its spell before vanishing once more.

He did not glimpse the possible truth of the matter until he was invited to a reception Pavel Gvishiani was holding for a few specialists who had earned commendations for their work. Simply putting the commendations into the public record would have been enough, but Pavel had decided that a celebration was in order. Tea, cakes, small pastries, and meat dumplings were set out on tables in a courtyard near the Administrators' ziggurat. Hassan, with his bondmate Zulaika Jehan at his side, drew himself up proudly as Administrator Pavel circulated among his guests in his formal white robe, his trusted aide Muhammad Sheridan at his side.

At last Pavel approached Hassan and touched his forehead in greeting. "Salaam, Linker Pavel," Hassan said.

"Greetings, Hassan." Pavel pressed his fingers against his forehead again. "Salaam, Zulaika," he murmured to Hassan's bondmate; Hassan wondered if Pavel had actually recalled her name or had only been prompted by his Link. "You must be quite proud of your bondmate," Pavel went on. "I am certain, God willing, that this will be only the first of several commendations for his skill in managing his team."

"Thank you, Linker Pavel," Zulaika said in her soft musical voice.

Pavel turned to Hassan. "And I suspect that it won't be long before you win another commendation for the credit you have brought to the Project."

"You are too kind," Hassan said. "One commendation is more than enough, Linker Pavel. I am unworthy of another."

"I must beg to contradict you, Hassan. *The Dream of Venus* has been one of our most successful and popular entertainments." A strange look came into Pavel's dark eyes then; he stared at Hassan for a long time until his sharp gaze made Hassan uneasy. "You did what you had to do, of course, as did I," he said, so softly that Hassan could barely hear him, "yet that first vision I saw was indeed a work of art, and worthy of preservation." Then the Administrator was gone, moving away from Hassan to greet another of his guests.

Perhaps the Administrator's flattery had disoriented him, or possibly the wine Muhammad had surreptitiously slipped into his cup had unhinged him a little, but it was not until he was leaving the reception with Zulaika, walking along another path where he had so often walked with Miriam, that the truth finally came to him and he understood what Pavel had been telling him.

Their original mind-tour might be where it would be safe and appreciated; Miriam had admitted that much to him. Now he imagined her, with nothing to lose, going to Pavel and begging him to preserve their unedited creation;

the Administrator might have taken pity on her and given in to her pleas. Or perhaps it had not been that way at all; Pavel might have gone to her and shown his esteem for her as an artist by promising to keep her original work alive. It did not matter how it had happened, and he knew that he would never have the temerity to go to Pavel and ask him exactly what he had done. Hassan might have the Linker's public praise, but Miriam, he knew now, had won the Linker's respect by refusing to betray her vision.

Shame filled him at the thought of what he had done to *The Dream of Venus*, and then it passed; the authentic dream, after all, was still alive. Dreams had clashed, he knew, and only one would prevail. But how would it win out? It would be the victory of one idea, as expressed in the final outcome of the Project, overlaid upon opposed realities that could not be wished away. To his surprise, these thoughts filled him with a calm, deep pleasure he had rarely felt in his life, and *The Dream of Venus* was alive again inside him for one brief moment of joy before he let it go.

At Tide's Turning

LAURA J. MIXON

A graduate of the 1981 Clarion writer's workshop, Laura J. Mixon has worked as a chemical engineer in polymer research, a Peace Corps volunteer in East Africa, and a corporate VP for a New York–based financial and energy trading corporation. Her short fiction has appeared in Analog, Asimov's, Wild Cards, *and elsewhere. Her books include the novels* Glass Houses, Astropilots, Greenwar *(in collaboration with Steven Gould), and, most recently,* Proxies. *Upcoming is a major new terraforming novel, related to her story in this anthology, called* Burning the Ice. *She lives in Albuquerque, New Mexico, with her husband, author Steven Gould, two children, a dog, three guinea pigs, and assorted tropical fish.*

Here's a powerful and eloquent study of technologists in a race with death, who must push on with terraforming an icy world at any price if they want to stay alive. In such life-and-death circumstances, under such extreme pressure, family relationships may come to seem unimportant, almost an unwelcome distraction. Until someone's trapped and dying in the dark, that is. . . .

> "People can't die along the coast except when the tide's pretty nigh out. They can't be born unless it's pretty nigh in—not properly born till flood. He's a-going out with the tide. . . . If he lives till it turns, he'll hold his own till past the flood, and go out with the next tide."
>
> —Mr. Peggoty to David Copperfield,
> from *David Copperfield* by Charles Dickens (1850)

After breakfast that morning, Manda CarliPablo headed to her work chamber to check her marine-waldos' night's work. The chamber was an ugly, rock-hewn room with fluorescent lighting and a thatch floor, with what looked like a hiker's daypack hanging from a rod in the room's center that rode across a wire web suspended just below the rough ceiling.

Decked out in her livesuit and -hood, Manda hooked the livepack onto her yoke's leads, slipped on the pack's straps, and then buckled it around her chest. Her liveface appeared before her as she did so, rendered on her retinas by lasers built into the specs set in her livemask. Glamour filled the room, a glowing sphere that defined her projection pod, and a host of 3-D icons appeared: shiny, translucent satellites locked in Manda-static orbit.

First Manda touched her communications-cube, and it expanded into a thicket of geometric shapes. She checked her mail and messages. LuisMichael hadn't sent her his new seismic data yet. So she folded the commcube up and started calling up her marine-waldo data. It blossomed around her in glistening bouquets and thickets of numbers, charts, and graphic landscapes, and she began to sort it all. Her handcrafted fleet of eight marine-waldos, the *Aculeus* series, collected a lot of information, and she had a lot of data to get through since she had taken the evening off yesterday.

But it wasn't long before fingers of cold seeped in, disrupting her concentration. Beneath all the protective layers Manda had on—layers of plastic, organic, and metallic fibers, one after another till she could scarcely bend elbow or knee—she shivered, nicking virtual icons with cold-clumsy hands and elbows. Data strands fragmented and cascaded around her down the inner boundaries of the projection pod like ice crystals flung by a storm.

"Shit."

With a sigh, suppressing both her frustration and the shivers, she recovered the data, reconstructed it, and started again—dancing her marine-waldo control dance, working her fingers, arms, legs, and torso to guide her fleet of machines across the dark, cold floor of the ocean, to read its secrets with their instruments.

She was the colony's best waldo pilot. The best. Amid the billions back on Earth, how could any single human presume to be the best at anything? For that, at least, she was glad to be one of the handful who lived on this freezing, barren world. She hadn't lost a machine yet, in almost six seasons of piloting in some extremely dangerous environments.

Manda's siblings Arlene and Derek, the oldest set of twins of the CarliPablo nineclone, had suggested the ocean search project to Manda, while they and the rest of the clone geared up on Project IceFlame. Whatever secrets lay beneath Brimstone's icy crust had stayed hidden ever since the colony's inception eighteen seasons before. They knew little about this world they inhabited: Brimstone, the biggest moon of the gas giant Fire.

When Derek and Arlene had suggested it, the assignment had seemed ideal. Manda hadn't been especially interested in attempting a collaboration with the rest of her much more experienced, tightly-knit sibling group—even if it would have put her at the controls of the winged waldos that would shortly be strafing the methane-laced ice at the poles, putting carbon dioxide and methane into the air to start a cascade of global warming and make this moon more than marginally habitable.

But was this really any better? All she was finding down in the ocean depths was dark and cold, and she'd had her fill of those. At least her prior assignments—flying the jet-waldos up to the poles, and using land-explorer equipment to take ice and air samples there—had turned up interesting data to analyze. Even her first assignment, driving an archaic and clumsy tractor-waldo across the rotten tropical ice floes, struggling to avoid being thrown into the brine by Brimstone's violent and chaotic tides while mapping the myriad island chains down there, beat this endless, oppressive nothingness.

She was a woman of planetshine, of air currents and ice fog and indigo sky. Out in the harsh, rock-cold winds—in air so thin that a brief walk *in corpus* left her panting and so frigid it burned the sinuses even through her fur-lined parka hood and nasal filters—the cold didn't bother her quite so much. In her aerial and terrestrial waldos she could outrun it . . . or so she pretended. Down here in the ocean there was nowhere to run. The chill pressed in all about. Thousands of tons of water and ice lay overhead. Even the sounds were oppressive, the gut-deep groans of shifting floes carried to

Manda's detectors across thousands of kilometers of gelid liquid: groans as deep and determined and agonized as those she'd heard some anonymous woman in labor make once, in a medical documentary. As if the world itself were trying to give birth.

And the dark, too, oppressed. Her fleet of marine-waldos had computer-enhanced vision; their visuals swirled with falsecolor images. But it was all unreal, no different than the hallucinations that swarmed behind her eyelids while she lay alone in bed at night—shivering, sweating—knowing nobody gave a fuck about her and she was going to die.

Her chest had grown constricted; through the pores of her livemask she gasped for air. With a pirouette that bordered on panic and a set of finger flicks on the translucent control icons that orbited her, Manda retreated from the waldo she rode—she wadded the whole thing up, shrinking its inputs till it was merely a shining ball of reduced data in her hands, and set it loose to float amid the other balls of compressed data at waist level. This took only a second to do. Then, with a word or two, she adjusted the livesuit settings, and bent over till the pressure eased.

Nerves, that's all, she told herself. She touched a different waldo's commandshape and the dodecahedron grew till it swallowed her, infusing her with its sensate data.

Maybe, she thought, calmer now, as a current lifted her marine-waldo, *Aculeus Quinque,* over a rise blanketed in faint, neon-green rocks—as she scanned the ocean floor with infrared skin-sense and magnified-light eyes and sonar ears, as she tasted the ocean currents with her waldo's thermocouples and chemical composition detectors—*maybe it really is time for a job change.* Moss or bamboo harvesting, polar duty—judah shit, even baby-tending—would be better than this endless, oppressive dark. (Okay—maybe not baby-tending.) Maybe Teresa was right and she should join the terraforming effort.

But if there really were vents down here, it'd change everything. All this work would have been worth it. She just didn't know if she could keep at it much longer. The work made her feel cold—oppressed—even more isolated than she already was.

It slowly dawned on her that she shouldn't be this cold—not *this* cold. She minimized the commandball again and then disconnected herself from the livepack that hung suspended in the middle of her projection pod. All her command-; program-, and databalls shrank, flattened, and moved toward the center of her vision, and the hazy boundaries of the light-sphere that defined her projection pod vanished.

Her older twins, Teresa and Paul, the youngest pair of the CarliPablo clone after Manda, passed by the doorway as Manda pulled off her livemask and tam.

Teresa and Paul were both tall and muscular, with smooth, almond-dark skin and yellow-green eyes, and kinky, ginger-blond hair—their faces and bodies an identical, exotic mix of African and Scandinavian features. The bristles of Paul's short hair stuck up through the mesh of his livehood; Teresa's hair was longer, pulled back in a severe ponytail pressed flat under the translucent mesh of hers. Otherwise they were the exact image of each other—and of Manda too, other than the eight seasons of age they had acquired that Manda hadn't yet. Their livesuits, or what she could see of them, protruding from the sleeves and necks of their cable-knit sweaters, glistened on the backs of their hands and on their cheeks and foreheads like a film of mother-of-pearl.

"Talking to yourself again?" Teresa asked with an arch smile. Manda realized she'd been vocalizing her unhappiness. And as usual, Teresa's teasing stung, probably more than she intended it to. It resonated with insults others had leveled at Manda recently, implying that there was something wrong with her for being a singleton. As if it were her fault somehow that her brother had died shortly before they were scheduled to be decanted, twenty-one seasons, or Earth-years, ago.

"I'm trying to work. Leave me alone."

Teresa's expression went flat and angry. Paul pointed a finger in Manda's face. "Lay off my sister."

He followed his vat-twin away.

"She's my sister, too, asshole," Manda said to his back. Then regretted her testiness. *Warm it up a degree or two, Manda. Your clone is just about the only friend you've got.*

This irritable back-and-forth between her and Teresa-and-Paul was a stupid pattern, but one Manda seemed helpless to change. From childhood, when Teresa and Paul were adolescents and Manda was "the baby," they'd always fought too damn much. Teresa was always provoking her, scolding or teasing—and Manda usually insulted her in response. Which invariably brought Paul to Teresa's defense.

Round and round we go, Manda thought. She'd have to apologize later.

Manda watched Paul catch up with Teresa, down the corridor: watched them walk away, fingers loosely interlaced.

Vat-mates. Rarely apart. Always there, an extension of each other—a remote limb, another self—since before awareness stirred in their cerebral cortices, before their nerve endings began to form and send signals to their nascent brains.

Self and other: the boundaries blurred, between clone siblings. Especially you and your vat-mate. Your vat-mate was part of you. When one died, the other committed suicide shortly thereafter. Almost without exception. No point in going on, when half of yourself had been amputated.

Or so she'd been told. Manda wouldn't know. Her vat-mate had died as a fetus, shortly before they were scheduled to be decanted, twenty-one seasons ago, as they'd neared this solar system. An accident; equipment failure or something.

This kind of thing happened a lot. All the machines were ancient, built back on Earth long ago. And even though they'd been designed for longevity in severe environments, and even though Manda's people had learned how to fix just about anything, entropy always took its cut. It was pure luck that Manda herself survived.

She remembered none of it, naturally. She'd always been alone. She was used to it.

She smiled at the retreating figures. *You'll never know the freedom of being a single,* she thought. Except that it wasn't joy that coursed through her now, but a bolt of fierce hatred, as she watched their casual closeness: so much a part of their world they would never even know enough to take it for granted.

A wave of nauseated guilt followed. Without her clone, she had nothing. Teresa, especially: she was the only one who'd ever stuck up for Manda, when the other kids had tormented her for being a single. (And then turned around and demanded to know what Manda had done to provoke them—but hey, it was more than anyone else had ever done.)

Then Manda noticed the rock wall, which was beaded with frozen condensate.

Frozen?

The readout above the thermostat on the wall read two degrees Celsius; that couldn't be right. Striding over to the wall, she ripped off a fleece-lined shell and nylomir mitten and her liveglove and touched the wall's white, chalky surface with her bare left hand. Ice cold. Sticky-cold, as the sweat from her fingertips froze. More like minus fifteen. The heaters had failed, again. No wonder she was so cold.

With a sigh of disgust Manda recoiled her short, frizzy braid. She pulled the cool, slick-soft mesh of the livehood down over her head and face again, dragged the tam's cuff down over her ears, and plugged back into the livepack. The large sphere of soft light reappeared around her. With her right, swathed hand she stabbed at a shiny icon that now hovered at shoulder height, which solidified as she focused her sight on it.

"*Damn* you, ObediahUrsula!" she snapped at the young, round face that materialized. "I can't work with the heaters failing all the time."

ObediahUrsula's brow puckered and his eyes widened. So young. What was a child doing, in charge of something as critical as the heaters?

"It's, it's just that the thermostats are—"

The words darted out of Manda's mouth in explosive puffs, like little ice daggers. "Don't. Give. Me. Another *fucking* sob story about equipment breakdown. Just fix it. If I lose a waldo, I'm going to put your name down as the cause."

She stabbed the comm icon off in the midst of his reply, and rubbed her hands over her painfully spasming stomach. A knot in her throat formed, swelled, threatened to burst.

"Goddammit." She swallowed the knot, washed it down with a dose of anger. "Damn it to hell."

Someone passing by in the corridor glanced in at her and shook his head in disapproval. PabloJebediah: one of Jack and Amadeo's younger sibs. Jack and Amadeo, along with Arlene and Derek and the senior twins or triplets of three other clones, ran Amaterasu's governing council. And, Manda remembered belatedly, PabloJebediah and ObediahUrsula were closely allied. Manda had probably just disrupted some sort of delicate, interclone power balance, or given Derek and Arlene some kind of coup-related headache. Too bad. She glared at him until he went away, then pulled her livehood back over her head, adjusted her specs and mic, and hooked back into her livepack. Her data- and commandballs reappeared, within the confines of her sphere of light.

All right, she admitted to herself. *It isn't ObediahUrsula's fault the heating systems are failing. But if I didn't yell about it nothing would get done, and we'd all freeze to death.*

She reconsidered and started to disconnect; she needed to calm down. She couldn't work when she was this upset. But a glimmer in one of the dataglobes at waist level caught her eye. Probably nothing—another false alarm; *Aculeus Septimus's* visuals might need calibrating again.

Or.

Maybe this time it was the hydrothermal vent she was looking for. The place where, if this frozen, forsaken pissball of a world had any remnants of life left, it would probably be.

Yeah, right. Shaking her head at her own optimism, Manda reached out for the little sphere, which showed a snippet of ocean floor with a bit of flickering red in it.

●

She spent the rest of the first-watch work shift trying to figure out what was going on with *Aculeus Septimus.* Hours—and countless tedious cross-checks and equipment calibrations—later, as she'd expected, the temperature anomaly turned out to be a false reading. *Aculeus Septimus,* which had reported the last two anomalies, was malfunctioning again. Time to haul it in for a tune-up. *Or better yet,* she thought irritably, putting away her icons, *maybe I'll just junk it.*

●

Manda had her own little space, separate from the rest of her clone. It wasn't supposed to be like that but she'd held out against all the recriminations and insinuations, back when, and eventually people had stopped making a fuss about it. She woke up from her first-watch sleep to find Paul and Teresa at the craggy entrance to her nook.

"Lights up," she said, sitting. A bulb burned out with a flash and a pop. Manda swore. Finding a replacement was going to be tough. She wrapped the fur about herself and eyed her older siblings in the dim light. "What's going on?"

Paul held out a data crystal, which she took. "Here's some stuff Arlene wanted you to look over," he said. "Inventory and loading schedules for Project IceFlame," Teresa added. Manda was going to be their primary co-ordinator Amaterasu-side, once the terraforming team headed for the poles. Paul said, "They'll need you in Stores tomorrow, to double-check everything."

"All right." She stood and tucked the crystal into a pocket of her pullover, which hung on a hook by the head of her sleeping mat.

But the data could just as easily have been transmitted online. Something else was up.

Their gazes pressed on her back. Ignoring them, she triggered her livesuit's don-routine and stepped into the center of the suit as footprints formed in it. The livesuit rippled up her form like liquid metal. She pulled her long-johns on over it, then lowered the yoke over her head, plugged it into her livesuit, slid on her gloves, and fitted them to the sleeves' leads. Finally she turned with an exhalation, bracing herself.

"Go ahead and break it to me," she said.

Teresa started: "We want you to—"

"—stay with us tonight," Paul finished. "For a while."

"We're holding a covalence ceremony," Teresa said. Which meant someone had a new exo-bond—a sexual pairing.

It had to be *really* important for them to be here. She'd refused to participate every single time they'd asked in the past six seasons, since her disastrous experience with JebediahMarshall. Curiosity overcame her initial impulse to simply refuse and kick them out.

"Who?"

Teresa and Paul exchanged a look. "JennaMara," they both replied. One of the other clones on the governing council.

Manda's eyes widened. "For real?"

"For real."

Wow. Major coup is in play, then. She started to ask, *Which ones?* Paul anticipated her. "Janice, on our side. You know Charlotte?" Manda shook her head. She didn't really know JennaMara, except for its prime, Lawrence. He was okay.

Manda worried a hangnail. "How is Farrah?" Farrah was Janice's vat-twin.

"She's dealing with it," Paul said, tersely.

About six seasons ago there'd been a pairing between Teresa and a ByronMichael. It had been really hard on Paul. The exo-bond had been Teresa's first—and only—serious one. All his anxiety and anger over it Paul had taken out on Manda when she'd refused participate in the covalence ceremony.

Teresa had somehow gotten Manda off the hook with ByronMichael and Paul, and the exo-bond with ByronMichael had eventually dissolved. But Teresa had extracted a promise from Manda to attend the next covalence she asked her to, and Manda had agreed. Until now, Teresa had been careful to avoid calling Manda on it—which had only increased Manda's indebtedness to her.

"I hate this," Manda said. She couldn't get away with a flat refusal. Still, it was worth a try. She gave Teresa a pleading look. "Can't you—"

"No." Teresa's tone was sharp. "Charlotte has asked for you."

Manda was surprised. "She did?" Paul and Teresa both nodded. "Why?"

"We don't know," Teresa replied, "but JennaMara wanted us *all* to be there."

"JennaMara really put its coup on the line for IceFlame," Paul added.

"So that's what this is about."

Paul frowned. "It's not just that. Don't be so fucking cynical, Manda." "Janice really has a thing for Charlotte," Teresa interjected. "She needs you to help make it okay." Paul went on, "If you're there, it'll mean major coup for us. Everybody knows—"

—*how you are.* Manda heard it without him saying it, and glared, but he stared steadily back.

"And Farrah needs you," Teresa said. Paul nodded. "She's taking it hard."

"She is?" Manda felt a twinge of sympathy. It hurt—she was told—when your vat-mate took a lover. The covalence ceremonies were supposed to salve anxious feelings and resentment between the unpaired vat-siblings on each side.

She thought, *At least Farrah has a vat-mate. She doesn't give a shit about me. None of them do.*

Try not to be a bigger asshole than you can help, Paul's gaze said. And, *you owe me,* said Teresa's. *You promised.*

Manda's heart fluttered painfully. No clean way out.

It was just a formality. It wouldn't take too long. She'd participated once or twice when she was younger, before she'd worked up the nerve to refuse. And at least Janice was showing good taste.

Manda sighed heavily. "All right. This once."

Relief spread onto their identical faces. Teresa hugged her and Paul gave her shoulder a squeeze.

"Thanks," they said in unison.

"When and where?"

Paul said, "Arlene has prepared—"

"—a meeting space on the Mound," Teresa added. "See you there," they both said, and finished, as Manda opened her mouth to ask when, "at twenty-seven o'clock tonight."

➤

Manda arrived a few minutes late to the IceFlame project meeting.

"Well, this is it," Arlene was saying, as Manda entered. "The council has settled on a final launch date for the polar expedition."

The entire project team was there. Manda's clone sat in front, seven of it, not counting Arlene and Manda: three men and four women. The others were all at least eight seasons older than Manda. At sixty seasons, Arlene and Derek were the eldest. Several other clones were also present, including those who, like Manda, would be providing Amaterasu-based support.

"We ship out in eight days. I've got everyone's assignments."

An excited murmur broke out.

Eight days? Manda felt a pang of anxiety. She hadn't expected things to happen so quickly.

She seated herself next to Teresa and Paul, and listened with perhaps half an ear while Arlene went over the initial setup stages of the project. Her role in that would be minimal. The other attendees were more attentive as with an economy of word and gesture cultivated by genetics and upbringing, honed to a high gloss over decades of working together, her siblings went over each phase of the assignment with the other team members.

Project IceFlame had two main thrusts. The first, which had been going on for several seasons, was a massive drilling effort: at twenty-eight locations strategically placed around the moon's surface—primarily in the upper latitudes, where most of the Moon's carbon dioxide was stored, in deadly, smoking-cold glaciers of CO_2 and methane-hydrate ice—drills would pierce the crust and tap into the magma, creating vast fields of lava "irrigation." These would serve as the ongoing energy source to keep Brimstone's many fields of methane-hydrate deposits burning, with fleets of air-avatars controlling the intensity and spread of the burns.

During the town meeting last month, at which the colonists had debated whether to carry on with IceFlame, those opposed had pointed out the risks of piercing the Moon's crust. There was a small risk it could set off a series of major quakes that could jeopardize the colony, and a greater risk that their precautionary tamps would fail: that the terraforming fires would burn out of control, put toxic amounts of carbon dioxide into the air, or melt the ice caps to the point that Amaterasu would be inundated.

It had been decided that the risks were worth it. Their equipment was slowly breaking down around them; their population was dwindling, as dozens of colonists a year died of exposure or cold-related accidents. They needed to get out of these caves.

"Bart and Charles will give us a status report on the magma drilling," Arlene said. The middle-aged CarliPablo twins came to the front of the room.

"The first drill is scheduled—·" "—to penetrate the crust and reach magma—" "—at thirty-six o'clock tonight," they said, trading off with such natural ease that it didn't matter who was talking. "The other twenty-seven should be breaking through the crust—" "—over the next six to eight days." "Any delays in drilling will result in a delay in the polar expedition's launch."

Others raised questions and brought up technical points; the discussion continued. As Manda watched her clone siblings and the other teammates, a sour feeling settled into the base of her gut. Once they left, she'd be all alone among the others, not one of whom cared whether she lived or died.

Well, it was too late to change her mind about joining IceFlame now. Even if she'd wanted to.

$\Rightarrow$

Gift. I need a gift. That evening after her second-watch work shift, while hurrying down through the colony tunnels from her work station to the Mound, she remembered and reversed her direction. It had to be something valuable. Something with personal meaning.

At her cubby, she picked hurriedly through her few belongings, set in the niches around the small room's perimeter. Then she spotted her rock collection. Perfect. She'd gathered all sorts of interesting specimens over the years.

Manda picked up a geode she'd found once. Its crystal interior caught the light in many small, rosy prisms. She remembered how when she'd broken the egglike rock open, she'd exclaimed with delight. How could such a rough, ugly exterior hide such inner beauty? She'd spent many a time gazing at it, imagining she had discovered a tiny fairy city in its depths. She loved it.

Then there was her lichened shale. She fingered the pale, grey-green, lacy growth that covered the rock, and bits of lichen and rock flaked off onto her fingers. She rubbed her fingers together, smelled its dust: imagining the rich scent of topsoil the lichen was building, molecule by molecule.

As a child, during a stint helping the herders with their reindeer, Manda had discovered a small outcropping blanketed with the stuff. The lichen growth was a volunteer—not planted by the colonists and not expected. Everyone had gotten excited. It was one of the first indicators that their early terraforming efforts were taking hold. The geologists she'd reported her find to—LuisMichael: Jim, Brian, and Amy's two older sisters, back when they were still alive—had given her this small piece in thanks.

It was that incident as much as anything else that had filled Manda with a desire to explore this icy moon they inhabited. Though several efforts had been made to explore overland and aerially, the colony's early efforts to explore the ocean floor had ground to a halt, back when Manda was little, when the JebediahMeriwether twins had died. All kinds of wonders might await them. Even Brimstone-based life.

Manda hesitated, then put the lichened rock back onto her shelf and took the geode.

She didn't want to lose her lichen. The stuff was all over the place now, and the geode was her rarest and prettiest stone—unusual enough to buy a lot of coup, at the upcoming ceremony. But to Manda, the lichen and the memory it stood for was worth more.

☕

The Mound lay in almost the exact center of the great cavern that held Hydroponics and the bulk of the bamboo forest: the lowest inhabited level of Amaterasu.

The bamboo forest itself grew in a series of dozens of interconnected large chambers, each in different stages of growth or harvest. These crop chambers surrounded a single, vast chamber—the second biggest in all of Amaterasu, after Hydroponics—that had a naturally-formed low hill in its center.

The eco-engineers had worked hard to grow a wild meadow and tree forest there, out of the barren, metal-salt–laden dust of Brimstone. And they'd been reasonably successful. Though marred in a few places by bald or sickly patches, in the main it was a lovely spot: a big, gentle hill shot through with wandering stands of ash and birch and black spruce (albeit dwarfish and spindly compared to the majestic virtual specimens in their Earth archives), and covered with silvery, cold-resistant, drought-resistant, metal- and salt-tolerant grasses, spritzed with pink, gold, and white wildflowers (-resistant, ditto) pollinated by bees and butterflies.

The lights set way overhead created a shadowless twilight—a dim setting, which left enough light to see by but gave the nocturnal animals time to come out of their burrows, to mate and graze and collect seeds. The acoustics were excellent here: bamboo leaves whispered; birds chirped and cats yowled; distant machinery in the hydroponics and machine-shop caverns echoed their arrhythmic, dissonant clanking; the soft lowing and yipping of the domesticated animals in their stables up and down the cavern walls wove a unifying harmony for the other sounds.

In the Mound's center lay the ceremonial circle where many of the colony's major fertility and harvest rituals were held. The circle was defined by a ring of carved stalagmites and rocks. She'd been told its design harkened back to some ancient sacred places on Earth. The carvings were geometric patterns, some of them, while others sported an assortment of caricaturish faces.

From the forest's edge, Manda saw that everyone else from both clones was there: CarliPablo seated on the far end of the circle, and JennaMara, an eightclone, seated on the near side. Farrah and Janice both wore long white gowns, as did Paul and Arlene, and of Janice's clone, Lawrence's vat-mate Donald and Janice's two vat-mates: a man and a woman whose names Manda didn't know. There must have been a drawing to see who would be the main participants. Manda felt a twinge of gratitude that they had left her out of it. Her role would be minimal.

Teresa held bamboo clavés in her hands and one of Janice's younger siblings had a multireed flute. Stacks of blankets and large cloths lay around the circle, behind the main participants. Both clones had arranged themselves by age. Manda stepped between the tall stones and crossed over to where her siblings sat. As she passed around the outside of the circle, she overheard Bart and Charles whispering to Derek in excited tones, "Drill eighteen broke through, eleven hours early!" "Fourteen and one are scheduled to hit magma in the next few hours."

"Excellent," Derek replied. "Great news."

Manda pressed her hands on her stomach as another wave of anxiety hit, followed by anger at her weakness. *Stop being a wimp. You don't need them. You don't need anybody.* She just wished it were true.

"Any tremors?"

"A few small ones. Nothing serious so far." "We're keeping a close eye on things."

"Good. Good. . . ."

She passed behind Janice and Farrah, and then Paul, who spared her a rather curt nod (what had she done to anger him this time?) and sat cross-slegged at the end of the line, next to Teresa. Janice was holding Farrah's hand but looking across at Charlotte, who gazed back at her as if no one else were present. Farrah's face was stony. Manda thought, *That's not an auspicious start.*

At a glance from Arlene, Teresa started a syncopated beat on her clavés. The wooden sticks *clack-a-clack*ed a short, repeating pattern, while the JennaMara flutist played a cheerful little tune. Manda winced. JennaMara apparently didn't have much native musical ability.

Arlene, taking prime for CarliPablo, and Donald, acting as prime for JennaMara, both stood and came to the center of the circle. Arlene carried a huge, stemmed bowl of mead, and Donald carried a burning taper and a meterlong waterpipe filled with tobacco and cannabis.

Arlene held the cup up. "I—we bless the joining of Janice and Charlotte." Then she took a sip of the liquor and dabbed at her lips with a long cloth napkin she had draped over her arm. From his seated position near her, Derek mimicked her gestures in miniature, moving his lips in synchrony with her words. Manda was sure he wasn't conscious of it. None of the others ever were, either. She felt that familiar old pang of isolation.

Donald, an older man with black skin and hair and a cordial gaze, lit the ceremonial herbs and sucked on the pipe till tendrils of smoke curled upward. The air above the water in the bulb filled with smoke. He lifted the pipe. "I—we celebrate this union of JennaMara and CarliPablo." Then he inhaled deeply. After this, he ground the taper out in the dirt and then exchanged pipe for stemmed bowl with Arlene, as twin streams of smoke trickled from his nose.

"My-our thanks to CarliPablo for this drink," he said, and took a deep draught of mead from the ceremonial cup. He coughed a bit, and wiped his mouth on his sleeve.

"And my-our thanks to JennaMara for this smoke." Arlene put her lips on the mouth of the waterpipe and inhaled. Then they traded back. Donald brought the pipe of herbs over to CarliPablo while Arlene went to JennaMara with the liquor. Manda watched while Donald handed the pipe to each of her siblings. Her turn came last. Donald gave her a nod as he held out the pipe. She drew a deep breath, and coughed, as the cool, sweetish smoke scoured her throat and bronchia.

Arlene had finished sharing mead with the youngest of JennaMara, adolescent male twins perhaps fifteen seasons in age, who were avoiding meeting anyone's gaze. Manda guessed they'd never attended a covalence before; they were barely old enough. Children, for obvious reasons, weren't expected to participate.

Now Arlene came across to Manda and knelt, putting the stemmed bowl of mead to Manda's lips. Manda took a big swallow, and managed to keep from sputtering as the liquid scorched her throat.

"Thanks," Arlene whispered, as she dabbed Manda's lips. *Thanks for coming,* she meant. The remark only annoyed Manda.

What the hell am I doing here?

If only she'd had the nerve to renege on her promise to Teresa. She didn't believe in any of this mystic shit. It was a all a big lie. Nobody really cared about anybody. They just wanted her to pretend. Don't make a scene. Pretend to be like the rest.

The gift exchange came next. Manda presented her geode to the youngest JennaMara vat-twins, who thanked her nervously. One of them gave her a framed photo of a dog, and the other gave her a bamboo boothorn he'd made. She muttered thanks and tucked them into her pockets, but instead of sitting next to the young JennaMara twins, she went back over to her original spot, and ended up next to Teresa, who was chatting with her own JennaMara counterpart.

I'm acting like a nervous adolescent myself, she thought. *What's the big deal? They're certainly cute enough, and I could probably teach them a thing or two.* (Not that she was all *that* experienced.) But she didn't get up and go over.

Several more passes were made of liquor and smoke, and Manda was getting dizzy. The music seemed to be getting better. She listened for a moment. Yes. Definitely improving. But the rest of it still infuriated her. People were talking in whispers, laughing. Manda merely sat there, arms folded. The twins were eyeing her. She studiously avoided their gazes—looked instead at the glistening stalactites far overhead, and the bamboo stairways and bridges that conjoined the holes along the walls, along which distant human and animal figures moved.

Bowls of curried ox-steak with bamboo shoots were served with *mana* bread, and afterward more alcohol and smoke was dispensed. Some sweets went around. Manda relaxed a bit, and chatted with Teresa and Paul, and with the two young men, who had moved over at some point. They seemed nice enough, and eager to please. They made a big deal over the geode and asked her where she'd found it. She told them the story, and they shared anecdotes about their experiences upside.

After a while, Arlene and Donald called for everyone's attention. Janice and Charlotte came to the center and kissed each other, lingeringly. Everyone whooped and clapped. They looped strips of leather over each other's wrists. Meanwhile the other active participants stood up and came to the center as well. Everyone was a little drunk or a little high, or both, and their gaits weren't too steady—except for Farrah, who looked stone-cold sober, and a lot like she was going to explode.

I know just how you feel, Manda thought. But she didn't, really. She didn't have a vat-twin to be jealous over, and wasn't all that angry anymore. Just anxious, and—for some reason—sad.

Arlene joined Farrah's left wrist to Charlotte's right with the leather strap, saying, "CarliPablo embraces JennaMara through its member Charlotte. Share you-yourself with each of me-us as you have with one."

Donald JennaMara joined Janice's wrist to one of Charlotte's vat-mates', the male one. "JennaMara embraces CarliPablo, through its member Janice. Share you-yourself with each of me-us as you have with one."

Next Arlene gestured at Paul. "Since Janice is a two-mate and Charlotte is a three-mate, Paul has agreed to covex with Martha for CarliPablo." She joined his left wrist to the right wrist of Charlotte's female vat-mate, saying, "CarliPablo embraces JennaMara through its member Paul. I-we share ourself with you-you through you-your member Martha."

The bindings were only ritual, and fell away as Charlotte reached up to kiss Farrah. Manda watched some of the tension leave Farrah's body as she released herself to Charlotte's passion. Everyone applauded and laughed. When the kiss ended, Farrah bowed her head, dashing away tears.

With a tender smile, Charlotte put an arm around her, picked up a blanket, and led her away from the circle. Janice watched them go with an expression of relief and approval. Then she kissed her own partner, Charlotte's triplet brother, while Paul kissed Charlotte's triplet sister Martha, and both couples got much appreciative applause. They also took blankets and left the circle.

More food, mead, and smokes went around. Manda got woozy. A while later, she found her head in the lap of one of the youngest boys. His twin was stroking her thigh while the first fondled her breast, smiling down at her. A very pretty young man, whose eyes were as dark and friendly as those of Donald. Still, terror lanced her, sharp and hard as a knife blade, dispelling the pleasant ache of desire low in her belly.

Shit.

She sat up and pushed them away, and staggered to her feet. Concerned and confused faces swarmed around her—*what's wrong? are you okay?*—as, swearing, she stumbled out of the stone circle and off into the bamboo forest.

Teresa came after her and grabbed her arm.

"You promised!" she said. Her speech was a bit slurred but her gaze was piercing.

"Leave me alone!" Manda threw off her grasp.

"You owe me this."

"I don't owe you a fuck with strangers. They aren't *my* exo-bond."

"You don't have to do anything with them. Nobody made you. But you shouldn't leave alone like this, before we do the wrap. It's rude."

Manda shook her head slowly, confused. She heaved deep breaths, trying to clear her head. Her heart was thumping, striving for her attention. Somewhere off to her left, one of the couples was engaged in lovemaking. Their moans and rustlings made her aware again of the ache throbbing low in her belly.

"I don't belong here," Manda said, wiping away tears. "This is hurting me." She grabbed Teresa's hand. "Please release me from the promise. Please."

Teresa glared at her, and snatched her hand away. She stalked back toward the circle, with a "Go, then," flung over her shoulder. Manda lifted a hand after her, then dropped it. She turned and made her sad and drunken way back to her cubby, where she relieved her unrequited desire with her fingers, thinking of those two lovely young men she couldn't bring herself to covex with.

◆

She woke in the morning with a slight hangover. The prior night's events had taken on, mercifully, a dreamlike vagueness. The absence of her clone in the crowded, noisy mess hall at breakfast—they were probably hungover or sleeping in with their lovers or something—anyway, their absence, and the absence of any JennaMaras, made it easy to put it all out of her mind. Besides, she had work to do.

Back at her work station, Manda saw the seismic data she'd been waiting for had come in. She set it aside for the moment, first slipping into the liveface pack and hooking up the leads. Instantly her liveware interface reconfigured itself around her to a higher-resolution, more sensorily based mode.

Her icons floated in the middle distance. She pivoted until she located the dodecahedral commandball from the signaling waldo, gestured to bring it closer, and when it was in range, reached out to touch it; instantly its data exploded into assorted complex shapes that moved to the periphery of her vision. A model of the waldo unfolded around her, as if she were a clear glass version of it, surrounded by the cold, deep, falsecolor sea. Her arms were enfolded in *Septimus*'s pair of rotary blades, her fingertips were transparent wires that connected to the key sampling and communications controls, and her feet became glacine connectors to steering, speed, and other controls. She was Manda-*Septimus*.

First she noted, with a frown of surprise, that *both* of *Septimus*'s thermocouples were reading higher than normal this time, not just one. Not much higher. Nothing to call the council about, but there was one other thing: the readouts didn't appear all that different from usual, but the current's tug *felt* just a tad stronger than usual against her-*Septimus*'s skin. It was nothing her engines couldn't easily handle, but the two of these factors together *could* mean that undersea volcanic activity somewhere in the vicinity was creating convective cells of warmer water within the trench. Her heart started beating a little faster.

Easy, Manda; don't set yourself up for disappointment. Confirm it. Her-*Septimus*'s rotors hummed, keeping her-it in place, as she disengaged from the view of the ocean floor and brought up the marine-waldo's assorted datashapes.

This data was mostly several hours old. Her marine-waldos were hundreds of kilometers away—or more—beneath a kilometer and a half of ice and many kilometers of water. Early during their occupation of Brimstone, the colonists had installed a series of phased-array sonar transponders beneath the ice layer just offshore, and had used them to locate a large, shallow deposit of crude oil. Beneath the crust of ice, about five or so vertical meters of chilly salt water lay atop the continental shelf with its crude oil deposits.

The refinery had long since abandoned the drill hole, since its location hadn't been ideal for tapping into the reservoir. But the drill hole had been ideal for Manda's purposes. Three seasons ago, when she'd first started this project, she'd pulled up the sonar transponders, refurbished them, and configured them in a phased array that would relay sonar signals to and from a fleet of marine-waldos. Manda's commands were processed by the colony computers and broadcast via radio to an exploratory drill site near the colony's petroleum refinery, which squatted in a valley three hundred kilometers east of Amaterasu, near the mouth of a glacier on the larger of Brimstone's two major continents, Arcas. It was a crude setup, compared to some of the elaborate computational links she had used with other explorer waldos in the past, but it worked.

Its main disadvantage was that sonar was not an information-dense medium. Even a phased-array setup—and even with the signal-boosting buoys she had planted here and there—didn't allow for a lot of information to be transmitted at once, since the frequencies she had to use were low ones. The link between Manda and her marine-waldos was a mere trickle of information across a very large expanse, and the inevitable errors in transmission and interruptions slowed things down even more. When she issued a command—to sample salinity, for instance, or descend or turn—her waldos might receive those commands several minutes—or even an hour or more—later. But her software compensated as best it could for this very long lag, and Manda's doggedness and ability to anticipate her waldos had served her well.

Manda called up some empty, transparent boxes, then grabbed the datashapes orbiting her-*Septimus*, and dropped them into the boxes. Three-dimensional brightly colored charts unfolded inside the boxes, positioning themselves around her.

She massaged the data, quite literally, moving variables and recharting them and changing the axes around, and then stepped back and eyed the brightly colored datascape around her. She wandered through them, running her fingers over the results, and listened to the harmonics that fluctuated as she moved.

Yes!

Over the past half hour, the waldo had wandered in and out of currents a few hundredths of a degree Celsius warmer—and about a twentieth to a tenth of a knot faster—than ambient. Sonar soundings of the vicinity revealed nothing new, merely a rocky bottom with some silting, and a fairly featureless cliff face to the west—but the chemical screens showed slightly elevated concentrations of manganese and particulates in the warmer, faster-moving eddies.

This was all very suggestive—still, she couldn't bring it to the council until she had something more substantial to show them. They wouldn't care about some little bumps that lined up. She needed more.

Manda called up a map of the region she was currently exploring, and checked the approximate location of all her marine-waldos. They were spread out over almost five thousand kilometers, at varying depths but most within thirty meters of the ocean floor. *Aculeus Septimus* had been exploring a deep sea trench extending roughly north-to-south, several hundred kilometers to the east of the coast. Its precise location at the moment was— *How interesting!* She increased the map's resolution. *Yes, it's just south of the equator.* According to Jim, the equator was a highly likely location for geothermal activity, due to rotational and tidal stresses on Brimstone's crust.

She noted that the bottom of the trench had been increasing in depth as *Septimus* proceeded southward; in this vicinity it went down to about four kilometers below sea level. *Septimus* had been exploring along the lower eastern edge of the trench, cruising near the bottom of its design depth of four kilometers below sea level. The drop seemed to continue to the south, at about two degrees per kilometer.

This posed a difficulty. If the source of the thermal activity lay much further south, and the trench continued to increase in depth, the heat source would be below the range of her marine-waldos' detectors. Meaning she'd either have to risk losing the waldos to implosion, or give up the search.

Give me time, she thought, rubbing at the livemesh over her upper lip; *I'll come up with something.*

When she overlaid her search grid onto the ocean-floor map she'd been building, she saw that *Septimus* had entered a large, virtually unmapped section of seafloor that extended south from the equator.

She called the four closest waldos, *Aculei Duo, Tres, Quatuor,* and *Octo,* to assist *Septimus.* It would take a day for the nearest of them to arrive; in the meantime she needed to come up with a good search pattern. This was no time to get sloppy. And she should let someone know what was going on.

She smiled fiercely into her livemask. Success was finally—if not yet hers—at least flirting with her for a moment or two.

Manda put a call in to Jim LuisMichael, the geophysicist who had helped her develop her original seamap routines. He materialized beyond Manda's livemask, grinning through his bushy, black, ice-encrusted beard. His eyebrows and nose hairs were also iced-over and his eyes made invisible behind a pair of small dark goggles. His microphone, a thick line, snaked across his cheek below the edge of his livemask, to perch beneath his lower lip; his radiation-alert badge was a blinking green LED at his collar. He must be using a wristband video transceiver, since his forearm, huge and near, faded into nothing at the periphery of her vision on the left, and the outsized tip of his mitten appeared at the periphery on her right.

She felt like a mote standing on his arm. In the background she could see pipes, distillation columns, and a portion of a petroleum storage tank.

"Manda!" he shouted over the wind. "What can I do for you?"

"I got your seismic data—thanks."

"Sure! Was it a help?"

"Oh, yes! In fact, I need your help refining my sea-mapping searches. Are you available to give me a hand?"

"Not right away. I'm out at the refinery. Won't be back for several days. We're finishing up some repairs out here. Can it wait till I-we get back?"

Manda gnawed her lip. She hated the idea of sitting idle for even just a few days, this close to her goal. But without his help developing a good search, based on the geology of the area, she'd be wasting her time. "Not if it can be avoided. Could you link in tonight, after sunset? Just for a little while?" She hesitated. "I think I'm on to something, Jim."

His eyebrows rose. "Oh?"

"Yes."

"Hmmm." He nodded. "All right. I'll try. Depends on how repairs go."

As he was talking a deep rumble came up through her soles and rattled her chest cavity. Her eardrums itched and popped. It went on longer than usual, and built in strength rather than fading, in a series of jerks that knocked her to her knees.

"What is it?" Jim asked.

"A quake," she gasped, scrambling for purchase on the thatching. "Hang on."

The jerking seemed to last forever, though certainly it must have been less than a minute. As the quake began to finally subside, a muffled *crack* shook dust off the walls, followed by a loud *whooomph*.

Shit. It's big—and close. She yanked her livesuit connectors loose and struggled out of the livepack. Jim's image depixilated to a lower resolution. He read her expression. "What now?"

"Cave-in. Big one. I'll call you back." She cut the connection as she ran down the corridor, and called the colony's support-systems syntellect. Its icon appeared before her.

"Where is the cave-in?" she asked.

"Specify cave-in."

"The cave-in that just happened, you dipshit!"

After an unusually long pause, it gave her the coordinates. The collapse had happened in a bad place, logistically: in the main traffic corridor at the colony's lowest level, which led to two of the colony's three major agricultural caverns. The livestock themselves wouldn't be affected by this, but the bamboo forest and Hydroponics might be. As well as the Fertility Labs and the nurseries and Child-Rearing.

Abruptly everything went dark but her liveface, which flickered as it switched over to battery and to an even lower-rez mode. The livesuit was now running from its own processor, no longer hooked up by radiolink to the Amaterasu net. Power and communications were down.

Someone collided with her, and swore. She pulled her flashlight from her belt. Other flashlights flicked on. The array of bouncing, caroming lights added more confusion, not less. Work-waldos now unpiloted milled about, crashing into the humans, or froze, blocking passage. She got pushed along a set of corridors and around turns till she wasn't sure where she was.

Manda stumbled along with the rest, bumping into stray people and equipment that fell across her path, until she caught a glimpse of a staircase ahead, and recognized her surroundings. She and others crowded down the nearest spiral staircase into the catecombs on the level below. A crowd was gathering at the intersection ahead. She rounded the corner there. Several adults were herding children this way. People were shouting. Two lines were forming—rubble clearance brigades—while through the middle of the corridor other adults and teens were helping the survivors—most of them kids—out.

The children looked confused; several were crying. A couple were injured—she couldn't tell how badly; she could only catch glimpses in the poor lighting—and being carried out. She sneezed: dust and a solvent mist stung her nose. Steam, rubble, and poor lighting obscured her view, but it looked as if the collapse had occurred a few meters ahead, just beyond the child-care area. About ten meters beyond the children's suites the corridor branched and opened up onto the caverns containing the Hydroponics gardens and the bamboo. The Fertility Center was in a set of caves off of the bamboo fields. If any of the three areas had been badly damaged, the colony was in trouble.

She strapped her flashlight to her head with a strip of cloth torn from her shirt hem, and then joined the brigade. It was filthy, mindless work: take the boulders and dirt and buckets of rubble from the person ahead of her, hand them to the person behind. Some of the rocks started coming out stinking and slippery, and she realized it was blood. Or worse.

Manda grew dizzy and her vision blurred—from the shock, from the effort, the smell, and the damp heat slowly building up in the corridor from the steam-line leak. But she kept going, doggedly, passing rock after bucket after rock. Her arm muscles shrieked their agony along her nerve endings. She hurled the fury that filled her into her brigade work, grab and pass, grab and pass, snarling at the others in the line—*Hurry it up, you lazy shitheads. Move it.* She knew she shouldn't, but she couldn't help it. The rage was just there, boiling inside her like a hydrothermal cauldron. It had to go somewhere.

A couple of mangled corpses came through the line, bundled in blood-stained sheets. Their faces were partially exposed and she knew them; everybody knew everybody—if not their given names, at least their clones. The first was a young JoeUrsula, who worked—had worked—in Child-Rearing. The second was Teresa.

Numbly, Manda took her sister's torso and looked at it, trying to make it be someone else. But the features of the dead woman in her arms refused to change.

Manda could tell by the way her fingers sank in at the back of Teresa's head, even through the bundling, that Teresa's skull had been crushed. Bile rose in Manda's throat. Teresa's body was so terribly battered that Manda was grateful for the bundling.

She hugged the body tight, spasmodically, trying to ignore the strange contortions and parts that weren't where they should be beneath the sheet. Then she looked at the face again, stroked the corpse's torn, bruised face. It was like looking in the mirror and seeing herself as a corpse—but at the same time it didn't even look like *Teresa*, much less a carbon copy of Manda.

"I'm sorry," she whispered, remembering their argument this morning. She felt dizzy. The world receded to the end of a long tunnel. She looked around, confused, half forgetting where she was.

The man directly behind her was looking at her with a pitying gaze.

"Take it!" She forced Teresa's body into his arms. Then she tried to rub the brown, sticky, drying blood off her palms, arms, and face before the next horrible load came down the line. She found it hard to breathe. But it wasn't till several drops struck her hands that she realized a stream of tears was flowing down her face, which had contorted into a taut mask.

Where's Paul? Does he know? Oh, God. My siblings, my siblings! Where are you?

She found herself sitting down, trembling like an ice-sprite. A woman was giving her oxygen from a portable unit. She'd been dragged out of the brigade. The woman was a young RoxannaTomas. Manda took several deep breaths into the mask, then signaled enough and struggled to her feet.

"You gonna be okay?" the other shouted over the din. Manda couldn't find the words to answer. She only returned to her place in line.

Gradually, the rocks began to come out clean and hot and wet: steam-blasted. Communications came back online. A kind of numbness settled over Manda. Her thoughts came more clearly.

She remembered the extra waldos and spare parts sitting in the equipment hangar. She should check, see what kind of equipment she could throw together. The digging could go much faster. Lives could be saved.

"Who is the cave-in rescue coordinator?" she asked those coming out, repeating the question until someone finally answered. It was Arlene. She spotted her up ahead, just this side of the cave-in.

Manda left the brigade and pushed through the crowd till she reached Arlene. Her older sister was directing people who had crawled into the make-shift tunnel with beams and were stabilizing it. The steam leak had been fixed, or the line closed.

They looked at each other, and Manda saw Teresa in Arlene's face. As Arlene looked away, Manda lowered her own gaze, shoving down the horror and nausea that tried to muscle its way up again. *Will any of us be able to bear to look at each other, after this?*

Other colonists had been lost over the years, too many of them, in too many different kinds of calamities. *But never one of us. Never one of us.*

"I can bring some machines in," she said.

"What?" Arlene squinted at her, clearly distracted.

"I can slap some big construction-waldos together to help with the digging."

Arlene frowned. "We're too cramped already. Several small rooms and corridors need clearing-out and we need to go very carefully. Your waldos are too big for this work, until we get into the caverns." She paused, thinking. "But you're right that we'll need the heavy equipment soon enough. Go see what you can come up with."

Manda turned to go, but someone up ahead, someone inside the hole, shouted, "We're through! We're into the caverns!"

Word traveled back along the line; everything grew hushed. Manda strained to get a glimpse; it was impossible to see what was going on in there, with the dust and dancing lights and workers obscuring the view.

The word came through: "The bamboo is intact!"

A murmur of relief rippled around them.

"What about the babies?" someone shouted, and someone else said, "What about Hydroponics?"

Arlene put in a call. Twin GeorgJeans appeared in front of them, crouching, out of breath. They were broadcasting on a public channel: not only could Manda see their filthy, fatigue-lined faces, several other people also gathered around. Dust motes drifted around the GeorgJeans. The female spoke loudly to be heard over the digging and shouting going on around her. "The Fertility Center is cut off by rubble but we're talking to them through the vents." "There are no adult casualties yet," the male said, and both finished, "We're confident we can get them out."

"The fetuses?"

Both shook their heads. "Their backup power unit was smashed up and a lot of the fetal-support equipment has been damaged as well." "Most of the vats are intact, but they have no working life support, and it's getting cold in there without the heaters." "The workers are trying to save the ones closer to term but it looks like we're going to lose a lot of them."

Arlene wiped a weary hand across her brow, leaving a smudge. Manda remembered her undecanted siblings, the new twins. A sharp pain lanced her through the midsection, piercing her armor of numbness.

Please, she thought. *Please.*

Arlene asked, "What about the gardens?"

The GeorgJeans grimaced. "We've got a lot of damage in Hydroponics. But the power plant took a hit, too." "We've got power out everywhere—" "—and we're not in communication with any survivors." "We won't know exactly how much damage there is for a while."

Arlene sighed and exchanged a grim look with Manda.

"Okay," she told the GeorgJeans, "the Fertility Center becomes our top priority. Give me regular reports. Manda," she said, as the GeorgJeans' images dissolved, "once we finish getting the Fertility Labs cleared out we'll need your waldos for the Hydroponics cavern."

"On my way." She started to go, then looked back. "Was it the terraforming drilling? Is that what triggered it?"

Arlene stared at her. They both knew the answer.

No way to be absolutely sure. But probably. Probably.

Rage flooded Manda: rage at Arlene, at Derek—at all her clone. *If not for your fucking IceFlame, Teresa would still be alive.* Manda stood there staring at her eldest sister for several seconds, shaking with the need to scream at her. To accuse. To denounce. Only the anguish twisting Arlene's face stopped her.

Finally Manda turned, with a smothered cry, and hurled herself down the corridor toward the lifts to the equipment hangar, as fast as she could.

◆

The team managed to rescue all the Fertility personnel, and those of their fetal charges still hanging on to life, within a few hours. Manda didn't ask about the baby CarliPablo twins right then. She couldn't handle losing more siblings, just yet.

Instead, she and the rest of the team got started clearing away rubble, building makeshift tunnels and valleys through the great mounds of debris that had dropped onto the gardens in the Hydroponics cavern. Power and the local network were brought back up after a while, which made things easier. Still it was tedious and gruesome work—there were too few living and too many dead—and the fact that she was only present in proxy, piloting a team of three construction-waldos, didn't make it any less dreadful. Still, she pushed herself—and the others—very hard.

As long as she stayed busy, she didn't have to think. She didn't have to remember.

She and two other waldo pilots did the heaviest work with their six big, lumbering machines, aided by almost three dozen workers present *in corpus*. In the middle of that first night after the cave-in, the council appointed DaliaMarshall to replace Arlene as leader of the rescue effort. The fourclone spread out, each taking charge of part of the cleanup. Manda's crew leader was Abraham DaliaMarshall, a large, bluff man two or three seasons older than Manda. Abraham been among her worst tormentors, growing up. A sneaky, vicious, backbiting bully. The rest of his clone was no better.

But this was no time for old grudges. So she worked with him. And her focused intensity caused the other workers to turn to her for guidance and ideas at least as often as to DaliaMarshall. When they grew discouraged or talk of quitting, she harangued them, admonished them, reminded them that there could still be survivors—asked how they'd like to be trapped in the rubble, knowing their fate depended only on the perseverance of the rescue team? For once, no one argued with her or told her she was being rude.

The LuisMichael threeclone soon returned from the refinery and pitched in, using sounding equipment and Jim's seismology expertise to listen for sounds coming from any survivors. With LuisMichael's help they located fourteen people trapped alive in various pockets of air under the rubble. But afterward, more than eighteen hours passed and several tons of rubble were cleared with no other survivors found, only scattered remains.

Finally they uncovered a large cache of dismembered bodies. They shipped as many of the remains as they could to the genetics people, who were getting the Fertility Labs cleaned up, and they also did swabs everywhere they saw a speck of blood or other apparent animal matter. Genetics reported back early second-watch on day two that they'd identified four different DNA signatures. Since two of the DNA sets were for two different pairs of clone-twins on the missing-persons list, this meant that between four and six more people were accounted for. Probably six, since the twins were probably working together when the cave-in had struck.

In which case, all were now accounted for except the UrsulaMeriwether threeclone: Helen, Jessica, and Rachel. The heart—and brain—of the Hydroponics effort.

Looking across at the wreckage of the gardens, mottled by debris-fragmented beams of light from the searchers' lamps—the broken, bone-colored remains of stalagmites and chunks of shale-like rock that lay like a stifling, multiton blanket over the shattered trays and tubes and wilted vegetable matter—Manda had to admit, if only to herself, that there were probably no more survivors. UrsulaMeriwether was dead.

With a sigh, she wheeled Mole and Crane over to join Scaffold, whose rear right tire had gotten stuck in a hole. The workers building a permanent embankment there needed the scaffolding-waldo out of the way to finish their task, and her efforts to unstick it under its own power had failed. She-Crane lumbered up, latched on to her-Scaffold with her-its hook, and lifted her-Scaffold up and out of the way. The workers below waved weary thanks as she-Crane set her-Scaffold down. Meanwhile, she-Mole caught a glimpse of the hole she-Scaffold had been stuck in. It was a floor drain whose grating had buckled under the bulky waldo's weight.

A *floor drain?* A *floor drain.* Back in her projection pod, Manda frowned, and detached from her livepack leads for a moment. Her liveface diminished in scope to a simple 2-D display. She stretched with an enormous yawn and took a long drink of water from her bottle, then sat down on the floor and did some yoga stretches to invigorate herself.

She was so tired it was hard to think, but there was something important about this. The drains.

A floor drain, she realized suddenly, meant that there were conduits or trenches under the floor. Tunnels perhaps big enough for a human to crawl into and avoid being crushed, if that person were a quick thinker. Which UrsulaMeriwether was.

DaliaMarshall—Abraham's vat-twin Robert, to be precise—showed up in her work station as she was calling up schematics for the lines under the gardens. His eyes were sunken and dark with fatigue and his face was dirty, gaunt, and lined. Manda stood to face him, and stiffened when she read his expression. She knew why he was here.

"Manda . . ." He sighed at the look on her face, and started again. "It's time to give it up. We've done all we can."

"I have an idea," she said. "I think I know where UrsulaMeriwether might be."

He groaned. "Not another one."

"Listen to me—there's a drain—"

DaliaMarshall talked over her. "We've chased down two of your possibilities already and hauled tons of junk for nothing. It's been too long. They're all dead. It's time to quit."

She stared at him coldly. "You give up, then. There are still at least three unaccounted for. I'm not stopping till we find them—alive or dead."

"You are fucking *impossible!*" he exploded. "Abraham's right about you."

"And you're a coward," she said. "Afraid to finish the job you-you started. Why the council would put your clone in charge, I have no idea."

He went pale and his lips thinned. "I-we am pulling the crew. You do whatever the hell you want. And the council will hear about this."

"Fine. Give them my love."

He gave her the fist of contempt and stalked out. Manda slumped against the wall and laid her forehead on her arm, feeling quivery and empty.

What am I trying to prove? she thought. She was exhausted, too.

This one last time, she thought. *I'll check this one last thing. The floor drains.* She dragged herself back to her feet and jacked into her livepack, and the full-sensory interface bloomed around her. When she faced into Mole, DaliaMarshall, the other three members of it, was overseeing the equipment cleanup. Most of the workers were already leaving. The other three big machines were gone.

A cold, hard pain squeezed her chest.

"Go, then!" she yelled. "Give up when there may still be people alive in there! Cowards! Go ahead and go."

She split her liveface into three and faced into Scaffold and Crane as well as Mole. Turning her-waldos' backs on the departing workers, she switched on her headlights and sent the three of them lumbering clumsily and faithfully back into the rubble mounds.

To her surprise, one of the LuisMichaels followed her. It was Jim! It must be. His clone-sibs, Amy and Brian, hesitated only for an instant before following as well.

Once they reached the end of the tunnel, Manda-Mole called them over. They crouched in a pool of light cast by Scaffold, amid clouds of dust and piles of loose debris, and she replaced her own image on Mole's belly screen with a schematic of the Hydroponics cavern, pre-collapse. Then she superimposed a rough sketch of the rubble; it blanketed the schematic like a foul mirage. The mirage had red veins running through it, which she-Mole traced with her-its claw hand.

"We've dug tunnels and set up listening equipment here, here, and here," she-Mole said. "But this large section over here, near the offices where the worst of the collapse was, is unexplored. And it's also most likely where UrsulaMeriwether and some of its top people were."

LuisMichael frowned at the schematic, and shook its heads. "But the offices abut the bamboo caverns right here, see?" Jim told her. "I've listened on the other side of the wall. I didn't detect any sound, not even breathing." "And our seismic tests of that area made it clear that there are no air pockets of any size in that vicinity," Brian pointed out.

"Not in the offices, no. But see this subterranean line right here? It's a floor drain, and see?—there's grating on the floor just outside the office. The quake lasted for several seconds before the cave-in occurred. It's possible they had time to make it to the drain."

"In which case they'd have run out of air by now," Amy said.

"Not necessarily. Not if they belly-crawled through to here." She pointed.

"The runoff catchment sump?" Amy asked, dubiously. "That's a good twenty-meter crawl, with two grated openings between the office and the sump." Brian went on, "The drain would be blocked by debris."

"I don't think so," Manda replied. "At least, there's a reasonable possibility it wasn't. A lot of the rubble has been larger than the grating gaps. And they could dig some, if they had to."

The three exchanged a glance.

"And look," she went on. She changed the overlay to a schematic of the level just beneath the floor. "All these utility pipes run on top of the sump. They're undamaged and some are still operating. Adding up to lots of vibrations from fluid flow and transmission of engine noises. They would mask any sound the survivors might make."

Brian and Amy shook their heads, but Jim nodded, slowly, after a moment. "It's worth a try. Where are we, in relation to the sump?"

Manda-Mole pointed straight down between its tractor treads. "Almost directly above it, according to my calculations."

Brian jumped up. "I'll get the utilities shut off—" "and we'll bring plumbing equipment back with us," Amy finished. They ran off, while Jim started setting up his sounding and seismic detectors.

Let this work, Manda thought. *If it doesn't, I'm out of ideas.*

◆

It didn't take long for Manda-Mole to tear through the thatch floor and the dust and rock layers, to reveal the utility pipes that overlaid the drainage conduit about a meter-and-a-half below the floor.

"There it is," she-Mole said. In the dimness, numerous utility pipes ran on top of the concrete floor drain, both parallel and crosswise to the drain. She saw no indication that the floor drain discharged into a sump within the confines of the large hole they'd dug. "We're not as close to the sump as I thought."

"That's okay. If they're anywhere in the vicinity, with the utilities turned off I should be able to hear them." Jim scrambled down into the hole, aided by Brian, while Amy loaded the seismic and other sounding equipment onto a pallet. The triplets worked with a silent, intent efficiency that gave Manda a pang of envy.

Back in her work station, Manda disconnected from her livepack and then made her way to the caverns. She could be more use *in corpus* for the finer-scale work, and if more heavy work was necessary, her lower-rez interface was adequate for controlling her waldos on-site.

Besides, she wanted to be there, in person, when—if—*when* survivors were found.

By the time she arrived, Jim had climbed down among the pipes and was brushing away soil. Amy and Brian were lowering his sonar equipment down to him on a rope.

"I'll need more light," he said. Manda-Scaffold shuffled over to shine lights inside the hole. A rumbling started. Terror knotted in Manda's throat, and she looked up at the cave ceiling, then around at the swinging lights, at the clouds of fine dust that rose. Small rocks pelted the ground here and there, with a sound like hail. The air choked them with fine dust and the smell of ruined vegetation. LuisMichael's gazes met hers, its own eyes wide with fear.

But it was just the usual small-scale tremors, and they died away in sec-

onds. Amy and Brian continued lowering the equipment. Manda recon-
nected to Scaffold and adjusted the lighting at Jim's direction. Then they
three waited, while Jim placed leads among the pipes.

"Turn on the detector," he said finally. Amy squatted next to the sound
detector and turned it on. Lines appeared on the screen. "I want everyone
to be very still." The lines on the screen peaked and bounced in response
to his words. "No talking, no shuffling, and breathe as quietly as possible."

They fell quiet, and the squiggles died down to small, occasional wiggles.
Manda resisted scratching a sudden, fierce itch on her leg. Her heart was
beating harder than usual, a response to the tremors as well as the thought
of finding UrsulaMeriwether. The noise was loud enough that Manda half
expected the detector to pick it up.

"Nothing unusual," Amy said after a few moments. "You want to come
check it out?"

"No. You know what to screen for. I'm going to move the leads. Any idea
which way the sump might lie from here?" he asked Manda. She checked
her maps once more, and leaned over the edge of the hole to check the
pipes. It was too hard to tell precisely where they were, in the midst of such
ruin, but the sump *should* be almost directly below. Somehow, her calculations were off.

She chewed her lip, then pointed. "Let's try that way."

Again Jim set the leads, this time at the edge of the hole where she'd
pointed, and again asked for silence. After a moment, Amy exclaimed, "I
think we have something!"

Jim climbed up out of the hole and hurried over. All four crowded around
the readout screen.

"See here?" Amy whispered, pointing at one set of squiggles. "And here."

"I see. Shh." Jim studied the lines, wearing a deep frown. "Well, it's something. Hard to say what. It could just be microtremors. Manda, do you think
you could clear away that section of flooring there?"

Things proceeded like this for some time, with Manda digging and scraping, and the other three moving the sound equipment and listening, with
equivocal results. They couldn't seem to locate the sump. They were all so
exhausted that the mere act of lifting an arm or speaking a few words had
become too great a chore. The hint of sound Jim had detected never panned
out into anything. They were all growing discouraged. Manda suggested they
take a short break, and volunteered to bring back food and water for everyone.

⬥

The mess was full of people, but no one said much. She tossed two decachips
onto the counter next to the cashier syntellect. The syntellect told her, "The
colony is on emergency rations. No one may have more than six chips' worth
of dinner."

Manda wasn't surprised; the destruction of the gardens was an extremely
serious loss. The colony might not survive it. "I'm collecting for LuisMichael,
also," she said.

"How many people total?"

"Four."

After a brief pause, the syntellect approved the additional purchases. Manda looked at the food on the tray. *Going to be a lot of hungry people around here.* She took the water bottles, fruit, and crispy duck–and–bamboo shoot *mana*-rolls the robotic arms had assembled and headed back to the dig.

Her companions took the food and ate greedily. It was all gone too quickly. After a few moments of silence, Brian took a slug of water and then said, "We've been talking it over, Manda. It's almost fifty hours since the cave-in." "We can't locate the sump, and even if they made it there, they've probably run out of oxygen or died of exposure by now," Amy said.

All three LuisMichaels looked so tired. Her own limbs felt like they were made of jelly. It was all too much. Too much for such a small group to do alone. "The others should be here helping," she said, and slumped over her knees. "It's a big sump. There could still be some air left."

LuisMichael stood and brushed itselves off. Jim said, "Come on, Manda. Time to call it quits."

The pause lengthened as she looked up at them. The familiar anger came on, and abated.

Manda, you know they're right. She really had given it everything she had. With a sigh, finally, she opened her mouth to say so.

Then closed it.

Then shook her head.

"I can't quit. Not till I find the sump."

The others exchanged glances filled with depths she couldn't read. When Manda next looked up, Jim was still there but the other two had gone.

"Till we find the sump," he said. "And that's it."

"Thanks, Jim," she said hoarsely, and blinked away tears.

They did extensive sonar soundings along all sides of the trench they'd dug, and Jim finally reported that there *might* be a large air pocket not beneath *this* floor drain, but beneath the one on what would be two aisles over. "*May*," he emphasized. "I could just be picking up empty piping or a crack that formed in the floor and didn't get filled in."

This meant excavating several cubic meters of rubble before they even got to the floor. Manda eyed the mounds she must move—mounds of dirt that were even higher than they had been before she'd started—and a feeling of futility rose in her chest. The fucking sump could be anywhere.

But if it were one of her own siblings, she'd work till she collapsed. Would she do less for UrsulaMeriwether?

"This will take awhile," she told Jim. "Why don't you get some rest, and I'll call you when I reach the pipes under the floor." He gladly took her up on the offer.

She first made a very careful study of the maps. Then she started digging.

Those next four hours she worked alone in the enormous cavern were the longest yet. She felt more tired than she ever remembered being—it took all she had to remain awake, huddled in the rubble surrounded by shattered Hydroponics equipment, in a dusty, fragmented pool of light, while Mole and Crane and Scaffold's grinding, hammering, clanking chorus echoed against the dark upper reaches of the cavern, and returned to her in wobbly, staccato mimicry of itself.

Yet she found a certain peaceful rhythm to the task. Several times she dozed off and reawakened to find her waldos standing lifeless nearby. She got up and paced as she worked, shaking her head, slapping her cheeks, swinging her arms—willing herself to stay awake as her three massive machines clanked and rumbled and bucked, first one, then two in concert, then the third, clearing away the rubble.

And finally she reached the floor, one aisle over. She-Mole tore through the thatch and rock and dirt, and she-Crane lifted the chunks of debris away, and now she was down to the piping. She was tired enough that she misjudged the depth and marred the pipes, rather than just skimming dirt from them. *Fuck it,* she thought. *It's a small price to pay.* The rubble she had moved to get there made a dark mountain beyond Scaffold's stick legs. She called Jim.

"I'm ready," she said. He rubbed his eyes and sat up, blinking blearily, in his quarters.

"Be right there." His words were slurred by fatigue.

Jim came, and so did Amy and Brian. As they were setting up, most of the other rescue workers who'd left earlier trickled in. And Derek and Arlene. Word had apparently gotten around.

"LuisMichael told us about your idea," Derek said, at Manda's curious glance, and Arlene said with a shrug, "It's worth a shot."

Jim climbed into the hole and squatted on the piping. Beneath his feet, the curved, bone-colored sump lay. He took out a wrench, reached down between the pipes, and tapped on the sump. It rang hollowly. Everyone waited. Nothing. After a long pause he tapped again. And there was an answering thump. And more thumps. And muffled voices.

Cries of excitement went up. Several people jumped into the hole and began trying to pry the pipes out of the way, while others started hammering and banging shovels on the floor drain. Manda whistled for attention, and she-Crane lumbered up.

"This will be quicker," she said. "Everyone out of the hole."

Jim shouted, as much for the sump's occupants as the workers, "Stand clear!"

Manda-Crane grabbed the pipes and floor drain with her-its claws and tore a two-meter segment of conduit away, with torn pipe segments trailing streams of fluid. When she-Scaffold rolled over to the hole and shone her-its lights back into it, the sump had an opening in its top, which had formerly been connected to the concrete floor drain. Manda jumped down into the hole with the LuisMichael triplets. She and Jim climbed down among the severed utility pipes and shone their flashlights into the sump, and their beams glinted off the upturned faces of four very dirty, shivering people: the UrsulaMeriwether sisters, and a JennaByron—one of the clone-siblings presumed dead.

Manda stumbled over to Arlene and Derek, while others moved in to help the survivors out. Derek opened his arms and she walked into them; they gave each other a long, wordless hug, and Arlene wrapped her arms around both of them. Manda pulled back and eyed her older siblings.

You saved the colony, Manda.

They didn't have to say it. The pride and love they felt gleamed in their gazes, even amid the still-raw sense of loss.

It was time to ask. "The twins?"

"We lost the girl," Derek said. "The boy is hanging on. They have him in intensive care. It . . ." His voice broke. Arlene finished in flat tones, "It doesn't look so good."

Manda pressed herself against them again, and hung on tight. She felt as if the world were coming to an end. Perhaps it was.

◦

Two days later Manda visited her little, unnamed brother. Paul was inside the intensive-care unit, masked, holding the baby in his gloved hands under a bank of warming lights. The baby was hooked up to an IV and several monitoring wires. The infant looked so pitiful, punctured and wired as it was; Manda cringed. (*Not it*, she reminded herself, sharply; *him.*) And the look on Paul's face was so intensely sorrowful that Manda couldn't bear to look directly at him, either.

She grabbed a mask and entered the room, and sauntered rather too casually over. "Hi."

He didn't even glance at her as she approached. She saw that Paul's right hand cupped the baby easily; he was that small.

"How is he doing?"

"I talked to the doctor. They say he's stable, he's gained a little weight, and his lungs are in better shape."

"He's a fighter," she said. Paul nodded.

"He might make it." Paul stroked the baby's hair with a thumb. "Poor little guy."

Manda realized he meant, *Poor little guy is going to* live. And that Paul was here to say goodbye to him.

"Being a single isn't *that* bad," Manda said mildly. He gave her a raw, shocky look; Manda guessed he hadn't slept at all in the three days since Teresa's death. He opened his mouth; *You don't know what it's like.* But of course, in her own fashion, she did. He closed his mouth and looked at the baby again.

"It's different when you grow up together, I guess," Manda said.

Paul nodded, swallowed convulsively. "Perhaps you're right. He won't know this." His voice cracked and bled. "This pain."

Fear grabbed Manda—fear of saying the exact wrong thing; fear of what would happen if she remained silent. She took a deep breath. "Paul, we need you."

Surprise and anguish flicked across his face. He slipped his hands out from under the baby and turned away from her.

"I can't, Manda. I can't. Part of me is already dead." He paused. "I reach out," he said, lifting a hand to empty air, "and—where she was, I reach for her and—nothing's there. I'm hollowed-out. I'm nothing." He closed his hand and brought it to his chest. "Teresa. Oh, God. Help me." He doubled over, and his voice became a growl of pain, a mantra. "I can't. I can't."

So Manda took hold of him, and they sank to the floor together. He howled his anguish. His fingers gouged into her and his tears poured out and soaked her sweater. Then he tried to silence himself, and bit her shoulder so hard it hurt even through the multiple layers she wore. She saw staff come running, and shooed them out.

Once Paul's grief had abated, she took his face in her hands—his face so like lost Teresa's.

Teresa. Teresa. As you love Paul—as you love me—give me the words.

And the words came. "Listen. Right now I know you don't care. Not about yourself, not about me, or our clone, or the colony. You don't have to promise me you won't ever do the recycler dive, or go walkabout without your gear. Just give me this one day. Just hang on till tomorrow."

He shook his head like a musk ox plagued by a shepherd dog's nippings. "Can't," he whispered. "Can't."

Manda gave his shoulders a shake. "You listen to me. You think I don't know the pain you're feeling because my own twin died before I was decanted and I don't remember him. Well, guess what. I live with that loss every fucking minute of every fucking day of my life, ever since I was old enough to understand why everybody thought I was a bizarre and useless freak.

"Well, I'm going to prove to them how wrong they are. This colony needs me, Paul, whether they know it or not. And they need this little baby. And they need you, too."

Paul had gone limp and unresponsive. After a moment Manda released him and draped her arms about her knees, sitting on the cold floor, eyeing the banks of equipment and the three other babies struggling for their lives.

"Teresa cared about this colony," she went on more quietly. "More than anything else. More than even her clone. If it had been you who had died, she would have hung on anyway, through the pain. I know it."

Paul just looked at her.

"You know good and well," Manda went on, "she would rather you suffer every ounce of this pain you're feeling than throw your own life away. She cared about the colony more than anything in the world." *She cared about me.* "She cared about you."

Anger coursed across his face. "What the fuck do you know about it? About her? You, with your selfish, loner attitude—you've always refused to have anything to do with me-us. With her. All you ever did was bring her grief. How can you possibly know what it's like?"

Then he lowered his head and hunched his shoulders and sobbed again: this time a child's helpless, heartbroken tears. Manda felt abashed. She watched him for a moment, touched his head. Then she stood up and took the infant in her own right hand.

It terrified her, how tiny he was. It awed her, that a human could be this small, this unformed, yet live.

"His name will be Terence," she said, and knew then that he would defy the doctors' worst predictions and live. As had she.

She held out her hand to Paul, who had grown quiet. He gripped her hand in his own—as tightly as if he were clinging to life itself—and stood up beside her. His face went through several contortions.

"A good name," he said finally, his voice hoarse.

"Give me till tomorrow," Manda said, and gave Paul's hand a last, hard squeeze.

He didn't answer or even look at her, but she sensed a softening in his resolve, and clung to that, watching him leave.

Brimstone's tides were powerful and chaotic, much more so than Earth's. During Brimstone's long summer season they wracked the coastlines, tossing massive chunks of ice up onto the land as if they were a child's blocks. And death, it seemed to her, came on like the tides. It bore down—unstoppable: sweeping its victims away, pounding the survivors into numbed, mindless submission, leaving a heap of wreckage on the shore, of chaos, pain, shattered lives. Leaving the survivors to sort it all out and find a way to go on.

The tide had taken something else away from Manda, she realized, besides Teresa. It had reached in and dragged away Manda's most secret and terrible anguish. She'd done something worthwhile for the colony. For the first time, *she* knew—if they did not, yet—that they were wrong about her.

She discovered in herself a renewed determination to continue her undersea mapping. She'd keep at it till she found the seafloor vents. She'd take her marine-waldos to that dark and cold and lonely place and return with whatever glorious secrets, whatever marvels, whatever treasures of alien knowledge Brimstone might harbor.

Her gaze went to her infant brother Terence. Though Brimstone's tidal quakes had undoubtedly contributed, their penetration to the mantle—the terraforming effort—had certainly triggered the cave-in. Death had exacted a terrible price for Project IceFlame: a blood sacrifice. But terraforming also meant that Terence and future generations would be able to walk and work and love freely on the surface of Brimstone someday. Teresa hadn't died for nothing.

It mattered, somehow, too, that Terence had come into the world even as Teresa had left it. His presence—his struggle to live—gave Manda hope. If she could just hold on long enough, some tomorrow down the line would be better than today.

She'd give it till tomorrow. As many times as it took.